## "Why was I brought here? There must be other mentaths—"

"Well, you have been quite useful in Her Majesty's service. There's no doubt of that." Grayson paused, delicately. "There is the little matter of your registration. Bring this matter to a satisfactory close, and...who can say?"

Ah. There was the sweet in the poison. Clare considered this. "I gather Miss Bannon is just as insubordinate and intransigent as myself. And just as expendable in this current situation."

Grayson actually had the grace to flush. And cough. He kept glancing at the sherry as if he longed to take a draft himself.

*I thought he was more enamoured of port. Perhaps his tastes have changed.* Clare shelved the idea, warmed to his theme. "Furthermore, the registered mentaths have been whisked to safety or are presumably at great risk, so time is of the essence and the need desperate—otherwise I would still be rotting at home, given the nature of my...mistakes. I further gather there have been corresponding deaths among those, like myself, so unfortunate as to be unregistered for one reason or another."

Grayson's flush deepened. Clare admitted he was enjoying himself. No, that was not quite correct.

Clare was enjoying himself *immensely*. "How many?" he enquired.

"Well. That is, ahem." Grayson cleared his throat. "Let me be frank, Archibald."

*Now the game truly begins.* Clare brought all his faculties to bear, his concentration narrowing. "Please do be, Cedric."

"You are the only remaining unregistered mentath-class genius remaining alive in Londinium."

Archibald's fingers tightened, pressing against each other. "Ah." *Most interesting indeed.*

Praise for the
# Bannon & Clare Series

### The Iron Wyrm Affair

"Saintcrow scores a hit with this terrific steampunk series that rockets through a Britain-that-wasn't with magic and industrial mayhem with a firm nod to Holmes. Genius and a rocking good time."
—Patricia Briggs

"Saintcrow melds a complex magic system with a subtle but effective steampunk society, adds fully fleshed and complicated characters, and delivers a clever and highly engaging mystery that kept me turning pages, fascinated to the very end."
—Laura Anne Gilman

"Innovative world-building, powerful steampunk, master storyteller at her best. Don't miss this one.... She's fabulous."
—Christine Feehan

"Lilith Saintcrow spins a world of deadly magic, grand adventure, and fast-paced intrigue through the clattering streets of a maze-like mechanized Londonium. The *Iron Wyrm Affair* is a fantastic mix of action, steam, and mystery dredged in dark magic with a hint of romance. Loved it! Do not miss this wonderful addition to the steampunk genre."
—Devon Monk

"Lilith Saintcrow's foray into steampunk plunges the reader into a Victorian England rife with magic and menace, where clockwork horses pace the cobbled streets, dragons rule the ironworks, and it will take a sorceress's discipline and a logician's powers of deduction to unravel a bloody conspiracy."
—Jacqueline Carey

# By Lilith Saintcrow

*Afterwar*
*Cormorant Run*

### GALLOW AND RAGGED

*Trailer Park Fae*
*Roadside Magic*
*Wasteland King*

### BANNON & CLARE

*The Iron Wyrm Affair*
*The Red Plague Affair*
*The Ripper Affair*
*The Damnation Affair* (e-book only)
*The Collected Adventures of Bannon & Clare* (omnibus)

### DANTE VALENTINE NOVELS

*Working for the Devil*
*Dead Man Rising*
*The Devil's Right Hand*
*Saint City Sinners*
*To Hell and Back*
*Dante Valentine* (omnibus)

### JILL KISMET NOVELS

*Night Shift*
*Hunter's Prayer*
*Redemption Alley*
*Flesh Circus*
*Heaven's Spite*
*Angel Town*
*Jill Kismet* (omnibus)

### ROMANCES OF ARQUITAINE

*The Hedgewitch Queen*
*The Bandit King*

THE COLLECTED ADVENTURES OF

# BANNON

# &

# CLARE

## LILITH SAINTCROW

www.orbitbooks.net

Omnibus copyright © 2018 by Lilith Saintcrow

*The Iron Wyrm Affair* copyright © 2012 by Lilith Saintcrow; *The Red Plague Affair* copyright © 2013 by Lilith Saintcrow; *The Ripper Affair* copyright © 2014 by Lilith Saintcrow; *The Damnation Affair* copyright © 2012 by Lilith Saintcrow
Excerpt from *Afterwar* copyright © 2018 by Lilith Saintcrow

Author photograph by Daron Gildrow
Cover design by Lisa Marie Pompilio
Cover images by Shutterstock
Cover copyright © 2018 by Hachette Book Group, Inc.

Orbit
Hachette Book Group
1290 Avenue of the Americas
New York, NY 10104
orbitbooks.net

First Omnibus Edition: August 2018

Orbit is an imprint of Hachette Book Group.
The Orbit name and logo are trademarks of Little, Brown Book Group Limited.

The publisher is not responsible for websites (or their content) that are not owned by the publisher.

The Hachette Speakers Bureau provides a wide range of authors for speaking events. To find out more, go to www.hachettespeakersbureau.com or call (866) 376-6591.

ISBN: 978-0-316-41945-1 (trade paperback)

Printed in the United States of America

LSC-C

10 9 8 7 6 5 4 3 2 1

# Contents

# THE
# IRON WYRM
# AFFAIR

*For those who serve in shadow*

# Prelude

## A Promise of Diversion

When the young dark-haired woman stepped into his parlour, Archibald Clare was only mildly intrigued. Her companion was of more immediate interest, a tall man in a close-fitting velvet jacket, moving with a grace that bespoke some experience with physical mayhem. The way he carried himself, lightly and easily, with a clean economy of movement – not to mention the way his eyes roved in controlled arcs – all but shouted danger. He was hatless, too, and wore curious boots.

The chain of deduction led Clare in an extraordinary direction, and he cast another glance at the woman to verify it.

*Yes.* Of no more than middle height, and slight, she was in very dark green. Fine cloth, a trifle antiquated, though the sleeves were close as fashion now dictated, and her bonnet perched just so on brown curls, its brim small enough that it would not interfere with her side vision. However, her skirts were divided, her boots serviceable instead of decorative – though of just as fine a quality as the man's – and her jewellery was eccentric, to say the least. Emerald drops worth a fortune at her ears, and the necklace was an amber cabochon large enough to be a baleful eye. Two rings on gloved hands, one with a dull unprecious black stone and the other a star sapphire a royal family might have envied.

The man had a lean face to match the rest of him, strange yellow eyes, and tidy dark hair still dewed with crystal droplets from the light rain falling over Londinium tonight. The moisture, however, did not cling to her. One more piece of evidence, and Clare did not much like where it led.

He set the viola and its bow down, nudging aside a stack of paper with careful precision, and waited for the opening gambit. As he had suspected, *she* spoke.

"Good evening, sir. You are Dr Archibald Clare. Distinguished author of *The Art and Science of Observation*." She paused. Aristocratic nose, firm mouth, very decided for such a childlike face. "Bachelor. And very-recently-unregistered mentath."

"Sorceress." Clare steepled his fingers under his very long, very sensitive nose. Her toilette favoured musk, of course, for a brunette. Still, the scent was not common, and it held an edge of something acrid that should have been troublesome instead of strangely pleasing. "And a Shield. I would invite you to sit, but I hardly think you will."

A slight smile; her chin lifted. She did not give her name, as if she expected him to suspect it. Her curls, if they were not natural, were very close. There was a slight bit of untidiness to them – some recent exertion, perhaps? "Since there is no seat available, *sir*, I am to take that as one of your deductions?"

Even the hassock had a pile of papers and books stacked terrifyingly high. He had been researching, of course. The intersections between musical scale and the behaviour of certain tiny animals. It was the intervals, perhaps. Each note held its own space. He was seeking to determine which set of spaces would make the insects (and later, other things) possibly—

Clare waved one pale, long-fingered hand. Emotion was threatening, prickling at his throat. With a certain rational annoyance he labelled it as *fear*, and dismissed it. There was very little chance she meant him harm. The man was a larger question, but if *she* meant him no harm, the man certainly did not. "If you like. Speak quickly, I am occupied."

She cast one eloquent glance over the room. If not for the efforts of the landlady, Mrs Ginn, dirty dishes would have been stacked on every horizontal surface. As it was, his quarters were cluttered with a full set of alembics and burners, glass jars of various substances, shallow dishes for knocking his pipe clean. The tabac smoke blunted the damned sensitivity in his nose just enough, and he wished for his pipe. The acridity in her scent was becoming more marked, and very definitely not unpleasant.

The room's disorder even threatened the grate, the mantel above it groaning under a weight of books and handwritten journals stacked every which way.

The sorceress, finishing her unhurried investigation, next examined him from tip to toe. He was in his dressing gown, and his pipe had long since grown cold. His feet were in the rubbed-bare slippers, and if it had not been past the hour of reasonable entertaining he might have been vaguely uncomfortable at the idea of a lady seeing him in such disrepair. Red-eyed, his hair mussed, and unshaven, he was in no condition to receive company.

He was, in fact, the picture of a mentath about to implode from boredom. If she knew some of the circumstances behind his recent ill luck, she would guess he was closer to imploding and fusing his faculties into unworkable porridge than was advisable, comfortable . . . or even sane.

Yet if she knew the circumstances behind his ill luck, would she look so calm? He did not know nearly enough yet. Frustration tickled behind his eyes, the sensation of pounding and seething inside the cup of his skull easing a fraction as he considered the possibilities of her arrival.

Her gloved hand rose, and she held up a card. It was dun-coloured, and before she tossed it – a passionless, accurate flick of her fingers that snapped it through intervening space neat as you please, as if she dealt faro – he had already deduced and verified its provenance.

He plucked it out of the air. "I am called to the service of the

Crown. You are to hold my leash. It is, of course, urgent. Does it have to do with an art professor?" For it had been some time since he had crossed wits with Dr Vance, and *that* would distract him most handily. The man was a deuced wonderful adversary.

His sally was only worth a raised eyebrow. She must have practised that look in the mirror; her features were strangely childlike, and the effect of the very adult expression was . . . odd. "No. It *is* urgent, and Mikal will stand guard while you . . . dress. I shall be in the hansom outside. You have ten minutes, sir."

With that, she turned on her heel. Her skirts made a low, sweet sound, and the man was already holding the door. She glanced up, those wide dark eyes flashing once, and a ghost of a smile touched her soft mouth.

*Interesting*. Clare added that to the chain of deduction. He only hoped this problem would last more than a night and provide him further relief. If the young Queen or one of the ministers had sent a summons card, it promised to be very diverting indeed.

It was a delight to have something unknown, but within guessing reach. He sniffed the card. A faint trace of musk, but no violet-water. Not the Queen personally, then. He had not thought it likely – why would Her Majesty trouble herself with *him*? It was a faint joy to find he was correct.

His faculties were, evidently, not porridge *yet*.

The ink was correct as well, just the faintest bitter astringent note as he inhaled deeply. The crest on the front was absolutely genuine, and the handwriting on the back was firm and masculine, not to mention familiar. *Why, it's Cedric.*

In other words, the Chancellor of the Exchequer, Lord Grayson. The Prime Minister was new and inexperienced, since the Queen had banished her lady mother's creatures from her Cabinet, and Grayson had survived with, no doubt, some measure of cunning or because someone thought him incompetent enough to do no harm. Having been at Yton with the man, Clare was inclined to lean towards the former.

And dear old Cedric had exerted his influence so Clare was merely unregistered and not facing imprisonment, a mercy that had teeth. Even more interesting.

*Miss Emma Bannon is our representative. Please use haste, and discretion.*

Emma Bannon. Clare had never heard the name before, but then a sorceress would not wish her name bruited about overmuch. Just as a mentath, registered or no, would not. So he made a special note of it, adding everything about the woman to the mental drawer that bore her name. She would not take a carved nameplate. No, Miss Bannon's plate would be yellowed parchment, with dragonsblood ink tracing out the letters of her name in a clear, feminine hand.

The man's drawer was featureless blank metal, burnished to a high gloss. He waited by the open door. Cleared his throat, a low rumble. Meant to hurry Clare along, no doubt.

Clare opened one eye, just a sliver. "There are nine and a quarter minutes left. Do *not* make unnecessary noise, sir."

The man – a sorceress's Shield, meant to guard against physical danger while the sorceress dealt with more arcane perils – remained silent, but his mouth firmed. He did not look amused.

*Mikal.* His colour was too dark and his features too aquiline to be properly Britannic. Perhaps Tinkerfolk? Or even from the Indus?

For the moment, he decided, the man's drawer could remain metal. He did not know enough about him. It would have to do. One thing was certain: if the sorceress had left one of her Shields with him, she was standing guard against some more than mundane threat outside. Which meant the problem he was about to address was most likely fiendishly complex, extraordinarily important, and worth more than a day or two of his busy brain's feverish working.

*Thank God.* The relief was palpable.

Clare shot to his feet and began packing.

# Chapter One

## A Pleasant Evening Ride

Emma Bannon, Sorceress Prime and servant to Britannia's current incarnation, mentally ran through every foul word that would never cross the lips of a lady. She timed them to the clockhorse's steady jogtrot, and her awareness dilated. The simmering cauldron of the streets was just as it always was; there was no breath of ill intent.

Of course, there had not been earlier, either, when she had been a quarter-hour too late to save the *other* unregistered mentath. It was only one of the many things about this situation seemingly designed to try her often considerable patience.

Mikal would be taking the rooftop road, running while she sat at ease in a hired carriage. It was the knowledge that while he did so he could forget some things that eased her conscience, though not completely.

Still, he was a Shield. He would not consent to share a carriage with her unless he was certain of her safety. And there was not room enough to manoeuvre in a two-person conveyance, should he require it.

She was heartily sick of hired carts. Her own carriages were *far* more comfortable, but this matter required discretion. Having it shouted to the heavens that she was alert to the pattern under these occurrences might not precisely frighten her opponents, but it would become more difficult to attack them from an unexpected quarter. Which was, she had to admit, her preferred method.

*Even a Prime can benefit from guile,* Llew had often remarked. And of course, she would think of him. She seemed constitutionally incapable of leaving well enough alone, and *that* irritated her as well.

Beside her, Clare dozed. He was a very thin man, with a long, mournful face; his gloves were darned but his waistcoat was of fine cloth, though it had seen better days. His eyes were blue, and they glittered feverishly under half-closed lids. An unregistered mentath would find it difficult to secure proper employment, and by the looks of his quarters, Clare had been suffering from boredom for several weeks, desperately seeking a series of experiments to exercise his active brain.

Mentath was like sorcerous talent. If not trained, and *used*, it turned on its bearer.

At least he had found time to shave, and he had brought two bags. One, no doubt, held linens. God alone knew what was in the second. Perhaps she should apply deduction to the problem, as if she did not have several others crowding her attention at the moment.

Chief among said problems were the murderers, who had so far eluded her efforts. Queen Victrix was young, and just recently freed from the confines of her domineering mother's sway. Her new Consort, Alberich, was a moderating influence – but he did not have enough power at Court just yet to be an effective shield for Britannia's incarnation.

The ruling spirit was old, and wise, but Her vessels . . . well, they were not indestructible.

*And that,* Emma told herself sternly, *is as far as we shall go with such a train of thought.* She found herself rubbing the sardonyx on her left middle finger, polishing it with her opposite thumb. Even through her thin gloves, the stone prickled hotly. Her posture did not change, but her awareness contracted. She felt for the source of the disturbance, flashing through and discarding a number of fine invisible threads.

*Blast and bother.* Other words, less polite, rose as well. Her pulse and respiration did not change, but she tasted a faint tang of adrenalin before sorcerous training clamped tight on such functions to free her from some of flesh's more . . . distracting . . . reactions.

"I say, whatever is the matter?" Archibald Clare's blue eyes were wide open now, and he looked interested. Almost, dare she think it, intrigued. It did nothing for his long, almost ugly features. His cloth was serviceable, though hardly elegant — one could infer that a mentath had other priorities than fashion, even if he had an eye for quality and the means to purchase such. But at least he was cleaner than he had been, and had arrived in the hansom in nine and a half minutes precisely. Now they were on Sarpesson Street, threading through amusement-seekers and those whom a little rain would not deter from their nightly appointments.

The disturbance peaked, and a not-quite-seen starburst of gunpowder igniting flashed through the ordered lattices of her consciousness.

The clockhorse screamed as his reins were jerked, and the hansom yawed alarmingly. Archibald Clare's hand dashed for the door handle, but Emma was already moving. Her arms closed around the tall, fragile man, and she shouted a Word that exploded the cab away from them both. Shards and splinters, driven outwards, peppered the street surface. The glass of the cab's tiny windows broke with a high, sweet tinkle, grinding into crystalline dust.

Shouts. Screams. Pounding footsteps. Emma struggled upright, shaking her skirts with numb hands. The horse had gone avast, rearing and plunging, throwing tiny metal slivers and dribs of oil as well as stray crackling sparks of sorcery, but the traces were tangled and it stood little chance of running loose. The driver was gone, and she snapped a quick glance at the overhanging rooftops before the unhealthy canine shapes resolved out of thinning rain, slinking low as gaslamp gleam painted their slick, heaving sides.

*Sootdogs. Oh, how unpleasant.* The one that had leapt on the hansom's roof had most likely taken the driver, and Emma cursed aloud now as it landed with a thump, its shining hide running with vapour.

"*Most* unusual!" Archibald Clare yelled. He had gained his feet as well, and his eyes were alight now. The mournfulness had vanished. He had also produced a queerly barrelled pistol, which would be of *no* use against the dog-shaped sorcerous things now gathering. "*Quite* diverting!"

The star sapphire on her right third finger warmed. A globe-shield shimmered into being, and to the roil of smouldering wood, gunpowder and fear was added another scent: the smoke-gloss of sorcery. One of the sootdogs leapt, crashing into the shield, and the shock sent Emma to her knees, holding grimly. Both her hands were outstretched now, and her tongue occupied in chanting.

Sarpesson Street was neither deserted nor crowded at this late hour. The people gathering to watch the outcome of a hansom crash pushed against those onlookers alert enough to note that something entirely different was occurring, and the resultant chaos was merely noise to be shunted aside as her concentration narrowed.

*Where is Mikal?*

She had no time to wonder further. The sootdogs hunched and wove closer, snarling. Their packed-cinder sides heaved and black tongues lolled between obsidian-chip teeth; they could strip a large adult male to bone in under a minute. There were the onlookers to think of as well, and Clare behind and to her right, laughing as he sighted down the odd little pistol's chunky nose. Only he was not pointing it at the dogs, thank God. He was aiming for the rooftop.

*You idiot.* The chant filled her mouth. She could spare no words to tell him not to fire, that Mikal was—

The lead dog crashed against the shield. Emma's body jerked

as the impact tore through her, but she held steady, the sapphire now a ringing blue flame. Her voice rose, a clear contralto, and she assayed the difficult rill of notes that would split her focus and make another Major Work possible.

*That* was part of what made a Prime – the ability to concentrate completely on multiple channellings of ætheric force. One's capacity could not be infinite, just like the charge of force carried and renewed every Tideturn.

But one did not need infinite capacity. *One needs only slightly more capacity than the problem at hand calls for,* as her third-form Sophological Studies professor had often intoned.

Mikal arrived.

His dark green coat fluttered as he landed in the midst of the dogs, a Shield's fury glimmering to Sight, bright spatters and spangles invisible to normal vision. The sorcery-made things cringed, snapping; his blades tore through their insubstantial hides. The charmsilver laid along the knives' flats, as well as the will to strike, would be of far more use than Mr Clare's pistol.

Which spoke, behind her, the ball tearing through the shield from a direction the protection wasn't meant to hold. The fabric of the shield collapsed, and Emma had just enough time to deflect the backlash, tearing a hole in the brick-faced fabric of the street and exploding the clockhorse into gobbets of metal and rags of flesh, before one of the dogs turned with stomach-churning speed and launched itself at her – and the man she had been charged to protect.

She shrieked another Word through the chant's descant, her hand snapping out again, fingers contorted in a gesture definitely *not* acceptable in polite company. The ray of ætheric force smashed through brick dust, destroying even more of the road's surface, and crunched into the sootdog.

Emma bolted to her feet, snapping her hand back, and the line of force followed as the dog crumpled, whining and shattering into fragments. She could not hold the forcewhip for very long, but if more of the dogs came—

The last one died under Mikal's flashing knives. He muttered something in his native tongue, whirled on his heel, and stalked toward his Prima. That normally meant the battle was finished.

Yet Emma's mind was not eased. She half turned, chant dying on her lips and her gaze roving, searching. Heard the mutter of the crowd, dangerously frightened. Sorcerous force pulsed and bled from her fingers, a fountain of crimson sparks popping against the rainy air. For a moment the mood of the crowd threatened to distract her, but she closed it away and concentrated, seeking the source of the disturbance.

Sorcerous traces glowed, faint and fading, as the man who had fired the initial shot – most likely to mark them for the dogs – fled. He had some sort of defence laid on him, meant to keep him from a sorcerer's notice.

*Perhaps from a sorcerer, but not from a Prime. Not from me, oh no. The dead see all.* Her Discipline was of the Black, and it was moments like these when she would be glad of its practicality – if she could spare the attention.

Time spun outwards, dilating, as she followed him over rooftops and down into a stinking alley, refuse piled high on each side, running with the taste of fear and blood in his mouth. Something had injured him.

*Mikal? But then why did he not kill the man—*

The world jolted underneath her, a stunning blow to her shoulder, a great spiked roil of pain through her chest. Mikal screamed, but she was breathless. Sorcerous force spilled free, uncontained, and other screams rose.

She could possibly injure someone.

Emma came back to herself, clutching at her shoulder. Hot blood welled between her fingers, and the green silk would be ruined. Not to mention her gloves.

At least they had shot her, and not the mentath.

*Oh, damn.* The pain crested again, became a giant animal with its teeth in her flesh.

Mikal caught her. His mouth moved soundlessly, and Emma

sought with desperate fury to contain the force thundering through her. Backlash could cause yet more damage, to the street and to onlookers, if she let it loose.

A Prime's uncontrolled force was nothing to be trifled with.

It was the traditional function of a Shield to handle such overflow, but if he had only wounded the fellow on the roof she could not trust that he was not part of—

"*Let it GO!*" Mikal roared, and the ætheric bonds between them flamed into painful life. She fought it, seeking to contain what she could, and her skull exploded with pain.

She knew no more.

# Chapter Two

## Dreadful Aesthetics

This part of Whitehall was full of heavy graceless furniture, all the more shocking for the quality of its materials. Clare was no great arbiter of taste – fashion was largely useless frippery, unless it fuelled the deductions he could make about his fellow man – but he thought Miss Bannon would wince internally at the clutter here. One did not have to follow fashion to have a decent set of aesthetics.

So much of aesthetics was merely pain avoidance for those with any sensibilities.

Lord Cedric Grayson, the current Chancellor of the Exchequer, let out a heavy sigh, lowering his wide bulk into an overstuffed leather chair, perhaps custom-commissioned for his size. He had always been large and ruddy, and good dinners at his clubs had long ago begun to blur his outlines. Clare lifted his glass goblet, carefully. He did not like sherry even at the best of times.

Still, this was . . . *intriguing*.

"So far, you are the only mentath we've recovered." Grayson's great grizzled head dropped a trifle, as if he did not believe it himself. "Miss Bannon is extraordinary."

"She is also severely wounded." Clare sniffed slightly. And *cheap* sherry, as well, when Cedric could afford far better. It was obscene. But then, Grayson had always been a false economiser, even at Yton. *Penny wise, pound foolish*, as Mrs Ginn would sniff. "So. Someone is killing mentaths."

"Yes. Mostly registered ones, so far." The Chancellor's wide horseface was pale, and his greying hair slightly mussed from the pressure of a wig. It was late for them to be in Chambers, but if someone was stalking and killing registered mentaths, the entire Cabinet would be having a royal fit.

In more ways than one. Her Majesty's mentaths, rigorously trained and schooled at public expense, were extraordinarily useful in many areas of the Empire. *Britannia rests on the backs of sorcery and genius*, the saying went, and it was largely true. From calculating interest and odds to deducing and anticipating economic fluctuations, not to mention the ability to see the patterns behind military tactics, a mentath's work was varied and quite useful.

A *registered* mentath could take his pick of clients and cases. One unstable enough to be unregistered was less lucky. "Since I am not one of that august company at this date, perhaps I was not meant to be assassinated." Clare set the glass down and steepled his fingers. "I am not altogether certain I was the target of *this* attempt, either."

"Dear God, man." Grayson was wise enough not to ask what Clare based his statement on. This, in Clare's opinion, raised him above average intelligence. Of course, Grayson had not achieved his present position by being *completely* thickheaded, even if he was at heart a penny-pinching little pettifogger. "You're not suggesting Miss Bannon was the target?"

Clare's fingers moved, tapping against each other restlessly, precisely once. "I am *uncertain*. The attack was sorcerous *and* physical." For a moment his faculties strained at the corners of his memory of events.

He supposed he was lucky. Another mentath, confronted with the illogic of sorcery, might retreat into a comforting abstract structure, a dream of rationality meant to keep irrationality out. Fortunately, Archibald Clare was willing to admit to illogic – if only so far as the oddities of a complex structure he did not understand *yet*.

A mentath could not, strictly speaking, go mad. But he could *retreat*, and that retreat would make him unstable, rob him of experiential data and send him careening down a path of irrelevance and increasing isolation. The end of that road was a comfortable room in a well-appointed madhouse, if one was registered – and the poorhouse if one was not.

"If war is declared on sorcerers too . . ." Grayson shook his heavy, sweating head. Clear drops stood out on his forehead, and he gazed at Clare's sherry glass. His bloodshot blue eyes blinked once, sadly. "Her Majesty is most vexed."

Another pair of extraordinarily interesting statements. "Perhaps you should start at the beginning. We have some time while Miss Bannon is treated."

"It is exceedingly difficult to keep Miss Bannon down for any length of time." Grayson rubbed at his face with one meaty paw. "At any moment she will come stalking through that door in high dudgeon. Suffice to say there have been four of Her Majesty's registered geniuses recently lost to foul play."

"Four? How interesting." Clare settled more deeply into his chair, steepling his fingers before his long nose.

Grayson took a bracing gulp of sherry. "Interesting? *Disturbing* is the proper word. Tomlinson was the first to come to Miss Bannon's attention, found dead without a scratch in his parlour. Apoplexy was suspected; the attending forensic sorcerer had all but declared it. Miss Bannon had been summoned, as Crown representative, since Tomlinson had some rather ticklish matters to do research for, cryptography or the like. Well, Miss Bannon arrived, took one look at the mess, and accused the original sorcerer of incompetence, saying he had smeared traces and she could not rule out a bit of nastiness instead of disease. There was a scene."

"Indeed," Clare murmured. He found that exceedingly easy to believe. Miss Bannon did not seem the manner of woman to forgive incompetence of any stripe.

"Then there was Masters the Elder, and Peter Smythe on Rockway – Smythe had just arrived from Indus, a rather ticklish situation resolved there, I'm told. The most current is Throckmorton. Masters was shot on Picksadowne, Smythe stabbed in an alley off Nightmarket, and Throckmorton, poor chap, burned to death at his Grace Street address."

"And . . .?" Clare controlled his impatience. Why did they give him information so *slowly*?

"Miss Bannon found the fire at Throckmorton's sorcerous in origin. She is convinced the cases are connected. After Masters's misfortune, at Miss Bannon's insistence sorcerers were hastily sent to stand guard over every registered mentath. Smythe's sorcerer has disappeared. Throckmorton's . . . well, you'll see."

This was proving more and more diverting. Clare's eyebrow rose. "I will?"

"He's in Bedlam. No doubt you will wish to examine him."

"No doubt." The obvious question, however, was one he was interested in Grayson answering. "Why was I brought here? There must be other unregistereds eager for the chance to work."

"Well, you have been quite useful in Her Majesty's service. There's no doubt of that." Grayson paused, delicately. "There *is* the little matter of your registration. Not that I blamed you for it, quite a rum deal, that. Bring this matter to a satisfactory close, and . . . who can say?"

Ah. There was the sweet in the poison. Clare considered this. "I gather Miss Bannon is just as insubordinate and intransigent as myself. And just as expendable in this current situation." He did not think Miss Bannon would be *expendable*, precisely.

But he did wish to see Cedric's reaction.

Grayson actually had the grace to flush. And cough. He kept glancing at Clare's sherry as if he longed to take a draught himself.

*I thought he was more enamoured of port. Perhaps his tastes have changed.* Clare shelved the idea, warmed to his theme. "Furthermore, the *registered* mentaths have been whisked to safety or are presumably at great risk, so time is of the essence and the need desperate – otherwise I would *still* be rotting at home, given the nature of my . . . mistakes. I further gather there have been corresponding deaths among those, like myself, so unfortunate as to be *unregistered* for one reason or another."

Grayson's flush deepened. Clare admitted he was enjoying himself. No, that was not quite correct. He was enjoying himself *immensely*. "How many?" he enquired.

"Well. That is, ahem." Grayson cleared his throat. "Let me be frank, Archibald."

*Now the game truly begins.* Clare brought all his faculties to bear, his concentration narrowing. "Please do be, Cedric."

"You are the only remaining unregistered mentath-class genius remaining alive in Londinium. The others . . . their bodies were savaged. Certain parts are . . . missing."

Archibald's fingers tightened, pressing against each other. "Ah." *Most interesting indeed.*

# *Chapter Three*

## *Theory and Practice*

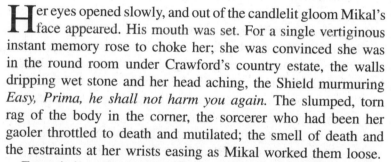

H er eyes opened slowly, and out of the candlelit gloom Mikal's face appeared. His mouth was set. For a single vertiginous instant memory rose to choke her; she was convinced she was in the round room under Crawford's country estate, the walls dripping wet stone and her head aching, the Shield murmuring *Easy, Prima, he shall not harm you again.* The slumped, torn rag of the body in the corner, the sorcerer who had been her gaoler throttled to death and mutilated; the smell of death and the restraints at her wrists easing as Mikal worked them loose.

Emma's heart leapt into her throat and commenced pounding with most unbecoming intensity.

She returned to the present with a violent start, disarranging the damp handkerchief on her forehead; a draught of violet and lavender scent unsettled her stomach even further. Mikal's hands descended on her shoulders; he pushed her back on to the divan. "Lie still." It was amazing, how he could speak through tight-clenched teeth. "The mentath is with Lord Grayson, he is safe enough. *You*, on the other hand, took a lead ball to the shoulder."

It mattered little. If she was still alive and Mikal was alive *and* conscious, her shoulder was a small problem already solved. Furthermore, she was *not* trapped in the small room that featured in her nightmares.

The relief was, as usual, indescribable. A mere month ago she had emerged from that stone-walled room, the torn and rotting bodies of her former Shields strewn in the hall like so much rubbish, and had not wept. Even after her nightmares, she did not.

The tears would not come. And *that*, she reminded herself, was what truly made her Prime. The capacity to split her focus was only a symptom.

"Was that what it was?" She peeled the handkerchief from her forehead. It was one of her own, and doused with *vitae*. That accounted for the violet-lavender. Her stomach twisted again.

"I drained the overflow. And attended to your wound." His eyes gleamed in the dimness. "I would counsel you not to move too quickly. You will likely ignore me."

She crushed the scrap of linen and lace in her palm. Her dress jacket was undone, her camisole sticky with sweat and blood; her loosely laced corset was still abominably tight, and the tingle of a limited healing-sorcery itched in her shoulder. This was one of the dusty, forgotten rooms of Whitehall, full of whispers it did not do to listen overmuch to. The furniture was exceedingly awful, though modern, and she immediately guessed this was part of Grayson's offices. The dimness was a balm to her sensitised eyes.

"I cannot protect you," Mikal continued. Under his colouring, he was remarkably pale. None of the blood or gunpowder had tainted his clothes, but a pall of almost visible smoke cloaked him. Or perhaps it was his anger. "You would do better to cast me off."

*Not this argument again.* "If you were not in a Prime's service, you would be executed in less than a day. In case you have forgotten that small detail, Mikal."

A half-shrug, his shoulder lifting and dropping. "You do not trust me."

She could hardly argue with the truth. *If you throttled one sorcerer you swore to protect, another would be a small matter, would it not?* "I have little reason to distrust you." The lie tasted of brass, and she suddenly longed for a glass of decent wine and an exceedingly sensational and frivolous novel, read in the comfort of her own bed.

Mikal grimaced slightly. He settled back on the stool placed precisely by the divan, glanced at the door. A Shield's awareness, marking the exit though he had never forgotten it. "I murdered my last sorcerer with my bare hands, Prima. You are not stupid enough to forget."

*Hence, you must be lying,. Emma, and I know it.* But, as always, it was left unsaid.

So she chose truth. "I might have murdered him myself, had you not." She held out the handkerchief. "Here. *Vitae* unsettles me a little, I fear"

"There was no rum." A slight, pained smile. He took the linen, calloused but sensitive fingers brushing hers.

An unwilling smile touched her lips as well. "We make do with what we have. Now let us have no more of this *cast off* business. We have other matters to attend to."

His chin set. When he scowled, or practised his stubborn look, he was almost ugly. He did not have a pretty face.

Then why did his expression make her heart leap so indiscreetly?

Emma pushed herself gingerly up, tilted her chin down to examine her shoulder. Under the shredded green silk and the torn and stained bit of her camisole showing, pale unmarked skin moved. The tingle-itch of healing had settled more deeply, flesh and bone protesting as it was forced to knit. *Well. That was instructive.*

"I am sorry. I took the ones on the east side of the street; then there were the dogs. That particular threat was the most critical."

She nodded. Her hair had come loose, her bonnet was missing, and the silk was ruined. Now would come her admission of mistrust, and his . . . possible hurt. Or did he care so much what she thought?

Why *she* cared about a Shield's tender pride was beyond her. The Shields were to protect a Prime from physical threats and bleed off backlash, nothing more.

*Come now. In theory, yes. In practice, no. All we care about is practice, correct? We have not achieved our position by being impractical. And yes, that is a royal "we", isn't it, Emma?*

One day, that nasty little voice in her head might swallow its tongue and poison itself. Until it did, however, she was forced to endure its infuriating habit of being correct, as well as its habit of being singularly unhelpful.

She eased her legs off the divan, skirts bunching and sliding. A moment's work had them assembled correctly. She'd bled down the front of her dress, splashes and streaks caught in the material, her hems torn and singed. The edges of her petticoats draggled, also singed. Her boots were spattered with mud and spots of blood, but still serviceable.

Anger was pointless. Anger over some stained cloth was doubly so. She swallowed it with an effort, turned her attention to other things. "The man who fired the initial shot – most probably to mark us – had a protection. I lost him in an alley, but we shall find the trail after we visit Bedlam."

"The mentath seemed to have some ideas. No doubt he will have more after visiting Grayson."

*Always assuming we can believe a single word spilling from the Lord Chancellor's forked tongue.* Her dislike of the Chancellor was unreasoning; he was a servant of Britannia just as she was.

Still, she did not have to enjoy his company. After all, Crawford had been a servant too. A treacherous one, but a servant nonetheless.

Mikal was indirectly reminding her of the mentath's capacity as a resource, with a Shield's infinite tact. She nodded, patting at her hair. A few quick movements, pins sliding in, and she had the mess reasonably under control. *Bloody hell. I liked that bonnet, too.* "I am sending Grayson an itemised bill for *every* dress ruined in this affair." She gained her feet in a lunge, swayed, and sat back down on the divan. Hard.

Mikal's eyes glinted, yellowish in the dimness. He did not have to say *I told you so.* He merely steadied her, carefully keeping the *vitae*-soaked handkerchief away. "You look lovely."

Heat rose on the surface of her throat, stained her cheeks. "You prefer the dishevelled, then?"

"Better dishevelled than dead, Prima. If you are careful, I believe you may stand now."

He was correct once more, damn him. As usual. Her legs trembled, but they held her. Mikal rose too, hovering, his hand near her elbow.

"I shall manage quite well, thank you." Emma exhaled sharply, frustration copper-bright to Sight cloaking her before she pushed it down and away. It was merely another weakness training would overcome. "Let us collect the mentath, then. I am loath to lose him now."

"Emma." Mikal caught her arm. "Did you think I had deliberately left the one who shot you?"

His mouth shaping her Christian name was a small victory, one she decided not to celebrate even internally. *The thought crossed my mind, Mikal.* "I was too busy to think such things. Come, leave that rag and let us find our mentath."

He did not turn loose of her. Instead, he held her arm – perhaps to steady her, perhaps for some other reason. Emma pulled against his fingers, silk slipping on her bruised arm.

"You need another Shield. *More* Shields." Said calmly, matter-of-fact. "A half-dozen at least. A full complement would be better."

*I had four, Mikal. They died protecting me.* "I *need* you to burn that *vitae*-infested rag and accompany me to wherever Grayson is filling that mentath's head with useless supposition," she snapped. "If you are *unhappy* with my service, Shield, then by all means remove yourself from my *aegis* and present yourself to the Collegia for extermination."

He turned pale. Such a thing did not seem possible, given his colouring. "I would that you had at least a single Shield you could trust, instead of losing precious time to backlash sickness because you will not let me perform my function."

Oddly, it stung. Perhaps because he was correct. Again. "We have no time for this argument." The divan groaned slightly; she could have sliced ice with the words. Emma took a firmer hold on her temper. It was her besetting sin, that temper. "When this mystery is solved, we shall approach the question of whether *I decide* to take the responsibility of another Shield or three, or twenty, *in addition* to my current intransigent Indus princeling. We will make a fine meal for our enemies, yours no less than mine, should we continue in this manner. Now *shut up* and rid me of that handkerchief, Mikal. I shall find Lord Grayson and Mr Clare, and I expect you to accompany me."

She tore her arm from his grasp, set out for the door. Her skirts rustled oddly, and the floor was moving most strangely beneath her boots.

The amber *prie-dieu*, dangling at her breastbone from a silver chain, turned into a spot of warmth. There was enough force stored in it for two strong minor Works, a multiplicity of Words, or merely to keep her upright until dawn's Tideturn renewed the world's sorcerous energies. Her sardonyx was drained, and should there be more unpleasantness in store tonight . . . well.

It did not matter. The best thing was to go from one task to the next, as quickly and thoroughly as possible.

There was a *fsssh!* and a pop behind her as Mikal called flame into being. The skin between her shoulder blades roughened instinctively. He was armed, and—

It was ridiculous. If he wished her death, he had many opportunities on a daily basis to gratify that urge. She was stupid to waste time and energy fretting about it.

*Unless that is part of the plan, Emma. How long would* you

*wait, for a vengeance? And you cannot credit any reason he might give you for how he became your Shield.*

Yet had Mikal not betrayed his sworn oath to the sorcerer who had almost killed her, she would be dead, and all this academic.

She twisted the crystal doorknob and stepped into the hall. The dead clustered here, diaphanous grey scarves of ill intent or mere confusion, soaking into the walls. Lamplight – Whitehall was now fitted with gas – ran wetly over every surface, and she heard voices not too far away. One, no doubt, was the mentath. Who had dealt with a sorcerous attack with far more presence of mind than she would ever have expected from a logic machine trapped in ailing flesh.

"Emma." Mikal, from the darkened room behind her. "I wish you could trust me."

She did not dignify it with a response, sweeping away. *Oh, Mikal. So do I.*

# Chapter Four

## In One Fashion or Another

The door was swept unceremoniously open, and Grayson visibly flinched. Clare was gratified to find his nerves were still steady. Besides, he had heard the determined tap of female footsteps, dainty little bootheels crackling with authority, and deduced Miss Bannon was in a fine mood.

Her sandalwood curls were caught up and repinned, but she was hatless and her dress was sadly the worse for wear. Smoke and fury hung on her in almost visible veils, and she was dead pale. Her dark eyes burned rather like coals, and Clare had no doubt that any obstacle in her way had been toppled, uprooted or simply crushed.

Green silk flopped uneasily at the shoulder, a scrap of under-clothing tantalisingly visible, but there was no sign of a wound. Just pale, unmarked skin, and the amber cabochon glowing in a most peculiar manner.

Grayson gained his feet in a walrus lunge. He had turned an alarming shade of floury yeastiness, but most people did when confronted with an angry sorcerer. "Miss Bannon. *Very* glad to see you on your feet, indeed! I was just bringing Clare here—"

She gave him a single cutting glance, and short shrift. "Filling his head with nonsense, no doubt. We are dealing with conspiracy of the blackest hue, Lord Grayson, and I am afraid I may tarry no longer. Mr Clare, are you disposed to linger, or would you accompany me? Whitehall should be relatively safe, but I confess your talents may be of some use in the hunt before me."

Clare was only too glad to leave the mediocre sherry. He set it down, untasted. "I would be most honoured to accompany you, Miss Bannon. Lord Grayson has informed me of the deaths of several mentaths and the unfortunate circumstances surrounding Mr Throckmorton's erstwhile guard. I gather we are bound for Bedlam?"

"In one fashion or another." But a corner of her lips twitched. "You do your profession justice, Mr Clare. I trust you were not injured?"

"Not at all, thanks to your efforts." Clare recovered his hat, glanced at his bags. "Will I be needing linens, Miss Bannon, or may I leave them as superfluous weight?"

Now she was certainly amused, a steely smile instead of a single lip-twitch, at odds with her childlike face. With that spark in her dark eyes, Miss Bannon would be counted attractive, if not downright striking. "I believe linens may be procured with little difficulty anywhere in the Empire we are likely to arrive, Mr Clare. You may have those sent to my house in Mayefair; I believe they shall arrive promptly."

"Very well. Cedric, I do trust you'll send these along for me? My very favourite waistcoat is in that bag. We shall return when we've sorted out this mess, or when we require some aid. Good to see you, old boy." Clare offered his hand, and noted with some mild amusement that Cedric's palm was sweating.

He didn't blame the man.

Mentaths were not overtly feared the way sorcerers were. Dispassionate logic was easier to swallow than sorcery's flagrant violations of what the general populace took to be *normal*. Logic was easily hidden, and most mentaths were discreet by nature. There were exceptions, of course, but none of them as notable as the least of sorcery's odd children.

"God and Her Majesty be with you," Cedric managed. "Miss Bannon, are you quite certain you do not—"

"I require nothing else at the moment, sir. Thank you, God and Her Majesty." She turned on one dainty heel and strode away, ragged skirts flapping. Clare arranged his features in something resembling composure, fetched the small black bag containing his working notables, and hurried out of the door.

His legs were much longer, but Miss Bannon had a surprisingly energetic stride. He arrived at her side halfway down the corridor. "I know better than to take Lord Grayson's suppositions as anything but, Miss Bannon."

Miss Bannon's chin was set. She seemed none the worse for wear, despite her ruined clothing. "You were at school with him, were you not?"

*Was that a deduction?* He decided not to ask. "At Yton."

"Was he an insufferable, blind-headed prig then, too?"

Clare strangled a laugh by sheer force of will. *Quite diverting.* He made a *tsk-tsk* sound, settling into her speed. The dusky hall would take them to the Gallery; she perhaps meant them to come out through the Bell Gate and from there to find another hansom. "Impolitic, Miss Bannon."

"I do not play *politics*, Mr Clare."

*I think you are a deadly player when you lower yourself to do so, miss.* "Politics play, even if *you* do not. If you have no care for your own career, think of mine. Grayson dangled the renewal of my registration before me. Why, do you suppose, did he do so?"

"He does not expect you to live long enough to claim such a prize." Her tone suggested she found the idea insulting and likely all at once. "How did you lose your registration, if I may ask?"

For a moment, irrationality threatened to blind him. "I killed a man," he said, evenly enough. "Unfortunately, it was the *wrong* man. A mentath cannot afford to do such a thing." *Even if the beast needed killing.*

*Even if I do not regret it.*

"Hm." Her pace did not slacken, but her heels did not jab the wooden floor with such hurtful little crackles. "In that, Mr Clare, mentaths and sorcerers are akin. You kill one tiny little Peer of the Realm, and suddenly your career is gone. It is a great relief to me that I have no career to lose."

"Indeed? Then why are you—" The question was ridiculous, but he wished to gauge her response. When she slanted him a very amused, dark-eyed glance, he nodded internally. "Ah. I see. You are as expendable as I have become."

Her reply gave him much to think on. "In the service of Britannia, Mr Clare, *all* are expendable. Come."

# Chapter Five

## An Insoluble Puzzle

"I cannot understand why it is often so difficult to find a hansom," she muttered, as she reclaimed her hand from Mikal's.

"I have applied logic to the question." Clare's tone was thoughtful. He shook his top hat, removed a speck of dust from the brim, and replaced it on his head with a decided motion. "And, to be honest, I have never arrived at a satisfactory answer."

The driver, his own battered stuff hat set at a rakish angle and his rotund body wrapped against the chill, cracked his whip over the heaving, coppery back of his clockwork horse, and hooves clattered away down the dark street. Tiny sparks of stray sorcery winked out in their wake. Gasflame flickered, wan light hardly licking the surface of the cobblestones, not daring to penetrate the crevices between.

"At least we were not attacked during this short voyage," Clare continued. "I must confess I am relieved."

*Are you? For I am not.* An enemy resourceful and practised, not to mention financed well enough to send sootdogs and hired thugs, was likely to have an idea of the finitude of even a Prime's power. The Tideturn of dawn was distressingly far away, and even that flood of sorcerous energy would not stave off the effects of fatigue and hunger.

*Worry about such an event when it becomes critical, Emma. Before then, simply do what must be done.* She straightened her back. For Bethlehem Hospital crouched before them, a long pile of brick and stone shimmering with misery.

The very bricks of Bedlam were warped, but had nevertheless been carried from the old site in Bishop's Gate two decades ago with the Regent's false economy. Sorcerers had warned against reusing the building materials, but it had done little good.

The sprawling monstrosity, its cupola leering at the sky and running with golden charter-charms, took up a considerable space – physical as well as psychic layers accreted for a good two hundred years since the insane had begun to be "treated" rather than merely confined or executed. In the near distance, the smoke of the Black Wark rose, the kernel of Southwark with its cinderfall and pall of incessant gloomy smoke.

Emma swallowed drily, and Mikal's hand closed over her shoulder. She stepped away. Any Shield would not like a sorcerer setting foot in this place.

Of course, Mikal was not *any* Shield, any more than she was *any* sorceress. There was a time when a sorceress of her Discipline would have been executed as soon as certain proclivities and talents began to show, whether she was Prime or merely witch. A man whose Discipline lay in the Black, rather than the White or Grey, had less to fear.

Men always had less to fear.

Emma raised her chin. Gaslamp glow picked out screaming faces swirling in the brick wall, and for a moment it was difficult to separate the audible howls from the silent ones. It sounded a merry night in Bedlam, cries and screams from the depths of the building muffled by stone, a seashell roar of discontent. The ætheric protections set on the place resounded, a discordance of smashed violins and overstressed stones.

Her *prie-dieu* warmed further against her chest. It would have to be enough.

She set off for the postern, her heels clicking against cobbles.

Her skirt was ragged, and its hem was torn. She must look a sight. Irritation flashed through her and away.

Clare fell into step beside her. "Why is a sorcerer in Bedlam, may I ask? Was there no other sanatorium?"

Her jaw was set so tightly she almost had difficulty replying. "Not with a fully drawn Greater Circle free, no. Llewellyn is no witch or Adept. He is – *was* Prime; even mad or broken he is not likely to be amenable to containment."

"Ah. *Was* Prime?"

*Will I have to teach him the classes of sorcerer?* "Sanity is a prerequisite for carrying the title. However disputable one considers the term when applied to a sorcerer." *And he is a peer; he cannot be thrown in a common prison.* For a moment her skin chilled, and Mikal was close enough that she could feel the heat from him. She knew without looking that his mouth would be set tight in disapproval. So was her own.

"I see." Clare absorbed this. "Miss Bannon?"

*For the love of Heaven, will you not be quiet?* "Yes, Mr Clare?"

"Is it advisable to enter through the side door?"

For a man who functioned by logic and deduction, he certainly seemed thick. "The main entrance is closed and locked at dusk. I do not relish the idea of wasting time waiting for the head warden to be called from his *divertissements*. Also, the more unremarked we can be, the better."

"I hardly think we will pass unremarked."

A sharp retort died on Emma's tongue. Perhaps he was simply making conversation, seeking to set her at her ease. Or he wished to find out if she was as empty-headed, as most men, even fleshly logic engines, considered women to be. "Llewellyn is being held near this door."

"I see."

*Do you? I fear you do not.* The outside guard was half-asleep, propped in the doorway at the top of a short flight of uneven stairs. Heavily bearded and reeking of gin, he blinked as the trio approached, and by the time Emma had set foot on the first step, bracing herself, his eyes had widened to the size of poached eggs and he had straightened, pulling at the high-collared broadcloth of his uniform coat. "Visitin' hours is one to three—"

Mikal was suddenly *there*, shoving him against the wall and making a swift movement. The *ulp* the man made was lost in the sound of the double blow to chin and paunch. Mikal's fingers flicked, subtracting the ring of heavy iron keys from the broad leather belt. There was a gleam of sharp metal, and the sliced belt thudded to the top step. The man slumped; Mikal lowered him fairly gently.

Clare's eyebrows nested in his hairline. "Is this really necessary?"

Paused on the second step, Emma strangled a flare of impatience. *You are an irritant, mentath.* "If Mikal is doing it, yes."

Mikal already had the correct key selected and inserted into the postern door. "The man reeks of gin," he remarked. "He was disposed to be troublesome. Petty authority." His lip curled, disdain clearly visible in the set of his shoulders as well. "He will not remember us."

"Let us hope as much." Clare did not sound convinced.

The door opened with a small groan; Mikal glanced inside. He nodded, once, and Emma continued up the stairs.

They plunged into Bedlam's grey confusion. Gaslamps hissed down the long hall, and she braced herself. For a moment the walls rippled, the entire hungry, semi-sentient pile of stone resonating as it took notice of what she was.

*The Endor! The Endor is here!* A mouthless, windless whisper, unheard by living ears, brushed against the surfaces of her skin and clothing. Grey smokelike figures crowded close, their sighs rising in volume as they sensed she could hear them. Ghostly fingers brushed her, slipping over the smooth, hard shell of a Prime's will; Mikal half turned and caught her arm. At the Shield's touch, the entire hallway clicked back into place with a sub-audible thump.

Another of a Shield's functions – an anchor. The more ætheric force a sorcerer could carry, the more danger of being lost on the currents the rest of humanity could not feel.

"Miss Bannon?" Clare, with a faint touch of concern. "You've gone quite white."

"Quite well," she murmured. Found her usual crisp tone again. "I am quite well, thank you. Mikal? Llewellyn is down the hall to the right. Fifth door, I believe."

"He will not be happy to see us," Mikal observed, but his grip was bruising-hard.

No, he did not like his Prima setting foot in this place. She was a fool to mistrust him. A traitorous warmth bloomed in her belly, was sternly shelved. And yet, how long before he decided she was as expendable as Crawford had evidently been?

*Now is not the time for that thought.* "We are not visiting him for tea." She followed his pressure on her arm. Surely it was not weakness to feel grateful. Entering Bedlam by herself would be . . . uncomfortable. "All the same, Mikal . . ." *Be prepared, for I am exhausted. And more than that, Llewellyn would like nothing better than to injure us both.*

"Say no more." He slanted her a deadly unamused glance, his mouth a thin straight line. Shortened his stride to match hers, while the mentath trailed in their wake. The corridor was stone-floored and reeked of pain and filth. At least it was swept, and the barred iron doors to either side merely vibrated uneasily. The place had quieted, at least physically, only faint echoes of faraway moans piercing the hush.

Other senses were not nearly so easily lulled. She folded her free hand over Mikal's, ignoring his second, slightly startled glance. The added contact helped shunt aside the screaming rush of whispered agony roaring through the hall, lifting strands of her hair on an unphysical breeze.

"Something's amiss." She was barely aware of speaking. "Badly amiss."

Mikal slowed, tense and alert. Their footsteps echoed. "I suppose it would do no good to ask you to—"

*Retreat? In the service of the Queen? I hardly think so.* "No good at all, my Shield."

"Miss Bannon?" Clare had caught up, and offered his arm on her other side. "May I be of assistance?"

It was a curious gesture, but one she appreciated. She loosed her grip on Mikal's hand and took Clare's arm as well. After all, she was a lady now. No matter how often she had the urge to repeat blue words. "Thank you, Mr Clare. This place is . . . distressing, to any sorcerer."

The hallway swayed under her feet, but Mikal's arm was steady, and so was Clare's. The misery of this place was dark wine against her palate, stroking against her will with a cat's-tongue rasp.

"Fifth door." Mikal's tone suggested he was extraordinarily alert. His arm was tense, muscle standing out under her fingers, and he slowed. "Mentath. The key is on a hook, just there."

"Ah. Yes." The mentath's long face pinched together, a change from its usual bright interest. Faint distaste swirled from him, a powdery blue to Sight, and Emma's *prie-dieu* sparked. It was taking more force than she liked to insulate herself from the dead crowding these halls, and the despair locked in the fabric of the building was troubling as well.

If Llewellyn Gwynnfud, Lord Sellwyth, had any sanity remaining, this place might well rob him of it.

The door was locked and barred, rivulets of golden charm and charter symbols sliding down its scarred iron surface. Clare peered through the observation slit, studiously avoiding touching it. He blinked, absorbing whatever vista the slit presented for a long moment. "Miss Bannon? Is it safe to unlock the door?"

"The charm and charter won't harm you, Mr Clare." Her voice came from very far away, but it carried all its usual briskness. *Thank Heaven for that.* "Its only function is to *contain*."

"Very well, then." He settled back on his heels and inserted the clumsy key into the lock. He even lifted the iron bar out of its brackets and set it aside, handling the bulk with startling ease for such a lean man. "I should warn you, it appears the patient is awake and expecting us."

"Well, good." Asperity tinted her tone. "I would hate to have to disturb a gentleman's slumber. Or question his corpse."

The air quivered as Clare gingerly folded his hand around the door handle; he pulled and it slid open with little trouble, well oiled. The charter symbols runnelled uneasily, but Mikal exhaled very softly and they calmed.

Llewellyn was indeed awake.

The stone cube was comfortless, and chill. A straw pallet was tossed in one corner, but it would do no good to a man trapped inside ætheric containment in the middle of the floor. Charm and charter wandered golden over the walls, and Emma blinked. *Most odd. Most exceedingly odd – who closed him in here? Old work, very old.*

The sorcerer sat in the exact centre of the Circle, its blue lines shifting over stone flagstones. He was shockingly dirty, as if he had rubbed filth into his own garments – the remains of an opera suit, draggled with dirt and torn in interesting places. His face was streaked with grime, and it was difficult to ascertain his features for a moment. They smeared like ink on wet paper, but perhaps it was only her vision blurring with fatigue.

Mikal's arm tightened. She knew what he was thinking – *Where are his Shields?*

She had seen no profit in informing him that the Shields had been found disembowelled. Which was, if one thought about it, the only way to cause enough damage to keep a Shield truly incapable of combat for long enough to kill him.

"Good evening, Llewellyn." *I sound quite calm. Very well, that.*

For he needed precious little of an opening to rob her of her composure.

His head lifted, strings of decaying blond hair twining with a life of their own, mixing with a grey Gwynnfud would have been infuriated with. With no charm to keep the colour its usual parchment pale, and none of the enhancements he favoured, he looked much less prepossessing than usual.

His long fingers spasmed, twisting together, and a glimmer of charm appeared on them. She tensed, and so did the Circle, its blue lines cavorting in intricate knots. It ran over the floor in wet streaks, and something about it was not as it should be, either.

"Emma." The word echoed through shifting veils of sorcerous interference. He *sounded* sane, at least. Terribly, calmly sane. Which was perhaps the worst that could befall them.

For while Emma Bannon was certain she could handle a sorcerer gripped in madness, a sane and mocking Llewellyn was another matter entirely.

Her grip on Mikal's arm loosened. If there was an event here, he had to be free to fight. Her chin lifted as she examined the Circle's work, storing away the odd peculiarities of personality visible in the strands. A sorcerer's memory was trained just as ruthlessly as her ability; in some cases, even more. And this was work she had not seen before. "Rather bad accommodations, I'm afraid. Are you well?"

His laugh came from the bottom of a dark well. Veils of sorcery shifted, keeping a Prime's force contained. His will, even broken or twisted, would fight any containment laid upon it; a Prime did not take a bridle well, if at all. Hence the hardening of the air, alive with ætheric force, blurring his outlines as if he sat behind a screen.

"I'm locked in a cell in Bedlam, Emma. Obviously I am not *well*." His dark eyes glimmered through the strings of hair. "And I have not even a change of linen. Barbarians."

*Your household should have bribed someone to bring such things to you.* Her wariness increased, if that were possible. "If you will waste my time, Lord Sellwyth, I shall go elsewhere."

It was a gamble, of course. It could prick his pride, and he might well refuse to say anything now. It could also trigger whatever unpleasantness was waiting around the corner, making the charm and charter react oddly. She was passing familiar with most native-Britannium sorcerers' work; sorcery always carried the stamp of its channel. But this was . . . odd.

And, as she had suspected, the thing Llewellyn feared most was the loss of his audience. "I would not want to waste *your* time, dear Bannon." He made the words a sing-song, rolling his head on his shoulders. Strings of hair crawled against each other and the cloth of his coat with bloated little whispers as sorcery crackled. "Especially when you've brought a snake-charmer and a lapdog with you."

Fortunately, Clare had enough presence of mind to hold his peace. Mikal almost twitched, restlessly, and Llewellyn's smile widened. "How long will it be before he strangles you, just like he did Crawford? And you, Emma. Queen and Country, how *boring*. Wouldn't you like some *real* power?"

*How very unlike you to be so direct.* Emma's concentration narrowed. "Throckmorton, Llewellyn. Your charge. You undertook to guard him at Britannia's request; he is dead, your Shields are dead, and you are . . . here. Whatever could have happened?" Precise, drily astonished, for all the world like a professor mocking a slightly dim student. Llewellyn hated that tone, especially when it was delivered by a woman.

His face contorted for a bare moment. The sorcerous interference intensified, streaks of shimmering painting the outside of a perfect, invisible globe as a Prime's will reflexively sought to break its cage. "Mentath," he whispered. "*That's* a mentath; some fool's let you get your hands on one. *Stupid—*"

*Get my hands on—* But the physical structure of Bedlam tolled once, a giant bell shivering as a hammerstroke echoed through the lattices of probability, and something hit her from the side, driving her down.

# Chapter Six

## Reflexes and Temper

It was a most interesting conversation, layers of inference and deduction ticking below the conscious surface of Clare's faculties, and he wondered briefly just when the sorcerer trapped in the Circle had ceased to be Miss Bannon's lover. Well, at least they had most certainly been intimate at one time, and sorcery's children had far different standards than the common crowd, but still, quite interesting. And from the sound of it, Miss Bannon had broken the attachment, yet there was no lingering of regret in her.

Clare's wonderings were interrupted by an odd scent. *Brimstone, perhaps?* And a faint low scraping, like a match swept across a strikeplate. The space inside the circle rippled, oddly, becoming no more than a painted screen for a bare moment.

He leapt, knocking Miss Bannon down. A moment of excruciating heat kissed the back of his coat. Then he was rolling, a confusion of shadows flickering as someone hurtled over him, deadly silent with flashing blades. Stink of wet, smoking wool, Miss Bannon struggling to her feet, the amber suddenly a glowing yellow star in the dimness as she snapped two words. Her hands flung themselves out, white birds, slim fingers fluttering. There was a crack, and a sudden showering smell of wet salt.

"Mikal?" Bannon, breathless in the sudden quiet.

"Here." The single word was so grim Clare tensed.

"The mentath—"

"Well enough." Clare finished shrugging out of his jacket. The wool was smoking, a dull, unpleasant fume. "Well. *That* was entertaining."

"Quick reflexes." The other man bent down, offering his hand. "For one of your kind."

*He means it as a compliment.* "And your own reflexes?"

The sorceress murmered. Thin threads of smoke traced up from her dress. The yellow-eyed man glanced at her. "Not quick enough, apparently. No—" He caught Clare's shoulder. "Do not approach her just now."

The sorceress's jaw worked, and for a moment Clare had the uneasy feeling of lightning about to strike – a raising of fine hairs on his arms and neck, his glands responding to some feral current.

He decided she was indeed not to be approached. "That must have been heard. We shall have guards here in a moment, and explanations to be made."

For there was a large smoking hole in the wall, odd twisted writing scored around its edges. Bedlam had sorcerous protections, but this did not seem to be one of them responding to Miss Bannon. Of course, Clare admitted, he could not be certain. But Miss Bannon would have no doubt alerted him, would she not?

The Shield's next words placed all doubt aside.

"A cunning trap, and well laid. We shall indeed be going." Mikal's lean face set itself, lines bracketing his mouth. "But my Prima has a temper, mentath. Wait just a moment."

The sorceress, indeed, was trembling. She stared at the hole in the wall to the next cell's blackness, her lips now moving soundlessly. The writing scored around the edges of the hole burned with sullen foxfire.

Clare cast a nervous glance at the steel-framed door. Grayson had indeed had worthless suppositions, but not as useless as Miss Bannon had supposed. One or two of them were quite reasonable, given the Chancellor's knowledge of events. And the encircled sorcerer's words had been most peculiar indeed.

But *this* was something altogether different. And troubling. "Does Miss Bannon have enemies?"

Mikal's profile vaguely reminded Clare of a classical statue. The Shield leaned forward, weight on the balls of his feet and his long coat oddly pristine. His attention was focused on the woman, whose trembling had spread into the air around her. Rather like the heat haze above a fire, air almost solid and shimmering as something invisible stroked it.

"She is *Prime*," the Shield said, quietly, as if that should be explanation enough. "And she does not suffer fools gladly."

"Well, I could see that." Clare stamped on his jacket once or twice more, to make certain it would not combust, and picked it up. Shook it out, shrugged into it. His hat had flown away; he found it in the ruins of the straw pallet. He glanced through the hole in the wall as he did so, but the uncertain light permitted no disclosing of its secrets. It was an oubliette; it might as well have been a painted-black circle. "Miss Bannon? Miss Bannon. If you please, we should be going now."

The yellow-eyed man inhaled sharply, but when Clare glanced up, he saw the sorceress had regained her composure. She clutched at her shoulder as if it had been re-injured, and red sparks revolved in her dilated pupils for a moment before winking out.

"You're quite right." Curiously husky. "My thanks, Mr Clare. Mikal, let us be gone from here at once."

"The sorcerer—" Clare did not relish the thought of giving her the news, but it had to be said.

For nothing remained of Llewellyn Gwynnfud but a rag of flesh and charred, twisting bone splinters, still trapped inside the circle of blue flame and heavy, rippling shifting.

"Appears dead, of course." She inhaled sharply and sagged,

and the yellow-eyed man apparently judged her temper safe enough, for he stepped forward and took her arm again. As soon as he did, Bannon swayed further, the tension leaving her. "And good riddance. Though I suspect he did not think they would deal with him in quite this manner."

*They?* "Which manner would that be?" Clare enquired, as Mikal ushered the sorceress to the door and glanced out into the hall.

"As bait." Miss Bannon's tone was passing grim. "Now they know *I* am at their heels, and in no uncertain fashion. Mikal?"

He all but dragged her along. "I hear footsteps. Out the same way we entered, and step lightly."

Miss Bannon, however, swayed drunkenly, her chestnut hair slipping free of pins. "I . . . I cannot . . ."

Her eyes rolled up, their whites glaring, and she went completely limp. The Shield did not pause, simply swept her up in his arms and cast a grim glance at Clare. "She has exhausted herself."

"Quite," Clare agreed as he followed, out into the hall. Bedlam was alive with screams and moans, a ship rocking on a storm sea of lunacy. "How long has she been baying at foxes in this manner?"

"Since before dawn yesterday; no sleep and very little food. Before that, a week's worth of work."

Clare jammed his hat more firmly on to his head. "That does not surprise me. Where are we bound?"

"For home." And the man would say no more.

# Chapter Seven

## Breakfast in Mayefair

Dawn rose over Londinium like thunder. Tideturn roiled through the streets, every witch and sorcerer, not to mention the charmers and sparkpickers, pausing to allow the flood to fill them. The Tide flowed up the river, spread through the streets with dawn's struggling glow through a curtain of soot, and Emma half woke for long enough to turn over, lost in her own familiar bed. She struggled to rise through veils of half-sleep, but even though Tideturn replenished sorcerous energy, she had abused her other resources far too thoroughly, and sleep dragged her back down.

When her eyes would finally open, she was greeted by her own room, dimly lit, the blue velvet curtains tightly drawn and the ormolu clock on the mantel ticking away to itself. A softly shimmering ball of witchlight hung caged in silver over her vanity, brightening as she pushed herself up on her elbows and yawned.

Sensing her return to consciousness, the room quivered. She made a gesture, fingers fluttering, and the drapes slowly pulled back, the charm on them singing a low humming note of satisfaction. Filmy grey Londinium light spilled through the window. The house resonated, its mistress awake, and she heard footsteps in the hall.

"*Bonjour!*" Severine trilled, sweeping the door open. Her plump face opened wide in a sunny smile, and her starched cap was shockingly white. "*Chocolat et croissant pour ma fille.*" Her skirts swept the royal-blue carpeting, and her eyes danced with good humour. The indenture collar rested against her throat, a soft foxfire gleam, the powdery surface of the metal lovingly polished.

One could tell a great deal about a servant from the state of their collar. And an indenture provided a degree of status; it meant References and certain legal rights. Most sorcerers above Master level could and did engage *only* indentureds; it was a question of safety and loyalty.

There were other, darker reasons for such a preference, but Emma preferred not to think upon them. Not in the morning, at least. She stretched, wincing as several muscles twinged. "*Bonjour*, Severine. Has your goddaughter had her baby yet?"

"Not yet, not yet." Fragrant steam rose from the silver tray balanced in her plump paws, and behind Severine trooped Catherine and Isobel, lady's maids both scrubbed clean and cheerful. The scar tracing down Isobel's face was responding very well to the new fleshstitching treatment, and Emma nodded as they both dropped a curtsy. "*Monsieur le bouclier* is in the salle with our guest. Such a breakfast they had, too! Cook shall have to send out for more ham."

"I leave that in Cook's capable hands." Emma yawned again and slid free of the bed. Everything on her ached, and her hair felt stiff with grime. "Isobel, my dear, draw me a bath. Catherine, something dowdy today, I am going through dresses at an alarming rate."

"The green silk's fair done for, mum." Catherine's fair freckled face pinched in on itself as soon as she'd spoken, her collar glowing as well. She often flinched at the end of a sentence, despite the indenture here being relatively easy. Or at least, Emma thought it should be regarded as comparatively easy. Mistreated underlings stood a higher chance of being disloyal underlings even with the insurance of a collar; she had seen enough of indenture to know *that*.

Catherine had come to her Without Reference, and Severine had much protested indenturing a girl who had no papers. Finch had been against the notion too.

But they were not the mistress at 34½ Brooke Street. Catherine's doglike fidelity and skill with a needle – she was a sempstress of no mean ability, so much that Emma suspected her of a limited needle-charmer's talent, though not enough sorcery to make it illegal to indenture her – not to mention her untiring capacity for work, had proven said mistress right in this instance.

Had she been proven wrong, she was more than capable of punishing the transgressor in her own fashion.

Severine busied herself at the tiny table near the window, fussing until everything was just so. "You are pale, *madame*. You work too hard. Come, the *chocolat* is hot. And the croissants fresh! Very fresh."

"Just a moment, *cher* Severine." Emma stretched again, luxuriously, as Catherine disappeared into the dress-house and Isobel's humming started up in the bath room over a cascade of falling water. The girl was always singing something or another. Today it was a tune much heard on Picksdowne, a country girl bemoaning faithless love and a city gent. It was vaguely improper, but Isobel was a good girl. She and Catherine reworked and shared Emma's cast-off dresses, though not the burnt and battered ones, and more than once they had performed last-minute miracles when Emma's wardrobe required such.

To be a servant of Britannia of Emma Bannon's stripe could – and sometimes did – require going with little to no notice from a filthy back alley in Whitchapel or Seven Dials to a Grosvenor Square ball.

Both environments had their dangers, certainly. There were others in the service of the ruling spirit much as Emma was, but she eschewed any contact with them. Murky secret societies were, in her opinion, only to be infiltrated. Besides, there was certain latitude granted her as a soloist, so to speak.

And not so incidentally, even other sorcerers would feel trepidation at the prospect of dealing with a woman who was both Prime and of a Black branch of Discipline. Even if she kept her *exact* branch a fairly close secret, she would be hard pressed to pass as even one of the Grey, let alone the White. For one thing, she was too bloody practical.

And for another, she did not mind the blood and screaming as a proper woman should.

Emma touched the obsidian globe on her nightstand. The globe's surface, chased with silver in fluid charter symbols, rippled and trembled like water. Her fingers stroked, soothing, and the house vibrated again. Every ætheriel protection on her home was clear and tight, a Prime's will and ætheric force coursing in channels laid through physical substance, tied swiftly and efficiently with complex invisible knots, and all as it should be.

The novels stacked around the obsidian globe were all exceedingly improper and sensational, and she smiled ruefully at them. *When this is all over, I'll lie abed and read for a week.*

She had been making herself that promise for months. There was always a fresh crisis brewing. The Prince Consort was inexperienced and the Queen was still young, even though she *was* Britannia, and there was no shortage of intrigue. Victrix's lady mother had only recently been prised from her daughter's tender back, her influence slowly leaching away from the young Queen, who had not proved amenable to being ruled by Dearest Mum (as she was irreverently but very quietly called) after all.

If not for a dedicated few interested in serving Queen Victrix rather than her mother . . . well, who could say? Britannia would reign, no doubt, long after her current incarnation fell prey to old age, and after Emma's long life as a Prime was finished as well.

Still, it did not mean she could neglect her duty.

*Queen and Country, how boring. Wouldn't you like some real power?* And Llewellyn's parting words – Emma did, indeed, have her hands on a mentath.

No doubt Mr Clare would have some ideas. She had a few of her own, including where to start the next day's unravelling of this tangled web. But for the moment, she shrugged into her robe and settled at the small table, and Severine clucked over her while she had her morning *chocolat*. In short order she was finished, the day's gown was chosen, and the luxury of hot water was not nearly savoured enough before she was in her dressing room, being loosely corseted and encased in a high-collared almost drab brown velvet, her hair chafed dry and lovingly pinned up by Isobel's quick fingers, a little parfum dabbed behind her ears and her jewel cases opened, plundered, and put away. Catherine retreated to the bath room and Isobel to the bedroom, to set both to rights before the chambermaids came along to clean.

Thus fortified, and her thoughts somewhat rearranged, she checked herself in the large mirror over her white-painted vanity and frowned slightly. Slightly dowdy, yes. But at least if *this* dress were ruined, she would not feel so bad. "Severine. Do have Catherine report to Mr Finch on the frocks I've had damaged in the past week, and ask Finch to prepare a bill, itemized, for each. And for the ones I will no doubt ruin in the near future."

"*Oui, madame.*" Severine clasped her plump hands, standing near the door. "Cook will want to know the menu—"

"I'll be leaving the menu in your and Cook's hands for the upcoming week. Mr Finch should know I am not receiving for the time being, as well."

"*Oui, madame.*" Severine's cheeks had turned pale. When the menu was left to her and Cook it was always acceptable – but still, the housekeeper was terrified of a misstep, as well as breathless with fear for her mistress.

Severine's last indenture had not been pleasant. Emma had learned it was best not to reassure her overmuch; such coddling only made her more nervous. Like mastering a high-strung unAltered horse, it was best to be firm and brisk, but gentle.

"And please do have Finch secure more linens for our guest, and find him a suitable valet among the footmen. I rather think Mr Clare may be stopping with us for a while."

The salle was long and drenched with sunlight as well as the directionless glow of witchballs caged in filigreed aluminium, the floor mellow wood occasionally covered with rough mats supposed to make a fall during Mikal's daily practice less dangerous. Of course, the idea of Mikal *falling* was preposterous. Rather, the mats were a gesture.

Or they were for the infrequent times when she had company capable of sparring with a Shield. Like today.

Well, perhaps *capable* was too generous a term. For Mikal moved almost gently, deflecting the mentath's flurry of blows. Clare was not untrained, but to an eye used to the Collegia's classes of practising Shield candidates he appeared slow and graceless. Still, he was sweating, stripped to the waist, and surprisingly muscular. Emma folded her arms, watching Mikal as he gave ground, pivoting neatly and pulling the mentath off balance. A single strike, and Clare doubled up, losing most of his air. Mikal wore an odd little smile, one that meant he was enjoying himself.

Emma took notice of her unladylike posture, and clasped her gloved hands before her. The sardonyx ring prickled, and she had kept the amber prie-dieu, freshly glowing with a charge of sorcerous power from Tideturn. Today, though, the earrings were long jet daggers, and the cameo at her throat could hold a great deal of charge. Two more rings – one ruby, another a thick dull golden band – completed today's set. She was as prepared as it was possible to be.

*He will not like this.* She waited patiently, watching Mikal's smile deepen a trifle as Clare levered himself up from the mats.

"You do *not* have to look so bloody entertained, sir," Clare panted.

"My apologies." Mikal's grin widened. "Another round? You are quite agile, mentath."

Clare waved the compliment away. "No, no. I fear I am done. And Miss Bannon has made her appearance."

*Oh, so you remarked my absence, did you?* "Gentlemen." She accepted Mikal's traditional bow and Clare's slightly less formal movement with a nod. "Did you sleep well, Mr Clare?"

He flushed, all the way up to the roots of his sandy hair. "Quite well, thank you. And you, Miss Bannon?"

"I am well enough, thank you. I shall be gone for the day, hunting some rather interesting loose ends of this conspiracy. Here is the safest place for you, Mr Clare, and with Mikal to watch over you—"

"Prima." Just the one word, but Mikal's face was a thundercloud.

"Do not interrupt, Shield." She let the sentence carry its own warning. "Your charge is to protect the mentath. It appears mentaths are central to this series of events; therefore, he shall be as safe as I may make him while I hunt in other quarters. I shall hopefully return in time for dinner – Mr Clare, we dine a trifle early, I do hope that won't inconvenience you?"

"My digestion agrees with the notion." But his long, sweat-greased face had returned to mournfulness, and he shrugged into a threadbare shirt, folding down the turnover collar precisely. "However, Miss Bannon, I am not at all certain that I am the only target of the attacks we have endured so far. Last night—"

*There are other reasons for me keeping you mewed here, thank you.* "These foxes now know I am at their heels. My barouche is making deceptive rounds today, and I shall slip about largely unseen." She loosed her fingers with an effort, ignoring Mikal's tension, a powder-bloom of deep bruiselike colour visible to Sight. "I assure you, Mr Clare, I am *quite* capable of performing the duty Her Majesty has assigned me – namely, protecting a mentath, and ferreting out the source of this unpleasantness." Her shoulders ached; she relaxed them with an effort. "My staff has been set to procuring you fresh linens – yours have arrived from the Chancellor's care, and been laundered – and providing you with a valet, since you may be my guest for some small length of time. Would you be so kind as to accept Mr Finch's questions on those matters, once you have refreshed yourself?"

"Delighted to." The look on his face shouted that he would be anything but. Still, he did not waste time. He simply shook hands with Mikal and left the salle. Of course, he would think her terribly unfeminine.

*Let him. His opinion matters little; his continued existence is what I am to protect.* She held Mikal's gaze as the salle door closed with a decisive snick, and the Shield's cheekbones were flushed with ugly colour under their copper.

Fighting did not make him blush so.

"You will guard the mentath." Even, level, her tone neverthe-less paled the sunlight coming through the long upper windows. The witchballs shuddered, one of them spitting a few blue sparks.

"My Prima." His jaw set. A fine thin tremor ran through him as her will hardened, the link between them painfully taut.

*My Prima. As in, it is my duty to guard* you. "He is in more danger than I am. And I have my reasons, Mikal."

A small, restless movement. If he dared, she almost thought he would *argue* with her.

And that could not be allowed.

"Good." She touched her skirts, her reticule brushing against velvet. The bonnet she'd chosen was far worse than dowdy, but at least she would feel no sting if it was lost or damaged, and it did not interfere with her peripheral vision. "Until dinner, then."

And there she would have left it, but for his stubbornness.

"Emma." Tight-clipped, her name, forced from his throat. "Please."

Sorcerous force flared through her. He fought it, but she was Prime, and her will forced his knees to bend. When he was in a Shield's abeyance, kneeling with his hands resting loose against his thighs, head bowed and almost every muscle locked, she let out a soft sound between her teeth.

"I am *Prime*." The words turned to gall, scorching her throat. "I am not some hedge-charmer to be ordered about. I *allow* you a great deal, Mikal, but I will not abide disobedience. You will guard the mentath." *The threat of you strangling me as well is not enough to make me tolerate an order from a Shield. Not nearly enough at all.*

The struggle went out of him. He slumped inside the cage of her will. "Yes," he murmured.

"Yes . . .?"

"Yes, my Prima."

It was a wonder he did not hate her. Of course, he very well might. But as long as he was desirous of continued survival, they were allied. Hatred mattered little in such an alliance.

*Or so I tell myself. Until he finds a better treaty to sign, and then? Who knows?* "Good." She turned, skirts swishing, and set off for the door. Her will slackened, but Mikal did not move.

"Emma." Softly, now.

She did not halt.

"Be careful." A little more loudly than he had to, making the salle's bright air tremble, dust swirling softly. "I would not care to lose you."

Sudden self-loathing bit under her breastbone. It was a familiar feeling. "I have no intention of being lost, Mikal. Thank you." *I should not have done this. Forgive me.* The words trembled just on the edge of her tongue, but she swallowed them, and left him behind in the sunlit salle.

# Chapter Eight

## You Will Do, Sir

The sorceress's house was odd indeed. It was a good address – Mayefair was a *very* respectable part of Londinium, and Miss Bannon was of course comfortable. Rare indeed was the sorcerer with bad business sense, though most of them affected a high disdain for such matters. To be in trade carried its own shame, sometimes worse than the stigma of sorcery.

The house seemed far larger than its exterior would have given one to surmise, and he did not like that illogical notion at all. It caused him some discomfort until he consigned it to his mental drawer of complex problems judged worthy of further investigation at some later date, if at all.

The suite he had been shown to by the cadaverous Finch – tall, thin, marks of childhood malnutrition around his jaw and evident in his bowed legs, dressed in dusty black but with his indenture collar lovingly polished – was furnished spare, dark, and heavy, but the fume of scorched dust told him hurried cleaning charms had been applied just prior to his residence. Dark wainscoting, leather and wine-red upholstery, but the bed was fresh and its linen crisp. Fire crackled merrily on the grate, and he was gratified to see that during his morning's exercise newspapers and periodicals had been brought, stacked neatly on the huge desk. Plenty of paper had been provided as well, and a complete set of *Encyclopaedie Britannicus*, in fifty-eight volumes, was arranged on the bookshelf, along with two dictionaries and a chemist's arrangement of reference works.

Miss Bannon must have given orders. It would do to keep his faculties occupied for a short while.

The servants were proud, but they spared no effort. Each one had a burnished indenture collar, and they were an odd assortment. Finch, for example, spoke with a laborious upper-crust wheeze, but Clare's trained ear caught traces of a youth spent mouthing Whitchapel's slur and slang. The man's musculature was wasted, but several of his mannerisms led Clare to the conclusion that Finch was familiar with the ungraceful dance of a knife fight or two in the darkness of a forgotten alley.

Then there was the pair of chambermaids – one with long chestnut ripples pulled tightly back, all elbows and angles in her brushed black gown, the other a short, plump, fair Irish colleen – who descended on his room to put it to rights a few moments after he pulled the bell-rope upon awakening. And the housekeeper, a round merry-eyed Frenchwoman with an atrocious Picardie accent, who had fussed him into a Delft-and-cream breakfast room and *tsk*ed over him.

The chambermaids both flinched at odd moments, and the housekeeper compulsively straightened everything she could lay her hands upon, tweaking with deft fingers. Yet they did not seem precisely *afraid*; Clare's sensitive nose caught no acrid note of fresh fear. The food, of course, was superlative, for all that Miss Bannon made no appearance until mid-morning in the salle.

And what an appearance that had been.

The man Mikal was still a puzzle. Clare settled in a chair next to the fire and lit his pipe, puffing thoughtfully. He was ready to turn his entire attention to the problem of the Shield, but there was a tap at the door.

A pleasure foregone was enough to irritate him at the moment. "Enter!"

The door opened and the Shield appeared, his yellow eyes flaming and his entire body stiff. "I hesitate to disturb—" he began, but Clare brightened and waved him further into the room.

"Come in, come in! You will do for a half-hour at least. Is Miss Bannon gone?"

"I saw her to the door." The man's jaw set, and Clare deduced he was most unhappy with this turn of events. It was, from what he could remember, not at all usual for a sorcerer, especially a powerful Prime, to set foot outside without a Shield or three, or more.

Of course, what Clare knew of sorcery was little more than the average man would. It did not do to think too much on the illogical feats such people were capable of performing. On the other hand, a surface study of such things would have armed him with enough to make workable deductions about Miss Bannon's character.

*Let us test the waters.* "No doubt you can tell me her true motivation in leaving the pair of us mewed here." He took a mouthful of smoke, tasted it speculatively, and almost smiled at the sensation. Mentaths did not feel as others did; logic was the pleasure they moved towards, and irrationality or illogic the pain they retreated from. Emotions were to be subdued, harnessed, accounted for and set on the shelf of deduction.

Privately, Clare had decided that few mentaths were completely emotionless. They simply did not account fully for Feeling, it being easier to see the occlusion in a subject's gaze than in their own. It was simply another variable to guard against, watch for, and marvel at the infinite variety of.

"She thinks to protect you." The Shield lowered himself into the chair across the fire, sat bolt upright, his hands resting on his knees. His long grey coat, buttoned all the way to the neck, did nothing to hide the muscle underneath. Outside the window, Londinium continued its morning roil under a blue spring sky lensed with coal-smoke fog. Shafts of smoke and steam rose; the note of copper from the Themis told Clare there would be clouds by afternoon and fog tonight. "Since the Queen, via Lord Grayson, consigned you to her care."

"Fetching concern," Clare murmured, puffing on his pipe, his eyes half lidding. The mournfulness of his features was accentuated by this manoeuvre. "Tell me, Mr Mikal—"

"Just Mikal." The man's chin lifted slightly.

*Aha. Jealous of our pride, are we?* "Mr Just Mikal, how many Shields does a sorcerer of Miss Bannon's stature – that is to say, a Prime – normally employ?"

Mikal considered this. His short hair was mussed, as if he had run his hands through it. When he visibly decided the information could do no harm, he finally responded. "A half-dozen is the normal minimum, but my Prima keeps her own counsel and does as she pleases. She had four Shields some time ago, and . . . well. It is a dangerous occupation."

"Four Shields. Before you?"

"Yes." Mikal's face visibly closed. Clare could almost hear the snap. Most interesting.

"And she has been chasing this conspiracy . . ."

"Three days. Sir. Since she was called to examine a mentath's body *in situ*—"

"That would be Tomlinson, I take it. The first to die."

"The first she was called to examine." Those yellow eyes glittered. Their colour seemed much more pronounced now, as the Shield gave Clare his attention.

*Very good. You are not stupid, nor do you assume much.* "Your lady suspects there must be more."

"She has not seen fit to share her thoughts with me."

*Well. This is a pleasant game.* "We will get exactly nowhere should you continue being obstreperous."

"Or should you continue seeking to bait me."

An extraordinary hypothesis presented itself. Clare held his silence for a long moment, puffing at his pipe. Hooves and wheels rumbled outside through the city's arteries, an ever-present muted Londinium song. "You do not trust me."

A single shrug.

"It has occurred to you – or perhaps to Miss Bannon – that a mentath, or more than one, may be involved in this conspiracy not just as a victim, but as a conspirator."

Another shrug.

*Well. You are even less stupid than I initially supposed.* "May we at least for the moment proceed under the assumption that I am not, supported by the evidence that I have been almost murdered in the past twenty-four hours?"

A grudging nod.

*Well, that's half the distance to Noncastel.* "Many thanks, sir. So. Start at the beginning, and tell me what occurred from the moment our dear sorceress was called from her usual work – which no doubt involved driving herself to exhaustion – to the scene."

Mikal gazed at him for a long moment. Thoughts moved behind that yellow gaze, and the planes of his face took on a sharper cast. "My Prima was called to a house at Elnor Cross; she arrived to find the body of a mentath and fading marks of sorcery. The attending forensic sorcerer had blurred several traces and my Prima was in a fine mood—"

"No, no." Clare waved his pipe. Sweet smoke drifted, taking angular shapes as if it sensed the tension radiating from the other man. His colouring was not nearly dark enough to be Tinkerfolk, Clare decided. Indus, most likely, but the shape of his cheekbones was . . . odd. "The *house*, first. Precisely where is it located? Give me the street address and the number of rooms, then describe to me which room the body was in. Then you will give me the name of the sorcerer, and *only then* proceed to our Bannon's arrival and what transpired then."

Mikal blinked. "You wish for a Recall, then?"

*How very interesting.* "A Recall?"

"A sorcerer may need to use a Shield's eyes. There are two ways of doing so, a Glove and a Recall. We are trained to observe and offer only what we have observed. That is Recall."

The fascinating question of just what a "Glove" consisted of could occupy him another time, Clare decided. "Very well, then. May I question you during the process, or must I save my questions for afterwards?"

A single economical movement. "Save them. You do not know how to question properly."

*I doubt you would teach me to do so, sir.* Clare puffed on his pipe again. The tobacco was fine, and for a moment he considered a fraction of coja to sharpen his faculties. Discarded the notion – for if he paused, he suspected Mikal might think better of this offer. "Very well. Proceed when you are ready, sir, and I shall pay most close attention."

*Tomlinson was found slumped in a heavy armchair, his dressing jacket unwrinkled, no visible sign of foul play. It seemed a routine case of apoplexy – not common in mentaths, but also not unheard of, the logical patterns of the brain snarling and melting, stewing in irrationality. Tomlinson, however, was busy amid several cases that should have kept his faculties sufficiently exercised.*

*The attending Master Sorcerer, a certain Hugh Devon, seemed surprised when Miss Emma Bannon made her appearance as the Crown's representative. He seemed even more surprised when she took him to task for smearing the delicate ætheric traceries rumbling and resonating inside the room: "Bumbling like an idiot; now we cannot rule out foul play!"*

*At which point Mr Devon turned apoplectic-red himself, sputtered, and one of his Shields – a tall, lean blond man – stepped forward. Mikal had merely watched. Miss Bannon had arched one elegant eyebrow. "Leave." Just the one word, but it cut through the other sorcerer's sizzling and transformed the air in the overcushioned sitting room to ice.*

*Devon and his pair of Shields quit the room, and once they did, Mikal watched as his Prima stalked to the bookcase and pulled free three redrope folders, of the sort solicitors and barristers used. She checked them, one eye on Tomlinson's stocky corpse, and suddenly fixed her own Shield with a searching gaze. "He is without his slippers, Mikal."*

*She was correct. A pair of tattered woollen socks clasped the mentath's limp feet.*

*"And I cannot even question his shade, for that fool Devon has tangled everything beyond repair. Come, Mikal. We must examine the room and then seek out the Chancellor; there is something odd afoot."*

*Masters the Elder, shot on Picksadowne Street between numbers 14 and 15½; there were no witnesses to speak of. Certainly there were onlookers, but none would swear to a description of the shooter. In that part of town, that was very little mystery. The mystery lay in what on earth Masters was doing there, and why he was shot three times – once to the heart, and two bullets shattering his skull. Which meant his shade could not be questioned either, Miss Bannon noted aloud to her Shield.*

*Very interesting indeed.*

*Smythe was stabbed near Nightmarket, just before Tideturn. Again, onlookers but no witnesses, and by the time Miss Bannon had arrived his body had been picked clean – and the ætheric traces were smudged as well. It could have been by the pickers; rare was the corpseduster who wished to be found guilty of such a thing.*

*The sorcerer set to watch Smythe, a certain Mr Newberry, was nowhere to be found. Miss Bannon had commanded Mikal to stand guard over the body and disappeared into the nearby alley, emerging startlingly pale. She did not grant him leave to view the alley for himself, but he did see bodies carried forth from it when help arrived.*

*He could not swear they were Shields, yet . . .*

*Throckmorton's house was still blazing when they arrived. Miss Bannon had quelled the fire with surprising difficulty, sorcery fuelling the twisting flames and fighting her control. A crimson salamander, its forked tongue flickering white-hot, had launched itself at Mikal's Prima, and he had killed it. Its ashes, treated with* vitae, *glowed blue, proving it had been controlled. Which made the fire sorcerous in origin, and the entire chain of events began to take on a disturbing cast. Throckmorton's corpse was corkscrewed and charred, flesh hanging in ribbons. Either the salamander had been feasting on his remains, or he had been tortured before his death.*

*Or both. The heat-shattered skull and cooked brain meant his shade could not be questioned either, and that put the sorceress in a fine mood as well.*

*The Prime who was to be watching the unfortunate Throckmorton, Llewellyn Gwynnfud, was found causing a scene in a Whitchapel brothel, gibbering and Shieldless, and transported to Bedlam by a contingent of nervous hieromancers. And then the first dead unregistered mentaths were found, their bodies terribly mutilated, and Miss Emma Bannon's temper had passed beyond uncertain to downright combative.*

*She had begun, it seemed, to take something personally.*

"Most interesting." Clare relit his pipe. "And did Miss Bannon also search Throckmorton's house?"

"Thoroughly. What little was left of it."

*Mutilated if unregistered. How unpleasant.* His skin briefly chilled, and he set the thought aside. There were other questions to answer first. "And . . . you will pardon my asking, but what is Miss Bannon's Discipline? Every sorcerer has a Discipline, correct?"

Mikal nodded. His straight-backed posture was the same, but his face had eased slightly. "Yes."

"And Miss Bannon's is . . ."

Mikal's mouth turned into a thin straight line.

*Do not insult my intelligence.* "Oh come now, man. If I had not guessed her to be one of the Black, I would have to be thick indeed. A sorcerer does not so cavalierly mention questioning shades unless their Discipline overlaps with the Black, correct?"

It was not so outré a guess. Sorcerers were not overly social, but Miss Bannon seemed standoffish even by their standards. She behaved as a woman who was accustomed to having others fear her, and Cedric Grayson had turned pale and sweating. The three branches of sorcery were supposedly all equal, but whispers swirled about the Grey, and swirled even further about the Black. Nothing concrete, certainly . . . but *something* could be inferred even from rumour.

Another small, grudging nod from the Shield.

Clare had to restrain a sigh. "I am not one of the callow multitudes, Mr Mikal. Logic dictates that the service of Britannia's incarnation must hold those the common man perceives to be dangerous. Miss Bannon may be exceeding dangerous, but she is not an ogress, and she does not represent a danger to *me*. I ask about her Discipline only to clarify a point or two to myself and to found my chain of deduction on solid—"

"She is of the Black." Mikal propelled himself to his feet. "There. You know now, mentath. Tread carefully. *She is my Prima.* If you threaten her, I shall find ways to make you regret it."

*Threaten her?* Clare lowered his pipe. "Who was Crawford?" The name was common, but something nagged at his memory. A recent scandal, perhaps?

The colour drained from Mikal's face, leaving him ashen under the copper. His eyes lit, venomous yellow irises glowing. One hand twitched, a subtle movement.

Clare tensed. He was no match for the Shield, but the sorceress's orders were for Clare to be unharmed.

At least, he *assumed* those were her orders. The threat of some dire consequence that would leave Clare physically unmarked was not to be taken lightly.

"Crawford." The ghost of an accent tinted the word. "He was the first man I killed for her." Mikal's tongue darted out, wetted his thin lips. "He was not – and shall not be – the last."

And with that, the Shield stalked across the room, swept the door open, and stepped into the hall. He would stand guard there, probably the better to keep his temper.

*Dead, then. This requires thought.* Clare puffed on his pipe. A slight smile played about his mouth. A very successful chain of deduction, far more data than he'd had before, and much was now clearer about Mikal the Shield.

What an extraordinarily diverting morning this was proving to be.

# Chapter Nine

## The Abortionist

Tideturn had laid smoking gossamer fabric over the traces of the ætheric protection on last night's luckily escaped assassin. Emma clasped her hands before her, lowering her head as she concentrated, invisible threads singing as she handled them so, so delicately. There was joy to be found in the complexity of such an operation, her touch deft and quick.

Like the scales on a butterfly's wings, the imprint of a sorcerer's work on the fabric of the visible world fluttered. Her memory swallowed the pattern whole, comparing it to the thick ætheric tangles laid over Llewellyn Gwynnfud last night.

There was no overlap. Well, it was hardly a surprise that more than one sorcerer was involved in this.

The climax of last night's events bothered her, though. She should have been able to guess the irregularities in the charm and charter symbols would act so vigorously, and perhaps taken steps to keep Llewellyn alive for further questioning.

*But you did not, Emma. Was it because the thought of him dead did not distress you at all? It is rather a relief, isn't it? Come now, be honest.*

Well, if she had to be *absolutely* honest, she would have preferred snuffing Llewellyn's candle herself. Yet another unfeminine trait. Or was the desire to be thorough and tidy so unlady-like? Llew had been a loose end.

He had almost certainly suspected what had happened in Crawford's round room, and further suspected that Emma would be vulnerable. He was far too dangerous to possess knowledge of a weakness of that magnitude.

*It is well that he is dead, and we have business with the living.* She returned to herself, shaking her head slightly. The alley was piled with refuse, and if not for the air-clearing charm every Londinium sorcerer with any talent learned early and used religiously, it would be easily ripe enough to turn her stomach. The cobbles underfoot were coated with slick foulness, and she edged forward cautiously.

*There.* She caught sight of a gleam – a copper disc and a broken ribbon, tossed aside as soon as it was used. *Oh, you idiot, whoever you are. Bless your stupidity, for you have given me an opening.*

Here in the sunlight, without a single Shield, she would have to use all appropriate caution. She picked her way over the slimy stones, keeping her breathing even with an effort. Sarpesson Street was quieter at this hour, but traffic still rumbled past, whipcracks and clockwork sparks echoing oddly in the alley's choked confines.

*He came down there, triggered the protection, flung it away. Hard to see in the dark, and hoping the refuse would cover it. Then . . . where would he go?*

She bent, her stays digging briefly even though she was only loosely corseted – there was fashion and there was idiocy, and while she was vain enough to love the former, she was not willing to indulge the latter. A stray shaft of weak sunlight pierced the alley's roof, buildings sloping together alarmingly overhead, and even that was enough to jab at her sensitised eyes.

*Blast and bother.* She tweezed the ribbon carefully between gloved fingers and slowly straightened, holding the protection disc stiff-armed away from her body as it glowed dully. The charm had been well made, even though its physical matrix was flimsy and disposable. It was at the very least the work of a Master Sorcerer, and as she examined it more closely, Emma realised it was familiar.

She breathed a term a respectable lady would faint upon hearing, then cast a squinting glance over her shoulder as if someone might witness her lapse. No, the alley was deserted. So why the sudden sense of being observed, lifting the fine hairs on her nape and tingling down her spine under the drab brown velvet?

*Proceed very carefully indeed, Emma. He is bound to guess you will show up at his door, unless you are dead.*

And Konstantin Serafimovitch Gippius would not trust a rumour of Emma Bannon's demise until he could see her mutilated body.

Perhaps not even then.

Even this early in the day, Whitchapel seethed with a crush of stinking humanity – ragpickers, pickpockets, loiterers, day labourers, streetmerchants, hevvymancers and drays, public houses doing a brisk trade in cups of gin and tankers of beer, washerwomen and ragged drabs, stray sparks and flicks of charm and sorcery crackling along the filthy street. Pawnbrokers' coloured signs flashed with catchcharms, their infrequent windows glowing with lightfinger wards and their doors re-inforced. Clockhorses strained and whinnied, shouts and cries echoed, and the entire squeezing, throbbing mass teemed not only with the living but the vaporous dead. Ragged children darted through the crowd; at the corner of Dray Street and Sephrin a cart carrying a load of barrels lay sideways, a man lying groaning, half crushed under one side and the onlookers jostling to get a better view as a gang of labourers – not a hevvymancer in sight – struggled to heave the cart away. Clockwork horses screamed, their gears grating and sorcerous energy spilling dangerously uncontrolled.

It would have taken mere moments to restore some order, but any disturbance of the æther here would warn her quarry.

*The carter will be dead within a quarter-hour anyway,* she told herself sternly as she threaded through the crowd, the cameo at her throat warming as thin filaments of glamour turned her into anything other than a respectable woman sliding into Whitchapel. *The greater good of all demands I do not become distracted here.*

Still, the screams and moans rang in her ears as she turned on Thrawl, slowing as a press of human flesh choked about her. A pickmancer's nimble fingers brushed for her skirt pocket, but her sardonyx ring sparked and the touch was hurriedly drawn back. A raddled drab, her ruined face turned up to the morning light and runnelled with decaying powder, sang nonsense in a cracked unlovely alto, while a mob of flashboys whooped near the low sooty entrance of the Cross and Spaulders, their draggled finery sparking slightly with sartorial charms. Alterations gleamed – any flashboy worth the name would have an amendment, the more visible the better. One had a blackened clockwork hand that spat sparks from its hooked fingers, another a green-glass eye rolling in an exposed, bony socket. Cheap work, that, but this was Whitchapel.

Everything was cheap here. Including human life.

Already the sky was hazed – not nearly enough; the light speared through her skull. This would be so much *easier* after dusk.

It would be easier for Gippius too. So Emma blinked furiously, did *not* lift her handkerchief to her nose, and kept the subtle threads of glamour blending together. Some few of the slightly sorcerous on the street glanced at her once or twice, but she was Prime and they were merely sparks. They would not see what she truly was unless she willed it.

A venous network of alleys had grown around Thrawl, slumping tenements festooned with sagging laundry hung on lines despite the coal dust, refuse packed into corners. Children screamed and ran about, playing some game that made sense only to them, the slurring drawl of the Eastron End already evident in their joyous accents. Malnourished but agile, they were more problematic than the adults – sometimes a child's gaze would pierce a glamour where even an Adept's could not.

She found the rat's nest of alleyways she was looking for, and plunged into welcome gloom. Some doors hung ajar, shadows flitting through them; a colourless vapour of gin and hopelessness rose. A baby cried, wheedling and insistent, somewhere in the depths of a building. A man crouched on a low step in front of a battered, dispirited wooden door. Muffled cries were heard from inside, and the man's eyes followed Emma's shadow as he peeled his nails with a short, wicked knife, taking care to palm the filthy clippings up to his mouth as an insurance against charming.

At the far end of the alley the abortionist's door, studded with iron nails, grimaced. Emma braced herself and strode for it, her boots slipping a little against the crust coating the alley floor. No wonder Gippius had sunk into this quarter of the city – few constables would brave this hole.

Few sorcerers would, even.

Invisible strings quivered under the surface of the visible. The cameo warmed at her throat, and the ætheric protections in Gippius's walls resonated slightly.

*That is not a good sign.* The door had no knob; she simply *focused* – and stepped through, a shivering curtain of glamour sparking and fizzing as her will shunted the river of charm and charter aside.

Gippius was quick and deadly, but he was not native. In his country, she would be the sorcerous stranger, and the resultant struggle might have had a different outcome. As it was, she flung out a hand, the Cossack who did a Shield's duty for Konstantin stumbled back into a mound of clothing waiting for the ragpickers, and Emma's other gloved hand made a curious tracing motion as she spoke a minor Word. Witchlight flared, and Konstantin Gippius stumbled back, clutching at his throat. A single line of chant, low and vicious, poured from Emma's mouth, a fierce hurtful thrill of sorcery spilling through her, and the Cossack shrieked as ætheric bonds snapped into place over him.

The chant faded into the humming of live sorcery. Emma climbed to her feet, brushing off her dress. The Cossack's shriek was cut short on a gurgle; she grimaced and made certain her bonnet was straight. The huge glass jars filling every shelf chattered and clattered together, the abominations inside twitching as dark, pudgy Gippius thrashed on the trash-strewn floor. He was turning a most amazing shade of purple.

"Behave yourself," she said sternly, and flicked her fingers, releasing the silencing.

Gippius's throat swelled with sound. Sorcery flashed towards her; she batted the venomous yellow darting coils aside and tightened her gloved fist, humming a low sustained note. The silencing clamped down again, the cameo a spot of scorch against her chest. "I said *behave yourself*, Gippius! Or I shall choke you to death and go a-traipsing through your house for what I wish."

Spluttering, the Russian thrashed. His boots drummed the floor. When she judged she had perhaps expressed her seriousness in terms he could comprehend, she fractionally loosened her hold once again.

The abominations in the jars moved too, slopping their baths of amber solution against dusty glass. Tiny piping cries echoed, their large heads and tiny malformed bodies twitching. Metal clinked – some of them had been Altered. Gippius's science was inefficient, and disgusting as well.

*It is a very good thing I have a strong stomach.* Emma eyed Gippius as he lay quiescent, glaring balefully. Greasy black hair hung in strings, sawdust from his rolling about griming the curls. A crimson spark lit in the backs of his pupils, but quickly dimmed and was extinguished as his face grew more and more plummy.

She eased the constriction, in increments. It took a good long while for his tortured gasps to even out, and the Cossack moaned to one side. Emma spent the time eyeing the jar-living abominations, examining the filthy curtain drawn to mark the entrance to Gippius's surgery, the low sullen light of malformed witchballs sparking orange as they bobbed in cheap lantern-cages. The stove in the corner glowed sullenly as well, and the large pot bubbling atop it reeked of cabbage.

When she judged it safe enough, and further judged she had Konstantin's entire attention, she drew the protection disc and its broken ribbon from her skirt pocket.

"Now," she said quietly, for it did not do to shout if there was no need, "I am about to question you, Konstantin Serafimovitch. If you do not have proper answers – or if I even *suspect* any impropriety such as dishonesty in your answers – first I will kill your Cossack. If you continue to be remiss, I shall shatter all your jars. If you are *still* remiss, I shall be forced to make things very unpleasant for your *corpus*." She paused, let him absorb this. "And I do not have to cease when you expire, either."

Now he was moaning as well. The counterpoint of male agony was almost musical.

She began working her gloves off, finger by finger, though her flesh crawled at the thought of touching anything in this hole with bare flesh. "Now. Let us start with this protection charm."

# Chapter Ten

## Tea and Data

Newspaper clippings scattered over the table, turned this way and that as he tested connections between them. Two volumes of the *Encylopaedie* stood open as well, a further three stacked on the chair, and he paced between the fireplace and the window. More papers, covered with his cramped handwriting, fluttered as he passed the table. The desk was snowed under with a drift of notes and more volumes.

Occasionally he stopped, running his hands through thinning hair. His pipe had long since gone out.

"The connections," he muttered, several times. "I *must* have more data!"

He had endured the visit from Mr Finch, interrupting his research with idiocy about linens and a valet, and further endured the measuring-charms and queries of the footman chosen to do valet duty. His freshly laundered linens, sent by an obliging Grayson, had been delivered and stowed away. Then, thankfully, they had left him in peace – what peace there was, for he was beginning to be sorely pressed.

The door resounded under a series of knocks, and when it opened, the Shield took in the explosion of paper and Clare's pacing. "Tea," he said, the single word as colourless as it was possible for a syllable to be. His mouth turned down at the corners, and he was actually grey under his copper hue. "In the conservatory."

"*That's not where she takes her tea!*" Clare cried, turning in a jerky half-circle. "I know that much! I am engaged on deducing much more. But there's one piece, *one critical piece* – or maybe more than one. I cannot tell. I must have more data!"

Mikal's features betrayed no surprise. Just that grey, set monotone. "My Prima takes her tea in her study, but you are a guest, and the conservatory is made avail—"

Clare halted, staring at him. "My God, man, you look *dreadful.*"

The Shield's head dipped, a fractional nod. "Thank you. Tea, mentath. Come along."

"Why do you—" Clare stopped short. His head cocked, the chain of deduction enfolding. "Surely you are not so worried for Miss Bannon's safety that you—"

"Tea," Mikal repeated, and retreated into the hall, pulling the door to but not latching it. Which effectively halted the conversation, though only until Clare could exit his suite.

Unfortunately the Shield had taken that into account, and was at the other end of the hall before Clare could gather himself. He led Clare through the house, always just at the end of a hall or at the bottom of stairs, and did not slacken the pace until Clare stepped into the largish conservatory's pearly glow. A thin dusting of rain streaked the glass walls, rippling panes held in filigreed wrought-iron, charter symbols falling through the metal like golden oil. The day had turned grey-haze, but the collection of potted plants and small, ruthlessly pruned larger bushes – orange, lemon, lime, false lime, rosemary, bay laurel, and the like – still drank in the light greedily. The north end was given to straggling, rank, baneful plants – rue, pennyroyal, nightshade, wolfsbane, nettle, hadthorn, and more. East and west held common herbs – feverfew, a few mint species, chamomile, costmary and other culinary and common-charm plants. The south end was given to exotics – a tomato plant, green unripe fruit hanging on charter-charm-reinforced green stems, orchids Clare could not name, a small planter of fiery scarlet tulips, a dwarf rose whose petals were a velvety purple very close to black. Each was covered by a crystalline dome of sorcery, ringing with thin, gentle sounds when the atmosphere inside stirred the leaves – a quite pleasant sound, like faraway bells.

To properly examine every plant would take perhaps an hour and a half. Here was another unexpected richness. It was not the sort of room Clare would expect to find Miss Bannon in, and his estimation of her character went through a sharp change as a result. Which led him down several interesting and troubling roads all at once.

The furniture was white-painted wicker, the chairs cushioned with rich blue velvet. A snow-white cloth trimmed in scallops of blue lace covered the tabletop, the service was burnished to within an inch of its silvery life, and a full tea was arranged on three tiers, the shimmer of a keeping charm visible over it. The air was alive with sorcery.

Mikal prowled near the northern end of the sunroom, pacing, his boots soundless on the mellow-glowing, satiny wooden floor. The light picked out red highlights in his dark hair, stroked the nap of his velvet coat, and made his colour even more sickly.

The housekeeper, her black crêpe rustling, hovered over the table bobbing a tiny curtsey. Her cap was placed so precisely he half expected it to bow as well. Her round face lit with genuine pleasure, and not a single lock of dark hair was out of place. Her indenture collar glowed. *"Bonjour, Monsieur Clare!* Tea is generally mine, *madame* prefers it so. Shall I pour for you?"

He could very well pour for himself. But here was another opportunity for deduction and questioning. "I would be delighted, Madame Noyon. Please, join me. It seems Mr Mikal doesn't care for tea."

"He never does. *Madame* would make him sit, but he is not likely to now." Her plump nervous hands moved, and Clare laid a private bet with himself about which chair she would prefer him in.

"How often does Miss Bannon leave him behind to fret, then?"

That earned him a solemn French glance. Her collar flashed, and her daggered jet earrings swung. "*Monsieur.*" Sudden, icy politeness. She indicated the chair he had chosen, and at least his instincts were not off.

"Very well. I am only concerned for Miss Bannon's safety, Madame Noyon."

"Well." Slightly mollified, she began the ritual of tea with an ease that spoke of long practice. She made an abortive movement for the milk, and he deduced Miss Bannon habitually took some, and was often otherwise occupied while Madame Noyon poured. Some of the savouries appeared to be favoured by his absent hostess, too. "You have no need to fear, *monsieur*. Our *madame* is the finest sorcerer in Londinium. When she says a thing is to be done, *pouf!* It is done."

*Touching faith.* He added a few more links to the chain of deduction. "She rescued you, did she not?"

"*Ma foi*, she rescued us all! Lemon?"

"No, thank you. Rescued you all?"

"Finch, he was thief. Catherine, she was Without Reference, as you *Anglais* say. Wilbur in the stables, he was—"

Mikal was suddenly across the table, yellow eyes glowing. "Enough. The domestics are no interest of yours, mentath."

Madame Noyon gasped, her hand to her mouth. The tea service rattled slightly, the table underneath it responding to a feral current.

"You could sit and have tea," Clare returned, mildly enough. "The more I know, Mr Mikal, the more help I am to your mistress. A mentath is useless without data."

"You are worse than useless anyway." The Shield's graven face had lost even more colour. "If she is harmed while I am forced to sit—"

"*Monseiur le bouclie.*" Madame Noyon tapped the teapot with the lemon knife. "You are in very bad manners. Monsieur Clare is our guest, and *madame* left instructions. You sit, or pace, but do not loaf about table like vulture!"

Clare watched as the Shield's face congested, suffusing with a ghastly flush before the man turned on his booted heel and glided away towards the north end. The rain intensified, spattering glass and iron, the charter symbols sending up small wisps of fog as cold water touched them.

Madame Noyon swallowed, audibly. Her fingers trembled slightly before she firmed her mouth and put on a bright expression. "*Madame* returns soon, *monsieur*. Eat, eat. You are thin like Mr Finch, you must eat."

Clare certainly intended to. His landlady's teas were nowhere near as grand, and only a fool would let his digestion be troubled.

Yet he pushed his chair back and rose. He approached the north end of the conservatory, his hands clasped behind his back and the slap of rain intensifying again. Rivulets slid their cold fingers over the glass.

"Mr Mikal." He hoped his tone was not overly familiar – or overly distant. Dealing with this messiness was so *difficult*. "I beg your pardon, sir. I do not intend to be a burden, and my intent in questioning about Miss Bannon is purely so I may assist her in whatever way necessary, to the best of my ability. I may be useless, and own no sorcery, but I am striving to become *less* useless, and I very much crave your assistance in that endeavour."

Mikal had come to a stop, his head down, staring at a thorn-spiked, venomous-looking plant in a low earthenware pot. His shoulders hunched, as if expecting a blow, but straightened just as swiftly.

Clare retreated to the tea table. But halfway through his second scone, Mikal dropped into the chair across from him. Madame Noyon's eyebrows nested in her hairline, but she poured for him too. The Shield's face did not ease and his colour did not return. He was still grey as the rain.

But he drank his tea, staring up over Clare's head at an infinitely receding point, and Clare was hard pressed not to feel . . .

. . . well, extremely pleased.

# Chapter Eleven

## Unpleasantness is Not Over

*I must reach home.* The bright blood welling beneath her gloved hand clasped to her ribs splattered her skirt, and she was no doubt leaving a trail a mile wide. Ætheric strings quivered; the effort to mislead the parties searching for her consumed most of her waning strength. *Why is there never a hansom?*

She could barely hail one as it was, bleeding so badly. Not to mention a respectable driver might not stop, even if her glamour held. Another fiery pang rolled through her as the æther twisted, a screaming rush of air almost touching her disarranged curls, and for a moment the effort of blurring what an onlooker would see almost failed. Fresh hot claret slid between her fingers.

If not for her corset stays, she might well have been a dead woman. They had turned the knife a fraction, slowing it, and the man attacking her had died of a burst of raw shrieking sorcerous power. Konstantin had not lied; he had given her all the information she could reasonably suppose he had. But those who had engaged the services of one of the actual rooftop assassins – Charles Knigsbury was at least one of his names, a flashboy who had procured the protection from the abortionist on his own account – had also thought to ensure said assassin would not open his lips to one Emma Bannon.

Or indeed, to anyone.

The sorcery she had used on the small, rat-faced flashboy still stinking of gunpowder and terror had triggered a larger explosion of hurtful magic; Knigsbury's body had literally shredded itself to pieces, and a fine cloud of mist-boiled blood had coated the inside of his stinking Dorset Alley doss. The resultant ætheric confusion had allowed her to slip away, but moments later she had felt the passage of an invisible bird of prey, and deduced the flashboy was bait of a different sort.

*Well, I did think to spring a trap or two today.* An unsteady, hitching noise escaped her; she reached out blindly and braced herself against a soot-laden brick wall. It looked vaguely familiar, a corner she saw almost every day, albeit usually through a carriage window. The rain intensified, threading through her glamour with tiny cold trickles, and she was well on her way to looking like a drowned cat.

A drowned, *bleeding* cat. Her knees buckled.

*Emma, this will not do. Stand up!* The snap of command was not hers. For a moment she was in the girls' dormer at the Collegia again, her hair shorn and her skin smarting from the scrubbing, an orphan among the bigger girls who knew what to do and where to go – and how to bully the newcomer. And Prima Grinaud, the high magistrix of the younger classes, wasp-waisted and severe in her black watered silk, snapping sharply whenever Emma cried. *Stop that noise. Collegia sorceresses do not snivel.*

And little Emma had learned. Unfortunately, all that learning now seemed likely to pour out on to a filthy Londinium street.

*No, not filthy. There's the hedge. I am nearly home.* Instead of brick, her free hand scraped the laurel hedge, washed with rain and glowing green even through the assault of smoke. Was it smoke? It certainly clouded her vision, but she smelled nothing but the familiar wet stone and Londinium coal stink.

And the sharp-sweet copper tang of blood.

No, it wasn't smoke. Her sensitive eyes were merely failing her. It had been so bright earlier, even through the lowering clouds; her head hurt, a spike of pain through her temples. The gate quivered, iron resonating with distress; for a moment she was unable to remember the peculiar ætheric half-twist that would calm the restive guardian work wedded to metal and stone.

Either that, or she was clutching the wrong gate. But no, she blinked hazily several times and looked up as another wave of sorcery slid past her, ruffling her hair and almost, almost catching the edge of her skirts. When they found the blood trail—

*I am home.* Numerals made of powdery silver metal danced, charter symbols racing over their surface in golden crackles: *34½,* a sweeter set of digits she had never seen. The high-arched gate trembled until she calmed it and found the breath to hum a simple descant.

Or she tried to. It took her a long while of sipping in air suddenly treacle-thick.

Finally she managed it. The gate shuddered and unlatched, one half sliding inward; veils of ætheric energy parted just as the next wave of sorcerously fuelled seeking tore past, arrowing unerringly for her as she tipped herself forward. It nipped at her heels, the sympathetic ætheric string from her own blood yanking, seeking to drag her backwards into the street.

But she was safely inside her own gate, the defences on her sanctum snapping shut, and Emma Bannon went to her knees on the wet, pretty front walk, lilac hedges snapping and thrashing as the house recognised her and filled with distress. Rain pattered down; she went over sideways, her hand still clamped to the wound. Another hot gush of blood; she heard running feet and exclamations, and she struggled against the grey cotton cocoon closing around her.

*Thank goodness this dress was already ugly,* she thought.

And, *I must live. I* must.

*I know too much to die now.*

# Chapter Twelve

## Our First Dinner

Normally, Clare supposed, a woman half-dead of the application of a knife to her lung – discovered covered in blood and water at her own front door, no less – would be put abed for weeks. Certainly she would not appear, pale as milk and with one half of her childlike, almost pretty face bruised, at her dinner table in fresh dark green silk with *very* close sleeves and divided skirts, brushed boots, the cameo still caught at her throat and a new pair of earrings – sapphires in heavy silver – dangling with each turn of her head. Her ringlets were rearranged as well, and though she did not wear a bonnet, he was fairly certain one lay in waiting, probably in Madame Noyon's capable care.

It was no great trick to deduce that Miss Bannon's day was far from over.

The Shield, his jaw set so hard it looked fit to crack his strong white teeth, hovered behind her thronelike chair at the head of a long mahogany table, its legs of massive carved gryphonshape shifting restlessly. Against the Prompeian red of the draperies and the bronze walls, Mikal's olive velvet and yellow eyes were aesthetically displeasing but not altogether inappropriate. He was no longer grey, but boiling with tightly controlled fury.

At least, *fury* was the word Clare thought applicable. It could have been *rage*. *Anger* was altogether too pale a term for the vibrating, incandescent wrath leaking from his every pore.

Clare viewed his cream of asparagus soup with a discerning eye, tasted it, and discovered it was superlative. *That* was no surprise; Miss Bannon did not stint and Cook, like Madame Noyon, appeared to be French. The sideboard was massive but not overpowering; the large greenery in its Chinois-style pots was carefully charmed and rustled pleasingly. The folding screens were marvels of restraint, and he wished for the chance to examine them more closely. The epergne was *also* a marvel of restraint, its height managing to look graceful and lacy instead of massively overdone.

Of course, a sorcerer lived as flagrantly as he could, but Miss Bannon's discriminations appeared to be more in the realm of actual taste and quality, instead of fad and wild freakishness. The silver was of fineness, though plain, the linens snow-white.

He cleared his throat. "I take it your day was successful, Miss Bannon?"

"Quite." She was hoarse, and she flinched slightly as she reached for her water glass. As if her side pained her. "In fact, Mr Clare, I wish to put some questions to you."

*Oh, I'm certain you do.* "I have some questions as well. Shall we interrogate each other over dinner? You are likely to have some entertainment planned for the evening."

"If by *entertainment* you mean conspiracy-hunting and unpleasantness, as a matter of fact, yes." The circles under her eyes matched the bruising on her face; she winced again as she set her glass down. "I do beg your pardon. I hope my state does not interfere with your digestion."

"Madam, almost nothing interferes with my digestion. It is a great advantage to being a mentath." He savoured a mouthful of soup. "Here is an observation. There is a group of mentaths. Some are killed for one reason. Others are killed for a separate – but connected – reason, and mutilated in some fashion. Smythe had just returned from Indus, as Grayson commented. It makes little sense to think he was involved, unless—"

"Smythe was not in Indus." Miss Bannon's gaze flashed. Did she look amused? Perhaps. "That is where Grayson was *told* he had gone. In reality, he was in Kent, at a country house owned by the Crown."

"Ah." Clare's eyelids lowered. He savoured another spoonful. "You had various and sundry reasons for leaving me mewed in your house with your Shield, then, not merely my safety."

The barest flash of surprise crossed her bruised face. It looked as if someone had struck her violently, and also tried to throttle her. The marks were fading, her skin rippling a little as the ancient symbols of charter surfaced and dove beneath the paleness. Healing sorcery.

If he had not had such excellent digestion, the sight might have turned his stomach. Besides, it was ridiculous to let such a thing interfere with one's repast.

"I did," she admitted. "Though you must admit you are safest here, and—"

"Oh, tell him," Mikal snarled. "You cannot trust me, so you wander out into Londinium and find yourself a knife to fall on."

Clare was hard put to restrain a flash of most unbecoming glee at the rich new vistas of deduction *that* remark opened.

"If you will not let me eat my dinner in peace, Shield, you may wait in the hall." But Miss Bannon did not sound sharp. Only weary.

The Shield leaned over her shoulder. "What if you had died, Prima? What then?"

"Then I would be spared this most unwelcome display at the table." Miss Bannon gazed steadily at Clare. "My apologies, sir. My Shield forgets himself."

"I do not *forget*." Mikal planted himself solidly, folding his arms. The high carved back of Miss Bannon's chair did nothing to blunt the force of the ire coming from him. "Such is my curse."

"Should you truly wish a curse, Mikal, continue in this manner." Miss Bannon sampled her soup. Finch appeared, his thin arms bearing a tray with decanters; he busied himself at the sideboard. The footmen came and went, serving with clockwork precision and muffled feet. One of them was missing his left smallest finger, quite an oddity. "Mr Clare. Tomlinson and Smythe were given different . . . pieces, as it were, of a puzzle. They seemed to be very near to a solution in their respective ways. Masters and Throckmorton were apparently given parts of those separate puzzle pieces, and—"

*You are telling me a carefully chosen tale, which probably bears only kissing relation to the truth.* "I have the idea, thank you. What were they researching?" *And why were the unregistered mentaths mutilated? You avoid that subject with much alacrity, Miss Bannon.*

"If I were at liberty to disclose that, Mr Clare . . ." She needed say no more.

"Very well." He turned his attention to the soup, momentarily, while deductions assumed a different shape inside his skull. "That rather materially changes things. You are aware of the nature of this puzzle; Lord Grayson is now too. Which means the Chancellor is suspected, or your orders are from another quarter, or—"

"Or I am a part of the conspiracy, keeping you alive for my own nefarious reasons. Mr Finch? I require rum. Shocking at dinner, but my nerves rather demand it. Mikal, either *sit down* at the place laid for you, or go out into the hall. I will *not* have this behaviour at dinner."

"I prefer to wait upon you, my Prima." It was a shock to see a grown man so mulishly defiant, like a child expecting a spanking.

"Then you may wait in the hall." The dishes rattled, the table shifted slightly, and the plants whispered under their charm domes. Clare applied himself more fully to his soup.

The Shield pulled out the chair to Miss Bannon's left – the

right was reserved for Clare – and a servant hurried forward. Finch brought a carafe and a small crystal glass, poured something Clare's sensitive nose verified was indeed rum, and Miss Bannon quaffed it smoothly, as if such an operation was habitual.

Some colour came back into her face – natural colour, not the garishness of bruising. "Thank you, Finch. I shall relate to you the most interesting portions of my day, Mr Clare, since your digestion is so sound, and you shall analyse what I tell you."

"Very well." Clare settled in his chair. The gryphon-carved table legs chose to still themselves, which was a decided improvement. What she told him now would be as close to the truth as she could risk.

She wasted little time. "Last night a single one of our attackers escaped. I meant to trace his whereabouts after we visited Bedlam, but it was not possible. However, had I not waited for daylight, today's events might have gone in a very different direction. In any case, I found our attacker had received a protection from a certain sorcerer I am familiar with. I visited said sorcerer's domicile in Whitchapel and received the information that the man – a flashboy, if you are familiar with the term?"

"A man of the lower classes. One who has been Altered. Specifically, a type of petty criminal who takes it as a point of pride." Such men were dangerous. If the Alteration did not make them unstable, the crime they were steeped in would do so. Their tempers were notoriously nasty, and by all accounts extraordinarily short.

And Miss Bannon had ventured alone into the sink of filth, danger and corruption that was Whitchapel. _Most_ intriguing.

"Precisely." Miss Bannon gave a nod of approval, drained another small glass of rum, and the roast chicken was brought in. "I received the information that our flashboy had arrived, requested a protection, paid, and left."

"Exactly how much did he pay?"

"Two gold sovereigns, a guinea, and fivepence. One rather gets the idea he was pressed for time, and that he had so much as a mark of faith from his employer."

"It being Whitchapel," Clare observed, "the fivepence was no gratuity."

"No, the sorcerer squeezed for every farthing the flashboy was willing to part with. In any case, I found the flashboy's doss and persuaded him to give *some* information before he attacked me. I defended myself – *I* did not kill him – and in the process, a truly terrible amount of sorcery was triggered on him." She eyed Clare speculatively, and her colour was indeed better. She set to the roast chicken with a will, and Clare copied her example. "It was old sorcery, the same practitioner as last night's event in Bedlam. Our flashboy was no sorcerer, so it . . . the force tore him apart. It was intended to not only do so but also incapacitate any sorcerous visitor so his employer could discover any meddling in his business."

"His?"

"I find it extraordinarily unlikely this is a woman, sir."

Clare was inclined to agree, but Mikal could apparently stand it no longer. The Shield stared at the chicken on his plate, the potato balls drenched in golden butter, the scattered parsley, as if it were a mass of writhing snakes. "*Injured* you? Stabbed you in the lung, and—"

"Do *not* interrupt, Mikal." A line had appeared between Miss Bannon's arched eyebrows. "I am sure Mr Clare is aware of the extent of my injuries. So, mentath, your analysis, if you please."

Clare sampled a potato ball. *Most excellent.* "I have been reading the papers today. Your hospitality is wonderful, Miss Bannon. The *Encyclopaedie* was also useful, though I may need some other texts—"

She waved a hand, her rings sparkling. Fire opals this time, two of them set in heavy bronze and surrounded by what appeared to be tiny uncut diamonds. "Merely inform Mr Finch of your requirements. Analysis, please."

"You will not like it."

"That does not detract from its validity."

"You are a very managing female, Miss Bannon."

Thus ensued a very long silence as Clare's utensils made tiny noises against his plate. The ham arrived and was dealt with, a dish of *haricots verts* in a sauce full of lemony tang as well. No oysters, but he did not feel stinted.

It took until the sherbet for him to notice the uncomfortable quality of the silence. At least, a normal person might have called it uncomfortable. It was heavy, cold, and almost . . . reptilian. The gryphons carved into the table legs shifted, the table's surface completely level and the fluid motion underneath almost enough to unseat even *his* stomach.

The illogic of it bothered him. A table should not move so.

"My analysis—" he began.

"Is that I am a 'managing female'?" Miss Bannon enquired, almost sweetly. The tone alarmed him, and he diverted his attention from the exquisite bone-china sherbet dish.

He was right to be alarmed, for he noted Mikal had tensed. The Shield's head was up, and he stared at the sorceress with the leashed expectation of a bloodhound. The sorceress, her curls falling forward, toyed with a small silver spoon, tracing patterns through melting lemon sherbet.

*Aha. We have found a chink in your armour, Sorceress Prime.* "Is that you know far more than you are telling me, and hence your invitation to analyse is a trap. I shall at the very best look like an idiot, and at the worst waste precious time."

"Indeed." She settled back in her chair, and the sherbet was whisked away. So was Mikal's, untouched. "Excuse me. I have preparations to make before I leave the house again. Enjoy your coffee, Mr Clare." She rose, and Mikal all but leapt upright as well.

"I do hope I shall be able to accompany you?" Clare pushed his chair back and gained his feet. "Now that you have satisfied yourself that I am not part of this conspiracy?"

"I have not satisfied myself on that account, sir. But you may accompany me." She glanced once at Mikal. "I wish you precisely where I may watch you. We shall leave in a half-hour."

# Chapter Thirteen

## Britannia's Worst

Emma spent most of that half-hour roaming her study as the swelling on her face retreated, running her fingers along leather-clad spines and attempting to clear her mind. The skull on her desk creaked each time she passed, bone-dust rising and settling along its grinning curves. Mikal, by now well acquainted with this ritual, stood by the door, his hands crossed in a Shield's habitual pose.

Scraps covered with her handwriting scattered across the desk as well, different charm and charter symbols, experiments, notes and drawings arranged in a system no other person would be able to decipher. A globe of malachite on a brass Atlas's straining shoulders spun lazily, a small scraping sound under the rustle of her skirts. The long black drapes moved slightly as well, and witchglobes in heavy bronze cages sputtered, almost sparking and giving out a low bloody light that *precisely* matched her feelings at the moment.

The little sounds only underscored Mikal's silence. She finally halted next to the high-backed, severe leather chairs before the fireplace. Gripped the back of one, her fingers turning white. Her chest ached, so she squeezed harder. Healing sorcery could only do so much, and Mikal's facility with it was not infinite, though certainly not inconsiderable either.

The map of the Empire over the fireplace, etched on brass and framed in Ceylon ebony, glowed with soft golden reflections, showing the passage of sunlight over the Empire's dominions. The sun indeed never set; Britannia's sway was wide.

But even *she* was not infinite, or invulnerable.

Emma stared, stiffening her knees, and for a moment she considered retreating behind her walls and doing no more. God knew she had paid enough, over and over, for every scrap she had received.

But that would be treachery of a different sort, wouldn't it. To simply leave the Queen without a sorceress willing to do the worst.

And there was her regrettable pride, raising its head. There might be Primes more powerful than Emma Bannon, and a few more socially acceptable, and perhaps even one or two as loyal. Yet there was no Prime who would sink to the depths *she* would in service to the current holder of Britannia's essence.

Who was, after all, merely a girl who had been thrust on to the throne, and fought with surprising skill and ferocity to free herself from those who would use her.

*Is that why I find myself so inclined to settle in this harness?* Emma half turned, uncramping her hand with an effort. The Shield's gaze met hers.

What could she say? "Before I left . . . that was unjustified, Mikal. My temper is . . . uncertain."

A single nod. Perhaps an acceptance of the apology, perhaps simply affirmation of his hearing it.

Proud to the end, her Shield. At least the past month had taught her *that*. And today's events had been rather a slap of cold water. Since the Crawford . . . affair, she had been simply focused on her service to Britannia. As if working herself into a rag of bone and nervous ætheric force would somehow give her an answer.

*There may not be another time to ask.* "Mikal?"

"Prima."

"Why did you do . . . what you did?" *And what is the assurance that you will not violate your Shield oath again, if you judge me as you judged* him? *Or did you? I do not know enough to guess at the music that moves you.*

*Perhaps I should ask Mr Clare to deduce its measures.* For a moment, she thought of explaining to a mentath how she had been trapped in chains and a Major Circle not of her devising, close to having her sorcery torn out of her by the roots, and what she had heard as Mikal's fingers closed around Crawford's throat. The crackling of little bones, the awful choking noises mixing with her own panicked, ineffectual cries.

To be so helpless was enough to drive a Prime to the edge of sanity. Or past. And Emma wondered if she had been quite sane since the experience.

Perhaps Mikal chose to misunderstand her question. "It was a choice between service to another Prime or death." Calm, matter-of-fact, his expression set and unyielding. "You said it yourself, Prima. They would kill me if I were not in service to a sorcerer who could protect me, and you are the only one willing to do so."

*At least that you have found.* What was the danger of continuing thus? She braced herself, and took the next logical step. "You may, if you choose, leave my service and stay in my house as a sanctuary. The Collegia will censure me, but at least you will still be alive." *And I will not have to wonder when you will find me lacking and squeeze the life out of me.*

"No."

Well, at least she had made him express a preference. "Very well. You may decide otherwise at any—"

"No." His eyes flamed. She wondered, not for the first time, how much of what she suspected of his bloodline was true. "Do not ask again, Prima."

*Very well. I shall simply be on guard. As I have been. And look how satisfactorily* that *has proceeded.* Still, he had not turned on her yet. "You will need to be fully armed tonight."

The crimson light made him an ochre statue, except for the gleams of his eyes. "I am."

"Already?" She sounded mocking, she supposed.

"I do not take it lightly when *my* Prima is stabbed in the lung."

Your *Prima. Did you feel so proprietary of* your *Prime, lo that scant month ago?* "I returned, did I not?"

"Barely, Emma. Shall we continue this conversation, or would you like to bring me to my knees again and save time?"

*I apologised, Mikal.* "You say that as if you do not enjoy it." Sharp, a prick for his temper, no less regrettable than her own.

He chose not to give battle, for once. "No more or less than you do, Prima. Shall I ask where we are bound tonight? Tideturn is close. No more than a quarter-hour."

*I am aware of that.* She glanced at the softly ticking grandfather clock, its face showing the different hours of the day in jewelled simulacra of the Ages of Man. Sorcery bubbled in its depths, its wheels and cogs and springs measuring each second of eternity. Given proper care, the works would continue even when the thick oak casing, sheathed in chasing metal, turned to dust. The dealer had sworn it was from an alchemyst's laboratory, hinting that so august a personage as von Tachel had owned it at one time. Exceedingly unlikely . . . but still, Emma liked it, and the jewelled simulacra were a reminder.

Especially the dirty labourer at noon, lifting his mug of foaming beer to blackened lips, and the drab pleading with the gentleman at eleven.

The massive dragon's head carved above the face, its eyes glowing with soft sorcery, held its jaws in a constant, silent roar. *Time*, it said, *is a gaping maw like mine. You have escaped the worst.*

And she had, even before Miles Crawford had so neatly trapped her. But for an accident of fate, she could have ended as a drab herself, in the very slums she had been hunting through this afternoon.

"Southwark," she heard herself say. "We are visiting Mehitabel."

She had the satisfaction of seeing her Shield pale before she swept past him and through her study doors.

# Chapter Fourteen

## The Wark and the Werks

Clare offered his hand, but the sorceress put no weight on it as she climbed into the hansom, her petticoats oddly soundless.

"All the same, my good man, one shouldn't have to throw oneself into the street to attract a driver's attention." Clare looked back at the house – it appeared dark, closed up for the night, the gates to the front walk locked by invisible hands.

"I stops for my fares, I does." The driver's gin-blossomed nose and cheeks all but glowed in the ruddiness of dusk. The sun was sinking quickly, and the fog was rising. A regular Londinium pea-souper, creeping up the Themis. "You won't find no one else willin t'take you half-crost that bridge, no sir. Not Southwark, this close to Turn. Right lucky you are."

"Very lucky indeed, especially since we're paying double fare." The man was no use for deductive purposes; he was a cockerel Cockney with a war wound to his left leg, reeking of gin and married to a Stepney woman who tied the traditional ribbon in his buttonhole.

"Mr Clare." The sorceress leaned forward. Her swelling and bruising had gone down remarkably, and a crease of annoyance lingered on her forehead. "Cease arguing with the man and get *into* the carriage."

He complied, the door banged shut, and the heaving brass flanks of the clockhorse crackled under the whip. *Altered horse and Altered flashboy,* his brain whispered. *There is no connection, do be reasonable.*

He was uneasy. It was the gryphons at the table, of course. Irrationality bothered him as it would bother *any* mentath. That was all.

*No, it is not. You haven't enough information. Simply be patient.* It was hard to be patient, he acknowledged, when Miss Bannon so assiduously avoided the subject of the mutilations of unregistered mentaths.

That hit a trifle close to home, so to speak.

Mikal had disappeared, though Clare suspected further trouble would bring his reappearance. The Shield no longer looked grey and drawn, though grim enough, and the sorceress was still pale, wincing slightly when she had to move in certain ways. The wound could very easily have proved deadly.

*I did not kill him,* she had hurriedly said, as if he would suspect such a thing. The mental drawer bearing Miss Bannon's name had turned into a large bureau with several nooks and crannies. She was doing far more to keep his faculties exercised than the conspiracy.

Which was beginning to take on some troubling characteristics in its own right, to be sure.

The hansom jolted, Miss Bannon swayed into him, and Clare murmured an apology. "Close quarters."

"Indeed." She was rather alarmingly white, her curls swinging. "Mr Clare, I have not been entirely open with you."

"Of course. You are not entirely open with anyone, Miss Bannon. You have learned not to be."

"Another deduction."

"Have you read my monograph, madam? Deduction is my life. Any mentath's, really, but mine *especially.*" He permitted himself a sardonic raise of the eyebrows, glanced at her, and was gratified to find a slight smile. "I deduce you are more irritated with your own ill luck than with me *or* your Shield. I deduce you were an orphan, and your early life taught you the value of luxury. I *further* deduce this 'conspiracy' is actually a disagreement over a certain item mentaths have been engaged in—"

"Wait." She cocked her head, lifting one gloved hand, and shivered. Clare consulted his pocket watch.

Tideturn.

Charter symbols, glowing gold, crawled over her skin. Her jewellery boiled with sparks, the cameo becoming a miniature lamp, filling the cab's interior with soft light. Clare watched, fascinated, as the charter symbols dove into her flesh, stray sorcery dust puffing from the folds of her dress and winking out of existence in mid-air. Fresh charter-charm marks appeared, a river of runic writing coating her.

Miss Bannon exhaled, sharply, and the lights faded. She shook her fingers, and sparks popped. One of the clockhorses neighed, and the cab jolted. "Much better," she muttered, and turned her dark eyes on Clare. There was no trace of the horrific bruising on her face and throat, and she did not flinch at another jolt. "You were saying. A certain item?"

"A certain item mentaths have been engaged in building, but in parts, so none of them knows the whole." He tucked his watch away, carefully. Fresh linens of exceeding quality had magically appeared for him, and a permanent measuring charm had been applied to him and his clothes. The valet was, at least, dexterous and did not seek to engage him in superfluous conversation.

Miss Bannon's hospitality was proving itself legendary in stature.

"Hm." Neither affirming nor denying.

"An item Lord Grayson was deliberately kept somewhat unaware of." *Or you hope he is unaware.* "Which means you have been involved with these mentaths for longer than they have been dying, and your orders come from another quarter indeed."

"And who do you suppose could *order* me about, sir?" The cab lurched; she lifted her chin, but relaxed immediately. Clare's stomach somersaulted, perhaps expecting a repeat of last night's games.

"I have noted the royal seal on several items in your excellent library, which I availed myself of just before we left, and the statue of Britannia in your entry hall is of solid silver, as well as stamped with the royal imprimatur. No doubt you offered some great service and were given a token – but even if you had not been, you would have continued to serve. Your utterance of *God and Her Majesty* is sincere. And, one suspects, heartfelt."

Her lips pursed. Her hands clasped together, lying decorously well bred in her lap. Despite the likely chill of the evening, she wore no shawl. She was hatless as well, despite his guess to the contrary. She perhaps expected an unpleasant event during which a bonnet would be a hindrance.

He did not find this a soothing observation.

Silence stretched between them, broken only by the clopping of metal-reinforced hooves and the driver's half-muffled cheerful catcalls as they turned south. Other hackney drivers responded, and the crowded streets around them were a low mumbling surf-roar. Just after Tideturn the city was a freshly yeasted, bubbling mass, especially near the Themis.

"Let us suppose you are to be trusted." Miss Bannon peered through the window, watching the crowd whirl past. "What then?"

"Why then, Miss Bannon, we discover who has been killing sorcerers and mentaths, uncover the missing pieces of this item, learn who among Her Majesty's subjects is treacherous enough to wish to steal this item and presumably use it against Britannia's current incarnation, and—"

"Be home in time for tea?"

It took him by surprise, and his wheezing laugh did as well. He sobered almost instantly as the hansom slowed, swimming against the tide at the northern edge of the Iron Bridge. "One hopes."

"Indeed. Then let us proceed with this understanding, Mr Clare: I am responsible for your safety, and I do not forgive disobedience or incompetence. You are relatively competent; may I trust you not to question?"

*An* exceedingly *managing female.* "Until further notice, Miss Bannon, you may. Provided your requests fall within the compass of my ability."

"Fair enough. We are at the Bridge; no doubt our driver will be stopping soon. You are a gentleman, but pray do not precede me from the carriage. You are far more vulnerable than I."

A sharp bite of irritation flashed through him. He shelved it with difficulty. "Very well."

"Thank you." Primly, she gathered herself, and as if in response, the hansom halted.

Queen's Bridge – otherwise known as the Southwark or the Iron, to balance the Stone Bridge as one of Londinium's arteries – loomed in twilight, fog shrouding both of its massive ends. Black iron gleamed wetly, the Themis rippling with gold under its arches as Tideturn spilled and eddied back to sea. It was perhaps the ugliest bridge in Londinium, and the charter symbols cast into its long span crawled with touches of vermilion. Some said the Bridges kept the Themis under control, binding the ancient, hungry demigod sleeping in the river's depths.

Most illogical. Still, the cold iron was superstitiously comforting.

At the Bridge's southern end, the Wark sent up columns of dense smoke underlit with crimson, the unsleeping foundries audible even at this distance. Cinders fell like Twelfthnight snow there, and the bridge thrummed unpleasantly underfoot.

"'Tis as far as I go, worships." The driver was pale under his gin-touched cheeks. "The Black Wark's unsteady tonight. Feel it in the Bridge, you can."

Mikal had appeared at Miss Bannon's elbow, yellow eyes taking a last gleam from the Themis. He murmured to the sorceress, who nodded once, sharply, her earrings swinging. "Give him a further half-crown, Shield. He's done well. Mr Clare, come with me."

"Thank you. Good man." Clare dusted his hat. The Wark's cinders would perhaps ruin it. "Off you go, then. Mind you," he remarked to the sorceress, "I am still no closer to discovering why a hansom can be so bloody difficult to find."

Mikal tossed a coin, the flick of his fingers invisible in the uncertain light. The cabbie, however, plucked the half-crown from the air, and the coin vanished. He tipped his hat at the sorceress and winked before lifting the reins.

"Conspiracy." Miss Bannon watched as the hansom negotiated a tight turn, the clockhorse's Altered hooves clipping the bridge's surface. Stray sparks of sorcery winked out in its wake. The whip cracked, and their driver made good his escape.

"That could be so." Clare's dinner was not sitting so excellently at the moment. He put his shoulders back, seeking to ease the discomfort.

The middle of the Bridge was deserted. On either end, Londinium teemed; Queen Street's terminus on to Upper Themis was crowded with warehouses and sloping tenements. Lights winked among them, gasflame and the pallid gleams of the occasional witchglobe. On the other end, Southwark's bloody glow made a low, unhappy noise.

Miss Bannon did not relax until the hansom was out of sight, vanished on to Upper Themis Road. Even then, the tension in her only abated; it did not cease. "Safe enough," she murmured. "Come, Mr Clare. Listen closely while we walk."

He offered his arm. Stray cinders fluttered, a grey curtain.

"We are about to enter Southwark." She did not lean on him, though she rested a gloved hand delicately and correctly in the crook of his elbow. Mikal stepped away, turning smartly, and trailed on Miss Bannon's other side.

"Obviously."

"Do not interrupt. Once we step off the Bridge, no matter

how important, do not speak without express permission from me. The . . . lady we are visiting is eccentric, and much of the Black Wark is full of her ears. She is also *exceedingly* dangerous."

"If she is dangerous enough to cause you this concern, Miss Bannon, rest assured I shall follow your instructions precisely. Who is she?"

"Her name is Mehitabel." Miss Bannon's jaw was set, and she looked pale. "Mehitabel the Black."

"What a curious name. Tell me, Miss Bannon, should one fear her?"

Her childlike face with its aristocratic nose was solemn, and she gave him one very small, tight-mouthed smile. "You are sane, Mr Clare. That means *yes*."

The heart of Southwark was the Black Wark, grey and red. Grey from the piled cinders the shuffling ashwalkers pushed along with their long flat brooms, the wagons loaded with the stuff taken to the soap factories grumbling along on traditional wooden wheels. Red from the glow of the foundries, red for the beating heart under the Wark's crazyquilt of streets and jumbled alleys. The gaslamps here corroded swiftly from the cinderfall; yellow fog sent thin tendrils questing along the cobbles. The low red glow made the fog flinch, hugging corners and pooling in darker spots.

Between Blackfriar and Londinium Bridges, the Iron Bridge stood and the Themis was dark, great fingers combing its silk as the foundries drank and sent their products forth. Metalwork, mechanisterum used for Alteration, the huge warehouses for the making of clockhorses on the near side of High Borough, close to the Leather Market. Blackfriar, Londinium Bridge, Great Dover-Borough High-Wellington and Great Surrey to the west and east, Greenwitch at the south; these were the confines of the Black Wark. Some said those streets had powerful enchantments buried underneath, wedded to rails of pure silver, keeping the Wark contained. Whispers told of workshops in the Wark where workers so Altered as to be merely metal skeletons grinned and leapt, or streets faced in dark metallic clockwork that *changed* when the fog grew thick and the cinderfall was particularly intense.

The Wark's natives were Altered young. Immigrants, mostly Eirean, poured in to work at the foundries and warehouses, living twenty or more to a stinking room while gleaming delicate clockworks and massive metalwork were shipped out clean and sparkling on each tide.

If a gentleman went into the Wark, he hired Altered guides, native flashboys working in groups of a half-dozen or more who mostly took it as a point of rough pride to guard their employers. The Wark's flashboys were feared even in the Eastron End's worst slums, and rumour had it they were often contracted for shady work even a Thugee from darkest Indus would flinch at.

At the end of the Iron Bridge, Mikal stepped forward, and the veil of cinderfall parted.

"Passage a pence apiece!" a rough voice croaked. "Threepee for your worships!"

A bridgekeeper appeared in a circle of gaslamp glow, cinders shaking from the brim of his hat. Round and wrapped in odds and ends; metal gleamed as his Alterations came into view – a lobster claw instead of a left hand, soot-crusted metal gleaming in odd scraped-bare spots, and a glass eye lit with venomous yellow, like the fog. He moved oddly, lurching, and Clare's interest sharpened.

*He has been Altered even more thoroughly than that. Look, there. Wheels. He has wheels instead of feet.* They were not quality Alterations, either. Rough edges and clicking cogs caked with grease and cinders, no smoothly gleaming surfaces.

Clare held his tongue with difficulty.

"Mikal." The sorceress did not break stride, drawing him on.

"Ye'll be wanting guides, worships, specially after Tideturn." The bridgekeeper chuckled. "And wit a laddle too!"

Movement in the shadows. Clare stiffened, but Miss Bannon

simply tilted her head. "I require no *guide*, Carthamus, and you should polish that eye of yours. Give your dogs the signal to withdraw, or you'll lose a goodly portion of them to my temper."

Mikal's hand flicked. Three pennies chimed on the cobbled street, almost lost in a drift of cinders. The Shield stepped back, almost mincingly, and the bridgekeeper cursed.

"Watch your tongue," Miss Bannon snapped, and her fingers clamped on Clare's arm with surprising strength. "This way."

"There are quite a few of them." Mikal, hushed and low.

"Oh, I should think so. She's expecting me."

They plunged into the Wark, Clare's senses quivering-alert, and he almost wished he had chosen to remain in Mayefair.

# Chapter Fifteen

## Steelstruck Teeth

The jackals gathered the instant they stepped off the Bridge, and Emma didn't bother hailing one of the footcabs. Mikal was tense, his footsteps following hers and the scent of his readiness gunpowder-sharp, a different crimson than the low foundry glow. To Sight, the Wark was full of sharp-edged runic shapes trembling on the edge of the visible, an alien charter language wearing at the warp and weft of Londinium's ancient sorcery. The cinders whispered in toothless, burning voices, and she wished she had brought a veil. Sparks lifted lazily into the fog, the Wark still resonating from Tideturn like a giant bell shivering long after its vibration voice has dropped below the audible.

The taste of sorcery here was metallic, and there was so much interference it was almost a relief to feel Clare's arm solid and real under her hand. Mikal could not anchor her – he would be far more occupied if any of the jackal flashboys took it into their heads to make trouble for the trespassers.

*What a time to wish for more Shields.* The thought was there and gone in a flash; she had other matters to attend to.

The cinderfall changed direction, flakes of ash spinning though there was no wind. Londinium's fog kept creeping, sliding its fingers into the cracks, and was forced back by the intelligence in the Wark's red glow.

A sharp right, staying well away from the dark, toothless-gaping alleys; she set their course and decided to approach the Blackwerks from the north. It made sense, and the less time she spent in the Wark with a mentath at her sleeve, the better.

He was already looking decidedly green. She supposed she should have mentioned that the sorcery within the Wark's confines, not only illogical but *alien*, might discommode him.

Scuttling things moved in the shadows, clinking sharp edges dragged over cobbles and through filth. Whispers, gleams of eyes from the towering roofs. A small foundry opened on their right; glowing metal poured from one giant cauldron to another, sparks flying as the workers inside became cutpaper shadows. Tiny, paired gleams peering through grates and clustering in the alleys told her the rats were out in force, their sleek sides heaving and their naked tails leaving opalescent slug-sheens behind.

She had to prod Clare. He was slowing down, craning his head to take everything in. He would be straining to make sense of the cinderfall's eddies and flows, the light not behaving as it should, the little slithering scrapes in the darkness.

"Merely observe," she whispered, as if he was a Shield trainee and she was responsible for teaching him to Glove. "Do not analyse."

He gave her a wide-eyed look that qualified as shocked.

It would likely not fool the Black Lady. They turned with Park Street's sharp bend, and it was not her imagination – the gaslamps were dimming. The cinderfall was a curtain, sweeping closer. The tiny paired gleams slid free of the alleymouths, drawing closer as the cinders smoothed over their wet-gleaming flanks.

*Oh, for Heaven's sake.* She breathed a most impolite term, glanced at Mikal, and snapped her free hand out, fingers twisting as a half-measure of chant pulled its way free of her lips, sliding bloody and whole into the thick darkness.

Clear silver light flamed. A sorcerous circle smoked into being around them, familiar charter symbols flashing and twisting through the cinderfall, and the rats scattered. They were Altered too, clockworks spinning in their hindquarters, grease splashing from the gears and their little diamond claws skritching against the cobbles.

"*Enough!*" she snapped, and the gaslamps flared back into guttering light. Londinium's fog writhed, its tendrils thickening. "I am not to be trifled with, Mehitabel!"

All motion ceased for a moment, the cinders arrested in their slow whirling motion and sparkling in mid-air. The light faded, a witchball popping into being and hovering behind Emma, dimming slightly as her attention turned from it. And as she expected, when the world hitched forward and time began again, there was a flashboy just at the edge of her sphere of normalcy, his top hat cocked and his moth-eaten purple velvet jacket carefully brushed. His right hand was a marvel of Alteration, black metal that looked almost exactly like the appendage he had been born with, and the metallic patterns etched on his ageless-young face were familiar.

He was high in Mehitabel's favour, and would probably continue to be so for a long while yet. At least while his reflexes were good and his cruelty pleased her.

"Ladyname." He grinned, his teeth steel chips. That right hand flexed with a dry, oily sound, and Mikal stepped forward. Just one step, but it was enough. The flashboy gave him a brief glance, then addressed Emma again. "Ye use Ladyname. Billybong o'ye, laddle."

"She knows my name as well," Emma replied crisply. "I am on *business,* Dodgerboy. Bound for the Blackwerks, and I do not appreciate this nonsense."

"Guide ye, and for no fiddle e'en." The flashboy turned, the nails pounded into his boot heels striking a single crimson spark from a garbage-slick cobble. "Ladyname be specting."

She permitted herself a single, unamused chuckle. "Well, I would hardly dare call upon her otherwise. Lead on, Dodgerboy, and mind yourself. I suspect the Lady would hate to lose you."

"Oh, aye. 'M flash-quick. Pop yer farthings a' three paces,

leave cammie rag for the wisps." He waved his un-Altered hand, a flash of grimy pale skin.

Emma squeezed Clare's arm again. The witchball brightened. "He means he could pick your pockets clean at three paces and leave your handkerchief for lesser thieves. It is most likely no boast, so Mikal will cut off his fingers – *all* of them – should he approach us. Let us be along, I have other business to transact tonight."

The flashboy glanced once at Clare. "Deefer, that 'un?"

She tapped her foot, the gesture losing something under her skirts but still, she hoped, expressing her displeasure. "He is not deaf, *or* dumb, not that it is your *business*. Do we move along, or do I set your hair on fire and visit your mistress while in a bad mood?"

He gave no reply, just showed his steel-struck teeth again. For a moment Emma imagined those teeth meeting in flesh, blood squirting free and griming the bright metal, and quelled a shudder.

She had seen Mehitabel's flashboys feeding, once.

But Dodgerboy set off, and once Mikal nodded, his jaw set in a grim line, she propelled Clare along with the simple expedient of pulling on his arm, and they walked further into the Wark, followed by a bobbing silver globe of witchlight.

Two steps later, she noticed Mikal had disappeared.

Good.

# Chapter Sixteen

## Not You, Too

The Blackwerks rose, spines of black metal corkscrewed with heat and stress. Clare's skull felt tight, confining. There was simply too much illogic here. The cinders, for one thing – there was no way the fires of the Wark could produce this much matter. Yet it had to come from *somewhere*. And the rats – something so small should not be Altered. Their eyes glowed viciously, and they scuttled with quick, oily movements.

The young Altered boy walked ahead of them, whistling, hands stuffed deep in his pockets. Every once in a while he performed a curious little hop-skip, but to no rhythm Clare could discern. Miss Bannon's tension communicated itself through her grip on his arm. If this was a promenade, it was one through a Hellish underworld where every angle was subtly skewed.

As soon as the thought arrived, the squeezing of his skull ceased. He began seeking to catalogue the precise measurement in degrees of every angle, calculating the inconsistencies and attempting to apply a theory to them. It was difficult mental work, and he was faintly aware of sweat springing up on his brow, but the relief of having a task was immense.

A pair of huge spiny gates, their tops tortured by unimaginable heat, stood ajar. Ash piled high on either side, drifting against a gap-toothed brick wall. A painted tin sign proclaimed

*Blackwerks,* and the Altered boy minced through the gates, turning and giving a deep bow. "Enter, w'ships, Ladyname be bless'd. Step right inna the Werks." Two stamps of his left foot, his boot heel ringing against cracked cobbles, and he danced back into an orange glow.

The cavern of the Werks rose, its entire front open and exhaling a burning draught. Machinery twisted inside, cauldrons tipping and pouring substances he did not care to think too deeply on. Wheels ticked, their toothed edges meshing with others, huge soot-blackened chains shivering, clashing, or stretched taut. The cinderfall intensified here, Clare was glad of his hat. Somehow the falling matter avoided Miss Bannon, and the witchlight behind them made everything in the circle of its glow keep to its proper proportions. He wondered what effort it cost Miss Bannon to keep that sphere of normalcy steady, and decided not to ask.

A slim figure resolved out of the heatglare, gliding forward. *What is this?*

It was a woman. Or perhaps it had been once. Long swaying black bombazine skirts, stiff with ash, smooth black metal skin, an explosion of ash-grey horsehair held back with jet-dangling pins. Its arms were marvels of Alteration, metal bones and hands of fine delicate clockwork opening and closing as it – *she* rolled forward. The face was also blank metal and clockwork, the nose merely sinus caverns; the eyes were hen's-egg rubies lit from within by feral intelligence.

Miss Bannon squeezed his arm again, warningly. Clare stared.

The thing's mouth – or the aperture serving it as a mouth – moved. "*Prima.*" The voice held a rush and crackle of flame, and the skirts shuddered as whatever contraption was underneath them encountered an irregularity in the flooring.

*That dress was fashionable a decade ago.* He caught sight of a reading-glass dangling from a thin metal chain, hiding in the skirts. *Does this thing read? How long ago was it human? Does it have any flesh left?*

"Mehitabel." Miss Bannon nodded, once. "I have come for what I left."

A rasp-clanking screech rose from the thing's chest. It took Clare a moment to recognise that rusted, painful sound for what it was.

Laughter.

The hideous noise cut off sharply, and the boy who had led them here stepped back nervously, like an unAltered horse scenting the metal and blood of the pens. The thing called Mehitabel turned its head, servomotors in the neck ratcheting with dry terrible grace. The wretched imitation of a human movement made Clare's dinner writhe.

*Perhaps my digestion is not as sound as it could be*, he noted, and found himself clutching at Miss Bannon's hand on his arm. Patting slightly, as if she were startled and he meant to soothe. His throat was tight.

*Emotion. Cease this.*

But his feelings did not listen.

"Oh, Mehitabel." Miss Bannon sounded, of all things, saddened. "Not you too."

"*You do not know your enemies, sorceressss.*" Rust showered from the thing's elbow joints as it lifted its arms. Its mouth widened, a spark of glowing-coal red dilating far back in its throat. Miss Bannon stepped forward, disengaging herself from Clare with a practised twist of her hand, and the witchlight intensified behind them, casting a frail screen of clear silver light against the venomous crimson of the Werks. Machinery shuddered and crashed as Mehitabel's body jerked, and Miss Bannon yelled an anatomical term Clare had never thought a lady would be conversant with.

The crashing ceased. Mehitabel's metal body froze, in stasis.

"I may not know my enemies," Miss Bannon said softly, her hands held out in a curious contorted gesture, fingers interlaced. "But I am *Prime*, little wyrm, and you are only here on sufferance."

The metal thing shuddered. There was a flicker of motion, and Clare's blurted warning was lost in a draught of scalding air. Mikal was suddenly *there*, smacking aside Dodgerboy's hand with contemptuous ease, the slender gleam of a knife flying in a high arc to vanish into the ash outside. The Shield made another swift motion, almost as an afterthought, and the Altered boy flew backwards, vanishing into a haze of red light and confused, whirling cinders.

"*Sufferance?*" A low, thick burping chuckle rode the rush of hot stinking air out of the Werks. The voice was terrible, a dry-scaled monstrous thing approximating human words over the groaning of metal and crackling of flame, the sibilants laden with toxic dust. "*Oh, I think not, monkeychild. You are in* my *home now.*"

The witchlight blazed, sharp silver brilliance. "Mikal." Miss Bannon's voice cut through the thing's laughter. "Take him. And *run.*"

The descant scorched her throat, her focus splitting as the great twisting metal thing fought her hold. Her left hand cramped, burning as she held the rope of intent, the force clamped over Mehitabel's simulacrum fraying at the edges. She had to choose – the trueform or the metal echo, layers of the physical and ætheric vibrating as sorcery spread in rayed patterns, the Wark quivering as she forced its sorcery to her will.

*I will pay for this later.* A Greater Word rose within the fabric of the chant, weaving itself between the syllables. It settled on the metal form, which buckled and curled like paper in a fire.

A massive wrecked scream rose from Mehitabel's unseen trueform. *That must sting.*

But it freed Emma to bring her focus back to a single object, white-hot sorcerous force running through her veins. The Blackwerks seethed with running feet, shouts. Mehitabel's flash-boys and the antlike workers who crawled through the heat-shimmering cavern began to appear, flickering unsteadily through the cinderfall.

Emma's hands shot out, sorcery crackling between them. She *squeezed*, smoke rising from her rings and the scorched material of her gloves, and Mehitabel shrieked again. The flashboys froze, workers dropping where they stood. The chant died away now that Emma had her grip.

"I can crush flesh just as easily," she called, the words slicing through snap-crackling flame and shuddering metallic clanking. The simulacrum's face continued melting, runnels of liquid iron sliding down, its unfashionable dress a torch. "Even *your* flesh. Where is it, *Me-hi-ta-beh-ru-la gu'rush Me-hi-lwa?*" The foreign syllables punctured tortured air; Emma's throat scorched and her eyes watering as she accented each in its proper place.

Hours of study and careful tortuous work had suddenly returned its investment. Mehitabel had obviously never guessed that Emma might uncover her truename, much less *use* it.

A wyrm would never forget, let alone forgive such a thing.

The Blackwerks . . . stopped.

Sparks and cinders hung in mid-air. The burning simulacrum was a painting, flames caught in mid-twist, its face terribly ruined.

A huge, narrow head, triple-crowned and triple-tongued, rose from a crucible of molten metal, snaking forward on a flexible, black-scaled neck. The eyes were jewels of flame, matching the now-cracked rubies of the simulacrum, and leathery wings spread through the cinderfall, their bladed edges cutting through individual flecks and sparks held in stasis.

The tongues flickered, smoke wreathing the wyrm's long body in curiously lethargic veils. Mehitabel held the Werks out of Time's slipstream, her wings ruffling as they combed slumbering air. The heat was immense, awesome, the cup of metal holding the lower half of her body bubbling with thick tearing sounds. She turned her head sideways, one ruby eye glinting, but Emma leaned back, fingers burning, the thin fine leash of her will cutting across the dragon's snout.

*They are the children of Time,* her teacher had intoned long ago. *They are of the Powers, and their elders sleep. We should be glad of that slumber, for if those wyrms awakened they would shake this isle – and plenty more – from their backs, and the Age of Flame would return.*

Mehitabel's head jerked back and she glared, one clawed forelimb sinking into the edge of the crucible and digging in with another tortured sound. The tongues flickered. *"You* are dead."

"Not yet, wyrm." Emma set her boots more firmly. "Where is it?"

"It isss not here." Heat lapped Mehitabel's sides, her flexible ribs heaving bellows-like.

*"Where is it?"* Emma's hands clenched, pressure enfolding the wyrm. She bore down. The sensation was different from the crunch crushing of metal – slippery and armoured, giving resiliently and struggling to escape. The dragon could make another simulacrum, but its trueform was also vulnerable – especially to an angry sorceress who knew its name.

*That* was also what it meant to be Prime – to pronounce a name of such power without your tongue scorching and your eyes melting in hot runnels down your cheeks. Some were of the opinion that only a Prime's overweening pride shielded him from such agony. Others said it was the size of the ætheric charge Primes were able to carry. None had solved the riddle, and Emma's own research was inconclusive at best.

Had Mikal taken the mentath away? She hoped so. This much concentrated sorcery was dangerous, and what she was about to do with it doubly so. And they had a chance to escape Mehitabel's flashboys and the other dangers of the Wark *now*, while she held the wyrm captive.

The dragon hissed, lowering its head. Its teeth were slashes of obsidian, each one with a thin line of crimson at its glassy heart. "One came and relieved me of the burden. Shake in terror, little monkey—"

Emma's fists jerked. Mehitabel howled, a gush of rancid

oily-hot breath pushing Emma's hair back, wringing scalding tears free to paint her cheeks, snapping her skirts. When the wyrm was done making noise, Emma released the pressure. But only slightly, her concentration narrowing to a single white-hot point.

"Names, Mehitabel. Who came, and for whom?"

"I will kill you for thiss. You will *dieeeee*—" The word spiralled up into a glassine screech.

Her own voice, a knife through something hot and brittle. "*Names*, Mehitabel! Truenames! Or we learn the look of your insides, ironwyrm!" The force of Tideturn would start to fail her soon. The cameo was a spot of molten heat at her throat, and her rings glowed, finally scorching away the last of the kidskin on her fingers. The fire opals, shimmering charter symbols rising through their depths, popped sparks that hung restlessly for too long before dropping with languid grace.

Mehitabel gasped. *No flame without air*, Emma recited inwardly, and another chant filled her throat. This one was low and dark, a single syllable of the language of Unmaking, and before she had finished the first measure the dragon was thrashing against her hold as its ruddy glow dimmed.

When the dragon was limp but still burning, a sullen ember, Emma halted. "Names." She sounded strange even to herself, harsh and brutal. "Truenames. Now."

"Llewellyn," Mehitabel hissed. "Llewellyn Gwynnfud."

*This does not surprise me.* "Who else?"

"One of our—"

*Oh, you are not about to play a riddling game with me.* "Name, Mehitabel. Truename."

"A fat man, and sstupid. Graysson was the only name he gave—"

A chill knifed through her, her sweat turning to clammy ice. "Who *else*?"

"An Old One." Mehitabel chuckled. The sound was a scream of tortured iron. "*Him* you will not ssorcer so eassily, monkey-bitch."

The chant rose again. Her focus was slipping. Holding even a young wyrm was difficult, and she still had to escape the Wark. The silver witchlight behind her blazed, her shadow cut of black paper on the fine, soft ankle-deep ashfall.

Mehitabel thrashed, gasping soundlessly. Molten metal slopped against the crucible's sides. "*Who?*" Emma demanded again, when the dragon had quieted. There was precious little time left. Her arms trembled, and did her legs. A crystalline drop of sweat traced down her cheek; her hair was damp. Hot beads of blood welled between her clenched, smoking fingers, soaking into the shredded remains of her gloves.

"*Vortisss,*" Mehitabel hissed. "*Vortiss cruca esssth.*"

*That's not a name.* But Emma's hold slipped for a single heartbeat; Mehitabel slid free –

– and arrowed straight for her tormentor, head snaking, wings shedding globules of molten metal, jaws held wide.

# Chapter Seventeen

## It Discommodes Me

One moment the sorceress stood, slim and composed, between Clare and the abominable metal thing. There was a curious sensation, as if a thunderstorm threatened, the fine hairs all over his body standing up and a queer weightless vertigo filling him. Mikal was a shadow flicker in his peripheral vision, there and gone in less than a flash.

Then, confusion. The shock knocked him to the ground, foul heat showering over him in a gush of rank oily sweat. His hat went flying, and he had the pepperbox pistol free as soon as his head cleared, searching for somewhat to use the weapon upon.

The reptilian thing thrashed as Mikal leapt aside, his blades painting vermilion streaks through gouts of falling ash. The cavern was full of motion, tattered flashboys with gleaming Alterations seething like ants, the workers – scarecrow figures in shapeless grey smocks and draggling frocks, dull-eyed and vacant – crawling forward with odd jerky grace. The only still point was the sorceress, flung face-down in a drift of ash like a doll. Cinders gathered on her limp, bleeding hands, her gloves scorched and tattered, flesh flayed almost to bone.

Clare made it to her in a scrabbling scramble, as the reptilian thing gave out a choked terrible sound and Mikal's blades flashed again.

She was astonishingly light. Clare slid an arm under her, the ash smoking along his jacket sleeve. She coughed, her eyes welling with tears that streaked the soot on her face, and he congratulated himself. At least she would not suffocate.

A flashboy in a scarlet jacket leapt. Clare's arm jerked, the pepperbox pistol's first barrel spoke, but the crack of it was lost in massive, ear-grinding noise. The flashboy folded down, his Alteration – an arm that was no longer an arm, but a scythe of bone and iron – sending up one last bloody gleam before he fell into ash and the rest hesitated, uncertain, their eyes shining with pinpricks of mad red intelligence.

*Just like the rats.* Shudders worked through Clare's frame, but he ignored them. *Three shots left, then we shall be forced to improvise.* A thud rocked the entire Blackwerks, molten metal splashing in high scorching arcs, and he found himself dragging the sorceress's limp form towards the entrance, where a draught of cooler air poured the snowflake cinders into the Werks' maw. An instinctive move, the body seeking to protect itself, but that was acceptable because logic tallied with it, and—

The sorceress woke, her dark eyes snapping open and her ribs expanding as she drew in a long, gasping breath. Another massive crash shook the Werks. The cameo, askew at Miss Bannon's throat, filled with silvery radiance.

Mikal shouted, a wordless challenge, and Miss Bannon blinked. She stared up at Clare, her gaze so blank and terrible he wondered if she recognised him at all. A pin tumbled from her hair, losing itself in thick ash.

Her lips shaped a word under the noise. He had no trouble deciphering it.

*Mikal?*

Tension invaded her. She scrambled to her feet, and Clare did as well, though the ground quaked. The mob of flashboys and workers was now pressing close, streaming through the twisted machinery, intent on the sorceress – and by extension, on Clare himself.

*This will become quite unpleasant very quickly.* As if it was not already unpleasant *enough.*

The Shield shouted again, and the wyrm made a sound like half-molten metal tearing and bubbling. The sorceress threw out her hands, fingers flashing in a complicated gesture that ended in a contorted fashion Clare recognised as a faintly obscene gesture more suited to a hevvy or a dockmancer than a lady of quality.

Miss Bannon was becoming more and more interesting.

Sorcery crackled, a rain of crimson sparks bleeding from her pale fingertips, and the sorceress *leaned* as if pulling a heavy weight, her body arched and a word bursting free of her lips. Blood spattered from her flayed hands; Clare winced, his throat tightening with something suspiciously like fear, raising the pistol. Two more shots. Perhaps its menace would keep the gathering crowd back.

He needn't have bothered. For Miss Bannon moved, flinging her arms, her skirts swaying, and the long, black-scaled body of the wyrm was tossed aside like a wet sheet, directly into the crowd of flashboys and workers.

The Shield moved smoothly back, his curious glove-soled boots shuffling lightly through accumulating ashfall, and glanced back at them. His yellow irises glowed, and his lean face was bright with a fierce, devouring joy.

Shouts, screams, the wyrm's cheated howl. Mikal reached them, nodded once, ash crowning his dark hair and that terrible happiness glowing through his entire body. Miss Bannon turned, smartly, and her bloody hands were full of a low reddish light, somehow cleaner than the Wark's glow.

The light pooled between her fingers, and she cast it at the floor. Smoke roiled, puffing up, and Clare understood they were to flee.

His lungs were afire and his ribs seized with a giant gripping stitch. Clare wheezed, leaning against the alley's wall, desperately seeking to regain his breath. The ashfall had intensified, a soft warm killing snow. At least they would not freeze to death here, but suffocation was a real danger.

Mikal examined the sorceress's hands, his fingers tapping and plucking while charter-symbols bled from his flesh to hers. Clare did not wish to observe the way her rent flesh was closing, in violation of physical laws. He also did not wish to observe Miss Bannon's pinched, wan little face. The silvery witchlight had vanished, and so had most of the sphere of normalcy; every angle was off by a random number of degrees and the falling cinders obeyed no law that he could find, except the law of downward motion. Among these annoyances, the least was Miss Bannon's face.

"That is all I can do." The joy had left Mikal's lean features. His coat was torn and the ash in his hair turned him prematurely grey.

"We must escape the Wark." Miss Bannon closed her dark eyes, leaning wearily against the same wall propping Clare up. "*She* will have her eyes about soon."

"Which route?" Mikal did not let go of her hands, examining her palms critically. The cuts had been deep and were still flushed and angry-looking, despite the soft foxfire glow of charter sorcery stitching the flesh together.

"West." Bruised circles stood out underneath Miss Bannon's eyes. Her skirts were tattered, and there was a smudge of ash on her cheek. Still, most of the falling cinders avoided her; the grit clinging to her hair was perhaps from lying face-down on the Blackwerks floor. "Borough or Newington. Probably the former; but both pass by the gaols, and that is not *her* purview. At least, not while Ethes is present."

"Very well." The Shield finally let her blood-masked hands drop. "We shall not be free of pursuit for long."

"Oh, I know." A curl fell in her face; she wrinkled her proud nose. "The mentath?"

"Well enough." Mikal didn't even spare Clare a glance. "Do you need—"

"No, Mikal. Thank you." She finally opened her eyes. "Mr Clare. Thank you, as well."

His breathing had finally eased somewhat, and the stitch was slowly retreating. "Most . . . diverting." The pressure behind his eyes mounted another notch as he sought to find some pattern in the random angles, or the spinning flakes of ashfall. "Though I would very much like to exit this district, Miss Bannon. It . . . discommodes me."

"You have survived your first encounter with a dragon. They affect the orderly progression of Time most strongly, and the illogic you are seeing is a result of *her* presence." Bannon shuddered. "I will not take either of you to task for not fleeing when I gave the word."

"Good." Clare swallowed, hard. An illogic so strong it could affect Time itself? The very notion caused an uncomfortable sensation within the cage of his ribs. *I could live quite comfortably for the rest of my days without another such experience.* Still, having an explanation for the warping and strangeness helped. "For I believe we did very well indeed."

Mikal's head tilted. "Feet," he said, softly. "Small, and large."

"Newington it is." Miss Bannon straightened. The remnants of her gloves fluttered as she plucked gingerly at her torn skirts. "Come along, gentlemen. There is no time to waste."

The streets of the Black Wark trembled slightly, like a small animal. The buildings stood blank-faced, no light in any of the infrequent, often broken windows, their holes stuffed with various fabrics and papers to keep the elements at bay. Warehouses leaned against each other, slumping dispiritedly under the caustic unsnow. The roofs were steeply pitched, and the only sound was the kiss-landing of cinders or the sudden whispering slide of ash off a roof edge, landing with a soft plop on the street. The gaslamps here were infrequent, wan, sickly circles of orange glow pulled close about their stems.

Clare blinked away ash and followed the swish of Bannon's ragged skirts. He fixed his eyes on the draggled hem, cloth behaving very much as cloth should. A certain relief at the sight loosened the tightness inside his ribs and the iron band around his temples.

"How far?" Miss Bannon whispered.

"Three streets, I think." Mikal's footsteps were soundless. "The rats. Dodger, possibly. I do not think I killed him. Perhaps one or two others."

"She expected me to move in a different direction." Miss Bannon sounded thoughtful. "Which one, I wonder."

"Passing close to Horsemonger is also dangerous. Not to mention Queensbench." Mikal, soft and equally thoughtful. *Well,* Clare thought. *He obviously respects her ability. That is most heartening.*

"Ethes is no trouble, and Captain Gall even less. But I see your point." Miss Bannon halted. "Mr Clare? Are you well?"

It was becoming more difficult to draw breath. "Well enough. Damnable atmosphere here."

"Oh, good heavens." She half turned, snapped her fingers, and muttered a word he could not decipher. Immediately, the ash shook itself free of his hair, whirling away, and he no longer felt as if he were breathing through a damp woollen blanket. "Better?"

"Quite." He stared at her boot toes, peeping at him from her ragged hem. If he concentrated on those, on how they rested against ankle-thick ash that behaved as ash should near them, he could ignore the rest for a short while.

A soft, scraping sound. Metal, drawn from a sheath. "Go." Mikal, tense now.

"Take the mentath, I shall delay—"

"No." The Shield thought little of this notion. "They come to kill, my Prima. Take care near the prison; I shall be close."

"Mikal – oh, *bloody* hell."

Clare might have raised his eyebrows to hear such language from a woman, but he was too busy studying her boots. He could infer much from the way she stood, toes pointed slightly outward, the fractional favouring of her right foot meaning she was right-handed. *She must dance well, and lightly. And she can move very softly if she wishes. Best to remember that.*

Her toes were whisked away as she turned, and her hand crept into the crook of his elbow. She tugged him along, and Clare allowed himself to be led.

A low, grinding noise had begun, but Clare felt absolutely no desire to look up.

"I did not think it would affect you this badly. Come, Mr Clare. It shall be better very rapidly; the closer we are to the gaols, the less stray sorcery there is about to trouble you."

"Jolly good." His skull squeezed everything inside it, pressure building again. Every random angle he had measured since stepping into the Wark's confines, every calculation of the speed and drift of cinders falling, refused to snap together into a pattern. What *was* that hideous grinding noise? It could not be his teeth, for all that his jaw was clenched tight.

"Do *not* look up," Miss Bannon said softly, hurrying him along. Their steps were muffled in the ash, now above ankle-high. How often did they clear the streets here? It had to be frequently, else anything living would choke to death.

The terrible grating continued, and Miss Bannon muttered another highly colourful term. A hot, rank breath poured past them, tugging at Clare's coat and hat, flapping the sorceress's skirts. He did not raise his eyes, but his reasoning leapt ahead. *The street. The street is moving.* He could *imagine* it, from the ripples pouring through the field of cracked and rutted cobbles, walls receding and others pushed forward as the Wark reshaped itself. Miss Bannon exhaled quickly, a short sharp puff. "Tricksome," she muttered. "Very tricksome."

His stomach revolted. His digestion was not its usual capable self. But as they hurried on, Miss Bannon's boots now clicking faintly instead of muffled in ash, it settled remarkably. She was humming, a queer atonal melody looping on itself, and Clare found that the sound covered up the grinding tolerably well. It did not cover the choked cry from their left, or the rushing skitter of tiny metallic rodent feet. Miss Bannon's grip on him tightened, but whether that was for his comfort or her own, he could not guess.

The composition of the ash underfoot changed, slick and greasy instead of fine and dry, and Miss Bannon's humming grew strained. The grinding suddenly ceased to their left; the sorceress lunged forward, dragging Clare along. A subliminal *snap* echoed through Clare's entire body, the iron bands constricting his chest loosening slightly. He dared to glance up, and the grey bulk of Queensbench Gaol shimmered with pinpricks of light. The prison's massive gate yawned, the gibbet in the small square before it crawling with blood-coloured charter charms. Their pace quickened, ashfall turning to hard hail-stinging pellets. A sharp turn to the left, and he understood by the sudden close rumble of traffic that they were skirting a thoroughfare. Darkness pressed close, gaslights muffled, and they plunged into a maze of debtors' tenements. Another cry sounded to their right, ending with a clash of steel.

*Mikal.* The Shield was doing his best to hold back their pursuers. But the shadows were alive with tiny crimson eyes now, and small twitching metallic noses.

It was a dreadful time, he reflected, to wish Miss Bannon had more of Mikal's type about. "Miss Bannon?" Clare whispered, as their pace quickened still more.

"What?" Her tone could in no way be described as *patient*.

"I rather believe we should run."

# Chapter Eighteen

## We Use You Dreadfully

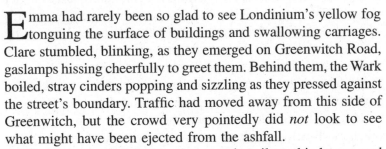

Emma had rarely been so glad to see Londinium's yellow fog tonguing the surface of buildings and swallowing carriages. Clare stumbled, blinking, as they emerged on Greenwitch Road, gaslamps hissing cheerfully to greet them. Behind them, the Wark boiled, stray cinders popping and sizzling as they pressed against the street's boundary. Traffic had moved away from this side of Greenwitch, but the crowd very pointedly did *not* look to see what might have been ejected from the ashfall.

The mentath stumbled again, went heavily to his knees, and proceeded to retch. Emma clamped a hand to her side, the freshly healed stab wound unhappy at rough treatment. Her corset, loose as it was, still cut intolerably. She shook her hair, spitting a clearing charm between her teeth, not caring if she would need the energy later. The dross of the Wark fell away in veils, grey matter shushing as the charm crackled it loose.

It would take more than a minor sorcery to get the burnt-metal tang of Southwark out of her mouth, though.

A clockrat spilled over the rim of the street, scuttling weakly as it fought the constraints of normal time. Emma's hand jabbed forward, the golden ring gleaming – but Mikal appeared. A quick hard stamp, a scream of tortured metal, and a puff of vile-smelling crimson smoke; and the rat was merely a twisted scrap of metal and moth-eaten fur. The Shield's eyes glowed furiously, and specks of blood and other fluids dewed his filthy coat. He looked little the worse for wear, despite being covered in Wark-ash.

She shuddered. Clare retched again, feelingly. "A *range!*" he choked. "From thirty-three to eighty-nine per cent! It can only be explained in a *range!*"

*Dear God, is he seeking to analyse Mehitabel? Or the rats?* "Clare." She coughed, caught her breath. *I think we may have survived. Perhaps.* "Clare, cease. There are other problems requiring your attention."

"Prima." Mikal's hand on her shoulder, his fingers iron clamps. "*Emma.*"

She swayed, but only slightly. "You've done well." *Well? More like "magnificently". One Shield, a small army of Mehitabel's flashboys, the rats – I cannot understand how we are not all dead*

Either she had hurt the ironwyrm far more than she thought possible or likely, or Mehitabel had expected Emma to flee in a different direction – perhaps north, the way they had entered the Wark. Or – most chilling, but a prospect that must be considered – Mehitabel the Black *let* them go for some wyrm-twisting reason, even though Emma had used her truename.

"Easy hunting." Mikal's mouth twisted up at one corner, a fey grimace. The ash gave him an old man's hair, caught in his eyebrows, drifting on his shoulders. "Her troops are clumsy, and loud, and had to check every dark corner."

"*What* problems?" Clare managed, through another retch. "Never. *Never* again."

"Oh, we shall brave the Wark again, if duty demands it." Emma let out a shaky breath. The idea of going home, throwing her corset into the grate, and watching it burn was extraordinarily satisfying. "But not tonight. At the moment, Mr Clare, we are on Greenwitch, and I wish you to help me find a hansom."

"Oh, excellent," Clare moaned. "Wonderful. What the deuce for?"

"To ride in, master of deduction." Her tone was more tart than she intended. "We have news to deliver."

It was past midnight, and the stable smelled of hay and dry oily flanks. Restless movement in the capacious stalls, half-opened eyes, the perches overhead full of a rustling stillness.

The gryphons were nervous. Iridescent plumage ruffled, spike feathers mantling; sharp amber or obsidian beaks clacked once or twice, breaking the quiet. Tawny or coal-dark flanks rippled with muscle, claws flexing in the darkness. Emma stood very still, carefully in the middle of the central passage, her skirts pulled close. Mikal was so near she could feel the heat of him.

Clare peered over one stall door, his eyes wide. "Fascinating," he breathed. "Head under wing. Indeed. The musculature is wonderful. *Wonderful.*"

The gryphon stable was long and high, dim but not completely dark. Britannia's proud steeds took sleepy notice, ruffling as they scented a Prime.

Of all the meats gryphons preferred, they adored sorcery-seasoned best.

Mikal's hand rested on Emma's shoulder, a welcome weight. A door at the far end opened, quietly, skirts rustling on a breath of golden rose scent, overlaid with violet-water. Emma stiffened. Clare did not straighten, leaning over the stall's door like a child peering into a sweetshop.

"Mr Clare," the sorceress whispered. "*Do* stop that, sir. They are dangerous."

"Indeed they are." A female voice, high and young, but with the stamp of absolute authority on each syllable. "No, my friend, do not courtesy. We know you must be uncomfortable here."

Emma sank down into a curtsey anyway, glad she had applied cleaning charms to all three of them. Mikal's hand remained on her shoulder, and Clare hopped down from the stall door, hurriedly doffing his hat. "And who do we have the pleasure of— Dear God!" He lurched forward into a bow. "Your Majesty!"

Alexandrina Victrix, the new Queen and Britannia's current incarnation, pushed back her capacious sable-velvet hood. Her wide blue eyes danced merrily, but her mouth turned down at the corners. "Is this a mentath?"

"Yes, Your Majesty." Emma forced her legs to straighten. "One of the few remaining in Londinium, Mr Archibald Clare."

"Your Majesty." Clare had turned decidedly pink around his cheekbones, though the sorceress doubted any eyes but hers would see it.

Emma's mouth wanted to twitch, but the business at hand dispelled any amusement. "I bring grave news for Britannia."

"Since when do you not? You are Our stormcrow; We shall have Dulcie make you a mantle of black feathers." The Queen's young face could not stay solemn for long, but a shadow moved behind her eyes. "We jest. Do not think yourself undervalued."

"I would not presume," Emma replied, a trifle stiffly. "Your Majesty . . . I have failed you. The core is missing."

The young woman was silent for a few moments, her dark hair – braided in twin loops over her ears, but slightly dishevelled, as if she had been called from sleep – glinting in the dimness. Even so, pearls hung from her tender ears, and a simple strand of pearls clasped her slim throat. The shadow in her eyes grew, and her young face changed by a crucial fraction. "Missing?"

"I left it with Mehitabel." Emma's chin held itself firmly high. "It was taken with her consent. She gave me names."

"The dragons are involved? Most interesting." The Queen tapped her lips with a slim white finger; under the cloak her red robe was patterned with gold-thread fleur-de-lis. The shadow of age and experience passed more clearly over her face, features changing and blurring like clay under water. The signet on her left hand flashed, its single charter symbol fluorescing briefly before returning to quiescence. "This was Our miscalculation, Prima. The Black Mistress has been true to her word before; it is . . . disconcerting to find she is no longer. What names were you given?"

*Some very uncomfortable ones.* "I almost fear to say."

"Fear? You?" The Queen's laugh echoed, an ageless ripple of amusement. "Unlikely. You wish more proof, and to finish this matter to your own satisfaction, if not Ours."

Emma almost winced. Britannia was old, and wise. The spirit of rule had seen many such as her come and go. She was the power of Empire; was a Prime, in the end, was merely a human servant. "She mentioned the Chancellor of the Exchequer, and Llewellyn Gwynnfud, Lord Sellwyth. And another name. *Vortis.*"

Feathers whispered like a wheatfield under summer wind as the gryphons took notice. Lambent eyes opened, lit with phosphorescent dust. Mikal's fingers tightened, a silent bolstering.

Yet a still small voice inside her whispered that Mehitabel's flashboys had not chased them nearly enough. And Llewellyn, of course. *How long will it be before he strangles you, as he did Crawford?*

"That name is . . . not well known to Us. But known enough." Deep lines etched themselves on the Queen's soft cheeks. The fine hairs on Emma's arms and legs and nape rose, tingling as if she stood in the path of a Greater Work or even the unloosing of a Discipline. The gryphons stirred again, and a blue spark danced in the Queen's pupils as the power that was Britannia woke further and peered out of her chosen vessel. "And the Chancellor, you say? Grayson?"

"A wyrm's word—" Emma began, hurriedly, but the Queen's finger twitched and she swallowed the remainder of the sentence.

"If he be innocent, he hath nothing to fear from thee, Prima. Thy judgement shall be thorough, but above all *unerring.*" The blue spark brightened, widening until it filled the Queen's dilated pupils.

*A not-so-subtle reminder.* Emma's mouth was dry. She had, indeed, lied to Victrix about Crawford, and by extension, she had lied to Britannia. The ruling spirit of Empire had either chosen to believe Emma's version of events in the round stone room, or – more likely – she guessed at the truth and reserved her judgement because Emma was useful. "I am uneasy, Your Majesty. Too much is unknown."

Britannia retreated like Tideturn along the Themis, a rushing weight felt more than heard. The Queen blinked, pulling her cloak closer. "Then you shall uncover it. And the mentath . . ."

"Yesmum?" Clare drew himself up very straight indeed, his long, lanky frame poker-stiff. "Your Majesty?"

The Queen actually smiled, becoming a girl again. "Is he trustworthy, Prima?"

*I am the wrong person to ask, my Queen. I do not even trust myself.* "I think so. Certainly he faced the ironwyrm with much presence of mind."

"Then tell him everything. We cannot finish this without a mentath; it would seem Britannia is favoured in these as well as in sorceresses." Victrix paused. "And Emma . . ."

Her pulse sought to quicken; training pressed down upon Emma's traitorous body. "Yes, Your Majesty?"

"Be careful. If the Chancellor is involved, Britannia's protection may . . . wear thin, and Alberich Our Consort is not overfond of sorcerers. Do you understand?"

*Britannia rules, but we cannot move openly against a Chancellor of the Exchequer without compromising the Cabinet. Your lady mother would love to intrude another of her creatures to said Cabinet, and your Consort is not only low of influence but also dislikes sorcerers with an almost religious passion. So it is quiet, and deadly, and everything must be kept as smooth as possible.* "Quite, Your Majesty."

*And, not so incidentally, if any part of this becomes a scandal, I will be the one to feel its sting.*

"We use you dreadfully." The Queen stepped back, a heavy rustle of velvet, and the gryphons murmured, a susurrus of sharp-edged feathers.

"I am Britannia's subject." Stiffly, she sank into another curtsey. "I am to be used."

"I wish . . ." But the Queen shook her dark head, her braids swinging, and was gone. The open door let in a draught of garden-scented night, tinged with the violet-water she favoured, and closed softly.

Clare's mouth was suspiciously ajar. "That was the *Queen*." He sounded stunned.

*Indeed it was.* "We are wont to meet here, when occasion calls for it." And God help her, but did she not sound proud? That pride, another of her besetting sins.

"Little sorceress." A rush of feathers ruffling; the voice was gravel-deep and quiet, but full of hurtful edges. An amber beak slid over the closest stall door, and Emma's knees turned suspiciously weak.

The eyes were deep darkness ringed with gold, an eagle's stare in a head larger than her own torso. Feathered with ink-black, the powerful neck vanished into the stall's dimness, and Mikal was somehow before her, his shoulders blocking the view of the gryphon as it clacked its beak once, a sound like lacquered blocks of dense wood slamming together.

"Close enough, skycousin," Mikal said mildly.

"Merely a mouthful." The gryphon laughed. "But I am not so hungry tonight, even for magic. Listen."

Clare stepped forward, as if fascinated, staring at the gryphon's left forelimb, which had crept up to the stall door and closed around the thick wood, burnished obsidian claws sinking in. "Fabulous musculature," he muttered, and the gryphon clacked its beak again. It looked . . . amused, its eyes twin cruel glints.

"Mr Clare." A horrified whisper; Emma's throat was dry. "They are *carnivores*."

"They look well fed." The mentath cocked his head, and his lean face was alight with something suspiciously close to joy. "Yes, that beak is definitely from a bird of prey."

"Enough." The gryphon's head turned sidelong; he fixed Emma with one bright eye. "Sorceress. We know Vortis of old." The claws tightened. "You go wyrm-hunting, then."

It was the gryphons' ancient alliance with Britannia that had held the island stable, as the Age of Flame strangled on its own ash and the dragons returned to slumber. Or so it was told, and any study of the beasts was hazardous enough that very few sorcerers would attempt it. Emma stared at the creature's beak – its sharp edges, the flickering of dim light over the deep-pitted nostrils. How the creatures spoke without lips fit for such an operation was a mystery indeed; gryphons were not dissected after their deaths.

No, they *ate* their own. She suppressed a shudder, grateful for Mikal's presence between her and the creature. "Perhaps. A wyrm's word is a castle built on sand."

"Or air." The proud head lowered in a terrifying approxima-tion of a nod. "You should have more Shields, sorceress."

"I have as many as I require at the moment." *The ironwyrm would have had me, but for Mikal. And yet.*

"We are many, and you are a tempting morsel." A laugh like boulders grinding. "But we are sleepy, too. You should go now."

*I think so.* For she noted the subtle tension in the beast's forelimb, raven feathers shading into blue-black fur. "Thank you. Mr Clare, do come along."

"A whole new area of study—" Clare, his sharp blue eyes positively feverish, stepped closer to the gryphon's claw.

Mikal lunged forward. The wood of the stall door groaned, splintering, and the Shield yanked Clare back, tearing his already worse-for-wear frock coat. The gryphon's claw closed on empty air, and the beast chuckled.

"Enough," Mikal said, pleasantly. "Stand near my Prima." He did not take his eyes from the beast. "That was unwise, skycousin."

"He is a mere nibble anyway, and unseasoned." The gryphon's eyes half lidded. "No matter. Take them and go, *Nágah.* Safe winds."

"Fair flying." Mikal stepped back. "Prima?"

"This way, Mr Clare." She made her hands unclench, grabbed the mentath's sleeve. "And do not pass too closely to the stalls."

Clare did not reply. But he did not demur, either. When they finally eased free of the stable's northern door and into the close-melting fog scraping the surface of the road and Greens Park beyond, Emma found she was trembling.

# Chapter Nineteen

## For My Tender Person

Greens Park was utterly deserted, yellow fog turning impenetrable black in places, licking the lawns and tangled trees. This close to the Palace, the shadows were free of thieves and thugs. Such would not be the case in other Londinium parklands.

They walked a fair distance to reach Picksdowne, Clare muttering to himself about musculature for a good deal of the way. It was absolutely *fascinating*, and he found himself wondering what discoveries one could make if a gryphon corpse happened to appear in one's workshop. He knew little of the beasts save that they were the only animals fit to draw Britannia's carriage; their riders were highly trained officers, and there had been corps of gryphon-riders used as sky cavalry in the battles with the damned Corsican—

Beside him, Miss Bannon cleared her throat. She was occupied in seeking to restore the ragged mass of her gloves.

"Oh yes." He had almost forgotten her presence, so intrigued was he by the glimpse of a new unknown. One that obeyed patterns, one that helped the hideous memory of Southwark recede. "There are things you no doubt wish to tell me, Miss Bannon."

"Indeed." Was there a catch in her voice? On her other side, the Shield stepped lightly, a trifle closer than was perhaps his habit.

The gryphons had severely shaken Miss Bannon. She was paper-pale, and her fingers nervously scrubbed themselves together while she sought to straighten her gloves. Still, she pressed onward over the gravelled walk, and her pace did not slacken. "What do you know of Masters the Elder? And Throckmorton?"

"Nothing more than their names: mentaths are acquainted with their peers only so far. I can surmise a great deal, Miss Bannon, but it is as the analysis you invited me to provide: a trap. Perhaps you should simply enlighten me."

The amount of shaky grievance she could fit into a simple sigh was immense. "Perhaps I should. In any case, the Queen commanded—"

"And she is not here to enforce said command."

A palpable hit, for she stiffened slightly before forging onwards, crisply and politely. "Pray do not insult me so, sir. Masters the Elder was engaged in building a core. Throckmorton had made a number of significant breakthroughs, and he and Smythe were brought together despite the danger. Certain advances were made."

Maddeningly, she ceased her explanation there – or perhaps not maddeningly, for his faculties leapt ahead, devoured this new problem, and his nerves sustained another rather unpleasant shock, adding to the night's already long list of unpleasantnesses.

"A core? Dear lady, you cannot possibly . . ." What was that cold feeling down his back? His jacket was ripped, certainly, but this was akin to dread. He noted the feeling, sought to put it aside.

It would not go.

"Throckmorton and Smythe, with Masters's core, achieved the impossible." She halted, but perhaps that was only because his feet had nailed themselves to the walk. Londinium's fog pressed close, and the Shield's gaze rested on his sorceress, yellow eyes lambent in the darkness. "A transmitting, stable, and powerful logic engine."

The fog had perhaps stolen all the air from the park. Clare stepped back, gravel grinding under his much-abused boots. He stared at the sorceress, who could have no possible idea what she was saying. He actually *goggled* at her, his jaw suspiciously loose.

"Such an engine . . ." He wetted his lips, continued. "Such an engine is not impossible. Theoretically, mind you. Extraordinarily difficult and never successfully—"

"I am *fully* aware it has never been done before. I am no mentath, but I have certain talents as a facilitator and organiser; much scientific work for the Queen can be and is done quietly. I am responsible for arranging such things. The mentaths who have been lately killed were all, in one fashion or another, involved in the making of said engine. The others . . . well. I am of the opinion many were murdered because of a particular note Throckmorton made of the peculiar nature of logic engines. They require a mentath to utilise them."

"Well, yes." Clare shivered. He was not cold. An ordinary person seeking to run a logic engine would be turned into a brain-melted automaton, injured beyond repair by the amplification. Lovelace had been the first to survive the wiring to a very weak engine; several geniuses had assumed that if a *woman* could endure it, a man's brain – even a non-mentath's – would have little difficulty.

The resultant casualties had been thought-provoking, the scandal immense. Some said the scandal had contributed to Lovelace's early death; others blamed the inefficiency of the engine – Babbage's work, true, but perhaps not up to the standards one would have wanted. There was, in particular, one scathing little paper written by Somerville, vindicating her pupil at Babbage's expense. Rare female mentaths were now required to be registered with the Crown as a result of the affair, and were wards of the Court until their marriages.

He heard his own voice, strangely strong and clear. "A . . . transmitting logic engine. Transmitting, I presume, to receiving engines. The amplification could save the trouble of murdering whatever mentath would wire himself to such a thing." *And the unregistered mentaths were mutilated.* He could not shake himself of the exceedingly unpleasant thought.

"Tests were made, at the country house in Surrey. It performed spectacularly well, from what the assembled reported. The engine is useless without Masters's core; I took the precaution of transporting the core to the Wark, where Mehitabel had agreed to hold it. Imagine my surprise when Masters and Smythe both turned up dead – they were not even supposed to be *in* Londinium. The engine has disappeared. Now it appears the core has disappeared as well." She paused. "Her Majesty is worried."

*As well she should be. Dear God.* "I presume you share her concern," he muttered, numbly.

"Oh, I do. The Chancellor, your Yton friend, may be involved. Llewellyn might have been a part of the conspiracy – for all I know, he may have killed Throckmorton himself. And yet several things do not make sense. The work was theoretical; a logic engine is valuable, yes, but all signs point towards the conspirators having *some* defined use for it already."

". . . It does. They do, rather." He was, he thought, beginning to recover from the shock somewhat.

"I suspect a military application." Patiently, as if she expected some further reaction from him.

Clare blinked. "I should think so."

"The question becomes, then, *which* military. You see the difficulty." Her hands still worked at each other, at odds with her calm, logical tone. The fire opals in her rings glowed dully, foxfire gleams.

"Britannia has many enemies. Any one of whom would not hesitate to use such an engine . . ." *But for what precisely?* "Even if there is not a military application *yet*, the consequences in manufacturing alone could be tremendous. And even in Alteration." His dinner, had any of it been left, might have tried for an escape at the last thought. "The unregistered mentaths. Their bodies were somehow savaged?"

"Certain pieces were missing, Alteration is not out of the question. I do not know enough yet." Emma Bannon's dark eyes glittered. "But now, Mr Clare, it is war. I will brook no treachery or threat to Britannia's vessel."

"Admirable of you," Clare muttered. "No wonder you locked me up in your house." *Keeping me safe, certainly. And any mentath is suspect. There is precious little I would not do to lay my hands on such an engine. The research possibilities . . . simply staggering.*

But it would not do to voice *that* particular thought.

"You may become extraordinarily *necessary*, Mr Clare." She finally stopped twisting at the ragged remains of her gloves. "If not, you are at the least useful. But in any event, you must be protected."

"I cannot quibble with *that* sentiment."

"Consequently, we are about to pay a visit." She dropped her hands, but her gaze was still level and quite disconcerting. It took Clare a few moments to discover why, exactly, he perceived such discomfort.

*A woman should not look so . . . determined.* "To gain some further variety of protection for my tender person?" He was only halfway flippant. Still, it gave him a chance to gather himself. The irrational feelings were highly uncomfortable, and he longed for some quiet to restore his nerves.

"Precisely. While we walk, occupy those admirable faculties of yours with the question of how you will uncover the whereabouts of a core and a transmitting logic engine. My methods have produced little of value at great cost, and I am needed to solve another riddle."

He found he could walk again. The Park was deadly still, but Londinium growled in the distance like a wild beast, and the

Palace was a faint smear of indistinct light behind the boiling-thick fog. If Miss Bannon took another four steps, she might well be lost to his sight entirely, so he hurried after her, his torn jacket flapping. "And what riddle would that be, Miss Bannon?"

"The riddle of a dragon, sir. Come along."

Arrowing north and west from St Giles, Totthame lay under a dense blanket of boiling yellow. The shops were closed tight against the choking fog – except for some of the brokers, low-glowing brass-caged witchballs barely visible above their doors and a flashboy or two often lounging on the step to keep the metal from disappearing. Side doors leading to individual closets for the gentler sellers to haggle privately were closed and bolted at this hour, but furtive movements could be seen in the shadows about them.

The swaybacked, dull-flanked clockhorse didn't even swish its ragged tail as they disembarked. The cab driver, swathed to his nose in oddments, was no trouble either, hiding Alterations from his misspent youth as a flashboy. Clare decided him as a Sussex youngblood come to Londinium to make good and only now as a man wishing he'd stayed where he was born. So much was obvious from the style of his dress and the broad accent in which he grunted the bare minimum necessary to secure their custom and give his price. Mikal appeared out of nowhere again and paid the man before they were allowed to alight, and Miss Bannon, still sunk in the profound silence she had spent the entire ride in, set off for the far side of Totthame with a quick light stride.

Mikal, silent as well, followed in her wake, glancing back at Clare as he hurried to keep up. The fog cringed away from her, curling in beseeching fingers. She was making directly for a broker's door, and the flashboys lounging there – one slim dark youth with half his face covered in a sheath of shining metal, the other just as dark but stocky, with gleaming tentacles where his left hand should be – elbowed each other. The thin one sniggered, and opened his mouth to address her.

Mikal's stride lengthened, but whatever the flashboys saw on Miss Bannon's face cut their ribaldry short. They hopped aside, the stocky one awkwardly, and the sorceress sailed past them, a slender yacht passing between battleships.

"Wise of you," Clare mumbled, and hopped up the biscuit-coloured stone step. The tentacle Alterations rasped drily against each other, scaled metal letting fall a single venomous-golden drop of oil, splattering on blue breeches. The stocky flashboy breathed a curse.

Inside, an exhaled fug of sweet tabac smoke, dust, paper, and the breath of mouldering merchandise piled in mountains enclosed them. Carpenter's tools beached themselves against the front of the shop; a pile of larger leather tack sat mouldering under hanging bridles and hacks. A cloud of handkerchiefs foamed over a long counter in front of the side door that would lead to the closets where the shy would seek to trade their wares.

Miss Bannon turned in a complete circle, her hands become fists and the sapphires dangling from her ears flaming.

"Twistneedle!" she called, and a mound of cloth moved near the back of the narrow shop. The shelves groaned with odds and ends – china, metal, clothing, a pair of duelling pistols in a long, dusty glass cabinet, a tangle of cheap paste jewellery and slightly less cheap snuffboxes threatening to swallow the gleaming barrels. Patterns formed with lightning speed, Clare's brain seizing on the sudden sensory overload and categorising, deducing, sorting puzzle pieces with incredible rapidity.

For the first time that long night, he was comforted.

"Don't *shout*, woman." A thready, reedy, irritable voice. More puffs of tabac smoke rose from the rear of the store. "I'm an old man. I needs my rest."

"Do not anger me, then. Ludovico. I want him."

"Oh, so many do. So many do." A wide, froggish face over a striped muffler rose peevishly from what Clare had taken to be a soulless mound of piled clothing in bundles; a polished brass earring gleamed. The round little man pushed aside a froth of calico petticoats and grinned widely, showing rotten stump-teeth. The pipe in his soft, round brown hand fumed extrava-gantly, while rings gleamed on the thick fingers. One was even a real diamond, Clare noted. "What will you give, miss? I don't hand out nothing for free, not even to those I fancy."

"Mikal." Deadly quiet.

The Shield glided forward, and the frog-man cowered, raising both plump hands. "None o' that! He's upstairs. Sleepin', most like."

Clare placed the accent – this man had probably never ventured more than a half-mile from Totthame in his life. Deduction ticked along under the surface of every item piled inside the narrow cavern. He wondered why he had never visited a pawnbroker's before – a single shop could keep him occupied for weeks. And with every deduction, Southwark retreated, more distant and dreamlike.

A movement behind a clutch of hanging frock coats in different colours, a slight twitching. *There's a door behind there,* Clare realised in a flash, but it was Mikal who moved, slapping aside the flung knife, its blade a blur in the smoke, burying itself in a pile of waistcoats tumbling off three narrow wooden shelves.

Some of the waistcoats still had traces of blood marring the fabric. Not just a pawner's, then. Clare's skin chilled.

A corpsepicker's shop.

"Ah." Miss Bannon sounded amused. "*There* you are."

"Call off your snake-charmer, *signora*." The frock coats twitched again. "I have the more knives, I use them, eh?"

*Naples*, Clare thought. *No more than twenty-six. And more afraid of the Shield than the sorceress.*

*Interesting.*

"He gets in rather a temper when you fling knives at me, *Signor* Valentinelli." Miss Bannon did not move; Mikal was now threading his way between two mounds of bundled, ticketed clothing. "I am not certain I should calm him."

The invisible voice let loose a torrent of abuse in gutter Italian, but Miss Bannon simply nodded and picked her way to the pile of waistcoats. Her mouth set itself firmly as she retrieved the flung knife, and Mikal halted before the hanging coats, tense and ready.

The cursing ceased. "Is there money, then?"

Miss Bannon straightened. "Haven't I always paid well for your services, *signor*? Be a dear and put a kettle on, I could do with a cup after the night I've had."

A sleek dark head appeared, pushing through the frock coats with a slightly reptilian movement. The face was still coarsely handsome, but ravaged with pox scars and bad living, and the close-set dark eyes flicked over the entire pawnshop. "What is it? Knife, *pistole*, garrotte?"

*Neapolitan indeed.* Clare placed the accent to his satisfaction. Miss Bannon was proving to have extraordinary acquaintances indeed.

"Maybe none, maybe all and more." Miss Bannon now sounded amused. "I bring you a chance to injure yourself in new and interesting ways. Do you really wish to discuss it here?"

Valentinelli let out a hoarse sound approximating a laugh. "Come up then. But keep *il serpente* away. He make me nervous."

"Poor Ludo, *nervous*. Mikal, keep a close eye on him." Miss Bannon held the knife away from her skirts, delicately, and shook a stray curl out of her face. "We would hate to have him faint."

The Neapolitan's face screwed itself up into a mask of dislike and disappeared, with a creak of leather hinges. Mikal pushed the frock coats aside, and Miss Bannon motioned Clare forward.

"Come, Mr Clare. *Signor* Valentinelli is to be your guardian angel."

# Chapter Twenty

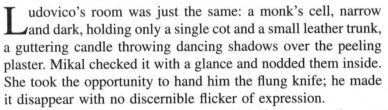

## More if I Die

Ludovico's room was just the same: a monk's cell, narrow and dark, holding only a single cot and a small leather trunk, a guttering candle throwing dancing shadows over the peeling plaster. Mikal checked it with a glance and nodded them inside. She took the opportunity to hand him the flung knife; he made it disappear with no discernible flicker of expression.

The Neapolitan promptly threw himself down on the cot, eyeing Emma speculatively. He was a quick little man, the efficiency of his movements lacking any sort of grace and bespeaking a great deal of comfort with physical violence. Sleek dark hair, those dark, close-set eyes in the scar-ravaged face – childhood smallpox had been vicious to him. Stretching his arms over his head and yawning, he settled his shoulders more comfortably. He looked like a hevvy, shirt and braces worn but stout, his trousers rough and his boots dusty.

The opening move was hers. "Not even a cup of tea. Your hospitality suffers, *signor*."

"You are here after hours, *signora*."

"You keep no hours. Do *not* annoy me. This is the man you'll be guarding."

Ludovico scratched along his ribs, tucking his other arm under his head. "Why? What's he done?"

"That is no concern of yours. You're to keep his skin whole while I'm occupied with other things." She paused as Mikal tensed slightly, the candleflame flinching and righting itself. "You may have to kill a sorcerer or two to do so."

The effect was immediate, and gratifying. Valentinelli sat straight up, eyes narrowing, and a dull-bladed stiletto appeared in his left hand. He spun it over his knuckles, and Emma did not miss Mikal's own hand twitching slightly.

It was a high compliment from her Shield.

"Why you no have more of *him* to watch *il bambino*, eh?" He jabbed a finger at Mikal, still spinning the knife over his knuckles, catching the hilt as it rocketed past. The grime under his short-bitten fingernails, black half-moons, matched the crease in his neck.

She forced herself not to swallow drily. "That is not your concern. Shall I go elsewhere, *signor*?"

"At this time of night? And Valentinelli is the best. I protect from *il Diavolo* himself; you pay me. In gold."

"In guineas, yes." The smile fixed to her face wasn't pleasant, Emma suspected, but it covered a set grimace of almost distaste. "Since you are a gentleman."

He jabbed forked fingers at her and hissed. "Not even for gold do I let a woman mock me, *strega*."

She gathered her patience once more. "I am not mocking, *assassino*. For the last time, shall I seek elsewhere?"

A supremely indifferent shrug. "I take the job. Twenty guinea, more if I die."

"Very well." She did not miss the way he blinked at her readiness to take his first price. It was bad form not to haggle, but she had no patience for his tender feelings at this point. "Bring yourself to me, *signor*. You'll be bound for this."

"Ai, you're serious." He heaved himself off the bed and paced towards her, graceless but silent. "What he do, you want him alive this bad?"

"Again, none of your concern." Emma held her ground,

suddenly very aware of the space between her and the Neapolitan. Mikal's eyes flamed in the dimness, matching the candle's glow. "Mr Clare, please come here."

The mentath stared at Valentinelli in the uncertain light, his eyes half closed. His colour was much better, and he seemed to have recovered from the shock of the Wark quite nicely. "You," he said, suddenly, "had a wife at one time, sir."

Valentinelli halted. Emma could have cursed the mentath roundly.

"She die," the Neapolitan said. "What, you a *strego*? Or you *inquisitore*?"

"Neither." Clare's eyelids drooped a bit more. "Your accent is really wonderful. There's something, though—"

"*Mr* Clare." Emma stepped forward and plucked the black-bladed stiletto from Ludo's filthy fingers. "Do stop carrying on, and come here. You know what to do, Ludovico."

"If he is *inquisitore*—" His voice rose, losing for a moment the soft singing of Calabria and becoming more clipped, more educated, and generally more dangerous.

"He is *not* one of the holy running dogs, *do* be reasonable! He's simply a mentath. Give me your hand, Mr Clare."

"I don't know what you mean by *simply* a—" Damn the man, he sounded *irritated*. Emma grabbed his hand, the knife flickered, and he actually *yelped* at the bite of the blade. "What are you *doing*?"

*Ensuring your survival despite your thickheadedness.* "You are an execrable nuisance, sir. Your hand, Valentinelli."

Mikal drifted closer. Ludovico glanced at the Shield, his jaw set and his grimy fingers working as if he felt a neck under them. A trickle of sweat traced down Emma's spine, cool and distinct.

"Mentath? *Mentale*? Ah." He smelled of leather and male, a sharp underbite of grappa and sour sweat. "I forgive him, then." His cupped palm was strangely clean, given the condition of his nails. But then, she had seen him in many different lights, and this was only one of them.

Her breath caught, her pulse threatening to gallop before she invoked iron control. The man unsettled her.

More precisely, he reminded her of certain childhood things. Things best left in the recesses of memory, uncalled and unmissed.

"Most civil of you," she murmured, and the knife bit again. A bleeding slash on the Neapolitan's palm matched on the mentath's, she pressed their hands together. Ludovico had done this before, but Clare resisted; she was forced to glare at him and make a sharp *tsk*ing noise.

When their palms were clasped together, the copper tang of hot blood reaching her sensitive nose, she closed her eyes, her own fingers a white cage around theirs. "*S——!*" she breathed.

It was a Greater Word of Binding, and even more of Tideturn's charge trickled free of her flesh, sliding into the two men and licking hungrily at the scant blood. She flicked her hands back, like a hedge conjuror flapping a handkerchief, and a brief gunpowder flash painted the peeling walls.

She swayed, and Mikal was there, as usual, bracing her. His jaw was set; Emma wondered just what her own face was expressing.

"There." She found, to her relief, that she could still speak in a businesslike manner. "'Tis done. Present yourself at my door no later than Tideturn next, Valentinelli, and afterwards Mr Clare shall not stir one step without you."

"How long?" The Neapolitan examined his palm – smooth, unbroken skin, criss-crossed by thin faint lines where other bindings had been sworn. He arched one sleek eyebrow, and his white teeth showed as his lip lifted.

"You have other pressing appointments, I take it? As long as it is necessary, Ludovico. Until I take the binding off. You'd best hope nothing happens to me, too." Even the candleflame stung her suddenly sensitive eyes. They squeezed shut with no prompting on her part, tears rising reflexively.

"Home?" Mikal pulled her away, and she made no demur.

"Yes. Home. Come along, Mr Clare."

"Yes, well." Clare cleared his throat. "Archibald Clare. Mentath. How do you do."

She prised one eyelid open enough to see Clare offering his hand to the Neapolitan.

"Ludovico Valentinelli. Murderer and thief. Your servant, sir." Those dark eyes had lit with something very much like amusement.

"Murd—" Clare audibly thought better of finishing the word. "Well. Very interesting. A pleasure. I shall accompany Miss Bannon to her home, then, and wait for our next meeting."

"Do that. And be careful with *la signora*; be a shame to lose her pretty face. Give me my knife, *strega*."

"Oh no." Her fingers tightened on the leather-wrapped hilt. *The blade's sensitised now; it could cut that binding I just laid on you. Try again, bandit.* "That wouldn't do at all, Ludo. Mikal shall leave you the one you flung at me, though. Pleasant dreams."

There was a sharp meaty sound as Ludovico's knife thudded into the wall aross the room, and Mikal's lip curled. The Neapolitan's curses followed them out of the door, but she could tell he was intrigued.

Good.

The hectic strength sustaining her after dancing with Mehitabel had largely deserted its post by the time they reached Mayefair. In any case, she could not search for more answers until morning and a visit to the Collegia. The darkened foyer was a balm, the house sleepily taking notice of her return. The rooms would be ready, since the servants were well accustomed to her appearing and disappearing at odd hours.

Emma could wish that it was not quite so routine. "I suggest you take some rest, Mr Clare." She could finally occupy herself in stripping the remains of her gloves from her aching hands.

The mentath was remarkably spry. "Oh, indubitably. I shall

no doubt sleep well. You have some interesting friends, Miss Bannon."

*I have few "friends", Mr Clare.* "Valentinelli is not a friend. He is more . . . a non-enemy. I amuse him, he is reliable. Especially once he is hedged with a blood oath."

"Yes, well, I am not at all certain I like the idea of a filthy Italian bleeding on me." Clare actually *sniffed*. "But if you say he is capable, Miss Bannon, I shall take you at your word. I shall expect him at dawn or shortly after."

She gave up on her gloves and leaned into Mikal's hand on her arm. "Breakfast will be shortly after Tideturn. I presume your agile faculties are even now turning over the question of how and where to—"

"Oh yes. In fact, I have tomorrow's investigation planned."

Her conscience pinched, but she was, blessedly, too tired to care. "Good." She took an experimental step toward the stairs; Mikal moved with her. The Shield's frustration and annoyance was bright lemon yellow to Sight; her temples throbbed as it communicated to her.

"Miss Bannon?"

*For the love of Heaven, what now?* "Yes?"

"You have suddenly decided this Valentinelli is sufficient protection for my fragile person. Either you have a high faith in his capabilities, or—"

*Or I shall dangle you in the water and see which fish rises. You do well to suspect me, sir.* "I have become a much larger threat to these conspirators than you, Mr Clare. And by now, they are informed of it. You may take some comfort, at least, in that."

Wisely, perhaps, Clare left it at that. Emma set herself to climbing the stairs and navigating halls. Her skirts dragged, the Wark's ash still clung to her despite carefully applied cleaning-charms, and her Shield was about to explode.

He had the grace to keep himself quiet until the door to her dressing room opened, and she moved as if to free herself from his grasp. Her bed had rarely seemed so welcoming.

"Emma." Quietly.

*Please. Not now.* But he had apparently decided that yes, now was the time for a discussion.

"A dragon, Emma."

*One of the Timeless, albeit a young wyrm.* "Yes." She fixed her gaze on the shadowed bulk of one wardrobe, the dressing room's interior faintly glowing from the pale grey carpet and the plain silk hangings. "You should have taken the mentath and fled."

"Leaving you to Mehitabel." A single shake of his dark head, one she felt through his hand on her arm. "You should not ask such things of me."

"What should I ask of you, then? I am very tired, Mikal."

"A *dragon*, Emma."

*You are repeating yourself.* "I am fully aware of what transpired at the Blackwerks. The ironwyrm had orders to kill me. Those orders could only have come from another of the Timeless; a dragon would not care to obey a sorcerer, even to kill another of our ilk." She stared at the wardrobe. "And Britannia herself warns me that if Grayson is in league with the wyrms, her protection may not be enough. They are dangerous, and her compact with them is old and fragile. To them, we are merely temporary guests, and our Empire a wisp of cloud."

"Then why should they care if . . ." It struck him. He stiffened, his fingers clamping her flesh. "Ah."

"Someone has *made* them care for this piece of mechanisterum, Mikal. I must find out precisely who and neutralise the threat they represent to Britannia, or even the possible military uses of a logic engine will be beside the point. I am extraordinarily fatigued. You may retire."

He still did not let go. "What if I have no wish to retire?"

"Then you may dance in the conservatory or paint in the kitchen for all I care. Turn loose."

He did, but when she paced unsteadily into her dressing room he followed, closing the door with a faint but definite *snick.*

Every piece of jewellery on her tired body was dark and dead spent. She was barely upright, and if he sought to free himself of the shackle of duty to another sorcerer, there was no better time. She halted, swaying unsteadily, in a square of moonlight from the glass panels set in the ceiling, charter symbols sliding sleepily over them in constellation patterns.

And she waited.

His breath touched her hair. The closeness was too comforting; she shut her eyes and thought of Ludovico's filthy fingernails, the healthy animal smell of him, alcohol and exertion. Mikal was perfumed only with soot and the familiar tang of sorcery, a faint hint of maleness underneath.

It was useless. The pointless urge, once more, rose in her throat. This time she did not bar it. "Thrent," she whispered. "Jourdain. Harry. Namal."

"They betrayed you." Intimate, the touch of air against her ear. She shivered, swaying again, but he didn't touch her. "That was why they died."

Tall, dark Thrent. Small, blond, agile Jourdain. Harry with his smile, Namal with his gravity.

"They did not betray me. *He* killed them." The last name. She licked her dry, smoke-tarnished lips, said it to rob it of power: "Miles Crawford."

"He hurt you." So soft. "So he died. And *they* allowed themselves to be taken by surprise; their betrayal was in their carelessness. I would have murdered them myself for it, if *he* had not."

*They eliminated the rest of* his *Shields while Crawford sprang his trap on me. It was my fault, of course. I judged myself too highly.* "Very comforting." But her breath caught. He leaned a little closer, the almost-touch paradoxically, exquisitely more intimate than his fingertips could ever hope to be.

"You know what I am." A mere breath.

*I am not certain at all.* "I have my suspicions."

And there was the *other* reason to mistrust him. For there

were certain troubling things she had observed in her Shield, and if her suspicions were correct, the ease with which he had throttled Crawford was a dire sign indeed.

"Easy enough to prove."

"What if I prefer them to remain suspicions?" Her voice did not sound like her own. It lacked utterly the bite Emma was accustomed to putting behind each word.

"You cannot abide mysteries, Prima. It is," he finally touched her, warm fingers sliding under the half-awry mass of her hair, stroking her nape, "a small weakness."

*That you have no idea of my other weaknesses is a very good thing.* She raised her chin, pushed her shoulders back, and stepped firmly away from Mikal's hand. "Thank you, Shield. You may retire."

His hand fell to his side. "Do you wish me to sleep at your door like a dog?"

*Would you? How charming.* Her shoes were filthy; she had tracked cinderfall and God alone knew what else into the house. The maids would have a time of it in the morning. Another dress ruined, too, and sending a bill to Grayson was not likely to gain her any remuneration.

And unless she wished to ring a bell and wake someone to help her undress, Mikal would. It was, after all, part of a Shield's function to act as valet – or lady's maid, as the case may be.

"D—n your eyes." Unladylike, yes. But her flesh crawled, and her temper had worn thin.

"Is that a yes or a no?" He even sounded *amused*, blast him to the seventh Hell of Tripurnis.

Her only answer was to tack for her bedroom. Her bedraggled skirts were lead blankets, her bloomers chafed, and she would have had a special demise planned for her corset, had she not been so utterly exhausted. Let him do as he pleased. She was far too tired to care.

Or so she tried to tell herself, as she heard his footsteps behind her.

# Chapter Twenty-One

## Becoming Acquainted

Tideturn came slightly after dawn, filling the city with humming expectancy. The fog had not lifted, and there was no steady rain to keep it in check, just a few flirting spatters every now and again. The city smelled venomous, an odour that penetrated even Miss Bannon's sorcerously sealed dominion.

Despite that, breakfast was, as Clare had come to expect, superlative. The only dimming of his enjoyment came from the presence of the pox-scarred Neapolitan, who strolled in with great familiarity and proceeded to show terrible manners. The man's nails were no longer caked with filth, and he had somewhere found a respectable black wool waistcoat and a flashboy's watch chain, as well as a stickpin with a small, vile purple gem of no worth whatsoever. His high-collar shirt was of fine quality, but he still looked almost like a carter uneasy with high company. It was, the mentath decided, a carefully chosen façade.

Valentinelli's boots had belonged to a gentleman once, and Clare found himself engaging in unsupported speculation about how they had found their way to the Neapolitan's clumping feet.

The man *could*, Clare thought, walk lightly as a cat. He was choosing not to, stamping around the exquisite Delft-and-cream breakfast room. The soothing jacquard of the blinds was probably wasted on the assassin, who gave the room a single glance

– rather as a general would take in the terrain – and grunted at Clare, before loading a plate with all manner of provender and leering at one of the maids. Who simply ignored him with a toss of her honeybrown head.

Clare took this to mean she had some prior experience of the man.

Very interesting indeed.

Valentinelli filled his mouth with sausage, crammed in an egg, and chewed with great relish. He slurped his tea, wiping his fingers on the fine waistcoat – all the while standing between two potted palms whose charmed crystal cover-globes sang a wandering, tinkling melody. Clare studied him for a few more moments, sipping his tea meditatively and nibbling at kippers on toast. The furniture here was surprisingly light and ladylike. From the size of the two small tables, Miss Bannon usually breakfasted alone.

Madame Noyon had left him to it after pouring tea; most likely she was attending to Miss Bannon's morning toilette and the business of running the house according to her employer's wishes. The breakfast table was of pale ash wood, its legs carved with water lilies and its cloth stunning white; the breakfast plate was delicate silver and stamped with a swan under a lightning bolt. Very Greque of the woman, indeed.

Clare crunched the last of his kippers and toast, washed it down with heavily lemoned tea, and decided to hazard a throw.

"I say, *signor*. You have quite the noble carriage."

The Neapolitan gave him one swift, evil glance. He took another huge bite of sausage, let his mouth fall open while chewing. His scarred cheeks had turned pale.

Clare dabbed at his lips with a napkin. "It is *marvellously* interesting that you are not a natural at rudeness. You were trained in fine manners. Your habit of performing the exact opposite of those manners gives you away."

A flush touched the Neapolitan's neck. Clare smiled inwardly. It was so *satisfying* to deduce correctly.

"A Campanian nobleman? Your accent, which you take pains to disguise, is too refined for anything else. But you left your homeland young, *signor*. You have adopted the English method of slurping tea, and you wear the watch chain as a costume piece instead of as a true hevvy or a carter would. And though you are no doubt very good with a dagger, it is the rapier that is your true love. Yours is an old house, where such things are still a mark of honour."

The Neapolitan grunted. His muscle-corded shoulders were tense.

Clare was actually— Was he? Yes. He was *enjoying* himself. The man presented a solvable puzzle, not without its dangers but well worth a morning's diversion.

"Very well then, keep your secrets." He considered another cup of tea, tapping his toe lightly. "This morning we shall go a-visiting. A friend of mine, or rather a close acquaintance. His is a respectable address; you may find yourself bored."

The Neapolitan swallowed a wad of insulted provender. When he spoke, it was in the tones of a wearied upper-class Exfall student, complete with precisely paced crispness on the long vowels. "If you keep talking, *sir*, I shan't be bored at all. Disgusted, perhaps, but not bored." No trace of Italy marred the words – the mimicry was near perfect. He grimaced, his tongue showing flecks of chewed sausage and crumbs of fried egg as he stuck it out as far as possible.

At that moment the door opened, and Miss Bannon appeared. There were faint smudges under her dark eyes, and she cocked her head as Clare rose hastily.

"Good morning. I see you two are becoming acquainted." Today it was dark blue wool, a travelling dress. The jewellery was plain, too – another cameo at her throat, four plain silver bands on her left hand and a sapphire on her right ring finger, her earrings long jet drops that would have been vulgar had she been wearing mourning. A brooch of twisted fluid silver alive with golden charter-charms completed the *ensemble*, and her hatpins dangled short strings of twinkling blue beads. The hat itself, small, blue, and exquisitely expensive, sat at a jaunty angle on her dark curls. It was *not* a bonnet, and he was obliquely gladdened to see so. Aesthetically, this was far more pleasing.

"I am gratified to see you well, Miss Bannon. Good morning."

The Neapolitan merely made a chuffing sound and buried his snout in more food.

"You seem to have disturbed Signor Valentinelli. Ludovico, *do* please come and sit down." She moved across the room, betraying no stiffness or injury, but she winced slightly as she sank into a Delft-cushioned chair opposite Clare, who lowered himself back down and eyed the teapot.

Mikal appeared, tidy dark hair and a fresh high-collared coat of the same dark green velvet, his glove-boots soundless as he nodded at Clare and began filling a plate.

Valentinelli glowered at the sorceress, swallowing another mass. "When you take the blood oath off, *strega*, I kill him." The Italian was back, singing under the surface of his words. Strengthening morning light fell pearly and pale across his scars, picking out the fresh grease stains on his waistcoat.

Miss Bannon examined him for a long moment, her hands motionless on the carved chair arms. "That would distress me," she remarked, mildly enough. The charter symbols cascading over the glass panels in the ceiling shivered, wheeling apart and coming together in new patterns. A brief rattle of rain touched them, steaming off immediately, leaving streaks of dust.

"Maybe I let him live. For you." The Neapolitan let out a resounding belch.

"Your magnanimousness fills me with gratitude." Miss Bannon accepted a plate of fruit and toast from Mikal. There was a small, very fresh and livid bruise on the side of her neck, low near the delicate arch of her collarbone, and Clare's eyebrows almost raised. It was extraordinarily uncomfortable to see such a thing.

*Well. She is sorceress, and may do as she pleases, but still.*

The Shield was the same, impenetrable. But his fingers brushed her shoulder as he turned away from serving her breakfast, and his yellow eyes were a trifle sleepy-lidded. Clare's estimation of their relationship twisted sideways a few crucial degrees. His organ of Remembrance, having had time to search through dusty vaults and cellars, served up something quite interesting.

The scandal surrounding Miles Crawford, Duke of Embraith and Sorcerer Prime, had been only glancingly mentioned by a former employer. Clare had simply stored the details and moved on, uninterested but unable to let any information leave his grasp unmarked. The Duke had been caught embezzling from the Crown, or some such; there were whispers of some *bad form*, which could mean anything from wiping his nose incorrectly at his club to the pleasures of Sodom. There had been no breath of sorcery surrounding his demise, which Clare had found a trifle odd at the time, but it did not warrant his attention. Sorcery was not a matter he found of great interest, and he had been . . . busy.

That had been the last time he crossed wits with Dr Vance, and the memory was pleasing and bitter at once. The pleasure of such an opponent and the bitterness of being outfoxed that once warred with each other most improperly.

Miss Bannon *tsk*ed at Valentinelli. "Must you behave in this manner? Mr Clare, I trust you slept well."

"As well as can be expected. There is a great deal to do today."

A small nod, very graceful. "Certainly. Mikal?"

The Shield poured his sorceress a cup of tea. As soon as he had delivered it, he produced a sheaf of papers. He handed them silently to Clare, gave the Neapolitan a single scorching look, and turned away to fill his own plate. His breakfast was just as hearty as Valentinelli's, but he managed it with infinitely more grace. For one thing, he sat to Miss Bannon's left side and used the silver.

"My, what is this?" The notations were interesting; Clare

scanned three pages and grew increasingly still, the breakfast room receding as he concentrated. All thoughts of Vance and old scandal fled. "Dear God."

"Indeed. That should aid your investigations – and I do not need to remark on the trust implied by even the simple admission of my possession of such papers."

"Working notes – these are Smythe's, I take it?"

Another nod, as she sipped tea with exquisite care. "I could not find Throckmorton's. There was very little left of his residence. There are also a few pages of Masters's notes on the bottom – they may be of some use as well."

"Undoubtedly. Thank you, Miss Bannon. This will aid my investigations immensely."

"There is one more thing." Her left-hand fingers flicked, the silver rings glinting dully, and a small crystalline pendant on a fine metal chain swung. It glowed even in the weak sunlight, a confection of silver wire and some colourless solid substance he could not immediately identify. "You shall wear this. If you are in dire need, I will be alerted, and I will offer what assistance I can at a distance, and furthermore make every effort to reach you. There is likely to be a great deal of annoyance involved in your investigations."

"I say. Is that an actual Bocannon's Nut?" Clare accepted the pendant, and Miss Bannon nodded before buttering her toast.

"With a few improvements, yes. They are time-consuming to create, and they can be broken, so do be careful."

Valentinelli pulled the last chair away from the small round table, dragging it along the carpet. He dropped into it, crushing the cushion, and banged his plate down on Miss Bannon's right. "Why you give him that, eh? I tell you I take care of him."

"Nevertheless." Miss Bannon's childlike face was unwontedly grave instead of simply set. "You may have occasion to thank me for it before this affair is finished. Do you recall the second time I made use of your services?"

The Neapolitan actually turned cheese-pale, his pockmarked

cheeks singularly unattractive as the blood drained away. "*Ci. Incubo, e la giovana signorina. E il sangue.* I remember."

"This is likely to be much worse." Miss Bannon applied herself to her toast and fruit, delicately conveying an apricot slice to her decided little mouth. "You may now leave the house at any time, Mr Clare, and return as you please. There is a brougham engaged and waiting at the front gate; you have the use of it all day." A final nod, the curls massed over her ears bouncing. "I suggest you do not loiter."

The driver was a broad-faced, pleasant man much exercised by the prospect of a full day's beneficent hire, and his maroon brougham was clean and well ordered. The clockhorses were freshly oiled and springy; the whip cracked smartly, and Valentinelli was suddenly businesslike. The sneering uncouth mask fell away, and what rose to replace it was a calm, unblinking, almost feline stillness.

The Neapolitan proved somewhat less terrible as a travelling companion. Clare had exited Miss Bannon's house with a shambling carter. Now he sat beside a dangerous man. He held his tongue, his attention divided between Valentinelli's immobility and the fog-choked, yellow-glowing street outside the window.

Sigmund Baerbarth's lodging in Clarney Greens was up two flights of stairs, the rooms spacious and well appointed but appallingly old-fashioned. The Bavarian kept them, antiquated as they were, because his workshop was situated directly behind the Queen Anne building holding his lodgings, in a long blue structure that had once been some manner of factory.

There was no chalked circle on the low wooden door inside the draughty building, so Clare tapped twice and entered. Valentinelli muttered a curse, shoving past him to peer at the tangled interior. A horrific noise was coming from the depths of the building, but that was normal enough. The Neapolitan finally nodded, curling a lip at Clare in lieu of simply saying it was safe to enter.

Shafts of sunlight pierced the dusty cavern, hulks of gutted machinery rising on either side. Metal gleamed, cogwheels as tall as Clare's leg or watchmaker-tiny, bits of oiled leather and horsehair, struts and spars, carapaces and wheels in unholy profusion.

"Sig!" Clare called. "I say, Sigmund! Put the kettle on, you've visitors!"

A clanking rumble was the only reply. A mass of metal jerked, shuddering, and Clare watched as it heaved three times, oily steam sputtering from overworked valves. The shape suddenly made sense as he saw insectile legs with high, black-oiled joints. The body, slung below and between them, twitched and shivered. Atop the metal beast's back, a short pudgy figure held on with grim determination, his arm rising and a monstrous black spanner rising with it. The man brought his arm down decidedly, a massive clanging resounded, and the pile of metal slumped, wheezing clouds of vile-smelling green steam.

The rotund man kept beating at the iron back, making a terrific noise, until it finally splayed on the sawdust-scattered floor, bleeding dark grease and panting scorched steam. A rich basso profundo voice rose, rumbling through quite a few scatological terms Clare might have blushed at had they been in Queen's English.

"Sig!" he called again. "Good show, I say! You've almost got that working."

"Eh?" Sigmund's seamed bald head jerked up, the leather-and-brass goggles clamped to his face making his eyes into swimming poached eggs. "Archibald? *Guten Tag,* man! *Wer ist das?*"

"Name's Valentinelli, he's my insurance. Bit of trouble, old man. I need your advice."

"Very good!" The Bavarian dropped the spanner with a clatter and hopped down, sawdust puffing from his boots. He wore a machinist's apron, and when he freed himself from the goggles one could see watery brown eyes under bushy iron-grey brows.

His moustache was magnificent, if a trifle singed, and his side whiskers were vast – to make up for his egg-bald head, since he was a vain man. "Come, I make you tea. And there is wurst! Cheese and your foul kippers, too. Come, come." He pumped Clare's hand with abandon, grabbed Valentinelli's and did the same. "You are small and thin. Italian, *ja*? No matter, you eat too. Baerbarth is not proud."

The Neapolitan gave a wolfish grin. "Neither is Valentinelli, *signor. Ciao.*"

"*Ja, ja,* come. This way, this way—"

He led them between stacks of machinery, into a section of smaller metal carcasses. The light came from gaslamps and high dusty windows, weakly struggling to penetrate the corners, glinting off sharp edges.

Four easy chairs crouched in front of a coal grate; a massive pigeonhole desk loaded with papers and smaller cogwheels and gears hunched to one side. This portion of the old factory was better lit and warmer, and a hanging rack constructed of scrap metal above the desk held loops of wurst links and a gigantic wheel of cheese in a net bag. The kettle near the grate was hot, and in short order a second breakfast was prepared. Valentinelli and Baerbarth set to with a will, while Clare contented himself with terrible, harsh tea cut with almost turned milk.

"Now." Sigmund's eyes gleamed with interest. "Tell me, Herr Clare. What is problem?"

There was nothing for it but to leap in, however indirectly. "I need Prussian capacitors."

Sigmund shrugged, chewing meditatively at a wurst as thick as his burly wrist. He was only a genius; his faculties were not quite mentath quality and he had failed the notoriously difficult Wurzburg Examinations twice. For all that, he was generous, loyal, and honest to a fault. If not for the efforts of his landlady McAllister and his sometimes assistant Chompton – a thin, half-feral lad with a near-miraculous affinity for clockhorse gears – he would probably have been cheated out of every farthing long ago.

"Capacitors." The great gleaming head nodded. "Prussians? Gone. Gentlemen bought mine month ago; none to be had, love or money. I could find you Davinports or some French ones, feh!" His face balled itself up to show his feelings on such a matter. To Sig, German mechanisterum was the apotheosis of the art, English was serviceable, and the French altogether too delicate and fancy to be considered proper mechanisterum at all. "But no, *mein Herr*, no Prussians. Not even my Becker haf them."

*Ah, so the trail is not as cold as I feared.* "Now that is very odd." Clare's nose sank into his teacup. His habitual chair was a wide broken-in leather monstrosity, smelling slightly sharpish with rot like everything in the factory. Valentinelli's head made a quick catlike movement, enquiring, as he perched on a wooden stool next to the grate – Chompton's usual spot. "And where is young Chompers today?"

"He is picking river-shore, like good boy. Back before Tide, I tell him, but he grunt and wave his arms. Young men!" He rolled his weak, blinking eyes. "I find you Prussians, but it take time."

"That's quite all right. I have another question, my friend—"

"Of course. You would like wurst, eh? Or cheese? Bread is good, I just scrape mould off. More tea?"

"No thank you. Sig, old man, how would one trace a certain shipment of Prussian capacitors? *Without* drawing attention to oneself?"

The Bavarian grinned widely. One of his front teeth was discoloured; he had a positive horror of toothcharmers. "Aha! Now is revealed!"

*No, but I would like you to think so.* "Indeed. And?"

Sigmund sank back in his faded blue armchair, blowsy pink cabbage roses blooming horrifically over its surface like spreading fungus. It squeaked as he settled his squat frame more firmly. "Difficult. Very difficult."

"But not impossible." The tea was almost undrinkable, but

at least it was strong. One could always do with a spot more to help a situation settle the proper way. "And if anyone can, Sig . . ."

"Archie. Is difficult, this thing you ask, *ja*?" Suddenly very grave, Sigmund took another mouthful of wurst and chewed. Like a cow, he thought best while ruminating.

A thin thread of unease touched Clare's nape. He glanced at the stool by the grate.

Valentinelli had vanished.

# Chapter Twenty-Two

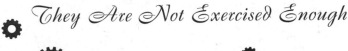

## They Are Not Exercised Enough

The dark green curricle was fast and light, especially with Mikal at the reins and the matched clockwork bays high-stepping. A trifle flashy, not quite the *thing* for a lady, but one had only to look at the witchballs spitting in their gilded cages, swinging from the swan-neck leaf springs, and the dash-charm sparking with crimson as it deflected mud and flung stones from the passenger, to know it was not just a lady but one of sorcery's odd children being driven by a nonchalant Shield through a press of Londinium traffic rather startlingly resembling the seventh circle of Hell.

The curricle took a hard left, cutting through a sea of humanity. Shouts and curses rose. Emma paid no attention. Her eyes shut, she leaned back in her seat, fine invisible threads flashing one by one through her receptive consciousness as she held herself still. One gloved hand held tight to the loop of leather on her left, her fingers almost numb. Mikal shifted his weight, the clockhorses so matched their drumming hoofbeats sounded like one creature, Londinium's chill fogday breath teasing at her veil. Even the strongest air-clearing charm could not make the great dozing beast of the city smell better than foul on days like this, when one of Dr Bell's jars had descended over everything from St Paul's Road to the Oval, and beyond. The night's fog crouched well past daybreak, peering in windows, fingering pedestrians, cloaking whole streets with blank billowing hangings of thick yellow vapour. Some, especially the ditch-charmers and hedgerow conjurors, swore Londinium altered itself behind the fog. Outside the Black Wark, the Well, Whitchapel's Sink or Mile End – or some other odd pockets – few believed them.

Still, those sorcery touched did not laugh at the notion. At least, not overloud, and certainly never overlong.

The avenues widened as they travelled north and west toward Regent's Park. Traffic thinned through Marylbone, taking the great sweep of Portland Place past terraced Georgian houses standing proud-shouldered, sparkling with wards and charms. Precious few were sorcerer's houses – no, the unsorcerous fashionable paid for defences, the flashier the better.

A sorcerer's defences were generally likely to be less visible and more deadly.

Mikal made a short, sharp sound, shifting again, and the horses leapt forward. Pelting up the Place was certainly one way to make a statement, and she did not wonder why he had chosen this particular route. She was to be as ostentatious as possible today, so her quarry would focus on her as the larger threat – and hopefully not notice Clare's poking about overmuch.

If they noticed *too* much, well, Valentinelli was the best protection she could provide, next to her own self. Ludovico might have made a fine Shield, if he'd been moulded earlier. He would have needed a light touch, though, and *that* was something very few sorcerers possessed.

Whoever rose to the bait of a mentath and an assassin would be interesting indeed. There was an art to preparing a hook without losing either hook or bait, and she intended to do so today.

The bay clockhorses, every inch of them gleaming now, ran like foam on crashing surf. Emma found the threads she wanted, her hands clenched before relaxing, fingers contorting and easing

as she made the Gesture, and the Word shaped itself on her
tongue.

"*Ex–k'Ae–t!*" As usual, the Word was soundless, filling her,
thunder in stormclouds. The curricle jolted, sparks fountaining
from clockhorse hooves, and the sudden eerie quiet as wheels
and hooves bit nothing but air enfolded them.

Her eyelids fluttered, daylight spearing into her skull, the
impression of Mikal standing, reins now loosely held as the
clockhorses settled into a jogtrot. Emma's own contorted fingers
held finer, invisible threads, snapping and curling, fresh ones
sliding into existence as the old tore.

The carriage *flew*.

Up they climbed, lather and sparks dripping, fog closing over
Park Crescent below them, its green sickly under the pall. Still
rising over Regent's proper, the only sound the curricle's wheels
spinning freely and one of the clockhorses snorting, tossing its
fine head. From the withers and haunches to the hooves,
cogwheels meshed and slid, the pistons in the legs working in a
simulacra of a flesh horse's bones, its skeleton sorcerously reinforced and the russet metal melding seamlessly into bay hide
lovingly tended by half-lame spine-curled Wilbur, the stable boy,
who stammered so badly he could not make himself understood.
The scar on his forehead perhaps showed why, but he had a
charmed touch with clockhorses. Yet another indenture she was
glad to have performed – her one-time kindness reaping a reward
out of all proportion. Harthell, her usual coachman, was another
– but she had no time to think on her collection of castaways.

For there, drifting as lightly as a soap bubble, the great
Collegia stood on empty air. The lattices of support and transferral cradling the massive tiered white-stone edifice were clearly
visible to Sight, but to the ordinary it seemed that the Collegia
simply . . . floated. It drifted in a slow, majestic pattern above
the Park, confined there to keep the Londinium rabble from
rioting at the idea that it could fall on their slums and tenements
– or vent its waste onto their heads.

Though they merrily shovelled excrement over each other, a sorcerer's dung was another thing entirely. None saw fit to tell them the waste was shunted into the Themis, just like their own.

The horses high-stepped up an invisible grade, turned as Mikal flicked the reins, and the Gates were open. Sharp black stone dully polished and sculpted with flowing fantastical animal shapes, running with bloody-hued charter symbols, the Gates had been the first thing built for the Collegia. They had stood open since the first stone had been laid by Mordred the Black, who had claimed descent from Arthur's left-hand line. Whether that was true, who could say?

The Lost Times were lost for a *reason*. Much as the records of the Age of Flame and the Age of Bronze were only fragmentary, or the records of the time during Cramwelle's Inquisition. Britannia, her physical vessel murdered and the shock of that murder reverberating through the Isle, had surfaced finally in a fresh vessel and halted Cramwelle's violent hatred of his sorcerous betters.

As the historial Lord Bewell had remarked, a little ambition could make even a hedge-charmer dangerous.

The most difficult part of entering the Collegia was landing on the slick marble paving. Even the cracking sound of transferring force away into empty air was to be avoided. Difficult, delicate, dexterous work; clockhorse hooves touched down soft as feathers, the curricle's wheels given a preparatory spin to match speed, and the gradually rising volume of hooves and wheels until every step rang on the cold white stone was a small triumph. The silver rings on Emma's left hand were warm, her attention rushed back firmly into her body and she cautiously opened her eyes.

The heavy veil took some sting from the foggy sunlight, much brighter here above the thicker soup of ground-level fog. Still, she squinted most unbecomingly before she half lidded her eyes languidly as a lady should. The curricle raced up the long circular drive; the massive fountain in the middle of the round garden played a sonorous greeting as multicoloured streams of light and prismatic water laved its surfaces. A half-nude Leda reclined under Jove in the form of a swan, blinding white; she chucked the snake-necked creature under its chin and for a moment the wings moved as her limbs did, dreamily. The light and water caressing them both made it far more indecent than the worst of the gentlemen's flash press.

It was, Emma reflected as Mikal steered the horses past the chill-white, massive Great Staircase, a very good metaphor for sorcerers in general.

The Library's white dome was low compared to the jabbing snowy enamel spires of the rest of the Collegia, but it was still large enough to swallow the Leather Market whole and ask for seconds. Mikal pulled the horses to a stop and a Collegia indentured appeared to take charge of them; her Shield leapt down from the curricle and Emma gathered her skirts.

*This should prove interesting.*

The Library's dome glowed, stone scraped thin enough to let sunshine through. In that drenching, directionless light, flapping shadows moved. They circled in small flocks, sometimes lighting on the tops of high shelves, other times fluttering toward the gigantic nautilus-curled circulation counter. A vast central well, five storeys of bookshelves rising around it and raying out in long spiralling stacks, was enough to make one dizzy. Balustrades of ivory and mother-of-pearl, the carpeting rich blue; the Library glowed with nacre, the smell of paper mixing with a faint breath of salt and sand. Thin cries could be heard as some of the books fluttered aloft, gaining altitude and swooping with gawky grace.

Mikal followed, perhaps more closely than was strictly necessary. But then, his life was forfeit here. A Shield could not be taken from a Prime's service and put to death, no matter the crime he had committed. The law was very clear on that point – even if the Shield in question had done the unthinkable and murdered his own sorcerer.

No other sorcerer was willing to run the risk of taking him in. None of her fellow Primes – indeed, no sorcerer, and no other person – knew *precisely* what had happened in that small room in the bowels of Crawford's palatial home, because she had steadfastly maintained her silence. As far as she could tell, so had Mikal. Yet the fact of his survival in her service, and Crawford's demise, could not be ignored; it shouted to the heavens what had most likely occurred.

*It is you, or the chopping block,* he had said, his jaw iron-hard and his eyes glowing venomously. *I prefer you. If you will not take my service, do me the courtesy of killing me yourself. I will let you.*

And Emma had believed him. Her fingers still tingled with the feel of his chest underneath her touch, the rasp of subtle scaling—

*Stop it. You are not here to daydream.* She stalked for the circulation desk, shaking herself out of memory with a sharp disciplined mental effort. It would be easy to believe Mikal felt . . . what?

Nothing she could trust. It was best to remember that.

Behind the desk, a tangle-haired witch in no-nonsense grey wool glanced up, startled by her approach. Of course, any livre-witch would feel a Prime's approach like a storm bearing down on a small sloop. Especially here at the Collegia, where sorcery vied for air as the most common medium.

This livrewitch was plump, her hazel eyes unfocused, and she swayed slightly as she gripped the desk's edge until she adjusted to the disturbance Emma represented. "Title?" she chirped, in a colourless little voice. Her dishwater hair was a rat's nest, matted locks hanging and others piled high with a collection of bones, small shiny bits of metal, and feathers. "Author? Catalogue number? Cover colour? Subject?"

"*Principia Draconis.*" Emma fought back a curling lip. Witches. Male and female both specialised young, and by the time they reached twenty their brains were capable of holding only their Discipline. Theirs were not the deep Disciplines of the Inexhaustible – fire, water, magnetism, creation, destruction – but the tiny niches. Swallows nesting in a cliffside, and never straying far from their tiny holes.

*Do not pity the witches,* a teacher had once intoned. *They are not less than sorcerers. They are far happier than you shall ever be – for they lack ambition. They find their joy in their Discipline, not their danger.*

ʼ "*Principia Draconis,*" the livrewitch repeated, slowly. A shuffling movement went through the flocks of books, shelves moving as the Library sought inside itself. "De Baronis, originally, 1533. Amberforth updated and glossed in 1746; James Wilson in 1801. Eight hundred pages, folio, cover is—"

"Bannon." The sneering behind Emma could only come from one man. "Still bringing trash into hallowed halls, I see."

"Lord Huston." She inclined her head, but did not turn. "Still unacquainted with basic etiquette, I see."

"*Ladies* are due etiquette, Bannon." The Headmaster's cane – an affectation, of course, with its silver mallard's head – hit the carpeting. He must have forgotten he wasn't in one of the stone-floored halls, where the tapping of his progress would send a wave of dread through the sensitised fabric of reality.

Mikal moved, a susurrus of cloth as he faced the Headmaster. Emma kept her gaze on the livrewitch, who was mumbling. At any moment the book would appear, and she could give the Headmaster short shrift before taking herself to a study table to do some quiet digging.

"And the trash seems to have ideas." Mock-surprised. "When *are* you going to take a proper Shield, Bannon? If any will serve with *that* murdering apostate behind you."

"Be careful, little man." Bannon allowed her right toe to lift and tap the carpet precisely *once*. Her skirts would cover it, but she was still annoyed at the movement. He was Prime, yes – but just barely. Had he not been extraordinarily lucky, he would be merely an Adept, or even a Master Sorcerer, since his Examination scores had been dreadful. "I am not a student."

"*A sorcerer who ceases to learn ceases to thrive,*" he intoned piously. "Whatever are you doing *here*, then, if you are no longer learning?"

"The Library is open to every Adept and above, at every hour." It was her turn to sound pious. "Or perhaps you'd forgotten that Law?"

A direct hit. "I forget no Laws," he hissed. "*You* are the one who has a Shield who no doubt murdered his charge. You should hand him over to justice."

Her temper stretched. "If you challenge me for one of my possessions, Huston, I might almost think you've grown tired of breathing."

The Library's rustling silence took on a sonorous, uneasy depth. *I do not have time for a duel today, Alfred, Lord Huston. Take advantage of that.* For a moment she considered how easy it would be to see him as a conspirator and administer appropriate justice.

The thought almost managed to soothe her.

"The *Principia Draconis* is not here." The livrewitch cocked her tangled head, the words a thin reedy murmur as she clasped her hands. Her gaze was already sliding away, uninterested in the drama before her. "It has been borrowed."

"That is quite impossible." Emma's temper rose afresh; she bottled it. Today was already unpleasant, and it was early for her to be so irritated. "It is one of the Great Texts; it is not to leave the Library."

Huston's sneer was absolutely audible. "Oh, the *Principia*? I believe Lord Sellwyth wished to peruse it at leisure; I gave my approval. Since he is such a *special* friend to the Collegia."

For a moment, Emma Bannon literally could not believe her ears. Books fluttered nervously, several taking wing from the carved banisters. Shadows darted, and she turned on her heel, the cameo at her throat warming dangerously. Her skirts belled, and Mikal took a half-step to the side, his broad back tense under green velvet. No blades were visible yet – of course, if he drew, she would be hard pressed to calm the layers of ancient stifling protection meant to safeguard students from misfired lessons.

Even the simplest spell could kill, here. Bloodlust on Collegia grounds carried a heavy price.

Huston, his scarecrow form in an antiquated black suit, collar tied high and snowy cravat under his chin as if Georgus IV was still Britannia's vessel, actually paled and stepped back. Thin strings of bootblack hair crossed his domed cranium, and if Emma had been a devotee of phrenologomancy she might well have decided to examine his skull for an organ of Cowardice and one of Idiocy to boot.

With a hammer, or another suitably blunt bludgeoning tool.

His breeches were spotless, and a perfumed handkerchief frothed in his free hand. The man even wore dandy boots, the toe pointed and heel arched. The clicking of his cane was usually followed by the soft tapping of his heels, a sound that featured in student nightmares. Long bony strangler's fingers, his right hand bearing the heavy carnelian Collegia Seal, spasmed on the silver duck's head.

The light in here was too damnably bright, but it was Emma's stinging eyes that reminded her of her priorities. The veil, thankfully, might hide her expression. "You . . ." She did not cough, but she did pause. "You allowed Llewellyn Gwynnfud to take a Great Text from the Collegia Library? The *Principia Draconis*?" She congratulated herself on only sounding mildly surprised. "When was this? I ask, Lord Huston, only to be quite accurate when I make my report."

"Report?" Now Huston was positively chalky. He would have no idea to whom she would make such a report, but the creeping cowardice of petty officialdom ran to his very marrow. The Seal made a scratching noise, the carnelian shifting from a carving of Pegasus to the double serpents of Mordred's time. It was, she reflected, far too large for his fingers.

"Yes." She also wondered – and not for the first time

– precisely which charm he used to colour his hair. The dual thoughts bled her anger away. A dangerous calm closed over her. "When was it, sir?"

"Well, let's see . . . hmmm . . . that is . . ." He tapped the head of his cane with one manicured index finger. "You know, I cannot quite—"

"*Principia Draconis.* Checked out. A fortnight ago exactly," the livrewitch said dreamily. "The Psychometry books were restless that day. So was the Bestiary section. It took some work to calm them. They are not exercised enough."

Huston's expression was priceless. Emma smoothed her gloves. "Thank you. That will be all. Come, Mikal." Dismissive, she set off for the entrance. *Well. A mostly wasted trip. But now I know you are to be mistrusted to an even greater degree than I did before.*

*And that is very valuable knowledge.*

Her Shield fell into step behind her. There was a sound from above – a student perhaps, witnessing the exchange. This would be round meat indeed for them. Only the almost randomness of Huston's malignancy made a revolt in the student ranks unlikely. Besides, he largely allowed the professors to do as they pleased, and they liked the power so much they kept him firmly seated at the helm of the Collegia.

Or what he believed was the helm.

"Harlot." Whispered just loud enough to be an insult. "*Whore.*"

It was the oldest insult hurled at a sorceress – or indeed, at any woman who did not do what a small man wished. Did he expect it to sting?

*If only you knew, you bastard bureaucrat.* Other words rose; she considered each one and decided a lady would not speak them, so *she* certainly would not.

Her back was alive with Mikal's nearness. She swept out of the Library with rushing blood filling her ears. Outside, the sorcerously cleansed air still reeked of Londinium's disease. Nevertheless, she stopped and took a deep breath.

"Prima?" Mikal, his tone promising vengeance, should she want it. She would be well within her rights to call Huston to the duelling ground – but she would have only Mikal and a livrewitch for witnesses. It would not do.

She would merely remember this, as she remembered so much else. A Prime's life was long, and she would see Huston falter one day. "Leave it." She did not have to try very hard to sound weary. "He is of little account. Besides, there is another copy of the *Principia*."

"Indeed? Where?"

"At Childe's. Fetch the curricle."

# Chapter Twenty-Three

## Better Your Sausage Than Your Life

The mystery of Valentinelli's disappearance was solved in spectacular fashion. At least, Clare decided that the body falling from the rafters was intimately connected to the Neapolitan's vanishing, even as he leapt – in a display of agility surprising even himself – and hit Sigmund squarely, knocking the burly Bavarian and his chair over. A tangle of arms and legs, Sig's wurst and cheese went flying, and the body thudded on to the carpet as the grate exploded with blue flame.

Clare freed himself with a violent, wrenching twist, losing his top hat, and made it up to one knee, his freshly loaded silver-chased pepperbox pistol out. Smoke billowed, and Sigmund had regained his breath, to judge by the volume of curses in German coming from his quarter. Already it was difficult to see, smoke stinging Clare's eyes, and for a terrible moment he was swallowed by the memory of last night's irrationality.

*LOGIC!* he bellowed inwardly, jerking to the side as something whooshed through the smoke near his head. *Smoke, a body from the ceiling – multiple attackers; the Neapolitan may be injured but I think it unlikely. The smoke is to confuse us.*

The motive was not simply murder, he decided. Which raised some interesting questions he had no time to consider, for there was a movement in the smoke. *Too tall to be the Italian, and moving incautiously. Do something, Clare!*

Sigmund was still cursing.

"*Quiet*, man!" Clare barked, and his free hand closed around one of Sig's spanners, dropped next to the spilled chair. He scooped it up and flung it, calculation flashing just under the surface of his consciousness so quickly he was barely aware of the motion. His aim was true; there was a muffled scream of pain, and Clare dived to the side, fetching up against the Bavarian again. "Stay low," he whispered fiercely, and his busy faculties cross-checked an internal dictionary. "*Unten blieben!*"

"*Ja!*" Sig whispered back, and they set off, crawling, away from the coal grate and its belching black smoke. "*Verdammt sie! Meine Wurst!*"

*Better your sausage than your life, man!* Clare kept the pistol pointed carefully away. "Crawl! *Kriechen!*"

"I remember my English, *mein Herr!*" Damn the man, he actually sounded offended. "My workshop! What do they do with my workshop?"

*I only have three shots. Choose them carefully.* "Weapons! Do you have any weapons?"

"I haf—" But whatever Sigmund had remained unsaid, for there was a scream and the sound of clattering metal. "No! *Scheisse,* not my *Spinne*! Bastard!"

Clare got a fistful of Sig's jacket, hauling him back. The Bavarian went down in a heap, another dark shape loomed through the acrid smoke, and Clare's hand jerked at the last moment, sending the shot wide.

"*Idioti.*" Valentinelli bent down. His shirt was singed, and there was a spatter of blood on one of his pocked cheeks. "Put that away! Come!"

"What is it?" Clare had a fair idea already, but it certainly never hurt to ask.

"*Alterato.*" His ruined face alight, the assassin held a knife with the blade reversed against his forearm. There was a dark stain on his left knee, whether grease or blood Clare did not wish to venture. "To capture, not kill. This way."

*Flashboys, perhaps. Come to kidnap me or Sig? We shall find out.* "Good show. Sig old man—" A fierce whisper. "Sigmund!"

"Aha!" The Bavarian appeared, crawling with surprising nimbleness for such a bulky man; he had found his wurst. He stuffed the remainder of the sausage in his mouth and scrambled after Clare.

The Neapolitan was a wraith in the rapidly thinning smoke, bent almost double and moving with jerky efficiency. One sleeve of his pale shirt flapped slightly; he cast a look over his shoulder at Clare and vanished again, stepping sideways into the vapour. Clare coughed, spat to the side. Bulky metal shapes loomed. Sigmund cursed again, but very low. A scraping sound – Sig had found a weapon.

Good.

His ears strained, eyes burning from the acrid vapour, his left hand scraping on packed earth and scattered straw as he endeavoured to keep the pistol free in his right, Clare realised he had not been bored *once* since Miss Bannon's appearance. Which was truly marvellous, and a relief for his busy faculties, but he could still wish things were not *quite* so bloody interesting.

And why had he thought of her? The crystalline pendant, snug under his shirt, was oddly cold. Was this a dire enough situation to warrant her attention? Probably not. He wished he had thought to find his hat before setting off at a crawl through Sigmund's workshop—

There was a wet crunching noise, and a soft cry. The smoke, draining in whorls and eddies, had lost none of its terrible stench. He motioned Sigmund aside; a huge metal carapace afforded a slightly safer hiding space. Inside, there was a tangle of sharp poking ends, but Clare pressed back nevertheless, and Sig crowded in beside him.

"*Mein Gott*, what smell!" he whispered, and Clare was forced to agree.

"Sulphur and agatesbreath, I believe." *Coal doesn't burn hot enough to ignite it; how did they? Must experiment later.* He readied the pistol, torn metal jabbing his jacket. "Be still."

More soft, stealthy scrapings. A clatter of metal; Sigmund twitched and breathed a rather filthy imprecation. The smoke became striations, behaving oddly, thick and greasy as it slid questing fingers over a broken clockhorse skeleton. The metal vibrated, resonating to a silent current of bloodlust, and Clare watched as a shape melted into view behind a screen of smoke.

He was Altered, but not a flashboy. Lanky, dark-haired, unshaven in ill-fitting grey worsted, he placed his shoes carefully and edged through the smoky fingers, moving with jerky, oily care. The Alteration wasn't visible, but Clare noted the irregularity under the rough homespun workman's shirt and his gorge rose. Limbs were all very well, but Alteration of the trunk of the body? Not only was it expensive and dangerous, it was simply *wrong*.

Sigmund, thankfully, had frozen. Whether he was immobilised by surprise or Teutonic rage was difficult to tell. Clare raised the pistol, the motion slow and dreamlike. The dry stone in his throat was unwelcome; it took effort to shelve the persistent nagging animal fear of being hunted. His mouth was dry, and his pulse pounded alarmingly. His ears heard each muffled beat, blurring together into a distracting roar.

The Altered stiffened, his head tipping back. Valentinelli's face appeared over his shoulder as his knees slowly buckled; the Neapolitan grabbed a fistful of dark hair and dragged the head back further. A swift jerking motion, then he slit the Altered man's throat. Arterial spray bloomed, smoke flinched away, and the assassin breathed a soft love word as the Altered slumped.

Valentinelli flicked the knife, bent down to wipe it on his victim's clothing. Clare lowered his pistol, silver glinting. His head was full of rushing noise.

*Why does this disturb me so?*

The Neapolitan's gaze was flat and blank. He looked, for all the world, like a man who was simply performing a mildly disagreeable but not very difficult task. "*Bastarde*," he said, softly. "Not even worth pissing on. Come to take Ludo's job away, eh? Not today. Is safer now," he continued, not even bothering to glance at the two men hiding like children. "Come out, little *polli*. Ludo has made it well again."

Acrid smoke thinned. Clare coughed, finding his eyes welling with hot water and his throat afire. "Sig?" he croaked. "Dreadfully sorry about your workshop."

"*Schweine*." The genius pushed past Clare, brushed himself off. He glared at the dead body, and as the smoke cleared, Clare found other lifeless forms scattered throughout the factory. "My beautiful wurst. And my *Spinne*. I hope she not damaged." He fixed Clare with a beady glare. "So, this is the trouble you bring to Papa Baerbarth, my friend? I find you Prussian capacitors. I help you. They pay for this, the *Schweinhunde*."

"Good show. I say, Valentinelli, very good." Clare emerged from the metal carapace, blinking. "Er, who were they after, do you think?" It was vanishingly unlikely they were here for Sig, but thoroughness demanded he ask. And his nerves required a question answered, *any* question, to steady them.

"Simple." The Neapolitan resheathed the knife. "If they after fat one there, I let them have him."

Clare swallowed. The crystalline pendant had warmed again, no longer a chip of cold metal ice under his shirt. His throat was amazingly dry. He could use even some of Sig's atrocious tea. "I see. Well, I thought as much. Sig, fetch your bag. We're going capacitor-hunting. Where do we start?"

Sigmund took his hat from his round head, dusted it fastidiously, and jammed it back on while setting off for the still smoking grate. "Docks. Always start docks first. Tell me *everything*."

The docks of Londinium seethed under a dome of sulphur-yellow fog. Here, the nerve endings of Empire sizzled with goods crated and bundled in every conceivable way, crawling with hevvy-mancers lifting loads or charming them into balance, sorcery spitting and crackling between the mountains of goods of every stripe, shipwitches wandering among them and laying carpets of charter charms. Tabac, indigo, flour, wine, carpets, chests, tea, coffee, cloth of every colour and description, spread and piled high over miles of timber. More hevvymancers charmed loads off the waiting ships, ship- and saltwitches humming in the rigging and calming restive breezes. The non-sorcerous carters, lifters, haulers, bullies, and half-clad ragged men looking to earn a few coins by shifting and hauling milled, choking the streets; warehouses stood tall and proud with Altered guards – some flashboys, others more serious and soberly modified – watching the crowded streets. No doubt many of them had a thriving trade in embezzlement to pay for their Alterations and the servicing of their metal, too.

They left the brougham and its driver at a nearby livery stable, the driver even more ecstatic that the day's work was proving so easy. Pressing forward on foot, Clare and Sigmund were soon lost in the crowd. Valentinelli drifted in their wake, and such was the confusion and clangour of Threadtwist Dockside that none remarked the blood on his clothes. To be sure, in the yellow glare it could be any dark fluid fouling him. Still, Clare found it difficult to look at the man.

Sigmund, still bemoaning the loss of his breakfast, kept up a steady stream of banter the entire way. Clare confined himself to non-committal responses, sunk in profound contemplation. He'd told the Bavarian the absolute minimum required, and they were now en route to a place where the tracing of a specific shipment of Prussian capacitors could begin. Miss Bannon's papers had included an invoice from a certain Lindorm Import Co., Threadtwist Dock, Londinium – an invoice that, when he had examined it after Miss Bannon's morning departure, had borne surprising fruit: a scrawl under "Rec'd of" he had more than a passing familiarity with.

After all, he had seen it many a time at Yton on Cedric Grayson's papers. The Chancellor of the Exchequer was involved indeed, and Clare could not wait to share the news with Miss Bannon. A dragon's word – he shuddered at the thought of the beast, hurried on – might not be acceptable proof to take Cedric to account, but *this* certainly was. And she had possessed it for who knows how long, without knowing its import.

*That* was satisfying in and of itself.

# Chapter Twenty-Four

## Never Aesthetically Lacking

Childe lived on Tithe Street; his wife was in Dublin and happy to remain there with his son. Mrs Childe had probably once thought to domesticate the man, but Primes were not easily tamed, especially one of Dorian's stripe. Still, she was a sorcerer's wife now, and did not want for support. At least Childe took care of his own, even if he also threw guineas over the young panthers of Topley like water. Whether he kept Mrs Childe well supplied because she had borne him a son who showed sorcerous promise, or because he had once cared for her, or because it was the decent thing to do, none could say. Emma was most inclined to believe the first, public opinion the second, and none but the extraordinarily naïve held to the last. A small contingent of fashionable opinion aired the view that since Childe was so busy buggering everything that moved, cash sent to Dublin was merely a means of keeping the woman away from his pleasures so she could tend to his son in magnificent seclusion.

Regardless, the Tithe Street house was magnificent; one of Naish's best, terraced and graceful, it rose for four storeys above the wide avenue, a low stone wall curving around it and containing a froth of gardens generally considered to be some of the finest in Londinium. Mikal paused before the gate as the invisible protections resonated – every knot and twist whispering

Childe's name to the extramundane senses, seashell murmurs of a Prime's disturbance in the fabric of the real.

Childe was at home. The defences swept aside, a not-quite-shimmering curtain, grandly theatrical like all his gestures. Mikal guided the high-stepping clockhorses on to the drive.

Emma's cheeks were damp. Achieving the Collegia grounds was one thing, descending was quite another. She blinked furiously, more tears sliding free. The blasted sun, just like everything else, was conspiring to fray her patience today.

Sometimes she wished her Discipline did not give her such an aversion to the daylight. Never for very long, and never very deeply, for on that path lay a danger she was unwilling to court. *A Prime should never doubt his Discipline*, the saying ran. Still, it would have been bloody lovely to be able to produce a Major Work that did not leave her half blind.

The stairs, a sweep of slick gold-veined marble with knife-sharp edges, marched to a huge crimson door. Only Childe would have such a *vulgar* thing. The urns lumbering up the steps held scarlet poppies, their blowsy heads nodding in unison, strangely bleached by the yellow cast of sunlight filtering through the fog. The air was deadly still, though a few stirrings promised rain later, perhaps at Tideturn. It might wash the filthy smell from the city, though Emma doubted it.

Inside, it was blessedly dimmer, the vast arching foyer was lit only by a few shafts of golden sunlight and several hissing witchballs in cages shaped like half-open amaryllis. Childe's long-suffering butler Mr Herndrop bowed, slightly and correctly, as he took the card from Mikal. His indenture collar was lacklustre, but his florid cheeks and nose more than made up for it. "He is in the front parlour, mum. Had quite a night of it."

*It is a wonder he is receiving, then.* But Childe very rarely turned *her* away. "Thank you, Herndrop. How is your arthritis?"

His chest puffed a little – not that it needed to; Herndrop possessed under his butler's black a barrel organ of a ribcage. "Tolerable, mum, thank you."

Emma nodded; he did not precede her to the parlour. That could be an indicator either of Childe's esteem for her, or of his incredibly foul mood. Or both. Besides, stationed at the door leaned a Shield of surpassing lankiness, his chestnut curls trimmed close but his moustache particularly fine.

"Lewis." Mikal, quiet and polite.

Lewis merely nodded. A flush had begun on his throat; he swallowed visibly. Few Shields would acknowledge Mikal openly now.

Not unless Emma forced them, and today she did not feel the need.

Emma, her skirts gathered and her stride lengthening, made straight for the door – white-painted, gold leaf trimming its rectangular carvings, the knob a carved crystal skull. *That* was a new addition – previously it had been red curtains and a pasha's fancy beyond. "Good heavens," she remarked, "I almost shudder to think of what's behind the door *this* time."

"Mum." Lewis sounded half strangled, but he reached for the knob anyway. Mikal did *not* let loose an amused half-chuckle, but it was very close.

The door swept open, bright light stung her eyes afresh, but Emma reached up to pull aside her veil. Childe had redecorated in bordello blue, with a French twist, Louis *L'Etat Quatorze* with curlicues, slim-legged tables, ormolu, and overstuffed furniture. Leaning on the mantel was a young man; Emma took him in at a glance and sighed internally. The loud coat, soft white hands, and scented hair all screamed a St Georgeth panther, brought home with Childe's usual utter lack of propriety or even good sense. This particular one had a fresh face still clinging to youth, but the sullen expression – no doubt charming when he was a lad – marred whatever remained of his attractiveness. He gave Emma an insouciant look, curling his lip and his little finger, and she suppressed a flash of irritation.

"*Well!*" Dorian Childe, sleek-haired, heavy-lipped, and one of the more powerful Primes of the Empire, was in a violently patterned green and black kimono, but his toilette was otherwise immaculate. "If it isn't my dearest Emma. Are you here for tea, or is this another of your flying visits?"

Emma gave him her hands, an unwonted smile curving her lips. A tear trickled from the corner of her right eye, and he *tut-tut*ted. "How silly of me. Here, darling—" A Minor Word slid free of his mouth, his lips shaping the sibilants sensually, and the indigo drapes freed themselves from their ropes, falling gracefully across the windows. The witchballs darkened, and the young man at the fireplace shivered. "Is that better? You must have had a morning of it. Come, sit down."

"I am here to plunder your library, Dorian. I see you've redecorated."

"You hate it, I can tell. Not all of us have your restraint, my darling. Still carrying your baggage around, I see." But his bright darted glance at Mikal held no malice. Just predatory interest, and Emma did not miss the reined distaste spreading from her Shield.

"Oh, don't start." Her shoulders relaxed, fractionally. Childe, at least, was a monster whose loyalty was not in question. Rather like a gryphon. "I saw Huston this morning. Do you know what charm he uses to colour his hair?"

"Whatever it is, I am certain it's dreadful. Do come and sit down; the library can wait a few moments while you refresh yourself. Paul, be a dear and fetch some tea. Cook knows what we like."

"I ent yer lady's maid," the panther at the fireplace sneered, but he peeled himself fully upright and slouched towards the door.

"Delicious, isn't he?" Childe stage-whispered. "And so tractable. At least, at this stage."

"You'll get a knife in the ribs one of these days," Emma murmured, as the tractable Paul banged the parlour door shut. "Where are your Shields?"

Childe magnanimously didn't note that said knife would have

to be applied while he was insensible not to earn its wielder a terrible sorcerous death, but the arch of his eyebrows and flare of his nostrils remarked for him. "Oh, around and about. You're a fine one to talk. I could give you Lewis, he's grown quite disapproving. Or even Eli. A lovely young thing like yourself shouldn't be wandering alone."

"Do I want the responsibility of another Shield? They require care and feeding, you know." *Eli. I remember him. Dark, and very quiet. He was with Alice Brightly, but she returned him to the Collegia. If he's returned again, it might be unpleasant.* "You've grown tired of Eli, then?"

"No, he's just so *serene* all the time. It interferes with my jollities. So, darling, my library. What are you after? A little bit of flash? Something no respectable girl should be reading? A novel or two?"

She restrained herself from remarking that she wished she had time to read the novels gathering dust on her nightstand. "Actually, I am after a Great Text. *Pricipia Draconis.* You have, I seem to recall, a rather fine edition."

"And you were at the Collegia earlier. Which means their copy has gone missing. How interesting." Childe's eyes all but sparkled. "My dear, what would you say if I told you that barely a fortnight ago, a dreadful little Master Sorcerer came with a letter from someone very important, asking me ever so nicely if I'd loan out my *Principia*?"

Emma blinked. *I wonder.* "Ah. It wouldn't by any chance be a rather slovenly fellow by the name of Devon, would it?"

"You've been divining, my dear." Childe's interest mounted another notch. "Can you guess who the letter was from?"

*Llewellyn?* She pretended to think it over, tapping at her lips with a gloved finger. "Hmmm. Would it be, by chance, Gwynnfud? Lord Sellwyth himself?"

"Oh no, darling. No indeed." Childe looked delighted to have feinted so successfully. He actually clapped his well-manicured hands, dropping into a chair as soon as Emma was settled on a settee swathed in gold-embroidered blue silk. "'Twas a wonder of penmanship from a certain Sir Conroy."

*Conroy? The Duchess's hangman. The Duchess – the Queen's mother. Oh, dear God.* Emma did not sway, though the world rocked slightly underneath her. "The comptroller? What use would he have for it?"

"Her Royal Matronliness herself, the Duchess of Kent, wished to peruse it." Childe positively wriggled with delight. "Oh, I've surprised you. How *delicious*. Tell me, is it high intrigue? Was I right to graciously refuse? I told Devon I couldn't *possibly* loan it, as it is a Great Text, but the Duchess was *more than welcome* to visit, at her convenience, to peruse it. At her leisure, too."

Emma was cold all over now. If she had to reappraise Childe's loyalty, this would be a dire situation indeed. "Did she ever accept your invitation?"

"No. Devon looked like he'd swallowed a stoat. After, of course, it had desperately battled with his hair. I tell you, darling, he could be so fetching if he simply took some care with his appearance."

"Intriguing." The relief of not having to suspect him was only matched in its intensity by fresh alarm. *How far is the Duchess involved? Or is it merely Conroy? Where he is, she isn't far behind, and she would like nothing better than to embarrass the Queen into compliance again.*

"No, he's rather boring, but he'd be decorative." Childe snorted.

"Not to my taste. What *precisely* did Devon say after you denied Her Majesty's darling mother the use of your *Principia*?" A touch of sarcasm here, for she knew it would please him.

So it did. His face lit with an expression of dawning *Schadenfreude*. "It *is* intrigue, then! You are never boring, my dear. He gave me to understand the Duchess would be most piqued at my refusal; I replied that I didn't care a fart in a windstorm – shocking I know, but he annoyed me; don't *laugh* so – if she was piqued or if she sang an entire aria in the water closet. Then the little hedge-charmer had the sheer effrontery to ask if he could *see* the book! I informed him I am not a lending library and the Collegia library is open for Master Sorcerers just as for Primes, though not, of course, at the same *time*." He almost wriggled with delight with the memory of the insult implied to Devon's status. "Did I do right, darling?"

"Oh, absolutely." Emma settled herself more firmly in her chair. "If I ask very nicely, Dorian dear, will you allow me to peruse the *Principia*?"

"My most enchanting Emma, you could set the damn thing on fire page by page in my bedroom while watching me disport with one of those boys you so highly disapprove of. *You*, at least, are never impolite *or* aesthetically lacking." He pantomimed a yawn. "But first let's have some tea. And really, darling, I was about to return Eli to the Collegia and pick out a more *active* Shield. Do you want him?"

Emma's heart pounded in her ears. Another Shield would not be a bad idea at all, in light of this news. She could not risk returning to the Collegia and publicly taking more of them into service, and Eli would no doubt be glad not to return to the Shields' dormitories in almost disgrace. "Yes." She folded her hands in her lap. "Yes, I rather think I do."

It was, she decided, probably a mercy she could not see Mikal's face.

After a very satisfying cup of tea, Dorian left her in his library, one of the few rooms he had never redone since his father had left him a good address and sorcerous ability but precious little else. Whether the room was left alone because Childe saw no need to alter it, or because he spent very little time among the rare texts he collected so assiduously, was a mystery Emma felt no need to solve.

Two storeys high, the ceiling frescoed with Grecque gods cavorting among pale nymphs, the library was dark heavy wood, comfortable leather furniture that had belonged to Dorian's father, a healthy fire in the grate, maroon drapes pulled against daylight. She breathed in the scent of paper, dust, old leather, smoky sorcery, and her shoulders eased still further. The other Prime was bursting with curiosity, and she had told him as much as she dared. The rumours he would start would be priceless in sowing confusion among her enemies.

At least Mikal waited until they were alone.

"Another Shield, my Prima?"

She turned away from the shelf, the *Principia Draconis* in her arms. It was a leather-bound monstrosity; this edition lacked Wilson's gloss, but she didn't think it would matter much. Wilson had simply cleaned up some of the archaisms. "I think it wise, if the Duchess of Kent and her hangman are involved. And I wondered where our conspirators received their money."

"Can you trust a Shield from *his* service?"

"Childe is loyal." *He has a great deal to lose under the sodomy laws if he dares to be anything less.* "And Eli is capable, from what I recall. Top of his year-class at the Collegia, rather as you were. Did you not recently seek to have me take on the responsibility of more Shields?"

He quieted, but the set of his chin was mulishly defiant. Emma sighed, hauling the book towards her usual table. The thing was as long as her own torso, and beastly heavy. Mikal let her take two steps before arriving to subtract the book from her arms. Surprised by its weight, he exhaled, shifted backwards and turned; she trailed behind, her skirts making a low, sweet sound.

The glow she had felt just before Tideturn, waking in his arms and feeling the rough texture of his skin against her back, was all but gone.

*I am Prime*, she reminded herself. *It is his duty. And I shall not make the mistake of acting like a silly girl over this.*

And yet. "Mikal—"

"Well enough. As long as he is *capable*." The *Principia* thudded on to a small rosewood table, and she winced.

"That is a Great Text, Shield. Pray do not injure it."

"Certainly. If you will take care not to injure *yourself.*"

"I am taking on an additional Shield, Mikal. One who will be glad of my service instead of Childe's, perhaps, and one who may have learned restraint and obedience." She tucked her veil aside, unnecessarily; it was still securely fastened. "Perhaps he can show you the value of such."

"Perhaps." He turned away. "Will he share your bed too, Prima?"

*Is that it?* For a moment, the silence was full of a resonant un-noise, as if the books had taken a collective breath after witnessing a sharp slap. Heat crawled up Emma's throat, stained her cheeks. Had he just called her a whore, too? From Huston, she had expected it.

*I am Prime. Your petty rules do not apply to me.*

But it did not salve the sting. Why should she care what a Shield thought?

*Because he is not merely a Shield, Emma. He is Mikal, and you are perhaps more grateful to him for saving your life and killing Crawford than you should be.*

She composed herself, took a deep breath, and sank into the chair. Her gloved hand passed over the *Principia*'s cover, and the two locks holding the book closed clicked. Green with age, they flew apart as if they had never intended to stay clasped. Sorcerous force rose, Emma's left hand flashing forward to curl around a slippery, not-quite-tangible armoured eel, as the book tested her will. It subsided quickly – after all, like every book, the Great Texts *wanted* to be read.

When she was certain the *Principia* knew who held the reins, she delicately lifted the heavy cover. Thick pages riffled.

"Prima." Mikal sounded oddly breathless. "I am—"

*About to apologise? That would imply I have taken insult, and from a Shield, no less.* "I have no wish to hear you speak." Her welling eyes fixed themselves on the *Principia*. Ink writhed, and the writing became clear. Serpentine illustrations flowed like water, bordering each page. She leaned closer, and breathed her query across the pages.

"*Vortisssss.*" The name trailed into a hiss, and the *Principia*'s pages riffled more quickly. A hot breeze lifted, touching her hair, fingering the entire library. The curtains rippled, paper on the gigantic desk near the fireplace stirred, the bronze-caged witchballs sizzled and turned bloody. Above the fireplace, a heavy-framed oil painting of Childe's father glowered, and the dark coat the man was encased in was suddenly alive with golden traceries of charter charm.

The pages slowed, the *Principia* humming as it woke fully and sought within itself. Finally they stilled, and Emma leaned slightly back, blinking back hot saltwater. Her throat was full.

The flush of anger and pain turned to ice. A cold metallic finger traced her spine. She had to swallow twice before she could clear her throat, not from hurt, but from another emotion entirely.

Two pages. On the left side, a woodcut of a vast black wyrm, triple-winged and infinite horned, wrapped about a hill with a white tower. On the right, closely packed calligraphy, the ink still remembering the quill that had spread it. The words runnelled together before her will flexed, then cleared. At the top of the page, gold leaf trembled as it shaped a word.

*Vortis* was merely a use-name. Emma's entire body quivered, and her earrings swung, tapping her cheeks uneasily. The cameo at her throat warmed, and she dimly heard the door open, Mikal saying something. Her well-trained memory dilated, the book speaking to her in its ancient language, her lips moving as the world hushed around her, motes of golden dust hanging suspended and the witchballs pausing in their spluttering hisses.

She was not one for prayer, except the fashionable sort uttered at conventional moments; besides, sorceresses were doubly damned by every church, Roman, Englican, or otherwise. But had she been the pious sort, Emma thought hazily, she might well start praying.

*Vortis cruca esth,* Mehitabel had hissed.

The *Principia* slammed shut, locks thudding closed. Emma

blinked. Her cheeks were crusted with salt, and her stomach rumbled. How much time had she lost, gazing at the pages, intuition and intellect communing directly with the Text?

Mikal's hand closed around her shoulder. "You are at Childe's, in Tithe Street. It is almost Tideturn." Did he sound ashamed? Did she care?

At the door stood another Shield. Dark-haired, a trifle shorter than Mikal but a little broader in the shoulder, a Bowie knife worn openly at his hip and his eyes closed. His features were even, regular, and as she shuddered, fully waking, his own eyes opened. He shifted forward incrementally, his mouth firmed. He looked just like a quick-fingered Liverpool bravo, though Childe, with his usual irritating attention to detail, had him in a flashy waistcoat over a fine white high-collared shirt. At least his cloth was good, even if the boots looked dreadfully impractical.

For a moment she could not remember who or what she was. It flooded back, and she shuddered again. Mikal's fingers tensed. She did not need the pain to steady herself, though the Duchess of Kent had suddenly become rather a small problem indeed.

*Vortis cruca esth.*

Or, if you did not speak the wyrm's slow sonorous hiss . . . *Vortigern will rise.*

# Chapter Twenty-Five

## Throckmorton, I Presume

As chance would have it, Sig's acquaintance Becker had lodgings near Thrushneedle Dock, a mean hole reeking of cabbage and gin but cleaner than one would suppose. There was much cheerful swearing in heavy German, Sigmund slapped the young hevvymancer's back, and glasses of beer were produced.

Becker was lean, in a hevvymancer's traditional red bracers and herringbone wool cap, heavy boots and a wide smile missing his front left canine. Perhaps he hated toothcharmers too, or could not afford one. Clare surmised that most of the young man's money went to his ailing mother in a lumpen shawl, who shuffled between the single cot and the ancient stove, poking at a pot of boiling something and gazing at her only surviving son with weak, misty eyes. The woman spoke no English, but Becker had been born in Londinium, and a good thing it was too. Had he been born in Germany itself, his hevvymancing would be unreliable here, and both of them might starve.

"Lindorm," Becker said, finally, standing because he had pressed Clare to take the only chair. Valentinelli stood by the door, examining his fingernails; the room was far too small for four males and the old woman's skirts. "*Ja*. Only open a fortnight and odd, taking deliveries." His accent was a mixture of his mother tongue and pure dockside nasal, a song of the displaced.

"We wondered. But they paid good bounty on Prussians, so they raked 'em in. No use sitting about when's shill'n to be earned."

"What bounty did they pay?" Clare settled himself carefully. The chair was alarmingly fragile, not to mention fusty, and the floor sloped.

"Two bob apiece, more for more. Heps over at Mockgale, he brought crates o' them, got a pound apiece. That fair made it scruth. Every jack and hevvy scramblin t' sell any bit o'metal an shine could be called Pruss." Becker's face twisted; he removed his cap and scratched along his hairline. "Made out fair m'self, I did. But legal-like."

*Oh, certainly. And I am a monkey's waistcoat.* "I am quite sure you were entirely legal. So, Lindorm closed after a fortnight and a few days?"

"Aye. 'Twixt one Turn and the next, pop! Gone like a skipper's goodwill. Never quite right, that place. We smells the odd, we do, and there was mancy there. Big, not like a hevvy or a shipwitch. Lord magic, that was. High'n mighty."

"Most curious. Who is buying Prussian capacitors now?"

"Naught. Some gents like to tear their own hair out waiting; some says they're in France somewhere, others say held up in the Low, one or two wot might know says the Pruss factories holdin 'em. Frenchie glassers and Hopkins shinies selling hand over fist now, since Prussians ent to be had."

Clare's eyelids dropped to half-mast; his thin fingers steepled under his proud long nose. Sigmund peered longingly toward the cauldron at the stove; Frau Becker muttered something and waved a wooden spoon as she advanced, menacing.

Sigmund sighed, heavily.

Clare absorbed the implications of young Becker's tale. "Would you happen to know where Lindorm sent the capacitors they had?"

"Oh, 'tis easy, guv." Becker's lean chest puffed, and he stuck his thumbs under his bracers. "Hired a crew of hevvy to charm a load of waggon, drays and all, four days' wages for two day haulin' to St Cat's, in the Shadow. Big warehouse there, black as sin, 'twas."

"Did you take advantage of this easy work?"

"Weren't *nuffink* easy 'bout it, sir. Nags were restless, loads kept slippin', heavy as churchman's purse each crate and bell. Each hevvy *earned* that two pound, sir."

"I see. Well, what particulars can you tell me of the gentlemen engaging your services?"

On this Becker was no fountain of knowledge; the work had simply been available, and he had taken it. By the time Clare had finished questioning and paid the man for his trouble – two guineas, part of the purse thoughtfully supplied by Miss Bannon that very morning against just such an eventuality – he was almost feeling cautiously cheerful. Becker gave one of the coins to his mother, who held it up and bit at it, though she was lacking teeth; the young man assured him that should he ever need a hevvy, Becker was *sienen Mann, ja.*

Outside, the street was still as throbbing-active as ever, carts rumbling by, hevvymancers chanting a song of harsh consonants and sliding nasal vowels. A line of yellow glare fell against the wall opposite, broken only by the low doors of public houses vying for trade, rollicking even at this early hour. A heavy-bearded Jack, fresh from the sea by the roll in his drunken gait, stumbled to a stop and began heaving up a mess of gin and somewhat else, to the amusement of passers-by and the great delight of a pair of ragged, bony curs, who immediately began lapping at the offal.

The Neapolitan, however, was not in the mood for sightseeing. He grabbed Clare's elbow. "Eh, *signor*, you are not planning a visit to *la Torre*?"

"If I must. Into the belly of Hell itself, Mr Valentinelli. Britannia is in need, and this is passing interesting."

"*La strega* said nothing about *la Torre*."

"If you feel yourself incapable, *signor*, by all means depart." Clare jammed his hat more firmly on his head. "Sig! Old man, find us some repast and a decent place to smoke a pipe. I must think."

But Valentinelli gripped his arm even more firmly. "You insult me."

*If I had, sir, you would already be attempting to kill me, blood oath or no.* "By no means, *signor*. Do you know what the most incredible part of young Becker's tale is?"

The Neapolitan's answering oath expressed that he cared not a whit, and Sigmund's florid face was suddenly drawn and grey as he witnessed this. The worthy Bavarian's hand was hidden in his coat pocket, probably preparatory to bringing forth his trusty clasp knife, and Clare decided he had best smooth the waters. People were so *difficult*.

"The incredible part, sir, is that young Becker is still alive." He met Valentinelli's gaze squarely. "Which means the feared Shadow of the Tower of Londinium is the least of our worries, for our greatest is whoever may be watching a hevvymancer or two, to see if they speak. Or to pay them for reporting any enquiries made about a certain load of goods. Or – and this is the idea I find most unsettling, sir – their plan is so near fruition they care very little about any hound on their trail."

The assassin halted. His pocked face was still and set, but the rigidity of his jaw had eased, and so did his hand upon Clare's arm.

Clare nodded, once. "You see. Very good. Come, my noble Neapolitan. I do need to think, and I'd prefer to do it somewhere a touch more comfortable." He paused. "And perhaps more defensible as well."

The Tower of Londinium was actually a collection of towers, held back from crashing down on the city by the grey arms of the Sorrowswall clutching at each rising spire. The White Tower rose above them all, sorcerously sheathed in glittering pale marble, bloody-hued charter symbols sliding in rivulets down its sides. Traitors met their end here, and those criminals judged too noble to be hanged at a common gaol. The fetid moat ran with murky oilsheen, and under its surface rippled . . . something. Rumour hotly disputed what beast it was, but all agreed it ate the bodies after the beheadings, and the heads sometimes after the showing.

And, occasionally, it took live prey.

But it wasn't the Dweller in the Moat Londinium's masses feared. It was the Shadow.

Sometimes it wreathed the towers, slinking along the walls, slithering down to brush the surface of the moat's oily water. It was not fog, or cloud – it was simply dark dank grey, and it prowled the neighbourhood of the Tower as a silent lumbering beast. Charm and charter did not hold it back – only a Master Sorcerer or above could make it seek elsewhere, by some means they kept hidden behind closed mouths.

Sorcerers disliked the Tower's environs too – the misery and death soaking it, perhaps. The quietest places in Londinium were under the Shadow's heel. Still, there were those who sought it as a sanctuary – those who needed to be certain of the law's reluctance to follow them.

Or those whose Alterations had gone badly. It was against the Tower's walls that the Morloks lived. During the day, one did not need to fear them overmuch.

Fortunately, the Shadow's grey bulk was clinging raggedly to the White Tower as the afternoon's yellow glare wore on. The light through the fog had deepened, the northern quarter of the sky bruising with weather approaching. It might almost, Clare thought, be a relief if rain would sweep in. Except in rainy weather, one could not be so sure of the Shadow's movements.

The warehouse Becker had described on Lower Themis Street, the Sorrowswall visible even over its bulk, was indeed black. Clare studied the structure as Sigmund burped contentedly. Feeding the Bavarian to make up for his thwarted breakfast had also given the mentath an opportunity to collect himself and smoke his pipe, and Valentinelli had applied himself to a quantity of coarse fare at a run-down public house a good distance from Becker's lodging. The dark, crowded interior had not been ideal, but at least Clare had gathered his wits and forced the spectre of agitation threatening his nerves away for a short while. The brougham driver would not approach the Tower this closely, and was left a few streets away, well satisfied with a tot of gin and a generously packed basket of dinner purchased at the pub with more of Miss Bannon's guineas.

The warehouse's stone walls had perhaps once been grey, but a patina of coal dust had packed itself on the rough surfaces. Normally the rain would streak such a building with runnels of acid-eaten paleness, but as Clare gazed, he caught a shimmer in the air around it.

Sorcery.

Valentinelli had either noticed it at the same moment he did, or waited for Clare's expression to change. "*Maleficia.*" His pocked face wadded itself up theatrically. "We wait for *la strega*, *ci*?"

"Miss Bannon has other difficulties." Clare did not see any reason to tell the assassin of the conclusions he had reached concerning Miss Bannon's likely availability to appear and deal with problems of a sorcerous nature. "Do you think we may enter that building? Is it possible?"

Valentinelli squinted. "*Ci.*" He rubbed at his forearm, meditatively, and Clare deduced there was a knife hidden in his sleeve. "But not for long, eh? Is work of large, very big *stregone*. Very nasty."

"Oh, I thought as much." Clare tapped at his left-hand breeches pocket, almost unaware of the motion. The tiny metal box of coja was safely stowed, and he felt soothed, even if the pendant under his throat was warming alarmingly. "Sig, this may be a bit dodgy. Are you sure you—"

"I go home, *mein Herr*, perhaps they try again? And not so politely." The Bavarian rolled his broad shoulders back in their sockets. "Is very interesting, this business of capacitors."

"Oh, very interesting indeed. Well, gentlemen, no time like the present."

Forcing a door was almost anticlimactic. Valentinelli sniffed, declared the shimmer in the air only dangerous to sorcerers, and stepped through. Two kicks and rotted wood shattered, he peered inside. "Eh. Come."

They plunged into a thick dimness, the dust and the smell of oiled metal mixing with an odd reek. The pendant was red-hot now; logic told Clare it would not burn him, and he kept his hand away from his chest with an effort. Sigmund choked back a series of mighty sneezes, managing to be almost as loud as if he had allowed them free rein. A close, clotted-dark hallway led along the outer wall for ten paces, then abruptly terminated, and the warehouse space bloomed, lit only by a few weak shafts of yellow Londinium glow stabbing down from high, papered holes in the roof.

They stood in serried ranks, each shrouded in canvas, slump-shouldered shapes three times as high as a man and broad as a shay. Two protuberances gleaming of metal peeked out from under each sheet of canvas, and Clare blinked fiercely, deducing. *I wonder—*

But there was no time for wondering. There was a fluttering motion atop one of the mysterious shapes. A small, definite click echoed through the dimness, and an unfamiliar male voice broke the hush.

"Move, and I shoot."

Clare's smile was broad – and, he hoped, invisible in the bad lighting. He lifted his own pistol, and noted, without any surprise at all, that Valentinelli had once again disappeared. "Mr Cecil J. Throckmorton, I presume?"

# Chapter Twenty-Six

## Introductions Can Wait

The curricle was left at Childe's excellent stable, and Bannon was glad she'd found her fellow Prime in a good mood. For not only did she have another Shield, but Childe had also pressed the use of a smart ivy-coloured landaulet on her; drawn by white and silver clockhorses, it was a darling little vehicle that had an absolutely bone-rattling ride. It mattered little at this speed.

For she had a rather pressing idea that Clare was in some trouble. The Bocannon she had given him was uneasy, scenting harmful sorcery in his vicinity and twitching the fine invisible thread tied to her consciousness. Which meant that, like a dach's-hund down a rathole, Archibald Clare had flushed prey she was interested in and would soon have a snout in dire danger of clawmarks.

Eli drove, and handled the carriage rather well. "Serene" was an understatement – the Shield looked half asleep, and only the grip of his hands on the reins betrayed him as, indeed, alert. His hair combed back from his face in the sulphurous breeze, the air bringing colour to his cheeks, and Mikal on her other side was a red and black thundercloud of tightly leashed frustration.

*Serves him right.* But she could not fault him overmuch. She was, indeed, a spectacular failure at femininity – except in the area of weakness. For last night had been merely that. Had she been born a man . . .

*What? Had you been born a man, you would be Llewellyn. That is what drew you to him, was it not? Deep down, Emma, you do not care.*

Then why did she put herself to this trouble?

*Enough. Think of what you will do when you reach the man you sent scurrying off with only Valentinelli to protect him. The situation has changed somewhat, even without the addition of a dragon so old he slept even before the Age of Flame. If the Duchess and Conroy have their fingers in this, it is not likely to end well. Victrix will not thank me if I injure – or, God forbid, murder – her mother, even if she hates the woman and Britannia would more than likely approve.*

The thin, fine invisible thread twitched again, more definitely this time. Her gloved hand flashed out, and a witchball sizzled into being. Her concentration narrowed as the globe of brilliance sped forward, settling in front of the clockhorses. Stray sparks of sorcery crackled, and traffic on the avenue drew away like water retreating from oil. Eli's chin dipped slightly, a fractional nod, and Emma settled back, impatience thinly controlled as the Shield piloted the juddering vehicle in the witchball's wake. The invisible strand twitched once more, more definitely, and the Bocannon she had given the mentath woke fully.

Clare was indeed in a great deal of trouble. Tideturn was approaching, and traffic was thick. Even with a Shield pressing the horses onwards and a free witchball before them warning all Londinium that a sorcerer was in a hurry, she would likely be too late.

The warehouse slumped under a bruise-ugly yellowgreen sky, banks of opaque fog drawing back as thunder rumbled uneasily. A storm coming up the Themis, perhaps, or a deeper unsettling. The elegant, powerful shell of sorcery laid over the building to disguise it would have been enough to make Emma's gaze simply slide past – if the Bocannon had not already been inside, and had she not been gripping Mikal's arm so tightly her fingers ached.

*There!*

The witchball sizzled, gathering momentum as Eli hauled back on the reins, Mikal flowing half upright, the veil plastered to Emma's damp face and stormlight prickling her tender eyes. Thunder rattled again, far to the north. The witchball arrowed forward, splashing into the glimmering not-quite-visible shield over the slumping warehouse, and fine silver traceries flashed, digging into the coaldust-sheathed sides. The horses pranced, more sparks snapping, and the landaulet jolted to a stop. Emma was already moving, gathering her skirts, and Mikal had antici-pated her. His boots hit the hard-packed dirt, he turned; his hands were at her waist and he lifted her down in one motion.

"Clare!" she snapped. "*Find* him, and protect him!"

A single yellow-fuming glance, and he was gone. One of the smaller warehouse doors had been broken in – Valentinelli, she would lay money on it – and the other Shield was suddenly beside her as she ran breathlessly in Mikal's wake.

The building shuddered as the defences on it woke fully, cracks veining the coaldust casing as she fed more force through the erstwhile witchball. An unsecured globe of sorcerous energy was difficult to control – but it was also plastic, and it reacted to the sudden cramping of the defences with a vengeance. Londinium fog flushed as the sun dipped, another peal of thunder resounded, and the coaldust cracked, shivering away from grey stone just before Mikal nipped smartly through the door in search of Clare.

Emma plunged into a close, stinking passageway, her eyes suddenly relieved of the burden of bright light and picking out details in the flimsy wooden walls. She skidded out into the warehouse itself, her skirts all but snapping as Eli's hand closed around her arm and gave a terrific, shoulder-popping yank.

The Shield pivoted, pulling her to the side as something

crashed into the wooden archway they had just cleared. The earth shook, and Emma groped to find the source of the attack. It was not sorcerous, she realised, just as Eli shoved her aside again and gave a short sharp yell.

*What in God's—*

It rose from wooden wreckage, gleaming and mechanical, its oddly articulated arms creaking as the man closed in its casing let out a piercing shriek of unholy glee. Emma screamed, terror seizing her, and sorcerous force struck. It was a blind, instinctive assault, force spent recklessly, and it had precious little effect.

The mechanical casing hunched, eerily mimicking the movements of the man inside it. The head was a smooth dome, its shoulders high so it shambled and slouched; its feet were oval cups. Cogs whirred and ground. Oil dripped from shining metal, and the thing screeched like a hound from brimstoned Hell.

The man shook his head, cogs sparking and grinding as the casing's domed top replicated the movement. It looked like a squat, bronze bald frog, especially as the controller sank back and it bent its oversized knees. The arms came up, fuming smoke pouring from the left, and a large hole pointed straight at her.

"*Hiiiiiii!*" The yell came from a human throat, but a grinding rumble swallowed the last of it. A metallic gleam lurched, and Emma's faculties almost deserted her as a second monstrosity shambled forward, its stubby arms rising in a weirdly graceful arc. The first thing's left-hand barrel was knocked skywards, a deafening roar sounded, and a hole opened in the roof. Stormlight poured in, and the sorcerous defences cracked yet further, sagging.

Emma backpedalled blindly, scrambling, her legs tangled in her skirts and her veil torn, her hat knocked askew, curls falling in her face. Eli yanked her again, and her abused shoulder flared with dull red pain. She realised she was screaming, could not help herself. The *thing* was not sorcerous; her mental grasp could not close around it and crush it. It simply shunted the force aside, spending it uselessly, and fresh terror clawed at her vitals.

The right-hand barrel lowered, pointing at her. The man inside the casing laughed, shrilly. There was a flicker of movement, bright knives lifted, and Mikal's feet slipped, seeking vainly for purchase on the thing's domed head. He fell, but twisted catlike in mid-air, and the knives flashed again as he drove both at the chest of the thing's internal rider. They missed, one skittering across the glowing golden disc; it cracked and fizzed, bleeding sparks.

The second metal abomination staggered, its dome head swivelling. But it lurched forward, and knocked aside the second gun just as it spoke.

Confusion. A massive noise, a geyser of dirt and splinters. And something else, invisible threads tightening.

The sorcerer was in the shadows, and she could sense his Shields. She recognised him just as Mikal hit the ground, curling and springing up. She saw messy tangled hair, fingers curled into a half-recognised Gesture, charter symbols spitting venomous crimson as they roiled between his palms.

*Kill his Shields. Don't kill him. You need him alive for questioning, and he is only—*

But before she could finish the thought, he cast the bolt of crimson charter charm. He could not have expected it to hold her or even damage her, for he immediately lunged backwards – but Eli knocked into her from the side as a flash of gunpowder igniting added to the confusion, driving the breath from her in a sharp huff and killing the chant rising to her lips.

One of the sorcerer's Shields had fired a pistol. And Mikal was otherwise occupied.

Gears screeched, grinding, and the falling-cathedral noise of a sorcerer's death filled the factory. *No! No, don't kill him, I* need *him for questioning, Mikal!*

Something atop her, pressing down. She struggled, treacherous skirts suddenly chains, her wrists caught in a bruising grip. "*Pax!*" someone yelled in her ear, her head ringing and swimming. "*Pax, Prima!*"

She went limp, ribs flickering as they heaved with deep drilling breaths.

*What was that? Dear God, what was that?*

Eli rolled aside, and as he pulled her to her feet Emma stared at the slumped mountain of metal. Its chest was empty now, the golden circle dead and cracked, lifeless. Shouts and clashing metal, Mikal's hissing battle cry rising over the din.

The second *thing* clicked, humming as its arms lowered, and Archibald Clare, his lean face alight with glee, hung inside its chest. It replicated his movements uncannily, a glowing golden circle strapped to his chest like a flat witch-ball. The glow threw his features into sharp relief, his hair blew back, and the metal structure around him creaked and shuddered.

The circle of light dimmed. Mikal appeared, glanced at Clare inside the metal abomination, visibly decided he was not a threat, and turned on his heel. Stopped, staring at Emma, whose knees were decidedly *not* performing their function of holding her up with their usual aplomb and reliability. Eli held her arm, not hard but very definitely, bracing her.

The light at Clare's chest snuffed itself. "*Most . . .*" The mentath's speech slurred. "Most intrig— Oh, *hell.*"

Ludovico Valentinelli, singed and bleeding, appeared out of the gloom. A stolid older man with massive side whiskers also appeared, and Emma blinked. *What in God's name just happened here? What are those . . . things?*

"Sig!" Clare sounded drunk, or perhaps so exhausted his lips were numb. "Come . . . damn straps, man. Help me."

"*Ja.*" The stranger, his whiskers half singed as well, climbed *up* the metal man-thing with quick dexterity. He began fiddling with the straps holding Clare inside it, and the mentath sighed wearily, closing his blue eyes.

Emma told herself firmly that now was *not* the time to engage in a screaming fit, or a swoon, though both would indeed be very welcome.

"Are you well?" Mikal was suddenly before her, his face inches from hers. "Prima? *Emma?*"

"Sorcery does not affect it," she managed, in nothing like her usual tone. "Dear gods. Sorcery did not even *touch* it."

That caught Clare's attention. "Rather . . . regrettable . . . side effect." The words slurred together alarmingly. Had the man been at gin? If he had, Emma rather hoped he had saved some. She could do with a tot of something stronger than tea at the moment.

Leather creaked, and the man with side whiskers cursed under his breath. Valentinelli peered up at the twisted ruin of the other metal monster, whistling low and tunelessly.

"Here." Mikal had a flask, held it to her lips. Rum burned; she took a grateful swallow. Her eyes stung, and it was a good thing Tideturn was soon. She had expended a truly ridiculous amount of ætheric charge on the thing, and it had not even affected it.

There were shapes under canvas standing in serried ranks all through the building's maw. They were all roughly the same size and shape as the mechanisterum abominations uncloaked before her. She took another long swallow of fiery liquid; it burned all the way down, and she handed the flask back to Mikal with numb fingers.

And . . . yes, her sensitised eyes pierced the gloom with little trouble. There was a body on the floor. She studied it and breathed a *most* impolite term. "That . . . is Devon. Hugh Devon." She sounded half witless, even to herself. "I needed him for questioning . . . oh, blast and bother and *Hellfire*."

"Rather . . . changes things." Clare almost fell; the side-whiskered stranger braced him, and they negotiated the distance to the ground more gracefully than seemed possible, given Clare's slurring and the portly stranger's girth. "Miss . . . Bannon. We need . . . to talk."

"Well, *rather*." The irritation was a tonic; she braced her fists on her hips and tilted her head. Whoever had been inside the wrecked abomination had made good his escape; *that* was an annoyance as well. "Someone will be along soon to see this mess. I suggest we repair to a far more suitable location. Where on earth is the brougham I engaged to—"

"*Strega*. I take them." Valentinelli did not turn away from the corpse. "What we do with body, eh?"

Clare leaned on his stout friend. The sulphurous glow sliding through the holes in the roof dimmed, and Emma did not like that, despite the comfort it afforded her aching eyes.

"Well, if he was alive I could question him." She tapped one gloved finger against her lips. *I sound as if my nerves are steady. Thank God. Who was in that . . . thing? And Devon, dead.*

"I broke his neck. But his head is still intact." Mikal's tone could best be described as *sullen*.

*Well, there is that.* "Ah. Yes. I see." She decided. "Very well, bring him. Ludovico, do take Mr Clare and his companion to my home. Formal introductions can wait until we are not *here*. We shall join you soon." She eyed the mentath, who swayed. His colour was *not* good at all, and his thinning hair stood straight up, grimed with soot. "And mind the mentath, he looks a bit—"

Clare's eyes rolled up in his head, and he collapsed. And Emma felt the chill along her fingers and toes that meant the Shadow had taken an interest in proceedings. She did not know how long they had before it arrived and must be dealt with, and she had expended far more force than she wished attacking the metal . . . *thing*.

"Oh, bloody *hell*," she breathed, just as the light failed completely.

# Chapter Twenty-Seven

## Unpleasant, but Instructive

Clare clasped the crackling brown paper, soaked with vinegar, to his aching head. "Unpleasant," he murmured. "Highly unpleasant. But instructive."

"I am glad to hear your afternoon went so well," Miss Bannon replied. "Mine was equally instructive, and it was very disagreeable dealing with the Shadow near the Tower. But, my dear Mr Clare, please answer me. What in the name of the seven Hells *were* those . . . things? Sorcery does not touch them; this upsets me a *great* deal."

He shifted on the fainting-couch. The sitting room was very comfortable, despite the tension sparking in every corner. "Obviously. I am trying to find a word that would explain them to a layman, but the best I can do is *homunculus* or *golem*. Neither is *precise*, mind you, but—"

"Mr Clare." Quietly, but with great force. "Kindly do not become distracted, sir. I have a dead body in my study that grows no fresher, and I cannot question the man's shade effectively unless and until I have some answers from you." Her tone grew sharper. "And Ludo, darling? *Stop whistling*, or I shall sew your lips together."

Clare peeled open one eye to see Miss Bannon perched on a low stool at his side, high colour in her cheeks and her hair most fetchingly disarranged. Behind her, Sigmund's wide faithful face loomed. The Bavarian was chewing on something that rather startlingly resembled a wurst and a slice of yellow cheese.

"Ah." Clare cleared his throat. "Miss Bannon, may I present to you Mr Sigmund Baerbarth, genius, and my personal friend? Sig, this is Miss Bannon, a most interesting sorceress."

"How do you do," Miss Bannon said over her shoulder, and Sig nodded, swallowing hastily.

"*Seer geehrte, Fraulein Bannon.*"

The sorceress returned her dark gaze to Clare, who had gathered himself sufficiently to face such an examination calmly. The vinegar did not help much. "Pray fetch me some ice and salt, if you would. My head aches abominably."

Bannon glanced over her shoulder again, her jet earrings swinging, and there was a murmur from the door. There seemed a large number of people crowding the sitting room. The rain had started, and its patter against the window panes was an additional irritation. When she again returned her attention to him, her mien had softened.

"You saved my life, Mr Clare." Her childlike face was sombre now. And yes – those were her gloved fingers, delicately holding his free hand. "That *thing* had cannons on its . . . arms, I suppose one would call them. Who was controlling the other one?"

"Hm. Well, yes." An uncomfortable heat mounted in his cheeks. Her little hand was trembling; he could feel it through the kidskin. "Bit of quick thinking, that. It was a mentath. Throckmorton."

"Remarkably spry for a dead man. He escaped. Helped by Mr Devon's Shields, I am told, which is shocking enough. I am *quite* put out that Mr Devon was not captured alive."

"Ah. Well. Miss Bannon, allow me to collect myself for a moment. Then I shall answer your questions. Is there tea?"

"Of course. Shall I fetch you some?"

*Well, she is remarkably calm, under the circumstances.* "With lemon, please."

The ice arrived in a well-scalded and proof-charmed cloth, and between that and a cuppa he was soon sitting upright, blinking in the rainy failing light. He did not care to know how he had been transported to Miss Bannon's house, other than to be grateful at the occurrence. The splitting pain of strained faculties inside his skull receded bit by bit.

Mikal hovered at Miss Bannon's shoulder as she sipped her own tea, thoughtfully, her little finger raised just so. The Shield's face was a thundercloud, and Clare suspected the reason was the *other* Shield, a dark-haired man who leaned almost somnolent at the mantel. The mystery of where Miss Bannon had acquired *him* could wait, Clare decided as his temples throbbed.

Ludovico Valentinelli, on the far side of the fireplace, was engaged upon cleaning his fingernails with another of his many knives, and glancing curiously at the new Shield. Sig was at the tea table, munching happily. Every so often the Neapolitan would drift to the table and help himself. It was a comfort to see their appetites undiminished, even if they were still soot-stained and faintly wild-eyed.

"Now," Clare said, finally, when he was certain his voice would remain steady. "It is much worse than either of us feared, Miss Bannon. Those things, the *mechanisterum homunculi,* for lack of a better term; Sig would merely call them *mecha*, dear boy that he is – do not run on Alterative sorcery. They can be run directly through the smaller logic engines inside their chest cavities. You will no doubt have noticed the glow at my chest while—"

"Yes. Proceed." One of her hatpins, he saw, had broken. He wondered if she had found the pieces; decided not to think on it too deeply lest overstress fuse his brain into uselessness.

"They *must* be run by a mentath. My current state is the cost of handling such an engine without preparation. The equations are . . . very difficult. But that is not what concerns us." He winced, took another swallow of tea. "Some toast, perhaps?"

"Of course. Mikal, please fetch him a plate." Visibly calmer,

Miss Bannon settled on the cushioned stool. Her skirts were arranged very prettily, Clare noticed.

It was the first time one of these episodes had not ended with her in tatters, he reflected. Doubtless she was glad.

He brought his attention back to the matter at hand. "The larger – the master logic engine, you see, would not be in that warehouse. It is being kept safe elsewhere. The master engine will be the transmitter. Those – the mechanicals you saw – are all *receivers,* with limited capability of being run directly. With a large enough transmitting engine, especially handling the sub-equations in a useful fashion, which is possible with enough power supplied through the core, the mentath wired to the transmitting engine will have control of an army."

Silence.

Miss Bannon had gone quite white. She stared not at him but *through* him, her gaze disconcertingly direct and remote at the same time.

"An army." Very thoughtful, and very soft. She took another sip of tea. "One that does not need food, or rest. One that sorcery does not touch."

"The field generated by the logic engines –"

"– rather makes it difficult for sorcery to penetrate. Yes, Mr Clare. And Mr Throckmorton alive." She continued, pedantically, after a long pause. "I wonder whose corpse was at Grace Street. And what Throckmorton was doing *there* with Devon."

"Standing guard, perhaps? Who would look for a mentath in the Shadow?" He suppressed a shudder at the thought. "I am not quite myself at the moment, Miss Bannon. Pray do not question me too much; it may overtax my faculties and I shall become a brain-melted embarrassment."

A fleeting, half-guilty smile greeted his sally. Mikal appeared, bearing a plate of provender. "Prima?"

"Hm?" She glanced up as Clare started gratefully on his toast.

"I have an idea."

"Yes?"

"I think it would be most instructive to learn the recent movements of a dead Master Sorcerer." The Shield straightened, folding his arms. "One who was running errands for Lord Sellwyth."

*Sellwyth? Yes, the dead Prime.* Clare winced again. Even such a simple act of memory strained the meat inside his skull most alarmingly.

"Quite." She took another sip of tea. She was still distressingly pale. "I wonder if anyone else has seen Mr Devon of late? Childe said a fortnight or so ago. The last time I saw him was at Tomlinson's. Where he had bungled the traces rather neatly, it now appears." She closed her eyes, gathering herself. When she reopened them, her gaze was very direct – and very, very cold. "Still, a corpse to mislead investigation is not difficult to procure, and the remains at Grace Street were so badly burnt . . . If Throckmorton is alive . . ."

Silence filled the room. Clare hoped she did not require his faculties to see her way through the tangle. He crunched on his toast, relishing the butter and the thick bread.

"I am very interested in Hugh Devon's movements," Miss Bannon continued. "However, following him is a waste of time, since he is dead. If Throckmorton is alive—"

"Cedric Grayson's signature is on the papers you gave me, Miss Bannon. You must not be as familiar with his hand as I am." Clare's attention snagged on a memory, and a braying laugh surprised him. "The sherry was poisoned. How *typical*."

"Sherry?"

*That was why it reeked as it did. It was cheap, yes, but also adulterated.* "When we visited the Chancellor. At the time I thought the sherry dreadfully cheap, but Cedric's aesthetics are so bad—"

"Poison. I see. A slow-acting one, no doubt, meant to preserve some parts of you."

"Preserve?"

"The other unregistered mentaths were missing their brains

and spinal cords. I rather thought it had something to do with a mad Alterations sorcerer."

"Oh." Clare shuddered. No wonder she had reserved that information. It changed the entire complexion of the affair, but his faculties were too aching and strained to make use of the revelation.

"And the trap in Bedlam," Miss Bannon continued daintily, "was meant to take care of *me*, possibly while I was occupied in ministering to you. Rather tidy. Which brings us to another interesting question."

*As long as you do not expect me to answer said query, dear God.* "Which is?"

"Where is Lord Sellwyn? If Throckmorton is alive, I find it hard to believe *he* is truly deceased."

*Indeed.* "Ah. Well. I cannot help you."

"No need." She sipped again, delicately, and he had the sudden fancy that there were very few places Lord Sellwyn would be able to hide once Miss Bannon took a serious interest in finding him. "Tell me, Mr Clare, how long will it take your faculties to recover?"

He cogitated upon this, carefully, wincing. "A few hours, and one of your most excellent dinners, should see me right as rain, Miss Bannon."

"Very well. Concern yourself with restoring said faculties, sir, and I shall speak with you after dinner." She opened her eyes and rose, waving at him abstractedly as he moved as if to rise as well. "No, no, *do* stay seated. You have done very well, Mr Clare. Very well indeed. After dinner, then."

He found his mouth was dry. "Certainly. But Miss Bannon?"

She was already halfway to the door, her teacup handed to Mikal and her stride lengthening, skirts snapping. "Yes?"

"The next time you use me as bait, madam, have the goodness to inform me. I do not mind being dangled on a hook. As a matter of fact, I derive a certain enjoyment from it. But I would rather not endanger my friends."

She paused. "You were not *bait*, Mr Clare. You were more of a dach's-hund, meant to flush the prey."

"Nevertheless."

A single, queenly nod. Did she unknowingly copy that movement from Victrix? Yet another question that could wait until his head ceased its abominable pounding.

"Yes, Mr Clare. You have earned as much. My apologies." And with that, she swept out through the door the new Shield held for her.

The door closed, leaving him with the assassin and Sigmund. Who crunched on something from his plate, licked his fingers, and belched contentedly.

"What a woman," he said, dreamily. "*Ein Eis Madchen.* Archibald, *mein Herr*, I believe I am in love."

The Neapolitan, upon hearing this, laughed fit to choke. Clare simply clasped the water-proofed ice cloth to his head and sighed.

Dinner, though superb, was a somewhat hurried affair.

Miss Bannon, appearing in black silk and even more fantastic jewellery, waited until the vegetable course. "I shall deal with Lord Sellwyth, Grayson, and Throckmorton. You, Mr Clare, shall deal with finding and – should it become necessary – destroying the larger logic engine."

"Splendid." He dabbed his lips with his napkin. Beside him, Valentinelli had dispensed with rudeness for once, and was partaking with exquisite manners. Across from him, Mikal and the new Shield – Eli – set to with a will. On the Neapolitan's other side, Sigmund expressed his admiration for the excellence of the dinner in mumbled German. He seemed supremely unconcerned with any larger questions, such as what his landlady and his apprentice would think of his disappearance and the state of his workshop. He had already dashed off a note for them penny-post, and then put them from his capacious mind, which was already busy worrying at other problems. "How do you propose I do so? I have my ideas, of course –"

"– but you would like to know if I questioned a dead sorcerer's shade, and can shed any light on the situation. I did, Mr Clare, and I can."

Clare noted that the new Shield turned pale and stared at his plate, before shaking his head slightly and renewing his interest in his food. *Interesting.* It was a pleasure to deduce again, without the inside of his skull feeling as if acid had been poured through it. The equations had nearly cracked him, the small logic engine cramming force through his capabilities until his head was a swollen pumpkin ready to burst. He had not felt so skull-tender since his Examination.

The new Shield was a Liverpool boy, dark-haired and not very comfortable in his high-collared coat that almost matched Mikal's. His boots were more impractical than Mikal's – or for that matter, the sorceress's – and Clare thought it likely Miss Bannon had not acquired his services as part of a well-laid plan. Another refugee, perhaps, to add to her household of cast-offs?

Or did Miss Bannon think the dangers of the situation finally required another Shield? Why not more than one, then?

The implications of *that* question were extraordinarily troubling. Just like the implications of the harvesting of other mentaths' nervous organs.

He brought his attention back to the matter at hand. Sometimes, after a violent shock, a mentath's mind wandered down logical byways, taking every route but the one most direct. "Please do."

"My method of procuring the information—"

"Does not trouble me at all, Miss Bannon. I believe I am past being troubled, at least for the next fortnight. After that, we shall see." His digestion, at least, was sound. It was a small mercy. "Nothing you could tell me would discommode me more than this afternoon's adventure."

Her pained half-smile told him she rather doubted it, but was too polite to say as much. "Very well. Mr Devon's shade, when pressed, informed me that the conspiracy is very near fruition.

It appears a single thing is lacking – a shipment of something from Prussia."

"Prussian capacitors, most likely." Clare nodded. "Especially if they intend to have a *single* mentath run the transmitting engine; each one will help with the subsidiary equations. I am not so sure what the nervous organs are for, but no doubt they have some function. The question of just *which* mentath they have to run the damn thing—"

"Is irrelevant at the moment. The Prussian things were delayed due to weather; they are to arrive in Dover tomorrow morning." Miss Bannon was pale again. "You and your companions shall intercept this shipment and do whatever possible to delay and disrupt the part of the conspiracy that hinges on them."

"And you will be occupied with?" Though he already knew, he found he wished to hear her say it. She was, he reflected, a most unusual woman, and it was rather nice to converse with someone who did not require intellectual coddling.

Someone who could *think*.

"It is high time Lord Grayson answered some questions." Level and chill, her gaze focused on the graceful silver epergne. The table's gryphon legs writhed, uneasily, but the snow-white tablecloth was flat and straight. The cadaverous Mr Finch, without asking, brought a decanter and a small glass to Miss Bannon's place; without looking, she accepted the glass and tossed its contents far down her throat with only a small ladylike grimace afterward. "Thank you, Mr Finch. Excuse me, gentlemen, but I require some bolstering. This is an unpleasant business."

"I agree." Clare found himself reaching for his wine glass. *I rather envy her the rum.* But it would dull his faculties, even as it afforded him some relief. A fraction of coja might help, but he could not take that at table. Later, then. "There is something that troubles me, Miss Bannon."

A slight lift of an eyebrow. "And what is that?"

"This is no ordinary conspiracy. What could these persons wish to accomplish with an army, even one so formidable as this? And where has the money to fund such a venture arrived from? This is most remarkable. I am very curious."

The rum seemed to make no impression on her. "There are things it is best for you not to know, Mr Clare. I am sorry."

"Ah. Well." He sipped at his wine. "I work best when I am informed, Miss Bannon. It is very unlikely that whoever wishes to unseat Britannia's current incarnation has merely *one* army or plan at their disposal. Even if that army is one sorcery will not touch."

The table rattled slightly. Even Sigmund looked up, his chewing halted for a moment.

Miss Bannon's childlike face turned even more set. Twin sparks of crimson flashed in her pupils for a few moments, then vanished. "We are not dealing with merely one conspiracy, Mr Clare. We are dealing with an unholy alliance of competing interests, none of whom are being exactly honest with each other. There is at least one party who wishes the destruction of Britannia Herself, one who possibly only wishes the damage of Her current incarnation to make said incarnation amenable to coercion, and a third who wishes to sow as much confusion and chaos as possible in order to impair the Empire in any way they may." Her long jet earrings swung even though she was motionless, and the large black gem on a silver choker about her slim throat flashed with a single white-hot charter symbol for a moment. Her curls stirred, on a slow cool breeze that came from nowhere and ruffled along Clare's own face. "I will allow *none* of this, and I *will* conclude this matter to my satisfaction and in the manner I deem best."

The silence was immense. Every gaze in the room had fastened on her. Ludovico Valentinelli seemed thoughtful, his pocked face open and interested. The Bavarian was still unchewing, his eyes wide like a frightened child's. The new Shield had turned cheesy-pale and laid his fork down. Mikal, on the other hand, simply watched her, and his expression was as unguarded as Clare had ever seen it.

*I wonder if she knows what he feels. I wonder if he does.*

Clare leaned back in his chair. He tented his fingers under his long sensitive nose and studied Miss Bannon's immobility. Finally he had marshalled his thoughts sufficiently to speak. *Be very careful here, Archie old man.*

"Miss Bannon. According to what I have seen so far, the Queen trusts you implicitly. This trust is well placed. You are neither stupid nor irresponsible, and you are, I daresay, one of the finest of Britannia's subjects. Despite the fact that you have suspected me and told me virtually nothing of the contours of this conspiracy, I find that I trust you implicitly as well. I am" – he untangled his fingers, lifted his wineglass – "your servant, madam. I shall do my very best to discharge the duty laid upon me, by God and Her Majesty. Now, do you view the situation as dire enough for us to pass over the sweets, or shall we partake, as this may be the last dinner some of us are fortunate enough to consume?"

Miss Bannon's mouth compressed itself into a thin line, and for a moment he was certain he had said exactly the wrong thing. People were so bloody *difficult*, after all, and she was a woman – they were noted for irrationality, never mind that this sorceress was one of the least irrational creatures he had ever known the pleasure of meeting.

But her mouth relaxed, and a smile like sunrise played over her face. "I believe the situation is dire enough on my account but not so dire on yours, so you and your companions will have to do justice to the sweets for me. I wish to see Lord Grayson as close to Tideturn as possible. Thank you, gentlemen."

She rose, still smiling, and the men leapt to their feet as one. She swept from the dining room, and the Shields hurried in her wake.

The Neapolitan breathed a curse. "Last time *la strega* look like that . . ." He lowered himself back into his chair as Mr Finch reappeared with two footmen bearing the sweets. The butler did not seem at all distressed or surprised to find his mistress had quit the table.

"What happened, the last time Miss Bannon looked like that?" Clare enquired.

Valentinelli allowed the scarred footman to clear his place. "Oh, nothing. Just Ludovico almost hanged, and *il sorcieri* laughing in the dark. *La strega*, the bitch, she save Ludo's life." A single shrug. "Some day I forgive her. But not today."

"Ah." Clare filed this away. Valentinelli's drawer in his mental bureau was almost as interesting as Miss Bannon's, by now.

But not quite. He could still feel her gloved fingers on his hand, trembling. And three separate interlocking interests making this conspiracy an even more troubling – and fascinating – puzzle.

Sig looked mournful. "We finish dinner, *ja?*"

"Indeed." Clare sat, slowly, and Mr Finch poured the sherry. "We finish dinner, dear Sig."

*It might indeed be our last one, if what I suspect is true.*

# Interlude

## The Cliffs Will Be No Bar

The rain had stopped as Tideturn swirled through the streets; but with the coming of night the fog resurged. It boiled down to the surface of the streets, and as the brougham thundered along at a steady pace towards the station, its driver occasionally cracking the whip, Clare steepled his fingers again and did his best to tease out the implications bothering him so.

This was difficult for a number of reasons, one of which was Sigmund, who could not or would not cease muttering about his new-found admiration for Miss Bannon. Valentinelli occasionally snorted, but otherwise held his tongue. The carriage roared along, clockwork hooves and the jolting a severe distraction – especially since Clare *had* taken his fraction of coja before setting out. The resultant sharpening of his faculties and dulling of his limitations would have been wonderfully soothing had he been alone.

"Such grace!" Sig muttered. "Baerbarth will be hero, yes! And so will Clare. Good man, Clare."

*Dear God, we are possibly about to die, and he cannot stop himself. Leave it be, Clare.*

Three players, then – or at least, three players that Miss Bannon was willing to admit to. A dragon, obviously. His reluctance to believe in such beasts had taken rather a shock lately.

Gryphons were all very well, but the wyrms who could halt Time itself, the harbingers of disaster and great concentrators of irrationality, the beasts supposedly responsible for teaching Simon Magister, the great mage who had offered gold to Petrus for God's powers, and been hailed by the surrounding crowds as a greater miracle-worker than a disciple of the Christos . . .

. . . that was a different thing entirely. Although the logic engines created a field of order and reasonableness sorcery would not penetrate, a dragon's irrationality was so vast it might not matter. The other conspirators might hope that it would – the question was, who exactly were those other conspirators? For Clare did not think even *he* could deduce a dragon's motivations.

Except Miss Bannon had already provided them. The destruction of Britannia? Was it even possible to destroy the ruling spirit of the Empire? She was ageless, changeless, accumulating knowledge and power with every vessel's reign. What was the nature of the dragons' quarrel with Her? He could not guess, and shelved the question for later.

*Cedric and a sorcerer – Lord Sellwyth. The Earl of Sellwyth, who I do not know nearly enough about. What would tempt Cedric? Power, obviously. And the sorcerer? Power as well. Ambition is a sorcerer's blood, they say.*

"A *Hexen*, yes. But that can be overcome, eh, Clare? I will build her something. What do you think *Hexen* want from *mechaniste*? Not my *Spinne*, no. But—"

"I rather think Miss Bannon is not the marrying type, old chap." *Why Prussian capacitors?* he wondered, suddenly. *They are of high quality, yes . . . but for the mecha I saw, not necessary to this degree. Davenports or Hopkins would work just as well, and could be transported with greater chance of secrecy. Why Prussians?*

Ludovico's lip curled. He maintained his silence, however, and Clare was suddenly glad. He longed for a few moments' worth of peace and quiet to follow this chain of logic. "Why

Prussians?" he murmured, staring out of the window at the gaslit fog, dim shapes moving in its depths.

Well, why not? Standardised to make the process of building the mecha easier – and there was another problem, Clare acknowledged. Who had *built* the damn things, including the smaller engines? Two or three mentaths were not capable of such a feat, and Miss Bannon's investigations should have uncovered a factory or two busily churning out the massive things if they were made in Londinium's environs – or even *shipped* to the city from elsewhere, a massive undertaking in and of itself.

Not to mention the . . . parts . . . of unregistered mentaths. Harvested.

*Something is very wrong here.*

He cast back through memory as Sigmund began meandering on about Miss Bannon's dark eyes again.

Becker. The hevvymancer. Something in that conversation . . .

*"Most curious. Who is buying Prussian capacitors now?"*

*"Naught. Some gents like to tear their own hair out waiting; some says they're in France somewhere, others say held up in the Low, one or two wot might know says the Pruss factories holdin 'em. Frenchie glassers and Hopkins shinies selling hand over fist now, since Prussians ent to be had."*

"Aha," he murmured, his fingers tightening against each other. The pleasure of a solution spilled through him, tingling in his nerves.

The second group, of course, would be a domestic party wishing Victrix controlled in some way – she was Britannia incarnate, of course, but while she had been unmarried she had been led by a coterie headed by her mother. The Duchess of Kent was banished to Balgrave Square, of course, and had been since the marriage. The Prince Consort was rumoured to be pressing for a reconciliation between Victrix and her mother, but so far it had come to naught.

The third party in Miss Bannon's allusions? Why, ridiculously simple once he considered it logically. Of course, this line of logic depended on much supposition—

"I shall build her lions!" Sigmund suddenly crowed. "What do you think, Clare? Lions to draw her carriages! Shining brass ones!"

"*Do* be quiet a moment, Sig." Rudely interrupted, Clare frowned. That was the problem with coja. If one was jolted free of the reverie, it was rather difficult to exclude all the endless noise about one and gather the traces again. "I rather think . . ."

"What is it you rather think, *mentale*?" For once, the Neapolitan was not sneering. "I tell you what I am thinking. *La strega* send me with you, she expect bad trouble. Everything to now, *pfft!*" A magnificent gesture of disdain was curtailed by the lack of space inside the brougham. "No, this is where trouble begin. Ludo has sharpened his knives."

"You may very well need them," Clare retorted. Would *none* of them grant him some time to think? "For I believe we may be facing not merely mecha, my dear Neapolitan prince, but perhaps, also, a deeper treachery."

*And the white cliffs of Dover will be no bar to it.*

# Chapter Twenty-Eight

## The Unforgivable

The Chancellor would not be at his *official* Londinium residence, of course. His unofficial residence was near Cavendish Square, a bloated and graceless piece of masonry with gardens clutched about it like too-thin skirts at the cold legs of a drab. Stacked precipitously tall and throbbing with sorcerous defences, the place was almost as ugly as the Chancellor's Whitehall offices.

Mikal handed Emma down from the hansom, Eli wide-eyed, for once, behind her. It felt like a lifetime since she had last had a Shield with her in the carriage and another running the rooftop roads.

She waited until the hansom had vanished into the fog before turning to look down the street, feeling Grayson's house pulse like a sore tooth. Along with the showy defences were one or two very effective ones, and if what she suspected she might find inside was indeed there, it was a very cunning and subtle way to camouflage it.

"Prima?" Mikal, carefully.

Tideturn had come and gone. The fog had thickened, venomous yellow with its own dim glow. Emma wondered, sometimes, if the gaslamps fed the fog's eerie foxfire on nights like this. The fog would suck on them like a piglets at a sow's teats, and spread a dilute phosphorescence through its veins.

"I expect this to be unpleasant." The stone at her throat was ice cold, and the rings clasping her fingers were as well. They were curious things, these rings – carved of ebony, silver hammered delicately into them, four rings connected with a bridge of cold haematite across the top pads of her palms. The haematite was carved with a Word, and from it clasping fingers held the ebony loops.

She did not like wearing the gauntlets, for the Word against the skin of her hands was a constant prickling discomfort. And they did not allow her to wear gloves.

Mikal made no reply. Eli shifted his weight, the leather of his boots creaking slightly. "How unpleasant?" he asked, in his light, even tenor.

Childe had perhaps chosen him for his voice. It would be just like the other Prime.

"We will find at least one dead man inside." She wore no shawl, no mantle, and no hat, either. A well-bred woman would not be seen on the street in such a manner.

*Then it is as well I am not one, for all I am a lady. Well, mostly a lady.*

She was procrastinating.

"Well." Eli absorbed this. "One less to kill, then."

"Not necessarily," she replied, and set her chin. They fell into step slightly behind her as she set off in the direction of the sparking pile of sorcery. "Not necessarily at all."

Fortunately, he did not ask what she meant. Emma was not sure she could have kept the sharp edge of her tongue folded away. She would not waste *that* on a Shield who was only seeking to lighten her mood. Perhaps Childe required banter of him.

And no doubt the exact branch of her Discipline had been a shock to the man.

An iron gate in the low wall surrounding the house was not locked, and Mikal gingerly pushed it open enough to slip through. Eli followed Emma, and gravel crunched underfoot as the circular drive trembled under the pressure of the fog. The gardens were indistinct shadows; the front door atop three worn steps was a monstrosity of steel-bound oak. It was there, before the steps, that Emma's heart thumped twice and turned to cold lead inside her chest.

For the left-hand door was open very slightly.

He was expecting her.

"Mikal?"

"Yes." He was in his accustomed place behind her right shoulder, and her flesh chilled.

For he had broken Devon's neck, keeping the head intact so she could question the man's shade, but robbing the body below it of the shade's control. As if he had anticipated she would wish to speak to the dead sorcerer, and provided the safest means to do so.

Which was . . . interesting.

"He is *mine*. You will confine yourself to the Shields."

"Yes, Prima." As if he did not care.

*We shall have a long conversation later, Mikal. But for now . . .*
"Eli."

"Yes, Prima?"

"Very carefully, open the left-hand door further. *Very* carefully."

There was little need for care, for the heavy oak and iron swung easily and silently. The darkness inside was absolute. The defences shimmering to Sight did not spark or tighten. Emma delicately tweezed them aside, tasting the unphysical traces of the personality behind them.

There was no need; she would recognise his work anywhere. It seemed yet another lifetime ago she had been learning the subtle twists, his habit of disdain, the serpentine shifts of his considerable intellect.

It had perhaps never occurred to him what he had been teaching her with every moment she spent in his presence. The lessons were many and varied. Dutifully, she applied one of them now.

*Do not spring a trap until you know exactly its manner and measure, dear Emma.* Slightly sarcastic, with the bitter edge; she could almost *hear* him. *But when you know, do it swiftly. So it knows it has been sprung.*

Chin high, she gathered her skirts and strode through the door.

For a moment the darkness stretched, a rippling sheet of black, but the spell was so laughably simple she broke it without even needing Word or charm, simply a flexing of her will. Of course, there could have been a more fiendish and complex spell behind it – but she did not think so.

And she was correct. The foyer was narrow but very high, the grand steps at its back managing to be the most utterly abhorrent piece of internal architecture she'd seen in easily six months. It was as if Grayson actively pursued the ugliest thing possible.

*Where would he be? Parlour or bedroom?* "Mikal?"

"They do not seek to be quiet," her Shield murmured. He pointed to the side. "There."

*Parlour, then.* Which meant a number of uncomfortable things.

"No servants to take one's wrap, even," she commented. "Dreadfully rude."

The parlour door's porcelain handle clicked. A slice of ruddy light widened as the flimsy door – painted with overblown cherubs, in a style that had not been fashionable even when it was attempted ten years ago – swung silently open.

*Cheap theatrics, my dear.* But she continued on, briskly, the two Shields trailing her. Her skirts rustled; there was no need for silence. She stepped over the threshold and on to a hideous but expensive carpet, patterned with blotchy things she supposed were an attempt at flowers.

The furniture was chunky and graceless, but again, very expensive. Someone had the habit of antimacassars and doilies, hand-wrought from the look of them, just the sort of meaningless thrift she would expect from whatever lumpen thing Grayson could induce to marry him. All Grayson's taste and judgement had gone into playing politics, and he was a keen and subtle opponent there.

But now, all his keenness and subtlety was splashed in a sticky red stinking tide across the terrible carpet. The brassy odour of death filled the stifling parlour, and from the least objectionable leather chair by the fireplace, licked by the glow and the furious heat given forth by a merry blaze, Llewellyn Gwynnfud chuckled. His long pale hair was pulled back, and for a dead man, he looked remarkably pleased with himself.

"Punctual to the last, dear Emma." The erstwhile dead Prime lifted a small cut-crystal wine glass of red fluid, and Mikal's sudden tension told her there were other Shields in this room. Hidden, of course, and she wondered if they knew of the fate of Llew's *last* crop of Collegia-trained protectors.

Grayson's twisted, eviscerated body was flung over a brown horsehair sopha, the tangle of his guts steaming. Now, as she spared it a longer glance, she wondered if the Prime had killed his Shields himself.

And if Mehitabel the Black had helped.

"A simulacrum," she replied. "And a fantastic one too, well beyond your power. Did you and your sleeping master truly expect the strike at Bedlam to kill me?"

A swiftly smoothed flash of annoyance crossed his face. Long nose, fleshy lips, his blue eyes a trifle too close together . . . well, he was handsome, Emma allowed, but only until one knew him.

Only until one saw the rot underneath.

"I have no *master*, my dear. One or two of our partners expected you to meet your doom before now, but they don't know you as I do." He twirled the small glass, the viscous fluid in its crystalline bowl making a soft sliding sound under the roar of the fire.

"Oh, you have a master. Not Mehitabel – she couldn't craft a simulacrum that fine, being of the Black Line." She tapped a finger to her lips, not missing Llewellyn's eyelids lowering a fraction. It was as close to a flinch as he would allow himself, facing her on this carefully set stage. "But no worries, I will settle accounts with your *master* soon enough. I have decided to deal with you first."

That produced a snarl, a flash of white teeth. "I'm flattered."

"Not at all. You are, after all, the smaller problem."

Sparks crackled, the breathless tension heightening a fraction. The fire was large, yes – but it was *not* large enough to produce such heat. There was the matter of the fluid in the glass, and the shadows clustering on the walls, any of which might hide a Shield or two. Or half a dozen. The eviscerated body of the Lord Chancellor was worrisome too, and the rest of Grayson's house ticking and groaning as nightfall settled and yellow fog began to press upon it in earnest was not quite as it should be. The sounds were too sharp, too weighty.

In short, Llewellyn Gwynnfud had prepared this for a reason. Emma took a half-step to her left, away from the ruin of Grayson's body. "The Chancellor did not expect this," she observed, as Eli and Mikal moved with her – Mikal soundless and Eli's boots creaking just a fraction.

Llewellyn didn't twitch. Instead, he lifted the cordial glass and stared into its swirl. "You found another Shield. Who did this one kill?"

Indirectly reminding her of Crawford, to see if he could unsettle her. Of course. "Not nearly as many as you have, I would fancy. Your former Shields, all dead and gutsplit in an alley." She indicated Grayson's indecently splayed body with a sudden sharp movement, and was gratified to see Llewellyn flinch. "Just like him. You're exhibiting a pattern, Lord Sellwyth." Her hand dropped. "That's right. *Sellwyth*. Dinas Emrys is part of your family's holdings, isn't it?" A long pause. "I've always wanted to visit it. Perhaps now's the time."

For in the lore of the Age of Flame, the ancient citadel of Dinas Emrys was tangled with the *Pax Draegonir*. It was where simulacra of the wyrms would meet in conclave, in the presence of their sleeping progenitor, the Third Wyrm, the one from who all the wyrmlings now were descended.

The first two Great Wyrms were either dead or sleeping so deeply they might as well be – or so sorcerers hoped. But Vortigern lay just under the surface of the Isle, and his might was such that even Britannia might not quell him.

The other Prime had gone very still. He made a slight *tsk tsk* noise. "You are *so* quick, dear Emma. Listen for a few moments."

"You have my attention." *For now.*

"It's one of your best features, my dear, that quality of wide-eyed listening you sometimes employ." His tongue stole out, wetted his fleshy lips. "A tide is rising." An eyebrow raise robbed the sentence of portentousness, but he was still, Emma thought, serious.

*Deadly* serious.

He continued, each word careful and soft. "How long will you spend chasing your hobbyhorse of duty, my dear? You are so talented, and lovely besides. I did not like our parting."

*You dropped me like a hot stone the instant you thought that French tart would give you an advantage, and I was unwilling to share your bed with another woman. Then there was Crawford, and you did not bother to show your face afterwards. No doubt you were busy with high treason and murder.* Emma merely tilted her head slightly. The stone at her throat was still ice cold, quiescent.

"You are here. But you haven't yet attacked me. Which means you need information you think you can force me to provide, or you're intrigued. Most probably the former. But just in case you are intrigued, my dear, how do you like the idea of immortality?"

*Oh, Llewellyn. A silly lure, even for you.* "Overrated. Primes have such long lives anyway, and any immortality has conditions. Try again, Gwynnfud."

"There is an immortality without conditions."

*Ah.* "A Philosopher's Stone." *That's what you were offered? Or you have been granted. If it's the latter . . .* "Am I meant to infer that you've been granted a Stone, in reward for services rendered, and *that*, instead of a simulacrum, is to blame for your wonderfully revived state? Oh, Llewellyn. *Really*. I abhor insults to my intellect."

"As soon as Britannia's vessel is breached and our great friend awakened, darling. The wyrms do not throw away a useful advantage."

*You would do well to remember that.* The heat was mounting, uncomfortably. "A Stone can only be made from a wyrm's heart. Slaying a wyrm brings a curse. Have you forgotten that?"

"Vortis has many children."

Under the close stifling heat, she was cold all through. "And he will slaughter a wyrmchild for *you*. Llewellyn, for God's sake, don't be an idiot."

"Two, actually. Two Stones. One was to be Grayson's. But since he's met with an accident, one will be in my power to give." Another quick wetting of his lips, and Emma's heart gave a shattering leap. "You are the only companion to hold my interest long enough to make such a gift worthwhile. *Think* of it, Emma. You, and me. Doesn't that sound lovely?"

*And you have convinced the Duchess of Kent that you will help her coerce her daughter. A pair fit for each other, indeed.* "You are," she informed him, "completely mad. I am Britannia's servant. Or have you forgotten?"

"You bow and scrape to that magical whore because you see no advantage elsewhere. Come now, do not play the high-and-mighty with me. I know you, Emma. Inside and out."

He was not precisely wrong. In fact, he was more correct than she cared to acknowledge, and the realisation was a slap of cold water.

"Apparently not." The water became ice, sheathing her. "You think I would betray Britannia for this pack of idiotic promises? I left you, Llewellyn, because you had grown *boring*." She took a deep breath, and uttered the unforgivable. "A Shield is far less trouble, and far more . . . *athletic*, besides."

The colour drained from Lord Sellwyth's cheeks. His eyes flamed, pale blue, and the cordial glass sang a thin note as his fingers tightened.

*Almost too easy. Every man has the same sticking point, and it nestles in their breeches.*

He gained his feet in a rush, flinging the glass aside. It hit the grate and shattered, the liquid inside blossoming into blue-white flame. Sorcery uncoiled, streaking for her, and Emma batted it aside with contemptuous ease. Part of the ceiling shattered, a flare of sorcerous flame breaking through four storeys and lifting into the fogbound Londinium night. Llewellyn's mouth shaped a Word, torn air suddenly full of choking dust. She was quicker, a half-measure of chant spat between her lips, warm and salt-sweet; it sliced the springing spell in half and knocked the other Prime back into the chair he had just leapt from. The chair skidded back, its legs tearing the hideous carpet, and smashed into the heavy oak wainscoting.

There were clashes of steel and sudden cries, but she ignored them. Llewellyn's Shields, bursting from their cocoons of invisibility, were not her worry. In a Prime's duel, her only concern was the other sorcerer. The Shields were left to make shift for themselves.

And, she thought, as the gauntlets warmed against her hands and Llewellyn rose out of the chair with a sound like a thunderstorm breaking, it was just as well.

For no Prime had ever duelled Lord Sellwyth and won.

# Chapter Twenty-Nine

## I Find Myself Reluctant to Disappoint

It was just as well he had taken the coja. If he had not, the ride would have been even *more* a nightmare. The knocking of the clocktrain's pistons, steam and charm working together to an infernal rhythm, was enough to drive a mentath's sensitive brain, recently bruised, into a state very near absolute madness. Still, the compartment was adequate, cushioned seats and a window he ensured was firmly shut – for he found he did not wish to see any of the flying cinders trains were famous for.

The difficulty of finding lodgings when they arrived in cold, fogbound Dover was most provoking. Valentinelli was little help, presumably because he cared not a whit where he laid his intriguing head, but Clare required a measure of comfort. There was the question of anonymity, too, but in the end, a respectable hotel was found, a room secured, and Clare gazed out of the window at the pinpricks of yellow gaslight receding down the slope of the town before the Neapolitan, making a spitting noise, shoved him aside and yanked the pineapple-figured curtains closed. Sig, who had napped on the train, took one of the beds, stretched out atop the covers without removing his boots, and was snoring within moments.

"*Porco,*" Valentinelli sneered, and took himself to a chair by the coal fire. Clare settled himself in the other chair, propping his feet on an uncomfortably hard hassock covered in the same pineapple fabric as the curtains. The coja still sparked, his faculties honed and extraneous clutter cleared away, every inch of his capability aching to be used.

He tented his fingers below his nose, and shut out the sound of Sig's noisy sleep. Valentinelli watched him, dark eyes half lidded and thoughtful. The lamp on a small table at Clare's elbow gave a warm glow, and the fire was delightful.

The entire jolting, unhappy experience of travel had almost managed to unseat the excellent dinner he'd finished. Miss Bannon's pendant was cold against his chest, and he wondered how the sorceress fared.

Clare closed his eyes.

"Eh, *mentale*." Valentinelli shifted in his chair. "Use the bed, no? I wake you, at time."

"I am quite comfortable, thank you. I wish to think."

"She got you too." The Neapolitan's chuckle was not cheery at all. "*La strega*, she get every one of us."

Clare's irritation mounted. "Unless you have something truly useful to say, *signor*, could you please leave me in peace?"

"Oh, useful." Valentinelli's tone turned dark. "We are *very* useful, *mentale*. She send us off to find a shipment of something. Bait again. Dangle *mentale* and Ludo, see what happens."

"We are not bait," Clare immediately disagreed.

"Oh no?"

"No. As a matter of fact, I believe we are Miss Bannon's last hope."

The Neapolitan was silent.

"Consider this, my noble assassin. We are three men against enemies who wish nothing less than the destruction of Britannia's Empire and quite possibly the murder of Her physical vessel. Given Miss Bannon's attachment to Queen Victrix, what does it tell you that she has left the defence of Her Majesty to *us*? For that is what she has done by sending us here. She is pursuing an enemy *more dangerous*, in her opinion, than rebellion or even assassination. The fact that she has left this part of the prosecution of said conspiracy to us I find outright disturbing in its implications. Also, did you notice the second Shield? You must have, for he was at dinner. For Miss Bannon to engage another of Mikal's type, when by all accounts she has resisted doing so quite strongly, makes me think this situation very dire indeed." He tilted his head slightly, his eyes still closed. The comforting darkness behind his lids held geometric patterns, interlocking vortices of probability and deduction. "Also, she left us at table and quit her home most ostentatiously, drawing off whatever pursuit she could and waving herself before possible attackers like a handkerchief fluttered out of a window. She has given us *every* chance, sir, and furthermore gave her word not to treat me as bait. No, my noble assassin, we are men Miss Bannon is relying upon. And I do not think that lady relies easily."

Silence filled the room to bursting. The quiet had several components – the whisper of the lamp's flame, the coal fire shifting and flaring briefly, a steady dripping outside the window. The fog here was not Londinium's yellow soup, but it still pressed down on the town from white cliff to railway station, muffling the dosshouses and rollicking publics where Jack Tar drank to dry ground. It muffled the sound of clockhorse hooves and rumbling wheels outside the hotel, and it gave even the warm room a dry, bitter scent tinged with salt.

Valentinelli breathed a soft curse in his native tongue.

"Quite," Clare commented, drily. "Now do be still, sir. I must cogitate. For I will be brutally frank: I do not see much hope of us fulfilling the task Miss Bannon has given us, yet I find myself most unwilling to disappoint her."

Not to mention that Londinium – and indeed, all Britannia – would be distinctly uncomfortable for a good long while if Queen Victrix was removed from the living and Britannia searching for another vessel, or if the Queen were unhappy under her mother's control again. *An unhappy vessel means an unhappy Isle*, whether from bad weather, crop failure, or the creeping anomie that would thread through every part of the Empire.

And, dash it all, this entire affair was simply an affront to the tidiness and public order any good subject of Britannia preferred.

Clare settled himself deeper in the chair. His breathing deepened.

*There are more logic engines. I must be prepared.*

An onlooker would think he slept. But it was a mentath's peculiar doubling he performed, half his faculties engaged upon the riddle of tangling the three parties wishing harm to Britannia in their own brisket; how best to bring this affair to a satisfactory conclusion. The other half, sharpened by coja and shutting out all distractions, embarked on a complicated set of mental exercises. The equations the logic engine had forced him to solve without preparation rested on a series of mental chalkboards, and he set himself to untangling them at leisure and learning the patterns behind their hot white glare.

Motionless, sweat beading on his brow, Clare worked.

He surfaced to the Neapolitan's grip on his arm. "Wake, *mentale*," the assassin whispered. "Ships coming in."

The lamp guttered, throwing shadows over the pineapple-embossed paper. The damn room was a shrine to tropical fruit, Clare thought sourly, and moved very gingerly, stretching his legs. The body sometimes protested after a long period of torpidity. After a few minutes of various stretches, watched by a curious and half-amused Valentinelli, he found his hat and was not surprised to see Sigmund yawning and scratching at his ribs, peering carefully out of the window.

"Too quiet," the Bavarian muttered. "I do not like this."

"Ludo doesn't either." For once, the assassin did not sound sour. "But it could be the tide. Or the fog."

Clare washed his face at the basin, and a quarter-hour

afterwards found all three of them outside in the thick fog, making for the docks. After a brisk walk, there were no more complaints of it being too quiet.

Ports, like Londinium itself, rarely slept, and the infusion of fresh seaswell into a harbour was a potent yeast. Even through the thick white-cotton vapour shouts and curses could be heard, the straining of hawsers and the heave-ho chants of hevvy-mancers. Saltwitches chanted too and wove their fingers in complicated rhythms, drawing the fog aside in braided strands and lighting the ships into port. Shipwitches would be standing at bows, easing the tons of wood and sail safely towards the docks; pilots cursed and spat, hawkers, merchants, and agents rubbed elbows. Bullyboys and Shanghai-men with fresh crops of charmed and coffled Jack Tars waited impatiently – they would be paid a shilling a head, in some cases, less for any with obvious deformities, and the tars would be trapped on a ship as crew for God knew how long. Those with even a small talent for sorcery were safe from the coffles; the tars were those born without. And there were many of them – for what else was a Jack Tar to do when the ship he had been chained aboard was in a foreign port? To sign on a trifle less unwillingly was his only option, either for the pay due at the end of the voyage or for the simple fact that the sea worked its way into a man's blood.

The crowd, in short, was immense, even at this dark and early hour. Some indirect questioning brought the news that the *Srkány*, sailing from Old Emsterdamme, had indeed docked.

As a matter of fact, it had docked last night, and had sailed on the outgoing tide; nobody knew where, and the harbourmaster's office was disinclined to answer such queries. Clare cared little, because Sigmund, with his usual genius for such things, struck up a conversation with a hevvymancer who had helped unload the *Srkány*'s cargo, among which were several crates bound for an estate near Upper Hardres. Heavy crates the hevvy-mancers cursed, for they behaved oddly under the lifting and settling charms.

Clare would hazard a guess that this was the very estate Masters had perfected the core at, never mind that it was a Crown property. Sig paid for the dour-faced hevvy's next pint of ale and they plunged back into the crowd, Clare nervous without good reason. Or, perhaps, the reason had not presented itself yet, struggling to rise from an observation he had not given proper weight to.

When he finally located the source of the unease, it was marked enough to force him to lay hold of Sig's arm and pull the Bavarian into a close, conveniently dark, reeking alley. "Look there," he muttered, and Sigmund knew better than to protest. "And there. What do you see?"

Valentinelli swore, melding with the dimness behind them. Clare was perhaps just the tiniest bit gratified that he had seen them before the Neapolitan.

Across the street, a heavyset man with tremendous sweeping whiskers stepped sideways, as if he did not quite have his land legs yet. His coat was of a cloth not often seen on Britannia's Isle, and his bearing was unmistakably military. He had, so far, wandered once up and down in front of the nameless inn already doing a brisk business in gin and merriment, and he turned to make another pass.

Once Clare's attention had snagged on him, other bits of wrongness blared like trumpets. "The man in grey, across the street. See how he holds his pipe? No Englishman does so. And his boots – Hessians, and shone to a fare-thee-well. Now, look there, chap. Another one, with Hessians and his coat. You'll notice it's turned inside out. There, the two men in the tavern door – the same boots, the same coats. They have sought to disguise themselves, one with a kerchief and another with those dreadful breeches. Look at their whiskers. Not the fashion *this* side of the Channel, dear Sig. What does that tell you?"

The Bavarian spread his hands, waiting for Clare to answer his own rhetorical question.

"Prussians, Sig. Mercenaries, I'd lay ten pound on it. Look

at the way those two hold their hands – they are accustomed to rifles. *That* one is a captain – he subtly presents his chest, so none below him in rank will miss the badge he has been forced to lay aside. And see, that one there? He is watching the street."

"This is Dover," Sigmund said heavily. "Different men from different countries come here, *ja?*"

"Indisputably." Clare frowned. "But there are *two* in the door, another *there* standing watch, and the captain is patrolling. Looking for stragglers, perhaps? Or making certain nobody remarks that the inn there, and probably all the rooms inside it, is full to the brim with Prussian mercenaries. *That* is why Prussian capacitors, and *that* is what else was on the ship. I expected as much."

Valentinelli swore again. "We leave now. *Now.*"

"Quite." Clare jammed his hat more firmly on his head. "We must find horses. I doubt the train runs to Upper Hardres before noon."

# Chapter Thirty

## Duel and Discipline

The Major Circle about her glowed, quicksilver charter charms inside its double circuit spitting and hissing as Llewellyn threw a Word at her. She batted it aside, her throat swelling with chant, and another hole tore itself in the parlour wall, narrowly missing one of Llewellyn's Shields as the man leapt for Mikal. Who turned, with sweet economy of motion, and drove a knife into his opponent's throat with a sound like an axe buried in seasoned wood.

Her fellow Prime was off balance; she had always been much better at splitting her focus. He was contaminated water, seeping at the borders of her will; she countered with clean lake and ocean, and a Word shaped itself under her chant, blooming hurtful bright as fire burst through the ocean's surface and scorched him. Llewellyn took a half-step back within his own Circle, his pale eyes narrowing, and his answering Word robbed the fire of breath, crushing blackness descending on Emma and *squeezing*.

She had expected that, though – it was one of his favourite tricks. A non-physical shift sideways, her hand flung out, and the curse jetted free of the gauntlets, the charter symbol sleek and deadly as it pierced veils of ætheric protections. Llewellyn almost did not hop aside in time, and his left arm whipped back, blood exploding from his shoulder. He ignored the injury, flicking his right hand forward, force expended recklessly to crack her own protections. Which shimmered, shuddered . . . and held, just barely.

Thick crimson, almost black in the uncertain light, flowed down Llewellyn's arm. His frock coat was going to be absolutely ruined. A sudden burst of amusement threatened to dislodge Emma's grip, but she recognised the attack and let it slide away, her chant taking on the sonorous ripple of a hymn. Llewellyn's face twisted, and she was certain her own countenance was not smooth either.

*It is a very good thing I am not a lady.* She pressed the attack, her will bearing down, the chant rising in volume as his faltered. The blood painting his sleeve dripped, but too slowly – globules hung in the air below his contorted hand, spinning gently in mid-air. The fine hairs all over Emma's body rose.

Llewellyn's spine twisted. The blood slowed further, and she scented the beginning of a Major Work, hovering on the edge of probability and possibility, its structure a glory of tangled crystal lattices calcifying with pure white-hot iron.

*He's using blood to fuel it; be careful, Emma!*

If she had not once been so close to Llewellyn, she would not have seen the weakness, carefully protected by a nest of thorn-burning spikes.

*Do not hesitate*, he had told her, over and over again, his hand on her hip, warm and safe in the nest of whatever bed they were sharing at the moment. *Hesitation in a duel is loss.*

She struck for the raw spike-choked gap, ætheric force turned to a shining-sharp blade that *bent*, a jolt pouring up her arms as her own Work mutated, responding to the shape of his. This was the critical juncture – if she misjudged, the force of her defence would be spent and his attack would strike her head-on.

But she had not misjudged.

Llewellyn's body crumpled, flung back like a rag doll as his own Work detonated beneath him. Broken charter symbols spun, spitting sparks in every shade, and the entire house shuddered on its foundations. The limp form of the other Prime crashed into the fireplace, a jolt of blue flame searing Emma's sensitised eyes, and two of his Shields dropped mid-motion as he shunted the backlash aside, sacrificing them.

*That's not a good si—*

Mikal screamed, inarticulate rage a bright copper note against the sudden throat-cut quiet. He launched himself at her, both knives out, and Emma's instinctive twitch to protect herself was unnecessary.

For Mikal was not striking at her. Instead, he had read the threat from Llewellyn far more accurately than she had, and reacted more quickly to boot. Frozen, her unneeded defence sparking as the stone at her throat warmed fractionally, Emma could only watch as Mikal flung himself past her –

– and straight into a scythe-storm of sorcery, as Llewellyn's black-shrouded form birthed itself from the ruin of the fireplace. Ætheric blades blossomed in a hurtful black rosette, and blood exploded for the second time as her Shield fell.

"Hold his head up." Emma's hands were slick with hot blood. "There. And *there*." Sorcerous force bled from her fingertips. Her earrings shivered, the charge contained in their long swinging beads delicately spinning down her neck, twining across her collarbones, and draining down her arms as she closed the rip in Mikal's belly.

Mikal's eyelids fluttered. Eli held his shoulders, pale cheeks spattered with blood and other fluids. Emma's concentration did not allow wavering. She smoothed the violated flesh, charter symbols flushing red as they sank into torn meat, the language of Mending forced to obey her foreign lips shaping its syllables. She was not of the White, whose branches of Discipline encouraged healing. She was not even of the Grey, the seekers of Balance. No, Emma's Discipline was deeply of the Black; the primal forces too great to be concerned with small things like ripped-wide skin and muscle.

At this instant, she did not care in the slightest. Mending would *serve* her, she had decided, and there was no room for disobedience. Flesh melded together, the spark of life within it responding with far more strength than she thought possible, and Mikal's eyes opened fully, yellow irises glowing with unholy fire. He cried out, a long, shapeless sound full of thunder, and she sat back on her heels. Plaster and brick dust coated her face – Llewellyn had blasted straight through walls in his hurry to flee her.

*And well he should,* she thought, grimly. But first things first. She looked up, met Eli's gaze. The younger Shield was wide-eyed and very pale. Childish of him, but she did not have the heart to take him to task. "He shall mend," she said, heavily. "Listen to me very carefully, Shield."

"I hear," Eli answered automatically. He was well trained, she decided, but not particularly imaginative. Mikal's eyes had closed again, and he slumped, bloody but whole, in his brother Shield's arms. Grayson's body was twisted wrack, the sopha it had been flung over smashed to flinders. She could not remember when during the duel *that* had happened.

It did not matter. Mikal was alive, and that had to be enough. Her damnable duty lay heavy on her shoulders.

"Take him to St Jemes Palace. Tell whoever is on guard duty that the Raven has sent you. You will be ushered into a certain personage's presence. Tell that personage that Lord Sellwyth is alive and treacherous. Say, *Dinas Emrys*. Furthermore, tell this personage everything you have witnessed so far, word for word, and Mikal shall add his own observations. Afterwards you are to stay with that personage, and guard that personage *with your very life*. Are my instructions clear, Shield?"

"Very." Eli swallowed hard. His clothes were in a sad, sorry state – all three of them were coated with ground-fine plaster, their faces garishly chalked with the stuff. "Prima, where—"

He sought to *question* her? "Cease your noise. I shall be pursuing Lord Sellwyth." She paused; decided he did, after all, require more explanation. He had only just arrived in the game. "Eli, I am about to open the gates of my Discipline. Keep Mikal here until he has Mended sufficiently to travel to St Jemes." Another pause, this one longer, while she touched the quiescent Shield's cheek. Her fingers left a bloody smear on the fine powdery grit. "I . . . do not wish him to see this. Nor you," she added, belatedly, and stopped herself from continuing. *If he does not reach St Jemes whole, if you somehow damage him on the way, I shall hunt you down. And what I do to Llewellyn shall seem a mercy compared to your own suffering.*

But that was not quite proper. She took her hand away and rose, shedding dust and dirt with the crackle of a cleansing charm.

The trail of destruction punched through walls, the entire house vibrating with the after-effects of a duel. Patches of plaster had turned to glass or smooth iron, chalky and inky feathers flew, irrationality transmuting the prosaic materials of the everyday into something else. Moisture dripped from the ceilings, droplets sliding upwards from the floor in some patches. The force of gravity itself was disturbed, and it would take time for the irrationality to bleed itself away through other sorceries worked in the vicinity.

She stepped through the outer wall, shaking her head slightly as the edges torn in the brick facing shivered. They had transmuted to a long red silken fringe, fluttering even in the still, fog-bound air, touching her cheeks and the backs of her hands with sinister, slippery little kisses.

Llewellyn and his remaining Shields had made for the stables. As Chancellor, Grayson had the right to have his carriage drawn by two gryphons on State occasions, as long as he defrayed the cost of their keep.

And of course, with his Shields, Lord Sellwyth could commandeer said beasts to effect his escape.

*I must have frightened him very badly.*

They had paused long enough to let the gryphons at the clockhorses. Shreds of horseflesh spattered the wrecked interior of the stable; the hot reek of offal and copper blood filled her nose. Shards of bone littered the floor. Grayson had possessed quite a collection, but every single clockhorse was a mess of bone, metal, and rent meat.

*It does not matter, Emma. It is time.*

She stood, her fists caught in her tattered skirts. The vision of Mikal's broken body rose before her; she banished it with an effort that caused sweat to spring free. The plaster dust turned to a slick coating, and she fought to contain the force rising in her.

When she had again mastered herself, she gazed about the stable as if seeing it for the first time.

*Death is here.*

Very well, then. She was of the Endor, and it was high time she reminded Llewellyn Gwynnfud of the fact. Incidentally, if he reached his destination and engaged on what she suspected his next step was, her Queen would be in danger.

Emma Bannon, Sorceress Prime, did not like that idea at all. She inhaled smoothly, disregarding everything about her, turning inward to the locked and barred door of her deepest self.

And her Discipline . . . unfolded.

There was the lesser sorcery, charter and charm of force stored and renewed every Tideturn. Then there was Discipline, the unleashing of power that did not follow the sorcerer's bidding. It simply *was*, working through the gateway suddenly opened for it until the strength of the conduit failed. When the gateway closed, the world was *changed*.

This, then, the danger of sorcery – a losing of oneself.

A fierce hurtful flower blooming in her, its barbs tipped with rotting dust and earth in her mouth. Leprous spots crawled over her skin, the taste of bones and bitter ash. "*Aula naath gig,*" she cried, a Language older even than Mending's mellifluousness, and the chant took shape, tearing itself free of moorings inside her. Sorcery rose, pure and unconstrained.

The bones and meat and metal bedecking the stable's interior . . . twitched.

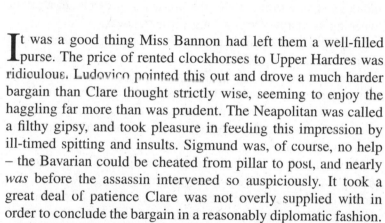

# Chapter Thirty-One

## Quarry and Quarry

It was a good thing Miss Bannon had left them a well-filled purse. The price of rented clockhorses to Upper Hardres was ridiculous. Ludovico pointed this out and drove a much harder bargain than Clare thought strictly wise, seeming to enjoy the haggling far more than was prudent. The Neapolitan was called a filthy gipsy, and took pleasure in feeding this impression by ill-timed spitting and insults. Sigmund was, of course, no help – the Bavarian could be cheated from pillar to post, and nearly *was* before the assassin intervened so auspiciously. It took a great deal of patience Clare was not overly supplied with in order to conclude the bargain in a reasonably diplomatic fashion.

Nevertheless, they were saddled by the time dawn broke over Dover's cliffs, and a half-hour later had quit the town's clutching limits.

The ride was a green and grey blur, Clare's attention turned mostly inward, equations filling his mental cauldron near to bursting. The pattern trembled just out of reach. He did not know Throckmorton's work, and there were other influences besides – he had read Roderick Smythe's monograph on logic patterns, but the crop of equations bore as much resemblance to Smythe's examples as a single fingernail gear did to Brocarde's Infinitude Audoricon.

The clutching fog tried to follow them, but five miles out of Dover they burst into watery grey sunlight. The waking world was hushed, even the birds forgetting to greet the sunrise.

Their view was for the most part trammelled by high green hedges on either side, and Valentinelli slumped in his saddle as if he wished he were elsewhere. Sigmund clutched at the reins and looked miserable. Clare would have quite enjoyed himself, if not for the incessant mental work. He was no closer to finding a pattern to the equations when they breasted a rise and looked down on the dual villages of Hardres, Upper and Lower. The estate was on the far side of the Lower town, a haze of coal and other smoke riding under the billows of grey cloud, weather sweeping in visible from a long distance away.

Despite his slouching, Valentinelli was a good horseman, and his bay clockhorse picked up the pace as much as was safe. Hoofbeats pounded steady time, jog-trotting, sometimes reaching a bone-rattling canter when the Neapolitan judged it appropriate. Time pressed down on Clare, ticking – there was only a limited amount of it before they reached the estate, and once there time would weigh on them even more heavily.

They passed a weather-beaten sign, proclaiming *Hardres Quarry Ltd 3mi*, proudly pointing down an overgrown track that had nevertheless seen hard recent use, if the state of the broken and battered herbiage on its floor was any indication. Clare noted this, and his uneasiness mounted. The Sun refused to show His face, and the air was heavy with the fresh greensap scent of rain.

"*Mentale.*" The Neapolitan glanced over his shoulder. "What we likely to find here?"

It was somewhat of a relief to turn his attention from the equations. The array of mental blackboards had changed into a forest of hideously twisted chalk scribbles. "More mecha, certainly," he answered, his faculties directed sluggishly at the new question. "Possibly a mentath to deal with the arranging of the fresh capacitors. What troubles me is that almost certainly we will find a few men in the trade of violence. We are not so very far from Londinium, and if Prussians have arrived in Dover, they have arrived elsewhere as well. Brighton and Hardwitch, of course." *The planning involved is tremendous. But they would not need many – just enough to hold the Palace and Whitehall, as well as the Armory at the foot of the Tower. Much will depend on exactly how they plan to incapacitate Britannia or Her vessel.*

The thought of Britannia incapacitated, or Queen Victrix somehow under duress, gave him a queer feeling in the region of his stomach. It could not have been his last meal, for that had been Miss Bannon's excellent dinner.

*Well, if it was the last, at least it was a fine one. And in good company.*

"Hmm." Valentinelli grinned, white teeth flashing in his dark face. "I tell you what. I kill mercenaries, you kill the other *mentale*. Simple."

"I cannot kill him until I know more of the plan."

The Neapolitan jerked his head in Sigmund's direction. "Is he any good at the torture, then?"

Sig piped up. "The bastards who broke my *Spinne*, yes, I torture them. Baerbarth shall invent *new* tortures!"

"I should think not, Sig old chap." Clare suppressed a sigh. "Dear heavens. A mentath does not respond to such things as a mercenary would."

Valentinelli's snort was a masterpiece of disdain. "A man feel pain, he answer questions. Especially when Ludo is asking, *mentale*. Never mind. We see when we arrive."

"If you would cease speaking like a bad imitation of a Punchinjude puppet, *signor*, we would deal much more easily with each other." For a moment Clare regretted saying it. His irritation had mounted to a considerable degree. Neither Sig nor the assassin was *logical*. Not like Miss Bannon. Of course, she was not logical either, so—

*Wait.* His attention snagged on the thought, but he was not given leave to follow it.

"So I should speak the Queen's tongue, should I?" The same clipped, cultured schoolboy tone as before. He sounded thoroughly nettled, and had ceased slumping atop his clockhorse. "If I was not blood-bound, *sir*, you and I would have an accounting."

"I am your man, *signor*," Clare returned rather stiffly. "As soon as this damnable affair is finished. In the meantime, can you *please* not insult me by speaking as if you are a dolt? I have rather a sizeable respect for your intelligence, and I wish not to waste time arguing you into acting as if you possess said intelligence."

Silence, broken only by the thumping of hooves. Clare blinked.

*I am very uncomfortable with the idea of Miss Bannon in peril. It is not logical, but . . . oh, good heavens, she is a* sorceress! *You are becoming ridiculous, Archibald!*

Valentinelli finally spoke. "It is a habit, sir. I wish everyone, without exception, to underestimate me. It makes my life much easier."

"Everyone? Including Miss Bannon?"

"I think she is the only one who never has." The soft, cultured tone was chilling. "And I hate her for it."

*Well.* "Ah." What could one say in response? "I should think it would be a comfort."

"A man does not like a woman he cannot surprise, *mentale*." *Much about you becomes clearer.* "I see."

Valentinelli kneed his horse into a canter, and Clare hastened to follow suit. Sigmund groaned, and their destination grew ever closer.

And Clare still had no pattern for the equations.

"There is no one here," Sigmund announced. He was flushed and sweating, his broad face shiny.

Clare hushed him, gazing at the crumbling manor from the shelter of an overgrown hedge.

It was of the flat *chateau* style, a box with a sadly punctured clay-tile roof, the gardens crumbling and overgrown, its windows lackadaisically boarded with worm-eaten wood. Weeds had forced their way up between flagstones, and the whole place had such an obvious aura of disrepair that he was half tempted to agree with Sig's assessment.

But only half.

Valentinelli merely pointed. The weeds were crushed where heavy cart wheels had rolled over them. The trail pointed directly to the three stairs leading to the chateau's fire-scarred front door.

*The fire was recent. And chemical in origin, from what I can observe. Which does not bode well.*

The Neapolitan cocked his head, his dark eyes taking on a peculiar flat shine.

Clare was suddenly cold, and very glad they had left the horses in a small copse outside the estate's fallen gates. The greenery hiding them seemed a very thin screen indeed.

For there was the sound of scraping metal, gears catching, and fizzing sparks. The manor house shuddered, its stone façade zigzagging with cracks. The earth rumbled, vibrating as if a gigantic beast slumbering in its depths turned over in its sleep.

In a blinding flash, Clare thought of the quarry down the road. *Yes. They would not need to dig far to stay hidden; and no wonder there were cart tracks. Building underground; now why did I not account for such a notion?*

The manor shuddered again, and masonry fell. A cavern tore itself in the front wall, belching steam, smoke, and blue-white arcing electricity. Clare's faculties supplied him with an observation he did not fancy *or* trust. He questioned it from every angle, and it became indisputable. He was not going mad.

A gigantic mechanisterum homunculus had been built *into* the house.

Sigmund's disbelieving laugh was lost in the thundering noise. "*Spinne!*" he yelled. "*Bastards! Schweine!*"

The mecha rose out of the manse, shedding bits of masonry

like rainwater from a duck's back. Clare's busy faculties swallowed every detail they could reach while the thing's legs unfolded, a mad dream of a mechanical spider taking shape before him on a lovely sunny afternoon. The appendages thudded down one at a time, while the cephalothorax and abdomen lifted, gleaming. Prussian capacitors winked in orderly rows along the bottom of its body, a constant whining hum rattling every tooth in Clare's head. The pattern behind the deadlights trembled on the edge of his comprehension. Steel-banded glass jars bubbled with green fluid atop the mecha's back, and in each one floated—

*So that is what they needed the brains and spinal cords for.* His limbs refused to move, his busy brain straining. *A mentath attempting some form of Alterative sorcery? But how? How is it possible?*

The ground would not cease its rumbling, and Clare's imagination served him a picture of other mecha, built in the depths of an abandoned quarry, golden discs on their chests sparking into life as the workers who built them – and he was suddenly quite sure they had been assembled by *things* very like the metal scarecrows in the Blackwerks' depths – capered with furious mechanical glee, their eyes glowing crimson with mad intelligence.

If a dragon could run the stink and clamour and hellish heat of the Blackwerks, one could easily induce its unsleeping metal minions to build in the dank darkness underground. Another thought turned Clare even colder: perhaps there was more than one of the beasts cooperating in this terrible mockery of the mechanisterum's art.

"*Get down!*" Ludovico yelled, shoving him into Sigmund. They fell in a rattling heap, Clare's hat disappearing into the overgrown shrubbery. The juicy green stink of broken sap-filled branches rose, struggling with the odours of ozone, heated machine oil, scorched metal, and stone dust.

The mecha was immense. *No wonder the equations are so complex. This rather changes things.*

Valentinelli crouched, his hip knocking Sig's shoulder. The Bavarian was pressed into the dirt, and Clare thought perhaps the Neapolitan enjoyed the chance to do so . . . but it did not work. For the gigantic mecha lifting its way up out of the ruins of the manse had some means of detecting them. The eyes on its arachnoid head dripped with diseased golden electricity, and the thing squatted over smoking ruins. Massive clicking noises assaulted the shivering air, and apertures slid open where a living arachnid would have spinnarets. Cannon shapes whirred down into place, and Clare's stomach gave a decidedly uneasy message to the rest of him.

The cannons swivelled, pointing unerringly at Clare and his companions. The Neapolitan cursed –

– and there was a booming so immense it robbed every other sound of consequence as the mecha fired.

# Chapter Thirty-Two

## Bannon's Ride

White bone, red muscle, dark metal. Stink-steaming hides of several colours twitching, shaking free of offal and straw. The hooves coalesced, metal shards bending as sorcery crackled, sliding up splinters of bone as they fused together to become legs.

Emma Bannon stood, her eyes open but sightless, black from lid to lid. Her outstretched hands were loose and cupped; she leaned forward as if into a heavy wind, but her curls only riffled slightly. Her ragged skirts fluttered, and her pale flesh marked itself with charter charms. The spiked glyphs did not glow.

Not completely. The symbols sliding against the texture of her skin were black as well, their sharp edges fluorescing with traces of eerie green foxfire.

The chant came from her slack mouth, but she was not voicing it. Her lips parted, her tongue still; the words swelled whole from her passive throat. The Language was not Mending or Breaking, not Naming or Binding or Bonding. It was not a Language of the White or the Grey. It was the deepest Black, that tongue, and it was given free rein.

Discipline was not entirely inborn, but it was not entirely chosen, either. Rather, the predisposition and character of witch, charmer, mancer or sorcerer narrowed choices until, in the last year of Collegia schooling, the practitioner arrived at the Discipline that in retrospect seemed a foregone conclusion.

The non-sorcerous feared the Grey and despised the Black, thinking the names meant things they did not. The White was often capable of causing the most harm as it sought to cure, and the Black was the restfulness of night after a hard day's labour – or so its practitioners said.

The White disagreed, vehemently. The Grey kept their own counsel.

And yet, even among the Black, the Endor were . . . well, not feared. But held in caution. Once, one of their kind had brought a shade back to flesh to answer a king, a feat still whispered of with awe.

The haunches built themselves, massive, meat rearranged and muscles attaching to re-fused bone. Clockhorse metal filigreed each bone, ran threadlike through the muscles, and crackled with the same rot-green foxfire as the charter symbols on Emma's skin.

A figure appeared behind her, indistinct through plaster dust and the smokegloss of sorcery. *Two* figures, one leaning heavily on the other, both tall, well-muscled men, picking their way through scattered bricks and the destruction of a sorcerer's passage. One man was dark-eyed. The other's irises burned yellow in the gloom.

Emma's delicate fingers tensed. The chant took on sonorous striking depth. The withers appeared, and the thing was unmistakably a horse, but too big. The stitched-together pieces of horsehide flowed obscenely up its legs, hugging naked iron-filigreed musculature. The neck lifted in a proud curve, the vertebrae knobs of glassy polished bone, lengthening to fine thin short spikes of mane. The tail was a fall of metal-chased hair, and its head was two clockhorse skulls melded together to create a larger, subtly *changed* thing. For it had sharp teeth no horse, Altered or pureflesh, would have, and its bone eyesockets were emptily, terribly dark.

The steed stood very still. A ripple went through it as the hide finished its patchwork. More metal quivered and flung itself from the floor, sorcerously magnetised into plates of armour. A saddle appeared, shaping itself from shredded leather tack.

The amalgamation of flesh, metal, bone, and sorcery became a massive destrier, its shoulders straining as ætherial force struggled to violate Nature. Armoured in metal barding and caparisoned in green and black, a gossamer fabric made of dust and foxfire cloaking the hurtful edges, it stood slump-shouldered and obscene.

The sorceress's fingers flicked. The chant halted, turned on itself inside her throat, and birthed a Word.

"*X——v!*"

It did not echo, but it continued for a long time, a hole torn in the world's fabric, a curtain pulled aside. And something . . . descended.

The *Khloros* lifted its massive head. Leaf-green sparks flamed in its eyesockets. A clashing ran along its length as the armour shifted, settling, under the fabric of dust and æther cloaking it.

Crackling silence. But the Work was not finished, for as the sorceress strode forward, the black gem at her throat gave a burst of radiant spring-green flame as well, scorching eye and mind alike. She leapt, caught the pommel, and her foot found one huge silver-chased stirrup. Light as a leaf she vaulted into the saddle, and as she did, spurs jingled, oddly musical. Her own armour appeared, metal striking her Black-charmed skin and spreading as if liquid, flowing up her legs to make greaves, rising to encase her thighs and torso. Her head tipped back, dark curls tumbling feather-free before the helm grew from spiked shoulders. The green became patterns of charter and charm, flowing through sorcery-blackened metal, and the sharp-scaled gauntlets creaked as her fingers flexed again, their paleness disappearing like birch twigs under a flood of ink.

From the helm's shadowed depths, the Word came again.

"*X——v!*"

The *Khloros*, the Pale Horse, neighed. The sound shattered what little of the stable's interior remained intact, and both onlookers flinched.

"*X——v!*" A final time, the Word resounded, full of the rush and crackle of conflagration.

The *Khloros* shook its spiked mane, and its front hooves lifted. It reared, its rider moving with fluid hurtful grace, melded to its sudden poisonous loveliness. By the time the Word's thunder died, the *Khloros* was an unholy, beautiful thing cloaked in twisting pale green fire. At the heart of every flame was the black between stars, a thin thread of utter negation.

The helm's triple spikes nodded among firefly flickers of stray sorcery. The *Khloros* wheeled, a caracole of exquisite, diseased elegance. Its hooves left frost-scorch on the shivering, unwilling ground. From the darkness under the three spikes came the sorceress's voice, and yet it was not hers. It was the lipless sigh of Life's oldest companion.

"*Death,*" she whispered.

The *Khloros* unleashed itself with a musical clatter of metal against stone, another shattering neigh blowing a hole in the only remaining untouched wall in the stable. It leapt forward in a foaming wave, and the two men had gone to their knees in the ruins. The roof creaked dangerously, but neither moved. The Shields clutched each other like children wakened from a nightmare. One was paper-pale, trembling as if with palsy, and he leaned aside to retch uselessly.

The yellow-eyed Shield swayed. His face was alight.

"Beautiful," Mikal whispered.

In the distance, the screams began.

*They rode.*

*The earth itself repelled the* Khloros, *so its hooves struck ash-green sparks from a cushion of screaming air. Its gait flowed, its neck arched and its metallic tail sparking on the wind of its passing. The Rider moved with the massive beast as one, and the breathless screams of Londinium were as music over the drumming hoofbeats.*

*For the Rider did not merely call forth the pale horse. The sorcery flowing through her had not reached its high tide yet. With every hoof-fall, the city quaked like a plucked string.*

*And the dead answered.*

*They rose from their graves, gossamer shades with wide-stretched rictus grins. The Khloros could not step above ground uncontaminated by Death; few places were closed to it. Sanctified ground was no bar to it, for the dead were part and parcel of the hallowing.*

*This was what caused the screaming. As the Pale Horse cantered, its Rider staring straight ahead under her triple-peaked helm, the dead within sound of their passing rose like veils. The stronger among the deceased, newly woken or newly buried, ran like dogs or rode horses of their own, spectral rotting things with soft pads instead of hooves.*

*For as long as there was Londinium, there were equines to serve, to labour . . . and to die.*

*The living cowered and fled, though the dead shied away from their warm breathing fear. Some few claimed to have seen the face of the Rider, but they all agreed it was a man. Those whose gaze did pierce the deep shadows of the helm stayed silent, for they recognised the white-cheeked, burning-eyed woman they glimpsed. The silent ones were those whose candles were already flickering, and within a week those few had been laid to rest in cold earth.*

*To the west the Dead Hunt rode, a freezing wind tearing shutters from stone houses, shattering windows, bursting chimneys and grinding cobblestones and brick facing in weird lattice patterns. The West End, the homes of the rich and influential, cowered under the lash of the Eternal. There were those on Picksdowne who claimed to see the insubstantial* dead rising from the street itself, and the clapperless, immense Black Bell hung in the Tower tolled once, sharply, the Shadow lifting its malformed head and staring with eyes like two flat silver coins. The dome of ætheric protection cupping the Palace of St Jemes lit like a white-hot bonfire, sensing something dreadful afoot.

The Rider cut through one corner of Hidepark, and for months afterward there was a black scar in the lush greenery near the Cumber Gate, one the quality affected not to see as they drove past on their daily promenades.

Then she turned, sharply, to the north, wheeling as a giant bird will. None but the tide of half-seen crystalline shades following her witnessed the helmed head lift, as if she studied the heavens, searching for . . . what? What could such a being be chasing, on such a night?

Whatever it was, she found it. For sudden tension bloomed in the Rider's figure, and her scaled gauntlets tightened on the reins. The Khloros's massive head rose, too, as if it could taste the spectral traces of a traitor's passage against the velvet-yellow clouds reflecting Londinium's nightly glow. The pale horse champed, and its hoofbeats took on new urgency.

A final Word broke free of the Rider's throat. It was feathered with diamond ice, a weightless sound, and the dead flowed forward, streaming around the Khloros. The Rider shimmered as if under cold heavy oil, fog flash-freezing and scattering sparks of foxfire sorcery. The Pale Horse's hooves hit a billowing cushion of vapour, and its bulk heaved up with a gasping-fish leap.

Khloros and Rider flew, on a white-billowing cloud of the dead. Their melting shadow touched the earth below, terribly black and crisp though there was precious little light to cast it. A withering stole through the dark hole of that shadow, and as they flew, the living in houses underneath cowered without knowing quite why.

It was over two hundred miles to Dinas Emrys, and the Rider

*had to reach it by dawn. As long as the strength holding the
ætheric conduit open held, the* Khloros *would bear her.*

   *Following a gryphon-borne traitor, Death flew from Londinium.*

# Chapter Thirty-Three

## Man Only Dies Once

Ears ringing, blood slicking his face, Clare staggered upright. *That is precisely the problem with cannon. Difficult to aim, especially when firing from a suspended carriage.* He shook his head, and Valentinelli was suddenly before him, crouching and bloody. The man's thin-lipped mouth moved, his dark hair half singed and wildly disarranged. Clare blinked, realising he was deaf.

*Temporarily, or . . .*

As if in response, the world poured into his ears once more. A sudden overwhelming welter of noise scored through his tender skull, threatening to turn his brain into thin gargling soup. His knees hit the smoking dirt, and Sigmund appeared, a thread of bright blood sliding down his filthy, soot-stained face.

Clare strained to deduce, but his faculties would not obey. The coja, false friend, had turned on him. Whatever bolt the immense arachnid mecha had fired at them was no help either.

*The bolt. Electrical in some fashion? The mecha was swimming in electrical force; the capacitors are maintaining at a high rate. The core! Masters's core!*

The thought was driftwood to a drowning man. He clung to it, his mental grasp tightening with the strength of desperation.

*A shifting stream of values! That's it!*

For a blinding moment he saw it all – the Blackwerks, where every difference was a *range*, not an orderly single value. The trouble was not irrationality. Rather, it was rationality not wide enough to contain what it saw.

*The world is wider, Horatio, than is dreamed of in your philosophy.*

The pressure in his skull eased all at once. Marvellous relief, sensory information behaving as it should now, and he opened his eyes to find the Neapolitan's pox-scarred face above his. He had fallen; the assassin had caught him, and even now held him. The ground was charred, soot rising in fine dancing black flakes, the hedges blackened and crisped, peeled back in a perfect circle that had *just* missed them. Had Valentinelli not knocked them aside and held Sigmund down, all three of them might have been caught in the blast, instead of on its smoke-crisped margin.

The earth was quiet now, settling itself after a violation. The only hint of thunder was far in the distance, and one could not be sure it was not merely one's nerves echoing after a sustained assault.

*Calculate the stride length. The arachnid will have to pace slowly for the smaller mecha, but they will not grow tired. Sub-equations in the core will take care of that – how is it speaking to the receivers? An invisible signal, bringing it into range – pure electricity? No, and not magnetism either. Perhaps some blend of the two? How? Is it sorcery? No, the logic engine will not allow for that; the brains in the casks atop it must not be Altered then. I must have more data.*

Valentinelli's mouth was still moving. Sigmund nodded, leaned down –

– and slapped Clare. Not lightly, either, his work-hardened palm cracking against Clare's cheek.

The shock snapped Clare's head aside, and he thudded back into his body with a sound akin to a carriage wheel jolting through a pothole. "Thank you," he gasped. "Dear heavens, *that* was uncomfortable."

The Neapolitan relaxed slightly. He swore in Italian, more as a means of expressing his happiness than anything else. Clare blinked and found his body would obey him, gained his feet with Valentinelli's help, and spotted his hat among some smoking shrubbery.

"*Spinne!*" Sigmund crowed. "Did you see that, Archie? Bastards built a *Spinne*! And what a beautiful beast. We hunt them down, *ja*? Hunt them and see how they made the *fräulein Spinne!*"

Bending over to retrieve his hat was problematic, but Clare managed it, and turned to survey the smoking pile of rubbish that had once been a reasonably nice, if somewhat decrepit, manor house. "Indubitably."

"*La strega* do not pay enough for this," the assassin muttered darkly. "That *thing*. *Diavolo*." And, of all things, the assassin crossed himself in the manner of the Papists.

"Twenty guineas," Clare reminded him, a trifle more jollily than he felt. "And you said you'd take on the Devil himself, my princely friend."

"Twenty guinea is *not* enough." The man's accent had settled into what Clare suspected might be his true voice – clipped and cultured, but with the song of his native tongue rubbing under unmusical Queen's Britannic. "That was not a cannonball, *signor*."

"Nor was it a kiss on the cheek." Clare jammed his hat atop his head. The reek of singed hair, singed greenery, boiled rock, and dust was immense. If Valentinelli knew he was missing his eyebrows, he gave no sign of it – and Clare wondered if he might be missing his own. "Come, gentlemen. We must find the horses, if they have not bolted. We have work to do."

"Wait. That – that *thing*." Valentinelli's hands were tense and his clothing still steamed. His coat was sadly the worse for wear, and his dark hair was scorched as well. All in all, they were a rather sorry and raffish bunch by now. "How you plan on stopping it? What it *doing*, eh, *signor*? And what you propose *we* do?"

Sig stared in the direction the vast mecha had gone, his broad rough hands working on empty air as if he had the builder of such a contraption by the throat.

Clare took stock of himself, patting his pockets. His pistol had not discharged, thank goodness. His watch was still in its accustomed place, and he drew it forth, noted the time, and wound it, a soothingly habitual set of motions. "First we find the horses." He replaced the watch and pulled his cuffs down, brushed at his frock coat. He stamped, doing what he could to rid his boots of dust and char. Miss Bannon's money was still secure. "Then we visit the quarry three miles from here. If luck is on our side, there will be a mecha there we can steal, for the range of values will no doubt have excluded some of those built." He paused. "If not, we shall think of something. Then we hie ourselves to Londinium and do our best to nip a rebellion in the bud."

There were Altered guards at the quarry's mouth, but Valentinelli left Clare and Sig in a shaded dell and disappeared around the bend in the cart track. He reappeared a few minutes later, wiping one of his dark-bladed knives on a torn rag he dropped without further ado in the dust. Clare did not overly examine the traces of crimson on it; it was enough to deduce the provenance – the shirt the Neapolitan had torn it from as soon as the owner had ceased breathing.

Mercifully, the corpses lay with their faces turned away from the entrance, their necks crooked oddly. Their Alterations were only hinted at – deformed ribs and too-thick legs insinuating changes to the human body that might sicken Clare, did he not have other things to focus on.

"Kielstone," he murmured. It *was* an underground quarry. Kiel could be cut in any direction, unlike slate, and it ran in odd veins, twisting and looping underground. It also was mildly resistant to sorcery, meaning it had to be extracted by hand. Even traces of kiel would camouflage the mechas nicely, before their logic engines turned on.

The entry was a cavern of pitch black, even under the strengthening daylight. The clouds were thinning, and it might turn into a beautiful Kentish spring day before long. The mecha would glitter under the sun as they strode toward Londinium.

Were there other quarries in the districts around the ancient city just waiting to birth a stream of metal monsters? Very likely. How many?

*More than will be comfortable, Clare. Concern yourself with the task at hand.*

"Archie." Sigmund had gone rather pale under his mask of soot. "In *there*?"

"Come now, Sig. You're a lion for Miss Bannon, aren't you? See there." Clare pointed. "We shall find lanthorns, no doubt. Or glowrock. Signor Valentinelli, if you would be so kind."

In short order they had glowrocks caged in steel, the surfaces of the stones dark and oil-slick as they absorbed sunlight. They seemed well charged, but just to be safe Valentinelli also found a lanthorn with a trimmed wick and plenty of oil. Clare thought to ask if the man had lucifers about him, but the gleam in the Neapolitan's dark eyes told him such a question was foolish.

They penetrated the cavern's black mouth. Twenty paces in it was dim enough that the glowrocks began to shimmer. The floor was stone, scarred and worn smooth, implements stacked against the walls – picks and shovels, rope, kegs of various sizes, scrap lumber, a small pile of miner's hats, candleholders. Fifty paces, and they walked in tiny spheres of silver glow, blackness pressing down all around. A hundred paces brought them to a junction. The main passageway continued down, terminating in what had to be some sort of caged hoist-lift; a much narrower passage veered sharply off to the right.

Valentinelli was a scarred caricature, glowrock light disappearing into his pupils and the pits on his soot-streaked face. "*Signor?*"

Clare swallowed drily, pointed at the smaller passage. "That one."

"How would they . . ." Sig coughed. "No, of course. That is for supplies. *This* is for people."

Pleased, Clare made a noise of assent. Valentinelli handed his glowrock cage over and edged into the small passageway. If there were more guards below, he did not wish to be blinded. It was a good idea. But they did not have to go far. The narrower passageway terminated at a wooden platform. Two frail guard-rails over a pitch-black pit, with the wooden struts of a ladder showing.

"Oh, *Scheisse*." Sig's voice struck the edges of the pit, and a faint echo drifted back up.

"Cheer up, Sig. Man only dies once, you know."

Valentinelli's humourless snigger echoed as well. "In that case, *signor*, you go first." But he shouldered the mentath aside with a small spitting sound of annoyance, grabbing the third glowrock cage and producing a handkerchief. In a trice the cage was tied to his torn waistcoat, and he tested the ladder with commendable aplomb. "Safe enough. Twenty guinea, *definitely* not enough."

The climb down was more arduous mentally than physically. Sig, sweating and muttering awful imprecations under his breath, nearly wrenched one of the ladders free, he trembled so violently. Every twenty feet or so the ladder would end, resting on a trigged platform of warped wood. The glowrocks' shimmer intensified as they descended, and Clare was seeking to calculate just what sort of foul air they might encounter in the depths when Valentinelli hopped off the ladder and on to solid ground. The Neapolitan sighed, a not-quite-whistle, and lifted his glow-rock cage.

A vast chamber tunnelled out of rock greeted them. It was mostly empty, but the scuffs on the dusty, dirt-grimed floor were fresh. To Clare's left, the other half of the large hoist-lift rested in a carven hollow. The sides and floor of the cavern were unnaturally smooth, almost glassy. The cavern's roof was ribbed like a cathedral's vault, but the ribs were odd. Almost . . . organic.

*Where did the workers who built this all vanish to?* For a moment he had an odd mental vision of them seeping through the cracks in the floor, metal become liquid and returning to earth's embrace. He shook it away, annoyed at the fancy.

Sig let out a bark of relief when his boots touched firm ground. Great pearls of sweat cut tracks through the ash on his face. "Archie. I hate you."

"Ha!" Clare's cry of triumph shattered the stillness.

Scattered on the floor of the cavern were a few bipedal mecha of the sort they had seen in the warehouse near the Tower. They slumped, curiously lonely, and from the way they all faced toward the deepest darkness at the back of the cavern, Clare could imagine the serried ranks that must have stood here before awakening to the invisible call.

"Ha!" he repeated, and actually bounced up on his toes. "As I suspected! Some of them did not receive that call, Sig. You and I are going to mechanister them, and then we will take them to Londinium." The only response his revelation garnered was frank, open-mouthed stares from his companions. "Don't you see? We will have mecha of our own!"

"Mad," Valentinelli muttered. "You are *mad.*"

Sigmund, on the other hand, stared for a few more moments. Then a smile spread over his broad face. *"Du prächtiger Bastard!"* He clapped Clare on the shoulder hard enough to stagger the mentath. "Only if I take it to workshop after. *Ja?*"

"Sig, old man, if we make this work, you will have a multiplicity of mecha carcasses to pick over at your leisure. We haven't much time; let us see what they have left us."

# Chapter Thirty-Four

## Always the Bloody Way

The first thread of grey on the eastern horizon was a silver ribbon under a heavy door of ink. It whipped the *Khloros* into a frenzy of speed, the countryside below running like a sheet of black oil on a wet plate. The Rider leaned forward, spiked helm nodding and armoured shoulders shaking with effort. The door of her Discipline was closing, and she could not stop it.

The tide of the dead who rode with her foamed in the dark-clouded sky, a crystal tracery of flung sea-waves. Under the shadow of *Khloros* and Rider they rose like smoke from grave-yards and ditches, fields and rivers, and joined the procession. The things they rode were vaguely horselike, or they ran in empty air, spirits whole as they had been while living or terribly disfigured as they had been at life's ending. The drowned and the murdered, the beaten and the lost, the starved and the glut-tonous, they ran in the *Khloros*'s wake.

This was why Endor was held in caution. Who could trust a man or woman who held congress with such a crowd? Or a Prime who could bring the *Khloros* to a night's unlife?

The Pale Horse arrowed down. The silvery ribbon in the east became fringes of grey. It lashed sensitive flanks, scored smoking weals in piebald, stitched-together horseflesh. The armoured barding sought to protect the sorcerous skin underneath.

*It does not matter. The journey is at an end.*

With the thought, consciousness returned to the Rider. For a moment she hesitated, trembling, on the threshold, nameless and irresolute. It seemed an eternity she had been riding, following the scentless trail of treachery borne on gryphon wings. Did he know she followed? Quite possibly; she was loud enough to be heard counties away.

Between one heartbeat and the next she was through the door, the memory of being merely a cup to pour meaning into mercifully evaporating. Even a sorcerer's finely tuned mind could not stand such a violation. Best it were forgotten, and soon.

A white sword coalesced at the eastern horizon. The grey light intensified, and the sound of waves crashed back and forth. *Khloros*, understanding her human need, intensified its speed again. It was graceful even in its desperate shambling, its armour and barding and flesh, bones and metal unravelling into pure æther. It burst into colour – the page written upon, the pallid light broken into its constituent parts.

The crystal wave clustered around the Rider, dead hands outstretched and fingers turned to vapour.

She fell.

Sunlight. Warm as oil against her cheeks, striking her sensitised eyes even through protective lids. She lay on chill dampness, various bits digging into her back and hair and skirts. She did not dare open her eyes, simply lay where she was for a few breaths, taking in everything she could of the space around her.

Morning chill, a damp saltbreath of the sea a distance away, flat metal tang of riverwater closer. The sunshine came in dappled patterns – she was under leaves. A faint breeze rattled them. What was that sound? It was not waves or the groaning crash of rent earth. It was not the hoofbeats of *Khloros*, and it was most *definitely* not her own voice.

Cries. The clacking of razor beaks, a voice raised high and furious in sonorous chant. A shuddering ran through the damp, hard ground underneath her.

*What?*

Sense returned. Every inch and particle of her savagely abused body hurt. To open the door to Discipline was never undertaken lightly. Things could happen to those whose will was not honed, and Discipline took a hard toll on the body as well as the mind. Emma Bannon sat up, blinking furiously, and found herself in a ragged ruin of a dress, her corset stays snapped and dark curls knocked loose, the morning dew gilding bracken and bramble. To her left a rocky hill rose, choked with vines. It was from the top of that hill that the sounds were pouring, screeches and nasty grindings.

She staggered upright, tearing herself free of clutching greenery. Her knees threatened to give; she silently cursed at them. That gave them some starch, but only *some*. Her rings ran with sparkling light – Tideturn had come while she lay senseless, and she carried a full charge of sorcerous force. It stung, like the touch of sun on already reddened skin.

She took stock. All in all, she was reasonably whole. The black stone at her throat was ice cold, her rings on numb fingers sparked with charter symbols, and her earrings quivered against her neck, brushing dew-damp skin. If she did not take pneumonia from lying on the cold ground for however long, it would be a miracle.

*That's Llewellyn up there.* She shook herself, cast about for a path. None was apparent.

*Oh, isn't that always the bloody way. Where am I? God alone knows where, with a mad Prime above and the fate of Britannia at stake, and not even a goat track in sight.*

"Bloody f—king *hell*," she muttered, and other words more improper, as she turned in a full circle. The clashing and scraping and cawing above her was mounting in intensity.

*Well. There is nothing for it, then.*

She waded through the bramble to the base of the hill, set her hands to the rough grey stone poking out through moss and vine, and began to climb.

# Chapter Thirty-Five

## Don't Touch the Contacts

Sigmund swore, hit the mecha's froglike head twice with the spanner. The resounding clashes filled the cavern. The glow-rocks were dimming. "There. Try now."

*Really? Banging it with a spanner? Sigmund, I am disappointed in you.* Clare, strapped into the mecha's chest, sighed and shook the jolting out of his bones. Each time Sig banged on something, he was half afraid he would end up skullsplit, sagging in the mecha's straps and buckles.

He curled his fists around the handles, turning his wrists just slightly so the metal plating had full contact with his skin. "I don't think it's going to—"

Golden glow burst from the circle over his chest. The small logic engine sputtered, and Clare was so surprised he almost sent the mecha tumbling over backwards. Ratcheting echoed, capacitors hummed. Clare's concentration narrowed. The equations ran smoothly, ticking below the surface of his conscious mind, as tingling ripples slid up his arms.

*Ha!*

He had solved the equations. It was now close to child's play to bend the mecha to his will. It took two steps forward, obedient instead of fighting him, and one impossibility followed another.

Around the cavern, humming clangour rose. Golden discs,

hanging slackly in the chests of the slumped mecha, flashed blue-white. *Aha! The variance, that's why they're responding to this one. Must be a redundancy built into their capacitation metrics. There's bound to be several that weren't within the large engine's tolerances but are within mine. Drop in the bucket, but still jolly good.*

"Clare?" Valentinelli sounded nervous.

"It's all right," he called. The words echoed internally, feedback mounting, but he dumped the superfluous noise with a repeating equation. Once one had the trick of it, surprisingly easy. "Climb into a mecha, but don't touch the contacts!"

Valentinelli's reply was unrepeatable, and Clare laughed. The fierce white-hot joy of logic took him, a razor-edged glow. "*Onward!*" he yelled, as the mechanisterum homunculi began to stamp. "*Onward to Londinium! But don't touch the bloody contacts!*"

To run with iron pistons for legs and a burning globe of logic for a pumping heart, faster than a thoroughbred or a sporty carriage, faster even than a railcar. To watch Londinium grow on the horizon, under a pall of smoke rising into the sky like a column of God's guidance, while metal legs tirelessly carried one forward.

This was joy.

Sigmund whooped almost the entire way, drunk with the exhilaration of speed. Valentinelli, his pocked face set and alarmingly pale, hung in the straps, jounced about like a Red Indusan papoose. The assassin had spent the last hour desperately seeking to avoid touching *anything*, not just the contacts.

Clare, overjoyed by the wind in his face and the logic humming through his bones, found himself laughing again.

They were half a mile from Londinium when it suddenly became more difficult to move. The equations tangled, snarling against each other, and sweat sprang on Clare's brow as he fought air gone suddenly glass-hard.

*Oh no you don't.*

The will pressing down on them was immense, and backed by a much larger logic engine, one powered by a core far more powerful than the tiny one at Clare's chest. But that much strength was clumsy, and created so much interference it was relatively easy to divert the force of its attack.

He had wondered if the mecha he had control of would respond to the larger logic engine's soundless call once they were awake. It appeared they would not – unless the mentath controlling the spider solved the riddle of the variances.

Clare devoutly hoped he would not.

And now the other mentath knew he was here. Clare's attention became fully occupied, his small band of a dozen mecha slowing, Sig finally catching the idea that something was amiss.

*Carry that over, dump the quad, string those together, there's the weakness, let it replicate, aha! Eat that fine dinner, sir!*

Were Clare to explain this battle, he would liken it to a game of chess – except with a dozen boards, each board in five dimensions, and each player with as many pieces as he could mentally support without fusing his brain into a useless heap of porridge.

There was, unfortunately, no time for comparison or explanation. He pushed the dozen mecha forward, a tiny piece of grit edging under Londinium's shell, metal creaking as he leaned forward, his body tensing inside the straps. Gears whined and ratcheted, fountains of sparks showering the paving of Kent Road.

Shimmering curtains of equations spun and parted, the world merely interlocking fields of force and reaction. For a moment the whole of the city spread below him, nodes and intersections, and he saw the thrust of the other mentath's attack.

St Jemes's Park lay littered with smoking mecha corpses. But there was an endless array of them, pressing north towards the Palace. Further clusters about Whithall and the Tower, and Clare had to decide which he was to strike for.

*Save Victrix. Nothing else matters.*

It was as if Miss Bannon stood at his ear, whispering. The pendant she had given him was quiescent, neither hot nor cold – of course, the field of an active logic engine would interfere with it somewhat. But ever afterwards, Clare thought it very likely that some quirk of Nature had spoken across time and space, telling him *exactly* what Emma Bannon would say. Perhaps it was only his deductive capability.

He did not think so.

The decision was already made. He quickly made the calculations, turning several of the necessary routines over to the logic engines and smaller subroutines to the glowing Prussian capacitors – their route was now fixed, pedestrians and carriages to be avoided if at all possible, the mecha not carrying himself and his companions striding ahead as pawns. Greenwitch Road, taking care to stay as far away from the edge of the Wark as was possible, then a cut through St Georgus Road; the Westminstre Bridge would be under attack but he would perhaps strike the invaders where they thought it least possible. If he could win the other side of the bridge, there was the battle at Whitehall to skirt and the park to traverse, then the Palace.

"Britannia!" he yelled, and the mecha screeched in reply, a hellish cacophony. "*God and Her Majesty!*" And the mecha leapt forward, just as the other mentath, its core-bloated intellect no longer resembling anything human, realised the small insect buzzing at the southeastron edge of Londinium was not smashed, and gathered itself to smite again.

"*Use the cannon!*" Clare bellowed, but Valentinelli had already – much to Clare's relief – decided that such an operation would be advisable. In any case, the cry was lost in the hullabaloo. Metal shrieked, groaning, and the peculiar discharge of the mechas' cannon – bolts of hot energy, crackling and spitting as they cleaved violated air – did not help matters. Valentinelli had torn the leather straps holding the contacts free of his mecha, as had Sigmund at some point in their wild career across

Londinium. The risk of one of the metal discs inside the leather
helmets touching their skin and inducing fatal feedback was too
immense.

Especially as the mecha were jolting as they fired. Clare had
eight remaining out of a dozen; four had been left at Westminstre
– one a shattered hulk, the other three under the control of some
doughty Coldwater Guards in their soot-stained, tattered crimson
uniforms who had been sent to hold the Bridge against this
menace. Good lads, they had ripped the contact helmets free
and taken the controls of the mecha in stride.

The Bridge had been littered with bodies and the smoking
remains of shattered mecha, some with intact golden cores glittering. Many of the bodies were sorcerers or witches and their
Shields; since charm and spell would not work, their only alter-
native had been to stand and die.

The Park was a wasteland of scorch and metal, trees stripped
of their leaves and blasted, the lake boiling from the weird
crackling cannon bolts. Clare stopped, wheeling; his fellow
mecha did the same.

*Wait. They are attacking Buckingham, not St Jemes.* That *must
be where the Queen is.*

Which was a more defensible palace, to be sure, but it rather
altered ·*his* plans. There was no time to explain; Clare urged
the mecha forward, taking over subsidiary control from his
companions. The earth quaked as their cuplike feet drummed,
mud and metal shards flying. Smoke wrung tears from his
stinging eyes, a minor irritant. The other mentath, behind his
massive logic engine, had ceased seeking to swat at Clare as
if he were a horsefly. Instead, the stirred-hive mass of mecha
were running together like sharp metal raindrops on a window
pane. Clare could *feel* them, a painful abscess beneath the skin
of Londinium. The city quivered, a patient under the tooth-
charmer's touch.

Force of numbers would drown what a battering of logic
could not. The other mentath's intellect was a smeared explosion

of living light, diseased and overgrown, swelling hot and painful in the mindscape of the glowing engines.

Mud sucked at the cuplike feet, the Park thrashed out of all recognition. The Palace lifted its brownstone shoulders, shattered windows gaping and bits of its masonry crumbling as the huge arachnoid mecha squatted, its spinneret cannon ready to fire. Squealing wraithlike howls, the ghost-snarled brains trapped in their sloshing jars atop the spider bubbling and struggling for release, their screams a chorus of the damned as the other mentath used them ruthlessly to amplify his own force.

*"ONWARD!"* Clare roared, releasing Sig and Valentinelli's mecha. It wasn't quite proper to force them into the charge, and in any case, he had more than enough to do with his remaining five passengerless mecha so near the immense core and engine burning in the arachnid's abdomen. Capacitors glowing, its eight feet stamping in turn, the gigantic thing braced itself as the spinneret cannon began to glow. The Other – for so Clare had christened the opposing mentath – woke to the danger a fraction of a second too late, and Clare's five mecha hurled themselves on the massive arachnid with futile, fiery abandon. Metal tore, screaming, Prussian capacitors shattering and overloaded cores howling at the abuse, and the Other engaged Clare with a burst of pure logic.

# Chapter Thirty-Six

## An Awakening

It was not the weakness in her limbs, Emma decided. The ground itself was quivering steadily, like a pudding's surface when the dish is jostled. Which was disconcerting, yes, but not *nearly* as disconcerting as the sounds from above.

Clacking razor beaks, the tearing-metal and crunching-bone cries of gryphons, hoarse male shouts, and a swelling sorcerous chant that ripped at her ears and non-physical senses. It was a complex, multilayered chant, a prepared Work of the sort that took months if not years to build. Consonants strained against long whistle-punctuated vowels and strange clicking noises, as if the peculiar personal language of the sorcerer had been married to an older, lipless, scaled tongue of dry fire and sun-basking slowness.

*An Awakening chant, of course.* She hauled herself up grimly, boots slipping on dew-wet rocks, vines tearing under her hands. The trick, she had discovered, was to push as hard as she could with her legs, silently cursing the extraneous material of her skirts. A minor charm to keep the skin on her hands from becoming flayed helped, but her arms shook with exhaustion, her fingers cramping and her neck afire with pain. *The dragon. Hurry, Emma.*

It was a surprise to reach the top of the rocky, almost vertical slope. She hauled herself up as if topping an orchard wall in the days of her Collegia girlhood, and lay full-length and gasping for a moment, protected by a screen of heavy-leafed bushes.

Shadows wheeled overhead, their wings spread. She blinked, sunlight drawing hot water from her unprotected eyes. The shapes were massive, graceful and fluid in the air, afire with jewel-toned brilliance.

*Gryphons. One, two, good heavens, six, seven – Grayson did not have this many!*

It did not matter. She rolled to her side, peering through the screen of brush. Exactly *nothing* would be achieved if she rushed into this. The chant was rising towards consummation, its broken rhythm knitting itself together, and she blinked back more swelling water, seeking to make sense of what she saw.

Lord Grayson's gryphon carriage lay smashed against the foot of an ancient, ruined, moss-cloaked tower. The hill shuddered, the tower flexing as if its mortar were some heavy elastic substance. A milky dome of sorcerous energy shimmered around an indistinct figure, whose posture was nevertheless instantly recognisable: Llewellyn Gwynnfud, Earl of Sellwyth, his pale hair crackling with sorcerous energy and his hands making short stabbing gestures and long passes as the passages of his memorised chant demanded. A prepared Work this long and involved required such a mnemonic dance, breath and movement serving to remind the vocal chords of their next assay.

She recognised the tower, too. *Dinas Emrys. That's where I am. Very well.*

The Prime's five remaining Shields were spread out in a loose semicircle, fending off angry gryphons. Three of the gryphons – two tawny, one black – bore shattered leather and wooden bits, the traces they had used to pull the dead Chancellor's chariot broken and useless, dragging them down. The remaining four lion-birds were slightly smaller, their plumage not as glossy. Wild, she realised with a shock.

*The gryphons are loyal to Britannia; they must guess his aim. This is bloody good luck.*

Two bodies – masses of fur and blood-matted feathers – lay on the stony ground. The Shields had managed to kill two lion-birds; or perhaps that black one had been lost in the chariot crash.

Emma forced herself to stillness. She breathed deeply, listening to the chant, judging the structure of the sorcerous dome protecting Llewellyn. The surface of the hill rippled, in a fashion that would make her ill if she thought too deeply on it, so she put it from her mind and concentrated.

*You are alone, and the gryphons will kill you as likely as Llew; their hunger for sorcerer flesh is immense and they are angry. Then there are the Shields; of course they will view me as a threat. That they are occupied does not mean they cannot spare a moment to slay me.*

Her fingers plucked at her skirts, thoughtfully. They felt something hard, plunged into the pocket, and brought forth Ludovico's dull-bladed knife. Mikal had found a leather sheath for it, and she had tucked it away, not trusting that the Neapolitan would not find some way of reacquiring it if it were not on her person. She had never underestimated the man, and she devoutly hoped she never would.

*Already sensitised. Ah.* The stone at her throat chilled further, ice banding her neck and her fingers aching as if she had stepped outside on a winter's day.

She drew the wicked, black-bladed thing from its dark home, tucked the sheath back in her skirt pocket, and worked her ragged left sleeve up. Braced herself and made a fist, then drew the razor edge lightly over the back of her forearm.

Blood sprang up in a bright line. A hiss escaped her taut lips. The knife vibrated hungrily, its dulled blade drinking in sorcerous force and the energy of spilled blood. The ground below pitched, a wave of fluid motion unreeling from the tower's flexing spike. Rock crumbled, and she was almost thrown over the edge of the hill. She jerked forward, the sound of her crashing progress through the bushes lost in a swelling cacophony. The chant swelled afresh, becoming something akin to Mehitabel the Black's long, slow metal-tearing hiss, and the gryphons redoubled their efforts. One of the Shields – a slim, tensile blond man – was distracted by her sudden appearance, and there was a tawny blur as one of the chariot gryphons darted forward, beak and claws striking with terrible finality. Human flesh tore like paper under iron spikes.

Emma ran, every step a jolt of silver-nailed pain up her legs, jarring her back, twisting her neck. The knife, held low, keened hungrily. She bolted for the space left by the Shield's death, and a shadow drifted over her as one of the wild gryphons dived.

Rolling. Razor claws kissing her tangled hair, shearing a few dark curls free. She spat a Word, sorcery striking snake-quick, and the gryphon screamed as it tumbled away, a spray of bright-red blood hanging in trembling, crystalline air. Gained her feet in a lunge, the Collegia's dancing lessons springing back to life in her abused muscles, and the shimmering globe over Llewellyn tensed, preparing itself for a sorcerous strike. The Shields cried out just as the other Prime's chant rose to a deafening roar, sliding towards a massive organ-noise of grinding conclusion. The tower flexed still further, and it was *not* her imagination – the masonry was running like water, shaping itself as one nail of a gigantic claw tensed.

*For Vortigern is the Great Dragon, the Colourless One*, the *Principia* had whispered, *and the Isle rides upon his back. When he wakes, half the Isle will crumble and Eire become a smoking wasteland. When Vortigern rises, Britannia dies.*

But not, she thought grimly, while Emma Bannon still breathed.

She went to her knees, skirts shredding against jagged rock, gryphons screeching and one of the Shields screaming a filthy word that did not surprise her one bit. Her left hand flashed out, the bright weak dart of sorcery spattering against the globe-shield. But that was merely a distraction. The Shield nearest her bolted in her direction, his broad hand reaching for her left wrist – but it was her *right* hand he should have worried about. It flicked forward, the motion unreeling from her hip just as Jourdain had taught her.

Even in death, her former Shields served her well. The memory of Jourdain's patience was a sting, there and gone, and she realised how much she missed them all.

The knife flashed, blood-sorcery on its blade shredding away as it passed through the globe-shield. The shield flushed red, but the knife itself, freed from its cage of ætheric energy, flew true, its dull blade eating a dart of spring sunlight . . .

. . . and buried itself to the hilt in Llewellyn Gwynfudd's back.

# Chapter Thirty-Seven

## Hardly Bad Company

*I know you*, Clare realised, as his mecha landed with bone-rattling force. The arachnid screeched, one of its massive legs twisted and hanging by a thread of metal. That thread was massive in its own right, but the gigantic mecha listed, its mass knocked off balance. Two of Clare's subordinate mecha tore at the Prussian capacitors lining its abdomen, glass shattering and bolts of energy sparking as they arced.

Sig's mecha crouched on the steps of the Palace below, its cannon crackling as he sought to hold back the tide of frog-headed, slump-shouldered mecha controlled by the Other. The Queen's and Queen's Life Guard – Beefeaters, Coldwater, and other regiments, scarlet and blue flashing through the smoke and dirt – was behind him, firing rifles in blocks and chipping away at the oncoming wall of metal. No few among them were sharpshooters, and the Bavarian had marshalled them to shoot at the golden discs; if the core was shattered, the mecha would engage in a jerky tarantella before it died, smashing its fellows before sinking to the ground in a crackling, dangerous mass of sharp quivering metal.

Valentinelli's mecha dangled, a mess of metal and glass, from the thread holding the almost severed leg. He could not see if the Neapolitan still lived, and in any case, it was academic.

Archibald Clare had tribulations of his own.

The arachnid heaved, and one of Clare's mecha flew, describing a graceful arc before crashing like a falling star in the mess of the Park, a geyser of mud vomiting up from its impact.

_This is not going well._

His own mecha, its cannon twisted into broken spars serving as grappling hooks, wheezed upright. He had been seeking to climb the leg in front of him and get to where he suspected the Other crouched inside the arachnid, contacts clasped to his own head, battering at Clare with streams of cold logic. If Clare could just get _close_ enough, there was a chance of wresting control of the larger logic engine away from the Other. Who was, he realised, Cecil Throckmorton, still not dead, forcing the brains of other mentaths to obey him, and still utterly bloody insane.

The oncoming horde of mecha could not be stopped, though Sig and the Guards were valiant indeed. There were simply too many, and Throckmorton's core was too vast.

Clare tensed every muscle, the mecha around him wheezing and grinding as its tired gears responded. _What am I planning? This is insanity. It is illogical. It is suicide._

It didn't matter.

Clare leapt, the mecha leaping with him. Shredded metal punched into the arachnid's leg; he pumped his arms, seeking to climb. Gears ground even further, pistons popping, the core at his chest furiously hot, shreds of his mecha falling in a silvery rain. Machines did not become tired, but Clare could swear the metal exoskeleton was exhausted. Shearing, fracturing, the rain of silvery bits intensified as capacitors bled away force, the equations multiplying so rapidly his faculties strained at the corners, seeking to juggle them all and push the Other away. It was a doomed battle, and when the core at his chest shattered Clare fell, narrowly missing spearing himself on spikes of discarded steel and glass. The force of the fall drove his breath out in a long howl, his head cracking against the paving.

It was a sheer, illogical miracle he didn't split his bloody skull.

The shock of the core's shattering caught up with him, drawing up his arms and legs in seizure. Hands on him, dragging, the smoke of rifle fire acrid, stinging his throat as he struggled to force air into his recalcitrant lungs. Equations spun inside his head, dancing, flailing like the thing above him.

He went rigid as they dragged him, staring at the massive bulk above him as it yawed, sharply, a ship sailing on thin legs. One leg spasmed, clipping the roof of the Palace, and stone shattered. There was an insect crawling on the vast shining carapace, a thin shadow against the glow of capacitors. Dust choked the daylight, but Clare squinted. He thought he saw—

"*Retreat!*" a familiar voice was yelling, a battlefield roar that would have done a Teuton berserker proud. Sigmund's mecha was a smoking hulk, and it was two of the Guards – hard-faced country boys, one from Dorset if his nose was any indication – dragging Clare along. He tried to make his legs work, but could not. They might as well have been insensate meat, for all his straining will could move them.

"*Inside!*" someone else yelled. "*Here they come! MOVE!*"

*That* was a familiar voice as well, and as Clare was hauled through the Palace's door like a sack of potatoes he wondered just what Mikal was doing here.

A deep, appalling cry rose from among the attacking mecha. "*Prussians!*" Mikal cried, as Sigmund cursed in German. "*Fall back! Brace the doors! Move, you whoresons!*"

*Well, at least Miss Bannon comes by her language honestly.* Clare's eyelids fluttered. Sig bent over him, something damp and cold swiping at Clare's forehead. It was a handkerchief, dipped in God knew what. *Prussians. The mercenaries. They must be very sure of overrunning us. And yes, mecha are not useful inside the Palace. Some part of the conspiracy wants Victrix captured alive, or proof of her death. A mecha cannot report on its victims as a man may.*

"Mentath." Mikal, hoarse and very close. "Why am I not surprised? And . . . where is the assassin?"

"Big *Spinne* outside," Sigmund gasped, for Clare's mouth wouldn't open. "Dead, maybe. *Wer weiss?*"

Now Clare could see the Shield. Grey-cheeked, blood-soaked, his yellow eyes glowing furiously, the man looked positively lethal. Behind him, Eli conferred with a captain in the Guards, glancing every so often at the straining iron-bound door.

"That won't hold for long," Mikal said grimly. "Bring him. Your Majesty?"

And, impossibility of impossibilities, Queen Victrix came into sight, her wan face smudged with masonry dust and terribly weary. An ageless shadow in her dark gaze was Britannia, the ruling spirit's attention turned elsewhere despite the threat to its vessel. "I must reach the Throne."

"Indeed." Mikal did not flinch as a stunning impact hit the door. Several of the Guards were still scurrying to shore its heavy oak with anything that could be moved, including chunks of fallen stone. "Come, then. Eli!"

"What next?" The other Shield looked grimly amused. Half his face was painted bright red with blood, but at least he had found better boots. He was alight with fierce joy, no measure of sleepiness remaining, and Clare found the iron bands constricting his lungs easing.

Sig walloped him on the back hard enough to crack a rib or two. Clare coughed, choked, and almost spewed on the Queen's dust-choked skirts. She did not notice, following Eli out of sight, and Mikal glanced down at Clare.

"Well done, mentath. One of the Guards will find you a weapon. We make our stand before the Throne."

*Oh.* Clare fought down the retching. "Yes." He coughed, violently, turned his head to the side and spat as Sig hauled him up and Clare found that yes, indeed, his legs would carry him. Shakily and uncertainly, but better than not. "Quite. God and Her Majesty, sir. Miss Bannon?"

"Elsewhere." Mikal turned on his heel and strode after the Queen. Sig clapped him on the back again, but more gently, thank God.

"Archie, *mein Herr.*" The Bavarian shook his filthy, bald-shining head. "You are crazy, *mein Freund. Du bist ein Bastard verrücht.*"

Clare coughed again, leaning on Sig's broad shoulder. "Likewise, Siggy. Likewise." *If I must die, this is hardly bad company.*

At his throat, the Bocannon turned to a spot of crystalline ice, and the skin around it began to tingle.

# Chapter Thirty-Eight

## A Life's Work

The globe of protective sorcery shattered, sharp darts of ætheric energy slicing trembling air. Emma skidded to a stop as Llewellyn staggered, the chant faltering. She intended to reach for the hilt, wrench it free, and stab him *again,* and *again*, as many times as it took to make him cease.

She did not have the chance.

A long trailing scream behind her, a wet crunching. One more Shield had fallen. She snapped a glance over her shoulder – the two surviving Shields were fully occupied now keeping the gryphons from their throats. The lion-birds darted in, the smaller wild ones swooping down in tightening circles. There were too many of them; even a Shield of Mikal's calibre would not keep that feathered tide back.

Britannia's steeds would not cease until this threat was contained and their furious hunger sated.

But Emma's immediate concern was the Sorcerer Prime collapsing to his knees before the tower. An altar – a plain slab of stone – glowed before him with hurtful dull-red ætheric charge, buckled and cracked. He struggled to hold the chant, but a gap of a single note opened and became an abyss, the complex interlocking parts shredding and peeling away.

Her throat closed. A moment's regret flashed through her

– with Sight, she could see the towering cathedral of the spell, beautiful in its wholeness for a single instant before cracks of negation raced up its walls and exploded through its windows, twisting and warping the flawless work of a Prime at his best.

A life's work. How long had Llewellyn been planning this?

Questions could wait. She reached for the knife again, but the Prime pitched violently backwards, his body lashed by stray sorcery escaping his control. It descended upon him, his flesh jerking, force a physical body was not meant to bear searching for an outlet and grinding the cohesion of muscle and blood away.

It was not a pleasant death. It replicated the dragon-fuelled simulacrum in Bedlam, shredding him to a rag of shattered bone and blood-painted meat, his eyeballs popping and his hair smoking as the spell, cheated, took its revenge. The knife fell free, chiming on rock; she bent reflexively to retrieve it, her fingers clamping on its slippery hilt. Something else rolled loose too, and her free hand scooped it up with no direction on her part, tucking it into her skirt pocket.

*Oh, Llew.*

The tower dropped back into its accustomed shape with a subliminal *thud*. No longer a single claw of a massive reptilian limb, it was now merely a shattered pile of masonry and moss, leaning as if into a heavy wind.

Shadows wheeled overhead as the gryphons dived, screaming triumphantly, and Emma turned away from the body on its carpet of boiling blood, her hand lifting to shield her face.

The ground settled as well. Vortigern, the colourless dragon, the Third Wyrm and mighty forefather of all the Timeless children still awake in the world, sank into slumber again, the Isle on his back pulled tight like a green and grey counterpane, upon which mites scattered and pursued their little loves and vendettas.

And Emma Bannon, Sorceress Prime, wept.

The silence was as massive as the cacophony beforehand had been, and she lifted her head, wiping her cheeks.

Most of the gryphons had settled into feeding at the fallen Shields and the three lion-bird corpses. The ripping and gurgling sounds were enough to unsettle even *her* stomach. No doubt even Clare's excellent digestion would have difficulty with this.

*Clare.* She swallowed, hard, invisible threads twitching faintly. Londinium was a fair ways away. She had ridden *Khloros* to bloody *Wales*, of all places.

One of the gryphons mantled, hopping a little closer. It was edging away from the carrion and eyeing her sidelong, its gold-ringed pupil holding a small, perfect image of a very tired sorceress armed with a toothpick.

*Oh dear.* Emma swallowed again, drily.

The gryphon's indigo-dyed tongue flicked as its beak opened. It was the remaining black from the carriage, its glossy feathers throwing back the morning sun with a blue-underlit vengeance.

"*Vortigern*," it whistled. "Vortigern still sleeps, sorceress."

*That was the whole point of this exercise, was it not? And now I have other matters to attend to.* The hilt, slippery with blood and her sweat, was pulsing-warm in her clenched fist. "Yes."

"We are *hungry*." Its beak clacked.

"You have the dead to feast upon," she pointed out. "And Vortigern sleeps."

In other words, *I have done you a favour. I am loyal to Britannia, as you are.* Or, more plainly, *Please don't eat me.*

It actually laughed at her. Its claws flexed, and the reek of blood and split bowel tore at Emma's nose. Blood could drive the beasts into a frenzy—

The invisible threads tied to a pendant twitched again. For such a movement to reach her *here* meant Clare was in dire trouble indeed.

"I am sorry," she told the gryphon, and her grip on the knife shifted. The stone at her throat, frost-cold, became a spot of ice so fierce it burned, and she knew a charter symbol would be rising through its depths, shimmering and taking form in tangled lines of golden ætheric force.

The beast laughed again, its haunches rising slightly as it prepared to spring. Its feathers ruffled, and its pupil was so dark, the gold of its iris so bright. "So am I, Sorceress. But *we are hungry.*"

Force uncoiled inside her. She was exhausted, mental and emotional muscles strained from the opening of her Discipline. Her sorcerous Will was strong, yes, but the toll of ætheric force channelled through her physical body dragged her down. It would slow her, just at the moment she needed speed and strength most.

*I am not ready to die.* She knew it did not matter. Death was here all the same, the payment demanded by *Khloros.* Death was inevitable.

Her fingers tightened on the knife's hilt. Inevitable as well was Emma Bannon's refusal to die quietly.

Even for Victrix.

The gryphon sprang.

# Chapter Thirty-Nine

## Who Dies Next?

The inner courtyard of the Palace, choked with drifts of dust and quaking underfoot, opened around them. The front door had broken, and the brown-jacketed Prussian mercenaries with their white armbands poured through, firing as they advanced. Many of the Guard fell, buying time for Victrix to flee through the halls. All that remained was to cross the courtyard and gain the relative safety of the Throne Hall.

Though how that great glass-roofed hall could shelter them was somewhat fuzzy to Clare. He suspected he was not thinking clearly.

Clare limped along, Sigmund hauling him, the vast shadow of the arachnid mecha stagger-thrashing above. Stone crumbled, the centuries of building and replacement work smashed in a moment. Something was wrong – the arachnid reeled drunkenly, shattering glass from its capacitors falling like daggers.

Victrix stumbled. Mikal and Eli all but carried her, one on either side, and the Guard fanned out. Rifleshot popped on the stones around them – the Prussians had gained height and were firing from the windows. The door to the Throne Hall had never seemed so far away.

They plunged into dust-swirling darkness just as a massive

grinding thud smashed in the courtyard. A gigantic warm hand lifted Clare and flung him; he landed with a crunch and briefly lost consciousness. He surfaced in a soupy daze, carried between Sig and a bleeding, husky Guard with a bandaged head and a limp, who nevertheless moved with admirable speed. Breaking glass tinkled sweetly overhead, and the Bocannon at his chest was a fiery cicatrice.

Shouts. Confusion. Mikal's hoarse hissing battle cry. Queen Victrix screamed, a note of frustration and terror as mercenaries poured in through the side doors.

Clare lifted his head. He blinked, dazed. There was another giant impact, and he realised he'd been half-conscious for too long. They were surrounded, Mikal and Eli flanking the Queen, whose young face was pale, one cheek terribly bruised and her dark hair falling in ragged strands.

*Miss Bannon looks much better dishevelled*, he thought, and the illogical nature of the reflection shocked him far more than the queer swimming sensation all through his limbs.

Sig had a pistol from somewhere. He was grim and pale, covered in dust and soot, and his mouth pulled down at both corners. A jab of regret stabbed Clare's chest. He should not have drawn his friend into this.

They were all about to die. Except possibly Victrix, whose face aged in a split second, Britannia resurfacing from wherever Her attention had been drawn, alert to the threat to Her vessel.

More shattering glass. The ground quaked violently, almost throwing Clare from his feet.

Then they descended.

The glass fell in sheets. The ancient roof of the Throne Room bucked, snapped, and fell, the shards – some as long as a man's body – miraculously avoiding the knot of Guards, Shields, and mentath-and-genius. The sound was immense, titanic, the grinding of ice floes, as if the earth itself had gone mad and sought to rid itself of humanity.

The gryphon was massive, and black. Its eyes were holes of

runnelling unholy red flame. Driven into the top of its sleek skull was a fiery red nail, a star of hurtful brilliance.

Perched on its back was a battered, wan, half-clothed Miss Bannon. Her dress had been ripped to tatters and her hair was an outrageous mess stiff with dirt, sticks, feathers, and matted blood. Bruising ran over every inch of flesh he could see, and the other shadows were more gryphons, breaking through the roof as Miss Bannon slid from the beast's back. The red flame winked out, and the deadwinged beast slumped to the strewn floor. It twisted, shrivelling, dust racing through its feathers and eating at its glossy hide.

The dead gryphon collapsed. Miss Bannon bent, wrenching the nail from its head.

It was a knife, and it dripped with crackling red as she turned. The Prussian mob drew back, the feathers in their hats nodding as her gaze raked them, slow and terrible.

"*Gryphons*," Britannia whispered, through the Queen's mouth. The single word was horrifying, as cold and ageless as the Themis itself, a welter of power and command.

Miss Bannon nodded, once. She did not sway, her back iron-rigid, but something was wrong. She held herself oddly, and her gaze was terrifyingly blank. Clare groped to think of just what was amiss.

The sorceress looked . . . as if she had forgotten her very *self*.

"Who dies next?" she murmured, very clearly, the words dropping into a sudden rustling silence as gryphons drifted down to land, their claws digging into stone and fallen timber, making slight scratching noises against steel. "*Who?*"

The first Prussian screamed.

After that, the gryphons feasted. But Clare gratefully closed his eyes, finally able to cease deducing. The inside of his skull felt scraped clean and queerly *open*. For once, he did not want to see.

The sounds were bad enough.

# Chapter Forty

## The Need Was Dire

B ritannia's vessel halted a fair distance away. "Emma?" Abruptly, Victrix sounded very young. Perhaps it was all the dust in the air. Or perhaps it was the ringing in Emma's ears.

She suspected she would pay for this episode very soon, and in bloody coin.

The gryphons pressed forward. They had made short work of the brown-coated mercenaries, and in the courtyard was a vast wreck of metal and glass she had only indirectly glimpsed as she struggled to keep the brain-stabbed gryphon in the air. It seemed Clare and company had endured their own travails.

"Your Majesty." She swayed, and suddenly Mikal was at her side. His fingers closed around her arm, and she leaned into that support, too exhausted to be grateful. She felt nothing but a vast drowning weariness. "I murdered one of your steeds, Britannia. You may punish me as you see fit. However, before you do, I beg leave to report that the Earl of Sellwyth is dead and Vortigern still sleeps. Your steeds had most of the stopping of Lord Sellwyth. I did not serve them well."

The body of the black gryphon – the knife, driven with exactitude into the tiny space between the back of the skull and the top vertebrae – bubbled as it rotted swiftly, the stresses endured by its physical fabric as she forced it to fly for

Londinium with its fellows in hot pursuit unravelling it.

The gryphons would not be able to eat their brother, and that was the worst that could befall one of their number.

They would not forgive her for this.

"Lord Sellwyth." The Queen's face was bruised, but granite-hard. Britannia settled fully into Her vessel and regarded Emma with bright eyes, glowing dust over a river of ancient power. "He sought to awaken Vortigern."

*I am not certain he was the only one who sought to do so. I do know he almost succeeded.* "I caught him at Dinas Emrys. Which is, I believe, part of his family's ancestral holdings." She fought to stay conscious, heard the queer flatness of her tone. Eli appeared on her other side, looking sadly the worse for wear. "I beg your pardon for the method of my return, but the need was dire."

*Where is Clare?* She glanced at Mikal, who stared at Britannia, a muscle flicking in his jaw. *I do not like that I cannot see him. And Ludovico, where is he?* The knife in her right hand dangled; she could not make her fingers unlock from the hilt.

A Word to steal the gryphon's breath, another Word to snap iron bands about its wings, and she had driven the knife into its brain and uttered the third Word, the most terrible and scorching one of all, expending so much of her stored sorcerous force she almost lost consciousness, holding grimly on to one single thought. *Londinium. Find the Queen.*

And the dead body had obeyed the Endor in her. It had *flown*.

"So it was. We shall inform you of any punishment later." The Queen nodded, slowly. "We do not think it will be too severe."

"*Blasphemy!*" one of the gryphons howled. They rustled, pressing close, and Mikal tensed next to Emma. She leaned into him even further, for her legs were failing her and even the dim, dust-choked light in the Hall was too scorch-bright for her sensitised eyes. "*She robbed the dead!*"

*I did so much more than that. The beasts will not forgive this, and their memory is long.* "Mikal." Her heart stuttered, her body finally rebelling against the demands she had placed upon it. "*Mikal.*"

He bent his head slightly, his eyes never leaving the Queen. "Emma."

*He would kill Britannia Herself, did he judge Her a threat to me.* The realisation, quiet but thunderous, loosed the last shackle of her will.

"I have been cruel to you." The whisper was so faint, she doubted he heard her. "I should not have . . . Forgive me."

"There is no—" he began, but darkness swallowed Emma whole.

# *Chapter Forty-One*

## *Amenable to Control*

"A nd this is the killer of that gigantic *thing*." Victrix inclined her head. "We are grateful, Mr Valentinelli. You performed a great service to Britannia."

The Neapolitan swept a painful, creaky bow. Both his eyes were swollen nearly shut, half his hair singed off, and his face was such a mass of cuts and welts it was difficult to see the pox scars. His clothes were in ribbons, and one of his boots was nothing more than a band of leather about his ankle and calf, the rest of it cut away and the stocking underneath filthy and draggled. "It is nothing, *maestra*. Valentinelli is at your service."

Clare's neck ached. The tension would not leave him. "Cecil Throckmorton. He was mad, Your Majesty, but he was also *used*."

"Used by whom?" The Queen half turned, pacing away, and Clare forced his legs to work. He and Sigmund held each other like a pair of drunks.

The smaller gryphons took wing, their shadows pouring over the glass- and rubble-strewn floor. The sound was immense, a vault filled with brushing feathers. The dust was settling.

Clare suppressed a sigh. But this was *important*; he must make the Queen understand. "There were three parts to this conspiracy. Miss Bannon dealt with those who wished Britannia and the Isle erased from existence; she judged that the larger threat. One part of the conspiracy simply wished Britannia inconvenienced, however they could effect that – I would look to the Prussian ambassador, who will no doubt deny everything, since they were mercenaries and, by very dint of that, expendable. The third part of the conspiracy troubles me most, Your Majesty. It wished *you*, personally, Britannia's current vessel, under control."

"Control." Victrix paused for a moment. Her shoulders came up, and she stalked for the high-backed Throne, the Stone of Scorn underneath its front northern leg shimmering soft silver as she approached. The Throne itself, undamaged, gleamed with precious stones.

It looked, Clare decided, dashed uncomfortable. But Victrix climbed the seven steps, turned sharply so her dust-laden skirts swirled, and sat. Sigmund might have gone up the steps as well, but Clare dug his heels in, and was strong enough to make him stop.

Victrix propped one elbow on the Throne's northern arm, rested her chin upon her hand. The Guards searching through the rubble for wounded compatriots were hushed, muttering among themselves. Men moaned in pain or shock. The Queen closed her eyes, and Clare could have sworn he felt the entire Isle shiver once as Britannia, enthroned, turned Her attention inward.

"And do you think," the Queen finally said, "that Britannia is amenable to *control*?"

"Not Britannia," he corrected, a trifle pedantic. "*Victrix*, Your Majesty. Wounded, frightened, faced with three conspiracies working in tandem? Your Majesty might well rely on . . . improper advice." Then he shut his mouth, almost . . . yes, almost *afraid* he had said too much.

"Well said, sir." Britannia sighed, Her chin sinking on to Her hand as if it weighed far more than it should. "Yet, as long as

We possess subjects of such courage and loyalty as yourself, We shall not worry overmuch."

"Miss Bannon deserves the credit, Your Majesty." He sounded stiff even to himself, but it was merely the agony of exhaustion weighing him down. Staying upright and speaking consumed a great deal of his attention.

A ghost of amusement passed over Britannia's closed, somnolent face. "No doubt she would lay it at your door."

"She is too kind."

"Not at all, mentath. We think it best you leave now. Our Consort approaches, and We wish a private word with him."

Clare thought of protesting. Valentinelli gripped his free arm, though, and it occurred to him that discretion was perhaps wiser than anything he might say, however well founded the chain of logic that led to his suspicions. "Yes, mum. I mean, Your Majesty. By your leave." *Oh, what* is *the proper etiquette for taking leave of one's sovereign in these circumstances?*

"Mentath. Mr Clare." Britannia's eyes half opened, and the aged face rising underneath Victrix's young countenance sent a most illogical shiver down Clare's spine. Her eyes were indigo from lid to lid, small sparks like stars floating over depths he found he did not wish to examine too closely. What would it be like to clasp such a being in one's arms?

No, he did not envy the Consort. Not at all. "Yes, Your Majesty?"

"Make certain Miss Bannon may find you and your companions. We shall wish to reward you, when We have sorted this unpleasantness through." Her eyelids fell again, and Clare heard the drumming of approaching feet, shouts, and crunching of glass.

What *did* one say in this exotic situation? "Yes. Er, thank you, Your Majesty."

Sig tugged him in one direction, Valentinelli in another. They finally decided on a course, Clare's head hanging so low he did not see anything but his own filthy boots dragged over rubble and dust. When he passed into a soup of half-consciousness, it was welcome, his overstrained faculties deciding they required a retreat from recent events. He heartily agreed.

The last thing he heard was Sig's muttering, and Valentinelli's non-committal grunts in reply.

"Just one," the Bavarian kept repeating. "You hear me, *Italiensch*? One mecha. We drag it to workshop. I feed you wurst. You help me."

# Chapter Forty-Two

## A Most Logical Sorceress

Emma slept for two and a half days, not even waking when Tideturn flushed her with sorcerous force. She finally surfaced to greet a fine clear Thursday dawn, spring sunlight piercing the haze of Londinium and the reek of the city cheerfully pungent, stray breaths of it creeping even into her dressing room.

The servants were slightly nervous, unused to seeing her in such a terrible state. Battered and tattered, of course, but even her corset stays had been broken, and she winced at the thought of the flesh she had shown. A hot bath, Isobel and Catherine's attentions, and a good dose of Severine's fussing brought her to feeling almost human again. *Chocolat* and croissants did *not* satisfy; her mirror informed her she was unbecomingly gaunt, even if the bruises had largely faded. She rang for Mr Finch as soon as was decently possible, and told him to send out for the broadsheets. Which arrived, ink still venomously wet, as she descended to a hearty breakfast.

Cook, it seemed, had missed her as well.

The story bruited about in the press was an Alteration experiment gone terribly wrong. It satisfied most and left the rest with a clear warning not to speak of their uncertainties. Emma found herself licking her fingers free of jam and contemplating another platter of bangers when the breakfast room door flew open and Mikal appeared.

He was just the same, from buttoned-up coat to flaming yellow eyes. Behind him, Eli ducked his dark head. They had evidently been at practice; the fume of recent exertion hung on them both. It was a relief to see Eli in proper boots; Mr Finch was a wonder.

Her heart leapt behind its cage of ribs and stays; the weight in her skirt pocket seemed twice as heavy. She ignored both sensations, though Mikal's gaze almost caused a guilty flush to rise up her throat.

"Good morning, Shields," she greeted them. "If you have not breakfasted, please do so. But I warn you, should you come between me and those bangers, I shall be *quite* vexed." She touched her skirt pocket, took her hand away with an effort. "Mikal. What news?"

"A pouch sent from the Palace, daily visits from the mentath enquiring after your health. He is due again for tea today. Valentinelli is still trailing him, despite being paid." Mikal filled himself a plate and glanced at Eli. "Eli finds your service most exciting."

"Too exciting?" She tried not to appear amused, suspected she failed.

"No, mum." The other Shield eyed the ravaged breakfast table. It was a relief to be in the presence of those who understood a sorcerer's hunger after such events. "Rather a change, that's all. Proud to be here."

*Well, that's good.* "Should you change your mind, Shield, do feel free to say so. I keep none in my service who would prefer to be elsewhere. Mikal, about Ludovico—"

"I gave him fifty guineas, Prima. Considering that he performed extraordinarily, killed Mr Throckmorton, and brought down a rather large mecha almost by himself. Would you care to hear of it now? Clare has given me the particulars."

She settled herself more firmly in the chair. "Certainly. Eli,

before you eat, please fetch the pouch from the Palace. No doubt
it is in my library . . .?"

"Of course." He was gone in a flash, closing the door quietly.

Mikal did not look at her. He settled in his customary seat,
his plate before him just so.

Emma waited. Silence stretched between them. The lump in
her pocket was an accusing weight.

He toyed with his fork, long, oddly delicate fingers running
over its silver curves. Still did not look at her.

*You will not make this easy.* "Thank you."

"No thanks are—"

"Accept my thanks, Shield."

That brought his hot yellow gaze up to hers. "Only your
thanks?"

Unbecoming heat finally rose in her cheeks. "At the breakfast
table, yes."

"And otherwise?"

*Otherwise? I do as I please, Shield. But let us speak of the
main thing.* "Sellwyth could have killed you."

"And he almost killed you. Do you think I do not *know*? It
does not *matter,* Emma. I am your Shield. That is *final,* so
whatever game you are pursuing, cease."

A faint smile touched her lips. "Did you just give me an
order?"

"If you are testing to see if I am *serious,* if I can be *trusted*—"

*I do not forget the sound Crawford made when you choked
the life out of him. But you did so for me.*

*Even a Shield may be, in the end, merely a man. Yet I am
grateful for it.* "I misjudged you once, Mikal. Never again."

"Are you so certain?" A spark in his gaze, one she found she
rather liked.

"Eat your breakfast." She snapped a broadsheet open and
examined it critically. "But leave those bangers alone. Else I
*will* be vexed, Shield."

"God save us all from that," he muttered. But he was smiling, she saw as she peeked over the edge of the broadsheet. A curious lightness began in the region of Emma's chest. She disciplined it, and returned to her work.

The solarium was drenched in golden late-afternoon light, the charter symbols wedded to the glass cooling the sun's glare enough to be pleasant. The plants sang in their climate globes, and Emma poured the tea. The wicker tables and chairs glowed, each edge clean and bright.

When she had handed the teacup over, she produced the parchment, rolled tightly and bound with red wax. "Your licence is reinstated. You are commissioned as one of the Queen's Own; also, you are to be knighted. Congratulations."

The mentath's long, mournful face pinkened slightly as he accepted the scroll, but he still looked grave. "There are still unanswered questions, Miss Bannon."

*And you do not like unanswered questions.* "Chief among them is the identity of Grayson's paymaster. Though he was Chancellor of the Exchequer, and had access to a variety of funds." Emma nodded, her curls brushing her cheeks. It was bloody *luxurious* to sit and have a quiet cuppa, and to wear an afternoon dress that had not been torn by some unpleasantness. "Suffice to say, there are personages we may not move directly against, no matter *how* high we may temporarily be in royal esteem. However, we have stung their fingers mightily, and now I may watch them. Which will be all the more easy, given recent events."

"Ah yes, your creation as Countess Sellwyth. Congratulations to *you.*"

*Britannia has her own strange sense of justice, and She wishes Dinas Emrys watched.* "That was not what I was referring to." She indicated the tiers of dainties. *And I do not want your nimble brain worrying at the question of who crafted the simulacrum in Bedlam. Even if it is a question that probably will not interest you, it is too dangerous for you to pursue.* "Please. You look rather not your usual self, Mr Clare."

He set to with a will. Apparently his digestion was still excellent. "There is something else that troubles me. Sellwyth's family held that place for generations. What made him think *now* was the proper time to unleash its, erm, occupant?"

*They offered him something his ambition could not refuse.* Emma shrugged. *And now I am left wondering what* my *ambition cannot refuse. We are alike, Llew and I, more than even he suspected.* "Who can tell? He was Throckmorton's paymaster, that much is certain; the mentath kept that secret very well. Pity Valentinelli killed him, though I understand it was necessary. Was he truly bollixing about with Alterative sorcery, I wonder?"

Clare looked a trifle uncomfortable for a few moments. "Mad. He was utterly mad. Throckmorton, I mean. Oh. Mr Baerbarth sends his regards, by the way. He was quite put out that he could not examine one of the mecha at leisure."

"Perhaps something can be arranged." The core and the large logic engine, of course, had been moved in secret. It was only a matter of time before someone else created something similar, and Emma half suspected Clare's first project as one of the Queen's commissioned geniuses would have something to do with preparing the Empire for such an eventuality.

"He would be most pleased. Also, Signor Valentinelli—"

"Will cease following you very soon; if he visits tomorrow, I may release the binding on him."

"Well, that's just the thing." Clare pinkened again. "He extends his regrets, but says he wishes no such thing. He rather likes the excitement, you see, though I've told him a mentath's life is usually deadly boring. He says he has grown too old for his usual line of work, and I apparently need some looking after. He sounds like an old maiden aunt, frankly, and the sooner you send him on his merry way the better."

"Ah." Her mouth wanted to twitch. *Oh, Ludo. You have ideas, I see.* "Well. He did seem to have taken a liking to you." She took a mannerly sip of tea, finding it had cooled most agreeably. The savouries looked very appetising indeed, and she was hungry again. It would take time to regain the lost weight.

"You mean, each time he threatens to duel me after your spell is taken off is a mark of affection? He is quite fond of that threat."

"He must enjoy your company." *And that bears watching too.* "How very droll."

The conversation turned to other things, and Clare did his best to observe the pleasantries. It irked him, though, and she could see the irritation rising in him. After another cup and a few pastries he began the process of taking his leave. He had a question of research waiting for him at his lodgings, and regretted leaving her so soon, et cetera, et cetera.

It was no surprise, though she did feel a slight sting.

Emma rose, and offered her hand. "Mr Clare, *Do* be reasonable. You have endured much in the service of Britannia, and I thank you for your courage and the care you have shown for the Empire's interests. You are under no social obligation to me. I know how sorcery . . . discommodes you."

He took her hand, pumped it twice. He was outright crimson now. "Not the case," he mumbled, swallowed visibly. "Not the case at all. Miss Bannon, you are . . . You are a . . ."

She waited, patiently. He did not turn loose her hand. There were many words he could choose. *Sorceress. Bitch. Whore. Managing female.*

He finally found one that suited him, drew himself up. "You, Miss Bannon, are a very *logical* sorceress."

Her jaw threatened to drop. Of all the epithets flung at her, she had never experienced *that* one. A second, very queer lightness began in the region of Emma's chest. "Thank you."

He nodded, dropped her hand as if it had burned him, and turned to leave.

"Mr Clare."

He stopped next to a false orange tree. The climate globe

around it jangled sweetly. His thinning hair did not disguise the way the skin over his pate was even more deeply crimson.

Thankfully, she had a gift she could offer to match his own. "I trust your digestion is still sound?"

"As a bell, madam." He did not turn to face her.

Emma took a deep breath. "May I invite you to dinner? Perhaps on Sunday? You may bring Ludovico, and Mr Baerbarth. If they wish to attend." *If they wish to avail themselves of my table without absolutely being required to do so. Odd. This is the first time* that *has occurred.*

Clare turned, retraced his steps, grabbed her hand, and pumped it furiously. "I say! Of course! Honoured to. *Honoured.* Sig will be beside himself."

"Sunday, then. Shall we say six? I dine early."

"Certainly!" And after a few more furious pumps of her hand, he was gone. She closed her eyes, tracing his progress through the house. Mr Finch let him out of the front door, and by the time Clare reached the laurel hedge he was whistling.

She brought her attention back to the sunroom. Mikal would be along at any moment. Her hand had slid into her skirt pocket, and she drew forth the stone that had fallen from Llewellyn's body. It had been on her nightstand when she awoke.

Had Mikal placed it there? Did he have any idea what it was?

It was deep red, flat on one side and curved on the other. Smooth and glassy, and when she tilted it, it throbbed. A pulse too deep for the stone's shallowness, a slow, steady beat.

Like a dragon's heart, perchance.

*Two stones, and he was reserving one? One stone gifted to him in advance, one later? Or there was only one stone to begin with, and he was paid at the beginning? But how could they be certain he would do what they wished? And who among the wyrms would have slain one of their own young for this?*

*Who crafted that simulacrum in Bedlam?*

She cupped the stone in her gloved hands. Its pulse slowed as it basked, drinking in the sunlight.

*The gryphons were at his body. And should I visit Dinas Emrys now, I would find nothing but anonymous bones. Still . . . it troubles me.*

Llewellyn Gwynnfud had always troubled her.

It was difficult to undo her bodice, but she managed. She slid the stone against the bare skin of her chest, tucking it securely under the top edge of her corset. Uncomfortable, but only temporary.

*You are right, Mr Clare. There are quite a few unanswered questions.*

She breathed out a long, slow, single sorcerous Word.

There was a melting sensation over her heart as the Philosopher's Stone sank into her skin. A flush of warmth tingled through every particle of her flesh. Her head tipped back, and the solarium dimmed. The rush of flame in her veins was a welcoming heat, gentle and inviting.

In the end, she decided, it mattered little. She was Prime and in the service of Britannia, and if another wyrm raised its head, she would crush it underfoot.

Smiling, Emma Bannon set her bodice to rights, and decided on another cup of tea.

# Rankes of those Sorcerousse

(taken from the Domesnight List)

**Minor:**     Charter[1] (lightfinger, bakewell)
Charmer (hedgecharmer, charing-charmer)
Mancer (hevvymancer, pickmancer)
Skellewreyn (not used past 1715[2])

**Commons:**  Witch[3]

---

1 The ability to draw a simple charter-symbol in charming is available even to the non-sorcerous. Those of very faint talent may perform the simplest of charter-symbols as long as said symbols are "married" to a physical item. A charmer must be able to hold a charter-symbol in free air for at least a few moments in order to be apprenticed; it is legal to indenture charters but not charmers or above.
2 The last Skellewreyn, the famous and rebellious Agnes Nice, was hung in 1712 in Hardwitch. Afterward, Skellewreyn – too much talent to be a mancer and not enough to be a properly-Disciplined witch, driven mad and physically twisted by their sorcery – did not appear, or if they did, they kept to certain shadows. Some of the Morloks are rumored to be of their ilk.

**Major:**   Sorcerer
        Master Sorcerer
        Adeptus
        Prime

---

3 Witches are held to be Common, since their Discipline fills their entire brain with no room left for the "splitting" of focus a Sorcerer or above must perform. A Sorcerer may perform a Greater Work without losing track of one's whereabouts; a Master Sorcerer or Adeptus may move physically while performing a Greater Work, and of course a Prime may successfully assay more than one Greater Work at once.

*. . . it is not required to possess a mentath's faculties in order to Observe, and to reap the benefits of said observation. Indeed, many mentaths are singularly unconcerned with any event or thing outside their chosen field of study, while a rich treasure trove of wondrous variety unreels before their very noses. A mere observer skilled in the science of Deduction may surprise even a mentath, and has the added benefit of a great deal of practical knowledge and foresight ever at hand. The faculty of Observation lies within each man competent enough, and taught to, read; it may be strengthened with practice, and indeed grows ever stronger the more one exercizes it.*

*If Observation is the foundation all Deduction is built upon, then the quality of Decision is the mortar holding fast the stones. Tiny details may be important, but it is of greatest necessitude to decide which details bear weight and which are chaff. Perfect, unclouded decision upon details is the purview of the Divine, and man's angelic faculties, wonderful as they are, are merely a wretched imitation. Even that wretchedness can be useful, much as the example of Vice's ultimate end may serve to keep Virtue from the wide and easy path to Ruin.*

*Much as Time seeks to bring down every building, and Vice seeks to bring down every Virtue, the treacherous Assumption ever seeks to intrude a detail's importance wrongly into Deduction. A proper Assumption may save a great deal of time and trouble, but an improper Assumption is a foul stinking beast, ever ready to founder the ship of Logic upon the rocks of Inaccuracy.*

*Fortunately, the weapons of Reason and Observation do much to overthrow the false faces of Assumption. The decision to carefully and thoroughly question each Assumption as if it is a criminal, or a fool who does not differentiate Fact from Fancy, will serve each person seeking to strengthen his habit of Deduction faithfully. As the organs of Reason and Observation strengthen, the art of quickly finding the correct details becomes natural.*

*We shall start with a series of Exercizes to strengthen the faculty of Observation any Reader assaying this humble work possesses. These Exercizes are to be done daily, upon waking and retiring, and at diverse points through the Reader's daily work as opportunity permits . . .*

— From the Preface, *The Art and Science of Deduction*, Mr Archibald Clare

# *Acknowledgements*

Thanks are due to the long list of the Usual Suspects: Miriam and Devi, for believing in my crazed little stories; my children for understanding why I hunch over typing for long periods of time; Mel for gently keeping me sane; Christa and Sixten for love and coffee. Thanks are also due to Lee Jackson for his love of Victoriana, and to Susan Barnes (soon to be a Usual Suspect) for putting up with me. And finally, as always, once again I will thank you, my Readers, in the way we both like best. Sit back, relax, and let me tell you a story...

*To the strangers*

# Historical Note

*I* *regret to inform the Reader that I have, as they say, played fast and loose with History. Being a subjective wench in several regards, History did not seem to mind, but some who peruse these books may. I can only say that whatever errors and inaccuracies are contained herein, they are for the most part lovingly and carefully chosen; any that are not, are the regrettable result of cracks and defaults that occur even in the best Research For The Purposes Of Almost-Historical Fiction, and the fault of Your Ob't Servant, namely, the Humble Author.*

*And now, my best and most faithful darlings, my Readers, let me welcome you once again into Londinium, where the smoke rises, the sorcery glitters, and the clockworks thrum . . .*

# Chapter One

## Not How Things Are Done

*I am too bloody old for this.*

Archibald Clare spat blood and surged upward. He gave the struggling fellow opposite him two quick jabs to the head, hoping to calm the situation somewhat. Foul knee-deep semiliquid splashed, dark as sin and smelly as the third circle of Hell. Clare gained his footing, unwilling to deduce what deep organic sludge his boots were slipping in, and retched painlessly. Blood from his broken nose, trickling down the back of his throat, was making his stomach *decidedly* unhappy.

*Where is that blasted Italian?*

He had no worry to spare for Valentinelli. For Clare strongly suspected he had other problems, especially if what his faculties – sharpened by coja and burning like a many-sided star of logic and deduction inside his skull –

were telling him was truly so. If, indeed, the man in the long academician's gown struggling in Clare's fists, spluttering wildly and half-drowned, was not Dr Francis Vance . . .

. . . Clare would not only perhaps have quite a bit of explaining to do, but would also have been bested *again* by the sodding criminal bastard.

The man in Clare's grasp ceased thrashing quite so frantically. Since he was being held under some of the foulest sewage drained nightly into the Themis, it was not so amazing. However, Clare judged that his opponent was about to drown, and further judged his own faculties were *not* stunned by the knock on the skull he'd taken earlier that night. Which made his opponent a potentially valuable source of information from whence to deduce Dr Vance's whereabouts and further plans.

Besides, drowning a man in shite was not, as Emma Bannon would say archly, how things were *done*.

*Now why should I think of her?* Clare freed the obstruction from his throat with a thick venomous cough, wished he hadn't because the reek was thick enough to chew, and dragged the false Vance up from a watery grave.

Choking, spluttering words more fit for a drover or a struggling hevvymancer than the man of quality Dr Vance purported to be, Clare's bespattered opponent hung in his narrow fists like wet washing. Clare's chest was uncomfortably tight, a rock lodged behind his ribs, and he wheezed most unbecomingly as his trapped opponent tried gamely to sink a knee into the most tender spot of Clare's anatomy.

*Bad form, sir.* So Clare took the man's feet out from under him and dunked him again, boots slipping in the sludge coating whatever passed as a floor to this foul tunnel. The echoes held a peculiar quality that made Clare think this part of Londinium's sewers were built of slowly crumbling brick, which made them not quite as ancient as those built by the Pax Latium. *Newer* often meant *sturdier*, but not always. The Latiums had believed in solid stone even for a cloaca on the benighted edge of their empire.

*An encouraging observation. Or not.* He hawked and spat again, grateful he could not see the colour of whatever bodily fluid he had just thrown into the dark. His face would be a mask of bruising upon the morrow.

He hauled the man forth from the sewerage again, and wished his sensitive nose would cease its operation for a few moments. "Be reasonable!" he barked, and the echoes gave him more of the dimensions of the tunnel. Quite large, really, and quite a volume of almost-fluid moving through its throat. His busy faculties calculated the rate of flow and returned the answer that Clare was lucky it was a slurry; he would have been swept off his feet and drowned had it been any thinner. "Vance! *Where is he?*"

The besmeared visage before him contorted; there was a sharp tooth-shattering crack. Another odd sound rose under the plashing and plinking. What little unhealthy gleaming there was showed a rather oddly coloured face under a stringy mass of black hair, a hooked nose decked with excrescence, and rotting teeth as the man Clare had been chasing howled with laughter.

*Dear God, what—*

The laughter swelled obscenely, and the man in his grasp went into convulsions. More filth splashed, and Clare swore with a ferocity that would perhaps have shocked even Miss Bannon, who could – he had discovered – let loose torrents of language that would make even the ill-tempered drabs of Whitchapel blush.

*Poison tooth, broken open. Of course.* And the reek blocked his olfactory capability, so he likely would not discover what variety of toxin in time to halt its progress.

Dr Vance was not above sacrificing a hireling or two. They were pawns, and life was cheap on Londinium's underside. For the promise of a shilling, much worse than this murderous diversion had been committed – probably several times over tonight, in the depths of the city. Or even in the past hour.

Clare swore again, dragging the suddenly stiff body towards the tunnel's entrance. He now remembered falling off the lip of the adjoining tunnel, splashing into this fetching summer garden of a place with a bone-rattling thump. The rock in his chest squeezed again, his left shoulder complaining as well. Perhaps he had strained it, in the excitement. He had chased the good Doctor from one end of Londinium to the other over the past two days, and at least denied the man his true prize – or so Clare hoped.

"Eh, *mentale*." A flat, queerly accented voice, falling against the thick water without so much as an echo. "You are *loud* tonight."

"Poisoned tooth!" Short of breath and patience, Clare was nevertheless gratified to find the Neapolitan assassin, as usual, did not ask useless questions. Instead, sleek dark Ludovico Valentinelli splashed into the muck a trifle more gracefully than his employer had, and relieved Clare of the burden of his erstwhile opponent. A different foul reek arose.

The man had voided his bowels. It was, Clare reflected, almost a cleaner stink. Certainly fresher, though hardly *better*.

He took in tiny sips of the fœtidness and choked. "Damn the man," he managed. "*Damn* him!"

"Too late!" Ludo was, as usual, infuriatingly cheerful. "He has risen to Heaven, *signore*. Or to Hell, who knows?"

"B-bring the b-body." Why were his teeth chattering? And his chest was even tighter, iron bands seizing his ribs. "D-dissection."

Ludo found this funny. At least, he gave a gravelly chuckle. "You are certainly no *Inquisitore*." He hauled the corpse to the entrance, heaving it up with little grace but much efficiency. Then, the assassin splashed back to Clare, who was suddenly much occupied in keeping upright. "*Mentale?*"

*How strange. I cannot breathe. Not that I wish to, down here, and yet . . .* "V-v-val—"

He was still seeking to speak Valentinelli's name when the pain clove his chest and felled him. The thick darkness was full of things no gentleman would wish soiling his cloth, and Clare's busy faculties, starlike, winked out.

# Chapter Two

## A Duke to Chastise

Inside the stoic, well-bred walls of 34½ Brooke Street, Mayefair, Londinium, a quiet bustle of orderly activity was shattered.

"*Strega!*" a familiar voice bellowed, and Emma Bannon, Sorceress Prime, arrived at the bottom of the fan-shaped stairs in a silk-skirted rush. Mikal was there in his tails and snow-white shirt, easing a dead man's lanky frame to the floor, and the smell hit her.

*Dear God, what is this?* Her half-unbuttoned dress whispered as she flicked her fingers, a cleansing charm rising with a Minor Word and scorching the air of her parquet-floored foyer. Her dark curls, almost-dressed in anticipation of Lady Winslet's ball, tumbled about her face as she recognised the long, beaky-nosed corpse who, contrary to her expectations, drew in a rattling breath, clutching at his left shoulder and jerking his limbs in a decidedly odd fashion.

Next to him, pock-faced and hollow-eyed Ludovico Valentinelli was spattered with effluvium as well, but she had little time to wrinkle her nose.

Her other Shield, tall dark Eli, arrived at a run. He was further along in the dressing process than Mikal, since both of them were to attend her tonight. Still, his starched shirt was unbuttoned, and his jacket knocked askew.

Clare's breath rattled. *Angina. It is his heart*, she realised, the spark of life in Archibald Clare's body guttering like a candleflame in a draughty hall. "Fetch me *crystali digitalia!*" she barked, and Eli leapt to obey, taking the stairs three at a time. Her workroom would admit him, and he knew enough to take care with any experiments in progress – especially the æthericial commisterum. "Ludo, what on earth?" She did not expect him to answer.

"*Strega—*" The Neapolitan was almost beyond words, but Emma was already on her knees. She was barefoot, too – the ball would not start for some while yet, and she had intended to be only *slightly* late. Only fashionably so, as it were.

Later than her night's quarry. It was always advisable to surprise one's prey.

Mikal, his yellow irises bright in the foyer's dimness, spared the Italian a single glance, bracing Clare's shoulders.

A Major Word took shape on Emma's lips, sliding free whole and bloody, red sparks of sorcery fountaining. The four plain silver rings on her left hand fluoresced as she pulled stored ætheric force from them, heavy garnet earrings swinging against her cheeks warming and sparking as well. She would, in all eventuality, need the force she was expending later tonight – but just at the moment, she did not care. Her right hand, a large bloody stone in its antique silver setting flashing on the second finger, clamped to Clare's chest and her senses dilated. She located the source of the distress, feeling about inside his flesh with several nonphysical senses, and determination rose bitter-bright inside her.

*Not your time yet, sir. Not while I am here to gainsay it.*

The heart, determined muscle that it was, twitched under her ætheric pressure. She forced it into a rhythm that matched her own, exhaling sharply as her concentration narrowed. There was some damage, true, but all in all the organ had carried on gamely.

She was not surprised. He could be provokingly stubborn, her mentath. "The golden orb in the library," she heard herself say, from very far away. "And three surdipped hawk feathers, Mikal. Bring."

He did not protest at leaving her alone and distracted with Valentinelli, for once. Which was very good, because Clare's tired heart began to resist the pressure of her will, and the sorceress was suddenly very occupied in keeping Archibald Clare's blood moving at its required pace. At least her Discipline, Black though it was, gave her sufficient knowledge of the body's processes to keep extinction from Clare's doorstep in *this* instance.

*I do hope his faculties have not been damaged.* The flow of ætheric energy through her hands intensified, scorch-hot. The mentath, a logic-machine trapped in frail, weary flesh, coughed and convulsed again.

*Strange, he looks old now.* Perhaps it was merely that his colour was very bad. Then again, he was not a young man. He had been a vigorous thirty-three when she met him, but the years since had kept up their steady wearing away at him, drop by drop.

And Clare was congenitally unable to cease pursuing trouble of the most exotic sort. He was not engaged in a life that would permit much rest, and the wear and tear on his physicality was marked.

A chant rose to her lips, the language of Mending forced to her will – for her Discipline was not of the White branch, and Mending obeyed her only reluctantly. Still, she was Prime, and such a designation required a will that brooked very little bridle – and could force even the most reluctant branch of sorcery to its bidding.

A rolling sonorous roil, the entire house suddenly alive with rushing crackles, its population of indentured servants so used to the feel of tremendous sorcery running through its halls they hardly paused in their appointed duties.

Eli arrived, not breathless but with his dark hair disarranged. He measured out two tiny venom-purple crystals of the *digitalia*, dropped them into Clare's fishworking mouth, and clamped the mentath's jaw shut for a few seconds to make certain they would stay in. Then he settled back on his heels, watching the Sorceress Prime's face, alight with crawling golden charter charms screening her flesh as she half sang, her evening dress pulled askew and white shoulders rising from a silver and blue froth of gauze and lace. The charter symbols, ancient runic patterns of Wheel and Plough, Stone and Blossom and others less willing to be named or pronounced, invaded Clare's pasty skin as well, and finally Eli glanced up at the Neapolitan assassin. "Looks as if you've had rather a night of it."

Ludovico shrugged. For once, he did not sneer, perhaps a mark of his agitation. Or perhaps his lips were sealed by the filth coating him, smeared on his face as if he had bathed in a foul-ditch. Under that mask, his colour was very bad indeed – not that his sallow, ratlike features would ever win regard for blooming beauty, indeed. At least the dirt masked the pox scars on his cheeks.

Mikal reappeared, yellow eyes alight as he shouldered his fellow Shield aside. In one hand he held an apricot-sized globe of mellow gold; the three feathers, coated with a black tarry substance, shivered in his other. The sorceress, dark gaze full of a terrible blank *presence*, swayed slightly as she chanted. The charter symbols glowed crimson as they ran down her left side, clustering high under the ribs, crawling over the pale slope of one breast like a cupped hand.

A shudder ran through her swelling song, the mentath's filth-caked bootheels drumming the parquet as his body thrashed, and Mikal leaned forward, offering the globe and the feathers.

Who knew what objects would be required for any act

of sorcery? It was, by its very definition, an irrational art. Many sorcerers were magpies, since one could not tell what physical item – if any – would be required for a Work. Some Primes sniffed disdainfully and said the best sorcery was unanchored in the physical . . . but those of a practical bent understood that the ease of a Work moored in an object of reasonable permanence was in most cases a desirable thing.

Sorcery flashed, ætheric energy coalescing into the visible for a brief moment, and Ludovico Valentinelli crossed himself, breathing a foul wondering curse in his native tongue. His pox-pocked face, under its splattering of black matter, was flour-pale.

The globe and feathers were gone, their physical matrices picked apart to provide fuel for the impossible. The chant relaxed, swimming bloodwarm through air suddenly prickling and vibrating. Clare, his eyelids fluttering, was no longer ashen. A trace of healthy colour crept back into his lean, lax face.

Easily, softly, the brass syllables wound down from Emma Bannon's lips. She leaned over the mentath, cradling him, and breathed in his face. His body jerked again and the sorceress relaxed slightly, uncurling her mental grip from the repaired clot of fibrous muscle in his chest. One final stanza, her nose wrinkling slightly as the acridity of some drug burned her sensitive palate, and the language of Mending fled her.

She sagged, and the almost-bruising grip on her shoulders was Mikal's hands, fever-hot and hard with callouses.

Emma blinked, shutterclicks of dim light stinging her suddenly sensitive eyes, storing away the taste of whatever substance had been running through Clare's blood. *Hmmm. No wonder he has looked rather ragged of late. It tastes dreadful, whatever it is.*

Mikal's face was tense and set.

"He will live." It was a relief to hear her usual brisk tone. For a moment, she had almost been . . . had she?

*Afraid.* And that could not be borne, or shown.

"He will live," she repeated, more firmly. "Now, let us be about clearing up this mess. I have a ball to attend and a duke to chastise."

Lady Winslet's dowry had restored the fortunes of her husband's family, and though she was not taken into *quite* the highest echelons of Society, her taste and judgement were considered quite reasonable. She had redone a fashionable Portland Place address – one of Naish's, of course – in a manner most befitting her husband's title. Of late she had taken to inviting an astounding mix to her Salons, patronising certain promising members of the Royal Society, and had garnered much praise for her dinners. In a few generations, the Winslets would be very proud indeed to have invited such a petty bourgeois into their hallowed family tree.

*If*, that is, she managed to produce an heir. Barry St John Duplessis-Archton, Lord Winslet, was a dissipate scoundrel, but he had ceased gambling and now only drank to a religious degree that might preclude fathering said heir. He had a nephew who showed some signs of not being an empty-headed waste of a few fine suit jackets, but, all in all, Emma privately thought the Winslets' chances rather dim.

And no breath of scandal attached itself to Lady Winslet; she did not seem the sort to have a groom provide the necessary materials to make a bastard either. Very sad; had she been just a trifle less extraordinary she would have more chances of success against the ravening beasts of Society and Expectation.

All of that was academic, however, for Emma had known the Duke of Cailesborough would be at the Winslet ball. One of his current mistresses was attending, and furthermore, Emma herself had carefully planted a breath of rumour that would interest him.

And he had taken the bait whole. Which led to her presence in this forgotten, cramped second-floor storeroom full of discarded bits of off-season furniture and rolled-up, unfashionable carpets. A single candle, stuck in a dusty candelabra probably dating from the time of the Mad King Georgeth, gave wavering illumination to the scene.

Eli straightened, exhaling sharply. He was not rumpled in the slightest, though there was a slight flush to his cheeks. Perhaps embarrassment, for the quality of Cailesborough's struggle had been quite unexpected.

Said Cailesborough, on the floor, trussed hand and foot and gagged with commendable efficacy with his own sock, glared at Emma with the one blue eye that was not swelling closed.

For a man of the aristocracy, he had put up a rather remarkable tussle.

That was immaterial. "Now," she said, softly, "what do we do with *you*?"

She had the dubious honour of addressing a Spaniard, moustachioed and of a small stature to inspire a touch of ridicule or pity, his right arm twisted behind him in an exceedingly brutal fashion by a silent and immaculate Mikal, who twisted his lean dark face and spat at her.

There was a creaking sound, and Mikal's other hand clamped at the small Spaniard's nape. "Prima?" The one word was freighted with terrible menace, and had Emma been feeling insulted instead of simply weary, she might have let her Shield do what he wished with the man. Mikal's eyes burned in the dimness, a flame of their own.

Outside the locked door, a hall and the cigar room away, the music swelled. Her absence would not be remarked during the waltz, but perhaps the Duke's would.

*They will be missing him a very long time.* A greater worry returned, sharp diamond teeth gnawing at the calm she needed to deal with this situation in its proper fashion. *Is Clare well? Resting comfortably, I should hope.*

She put the thought aside. He was as easy as she could make him, and she had other matters to attend to at this moment. Her regard for a mentath was one thing. Her service to Queen and Empire was *quite* another.

"On the one hand," she continued, suppressing a slightly acid burp – for Lady Winslet's cold supper tonight left a trifle to be desired – and clasping her hands prettily as she sank onto a small, handy-even-if-covered-with-a-dustcloth chair, "you are a diplomatic personage, sir, and Her Majesty's government does believe in observing proper forms. It would be a trifle awkward if a member of the august consulate of that pigeon Isobelia disappeared."

Don Ignacio de la Hoya went almost purple and cursed her in a whisper. He was emphatically not a Carlist, which was interesting indeed. The Spanish embassy had been rather a hotbed of anti-Isobelian sentiments for a long while, the round, benighted, silly Queen of the Spains had never had much of a chance against those who wished her a catspaw. Still, she was nominally in power, and Emma supposed the idea of royalty and majesty might have held a certain attraction for some of her subjects. Especially if they were as ill-favoured and ratlike as this specimen.

His throat had been almost crushed by Mikal's iron fingers, and now, the sharp stink of fear poured from him in waves.

The dustcloth would perhaps taint this dress. She should not have sat, and she was taking far too long over this part of the matter. Still, Emma tilted her head slightly and regarded the man. Don Ignacio writhed in Mikal's grip, and it would be merely a matter of time before he collected himself enough to raise a cry, bruised throat or no.

There was little chance of him being heard over the merriment and music, but why take the risk?

He stared at her, and the sudden spreading wetness at his crotch – it was a shame, his trousers were of fine cloth – sent a spike of useless revulsion through her. Champagne and terror were a bad mixture, and this man was no ambassador. He was a low-level consulate official, despite his *Don*; but, she supposed, even a petty bureaucrat could dream of treason.

"Did you truly think you could plan to murder a queen and go unnoticed?" She sounded amused even to herself. Reflective, and terribly calm. "Especially in such lackadaisical fashion? The weapons you brought for the planned insurrection will be most useful elsewhere, I suppose, so we may thank you for that. And *that* baggage . . ." She indicated the prostrate, struggling Duke with a tiny motion of her head, and Eli, well used by now to this manner of situation, sank a kick into Cailesborough's middle. He had not yet gone to fat, the Duke, but he was still softer than Eli's boot. ". . . well, he has some small value for us now. But you? I do not think you have much to offer."

Don Ignacio de la Hoya began to babble in a throaty whisper, but he told Emma nothing she did not already know of the plot. He had very little else to give, and fear would only make him too stupid for proper use. His replacement in the consulate was likely to be just as idiotic, but vastly less troublesome.

*His heart*, she found herself thinking. *What manner of substance was he using? The damage was much more than it should have been; thirty-five does not make a man old. Merely lucky, and somewhat better-fed than the rest.*

She brought herself back to the present with an invisible effort. Mikal read the change in her expression, and the greenstick crack of a neck breaking was very loud in the hushed room. The candle on the table guttered, but the charm in its wax kept the flame alive.

On the floor, the Duke moaned, his eyes rolling. He was to be delivered to the Tower whole and reasonably undamaged. For a bare moment Emma Bannon, Sorceress Prime in service to Queen and Empire, contemplated crushing the life out of him by sorcery alone. It would be messy, true, but also satisfying, and Queen Victrix would never have to fear this caged beast's resurgence. He had chosen ill in the manner of accomplices, but he was capable of learning from such a mistake.

*The decision is not yours, sorceress*, she told herself again. Cailesborough had been one of the few allowed near Alexandrina Victrix when she had been merely heir presumptive under the stifling-close control of the Duchess of Kent; of course he had not been a marriage prospect but he had no doubt been amenable to extending the Duchess's sway over her soon-to-be-crowned daughter. The old King's living until Victrix's majority had cheated the Duchess of a regency, and no doubt Victrix had cheated Cailesborough of some prize of position or ambition. Still, the Queen appeared to wish him dealt with leniently.

If the Tower could be called *lenient*.

De la Hoya's body hit a rolled up, unfashionable carpet with a thump, raising a small cloud of dust. Mikal glanced at her. "Prima?" Did he look concerned?

It had taken far more sorcerous force than she liked to lure them both to this room and to spring her trap. And the worry returned, sharper than ever. Clare was not a young man, and he seemed inclined, if not flatly determined, to do himself an injury.

"Bring the body, and the Duke." Londinium's fog was thick tonight, and it would cover all manner of actions. "The window is behind those dreadful curtains – and *do* make certain the Duke lands gently. Lady Winslet's gardens need no damage." She stood, a slight crackling as her finger flicked and a cleansing charm shook dust free of her skirts. The silver shoes with their high arches and spangled laces were lovely, but they pinched abominably, and her corset squeezed as well. *I would much rather have been at home tonight. How boring I've grown.*

"I'll fetch the carriage." Mikal paused, if she wished to tell him where they were bound. It was a Shield's courtesy, and a welcome one.

"We shall take both unfortunates to the Tower." *Though the body will go no further than the moat. The Dweller should be pleased with that.*

Eli bent and made a slight sound as he managed the Duke's bulky, fear-stiffened form. Mikal simply stood for a moment, watching her closely. She took back the mask of her usual expression, straightened her shoulders and promised herself a dash of rum once she returned to her humble abode.

And still, the worry taunted her.

*Something must be done about Clare.*

# Chapter Three

## Grief Is Unavoidable

Dark wainscoting, large graceful shelves crammed with books and periodicals, including an entire set of the new edition of the *Encyclopaedie Britannicus* – Miss Bannon's servants were, as ever, extraordinarily *thorough* – and the heavy oak armoire full of linens charm-measured exactly to Clare's frame. The rest of the room was comfortably shabby, rich red velvet rubbed down to the nub and the tables scattered with papers left precisely where he had placed them the last time he had availed himself of Miss Bannon's hospitality.

The oddity was the chair set by his bedside, and the sorceress within it, her slightness cupped in heavy ebony arms and her curling dark hair slightly mussed as she leaned against the high hard back, sound asleep, dressed in silver and blue finery fit to attend a Court presentation. Her childlike face, without her waking character to lend authority to the soft features, was slack with utter exhaustion.

Of no more than middle height, and slight as well, it was always a surprise to see just how small she truly was. One tended to forget as the force of her presence filled a room to bursting.

The other oddity stood at his chamber door, a tall man with tidy dark hair, an olive-green velvet jacket and curious boots, his irises glowing yellow in the dimness. The smell of paper, clean sheets, a faint ghost of tabac smoke, and the persistent creeping breath of Londinium's yellow fog alone would have told Clare he was in the room Miss Bannon kept for his visits.

Which had been rather less often than he liked, of late. The sorceress's company could not be called restful, precisely, but all the same Clare found it rather relaxing to have at least one person with whom he could feel a certain . . . informality?

Was *comfort* the more precise term?

The Shield, Mikal, did not stir. His yellow gaze rested upon Clare with distressing penetration.

*Lucid. But very weak.* He tested his body's responses, gingerly. They obeyed, grudging him as if he were an invalid. Fingers like sausages, toes swollen but movable, his chest sore as if a gigantic clawed hand had rummaged through the inside of his ribcage and left a jumbled mess behind.

*Now for the important part.* His eyes half-lidded, and he performed the curious mental doubling of a mentath. A set of mental chalkboards rose before his consciousness, and he began with the simplest exercises he had learned at Yton when his talent had truly begun to manifest itself. Mentath ability came to the fore during late childhood, scholarships were quite generous for any who showed considerable promise.

Said scholarships, however, were contingent upon that promise being fulfilled.

A quarter of an hour later, loose with relief but sweating from the mental effort, Clare let out a long, shaky sigh. His faculties were unharmed.

Miss Bannon, perhaps disturbed by the slight sound, shifted in the chair and fell back into slumber. Clare now had the opportunity to study her while she was deeply asleep, and it was so novel an experience he rather wished he had not been forced to forgo a portion of that time to making certain whatever had happened to him had not destroyed his capacities.

*You are avoiding, Clare. It was angina pectoris. Rather severe, too.*

Mikal's eyes had half-closed as well. The Shield leaned against the door, and he was perhaps almost asleep. Did he think Clare a threat to the sorceress?

She did rather manage to accomplish a fair amount of vexation. Especially to Britannia's enemies. And she did so with a disregard for her own safety likely to give the Shield, tasked with maintaining said safety, a bit of nervousness.

However, it was far more likely that Mikal was unwilling

to let Miss Bannon out of his sight for . . . *other* reasons. Quite personal considerations, one could say.

The question of Mikal had occupied Clare most handsomely at one time or another. Since the affair that had brought the mentath into the sorceress's circle – not that Miss Bannon had anything so social as a *circle*, it was rather the circle of her regard, which frankly interested Clare more – he had added tiny nuggets of information to the deductive chain Mikal represented.

*Your heart, Clare. Do not become distracted.*

He was clean, and in a bed which linens smelled of fresh laundering. The last event he remembered was the darkness of the sewers swallowing him whole. Slightly irritated, he shifted in the mattress's familiar embrace. How had he arrived here, of all places?

The answer was stupidly simple. Valentinelli, of course. Where else would the Neapolitan bring him? The man was as fascinated by Miss Bannon as Mikal was.

*Or as you are. You are seeking to distract yourself from a very important chain of deduction. Angina pectoris. A severe attack. You could have died.*

Yet here he lay, clean and safe. At least, it would take a great deal of unpleasantness before *this* house became unsafe.

*Miss Bannon no doubt performed some illogical miracle, and is sleeping at your bedside. In that dress, she was no doubt a-hunting in Society for a traitor, turncoat, criminal, or merely one who intrigued too openly against Queen Victrix. Yet here she sleeps, and you are . . . comforted? Troubled?*

The problem, he reflected, was that Emotion was insidious, and an enemy of Logic.

Item one: he had lost Dr Vance. Again.

Item two: the more-than-mild chest pains during the hunt for the blasted art professor were unequivocally symptoms of a much larger quandary.

Item three: Miss Bannon, breathing softly as she slumped in an uncomfortable-looking chair. She took very little care with her person, and it was not quite right for Clare to put her to such worry. It was not worthy of the regard he held for her, as well.

He had no family; his parents were safe in churchyard beds, and his siblings had not survived childhood. But had he been one of those blessed with surviving kin, Clare supposed he would have felt for them much the same way he felt for Miss Bannon. A rather brotherly affection, tinged with a great deal of . . . what was it? Worry?

He might as well worry about a typhoon, or houricane. Miss Bannon was eminently capable . . . but she was also strangely fragile, being female, and Clare was not behaving as a gentleman by putting her to such bother.

*You are being maudlin. Emotion is the enemy of Reason, and you are still distracting yourself.* Had he not been a mentath, Clare might have been tempted to stifle a groan. As it was, he merely swallowed the offending noise and set himself to exercise his reason, since his faculties appeared undamaged.

"Clare."

He almost started, but it was only Mikal, breathing the

single word from his place at the door. The gleam of his irises was absent; the foreign man – for Clare had deduced he was, in fact, of the blood of the Indus, even if he had been born on Englene's shores – had closed his eyes.

"Yes?" Clare whispered.

"You could have died."

*I am not an idiot, sir.* "Yes."

"My Prima greatly weakened herself to avert such an event."

*Obviously.* "I am most grateful."

Emma Bannon stirred again, and both Shield and mentath held their peace for a short while. When she subsided, sliding sideways to end propped against one side of the chair like a sleepy child during a Churchtide evening, Mikal let out another soft breath. His words took shape inside the exhale.

"She is . . . fond of you."

*Oh?* "Only a little, I'm sure." Clare shifted uncomfortably. Such swimming weakness wore on him; stillness was remarkably painful after a while. "Sir—"

"She is fond of very few."

"That I can believe."

Mikal arrived at the warning Clare had already inferred was his intention. "Do not cause her grief, mentath."

*I am a fleshly being in a dangerous world. Grief is unavoidable.* His answering whisper was as stiff as his protesting back. "I shall do my best, sir." Had he not just been reminded of his own perishability, in the most alarming way possible? And further reminded that he was not being quite correct in his treatment of his . . . friend?

Yes, Miss Bannon was a friend. It was rather like forming an acquaintance with a large, not-quite-tamed carnivore. Sorcery made for powerful irrationality, no matter how practical Emma Bannon was as a matter of course.

The Shield fell silent again, even the glimmers of his yellow irises quenched, and Clare lay in the dimness, studying one of Emma Bannon's small soft slumber-loosened hands, until fresh unconsciousness claimed him.

# *Chapter Four*

## *Breakfast and Loneliness*

The Delft-and-cream breakfast room was flooded with pearly, rainy Londinium morning light, translucent charm spheres over the ferns singing their soft crystalline lullabies. White wicker furniture glowed, and the entire house purred like a cat, content to have its mistress at home and the servants quietly busy at their various tasks.

"You could have sent me a penny-post," Emma remarked mildly enough, her hand steady as she poured a fresh cup of tea. "Or worn the Bocannon I gave you." Her back protested – sleeping corseted and slumped in one of the most uncomfortable chairs her house possessed was *not* likely to give her a happy mood upon awakening. She had chosen the chair deliberately, thinking its discomforts might stave off the resultant exhaustion of a night of hunting through the glittering whirl of a ball, waiting for her quarry to slip.

There was one duke fewer in Londinium this morning, and one more traitor in the Tower to be judged and beheaded as befitted a nobleman. The evidence was damning, and Emma knew every particle of it. Should Cailesborough somehow bribe his way free . . .

. . . well, there was a reason the Queen called on one such as herself to tidy loose ends, was there not?

Tidiness was one of Emma Bannon's specialities. It was, she often reflected, one of the few assets a childhood spent in a slum could grant one.

"I suspected you were rather busy yourself, Miss Bannon." Archibald Clare's lean mournful face was alarmingly pale. He accepted the cup, and there was no tremor in his capable, large-knuckled hands. "It seemed a trifle."

*Oh, yes, Dr Vance, a "trifle". Very well.* "No doubt it was." She poured her own cup, keeping her gaze on the amber liquid. "Did you discover what the trifle was after?"

"A certain artefact of Ægyptian provenance." Clare shifted, fretting at the rug over his bony knees. He was alarmingly gaunt.

Of course, he had not been a guest at her table as frequently as had been his wont, these last few months. She would have half suspected his friendship had cooled, had she not known of his obsession with Vance. "Hm." She decided the noncommittal noise was not enough of an answer. "Clare, if you do not wish to tell me, that is all very well. But do not oblige me to drag the admission from you by force. Simply note it is not my affair, and we shall turn to other subjects."

"Such is not the case at all." He shifted again. "I thought it would bore you. Your feelings on Dr Vance are known to me."

"My feelings, as you so delicately put it, are simply that you spend altogether too much time brooding over the man. Rather as a swain moons over his beloved." She set her cup down, delicately speared another banger with a dainty silver fork. Fortunately, her physical reserves were a fairly simple matter to replenish, and Tideturn's golden flood of ætheric energy had flushed her – and her jewellery – with usable sorcerous force. Any remaining exhaustion could be pushed aside, for the moment.

Clare's silence informed her she had hit a nerve. For a mentath driven by logic, he certainly was tender-skinned sometimes. A misting of fine rain beaded the windows, the droplets murmuring in their own peculiar Language as they steamed against golden charter charms.

"This artefact would not happen to be the Eye of Bhestet, would it?" She cut with a decided motion, her spine absolutely straight. *Tiny bites, as a lady should.* The ghost of a wasp-waisted Magistra Prima at the Collegia walked decorously through her memory: a familiar song of black watered-silk skirts.

Prima Grinaud had been a harsh teacher, but a consistent and ruthlessly judicious one. There was much to emulate in the woman, even if her cruelty was legendary among the Collegia's children. Primes were notoriously long-lived, but Grinaud seemed to be kept on this side of the great curtain of Being by sheer wormwood and gall.

Clare's silence deepened. He did look rather ill, she decided, glancing in his direction just briefly enough to ascertain this. *Perhaps I should not tell him.* Perhaps, instead, she could enquire as to the odd substance he had been dosing himself with? It had not tasted healthful at all.

He finally spoke. "Stolen. Of *course*. He must have given me the slip in Thrushneedle. Bloody *hell*."

"It was in the broadsheets this morning." And yes, she definitely regretted telling him. "The Museum is most embarrassed. Speculation is rampant as to the culprit. I am . . . sorry, Clare. If you like—"

"He is a *mentath*, Miss Bannon." Frosty, and polite, a tone he rarely used. He was pale, his eyes glittering harshly. The rug over his knees creased itself as he fidgeted precisely once. "Illogic and *sorcery* are not applicable tools to catch him."

*Well, you've been doing a fine job of it with your vaunted deductions.* She occupied herself with another nibble of banger. Greasy, satisfying, hot, delicious. Just what it should be. When she was certain she had a firm hold on her temper, she spoke. "Perhaps not. More toast? Cook remembers your fondness for kippers as well."

But Clare was staring morosely into his teacup. "So close," he mumbled. "And . . . ah, yes. Definitely in Thrushneedle. He was only out of sight for a moment, damn him. Even Ludo—"

"Yes, Ludovico." Irritation made her own manner sharper than she liked. "I told him to take great care with you, and *this* is what happens. You could have died, sir, and that would distress me *most* profoundly."

There. It was said. The entire breakfast room rang with uncomfortable silence. She speared another tiny piece of sausage with quite unaccustomed viciousness.

"I do not mean to be the source of distress." He still stared into his teacup as if he would find Vance's whereabouts in its depths. "I simply—"

"The man is not a danger to the Crown." She did her best to utter it as a simple statement of fact. "He is a thief. A passing-good one, a mentath who uses his talents for vice, but in the end, merely a thief. He is *not* worth such attention, Clare. Her Majesty would prefer your consideration turned elsewhere. You are, after all, one of the Queen's Own." She eyed the glittering ring on her second left finger, a delicate confection of marcasite and silver, ætheric force thrumming in its depths visible to Sight. "There are other matters to be attended to."

"I should simply let him go, after he has thumbed his nose at—"

"Clare."

"He stole from the Museum—"

"Clare."

"Damn it, the man is a menace to—"

"*Archibald.*"

He subsided. Emma found her appetite gone. She set her implements down and fixed him with a glare he might have found quelling had he not still been staring into his teacup. *Oh, for God's sake.*

"I would take it as a kindness," she informed him, stiffly, "if you would convalesce here. Ludovico was sent this morning to gather such of your effects – and such things pertaining to the cases you have been neglecting while you chase your art professor – as are necessary for your comfort during such an extended stay." She restrained herself from further lecture with a marked effort of will.

"I suppose the servants have been informed of my tender condition." He even managed to wheeze a little.

*And furthermore informed that you are not to stir one step outside this house unless it is under my care and my express orders.* "You suppose correctly. You have been fretting yourself absolutely dry over this Vance character, Archibald. Pray do not force me to immure you in your room like Lady Chandevault."

He finally looked directly at her, blinking owlishly, looking more mournful and basset-hound-like than ever. "Who? Oh, that. Miss Bannon – *Emma*. There is no need for concern. It was merely angina, which is common enough. I am not so young, and certain—"

Was she the only one to notice the lines at the corners of his mouth, the bleariness of his blue gaze? And the terrible fragility of him, hunched in a chair with the laprobe tucked carefully about him. Emma opened her mouth to take him to task and turn the conversation to what manner of substance he had been dosing himself with, but was interrupted by the door opening without so much as a polite knock to warn the room's occupants.

It was Mikal, his dark hair slightly disarranged and his coat somewhat askew. He must have been at a Shield's morning practice, for Eli was hard on his heels. "An envelope, Prima." Mikal's mouth was a thin line. "From the Palace."

"Ah." *So soon?* But treachery did not wait for mannerly visiting hours, she reminded herself. "Some fresh crisis, no doubt. Archibald, finish your breakfast. It seems there are other matters for me to attend to."

He looked strangely stricken, and sought to rise as she did. She waved him back down. "No, no. Please, do not. Concentrate on your recovery, or I shall be not only vexed but downright peeved with you. A fate worse than death, I'm sure." Her sally only received the faintest of smiles, but she had no time to remark upon his sudden high colour and the steely glint in his tired, bloodshot blue eyes.

For the envelope Mikal deposited in her hands bore a familiar hand on its front, and the seal – heavy and waxen – was Victrix's personal device.

The Queen called, and her faithful servant hurried to obey, leaving the mentath to breakfast and loneliness.

# Chapter Five

## With No One to Scold

*Shut me up like a child, will you?* Clare's pipe puffed fragrant tabac-smoke, furiously. He glowered at the grate, unable to enjoy the comforts of a charming, familiar Mayefair room. *There are other matters for you to attend to. More important ones, surely.*

He was, perhaps, being ridiculous.

*Perhaps? No. You are* definitely *being ridiculous.*

It did not sting so much that Miss Bannon had taken him to task. What pinched was that she was *correct* in doing so. He had been rather lax when it came to his duty to the Queen.

But Vance was such a damn nuisance. And it was *twice* now that Clare had been outplayed rather badly by the man. It most certainly did not help that there was no earthly reason why the sodding brute would want the statue of

Bhestet, carven from a single priceless blue gem. It was more of a gauntlet, a game, than an actual theft.

A game Clare had lost; a gauntlet he had not returned.

His pipe-puffing slowed, turned meditative. Tabac smoke rose in a grey veil, and near the ceiling it crackled, a charm activating to shape it into a globe of compressed mist, whisking it towards the fireplace and up the chimney. That was new, and he could almost see Miss Bannon's pleased expression when he mentioned that such a thing was dashed illogical but useful enough.

What was Vance, to him? Clare was one of the Queen's Own mentaths, his registration secure and his retirement assured by pension, since he had rendered such signal services during a few affairs of interest to the Crown. The first had, of course, been the most strenuous. And no few of the following affairs had involved Miss Bannon as well. They were rather an effective pair of operatives, Clare had to admit. Miss Bannon was very . . . logical, for a sorceress. Her capacity was admirable, her ruthlessness and loyalty both quite extraordinary, especially for a woman. Clare had his career, and Miss Bannon's regard, and his own not-inconsiderable list of achievements. What did Vance have? A chair at a university he had been hounded from, a dead wife and a respectable career gone . . .

. . . a criminal empire, and the Eye of Bhestet, now. And the satisfaction of winning.

Clare puffed even more slowly. Perhaps he should take a fraction of coja while he meditated upon the question of Dr Vance and his own response to the man?

At that precise moment, however, there was a token knock at the door, and Valentinelli slunk in, his pox-scarred face a thundercloud. He carried two Gladstones, and behind him trooped the cadaverous Finch supervising two footmen and a charm-cart carrying a brace of trunks.

*Horace, and Gilburn.* Clare found their names and the mental drawers holding their particulars with no difficulty. Like all Miss Bannon's servants, they had their peculiarities. Horace was missing half the smallest finger on his left hand, and Gilburn's slow, stately pace was less the result of decorum than of his Altered left leg – everything below the knee was gone, due to an accident Clare had not quite gained the details of yet, replaced with a tibia and fibula of slender dark metal chased with pain-suppressant and oiling charms; the limb terminated in a clockwork foot that was a marvel of delicate architecture. Miss Bannon had remarked once that she had contracted especially for the Alteration, since Gilburn had received great injury in her service, and the man had blushed, ducking his head like a schoolboy. For all that, he was quiet and well-oiled, and Horace often tucked his mutilated finger away or wore a glove with padding to hide it.

The more Clare saw of Miss Bannon's servants, the more he suspected quite a tender heart behind the sorceress's fearsome ruthlessness. Or perhaps Miss Bannon knew that there was no gratitude quite like that of a disfigured servant given back his or her pride and held to high expectations of performance.

And no loyalty like that of an outcast given a home.

It was a testament to the complexity of the sorceress's character that Clare could not quite decide which or what combination of considerations led to her policy.

"Eh, *mentale*." Ludovico dropped both heavy leather bags near the fireplace. "Where you want the trunks?"

"I am certain wherever those excellent fellows choose to set them will be *quite* proper." Clare made a small movement with his still fuming pipe. "Did you bring my alembics?"

"Am I your *donna di servizio*? Pah!" The Neapolitan made as if to spit, but visibly considered better of it. "Baerbarth will bring *those*. He is still packing."

*Dear God.* "I do not intend to abuse Miss Bannon's hospitality to such a degree—"

"Oh, what *you* intend and what *la strega* intend, they are not the same." Ludo waved one dusky, calloused hand. "I have letters, too." He toed one of the Gladstones and crouched to unbuckle it, keeping a wary eye on the two footmen. "Many, many letters."

Clare suppressed a groan.

"Will you be needing these unpacked, sir?" Gilburn said, laboriously seeking to disguise his heavy Dorset accent.

"Yes *indeed*." Valentinelli snorted. "*I* am not unpacking, and he is weak as kitten."

"For God's sake, I'm not an invalid!" Clare prepared himself to take issue with this treatment.

"Do you rise from that chair, sir, I shall make certain you reoccupy it just as swiftly." It was Clare's least favourite of Valentinelli's voices, the crisp consonants and upper-crust drawl of a bored Exfall student. The Neapolitan often employed such an accent when he felt Clare to be behaving ridiculously in some manner. "For the time being, we are abusing Miss Bannon's hospitality roundly." His tone changed a fraction as he dove into one of the Gladstones. "I thought we lost you last night, *mentale*."

"It was merely a trifle, my good man. Merely a bit of chest pain—"

"You make a bad liar, sir." Valentinelli nodded as the footmen began unbuckling the trunks. "Here, I bring your post to your chair, as good valet should."

*I do not need any damn letters* or *a thrice-damned Neapolitan valet. What I need is to catch Vance and put him in the bloody dock, and for you and Miss Bannon to cease this ridiculousness.* Still, duty called, and Clare's legs were decidedly unsteady. It was, he had to admit, a relief to have some of his effects brought to him. Except for the galling fact of Dr Vance's escape, a stay at 34½ Brooke Street did sound quite pleasant. Tonic, even.

But being treated like a child was insufferable. He sank into silence, even the soothing tabac smoke overpowered by quite reasonable irritation.

"Here." Valentinelli brought the lapdesk, a cunningly constructed item of wood inlaid with hammered brass. A fat sheaf of paper – envelopes, with varying handwriting, all addressed to *Mr Archibald Clare, Esq.* – landed atop it, and Valentinelli busied himself with exchanging the bowl of pipe ash at Clare's elbow with a fresh cut-crystal tray, then scooping up a pen, ivory letter opener, and a silver-chased ink bottle from the massive table in the centre of the apartment. "You are like *la suocera* with none to scold."

Clare could have cheerfully cursed at him, and perhaps would have, had they been at his own address. His landlady, the redoubtable Mrs Ginn, did not like Valentinelli, and Clare wondered what she thought of this turn of events.

With a sigh, he turned himself to the first envelope. It was addressed from Lancashire, the handwriting female and gently bred, even if the ink was cheap. Impoverished gentry, probably seeking some guess as to the whereabouts of a missing husband.

There were precious few surprises in any piece of mail he opened, and his faculties rebelled at the slow rot triggered by want of proper use. That was half the trouble – Vance and his exploits were, at least, *interesting*.

Another heavy sigh, and Clare opened the envelope. *Duty. Ever duty.*

Perhaps Miss Bannon's responsibilities weighed as onerously as his, but she certainly never seemed *bored*.

*Dear Sir, I am writing to you in great distress . . . my husband Thomas has disappeared and . . .*

Another deep, tabac-scented, involuntary sigh, and Clare set to work.

# Chapter Six

## One of Our Own

It was an occasion of little pomp, but great publicity.

"You may approach." Alexandrina Victrix, Britannia's chosen vessel, ruler of the Isles and Empress of Indus, sat straight-backed on her gem-laden throne, the Stone of Scorn underneath one leg glowing soft silver. The hexagonal Throne Room, its vast glass ceiling full of rainy Londinium mornlight, was nevertheless full of shadowed corners behind and between marble columns, and in one such corner was a deeper shadow.

Emma held the glamour soft and still, though an alert observer would catch any movement she made, or perhaps a gleam from her jewellery. True invisibility was difficult and painfully draining, but simply blending into shadow was so easy as to be childishly entertaining. Mikal was a soft-breathing warmth at her back, and Eli would be in the gallery above, moving silent as a fish in deep water.

He hunted best while drifting.

The Queen's dark hair frothed in ringlets near her ears, the back put up as a married woman's should be, and her soft face blurred like clay under running water. Her eyes had turned infinitely dark, tiny speckles of starlight in their depths as the ruling spirit of the Isle woke slightly and peered out of its vessel. The Queen's youthful figure had thickened, pregnancy swelling the outline of the girl Emma Bannon had sworn service to.

That oath was private and unspoken, and Emma was of the secret opinion that Britannia, as ageless and wise as She was, did not quite comprehend the nature of the sorceress's commitment.

Perhaps it was for the best. What queen would wish to know of the depths of service one born in the gutters could sink to?

Alberich, Prince and Consort, stood to the Queen's right, instead of using the smaller chair he was wont to occupy during interminable receptions or state business. The Consort, an aristocrat of Saxon-Kolbe, was a fine figure of a man with a lovely moustache and a dashing mien in the uniform he affected, but he took a dim view of sorcery in general and his influence upon Victrix, while of the moderating variety, was also . . . uncertain.

*He*, Emma thought, as she did every time she glimpsed him, *bears watching.*

There were few of the elect in the Throne Room for

this event, but at least two of them – Constance, Lady Ripley (christened "Constant, Lady Gossip" by the broadsheets) and the red-jacketed, portly Earl of Dornant-Burgh – could be counted to carry tales. That was their function, and Emma's shoulders were cable-tight under blue satin.

There, approaching the throne in a wide-sweeping formal dress of rose-coloured silk, was the reason for this concern: the Queen's formidable mother, the Duchess of Kent.

She was still a handsome woman, though growing much stouter as the years passed. An examination of her aquiline but pleasing face with its open, frank expression would lead one to believe her of a light and frivolous disposition, if one was extraordinarily stupid. There were plenty who ascribed to the view that the Duchess had been easily led by her comptroller Conroy into keeping Victrix under a stifling System of rules and etiquette that not so incidentally never allowed her contact with those her mother deemed unsuitable; others thought the Duchess's raising of the princess and later heir-presumptive merely suffered from a mother's natural but overly indulged desire to shield her child from all harm, real or imagined.

The truth perhaps lay somewhere between the two, on an island of ambition shrouded with syrup-sentiment and a frustrated will to rule. The Duchess would have made a fine prince of some foreign country, had she been chosen as a vessel . . . or a trouble indeed, if born a man.

Emma eyed the Duchess's stiff posture as the mother of the Queen made the merest courtesy demanded of a sovereign's family member. The necklace the woman wore, Emma decided, was far too gaudy to be anything but real gems; she was not wearing paste yet, this blue-blooded and cold-calculating princess. *Despite* Conroy's "management" of her estates and benefices, that was.

Victrix sat, utterly inhumanly still, only her eyes showing that Britannia was examining the woman who had given birth to her vessel, and examining her closely.

The sorceress's fingers tightened. The cameo at her throat warmed, ætheric force held in the piece responding to her mood. It would be so easy to strike the Duchess down, and she could even beg Victrix's forgiveness afterwards. Not every conspiracy threatening Victrix's rule had its origins in the Duchess's desire to bring her daughter back under her sway, true.

But the ones that *did* were . . . most troubling. There had been a certain affair involving a tower in Wales, a slumbering wyrm, and an army of unsleeping metal soldiers some time ago. It had also involved a Sorcerer Prime, and Emma's unease heightened another notch.

She *would* think of Llewellyn now, wouldn't she? There was a warm weight in her chest that grew a trifle heavier when she did. It was not the Stone that had been her private recompense for the affair, she had decided. Perhaps it was merely the consciousness of how close he had come to succeeding? Each separate part of that conspiracy had been working to different ends, but Llewellyn Gwynnfud's envisioned end had put the other parties to shame in sheer flamboyance and scope.

He would have been delighted to know she thought as much.

*Victrix will not take it kindly if I kill her mother, no matter what the woman has done. And no matter if Britannia roundly approves.*

Seen from this angle, the Duchess's beauty had faded considerably since her youth. Yet her eyebrows were the same high proud arches, and the long nose and decided chin were balanced by good cheekbones. A handsome woman, still.

Handsome enough to keep a lover, perhaps. Or her estates were certainly attractive enough to gain some attention.

Those in attendance had already noted that Conroy, normally his mistress's squire and shadow, was not present. If the pale-eyed, silk-voiced comptroller had decided to slip into the gallery to witness this exchange, Eli would neatly collar him . . . and Emma Bannon would have a small sharp chat with the man.

This was not Victrix's wish, but Emma had privately decided Sir John Conroy had become far too dangerous to wait upon handling. Perhaps it was arrogance on her part, to see so clearly a danger Victrix underestimated, and to set herself to drawing its venom. Or perhaps it was merely her duty. The two blurred together distressingly easily.

"Your Majesty." The Queen's mother repeated her courtesy, but more deeply. "It gladdens my heart to see my daughter."

Her words had an edge that only a sorceress, a lifelong student of tone and cadence and what remains unspoken, might hear.

No, that was not quite precise. It was also the tone a mother could use to chastise a grown child, treacle-sweet but loaded with private significance.

Emma's fingers twitched. At least Melbourne, nasty skinflint that he was, had given the young Queen her first taste of what passed for the freedom of rule. Victrix still believed most things possible, most things available, instead of seeing choice and circumstance narrow about her like a lunatic's canvas jacket.

Victrix raised her chin slightly. "Madam." Today she wore the Little Crown, its diamonds sparking as Britannia's presence spilled through her skin; she was not formally in state even though enthroned. To sit in state would have accorded the Duchess too much importance. At least Victrix had agreed when Emma made *that* observation. "We greet you."

*We.* Victrix hiding behind Britannia, or a sign that the ruling spirit was unwilling to take her gaze from a potential danger?

The Duchess's smile faltered slightly. "I would that I saw you more frequently, my dearest. But you have such important matters to attend to."

Emma was hard put to stifle a gasp. To speak so *familiarly* to Britannia might have earned one a spell in the Tower in less civilised days.

Victrix's head tilted slightly to the side, her features

shifting imperceptibly. To see the sweet face of a married-but-still-young woman age so rapidly, Britannia filling her vessel as the Themis filled its cold bed, was enough to send a chill through even the stoutest heart.

"Important matters." Victrix's fingers tapped the throne's arm, precisely once. She did not move to cover her belly with a protective hand, but it may have been very close. Rings glittered, scintillating not with ætheric force as Emma's jewellery might, but with a different brand of power. "Have you ever been to Wales, dear Mama?"

Emma's pulse beat high and hard in her throat. She had not expected this.

"Wales?" To her credit, the Duchess sounded confused.

"Dinas Emrys. A property of the house of Gwynnfud, or Sellwyth if you prefer their title." Victrix was pale now, and the depth of Britannia in her star-laden eyes spread, a haze of indigo fanning from the corners. Alberich made a restless movement, as if he longed to touch the Queen's shoulder, his white-gloved hand halting in mid-air and dropping back to rest at his side.

*Good. If he did not respect her, we would have even more trouble.* Respect was not quite enough, though. It would, she thought, do the Consort no end of good to outright fear his wife.

Sometimes a man's fear was a woman's only defence.

The Duchess was pale too. The lace of her cap quivered on either side of her face – she had affected a truly matronly headgear for the occasion. "I do not believe I have had the pleasure, my dearest." Not so vivacious now.

"I have not either, of late." Victrix's gaze swung away, roving over the few of the peerage who remained in the room – and her Chancellor of the Exchequer, Lord Craighley. The last Chancellor but one, Grayson, had vanished in mysterious circumstances; some whispered of embezzlement and of a retreat to the Continent. Others, very softly, whispered of sorcery.

It was Emma Bannon who saw to it they did not whisper overly loudly, or for very long. Sometimes it did not do to have the truth bruited about.

"I have not either," Victrix repeated, her tone sharpening. "But I think upon it often, Mother. The Sellwyths were treacherous *worms* of old, were they not?"

The Duchess of Kent trembled. It took a sharp eye to see, but Emma Bannon's gaze was indeed pointed, and she saw the quiver in the older woman's skirts. *Very well done, Your Majesty.*

"Alexandrina . . ." The Duchess's lips shaped a bloodless whisper.

"You may remove yourself from Our sight, Duchess." Victrix's tone took on new weight, and the shadows in the Throne Room thickened. Each gem on her chair or her person was a point of hurtful brilliance. "Thou'rt confirmed in thy titles and estates. But We shall not suffer thee in Our presence."

Emma loosened her fists, deliberately, one finger at a time. Had she truly doubted Victrix's ability to handle this confrontation? And so neatly, too.

The Duchess, to give her credit, paid a most steady

courtesy to Britannia. It was odd – the pale drawn look she wore now suited her, lending a shadow of slender youth to her features. Her dark eyes burned as live coals, and Emma wished she were more visible, so she could catch the lady's gaze. It was no doubt overweening pride . . . but she wished the Duchess knew she was witnessing this embarrassment.

The Queen's mother took the prescribed three steps backwards, her skirts swaying drunkenly. The shadow of Britannia retreated, pearly rain-washed morning light filling the vast glass-roofed expanse again. Victrix's gaze was no longer starred with the speckles of infinite night. No, it was human again, and her eyes were dark with very human pain.

"Mother," she said, suddenly and very clearly. "*I* am reconciled to thee. But *We* are not."

*Well, Lady Gossip and Lord Tale-A-Plenty will spread that far and wide. Good.*

Victrix rose, and there was a great rustling as all courtesied or bowed, and the Queen swept from the Throne Room on her Consort's arm. He murmured something to her, and Victrix's pained sigh was audible in the heavy silence.

Emma found herself smiling. It was, she suspected, not a pleasant smile, and she composed her features before allowing the glamour to fold itself away. There was no reason to remain in shadow now. It was against the spirit of Victrix's commands, and yet . . .

She needn't have bothered. The Duchess stalked from the Throne Room with her head held high, amid a wash of tittering whispers and buzzes. The morning's event would be digested and re-chewed in drawing rooms around Londinium by lunchtime, and halfway across the Continent by supper. Those who paid court to Kent, believing she had some influence, would fall away.

*This will only make her next gambit more subtle and hence, possibly more dangerous. And where is her hangman? Is he about?*

It was unlike Conroy to let an opportunity pass, and Emma had made certain that a delicate insinuation of the restoration of royal favour had dropped in his ear – and thus in the Duchess's. An effective feint, and satisfaction was had.

But he had not shown, which made the satisfaction tarnish slightly.

A tingle ran along her nerves. She raised her chin slightly, her gaze taking in the entire columned expanse of the Throne Room in one sweep. The brush of ætheric force retreated hastily, and her attention snagged on the opposite side of the room, where a gleam pierced another shadowed corner.

*Another player, or merely an onlooker? Interesting.*

She was now, after witnessing this exchange, to attend the Queen in private. There were other matters than a mother put firmly in her place requiring the attention of a Sorceress Prime in Britannia's service. Still, she lingered, allowing herself to become still and receptive, her consciousness dilating.

It was no use. The other sorcerer had felt her attention

shift, and was already gone. There was a side door close by, a twin to the one Emma stood near, and probably chosen for the very same reason she had selected this spot.

Something about such precaution did not quite sit well.

*Bother.* It mattered little; if there were another player at the table, soon enough he – or she – would slip and show a hand. Emma shelved the question and gathered her skirts, Mikal's step leaf-light behind her as she set a course for the door.

With a murmur of thanks, Emma lowered herself into the wide, heavy chair Victrix indicated with a wave of one jewelled hand.

"*Do* sit, Miss Bannon, that was *quite . . .*" Quite what, the Queen paused, as if unable to just yet define. Now, she clasped her hands over her rounded belly, wincing slightly. She had just begun to show, and so soon after the last. At least there was no shortage of prospective heirs, though Britannia had shown little interest in any of them to date. "Quite . . ."

*Uncomfortable? Liberating, and yet terrifying? I can only imagine.* Emma contented herself with a simple, "Thank you, Your Majesty." *After all, I have no mother or father, merely the Collegia. I cannot imagine.*

The Prince Consort, his features pale and mournful behind the fine moustache, busied himself at a rather grace-less mahogany sideboard. The hefty apple-figured drapes, overstuffed brocaded sophas and spindly gilt chairs were overdone, rather in the manner of a royal idea of what a respectable country gentleman's drawing room would contain, albeit envisioned without any proper visit to such a space to discern its peculiarities.

In short, it was very much like the doomed Queen Marette Antoinette's faux farm-village. The ruling spirit of France had not recovered from the bloody end its last vessel had undergone, and there were whispers that the freebooters first of the *Révolution* and then of the thrice-damned Corsican had slaughtered every child of the royal lines, both ancillary and direct, to keep Gallica from rising again.

Such things could happen without those strong, cunning, and yes, brutal enough to safeguard the vessel's person. No doubt another ruling spirit would rise, or Gallica would resurface eventually.

There were even whispers that some of the Corsican's line were showing . . . signs. Emma was still undecided whether judicious assassination should be suggested – oh, very delicately indeed. Victrix had certain regrettable qualms that would hopefully fade with the passage of time – and the lessons of ruling an Empire.

A weakened France was a help to Britannia, but not *overly* weak. Used as a shield and balanced against the Germans, not to mention Austro-Angary, she was a useful tool. A Gallican vessel sympathetic – or beholden – to Britannia, within reason, was an asset to be considered and planned for.

Emma folded her hands sedately. Victrix's long glittering earrings trembled as their wearer shook, and the sorceress averted her eyes, studying the curtains, counting the gold threads worked in stylised apple-shapes. The room was windowless, the drapes only softening bare stone walls. It was an apt metaphor for the illusion of absolute power. Trammelled in a stone cube, the ruling spirit of an Empire the sun never set upon was no more than a daughter reeling with helpless frustration and quite possibly a measure of despair.

Even the meanest of Britannia's servants were free to do things their monarch could not.

*That is a dangerous thought. Turn your attention aside. Is it safe here?* In the very bowels of Buckingham Palace, they could be reasonably certain of little physical threat.

Privacy was another issue entirely. Especially with a pair of unfriendly ears in the room.

Oh, the Prince Consort was not unfriendly to Victrix. Not at all. His animosity, tinged lemon-yellow and very visible to Sight, was directed to another quarter entirely.

"That went well." Victrix, softly. The Little Crown still perched, winking, atop her dark hair. She was pale, and her eyes were merely, humanly dark. "Rather well indeed."

Emma nodded. "Yesmum." Equally soft, her tone conciliatory and soothing as possible. She continued her examination of the drapes, the gaslamps hissing softly and their flames much better for her sensitive eyes than harsh sunlight.

"We think . . ." But the Queen did not continue. Alberich brought her a small glass – *vitae*, Emma discerned, smelling of lavender and threatening to unsettle her stomach. How anyone could drink *that* was beyond her. But it was a lady's draught, as popular now as ratafia had been during the time of the Mad Georgeth and his regent son.

Had Britannia felt the echo of her chosen vessel's madness? Did such a thing leach into the ruling spirit? Those she ruled might never know, and never know why Britannia chose not to leave Georgeth until the bitter end. Who were they to question the spirit of the Isles?

Who was anyone? Still, Emma found herself curious.

The Prince Consort sank into a chair at the Queen's side, picked up her small gloved and ringed hand, chafed it gently between his own. He cast a dark, disapproving glance at Emma, who affected not to notice.

"Emma." As if the Queen had to remind herself who precisely the woman sitting in one of her chairs was.

Now was the moment to turn her gaze to Victrix's face. So Emma did, wishing she had not left Mikal in the hallway outside. It would be . . . comforting, to have him close. Rather too comforting, and hence a weakness. She banished the thought, bringing all her considerable attention to bear. "Yes, Your Majesty. I attend."

"No doubt," the Consort muttered bleakly, as if he expected Emma not to hear.

"Alberich." Victrix's tone held a warning, but a mild one. "Lady Sellwyth is highly capable, and has earned Our trust in numerous affairs."

"Sellwyth. A worm's name." The Prince Consort patted her hand again. "You said so yourself."

An angry flush sought to rise to Emma's cheeks. She

quelled it, iron training denying flesh its chance to distract her. What would this princeling know of the battle atop Dinas Emrys, the knife sunk in the back of the only Sorcerer Prime who had ever matched her, and the danger she had averted? Had she failed . . .

. . . but she had not, and the little man was not the first to cast aspersions. *Sellwyth*, Britannia's fanged reward for her part in the affair, and an insurance that a possible key to the Colourless Wyrm's waking was in safe hands.

Safe, long-lived hands. Emma kept said appendages decorously loose in her lap. To take umbrage or even acknowledge the remark would overstep the bounds of propriety, but such a consideration did not halt her as much as it should. Instead, the genuine regard Victrix showed for the man made her refrain. *And* the fact that he seemed to wish to be a shield for her at Court and in the game of politics. Even though Britannia was the spirit of rule, there were still other factors to account for, and other centres of power to be balanced – and carefully stacked, so that the spirit of the Isle was not forced to certain acts.

No, the Saxon-Kolbe pretender to a seat less than an Englene county was not worthy of Emma's ire.

*Still, this will be added to the list of insults I remember. Odd, how that list grows and grows.*

"Alberich." The warning was less mild now. "Do not."

"Sorceress." The Prince Consort shook his head. But he subsided, and Victrix chose not to take him to task.

It was not, Emma reflected, that he found the arts of æther overly problematic. Charm and charter, sorcerers and witches, were to be found in his homeland as well. It was the fact of Emma's sex that gave the Prince Consort lee to insult, suspect and provoke her. She had long since grown as used to such treatment as daily exposure could make one.

"Emma." Victrix sighed, and Britannia rose under her features again. The sorceress held herself very still, but the ruling spirit retreated with an unheard rushing, a tide soughing back to the ocean's embrace. "One of Our Own is missing."

She absorbed the statement and its implications. "Sorcerer, or . . . ?"

"A physicker. Merely genius, We believe. A Mr John Morris. You are familiar with a certain Mr Rudyard?"

Emma nodded. Her curls swung, and the rings on her left hand sparked slightly. *Dear old Kim. Lovely.* "He is visiting again, then." Master sorcerers and Adepts lived long, but not nearly as long as Primes, of course. Rudyard courted death with a disdain and ferocity matched only by his single-minded dedication to Queen and Empire.

Slum-children, both of them, and if Rudyard despised Emma for the fact of her greater talent and the insult of her femininity, she could easily despise him in return for his violent arrogance, since she knew its source.

The trouble was, that arrogance sounded an echo in her own self, much as Llewellyn Gwynnfud's had. And Rudyard, well, had been *quite* attached to Llew in his own way.

Had he received word of Lord Sellwyth's mysterious

disappearance? It was very likely. And equally likely that he would suspect Emma of having a hand in said mystery.

For God – and Kim Rudyard – would both know that no other Prime could have faced Llew and survived. Or was that her own arrogance, again? Such an unfeminine trait.

"He is at the Rostrand." The Queen's expression suggested she was mystified, and Emma was hard put to hide a smile. "We are told he has . . . a monkey."

*I am certain he does.* Half-smile, half-pained grimace, Emma dispelled the expression before it could truly reach the architecture of her face. "How droll."

"He was the one to discover the physicker's absence. He will have the particulars for you."

*And that is very curious. Rudyard come to Englene's shores and discovering such a thing?* "Yes, Your Majesty." Emma waited. *Is that all? A physicker absconding, a mere genius? Not even a mentath?* But she did not press further.

She never had, beyond *by your leave* or *if I may*. If she could not guess, she would wait to be told, and keep her thoughts to herself. The principle had stood her in marvellous good stead in dealing with royalty.

It was also of good use when dealing with enemies, or potential enemies. Which covered a great deal of the globe's surface, no doubt.

The Prince Consort was breathing heavily through his nose, a huffing that denoted both unease with the proceedings and disdain for this common-born hussy who dared to sit, even when invited to do so, in the presence of Britannia.

Finally, Victrix nodded. She smoothed the fabric over her rounded belly, her fingers stippling over the loose corseting recommended at this juncture for supporting the distension of generation. "That will be all. Should you find Mr Morris, bring him to Our presence. But gently. We require him whole."

"I shall be as a mother cat with a kitten." Emma did not move. What would it feel like, to swell and split with a screaming little thing, a new life? Did she choose to breed, she would find out . . . but not yet. Though it was held to be a woman's highest happiness, she could forgo a little longer. "By your leave, then, Your Majesty?"

"Most certainly." Victrix's sigh was heavy. Even the Little Crown weighed terribly, and what was it like to host a being as ancient and headstrong as Britannia? Was it like a sorcerer opening himself to his Discipline, and becoming merely the throat a song moved through? At least a sorcerer knew the song would recede, and was trained to bear the shock of being simply an empty cup.

Emma Bannon rose, paid her courtesy. She did not acknowledge the Prince Consort. She left the room with a determined step and a rustle of skirts, uncaring if he took offence. It would serve the petty little man right.

*Victrix wishes me to find a man. I should find Clare's doctor as well, and make them both happy.*

She was, she realised, quite unsettled. It was not Alberich of Saxon-Kolbe's shot across her bow that worried her.

It was the fact that Conroy had not been in attendance this morning, and the Duchess of Kent had been far too easily disposed of.

*I smell a rat.* Later, of course, she would chide herself for being so exercised over what could have been coincidence . . . but at the moment, Emma Bannon was distracted, and in any case, how could she have known? Even a Prime could not tell the future with a certainty.

For now, she had her orders, the die was cast, and she winged towards her prey as a good merlin should.

# Chapter Seven

## An Admirer

Clare relit his pipe. Fragrant tabac smoke lifted, the charm near the ceiling crackling into life again. Afternoon light slanted through the window, past heavy wine-red velvet drapes and quiescent-glowing charter charms bleached by the sun's glow.

They had finally left him in peace. Valentinelli was no doubt in the kitchen, stuffing his pocked face and tormenting broad genial Cook; the footmen had gone about their business. The comfortable, dark-wainscoted room felt much smaller now, since his effects were unpacked over the table and into the capacious wardrobe. A full set of alembics brought by Sigmund Baerbarth – Horace would notify the cadaverous butler, Finch, to procure larger stands for them – and several of his journals were stacked higgledy-piggledy. Perhaps, if Miss Bannon wished him to remain hutched for a long period of time, she would make a workroom available? The sorceress's domicile often seemed larger inside than out, and there were curious . . . crannies, that sometimes seemed to change position.

His long nose twitched at the thought, as if he had detected an unpleasant odour. The irrationality of that thought was an itch under the surface of his skull. Once more he confined the irregularities of 34½ Brooke Street to the mental drawer of complex problems not requiring a solution at the present juncture. Several of Miss Bannon's peculiarities filled even that capacious space to overflowing.

There was a reason mentath and sorcerer did not often mix.

Clare puffed, and turned his attention to the most interesting letter – the one he had left unopened, setting it aside to savour.

It was a joy to have something unknown. The paper was heavy, linen-crafted but not bearing any of the characteristics of a maker Clare was familiar with. Privately made, then? Perhaps. The ink was bitter gall, and a ghost of . . . yes, it was myrrh, clinging to the envelope's texture. It had not been franked, either. Left with Mrs Ginn, for Clare spotted a telltale grease-spot on one corner; the redoubtable woman had been called from her pasty-making, no doubt. Although, Clare allowed, it could merely have been slipped into the postbox, for it was addressed to him very plainly, in a cramped hand that was certainly a gambit meant to disguise the sender. Male, from the way the nib dug into the paper. The simple trick of writing with one's left hand, unless Clare missed his guess.

*Oh, this is delicious.*

The seal was old-fashioned, a blob of scented wax. Clare inhaled delicately. Yes, that was definitely a breath of myrrh.

A church candle used for sealing. And not just any church, but Reformed Englican of the Saviour. *They* used such a blend of incense in their rituals; and there were only three of their ilk in Londinium, unless Clare had missed one springing up in the last ten years.

*Oh, careful, Archibald. Candle-wax is not enough to build a cathedral of reason upon. Remember your own words upon the matter of Assumptions, and how dangerous they are.*

The wax crackled and creaked. The symphony of its breaking proved its provenance, but a candle could be stolen. Or the envelope could have been left in a church to absorb its aroma.

Who would go so far?

He suspected. Oh, how he suspected! Another man, not a mentath, would have called the sensation a glorious tension, rather as the moment before a beloved yielded to his embrace. A swelling, a throbbing, a pleasurable itch.

He drew the letter forth. Expensive, to use an envelope rather than writing the address on the outside of a cunningly folded missive. But what was expense, between rivals or lovers? And the envelope would rob him of a deduction caught in a missive's folds.

He sniffed the folded paper, again, so delicately. That same breath of myrrh, with an acrid note that was not the gall of ink.

*Sewage. Oh, your escape was closer than I suspected. Good.*

A single page, and a message of surpassing simplicity.

*Dear Sir, your genius is much appreciated. Please do me the honour of considering me your Friend, not merely a Galling Annoyance. I remain, etc., An Admirer.*

Clare's entire frame itched and tingled with anticipation. He closed his eyes, and his faculties burned inside his skull like a star. The two sentences were layered with meaning; even the shape of the letters had to be considered.

"My dear Doctor," he whispered, in the smothering quiet of his invalid's room. "Another game? Very well."

The Neapolitan eyed him narrowly. "I know that look, sir."

"Hm?" Clare absently knocked ash free of his pipe, blinking. "I say, is it afternoon already?"

"*Ci.*" A pile of broadsheets thumped on the cluttered table, and Valentinelli turned slowly in a full circle, his flat dark gaze roving over every surface. "And you are up to mischief."

"I have been sitting here quietly for some hours, my good man." *Merely exercising my faculties in different directions, readying them for another go at the good Doctor.* "Very quietly. Just as an invalid should."

"Ha!" Ludo's hand whipped forward, flashing an obscene gesture very popular on Londinium's docks. "You complain and complain. *La strega* wish to take good care of you, sit and grow fat."

"I do not do well with idleness. You have been my man long enough to know as much." Even to himself he sounded peevish and fretful.

"Today I am not your man. Today I am your *dama di compagnia.*" A sneer further twisted his dark unlovely face. "She leave you in Ludo's hand because you are foolish little thing. I told you, a *pistole* would have solved all problems, *pouf.*"

*You think that if you repeat yourself, I will suddenly agree?* "I wished to *catch* the man, not kill him."

"So I shoot to wound. You must have more faith, *mentale.* It is your silly teatime. *La Francese* sent me to collect you."

"Madame Noyon is too kind." Clare stretched, the armchair suddenly uncomfortable as his lanky frame reminded him he had been wrapt in a mentath's peculiar trance for far too long. The flesh, of course, was no fit temple for a soul dedicated to pure logic.

Not that a mentath was purely a logic engine. Their faculties only approximated such a device; sometimes, Clare was even forced to admit that was best. The pursuit of pure logic had dangers even the most devoted of its disciples must acknowledge. Still, it was a frustration almost beyond parallel to feel the weight of physical infirmity as age advanced upon him.

He did not mind it so much as he minded the fear – and yes, it *was* fear, for a mentath was not devoid of Feeling – of the infirmity somehow reaching his faculties. Dimming them, and the glory of logic and deduction fading.

That would be uncomfortably like the Hell the old Church, and even the Church Englican, did spout so much about.

It took him far longer than he liked to reach his feet, setting his jacket to rights with quick brushing movements. His knees were suspiciously, well . . . wibbly. It was the only term that applied.

Ludovico watched, far more closely than was his wont.

"Good God, sir, I am not about to faint." Clare took stock. He was respectable enough for tea, at least.

"You look dreadful." But then the Neapolitan waved away any further conversation. "Come, tea. At least *la Francese* will have *antipasti*. Ludo is hungry. Hurry along."

#  *Chapter Eight*

 ## *Only if You Do Not Displease*

The Rostrand was not an old hotel, but it was fit for visiting royalty. Very few of Englene's natives would stay in its luxurious wallow; it was far too *Continental.* The walls were sheathed with kielstone, which meant the native flow of æther would not overly discommode foreign guests with any sorcerous talent. And, not so incidentally, so their own alienness would not create stray harmful bits of irrationality.

Rudyard was not a foreigner, precisely. He had been born in the glare and monsoon of the Indus. Which was practically Empire, true . . . but it still made certain of his talents unreliable when he ventured beyond the subcontinent's borders.

*How that must irk him.*

It was no great trick to locate him in the coffee room

off the cavernous overdone lobby with its glittering chandelier overhead sparking and hissing with repression charms. Mirrors in gilded frames reflected fashionable plumed hats atop women's curls, the height of Parissian fashion favouring dark rich jewel-colours this year, and men in sober black, a faint look of ill-ease marking every foreigner no matter how expensively dressed. The gaslamps were lit, their light softening each edge and picking out nuances of colour sunlight would bleach. The morning's glamour had not made her overly sensitive, but she still blinked rapidly. Even the rainy light outside was too much, sometimes.

The French were much in evidence today, and Emma's trained glance stored faces while her obedient memory returned names for some of them. Some of the guests here bore watching – the Monacan Ambassador, for one, oiled and sleek and quite fashionable to have in a drawing room lately. His tiny principality did not rate him such importance, and there were certain troubling rumours about his proclivities, both personal and professional, that would require attention sooner or later.

The coffee room was sun-bright and pleasant, done in a rather Eastern style. Sky-blue cushions with gilt tassels, a splendid hookah in a nook by a chimney – most likely defunct, a relic of some travel through a pawnshop – and cages of well-bred canaries cringing under a lash of high-pitched noise.

No, it was not difficult to locate Kim Finchwilliam Rudyard after all. For the small monkey, the ruff around

its intelligent little face glowing silver, was screeching fit
to pierce eardrums and shatter every single mirror and
glass in the Rostrand's atrium.

Several harried employees fluttered about carrying
different items perhaps meant to appease the howling beast
– or its master. Who sat, apparently unconcerned, in a large
leather chair near one of the fireplaces, one of the day's
broadsheets open before his lean tanned face.

His cloth was sober and surpassingly fine, his waistcoat
not disguising the taut trim frame beneath and his morning
coat no doubt the finest the Burlington Estate could
produce. Not for him the snappish newness of Savile Row;
Rudyard's taste for the most conservative of fashions was
an involuntary comment upon what he no doubt fancied
was a hidden desire. To be more of the Isle than Britannia
Herself would have suited him royally, for all Rudyard
was a young and bastard son.

A nose too hawk and cheekbones too broad, a skin
deeply tanned by the Indus's fierce sun – but not enough
to be native of that dark-spiced country, no. Later he would
be as seamed and rough as a nut, but for the time being,
he was merely unusual. A gold ring very much like a
Lascar's adornment dangled from one earlobe, and his hair
was too fair for the Indus and the wrong manner of dark
for Britannia. He wore no moustache, and though his colour
was not muddy as so many half-castes were, the exotic on
him was a dangerous perfume.

She did not see his *kukuhri*-knife with its hilt of sinuous
dark carven wood, but that did not mean he was not armed.

Emma took her time approaching him, taking note of the various glances and exclamations from the Rostrand's staff. Mikal touched her shoulder, a fleeting pressure, and she nodded.

*Of course he is armed somehow. And you can tell he is of the Indus. I wonder if you will recognise more of him?*

The question of how to deal with the screaming monkey was solved as soon as the creature sighted her. For it froze, its mouth wide open and sharp ivory teeth gleaming, its wide white-ringed eyes fixed on Emma.

No, not on her, but over her left shoulder. At Mikal.

*Well, that is very interesting.*

The sudden silence was almost shattering. The top edge of Rudyard's broadsheet trembled slightly, and Emma came to a halt at a polite distance, eyeing the monkey. It was an odd little creature, and idly she wondered if Victrix would enjoy such a pet. The shrieking might even be a side benefit, to drown out her Consort's gruff-grumbling displeasure. Did the expense of obtaining one balance the satisfaction to be had in its presentation?

Like Clare, she would have to postpone the question for further analysis. Her lips twitched slightly, and she dispelled the rising softness from her features, schooled them into an appropriately firm expression.

The broadsheet's top edge quivered again. Rudyard inhaled, smoothly and slowly.

"Like old dark wine." His baritone, lightly accented, was pleasant enough. "Sorcery's spice, and the dust of the grave. Can it be?" The paper lowered and Rudyard's odd hazel eyes, more gold than green, surveyed her from top to toe. Emma suffered it, the slight well-bred smile frozen to her face. "It can. Well, well." He unfolded himself in a leisurely manner and rose, and rose – he was quite *provokingly* tall.

"Sir . . . *sir.*" A rotund man in an ill-cut suit and moist paws for hands bustled officiously into range. "Sir, that *creature*—"

"Is enticing indeed, but I doubt you would wish to lay hand upon it. A poison bloom is she." Rudyard's teeth, just as white as the monkey's, gleamed in a smile, just their tips showing. "The female of her species is deadly."

"As is the assault upon the eardrums from your charming companion," Emma cut in, her tone light, arch, and amused. *Let us see how easy you are to provoke this time. It should lighten my mood immensely to darken yours.* "We shall require champagne, despite the hour, and a private room."

Rudyard's eyebrows lifted. You could see the echo of military bearing in his straight back, weight evenly balanced and his boots sharp-shining. He had been slated for a sepoy's life before his sorcerous talent had manifested itself. "Business, then. Very well."

"Sir . . ." The man – steward or head concierge, perhaps, with an incredibly harried air – next appealed to her. "Madam, that creature, the *creature*—"

She had very little patience for soothing him, though it was perhaps her female duty to do so. "I believe it is called a monkey, and it shall accompany us. Hurry along now, and prepare a private room. Champagne, and some light refreshment."

The man paused, taking stock of her jewellery, her frock, the charming and very expensive hat perched on her curls. Emma suffered this second examination with much less grace than the first, smoothing one gloved wrist with her opposite fingers. "I am not accustomed to such bold treatment, Mr . . .?"

He actually took a step back, paling as he realised his survey of her person was not genteel at all, and further taking note of the quality of her dress and posture, as well as her accent. "Yes. Of course, madam. Happy to. If you will follow me? Harold, champagne! Mr Bruin, refreshments to the Rose Room! I do hope you shall find it accommodating, Mrs . . .?"

"*Miss* Bannon. Mikal, my card." She held Rudyard's gaze with her own. The monkey still had not made a sound, but now it scrambled up the tall man's clothing and perched nimbly on his muscular shoulder. Its fur brushed his hair, and the contrast between the two textures was striking in its own way.

The concierge paled still further as he took in Mikal's leanness as well, the Shield's olive-green velvet coat and the knives worn openly at his hips, and finally realised – for he was no Clare, able to discern the facts of a situation at a glance – that Emma was not merely Quality but *sorceress*, and one powerful enough to require at least one Shield. Mikal produced a cream-coloured *carte* with a flick of his fingers and an unsettling, brilliant, white-toothed smile.

A curious crystalline silence, full of rustling, filled the

coffee room. Rudyard finally took notice of her Shield as well, and his colour underwent almost as interesting a change as the hapless little hotelier's.

The Indus sorcerer said something very fast and low, and – wonder of wonders – actually gave a half-bow, the monkey riding his shoulder with queer grace and managing to stay in place during the entire manoeuvre. It was the first time Emma had seen Rudyard perform such a gesture without a mocking edge, and she cocked her head, replaying the odd words.

*No language I know, and not a language of Discipline. Some tongue of the Indus, perhaps?*

Even more shocking was Mikal's reply. Her Shield sounded faintly pleased, but the edge to his tone was quite as intriguing as the words themselves. At least he spoke good Englene. "You are forgiven, *Kshatriya*. But only if you do not displease her."

"Your kind have no power on these shores. Nevertheless, I shall endeavour to be pleasant." Rudyard's eyes were suspiciously round, and he very carefully retreated, the broadsheet dropping from nerveless coppery fingers. When he blanched thus, he appeared paradoxically more Indus than Isle, and Emma's pulse leapt before her training flexed itself, controlling her heartbeat and glandular functions so she could act without her body's cries disturbing her concentration. "Come, Bannon." Rudyard reached for his brow, as if to lift a hatbrim, and visibly collected himself. "Your servant, ma'am. In every way."

It was a very good thing she was accustomed to the

Indus sorcerer's mercurial temper from their dual studies at the Collegia, for her jaw was suspiciously loose as the hotelier croaked a pale polite word and managed to bow and scrape the entire way to the Rose Room, whose only claim to roses was the overblown cabbagey herbage on the wallpaper. She observed a decorous pace, glad the coffee room was almost deserted, for this was a scene she would have rather avoided.

If Mikal's presence would frighten the Chessmaster of Lahore, it would certainly make questioning him much less tiresome. And perhaps, she reflected, it was time to turn her attention to the matter of her Shield's provenance.

She had put off that particular question long enough, and that it chose to rear its ugly head now was simply to be expected. The walk did her some good, therefore, since Emma Bannon's hands were, for the first time in a good while, not completely steady.

"Morris? Is that all?" A flute of champagne, bolted as common water might be and followed with a draught from a silver-chased flask, had done wonders to steady the half-Indus. Still, he was rather pale, and his tone far less biting than usual. "What a relief."

The monkey sat in his lap, shivering. Its fur bristled, grey sheen quivering with light that did not sting her eyes. Was it some manner of *animus*? She had read of the Indus sorceries of animal avatars, sometimes employed in place of a Shield to care for a sorcerer's physical well-being. She had never actually witnessed one, and probing at the creature with her non-physical senses would be . . . impolite.

Besides, it might make the man more difficult to handle.

"A guilty conscience, Kim?" She held her own flute, but had not sipped of it yet. The bubbling liquid within trembled slightly, and she studied its fluid gleaming. It was a good pose, and would perhaps hide her discomfiture.

Rudyard did not like being addressed by his Christian name – as an Indus boy instead of a *sir* – and Emma used the resultant pause to marshal her thoughts and calculate her attack. Mikal was at the door, arms folded and his yellow eyes half-lidded, his manner perhaps a trifle too tense to be called his habitual calm.

Perhaps the half-Indus sorcerer discommoded him.

The Chessmaster was a fortress, certainly. But Rudyard could be breached with relative ease. The problem was retaining enough civility to use him as a resource later.

Rudyard's face actually twisted, and he darted her a glance of such venom she was almost cheered to see it. "In the Great Lady's service, Bannon, such a thing is not uncommon. If you possessed such a thing as a *conscience*, it might well be uneasy."

She tilted her head a fraction. "Women are generally held to be creatures of sentiment and morality, albeit frail." *And your hatred of us is well known.*

"You are not properly a woman, are you? Not with *that* over your shoulder, and a Prime's will in you." But his voice dropped, and the monkey, its clever face a mask, grabbed his shirt-front with one tiny hand and patted at his lean dark face. "Never mind. Morris's working quarters are in Bermondsey. Faithgill Street. Twenty-seven, I believe."

*Just outside the Black Wark.* A chill traced its fingers down Emma's back, but her face gave no indication. She stored away the fascinating titbit of *that over your shoulder*, and continued studying her glass. "I see. And when was the last time you saw the good physicker genius?"

"When I returned from Keshmir, some weeks ago. He was engaged upon a commission that . . . overlapped with some of my concerns."

Emma waited.

Rudyard sighed, shook his head. "A problem of some bloody tribesmen, among others, and how to make them docile." Now he looked weary, lines appearing as he sagged briefly into the chair's embrace. "Some benighted folk do not see the benefit of being under Britannia's . . . protection."

*In other words, rather dirty business you don't care to speak of, even if it is your duty to Queen and Empire. And this genius has some part in it.* "I see."

The half-Indus sorcerer's head jerked up. He poured himself another generous measure of champagne. The monkey rode his lap with some aplomb, still silent. "How penetrating of you. Since you grasp all the complexities, let me add some advice, which you will no doubt ignore. Science for its own sake is as deadly as sorcery for its own end. The genius Morris, unprepossessing as he is, is a most dangerous man."

*Most intriguing.* "What, pray tell, is his speciality?"

"She didn't tell you?" His laugh was bitter as heavy day-old tea. The monkey hunched down, then half-turned, one beady little ancient eye fixed on Emma. "Poor Em, thrown into a *snake*-pit, blind. He's a genius of Biology. His speciality is tiny things, and he was working with an Alterator named Copperpot – a cracked man, to be sure. That's all I know. Go and see what you can accomplish, Bannon."

"Thank you." She set the alcohol aside, untasted. It was a shame, but her stomach had curdled. Passing too close to the Black Wark was not a thing to be desired, especially since Mehitabel's temper was extraordinarily uncertain. Not that it had ever been sweet . . .

. . . but the wyrm had cause to hate her openly now. It mattered little, Emma would brave much worse than a young wyrmling's ill-temper if necessary.

It was not quite craven to be glad that today, she did not have to, was it? Merely . . . wise.

"Good day, then, Mr Rudyard." She twitched her skirt aside as she rose, and for once, the man leapt to his feet instead of languidly unfolding. His face had suffused itself with ugly colour, and the monkey scrambled to his shoulder, a squeak escaping it.

"It's *good day*, is it? Something in return, *Emma*. What of that?" He pointed at Mikal with two spread fingers, rather as Valentinelli would avert ill-luck. "Do they know, at the Collegia?"

"My Shield was *trained* at the Collegia, sir. He is

properly native born." The cut was a trifle unjustified, but the idea of the Collegia perhaps investigating Mikal's background more thoroughly was a pinch in a sensitive spot.

Shields were taken young, and some of them, found or caught in the slums rather as Emma herself had been, were of uncertain parentage. The Collegia became mother and father to them as well as to sorcery's children, and their fleshly parents – if found – given remuneration. Some hopefuls even brought their babies to the Finding Festivals four times a year or to a sorcerer who could perhaps sponsor them – and add a shilling or two more to the recompense, ridding themselves of a mouth to feed in the process. "Are there none so well-trained in the Indus as to catch your fancy, that you must make eyes at mine?"

He took a step forward, and for a moment Emma thought Kim Rudyard might well strike her. His taste in lovers was easily indulged in some of the sinks of the Indus's dust-hazed cities, if *lovers* was a proper term for it. The gold hoop at his ear sparked angrily, foreign charter symbols running golden under the metal's surface, and her own necklace, a large oval cameo held to her throat by a black band of silver-threaded lace, warmed. The entire room rattled once, as if the hotel had forgotten it was stationary and had temporarily decided to become a train carriage.

It was, she thought, so *easy* to unsettle a man. Even a dangerous player in the great Game of Empire could be made to stumble in a simple verbal dance.

Rudyard recollected himself with a visible effort. Emma

was not surprised to find Mikal's warmth at her shoulder. "But," she continued, silkily, "perhaps I misunderstand you?"

"I hope you do." His white teeth showed in a smile that held no joy, a grimace of terribly amused pain. "Those *his kind* serve most often end envenomed. *Do* be careful. The Empire might hate to lose you."

*Is that a threat?* "I have no intention of being lost." She nodded, for that mannerly mark was all she would give him. If he was determined to be a rude beast, she was under no injunction to grant him more. "Thank you, Kim. You're a dear, sweet boy." The urge to pantomime a kiss at him rose and was ruthlessly quashed. "Good *day*." She turned on her heel, and Mikal stared past her for a moment. Her Shield's face wore a grinning grimace to match Rudyard's, and for a moment her breath caught in her throat.

There was a soft thump behind her, and Kim Rudyard made a curious, hurt little sound. Emma glanced back when she had reached the door, and found that he had gone to his knees.

The limp body of the monkey lay against the Rose Room's pink carpet. The thing lay on its side, its face turned towards her and its gaze, curiously filmed, had pinned itself to Mikal's back. Was it dead, or merely stunned?

*I did not do that.* Perhaps it was not an *animus* after all. Foreign creatures did not take well to the Isle's clime, and the thing's screeching no doubt had fatigued it. She fought the urge to curl her fingers in – a lady did not go about with fists clenched. She kept her head high and swept along at her accustomed brisk pace. Her Shield, trailing in her wake, said nothing.

Rudyard had recognised something about Mikal. Her own research and suspicions, while not quite inconclusive, now had a new direction to turn.

But first she would find this errant genius of Biology, and return him to Britannia. And she realised, once she had exited the Rostrand's glitter, that Rudyard had not mentioned Llewellyn.

Curious, and unsettling. It was turning out to be a dreadful day.

The bone-rattling ride in a hired hansom – for she had left her own carriage at home today, wishing to slip anonymously about – passed in almost complete silence, Emma staring thoughtfully out of the small window. Thankfully, it was Eli's duty to ride with her, as Mikal ran the rooftop road. The new Shield, for she still thought of him as "new" despite the considerable time he had spent in her service, was laconic in nature, and did not disturb her reflections, well used to her moods by now.

Emma roused herself as the hansom slowed, the driver chirruping to his mud-coloured clockhorse. Hooves struck the cobbles, and she glanced at Eli, whose attention was seemingly taken by the hem of her dress.

"Eli." As if reminding herself who he was. "How long has it been, now?"

"I couldn't say, Prima. Two years? Three?"

"Unlike you to be so imprecise."

"My former . . ." He halted. For all his dangerousness, he was still at bottom a quick-fingered ill-at-ease Liverpool bravo, who must have been a dark-eyed urchin on the Collegia's training grounds.

"Dorian asked you that, implying he would rid himself of your service? Charming of him." Emma sighed. "You are a good Shield, Eli, and *much* more suited to my temper than his. There's no danger of that." She chose her next words carefully. "I wish you to be very . . . observant, in the next few days."

As usual, when there was a task to accomplish, he brightened. "Glove, or Recall?"

"Neither. Merely . . . observe." *I am about to do something I may regret.* "It is Mikal. I wish your thoughts on him."

"I have thoughts?" He sounded honestly puzzled, and a flash of irritation boiled through her. But then he nodded, a curious expression crossing his almost-handsome face. "I shall observe him, Prima. Most closely."

"But without—"

"Yes. I am not *quite* thick-headed, though I am no mentath."

"I am no mentath either, Eli. We are in good company. Thank you."

He darted her a bright glance, and for a moment she wondered if he knew the nature of the . . . relations between Mikal and herself. And if he thought it likely she sought to replace Mikal in those particular relations with a more tractable Shield. Some of Emma's peers delighted in setting their complement of guards at each other in such a fashion, forcing them to vie for position within the closed circle of sorcerer and those who protected.

*I am Prime. It is beneath me to act in such a fashion.* Even though other Primes did not have the same . . . reluctance.

The hansom jolted to a stop and Emma alighted, Eli's hand warm and steady through her glove. Mikal appeared as the driver, a lean iron-spined old man in a tattered royal-blue coat and a voluminous red and yellow knitted scarf, popped the whip smartly over the clockhorse's dull flanks and drove his contraption away with a clatter and a grinding neigh of protest. The clockhorse was due for an oilbath, and Emma devoutly hoped the driver would give the poor creature one sooner rather than later.

To the west, a colossal lifting smudge was the perpetual cinderfall of the Black Wark. Daylight was the best time to enter that region of Londinium, but Emma was still secretly grateful she did not *have* to.

Twenty-seven Faithgill was a large slumping building, the district here sparsely populated due to the titanic stink from the Leather Market and the slaughteryards. Nearer the Wark, the clockhorse pens, where equine flesh was married to tireless metal in service to industry, gave out its own stench of coppery blood, terror, and the smokegloss of Alterative sorcery. The warehouses here would be full of spare bits for mechanisterum, to be hauled into

Southwark and given function before being shipped out, gleaming proudly, down the Themis to the sea.

No few of the vast boxlike structures would be stuffed with meat laid under slowly unravelling sealcharm, dripping ice and great fans wedded to cool charms to keep the interior of such buildings frigid. Catmeat and poor viands, true, but Emma always wondered how many of Londinium's finest ate this un-veal, unknowing. It was a good thing her own Cook was a canny marketer . . . and happy in her employ.

Mikal's face was a thundercloud, but she dared not acknowledge it. Instead, she gazed upon the rotting two-storey edifice, its brick crumbling and its timbers slumping dispiritedly. It looked to have been built in the time of Henry the Wifekiller, a vessel of Britannia who had paradoxically hated women almost as much as Kim Rudyard. Henry had also hated the Church, and had garnered the support of sorcery's children – even the females – by expelling the worst of the Inquisition from the Isle's shores along with the scarlet and black plague of Popish filth.

"I rather hope he is at home," she remarked, merely to break the tension. The sky was a mass of yellow cloud, Londinium's coal-breath holding the city under a lens. Perhaps after Tideturn it would rain. "Though it seems unlikely."

Both Shields gave her astonished glances. She shook her head, her curls bouncing against her ears and her peridot earrings swinging, a reassuring weight. "Never mind. Mikal, if you please. Eli, with me."

Her caution was almost useless. The inside of the warehouse consisted of two rooms – Morris's living quarters were tucked behind a sagging partition, spare as a monk's. A pallet, a small empty table that might have served as a desk or bedside table, and a single easy-chair in some hideous moth-eaten black fabric, and that was all. No wardrobe, no washbasin.

No means of storing food.

The workroom bore evidence of being lived in, but it was also full of disorder. Smashed glass smeared with various crusted substances lay everywhere, corroded brass fittings broken in piles on the floor, and scorching over everything as if a cleansing fire had been attempted. Emma wrinkled her nose at the stench. How had anyone *breathed* in here? More glass crunched like silver bones underfoot, and she did not bother to tell the Shields to move cautiously.

Later, she wondered if she should have. But she was too occupied with the new attention Eli was paying Mikal, and the deepening ill temper Mikal was barely – but thoroughly – keeping in check.

It was, indeed, a dreadful afternoon.

# ❀ *Chapter Nine*

---

## ❀ *Most Singular and Unnatural*

Miss Bannon's childlike face was unwontedly serious as she cut into her chop. "It is a puzzle, and one I should be glad of your help in solving."

"A physicker gone astray. Hmm." Clare applied himself to his own plate with a will. Miss Bannon's table was always superlative, and the graceful silver epergne had the air of an old friend. Even the carved gryphon legs holding the aforesaid table level, shifting occasionally as currents of sorcery or tension passed through the room, had become familiar. "Faithgill Street? Bermondsey?"

"Yes. Number twenty-seven. Very hard by the Leather Market." She was a little pale, and her tone had lost some of its usual crispness. Another might not have remarked upon it, but Clare's faculties had seized upon the tiny details as a distraction from the weary retreading of ground connected to Dr Vance.

And besides, he could flatter himself that after this much time he . . . did he? Yes. He could say he was well-acquainted with Miss Bannon.

He could even say he *knew* her. As much as a man could ever be said to know a woman whose trade was the illogic of sorcery.

"Very hard by the Black Wark." He paused again, as if thinking. The idea of that quarter of Londinium – the falling ash, every angle fractionally but critically off, and the *thing* that crouched inside its confines – tried to wring a small shudder from him. He controlled the movement, thinking of the equations he had arrived at to explain the range of degrees by which everything in the Wark had subtly *shifted*, and by consigning everything inside those ranges to a definition of "variable" soothed his nervousness most admirably.

"Yes." A tiny line had begun between her dark eyebrows. "Though during daylight, the Wark is . . . not very dangerous."

*The last time we ventured into that place, we barely escaped with our lives. And when I had a moment to reflect later, I arrived at the conclusion that you were the one most at risk.* But he contented himself with a noncommittal, "I see," and another pause, as if he needed further deliberation.

He sat, as usual, at Miss Bannon's right hand. Valentinelli beside him was applying himself to his plate with fierce, mannerly abandon. On Miss Bannon's left, Mikal ate slowly, rather in the manner of a cat who does not quite need the sustenance but likes the taste. Eli, dark and silent, had a high flush to his cheeks. Some manner of embarrassment between the sorceress and the men set to guarding her from physical danger, perhaps? The younger Shield merely toyed with his food, and Clare turned his attention in another direction.

"A genius of Biology. Hrm. Well. It seems he wished to stay hidden. That quarter of the city is rather notorious in that respect. And . . . the house was quite sound, you say?"

"Quite reasonably so, except for a great deal of broken glass in what I took to be his workroom. Shattered alembics and other curious pieces. Metal wiring, some brass pieces I took the liberty of sketching . . ." Miss Bannon lay her fork and knife down, with delicate precision. She took a sip from her water goblet, though a glass of mannerly hock stood by her plate; she held to the Continental custom of champagne as a dessert instead of to accompany the roast. "There are also some pieces in the workroom I have made available for you. Since I rather rudely assumed you would be disposed to shed some light on the matter."

"Quite disposed." The smile that stretched his lips was not unfamiliar now. "And you anticipated my likely request for such a space."

Across the table, Eli laid his own cutlery down. He had hardly touched his meat, and that was unlike him. The man liked his roast, and indeed ate such a goodly portion Clare was surprised he was not round as a partridge by now.

Of course, the daily sparring practice with Mikal was enough to keep anyone trim. Clare only occasionally partook of *that*, and the Shields treated him with a consideration he might consider insulting if he had not seen them in action against others of their ilk.

To see the Shields fight in deadly earnest was . . . distressing.

"Anticipation. A woman's sorcery." She toasted him with the water goblet, and he was surprised by the answering smile rising across her features. For someone with such a decided air, her face was oddly young, and yet Clare only sometimes saw flashes of the girl she must have been. "Mr Finch will show you to the workroom whenever it suits you."

"I take it this physicker is a challenging quarry." The salad, also in Continental fashion, had a tart tang that vied with the hock, but not displeasingly. "Since you are prepared to spend more than a day in seeking him."

She accepted the compliment with a slight queenly nod. "Any effects which might have told me the direction of his flight were quite provokingly absent. Questioning his neighbours led to nothing, as there were none. He has very few friends, and no tradesmen to question either, since any deliveries to said house left no scrap of bill or list."

"Very few friends?" *Speaks the sorceress who has none. Except, perhaps, myself.* As strange as it was, it seemed she valued his person far more than she valued even her fellow sorcerers. She had plenty of acquaintances, the better to hunt Queen Victrix's enemies in Society and elsewhere.

But very few ever saw behind the mask of manners and flashes of practical temper she chose to show.

She touched her glass of hock, thought better of it. "His disposition is said to be unpleasantly pedantic."

*Is it now.* "The same could be said of my own."

"You are *difficult.* Not *unpleasant.*" The sally was pale, but she was attempting to put him at ease.

And that was troubling. It was not at all her usual manner. "I am heartened to hear as much."

"His personal effects were thoroughly absent as well. There was not a scrap left behind to practise a sympathy upon, and I do not wish him alerted if he has engaged another of my kind to help him hide. I prefer to surprise him, since Her Majesty wishes him taken alive." She paused, as if waiting for him to comment. When he did not, she forged onward. "And undamaged."

His eyebrows threatened to rise. "She made a special point of those strictures? To you?"

"She did."

"Very interesting." He nodded, slowly. "The Crown requires information from him, but does not wish you to extract it."

"Insulting, but perhaps precautionary. Mine is not to question Britannia."

Was she aware of the clear note of pride ringing through the words, or the tilt of her head expressing even more pride in her chosen servitude? Perhaps not. "And the good physicker's disappearance was exceedingly well-planned. Which means he is in possession of something very valuable, something that could perhaps be used against our ruling spirit."

"Or Her vessel," she was quick to remind him, though her expression was suddenly very thoughtful. "Which concerns me more. Britannia . . . endures."

"And may She ever." The mumble was reflexive. Clare contemplated for a few further seconds, savouring every particle of the course before him. At least Miss Bannon did not press him – she knew that when he was ready, he would speak.

He did not, however, have the chance. For Eli pushed his chair back and rose, stiffly, his flaming cheeks and bright glassy gaze suddenly very pronounced.

The entire dining room drew a sharp breath. Or perhaps it was only Miss Bannon, whose earrings swung, spitting pale sparks, the profile on her large cameo running with pale foxfire as her mouth opened, her question – or irritable reproof – also unvoiced.

Eli collapsed, falling to the floor in a heap, and began to convulse, his entire body jerking to some music only its strained and tortured muscles could hear.

"High fever." Clare's sensitive fingers found the pulse in Eli's wrist, high and thready. "His heart is racing. No, those will do no good, cease waving them about."

The smelling salts vanished, one of the footmen whisking them away. Miss Bannon stood, her arms crossed over her midriff and a curious look on her childlike face. "It is not sorcerous," she said, numbly. "I cannot find its source . . . Archibald, what *is* it?"

Mikal's hand was on her shoulder, and the older Shield gazed down with a peculiar expression. Almost . . . amazed. And there was a flash of something very like fear; was this some dreadful fate that befell certain Shields? No, for Miss Bannon would know of its provenance and treatment.

Clare simply stored the observation away for later, being more occupied with the event before him. "I do not know yet." He peeled back one eyelid, stared at the fascinatingly thin greasing of blood over the white underneath. "Most interesting. Ludovico! Fetch my case, the one with—"

"Already here, *mentale*." The Neapolitan squatted on Eli's other side; he and Mikal had carried the fallen Shield into the adjoining cigar room, for the use of men during dinner parties Miss Bannon rarely, if ever, hosted. There was a soft confusion in the corridors – servants sent hither and yon, and the walls themselves resonating a trifle, as if feeling the pale, wide-eyed sorceress's distress.

"I can sense nothing," Mikal murmured, clearly audible. "Prima . . . *Emma*."

*Do keep her calm, sir.* "He was well enough this morning." Clare opened the small black Gladstone with a practised motion. "Let me see, let me see . . ."

Cholera? No, entirely wrong symptoms. Not flu, or dropsy – there were swellings under the chin, ruddy and vital, and when Clare touched one in the axillary region the sudden galvanic jerk running through the unconscious body informed him the bulges were painful. He next tried the inguinal fold, unconcerned at Miss Bannon seeing him handle the patient so familiarly. The same response, the same swelling. "Most intriguing."

"Burning up." Ludovico pressed his fingers to Eli's sweating forehead. The Shield's dark hair was sopping now, and the smell of his sweat was curiously sweet. Almost sugary.

"We shall need to make him comfortable. And ice, to bring the fever down." Clare settled on his heels, considering.

"How much ice do you require?" Miss Bannon's skirts made a low sweet sound, and Clare realised she was trembling.

*Most unsettling.* She was by far the woman least likely to engage in a display of fear or sentiment he had ever known. "Perhaps an ice bath? We must send for a merchant or charmer—"

She waved one small hand, visibly collecting herself. Her rings – two of plain silver, another a large ruby with a visible flaw in its centre that held a point of red light – glowed under the soft gaslight, and for a moment the atmosphere of the room chilled. "You shall have everything necessary or helpful. I shall also send for a physicker. Mikal, please inform Mr Finch to do so. Ludo, be a darling and tell Madame Noyon we shall need water boiled, and a tub brought to Eli's room. And you . . ." She pointed at one of the footmen, broad brawny Teague. Horace did not wait upon the table tonight. "Bring Marcus in to help carry him. Move along now, boys."

The Neapolitan and the Shield sprang into motion, and

Miss Bannon approached swiftly. She knelt, tucking her skirts back with a practised hand, and the edge of her new perfume – bergamot and spiced pear, odd but not unpleasing – brushed Clare's face. "I cannot Mend him effectively if I do not know what ails him. I cannot find a source for this distress." Her gaze was fastened to Eli's face. "In the absence of that, anything you need to discern the cause shall be provided. Archibald . . ."

"Don't fear, Emma." His hand clamped around Eli's wrist as the younger man began to thrash. "But do move back, he may harm you."

Physicker Darlington was a round jolly man in the long black stuff-coat of his trade, a throwback to the time when priests were the only legal medical professionals. At least he did not wear the bird-mask that had also been usual in those days, to protect from ill humours. Instead, he sported fine ruddy muttonchops and a gin-blossomed nose, and Clare caught a faint iron tang of laudanum in the man's scent.

*To soothe his nerves; perhaps it is why he smiles so.* "The swellings are of particular concern. They seem quite painful, and he is only semi-conscious."

"*Emma . . .*" the Shield moaned. "*Prima . . .*"

"I am here," she said from other side of the bed, quietly but with peculiar authority. "*Pax*, Shield. I am here."

He subsided, lapsing back into his delirium. The bed with its green-vined counterpane was narrow, and the Shield apparently had a fondness for botanical prints. His room was small but very well appointed, and Clare thought it was tiny because Eli preferred it so. The closeness perhaps reminded him of some childhood comfort.

Darlington felt the patient's pulse, and Clare's estimation of the man rose a notch as he noted the quality of the man's touch. His blunt fingers were surprisingly delicate, and he preferred the Chinoise method of seeking several "levels" of heart's-gallop, gathering information from each. The round man peeled back one of Eli's eyelids, just as Clare had, and almost recoiled from the thin film of blood over the eyeball. "*Most* unusual." He glanced up at Emma, his gaze bloodshot but bright blue. "Are you certain there is no sorcerous origin to this?"

Miss Bannon's gaze did not move from Eli's contorted features. "I can find no breath of sorcery about his illness. If there was, I would have already dispelled it."

"Well. Hrm. It is not consumption, not cholera . . . It is no doubt a miasma, or a form of pox, and a rubescent one at that." He tested one of the swellings again, and the Shield's body twitched. "Ice to bring the fever down. A preparation of laudanum to ease him and make him quiet. I shall lance one of these boils and see what manner of substance is contained therein."

There was another quiet commotion – a copper tub was being hauled through the door, and servants behind with buckets of steaming water. The tub was set just so, and Miss Bannon gestured. Gilburn and the black-haired Marcus set about stripping the Shield, being careful when he flinched, and Miss Bannon's fingers flicked. Sorcery hummed, the sound indistinguishable from the low contralto tone in her throat until her voice turned into words. "He shall not struggle so, now."

"I _say_ . . ." Darlington glanced at the sorceress. "_Do_ leave his undergarments in place!"

The hum vanished, replaced with the unsound-crackle of live sorcery. "I hardly think he is capable of shame, in this state." But Miss Bannon nodded, and the buckets, sloshing with catch charms to keep the water in place during its transport, were emptied with murmurs over the tub. It was quick work to fill it, running feet in the corridor from the washroom down the hall, and the house trembled again. Her small right hand sketched a symbol in empty air, and it flamed with a cold blue radiance; she uttered a short word Clare could not . . . _quite_ . . . remember once it had been spoken.

The copper tub creaked alarmingly, and frost traced tiny sharpfeather patterns on its sides. Horace and Marcus heaved, and thin threads of sorcery sparked and crackled as the deadweight of an unconscious body was eased.

"Gently," Miss Bannon murmured. "Let me adjust . . . there."

"Fascinating," Clare breathed. "You do not require an ice wagon then."

"Any competent charmer could do the same." Miss Bannon's gaze was fixed, a ringing in the air like a wet wineglass's rim stroked gently but firmly. "Do test it, physicker, and see if it . . . yes? Very good. Ease him in."

A splash and a howl as the shock of temperature change

met fevered skin. Clare might have winced, but he was observing events and effects with great interest. The physicker busied himself with a tray of shining implements, selecting a few that looked more like instruments of torture and laying them aside.

"Well, whatever comes from those swellings will give us a clue. A most singular illness." Darlington clicked his tongue twice, testing the sharpness of a lancet. "*Most* singular."

"There may be other remedies." Miss Bannon's queer flat murmur as she kept the sorcery steady was chilling. "You two shall keep my Shield alive while I pursue them."

Clare did not have the heart to tell her that he already doubted, very much, whether the Shield would survive the night. Later, he thought he had perhaps done both her and the young Liverpool man a grave disservice . . .

. . . but at that moment, all he felt was slight impatience, waiting for the body to be brought from the ice bath so he could gather more valuable data.

# Chapter Ten

## Coldfaith

The great Collegia, the massive main heart of Londinium's – and hence, of the Isle's – sorcerous population, seemed to stand on empty air. Charm-tangled lattices of support and transferral cradling its tiered white-stone edifices were clearly visible to Sight, but to the ordinary it appeared that the Collegia and its parklike grounds merely . . . floated. It drifted in a slow, majestic pattern above Regent's Parque, a nacreous glow in the dusk. Tideturn had come and gone, the golden flood of ætheric force sweeping up the Themis and filling every charmer, witch and sorcerer with a fresh charge to be used in service to their fellows – or in service to their selfish desires.

Emma normally almost-enjoyed visits to the Collegia's grounds. Tonight, however, she cursed inwardly and monotonously as she moved along a path of white crushed shell, her stride so energetic even Mikal sounded short of breath.

"Prima." Again, he attempted to engage her attention. "*Emma*. Listen to—"

"Cease your chatter." Sharper than she had ever addressed him, and breathless besides. "I am in a very great hurry, as you can see."

"The sorcerer. Half-Indus, correct? As you suspect I am. I would tell you—"

"No." She halted, her skirts snapping as her forward motion was arrested. Turned on one heel, and faced him fully. A curl had come free, it fell in her face. That was almost as provoking as his continued attempts to speak. "I do *not* wish to *know*, Mikal." *How much plainer can I be?* "Especially if such knowledge will force me to act in a . . . certain manner. Look about you, look where we *are*. Have you no sense?"

He stared at her, yellow irises alight in the gloaming. She studied him afresh, this Shield who had come to her service in the worst of ways.

"I have often wondered," she continued, in a much more well-bred tone, "why you killed Miles Crawford."

And there was another wonder: that she could say the name so calmly, robbing it of its power. Still, the memories rose – to be restrained, helpless, while another sorcerer prepared to tear one's ætheric talent out by the roots, was a thing almost guaranteed to drive a Prime past the brink of sanity. A Prime's will did not take a bridle lightly, if at all; it was that ill-defined quality of resolve that *made* a Prime, along with the ability to essay a split of focus and fuel into more than one Major Work at once.

To feel the bonds again, to hear her own despairing cries, to hear the sounds Crawford made as his throat was slowly crushed while water dripped and uncontained sorcerous force hummed its unformed song . . . it was enough to make one shudder, and it took all Emma's considerable willpower to quell the unwelcome movement.

Here between the House of Mending's white bulk and a low, sorcerously smoothed stone wall bordering a tidy herb garden, Mikal studied her for a long moment. Finally, his tongue crept out and wet his lower lip. "How long you have waited to ask me. I thought you knew."

*That is quite irrelevant.* "Answer me, Shield."

"He *hurt* you." Soft, sharp words, as if he had taken a strike to the midsection. "Is that not reason enough?"

*It is not a reason I may credit, though I might wish to.* She tucked the errant curl behind her ear, smoothing her hair with quick habitual motions. It displeased her to be dishevelled. "Surely you can see that Rudyard's dark hints would give me pause."

A short nod. "Nevertheless."

"What I wish not to know may still make me cautious, Mikal. Have I released you from my service? No. That should inform you of my continued trust in your capability." *It is not a lie*, she reminded herself. *He is capable, at least.* "Now come along, and do not be foolish."

She did not think it would soothe him, but it seemed

to. He followed in her wake, and she turned the corner. The House of Mending's front bloomed before her, its fluid lines pleasing even though the rivers of golden charter symbols held in its stone shivered uneasily at her presence.

For Emma Bannon's Discipline was not of the White, of which Mending was an honoured branch. Her sensitive eyes watered and stung slightly, and it would only be worse inside.

*Never mind that. Eli requires aid.* She moved forward, her back prickling instead of steadily warm with the consciousness of a Shield's presence. If Rudyard had meant to make Emma distracted and cautious, he had succeeded admirably.

The larger danger was, of course, that Rudyard would drop a quiet, envenomed word among her enemies . . . and Mikal's. There was no shortage of those, to be sure. The suspicion that Mikal was perhaps heir to a bloodline that should not under any circumstances be trained in the discipline of Shield was dangerous, for the only remedy – since he had *already* been fully trained, through what oversight Emma could not guess at, since there were many tests to avert such an occurrence – was a quick, nasty murder with all the force of law and Law behind it.

Even a Prime's absolute right over Shield and possessions could be . . . overcome . . . in cases of Law. Were she to halt and cogitate upon the problem, Emma would arrive at exactly where she had every other time she had considered this particular eventuality.

Even if Mikal was not what she suspected, she had

enemies enough; singly they were trifles, but together their collective force could rob her of Mikal's presence – and rob *him* of his very life.

*I do not wish to set myself against every Prime in the Empire just yet, thank you*, she might have said, were she possessed of breath and patience to spare. Which she was not, at the moment.

In any case, it was a calculated risk, bringing him onto the Collegia's grounds now.

*I do not care what he is*, she told herself. *I have trusted Mikal, and he has done nothing to change that. It is ridiculous to think that such an event as one of* those *could be trained as a Shield. It is simply not possible; the Shield tests are thorough and most thoroughly applied, as well.*

Then why had she asked Eli to watch him?

The Menders took bleaching as a matter of pride, hanging their Hall with swathes of pallid material and affecting spotless white-charmed linen. Marlowe had called them *whited bobbers* for their bowing and scraping to the Inquisition, a thing that had not been forgotten even today. Another name was less polite, and had to do with the process of bleaching involving vast quantities of urine and nasty herbs, not to mention charms that reeked of more urine and sulphur.

To be so pure required a great deal of stink. The Black, of course, did not seek to hide such rot. Or at least, Emma did not.

*If you had a conscience*, Kim Rudyard had sneered, and

she pushed the thought away. She blackened herself in Victrix's service, for while Britannia's current vessel had other sorcerers, including Primes, to work her will, she had none as thoroughly determined as Emma to do anything at all that might be required for that will to work. And if for that she was held in disdain, well, it would not kill her. It might even be useful.

*Careful, Prime. Do not lie to yourself. Of course some insults sting. Else you would not keep such a list of those deserving repayment.*

The Hall resonated as she stepped over the threshold, and the glare scoured her eyes. Hot water leaked down her cheeks, but she had not brought a veil.

She would not give them the satisfaction.

The entrance hall was hung with that rustling pale material, charter charms of Mending glowing golden on their rippling fluid lengths. The traditional white stone altar, carved with spirals and alive with golden light too close to sunshine for Emma's comfort, shifted uneasily in its seating. On its other side, the young student on receiving duty let out a squeak as the pressure-front of a Prime rippled through the sensitised air.

"Good evening." Emma came to a halt. "I require Mr Coldfaith, young one. Where is he?"

It was not quite polite, but there was no use in etiquette at this point. A fresh tear trickled down her cheek as she waited, her foot all but tapping under her skirts.

The student, a weedy young man with a prefect's patch and a bad case of spots that almost masked the fume of talent he gave off, swallowed visibly. He would no doubt be a Master Sorcerer, or more, someday. If he survived the Collegia. "Erm. Yesmum. Well. Sir is . . . well, he's . . ."

Emma grasped her temper in both mental hands and squeezed. *A lady must not shout.* She modulated her tone accordingly. "I am aware of the lateness of the hour, young one. If you are unable to point out Mr Coldfaith's location I shall go door to door through this House to find him. It is *quite urgent.*"

"No need to frighten the poppet," a deep bass rumbled from behind fluttering white. "Hullo, Em."

"Thomas." The tightness on her face was, she supposed, a smile. "I've something rather dire."

"No doubt. *C——x'y.*" The Word rolled free, silent thunder shaking through every bone and particle of stone, and the light dimmed.

Emma blinked, shaking her head slightly. It wasn't necessary for him to do such a thing, but it was, she supposed, a way of bringing home that he was Prime as well. And far more powerful than she. Though he would never stoop to duel, or unbend enough to act in any way unfitting the greatest Mender since Isabella de la Cortina – the Mad Hag of Castile herself might have been moderated by his influence.

No, Thomas Coldfaith was completely useless. And if it irked him to have no manner of pride in blood or matters of honour, none would ever know – except Emma herself.

*Does he still feel the same?* she wondered, not for the first time, as he moved past the fluttering material.

Mender he was, but no Mending would untwist his spine or remove the hump. One shoulder hitched on a muscled bulge higher than the other, his face almost a ruin except for two large liquid black eyes; he bore the stamp of Tinkerfolk in his colouring and dressed to it as well, in bright, oddly placed odds and ends. He was a scarlet jay among the Mender's monochrome, and the gold glittering at his thick throat and twisted fingers was an unwelcome echo of Rudyard's glimmering hoop.

Crow-black hair and those lovely eyes, skin scarred worse than Valentinelli's pox markings and his left arm twisted as it dangled from his high-hitched shoulder, fine legs that would have been the envy of many a man in the Wifckiller's time, when hose was the accepted means of clothing such appendages. His fingers were spidery, and his teeth picket-misshapen.

Such was the price Mending had demanded from its favoured Prime. Or perhaps the childhood accidents and beatings that twisted and so marked him had demanded it, and the Mending had rushed into him like water into a battered cup. *The light still shines, even though the vessel be oddened*, he had remarked once, and Emma, laughing, had kissed his bone-thick, fever-warm brow.

*You and your light. What good has it done you?* She had not missed the quick flash of hurt in his dark gaze then, but she had thought it of little account. Not until later, when she had seen him staring across the room at the last great Charmtide Ball of her school years, his face an open book in that moment – as Emma trod the measures of a dance in Llewellyn Gwynnfud's arms, laughing and blithe.

She did not often regret, but sometimes . . . well. And *after* that ball, Kim Rudyard and Llew had engaged in a screaming row inside the boys' half of Merlinhall.

*Kim would be happy to know he has unsettled me.* "Thank you." She found herself straightening her gloves, and forced the motion to cease. "I hoped you would be here."

"I am where you find me." Flat and ironic, his unamused smile showing the yellowed, stumplike teeth. "Fetch some tea, Straughlin, there's a lad. We'll be in my library." The Mender's hands tensed, knobs of bone standing out at each knuckle. Then he shook them out, his slight grimace so habitual she winced inwardly as well.

*They must still pain him.* There was a hot rock in her throat. "Thank you, but I may not be here long enough to partake. Time is short, and—"

"For a Prime, you are very rushed," he observed, mildly, as the student stammered out something affirmative and scurried away to fetch tea. "Bring your Shield. He looks like Folk, he does."

*He's not.* "He may be." She left it at that. It was polite of him to acknowledge Mikal – so few would, now. Since he had done the unforgivable, and was suspected of murdering the Prime he had been sworn to. "There is an illness. As far as I can tell it is non-sorcerous. It struck very suddenly, and—"

"Still the same." He had retained the irritating habit

of interrupting her. "Nothing ever Mends in a hurry. Come."

"I see." Thomas settled himself in the chair made specially for his twisted spine. His library was tall and narrow as he was broad and twisted, huge leather-bound books on the rosy-tinted wooden shelves vibrating with contained secrets. Plenty were Greater Texts of the White Disciplines – Mending, Making, Naming – though strictly speaking Naming had no colour, it simply served to *describe*. Mending's major branches were somewhat evenly repre-sented: the Trismegistusians, Hypokratians, even the almost-Grey Hypatians and the somewhat-embarrassing Gnosticans, who saw illness as something to be celebrated and sometimes fostered instead of treated.

Some of the smaller texts were jewel-bright and precious, herbals and treatises on the body and its humours, a folio of anatomical drawings from the great Michael-Angelo's corpse-studies, studies of various illnesses and illustrations of the body's attempts to cheat Death of its prize.

No novels, like those stacked on Emma's bedside stand. Nothing light or frivolous. A globe of malachite atop a straining, muscular bronze Atlas stood to attention on a desk with three precisely stacked piles of paper upon it; an inkwell and three pens in an ebonywood stand straight as rulers.

Thomas tapped his fingers once on the right arm of the chair, set lower than the left and curving further inward to support him. "Swellings, you say? At the armpit, the throat, and . . ."

"The inner hip. The physicker mentioned lancing them to see what they hold." Emma kept her tone even. He was disposed to listen, but also indisposed to move quickly. "It was so sudden."

"I see." This time he drew the two words out. They were not a question; they served to mark his place in the conversation while he thought.

The itching irritation inside her skin mounted another notch. *I have not the skill to Mend this. Tell me you do. Tell me you know what it is.* "I rather fear for him."

There. It was said. A shocked silence filled the library. Thank God there was no pale linen hanging from the vaulted white-stone ceiling; her impatience, tightly controlled, might have escaped her and shredded it. Or turned the strips to glass. Wouldn't *that* be a sight.

"Ah." Thomas's eyelids lowered a fraction. "And so you come to me."

Mikal, at the library's door, was deathly silent. She could sense his attention, and a sudden weary consciousness of being a woman in a world of silly but powerful men swamped her. They had to make everything so *difficult*.

And while Thomas perhaps wished to revenge himself in some small way for her treatment of him, Eli was suffering. A Shield, *her* Shield . . . and she was all but helpless.

Dear God, how she hated such a feeling. Was that why she served Britannia so faithfully?

Did she even wish an answer to that question?

She stood, ignoring his sudden twitch as if he would rise as a gentleman should. Gathered her skirts with numb hands. "Yes. It was rather foolish of me; I thought you would have some idea of how to combat such an illness."

"Combat? No. But Mend, perhaps. Emma—"

"I have had," she informed him, stiffly, "rather a trying day. I am concerned for my Shield. It is my duty to care for him, even as he risks death in my service. Which you disagree with the very *principle* of, well and good, but not all of us can wall ourselves up in our books and our mighty pacifism."

"Emma." Weary in his own turn now, as if she were a tantrum-throwing child. He succeeded in rising, with a walrus-lunge. His very gracelessness, and the placid acceptance of his body's failures, was yet another irritation. "I did not say I would not help."

*Then help, and cease being a hindrance.* "No, but while you reach a decision on the matter, my time is more profitably spent gaining every inch of aid I can muster." *I will not see another Shield die.*

If she thought of Crawford, she had to think of the four men who had vainly tried to protect her from him. And paid with their lives. Their twisted bodies, and the smell —

There was a flutter of movement as Mikal stepped aside, and a tremulous knock at the door. It opened to reveal the white-faced prefect, his spots glaring red. Why hadn't someone taught him the charm to rid himself of such annoyances, dear God? It was child's play for a *Mender.* There was a silver tea tray in his trembling hands, and from the look of it, someone had told him who she was.

*Emma. You are being ridiculous.* She took a deep breath.

Her corset, familiar as it was, cut most abominably, but it reminded her to stand correctly. The library was full of a rushing noise, but perhaps it was only the blood soughing in her ears.

Movement. Thomas had crossed the space between them, in his peculiar lurching way. "My God." A breath of wonder. "There is something you care for, after all."

*Did you ever think there was not?* But saying *that* was out of the question. Instead, she examined his countenance.

It would not have been half so horrid if his eyes had not been so beautiful. The Mending in him shone out, pale ætheric force behind the coal-blackness of his irises and pupils, luminescent jet beads. Those eyes belonged on a Grecquean urn, or to one of the marvellous statues of the great Samaritan, Simon Magister, who had swayed a crowd from a deranged prophet's ravings with beautiful sorcery. The language of Making even held a story of how one of the statues had fallen in love with an apprentice of the great Magister, and become flesh when he uttered her name . . .

. . . only to catch her dying beloved in her newly supple arms, for he had spent his entire life in those syllables to give her breath.

The story did not end, it merely halted, as if even a Great Language could not express what came next. Perhaps one of the Grey Disciplines had their own ending. Among the Black, the Magister was accorded high honour for several of his . . . *other* . . . researches.

Her teeth were clenched in a most unladylike fashion. "Of all people, Thomas, *you* should know how much I care." *And how little it matters when duty calls.* Though she could not fault him for thinking her cold and faithless. She had merely been young, and Llewellyn . . . and once again, the memory of a much younger Kim Rudyard rose, grinning and capering like a wraith. He had merely been finishing his studies, since any drop of good Englene blood, no matter what the admixture, was entitled to at least an Examination at the Great Collegia, the beating heart of the Empire's sorcery. No doubt in the Indus he was a *sahib*; just as among Menders, Coldfaith was a prince.

It did not seem to satisfy either of them. Her own dissatisfaction seemed a pittance compared to theirs; perhaps it was her sex that insulated her from such long-ings.

*Oh, Emma, you are engaged upon untruths with yourself. Do not.* "I am sorry for disturbing your rest. I shall be going now." Very evenly, very softly, her lips shaped the words, and she watched familiar pain rise in his gaze again.

"Emma—"

But she quickened her pace, and swept through the door. The teapot chattered on the tray, and she paused only long enough to speak the charm that would rid the boy of his spots, spitting each syllable as if it pained her and feeling the small words of Mending, a Discipline not her own, bitter as ash on her recalcitrant tongue. They were only a few – it was a child's charm – but when they passed, she found Mikal's hand on her shoulder, and the bright glow of the Hall's light stung her eyes so badly she was not ashamed of the tears.

# Chapter Eleven

## No Tongue Fit for It

Archibald Clare half lay, collapsed in the chair, staring at the grate. The coal burned grudgingly, hushed crackles from the charm drawing its breath up the flue scraping his sensitive ears.

He had spent many an hour here in the comfortable sitting room, conversing with Miss Bannon. The pale wainscoting was an old friend, and the paper above it, with its restful pattern of geometric gilt on sky blue, was particularly fine. The door was flanked by tall narrow tables, each holding a restrained alabaster vase with a plume of snowy ostrich feathers; the carpet was fashioned to seem a twilit pond with water-lily pads scattered thickly across it, clustering in the corners. The furniture, on slim birch stems, gave glimmers of paleness adding to the fancy, and two large water-clear mirrors held soft dancing luminescence in their depths, so the room was never entirely in shadow.

For all that, it was hushed and soothing, and it had the added benefit of being near the front door, so he could hear when Miss Bannon returned.

He had lost track of how long he sat there, staring at the coal as it grew a thick white coat.

The familiarity of the soft vibration running through the walls roused him from his torpor. He had never asked Miss Bannon if every sorcerer's domicile recognised the return of its inhabitant so joyously, trembling like a well-trained but excited dog. Perhaps he should. Her answer might be instructive, though often her replies clouded the issue rather than clarifying.

*How can I explain sorcery logically? Mr Clare, that is akin to asking the deaf to explain music, or a fish to explain dry land. There is no tongue fit for it but that of sorcery itself.*

His faculties were wandering. He shook his head slightly, heard the front door's opening, Mikal's murmur. No servants hurrying to greet her – would she guess?

". . . hear his heartbeat," Mikal said. He opened the door for her, and a very pale Miss Bannon stalked into the sitting room. Stiff-backed and dry-eyed, she nonetheless looked . . .

He groped for words, among all those he knew the permutations of. Yes, that was it. That was it precisely.

Emma Bannon looked as if she were weeping without tears.

Clare gained his feet slowly. They regarded each other, and the sorceress's childlike face grew set and still. And even paler, the delicate blue traceries of veins under her skin showing. A map of fragility, stunning in so iron-willed a personage.

His words did not stumble. "I sent the physicker home. After . . . Miss Bannon. *Emma*. You'd best sit down."

"He is dead, then." Quiet, each word edged with ice. The coal fire flared, its hissing whisper threading through the sentence. The entire house jolted, as if a train had come to rest, and Clare sighed. His chest pained him slightly, as did his joints.

"The boils burst. It was . . . there was a great deal of blood, and coagulated matter. Darlington admitted it was quite outside his experience; he was most vexed. The disease . . . we are not certain it is such, though it seemed . . ." For quite the first time in his life, Archibald Clare ran short of words, staring at Miss Bannon's small face.

Not much had changed. A ha'penny's worth of shifting, perhaps. But it had somehow altered the entire look of her. A pinprick of leprous green flared in each of her pupils, and Clare was suddenly aware of the nips and gnawings of exhaustion all through him. His collar was askew, and his hair was disarranged, and he had failed to roll his sleeves down. Where was his jacket? He no longer remembered.

Miss Bannon, still silent, studied him, rather as an astronomer would peer through a telescope. Her stillness was . . . uncanny.

"I drew samples." Clare decided that Eli's dying screams – *Prima! Emma!* – were best left undescribed. "The workroom is well-appointed, thank you. And I have examined the bits from your absent genius." He drew in an endless breath. "I am afraid we may have, erm, rather a problem."

She was so pale. Even in the midst of the affair with the dragon and a mad Prime, she had never looked thus. The burning coal whispered, mouthing a song of chemical reaction giving birth to heat. The sorceress's hair rose on a slight breeze from nowhere, curls over her ears stirring gently. Her hat was askew, Clare noted, and that pinprick of vaporous green in her pupils was almost as disturbing. She was normally so fastidious in matters of dress.

He forged onward. "The only conclusion I can draw is that this . . . illness . . . is somehow connected to the crusted substance smeared inside the glass canisters. Its source appears to be . . . Eli had suffered a small cut to his hand from the broken glass, and it is likely the . . . substance . . . was introduced. It is perhaps toxic – I took all appropriate caution, mind you, I suspected something of the sort – and, well. This genius Morris, he would not be engaged in manufacturing some manner of poison, would he? The implications are . . . distressing." *To say the least.*

"Poison?" A thin breath of sound. "His hand – a cut from the glass? You are certain?"

"It is the only conclusion I may draw at the moment. It presents very much as an illness, but it cannot be . . . I do not know." He searched for something to say. Why was this so difficult? He should be able to present the symptoms, explain his conclusions, and . . .

The damned angina intensified, but it was all through his chest instead of clustered high on the left. It was not, however, a physical ache. And its source was not his own organs of Feeling, but the look on the sorceress's face. The frailty of her shoulders, and those glimmers in her eyes. She would not weep, of course. Miss Bannon would not ever allow herself to do such a thing where it could be witnessed.

Perhaps he should have taken a fraction of coja to sharpen him, to make this less . . . messy.

"His body?" A shadow of her usual brisk tone, but he was heartened by it nonetheless.

"The cellar. Mr Finch said you would wish for it to be placed so."

"Yes." A single nod. Her earrings swung, the peridots flashing with far more vigour than the dimness of the room should allow. "Do *not*."

Mikal's hand fell back to his side.

"I am not quite . . . safe," Miss Bannon continued, in that same ghostly little voice. "Please do rest, Archibald. I am grateful for your pains in this matter, and I shall be calling upon your services tomorrow. We shall hunt this man, and I am not at all certain he will be returned to the Queen alive." A slow, leisurely blink, the green pinpricks staying steady though her eyelids closed, and Clare found he had to look away.

It simply was not *right* for such a thing to be seen.

Miss Bannon turned, sharply, and the house held its breath. She passed through the door like a burning wind, and it swung shut behind her, pulled by an invisible hand. Mikal, a curious expression on his lean face, stared after her.

*My Prima has a temper*, he had remarked once.

Her footsteps passed down the hall, and she must not have been able to contain her fury. For a single cry rent the nighttime quiet of 34½ Brooke Street, a sound of inhuman rage that would have blasted the house off its foundation had it been physical. It passed through Clare's skull without bothering to use his ears as a portal, and he staggered. Mikal's hand closed about his elbow, warm and hard against skin crackling with the dried blood from Eli's final convulsions, and the Shield steadied him.

"She will tear him to pieces," the man murmured, almost happily, and Clare was too shaken to enquire whom he meant. It was, in any case, perfectly clear.

The physicker Morris, wherever he was hiding, was about to find there was no hole deep enough to shelter him from Miss Bannon.

Morning rose grey and fretful over Londinium. Tideturn came slightly past dawn, soughing up the Themis's sparkle and spilling through the streets, filling the city with gold even the unsorcerous could see for a bare few moments.

Clare, roused from slumber by the consciousness of the hour more than by any real desire to be ambulatory, yawned and entered the breakfast room rubbing at his eyes in a decidedly ungentlemanly fashion.

"*Guten Morgen*, Archie!" Sigmund Baerbarth, round and ruddy as ever, his seamed head a boiled egg's proud dome, absently waved a teacup, its contents dangerously close to spilling. "I bring you letters."

"I say, good morning. More mail?" *Let me have breakfast first, old man.*

Baerbarth's face was grimed with soot, wiped clean hurriedly, and his fabulous sidewhiskers were tinged with black particles as well. "Serious, yes. *Frau* Ginn send for me, tell me hurry to you. Is from a man in top hat, she said. Very urgent. He pay her to give to you."

"Really." His skin chilled, reflexively. *It cannot be. Too soon.* "What did he pay?"

"Guinea." Sig set his teacup down, digging in his capacious pockets. Everything about him was rumpled and grimed with that same black dust.

*A guinea, eh?* "You have been at your *Spinne* again, haven't you." The huge mechanisterum spider was Baerbarth's true love, though he was also quite fond of Miss Bannon. *Un Eis Mädchen*, he called her, and paid her extravagant compliments. Yet he was forever taking the damn *Spinne* apart and putting it back together, with improvements and refinements.

Even a genius who had failed the notoriously difficult mentath examinations in his own country needed an obsession.

"She works!" Sig crowed, wiping his fingers on his jacket. "Archie, I make her work. She even make steam. Like tiny cloud for her to ride on." He kissed his blunt fingertips, then dug in his pockets some more. "Ah, here. Urgent letter. Important. But *Fräulein Eis Mädchen*, she said not to wake dear Archie."

"Miss Bannon? You've seen her this morning?" He accepted the missive – heavy paper, a folded envelope, a wax seal. *So soon? Well, well.*

"*Ja, ja.* She go out. All in black. Is *in Trauer*, the *Fräulein*?"

*Her variety of mourning is likely to be rather difficult for all concerned.* "I rather think so, old man." Clare settled himself, blinking as the rain fingered the windows. Londinium's yellow fog hunched under the lash of cold water. "Bit of bad business yesterday. Sig, did Mrs Ginn say anything about the gentleman who delivered this? Other than his hat?"

"Fine hat, top hat with feather. Blue coat. Muddy boots." Sigmund nodded, his poached-egg eyes behind their spectacles swimming a bit. He applied himself to the plate before him, heaped high with viands. Two different kinds of wurst, good plain bangers as well, and eggs. It was a wonder the lot of them didn't eat Miss Bannon out of house and home. "River mud. Saw it on the steps. *Mein Sohn*, he bring home mud like that every day."

Chompton, Baerbarth's assistant, a lean dark half-feral lad with an affinity for clockhorse gears, mudlarked about in the Themis, scavenging bits of mechanisterum and other things for Baerbarth's experiments – and to bring a few pennies in for his employer. If not for the young man's vigilance, Sig would no doubt be cheated of every farthing; the Bavarian was *incredibly* easy to separate from his coin.

"Ah." Clare settled himself further in the chair. The breakfast room, blue fabric and cream-painted wicker, was perhaps the most openly womanly of all Miss Bannon's chambers. He would not have put it past her to have weapons hanging in her boudoir; this and the sunroom were the only concessions to femininity she allowed herself.

The thought of a moment or two spent examining Miss Bannon's bedroom was extraordinarily pleasing. Such deductions he could make from, say, the shade of her draperies, or the contents of her—

*Impolite, Archibald.* He busied himself with arranging some provender on his plate. Sig was already snout-down in his own.

The door flung itself open just as Clare lifted the envelope again. Valentinelli stamped in, followed by a ghost-grey, burning-eyed Mikal. Who was dishevelled as he rarely appeared, hair disarranged and his shirt unbuttoned, a strange stippled pattern on his bare chest Clare did not have much time to examine before the man pulled the fabric closed, buttoning swiftly.

*How very odd. Burns? No, too regular. I wonder —*

"She did not tell *me*," the Neapolitan assassin snarled. "*La strega* go where she pleases. Threaten me again, *bastarde*. Ludo will answer."

*Wait.* Clare's jaw felt suspiciously loose. "Good God. Miss Bannon left without you?" She did not often do so, and with Eli . . . well.

The contours of this affair were beginning to take a shape Clare did not quite like.

Mikal cast him a single, venomous yellow glance. "Well before Tideturn. *He* saw her off."

"She go out in a carriage, black feathers and hats. *Ludo*, she say, *I do not wish to be followed. Tell Mikal.*" His imitation of Miss Bannon's softly cultured tones was almost uncanny. "I do, and he accuse me of—"

"I do not *accuse*," Mikal disputed, hotly, and a galvanic thrill ran through the entire house. The Shield turned on his heel, towards the door, and the betraying twitch in his shoulders told Clare he had been perilously close to sending his fist into the wall.

*How intriguing.* Clare settled himself to observe what would follow most closely. He was not disappointed, for shortly after, the mistress of the house appeared, her black watered-silk skirts dewed with droplets of gem-glittering rain.

She was in deep mourning, even a crêpe band at her throat holding a fantastic teardrop of green amber, softly glowing with its own inner light. High colour in her cheeks, and the slight untidiness to her hair, bespoke some recent exertion. Her rings were very plain, for once – bands of heavy mellow gold, one on each finger of her delicate, lace-gloved hands. Her earrings, long shivering confections of gold wire and small garnets, made soft chiming sounds as she halted, taking in the breakfast room with one swift glance.

"Good morning, gentlemen." She sounded exactly as usual, and that was the first surprise.

The second was the breath of sick-sweet smoke over-laying her perfume. Clare's sensitive nose all but wrinkled;

he took careful note of the circles under Miss Bannon's wide dark eyes and the decided set of her child-soft chin. There was a single tear-track on her cheek, brushed impatiently away, the lace of her glove had scratched and reddened. The redness rimming her eyes as well completed the picture of a woman fiercely determined not to let her grief consume her . . . but the mourning she wore all but flaunted it.

It was a response he would not have expected. His estimation of her character shifted another few critical degrees. Even after all this time, apparently, she could still surprise him.

*Bother.* He tucked the letter out of sight as he rose, and Sig dropped the wurst he had speared with a dainty silver fork as he hurried to his feet.

"*Guten Morgen, Fräulein.*" Sig's broad beaming smile was a flag. "Lovely, lovely. I bring Archie his mail, and supplies!"

"Thank you, Mr Baerbarth." Her small answering smile was a ghost of itself. "Ludovico, good morning. Mikal, have you had breakfast?"

"No." The Shield's face was a thundercloud. "I was too busy worrying for my Prima."

"Then by all means, please partake. I shall require you in readiness very shortly. Mr Clare? I have some rather—"

He had the most illogical desire to take her to task. "Have *you* had breakfast, Miss Bannon?"

The sorceress paused, her head tilted and the drops of rain caught on her dress each glimmering a slightly different shade. "No," she admitted, finally. "I have not. There were other matters to attend to." *And there still are*, her tone said, *and that is that.*

"I would take it as a kindness if you would join me," Clare persisted. "I would also take it as a kindness if you accept my services in finding this Mr Morris and bringing him to Her Majesty, as I am now quite intrigued. It is a fascinating puzzle."

She considered him, and he perceived how carefully Mikal was observing this interchange. Valentinelli, his back to the wall, had his eyebrows drawn together and one hand held oddly low at his side. There was a spark in the Neupolitan's gaze Clare had not seen in a long while – rather like a cat's expression as it crouches before a mouse-hole.

"Very well." Miss Bannon crossed the room with a determined air, her dainty boots click-tapping with their accustomed crispness. He had, Clare reflected, grown quite fond of that sound. "Do sit, gentlemen. Let us have a civilised moment before the day begins."

Mikal followed her, and Valentinelli peeled himself from the wall. Was it . . . yes, it was. The Neapolitan appeared slightly disappointed, of all things. What had he expected the sorceress to do?

The letter was a weight in Clare's pocket. To be caught with two items deserving his faculties was an unexpected gift, and as he settled to breakfast, Miss Bannon sinking gracefully into the chair a silently fuming Mikal held for her, he allowed himself a moment of quiet gloating.

Miss Bannon's next words, however, gave him much more to think upon.

"As a matter of fact, Mr Clare, I had hoped to see you before I left the house again. Do you think I might borrow dear Ludo from your service? Temporarily, of course."

"I stand right here, *strega*. You could ask me." Ludovico actually bridled, dropping into a wicker chair with a grunt that was only partly theatrical.

"Mr Clare is your employer. Please, do see if you can break another piece of furniture, I rather had the idea of replacing the entire house."

"If you like, Ludo break everything." His accent had thickened, and he looked well on his way to as foul a temper as Mikal.

"That will not be necessary, but thank you. I require you for something different today. We shall be visiting a certain sorcerer, and perhaps he will want . . . convincing, to give us whatever information he possesses." The smile that settled over her face was chilling in its good-humoured savagery, as unguarded an expression as Clare had ever seen. "And you are so *very* good at convincing, my *bastarde assassino*."

A pained silence descended on the breakfast table. Even Sigmund had ceased his chewing, staring at the sorceress.

Clare coughed, clearing his throat. "Yes, well. Quite. Some tea, Miss Bannon?"

The whip crackled, the matched black clockhorses with their ribbon-braided manes hopped, and Miss Bannon's carriage jolted onto Brooke Street. The sorceress sat bolt-upright on the hard red cushions, her right index finger tapping occasionally as she stared out of the window, her face set and bloodless.

"Who is this sorcerer?" Clare settled himself more securely – Valentinelli, jostled next to him, looked ill at ease with the sudden motion. Even the best of carriages jolted one about unmercifully, especially when its owner had told her coachman, *quickly, please.*

Said coachman, Harthell, a wizened nut of a man, was as adept at sailing a carriage through traffic as an experienced sempstress at threading needles. Shouts and curses outside, the carriage yawed alarmingly, then righted itself as the whip cracked again.

"Hm?" She stirred slightly, her hands decorously laid in her black-clad lap. The breath of smoke and roasting on her had faded, and her bergamot perfume was wearing through. It was easy to deduce she had consigned Eli's body to some form of flame; perhaps it was traditional to do so? Or perhaps it was a hygienic measure? "Oh. His name is Copperpot. He is a Master Alterator; I was at the Collegia this morning and took the liberty of checking the Grand Registry. His address was not quite correct, but there were enough traces at his former residence for me to acquire the location of his new domicile, which Harthell is following a tracer towards. It is quite possible there will be . . . unpleasantness."

*Oh dear.* "Dare I ask what manner of unpleasantness?"

"The usual manner, when we are hunting a conspiracy.

The quarter I received information from about Mr Morris had some dark hints, and he has quit his hotel. Perhaps he returned to his employment overseas, the better to avoid any further questioning."

"Ah." Clare absorbed this. "So, blood, screaming, and sorcery. And _Signor_ Valentinelli here . . ."

"Is to convince the sorcerer to tell all he knows." Valentinelli's grin was wolfish. He now looked supremely happy, even jolted and tossed as they were. "And even things he does not think he know, he will tell."

"Quite. I do not wish him dead until he has told all he knows, and I do not wish to question his shade, as such an operation takes precious time we may not have." Her lips compressed, and Clare's faculties woke and stretched more fully, inferences from her choice of words turning the picture several shades darker and more complex. "There are other considerations, as well."

_Oh, you are never boring, my dear Emma._ "I see."

"Good. By the way, Clare, you did not show dear little Sigmund the items from Mr Morris's home, did you?"

"Of course not. Sig would be of no use in . . . ah. I see."

"Precisely." Her hands clasped each other now, the lace digging and scratching as her fingers tensed, and she had gone quite pale. "I believe the fewer people who know of this affair, even in our small circle, the better."

"Good heavens." He could feel the blood draining from his own cheeks. "Surely you don't think Sigmund—"

"Of _course_ not." Irritated now, she made a small gesture,

easing her shoulders inside her dress, leaning into the rattling turn. "I merely wish him to be . . . safe. He did not see Eli's . . . well. We witnessed an event that no doubt has grave consequences. Mr Baerbarth does *not* need to be party to those consequences." Another pause. "Ah. We have arrived. Come, gentlemen."

## ☼ *Chapter Twelve* ·

---

### *Led to Regret*

Timothy Copperpot, Master Alterator and possessor of a very fine flat overlooking Canthill Square, was at home. Not only that, but he welcomed their visit with almost unbecoming enthusiasm. His narrow, nervous face bore a rather startling resemblance to a terrier's, since his whiskers were cut to resemble that animal's headshape.

"I say! Delighted! Charmed!" He was not sweating, and did not seem in the least put out that they had arrived unannounced. "Was just about to leave for the workshop, but would much rather a visit with another of the ætheric brethren. Tea? Something stronger?"

"Tea would be lovely, thank you." *This cannot be so simple.*

He had two Shields – even a low-level Alterator would need them for handling overflow if an Alteration went wrong or began twisting, the ætheric charge warping under concentrated irrationality. The idea of marrying flesh to metal was faintly distasteful, even if Emma could see the financial benefits available to those who could master the requisite Transubstantiation exercises. And Copperpot was no back-alley metalmonger; his cloth was fine and his flat was a wide, airy, pleasant one, on the third floor. His Shields – one dark, one fair – were neatly dressed, and they both eyed Mikal with a fair amount of apprehension.

Which meant they ignored Valentinelli, since the Neapolitan did quite a lovely job of slouching along behind Mr Clare, whose mournful basset face had brightened considerably as he glanced about the sitting room.

The curtains were pulled back, the coal fire built up and quite pleasant, the wallpaper a soothing blue and the wainscoting clean. Copperpot's taste ran to brass and a touch or two of the Indus, and Emma's gorge rose hotly, her breakfast staging a revolt. She quelled it with an effort, taking the seat Copperpot indicated with a smile and murmured thanks.

"Harry, old boy, do bring some tea, and the savouries! Had a spot of brekkie, of course, but never say no to more." The Alterator's delight seemed entirely unfeigned; to Sight he was a cheerful bubbling of low red, tang-tasting of the molten metal he charmed on a daily basis. The blond Shield glanced again at Mikal and hurried out of the room. Valentinelli hovered behind Clare, the very picture of a solicitous manservant to a not-quite-elderly-but-no-longer-young gent.

"Quite. I appreciate your hospitality." She tilted her head slightly as Clare settled in an easy-chair, Copperpot dropping into what must be his accustomed seat near the grate. "I do beg your pardon for the impoliteness, but I must come straight to the point."

"Oh, please do, then. Happy to help in any way, Prima! You have some work that needs doing, a spot of Alteration, or . . .?"

"I wish it were so simple. I must ask you about a certain genius, a physicker, Mr John Morris . . ." She left it open-ended. His response would tell her a great deal.

"Morrie? Oh, yes. Bit of a prickly chap. Had me make him lovely bits of metal and glass. Canisters, according to a set of drawings. Wonderful things, really. Tricky work, had to stand a great deal of pressure inside without leaking. Did he recommend me?"

*You poor man.* "He did, very highly." She settled her hands carefully in her lap. The dark Shield was not watching her. His attention was wholly occupied with Mikal. Clare leaned forward, his narrow nostrils flaring as his gaze roved every surface in the room. "How is his holiday progressing?"

"Saw him off to Dover this morning, matter of fact. A Continental tour, just the thing for his nerves. Rather raw, poor Morrie."

*Dover?* "He works too hard," she murmured. "Dover? I thought he was to be in town longer."

"No, no, he'd finished his masterpiece, he said. Saw him off at the station; made certain the canisters were loaded correctly and all. Taking two of them along, to show the Crowned Heads of Europe. *Quite* the thing, maybe even a patent!"

"Your maker's mark on the brass fittings," Clare interjected, suddenly. "The crowned cauldron."

"Too right!" The terrier-man beamed with pride. His fingertips rubbed together, and ætheric sparks crackled. "You've seen them, then? Pressurised canisters. A mixture of fluid and air, made into a fine mist – but it couldn't be steam. It couldn't be heated. Quite a puzzle, but Copperpot never gives up." He waved one finger, wagging as if to nag an invisible child. "I told him, I would make him a *thousand* once we found the right design!"

"Did you?" Clare leaned forward, and Emma could have cheerfully cursed him. She did not wish the quarry alerted just yet.

"No. Merely twelve, but the right design! Two sent overseas, with him. He said he'd show the remaining ten in Londinium, an Exhibition, he said, but I don't know . . ." Copperpot's smile faltered. He glanced nervously at Emma. "I say, what is it you're after, Prima? More than willing to help, but—"

"Master Sorcerer Copperpot." Emma's spine was rigid. An onlooker would not have been able to tell how her heart, traitorous thing that it was, had begun to ache. The chunk of amber at her throat warmed. "I regret this, I truly do."

Mikal *moved*. The dark Shield went down with the greenwood crack of a neck breaking, a sound that never failed to make Emma's heart cringe within her. Clare let out a sharp yell, Valentinelli was a blur of motion, and in short order the blond Shield, alerted too late, was down on the carpeting with Mikal's fingers at his throat. He had burst through the door, no doubt to save his master – who sat very still, with the edge of a knifeblade to his carotid and Valentinelli breathing in his ear.

"*Bastarde*," the Neapolitan whispered. "Move, or cast one of your filthy sorceries, I slit your throat."

"I advise you to believe him." Emma rose. Her skirts made a low sweet sound, and the curtains, fluttering, closed themselves without the benefit of hands. A Master Sorcerer was no match for a Prime, but still, caution was required. And the morning's light should not shine on this work. The sudden gloom was a balm to her sensitised eyes. "Now, Timothy – may I address you as such? Thank you. Timothy, Mr Clare and I require you to be absolutely truthful. And if you are absolutely truthful, you will survive this encounter."

It pained her to lie, but the man's face had turned cheesy-pale. He would be of absolutely no use if he knew the likely outcome of the morning's visit.

Britannia wished Morris taken alive, but she had said nothing about *this* man. And Emma was of the opinion that leaving behind anyone to be questioned was rather a bad idea at this juncture. It was *necessary*, she reminded herself, because she did not know if Kim Rudyard had left for his own part of the globe . . . or if he was still in Londinium, with a plan that hinged on some canisters and a certain physicker.

Clare glanced at her, but he did not, thank God, give voice to his plain certainty that she was being misleading.

"Mr Clare?" She kept her tone level. "Please question him thoroughly. I hope you don't mind if I interject every so often? Oh, but before you begin, one small thing . . ."

Mikal's fingers clenched. The crunch of cartilage collapsing was very loud in the hush. Emma's low hummed note caught the sound, wrapping the flat in a smothering veil.

It wouldn't do to have the neighbours inconvenienced.

The dark Shield suffocated, his heels drumming the floor, and Mikal glanced up. His gaze, yellow as the Ganges-dust of Indus, met hers.

Now that she had the attention of every man in the room, the business could begin. "What time did Mr Morris leave for Dover? And do tell me, what ship was he to board?"

Copperpot's eyes rolled. He was sweating now, and Valentinelli's hand was steady. The Neapolitan watched her too, his smile as tender as a lover's.

Ludo enjoyed this sort of thing far more than was quite *right*.

Timothy did tell them all he knew – which was quite a bit more than she had expected. And quite possibly, far more than the Alterator *knew* he knew. Clare grew paler and more agitated with each raft of seemingly innocuous or hopelessly complex questions, and Copperpot's visible hope that he would leave this flat later whole and breathing was uncomfortable to witness.

*If you had a conscience, Bannon, it might well be uneasy.*
Rudyard, damn him, had been utterly correct.

Clare looked rather green. His glance studiously avoided the stained armchair before the low-burning coal in the grate. "Are you familiar with the Pathogenic Theory?"

"Arrange it . . . yes, that will do." Emma shook her head. The silence cloaking the flat was well-laid; she checked its charter knots one more time, humming a sustained note that turned into the burring un-noise of live sorcery as she tweaked its contours, delicately, rather as she would smooth a dress's wayward fold. "No. I am not familiar, Clare."

"Illness – or at least, some illnesses . . . good God, man, did you have to do that to his hands?" The mentath shifted uncomfortably, tugging at his jacket and reaching for his pocket. His fingers brushed the material, then returned to the chair arms.

"When Ludo asks, he tell the truth." The Neapolitan settled the corpse's legs. "Ask *la strega*, she know."

"I am rather occupied at the moment." Emma sighed. Three bodies; she would have to expend rather more ætheric force than she liked tidying this mess up. "Do go on, Clare. Pathogenic theory? Is this Science?" *For if it were a branch of sorcery, we would not be discussing it thus.*

"There are beings invisible to the naked eye that may cause some illnesses. Science has suspected for a great while, but required proof – optics, and in particular, a certain Dutchman gave us the means of—"

"Do not become distracted. Perhaps you should wait in the carriage." There *was* rather a large bloodstain. "Put the Shields . . . yes, thank you, Mikal."

Mikal crouched easily over the bodies, his hands loose but his jaw tight. He did not question, but he was far too tense for her to believe the danger had passed.

"I am not *distracted*. Was it truly necessary, Miss Bannon?"

*Damn the man.* "Was Eli's death *necessary*, sir? Do not ask such silly, useless questions." The words had altogether far more snap than she was accustomed to hearing in her own voice. "We are dealing with some manner of poison, in canisters that will spray it in a fine mist. It must have been a virulent one."

"Perhaps not poison. The trouble taken to keep the temperature of the mist so rigidly controlled rather speaks against it. And poison does not *spread*. It is not a genius of Biology's likely method." As well as green, the mentath was decidedly pale. "Tiny organisms, Miss Bannon, are a possibility. The canisters are only a first step. No doubt the mist produced, drawn into the lungs . . . It would make precious little sense unless this Morris was certain the infection would spread."

Emma's hands dropped. She regarded him, the curious sensation of clicking inside her head as a piece of the puzzle fitted into place turning her to ice.

*Small things*, Rudyard had sneered. *Go and see what you can find.*

"Dear God. A weapon . . ." She halted herself with an

effort. Her lips were numb. In the closely packed streets of Londinium, such an infection could spread with hellish speed. And if its result was what Eli had suffered . . . "Eli . . . how . . .?"

"The crusted substance – introduced under the skin through the cut on his hand. There is much I can only surmise." Clare could not look away from the blood-drenched armchair. Even when Valentinelli hefted it with a grunt and dragged it to the arranged bodies, the mentath's blue gaze followed. "The canisters are no doubt already placed in public areas, in order to maximise the initial exposure." He blinked as the coal fire shifted, ash falling with a whisper. "And Eli had some few hours before he evinced symptoms. The first cases could be wandering the streets now. And infecting others."

"While the good physicker hies himself to the Continent and to whatever paymaster has turned him." *D—n the man. Oh, I shall give him an accounting soon enough. A right round one, too.* And *Rudyard. No matter how he hates me, this is quite beyond.*

It almost, she thought, bordered on the treacherous. *Almost*, and yet it was not in the Chessmaster's usual vein. This physicker genius was canny enough to hide his intent from Rudyard, if he had laid his plans with such care.

Clare's forehead furrowed. "I do not know if he has been turned. It seems unlikely."

She had to remind herself that her mentath did not say such things lightly, and that he was in all likelihood correct when he bothered to venture such an opinion. "Why?"

"To turn a man against his own country requires some manner of frustration, and Morris does not seem frustrated. Rather, he seems to be following a very logical path to its inevitable conclusion. He has made somewhat of a discovery and is testing it in grand fashion. Really, it is a magnificent and elegant—" He took note of her expression, and halted. "Ah, well. Yes. Clearly he cannot be allowed to proceed. But I do not find much evidence for *treachery*. Merely misguided genius."

"Yes. I was warned of that." *When next I see dear old Kim, I shall not be polite at all. First his monkey, if it still lives, then him.* "Mr Clare, can you find those canisters?"

"The sorcerer . . . yes, he has given me some ideas. Unknowing, of course."

"And discern the exact nature of this threat, poison or otherwise?" Did Britannia, Emma wondered, know the shape and danger of this weapon? The ruling spirit was ancient and wise, but Victrix was headstrong, and Science was new. Or was this a pet project of some minister gone astray?

*I do not know nearly enough of the roots of this matter.* She took a deep breath, seeking to still her quickening pulse and banish the prickle of sweat under her arms and against the curve of her lower back.

"I believe I may." He even sounded certain, thank goodness.

"Very well, then. I shall leave that in your capable hands."

"And meanwhile?"

*Why do you ask, sir?* "I shall be travelling. The man must be stopped."

"And brought to the Crown's justice?"

"Possibly." She did not sound convinced, even to herself. "He may be too useful for justice, Mr Clare." *No matter how I long to watch him die as my Shield did.*

She was rather becoming entrenched in the habit of lying to herself, was she not? It was an awkward habit for a Prime.

Awkward, and dangerous.

"As we are?" Thoughtfully, as he slowly rose. "Or am I?"

For a moment, she could not believe she had heard such a question. Her temper almost snapped. *I am standing over a pile of corpses, Archibald. Now may not be the proper time to accuse me of plotting* your *murder.* "If you are asking whether I would—"

"No. I do not think you would. Forgive me, Emma."

*Too late. It is said.* The pain in her chest would not cease. *And were you a danger to Britannia, I may well be led to regret.* "Certainly. Take the carriage, and Ludovico. Find those blasted canisters. And *do* be careful. For whatever you may think, sir, I am most loath to lose you."

Perhaps Clare would have replied, but Emma's attention turned inward, and threads of ætheric force boiled through her fingers. If she concentrated on the demands of the task before her, she could easily push away the jabbing beneath her ribs. It was perhaps merely her corset. A mentath's judgement should not sting so – he was only a man, after all.

*Oh, Sorceress Prime, lying to yourself is very bad form indeed.*

# Chapter Thirteen

## Don't Go that Way, Sir

Valentinelli, examining his dirty fingernails, looked supremely unconcerned as Miss Bannon's black carriage jolted into motion. In fact, he was humming an aria from *Ribellio*, of all things, and off-key as well.

It was, Clare reflected, like sharing a cage with a wild animal. Familiarity had allowed him to overlook just how dangerous the Neapolitan could be.

*And Miss Bannon?*

It was a very good thing mentaths did not often wince. For if they did, Clare was certain he should be wincing now at his own idiocy.

It was not the credence given to a controversial theory; there was no other way to account for the peculiarities the case presented. It was the flash of pain on Miss Bannon's features, swiftly smoothed away, when Clare had wondered aloud.

He had *meant*, of course, that Miss Bannon's value far exceeded his own in the current situation. It was quite likely that the Crown depended on her loyalty far more thoroughly than Miss Bannon ever guessed. Empire was maintained by those like her – proud servants, all.

Clare had often speculated upon the nature of the sorceress's attachment to Britannia's current incarnation, but had consigned it to the mental bureau-drawer of mysteries deserving close, thorough, and above all, *unhurried* contemplation at some later date. She did an excellent job of hiding her origins, did Miss Bannon, but he had the advantage of close acquaintance. The ghost of childhood want and deprivation hung about her, and her attachment to the Queen bespoke a battle against such a ghost within a person's character more than an avowed duty to Empire.

No doubt Emma would hotly dispute such a notion, or give it brisk short shrift. But Clare thought it very likely – oh, very likely indeed – that it was not Victrix the sorceress sought to insulate from harm. It was instead a young girl who had been saved from the spectre of a short brutal life in a rookery or worse, plucked from the gutter and set in the glitter-whirl of sorcery's proud practitioners. Of course nothing less than serving the highest power in the land would do for such a child's powerful wanting in a sorceress's body, and of course she would see an echo of her own struggles in Victrix's dangerous first years of reign.

In any case, this morning Miss Bannon had apparently not taken his meaning correctly, and Clare consoled himself with the thought that she was an exceedingly logical woman, and would not take umbrage at his indelicacy. Would she?

And yet, he had never quite seen her look . . . *hurt*, before.

The morning crush of crowd and other conveyances had thickened during the few hours spent in Copperpot's well-appointed flat. Rumblings, shouts, and curses filled the close-choking Londinium air. The wheels ground more slowly, and Clare's busy faculties calculated the likely rate of the sickness spreading and the resultant chances of sufferers surviving the boils.

*Could the Shield have spread the disease? Perhaps. Physicker Darlington? No, there was no break in his skin . . . but still.* Clare cursed inwardly. If the canisters dispensed a form of highly infectious illness, Eli may well have served the same purpose. Certainly very little of Morris's behaviour made sense unless he planned the sickness to spread from sufferer to sufferer.

Another jolt, and the carriage ceased its forward motion. There was a great deal of shouting and cursing – a blockage in the street, perhaps? Sunk in thought, Clare barely noticed when Valentinelli stiffened.

The carriage door was wrenched open, and Clare's short cry of surprise was drowned by Valentinelli's much louder bark. A confusion of motion, and the Neapolitan was thrown back, an elegant half-hand strike to the man's throat folding him up quite effectively. The attacker, stocky but long-legged in black, his top hat knocked askew, drove another fist into Valentinelli's groin, a swift blow that made Clare inhale sharply in male sympathy.

There was a click, and the door pulled closed. The man, with a speed that bespoke long practice, levelled the pistol at a cursing, writhing Valentinelli.

Clare coughed, slightly. "Well. A pleasant surprise."

Francis Vance, Doctor of Art and mentath, had a wide, frank, disarming grin. His moustache was fair but his hair had darkened as he aged, and one of the odd qualities of the man was his ability to change appearance at a moment's notice. He required no appurtenances to do so, merely his own plastic features. His eyes were variously hazel, gold, or green, depending on his mood, and at the moment they were quite merry. "Hullo, old chap.'"

"I *kill* you—" Valentinelli was not taking this turn of events calmly at all.

Clare cleared his throat. "Ludovico, please, he merely wishes to talk. Or he would have shot you with that cunning little pistol. A Beaumont-Adams, is it not? Double-action. And you only have two shots."

"Very good." Vance's smile broadened a trifle. "Two are all I require; normally it would be merely *one*. Your Neapolitan here is most dangerous, though. I have a high idea of him."

*So does Miss Bannon.* "You are not the only one who does. To what do I owe this pleasure, sir? I have been a trifle too busy to return your letters."

"If you *could* reply, I would be in Newgate by now. As it is . . ." Vance gauged Valentinelli with a sidelong look. The assassin had ceased sputtering and half lay, curled against the carriage's wall, glaring balefully at the uninvited guest. "I do apologise, *signor*. I did not think you would offer me a chance to speak."

"You were correct," Valentinelli snarled, and Vance's eyebrows raised a fraction.

"Indeed. You are *most* singular. Anyhow, Mr Clare, I have come to offer you my services."

"I would engage *your* services?" A queer sinking sensation had begun in Clare's middle.

"Oh yes." Vance apparently judged the moment to be less fraught, as he tucked the pistol away. His entire posture bespoke tense readiness, though, as Valentinelli slowly uncurled. "You are pursuing a certain Morris, are you not?"

*Dear heavens.* Clare's stomach was *certainly* sinking. "And you are as well? No. You cannot be. For one thing—"

"He came to my attention; I neither engaged nor funded him. His project is unprofitable, to say the least." Vance's smile faded. His changeable countenance became a statue of gravity. "For another, even *I* have some scruples, faint and fading as they are. This is dirty pool, old boy. Very dirty indeed."

"I see." Clare's mouth was dry. Of all the turns this case could take, this was perhaps the most surprising.

And he had not foreseen it. Perhaps his faculties were dimming.

"No, you do not. Yet. But, Mr Clare, might I suggest you tell your driver to direct us to Bermondsey? It seems a particularly profitable place to begin."

\*   \*   \*

Londinium's sky wept, a fine persistent drizzle tinted a venomous yellow as the sun began its slow afternoon descent. Between the buildings the fog rose in streamers, tamped down by the rain's catlike licking, the Themis breathing its vapour into street-arteries. Valentinelli slumped next to Clare, staring balefully at the mentath who had struck him.

Vance appeared at ease, having taken the entire seat for himself. "What do you know of Morris?"

Clare suspected he had gathered his faculties as much as he would be allowed to. "A genius of Biology. No more than thirty-three, and quite a disciplined student, though he failed any and all requisite mentath testing and consequently paid for his schooling by neighbourhood subscription and—"

"His childhood, Mr Clare." As if Clare were at Yton again, and Vance a patient instructor.

*I rather do not like this fellow.* "Londinium born and bred, south of the Themis in every respect until he was sent to school. I deduce his father died while he was young. His mother rather coddled him, and his schoolfellows did not like him."

"Consequently, he took refuge in his art. And in one other thing." Vance nodded. His eyes had darkened to hazel, the gold flecks in them shrinking. He observed a catlike stillness, but Clare had no doubt the pistol, especially filed by a gunsmith to rob the trigger of any stutter, would make short work of any obstacle in his path.

Clare's faculties helpfully supplied the answer. "Ah.

Religion." A few more scraps of information came together inside Clare's skull. "A Papist, quite possibly."

"Most certainly." Vance looked pleased. "And today is Monday."

*Of course it is. What does that have to do with—* But the carriage slowed its forward motion, Harthell calling and clicking to the clockhorses in the peculiar tongue of coachmen, and from the sound of the traffic outside, Clare decided they had reached Ettingly Street in Bermondsey.

*There is a church of the Magdalen here. I wonder . . .* "The Magdalen was Morris's church?"

"He visited regularly. Papists *can* be faithful, you know. Come, gentlemen." Vance's countenance had turned graver, and he now looked at least ten years older. "Let us discover if he was praying to a saint, or to Science."

Valentinelli's flat dark gaze met Clare's, and the mentath shook his head slightly. *No, my canny Neapolitan. Do not kill him. Yet.*

And Valentinelli subsided, his capable fingers retreating from the knife in his sleeve.

# *Chapter Fourteen*

## *Above Your Notice*

The stables were full of susurrus. Feathers rasped dry-oily against each other, and the clacking of sharp beaks snapping closed was like lacquered blocks of wood struck sharply together. The keepers, lean men in the traditional red bracers and high boots, were hard at work. They went in teams of two, one pushing the barrow, the other selecting chunks of red, dripping muscle and sawed-white bone, hefting it with an experienced grunt over the stall doors.

Gryphons were, after all, carnivores.

Emma stood very still, her hands knotted into fists. The smell – raw meat, the tawny flanks simmering with animal heat – scorched her throat, and the beasts craned their necks to see her, in the flat sideways way of birds. One hissed angrily, its feathered foreclaws flexing, and wood splintered.

"Best wait outside, mum." The head keeper, young for his post and with a livid scar across one wrist, shook his head. The beads tied into his hair made a clacking, just like the beasts' beaks. "Fractious today. And, well. Sorcery."

"Stay, Prima." Mikal, standing before her, did not precisely seem *small*, but he did look a very slender protection against the tide of feathers and gold-ringed eyes. "All is well."

*No, all is not well. Gryphons do not forget.*

"Ssorceresss." The sibilants were cold with menace. "*Deathsssspeaker.*" A black gryphon, a little smaller than its fellows but apparently the one appointed to communicate for them in this matter, clacked his beak twice. How the creatures used human language without lips to frame the syllables was a mystery, and one neither Science nor sorcery could solve. A dissection could have perhaps shed some light on it, but a gryphon's corpse was impossible to come by.

Theirs was a savage tribe, and it consumed its own dead. To be left uneaten by its fellows was the worst fate that could befall them, and Emma Bannon had caused one of their own to suffer it.

*I had no choice.* But gryphons did not understand such things. Or they would not, where a sorcerer was concerned. For of all the meats the beasts consumed, they liked sorcery-seasoned best.

"Speak to me, winged one," Mikal said, pleasantly enough. His back was tense under its olive velvet, though, and his feet were placed precisely, his weight balanced forward, his hands loose and easy. "My Prima is above your notice."

A ripple went through them, glossy, muscled flanks tensing. Emma set her jaw more firmly, and stared at Mikal's back.

Entering the stables was never pleasant. Even the smell of the creatures was dangerous, causing an odd lassitude that made anyone with ætheric talent prone to miscalculation. The effect on those without capacity, or on animals, was not so marked, but still enough to ensure wild gryphons did not often go hungry. They were Britannia's allies, and drew her chariot; they were also crafty, and exceedingly vicious. A better symbol of Empire than the ruling spirit conveyed by such beasts would be difficult to find.

The black gryphon moved forward. It had finished its meal, and an indigo tongue flicked, cleaning the sharp beak with a rasp. Traces of blood dappled its proud face, and the gold of its irises was a new-minted coin. The pupil of its nearer eye, black as ink, held a tiny, luminescent reflection. Over the reflection's shoulder peered a white-faced sorceress, her hair smartly dressed and the amber at her throat glowing softly as she held herself in readiness.

"Why are you here, *Nagáth*? We are hungry, and *that* issss prey."

"She is my Prima, and you will not taste her flesh. I require two of your brethren to fly swiftly at dusk, wingkin."

A sharper movement passed through the serried stalls and the overhead perches. If they decided to attack en masse, perhaps not even Mikal could hold them back. Emma had thought, when she had visited the Collegia that morning to consign Eli to the Undying Flame, to visit the barracks and select half a dozen Shields.

And yet, she had not.

*Thrent. Jourdain. Harry. Namal.* All murdered by Crawford. A litany of her own failures, men who had risked their lives in her service and paid the last toll. Now she could add another to that list, could she not? *Eli.*

Did Britannia feel this aching, when her faithful servants fell? Or had so many passed through her service that she no longer cared, and saw them as chess pieces – pawns could be lost, castles taken . . .

. . . and even queens could be replaced.

*A dangerous thought.*

"We sssshall not carry *her*." This from another gryphon, tawny with dappled plumage, its gaze incandescent with hatred. Its foreclaws gripped the top of a stall door, and the two keepers before it stumbled back, one of them with a dripping haunch clutched in both hands like an upside-down tussie-mussie for a sweetheart.

Mikal did not move, but a new tension invaded the air. "You shall carry whom I *command* you to carry. *Y béo Dægscield.*"

The ancient words resonated, the stable a bell's interior, shivering. The gryphons went utterly still.

*I am Shield.*

Their compact with Britannia was antique, true. But their compact with the brotherhood who guarded the workers of wonders was even older, brought from other shores with the wandering conjurers of the Broken City. Mordred the Black had given shelter to that brotherhood on the Isle's shores during the Lost Times. Mordred claimed descent from Artur's left-hand line; none knew the truth of that claim, none cared to dispute it, either. The Collegia itself, only recently tethered above Londinium, was a wonder of Mordred's age, its black gatestones crawling with crimson charter charms the first things laid. There was said to be a mist-shrouded mountain the Collegia had torn itself from the side of, long ago. A craggy peak whispered to have held another school where thirteen students were admitted, but only twelve left, and the last – either the best or the worst, according to which set of legends one excavated from antique dust – was taken as a toll.

"You are Sssshield." Grudging, the black gryphon lowered its head.

Mikal's tone softened, but only fractionally. "I would not ask, were the need not dire. Britannia requires, wingkin."

They moved again, restlessly, as the ruling spirit's name passed through them.

"*And we ansssswer,*" the chorus rose, as one.

*So do I, gryphons.* Emma's throat ached, the dry stone lodged in its depths refusing to budge. *So do I.*

# Chapter Fifteen

## Much Larger Problems

A thickly painted statue of the Hooded Magdalen smiled pacifically from her knees, beaming at the wooden, writhing holy corpse nailed to the *tau* above the altar. Clare blinked, his sensitive nose untangling odours – wax, incense of a different type than that perfuming the letter still in his pocket, old stone and damp, the ash of breathing, beating Black Wark close by providing a dry acid tang.

The church had stood before the Wifekiller's time, and those recalcitrant or conservative enough to remain under the command of the Papacy in matters of faith had preserved it fairly well. Well enough that Valentinelli, Neapolitan that he was, murmured a phrase in his native tongue and performed a curious crossing motion.

Clare caught Vance's glance at the assassin, and knew

the other mentath was storing away tiny bits of deduction and inference. Rather as he himself would.

He turned his attention away, examining the church's interior. Pews of old dark wood, each with a rail attached to its back for those who chose to kneel, the *tau* corpse lit from underneath by a bank of dripping candles. The altar was a tangle of dying flowers on a motheaten red velvet cloth; four confession-closets stood along the west wall, empty. On a workaday Monday, the stone-and-brick pile was full only of echoes. Generations of nervous sweat and the effort of pleading with uncaring divinity had imparted its own subtle tang to the still air, warmed by candle-breath. Another bank of candles crouched within a narrow room tucked to the side, under icons both painted and sculpted.

Vance exhaled, a satisfied sound. "Where would you say, old chap?"

Clare caught the first note of unease in the other mentath's tone. *Ah. You are not as certain as you would like me to believe.* "Certainly not the basement. Or the tower." He took his time, enjoying the sensation of pieces of the puzzle fitting together with tiny, satisfying unheard snaps. *Not under the altar, either.* He turned, smartly, and his steps were hushed as he entered the domain of the saints. Valentinelli drifted after him, and Clare was absurdly comforted by the Neapolitan's presence.

Vance had surprised the assassin once. Clare did not think such an event likely to occur a second time.

Paintings and small statues, the saints with their hands

frozen in attitudes of blessing and the thin crescents or circles of haloes about their heads worked in gilt, stared with sad soot-laden eyes. Clare stood for a moment, thinking.

*He is a genius, not a mentath. He is the prey of forces within himself he cannot compass, and they have driven him. The initial impulse came from another quarter, but he made the quest his own.* Clare nodded thoughtfully, tapping his thin lips with one finger. Ludovico, well used to this motion, stilled. Vance breathed out softly, perhaps in appreciation of the symmetry of this small room, a tiny gem of proportions tucked away inside the larger church. A pearl of a room, nestled in an oyster's knobbled shell.

"Only one possible choice," Clare murmured.

Under the painting of Kosmas and Demian grafting a leg onto one of their hapless patients – spoons and medicine boxes worked in gilt-drenched paint, the sufferer's mouth an elongated O of pain and the blood faded to a scab-coloured smear – was a shelflike table, its top a rack for a bank of small, cheap candles. The smoke from their tainted tallow was almost as foul as the yellow fog of Londinium's coal-breath: a miniature cousin.

Clare sighed. It was a sound of consummation, and he twitched aside the rotting cloth skirting the table's spindle-legs.

There, in the darkness, nestled in its hole, the canister sat. Perfect blown glass, still trembling with the breath of Alterative sorcery that had purged it of contaminants and occlusions, and the top, brasswork chased with charter symbols that winked out as he exhaled, their course run and their charge exhausted. Gears ringed the small perforated spigot at the top, each glowing with careful charm-ringed applications of neatsfoot oil.

"Ah," Clare murmured. "I see, I see. Here, before the saints of physickers. You *are* a doctor, after all."

"Not of Medicine," Vance corrected, somewhat pedantically.

*Miss Bannon would not like you at all, sir.* The thought, absurd as it was, comforted him. And how irrational was it, such comfort? To be a mentath was to largely forgo comfort.

Except the older Clare became, the less willing he was to believe such a maxim.

"Not of Medicine, no. But of Biology, that great clockwork of Life itself. Morris believes in the divine hand. He is merely a fingernail-paring upon it."

"Very poetic," Vance sniffed. "That is the mechanism?"

It was Clare's turn to become pedantic. "It is *a* mechanism. One used to contaminate those who came to pray to the saints of Physickers for aid. There are nine more scattered through Londinium, and there" – he pointed at the clockwork's bright-shining face – "there, you see, is the reason why we are too late. He set it to exhale just after Mass, when the devout would be praying to their saints. Then they go forth from the church, and carry death with them. The beast is loose."

"Dear God." Vance had actually paled. Clare ascertained as much with a swift glance, then returned to studying the clockwork.

*To measure off time, rather as one would measure boiling an egg. Very clever. And then . . . yes, pressurised, and there is the release. And it comes out. Not steam, though. High temperature presumably deadens the effect.*

He heard the soft thump and the sounds of struggle, but it was a predetermined outcome. Valentinelli had a matter of honour to avenge, and Clare perhaps should be grateful that the Neapolitan remembered Clare required the damn criminal taken alive.

"*Bastarde*," Ludo breathed, rather as he would to a lover, as Vance's struggles diminished. If a man could not inhale, he could not fight, and when respiration was choked off by Valentinelli's capable, muscle-corded forearm, even the most canny criminal mentath in the history of Britannia ceased his frantic motions very soon.

"Be careful with him, my dear Italian," Clare murmured. "I rather think I need his faculties to solve this puzzle."

"He is a motherless whoreson," the assassin spat, apparently unaware of the irony of such an utterance.

"That may well be." Clare sighed and reached forward carefully, touching the smooth, cold glass of the canister with one dry fingertip. "But at the moment, we have *much* larger problems."

# ✹ *Chapter Sixteen*

————————

*Barely, but Sufficient*

T he gryphon riders of the Skystream Guard were often chosen by the beasts themselves. It was not unheard of, even in these modern times, for a gryphon to descend from the sky and hover over a boy (or, very infrequently, a girl), buffeting them to the ground with wingbeats. To be plucked from a child's life and thrust into the training to ride Britannia's winged steeds was a shock some failed to endure.

Those who did found themselves with new names, scrubbed and shaven like a Collegia orphan, and drilled intensively before being allowed to see one of the creatures again.

Gryphons did not forgive a single mistake, and their riders had to be naturally resistant to the strange aura of lassitude that dropped over their usual prey. There was a martial practice of movement – the Shields were taught this, in addition to their other training – that allowed a rider certain advantages against even such a large, winged carnivore, and certain tricks with their traditional longcrook with its sharpened inner curve allowed them to direct the beasts.

The riders sometimes even slumbered with their charges, and there were stories of deep attachment between Guard and beast; from the gryphons they learned peculiar charter symbols that did not seem to disturb the æther but were nonetheless effective. Among the Skystream there were charioteers as well, those who could hold two or more of the beasts in check while they drew one of Britannia's shield-sided conveyances.

A gryphon chariot was light and afforded little protection from the elements. Boudicca had not been the first vessel to ride one into battle at the head of her armies, but it was said she had been the one to design better chariots. Certainly very little in their manufacture had changed since her ill-fated reign, and a citizen of the Isle from her time – or even Golden Bess's rule – would instantly recognise the high sides, rounded back and the queer metal-laced reins crackling with strange charter charms. Geared wheels and runners, cunningly designed to shift as the terrain made necessary or flight made *un*necessary, were alive with crawling coppery light.

Mikal leapt lightly into the chariot, his hand flicking out to take the reins from the charioteer. Muscle came alive on his back as the two gryphons – both tawny with white feather ruffs, their beaks amber and their wings moving restlessly – tested his control.

Shields, made resistant to the aura of lassitude by their membership in their ancient brotherhood, could commandeer a chariot. Carefully, of course, and only if the need was dire. Of course, very few of sorcery's children would consider such a conveyance under even the worst and most pressing circumstances.

There was no *time*. Rail to Dover and a ship from thence would simply not do. And the sooner Emma laid hands on the man, the sooner she could . . . do whatever was necessary.

"Prima," Mikal said, his head turned to the side. The gryphons heaved, and he stiffened, wrapping the reins in his fists. They settled, grudgingly – a Shield's strength was sufficient.

Barely, but sufficient.

The charioteer hopped down, his boots, with their curious metal appurtenances to keep them fastened to the chariot's floor, clanking briskly. He offered his hand, and Emma stepped gingerly up. She almost fell onto Mikal as the gryphons heaved, hissing their displeasure at being bridled and their further rage that they would be bearing her.

If Eli had been there, he would have buckled her in. As it was, the dark-eyed boy with an old, white claw scar down the side of his shaven head slid the straps over her, bracing her back against the front of the chariot and snugging the oiled leather across her shoulders and hips. Mikal slid the toes of his iron-laced boots through the iron loops on the floor and tested them as he kept the gryphons contained.

The charioteer glanced at her and she nodded. Anything she said would not be heard over the angry screeching. Unlike the Skystream, Mikal wore no goggles; his eyes hooded as Emma reached out, her gloved hand settling on his boot. A simple charm sprang to life, vivid golden charter symbols crawling over his cheeks – they would keep the wind from stinging his flesh too badly, and trickles of ætheric force would slide into him, easing the strain. Had she another Shield or two, they could have shared the burden.

But she did not. And now she wondered if her penance would be the death of her, and of her remaining Shield as well.

*How strange.* Her cheeks were wet, though they were not flying yet. *I do not believe Mikal can be killed.*

What a sorcerer could not compass was a weakness. To think the unthinkable was their calling; to lose the resilience of intuition-fuelled phantasy was to begin a slow calcification that was, to any Prime, worse than death and the precursor of annihilation.

"———!" Mikal yelled, and the charioteer sprang aside lightly as a leaf. The back of the conveyance latched shut, and gears slid. The great doors before them were inching open, and late-afternoon light scored Emma's tender eyes behind the leather and smoked glass of the goggles. The things were *dreadful*, but at least they kept the light at bay.

The chariot's runners squealed as the gryphons heaved. The ascending ramp, bluestone quarried and charm-carried across the Isle long ago, bore the scars of generations of gryphon claws and the scrape of numerous chariots, its slope pointing at a filthy-fogged Londinium sky.

Emma shut her eyes. The chariot jolted, and she felt the moment Mikal slightly loosened his hold, both psychic and physical, upon the beasts.

Motion. The straps cut cruelly as the beasts lunged, runners ground against oiled stone, and the great shell-shaped doors – their outsides still bearing the scars of the Civil War and Cramwelle's reign of terror – had barely finished creaking wide enough before the gryphons dragged their burden into the sky. The chariot's gears and wheels spun gently in empty air, the temperature dropping so quickly Emma's breath flashed into ice crystals before her face. Her stomach, left behind, struggled to keep up, and her fingers clamped on Mikal's ankle.

*No, I do not believe in his mortality. And yet I am afraid.*

# Chapter Seventeen

## A Process of Discovery

"We will not be torturing him. Why do you insist on making me repeat myself?" Clare tested the knot. No room for error when it came to their guest.

"He deserve it, *mentale*. A finger. One little finger, for Ludo's honour."

"I *can* hear you, you know." It was difficult to gauge Vance's expression under the blindfold, which was more a nod to Valentinelli's sense of propriety than an actual deterrent to Vance understanding which quarter of Londinium his captors had repaired to.

"Good." Ludovico was unrepentant, to say the least. He laid the flat of the razor-sharpened, slightly curved dagger along Vance's naked cheek.

A thorough search of the criminal's clothing and person had turned up several extraordinarily interesting items. One in particular had caught Clare's attention, and he slipped the small statue, cut from a single violently-blue gem, into a bureau drawer, deliberately making noise. There was no point in seeking to misdirect.

"You may return that to the Museum, Clare." Vance did not move a muscle. His tone was as if he was at tea, instead of with a sharp edge pressed to his flesh. "A sign of good faith, don't you think?"

"Ludo, fetch your instruments." *I sound weary.* Well, he *felt* weary. There were some terrible choices to be made soon. "We will in all likelihood not need them, but best to be prepared, don't you think?"

"*Ci.*" The Neapolitan was happier than Clare had ever heard him. "Do not start without me, *mentale.*"

"Wouldn't dream of it." He watched Valentinelli slink through the workroom's door, closing it with only the ghost of a click, and untied the blindfold. "My apologies, sir. He is . . . overzealous."

"But useful." Vance opened his eyes. He examined Clare from top to toe, then his gaze passed through the workroom Miss Bannon had placed at Clare's disposal.

Stone walls, sturdy enough to withstand all manner of experimental mishaps, showed grey and smooth, charm-brushed. One reached this room at the bottom of a long flight of stairs, and Clare had wondered if it was Miss Bannon's attempt to ease his mind at the incidence of such unnatural material in the walls and floor. The roof was heavy timbers, more than high enough for racks to dangle from them, hangman shapes with sharp and dull hooks Clare had not begun to fill yet.

The tables were heavy, solid pieces more likely to be found in a butcher's shop despite their fresh-scrubbed appearance, and the racks of alembics and other experimental minutiae gracing their surfaces were sparkling new. Clare's older glassware and materials did not look precisely shabby next to such equipment, but there was a glaring difference between the worn and the just-bought. Two capacious bureaus stood to attention, ready to receive larger items and racks. The desk, set with its back to one corner so Clare could see the door as he wrote, was a quite heavy oaken roll-top, with enough pigeon- and cubbyholes to satisfy the most magpie of mentaths.

"Very useful," Clare agreed. Whatever deductions Vance would make from the state of the workroom, he was welcome to them. "My hope is that you will prove likewise useful."

"If not, the Neapolitan prince is allowed to exercise upon me? Bad sport, old man." Vance's grin was untroubled. His eyes were now a cheerful hazel, and his moustache twitched slightly as he passed his gaze over the room's interior again.

"Almost as bad a sport as poisoning a decoy." Clare folded his arms, leaning one hip against the closest table, and examined his guest in return. He very carefully did *not* touch his pocket. "Or financing the lamentably missing Mr Morris."

"I did not *finance* him." Vance actually *prickled* at the notion, his eyes narrowing. A ghost of colour suffused his shaven cheeks. "He sought to engage some of my fellows in this work. But it is not *profitable*, and once I realised what he was about—"

*A weapon,* Miss Bannon said. *Now gone astray. Madness, sheer lunacy.* "And when was this?" Clare weighed every word, testing them for duplicity. "Your pangs of unprofitability, when do they date from?"

"Very recently, sir. I regret to say, very recently."

"It is, of course, an illness. Microscopic."

"Yes. And highly communicable. The Pathogenic Theory is borne out by my own experiments."

*Yes, let us hear more about those.* "You were working with Morris, and realised it was unprofitable only *lately*?"

"I was engaged on a process of *discovery*, Clare. Morris was merely a useful donkey to bear some bits of the burden. What he has done with it is sheer *folly*. He found others to finance his research, not the least of whom were the good offices of Her Majesty. Rather short-sighted, but they did not understand such a weapon will turn on its bearer as easily as onto Britannia's enemies." Vance's tongue flicked out, oddly colourless, and touched his dry lips. "Or even more easily, as it turns out."

"I see." *Miss Bannon was not told the nature of these experiments. Does the Queen know?* "Her Majesty's government was seeking a new weapon?" He said it slowly, as if not quite convinced.

Vance made a quick, impatient movement. "You are not dim-witted, sir, you understand this very well. Morris convinced a paymaster that such a weapon was efficient and controllable. He is wrong, very wrong. I am not certain whether he believed it himself, but it matters little." Vance had gone still, a flush rising in his cheeks. "What matters is finding a remedy."

"Indeed." Clare's chin dipped. He stood, sunk in deep thought, until Valentinelli's return was marked by a cheerful slam of the door.

"Ah, you must want to start with his eyes!" The Neapolitan thumped his own small well-worn Gladstone onto a free expanse of table, snapping it open with practised movements. "Not where I would choose, *mentale*, but very well."

"Hush for a moment, my dear bandit." Clare's eyelids had dropped halfway, and he longed for a fraction of coja to sharpen his faculties. Vance was still studying him, and the thought that the criminal mentath might be uncertain of Clare's next move was a balm indeed. "Yes," he said, finally. "Yes, we must find a remedy."

Valentinelli made a small spitting sound, and Clare turned his gaze upon him, noting afresh the man's pock-marked cheeks and calloused hands. *A prince? He is certainly noble, and his manners – when he chooses to use them – are exquisite. Very possible. Or perhaps Vance is seeking to misdirect. Either is possible, which one is probable?*

He brought his attention back to the matter at hand. He had noted this before – after a severe shock, sometimes the faculties wandered, taking every route to a problem but the one most direct.

"A remedy," he repeated, and stood straight, dropping

his arms. Vance twitched inside his casing of rope, and the assassin leaned forward. He had produced a knife with a dull-black, tarry substance smeared on the blade, and was examining the bound mentath with a wide white grin likely to cause no few nightmares. "Yes. We must consult Tarshingale."

# Chapter Eighteen

## How Well I Obey

The worst was landing on a steam ferry's heaving deck, salt spray and screaming. Gryphon claws dug into wood, Emma bruised and bumped about like a pea in a shaken pod, her numb fingers plucking at the buckles. The charm for loosing them almost would not rise past her chapped lips, and she felt *quite* dishevelled, thank you very much.

The screaming quieted as she rose from a tangle of leather. The sky was a sheet of bruised iron, rain slashing down in knife-sharp curtains. Mikal was fully occupied in keeping the gryphons under control as they screeched and beat their wings, and the ship's surface suddenly *far* too small for the chariot, the sailors, the winged beasts and those passengers unlucky enough to have paid only for deck-passage.

The captain hurried forward as Emma spat another charm, a hard bright jet of ætheric force opening like a parasol, shunting aside the restless rain. It was a simple act, but it saved *so* much explaining. Grizzled and bearded in his blue serge jacket and struggling-to-stay-aboard cap, the man opened his mouth to berate her, but shrank back as her status became evident and the gryphons almost bolted free of Mikal's grip.

"Good day," she shouted, over the incredible noise. "In Britannia's name, sir, I require your help."

She glanced behind him, just in time to see one of the deckside passengers edging for the railing. Tall, and wrapped in a long dark high-buttoned coat, the man lifted his hand to cough just as her attention came to rest on the furtive set of his shoulders, and intuition blurred under Emma Bannon's skin.

She flung out a hand as the captain began spluttering, and the gryphons ceased their noise. A great stillness descended upon the heaving ship; Emma pushed herself through air gone thick as treacle, humming a simple descant that nevertheless strained at her control. She was spending ætheric force recklessly, but cared very little. Her rings warmed, and the uneasy wind plucked at her skirts as rivers of charter symbols slid up her arms, circling her throat.

The man, caught in the act of turning, had ruddy, clean-shaven cheeks and a stained collar. His eyes were wide and dark, rolling as a horse's as he strained to reach the railing. In every particular, he matched the description of a certain John Morris, and Emma's throat filled with wine-red fury.

The descant took on an impossible, razor-edged depth, and Time snapped forward again. Only now, she was at his side, and laid her hand upon the man's arm.

"Sir." Very quietly, under the slap of rain and swelling of ocean-breath, the vibration of the steam engines a beast's slumbering rumble underfoot. "What is your name?"

The captain shouted behind her, and Mikal answered with an exceedingly impolite oath. That quieted matters somewhat, and he had the gryphons well under control. They clacked their beaks angrily, but did not cry aloud.

*Good. That was rather about to give me a headache.*

"*Prima?*" Mikal called, over the muted, returning noise of wind and waves.

Morris stared at her, glassy-eyed with terror. She would have to examine the passenger manifest and his papers, but she was reasonably certain it was he. The descant ended on a snapped note, cut off savagely, and she struck him across the face.

It was not ladylike to behave so. Just at the moment, however, it did not trouble her as much as it should. The weight of psychic force behind the blow knocked him to the deck like crumpled sodden cloth, and she inhaled sharply. *Consider yourself lucky your neck has not snapped, sir. When Britannia is finished with your services, I will find you. But for now . . .* She cast a glance over her shoulder, and every blessed soul on the deck was staring at her. *I am causing a scene. Do I care? No. It is enough that I have not killed him outright. Does Britannia know how well I obey?*

*Most likely not. And most likely, she does not care.*

For a moment the fury was crystalline, and she saw how easy it would be to shred this ship like a soap bubble, and consign every soul upon it to the Channel's uneasy depths. Child's play, for a Prime. And it would serve no bloody, God-be-d—ned purpose at all.

It would not bring Eli back from Death's domain. Nor would it bring Harry, or Jourdain. Or any she mourned.

*There is no remedy for what ails you, Emma. Save service, and protecting what still remains.*

Would that she had realised it before this morning, and Timothy Copperpot. Would his shade haunt her as well?

*It was necessary.* Yet that was the entire trouble with embarking upon a course of lying to oneself, she discovered. It meant one could no longer be so certain what was necessary . . . and what was merely, simply, vengeful pride.

"Madam." The captain stamped across the deck as the gryphons mantled nervously. They could not see her, or else they might strain more against her Shield's control. "I, erm. Yes. Captain James Deighton, at your service, mum." He touched his hatbrim with two calloused fingers, and she smelled tar, sweat and the iron note of charm-laced steam forced through metal throats to power the vessel. Some of the jacktars – no doubt those relieved she was not arriving to pursue *them* for any trespass, real or imagined – openly stared, no few of them conferring behind hands held to shield their mouths.

She gathered herself to deal with this fresh unpleasantness. Her throat was raw-scraped as if she had screamed, but it was merely the effort required to keep a civil tone that made it ache so. "Thank you. Miss Emma Bannon, sir, representative of Her Majesty. I require this passenger's records. If he is indeed the man I seek, I shall require any luggage of his brought forth and stowed upon the chariot, and a few of your sailors to bind him and place him on said chariot as well. Then I shall leave you be." She paused, then added judiciously, "You shall be compensated for the inconvenience, as well as the damage to the decking."

This news brightened the captain's outlook considerably, and smoothed the passage of events in a wondrous manner. In short order she had examined the passenger manifest and his papers to verify that it was indeed Mr John Morris, genius of Biology, who lay senseless and bound on the deck. He had not signed the manifest under his own name, of course, but the papers tucked into his folio proved his identity beyond a doubt.

Canny prey, yes. He had perhaps not thought he would be connected to the Alterator, or that Rudyard would be in the country to divulge Copperpot's name.

For a moment something – *oh, call it conscience*, she told herself irritably, *you might as well* – inside Emma twinged afresh, but she set that aside and returned to smoothing Captain Deighton's ruffled feathers. It was not a difficult task, and she turned down his offer of a cuppa as gracefully as possible.

In short order Morris's trunk was secured – there was no other luggage, which was a problem she would solve after she had brought him to Britannia. The unconscious man, his breathing coming laboriously, was placed carefully on Mikal's other side, strapped down like a prize pig meant for market, and Emma suffered the indignity of another jacktar, his bloodless face sweat-drenched even through the spray, buckling her into the straps again. Her bruised body ached, and the cold tingling in her fingers and toes told her she had expended perhaps a bit more force than was wise on this affair.

There was a lurch and a scrape, the gryphons screaming angrily as every sailor and passenger on the deck wisely flattened themselves, and Mikal managed them into the air again. If he was tired, his face gave no sign, and Emma's fingers curled around his ankle once more. The slow bleed of ætheric force through her hand resumed, and she fervently hoped it would drain her past the point of losing consciousness.

She had the uncomfortable idea only such an event would grant her any relief from the way her stupid, bloody, useless, and utterly infernal conscience was contorting.

# Chapter Nineteen

## A Fineness of Morals

"I do not like it." Valentinelli kept his tone low. The door to Clare's workroom, a sturdy strapping chunk of dark oak, was the only witness to their whispers. That and the short hall before the stairs leading to the hall from the sunroom, which Clare was *certain* had not sported this outgrowth before.

*Do not think upon that.*

"For the moment, there is much to be gained from his collaboration." Clare suppressed a sigh. "Simply watch him. When Miss Bannon returns, you shall give her an account of—"

"You shall not stir one step beyond this house without me, *mentale*." Ludovico was *most* troubled – the fact that he had dropped his Punchinjude accent *and* the Exfall crispness clearly said as much. "I am *responsible* for—"

"I am visiting an old friend. Tarshingale is a well-respected man, and he is exceedingly unlikely to put me in any danger, except perhaps the danger of being bored to death when he begins to go on endlessly about the wonders of carbolic." He lowered his voice still further. "I need you *here*, with both eyes on that mentath. Who knows what he will—"

The knob turned, the door's hinges ghost-silent as it swung open. And there, framed in the doorway, stood Francis Vance, arranging his sleeves as if about to sally forth through his own house door.

He had, apparently, shed the ropes binding him.

"Sir. And sir." He nodded to both of them. "Where are we bound, then?"

Valentinelli frankly stared. Clare sighed, a sound perhaps too much aggrieved. The damn man was a nuisance now, instead of an adversary. "I suppose it would be too much to ask for you to remain where I place you, Dr Vance."

"Oh, indeed." His smile was far too merry. "You are quite interesting, Mr Clare. I do not know how I have escaped you so far."

*Oh, you are a* bastarde, *as Ludo would say. And I shall call you to account for that remark at some other time.* "No doubt it is because of my fineness of morals allowing you an advantage." Bad-tempered of him, and ill-mannered, too. Not worthy of a mentath.

Or a gentleman.

"No doubt." Vance did not take offence at all. "Were it not for such a fineness, sir, you may well be my rival instead of my foil. I repeat, where are we bound? And I answer: to consult the controversial Edmund Tarshingale. You no doubt have an Acquaintance with the gentleman?"

"I do." Clare, nettled, glanced at Valentinelli. "Let us be on our way, then. You may be more useful where I may watch you, sir. And Tarshingale takes his dinner early."

Portugal Street was crowded even at this hour. Holbourne was famous for its taverns and divers entertainments, and additionally for closed-front houses where several fleshly pleasures of the not-quite-legal variety could be found – in a word, ancient mollyhouses, winked at even in Victrix's reign, reared slump-shouldered in the yellow Londinium fog. Their frowning faces were a reminder of their unhappy status, and the laws regarding such sport had not eased much, if at all.

However, since Tarshingale was not at his penitent Golden Square address among the musicians, it was to Holbourne that Harthell was directed to point his clock-horses' heads. And in the carriage Valentinelli glowered at Vance, who was silent, perhaps sunk in reflection.

Or turning some plan on the lathe of his nimble faculties. Who knew?

The tall narrow pile of King's College, its bricks pitted by corrosive rain, rose solemn and frowning as evening gathered in the yellow fog. If Tarshingale was not at home, he was here, treating all patients with polite, Scientific indifference in service to his theories. He was no mentath, charmer or Mender; no, Tarshingale was not even a genius.

He was dedicated, had graduated at the top of his class, and humourlessly insisted on muttering about carbolic at every possible juncture as well as lecturing his fellows about the requirement to serve all, even the meanest of Britannia's subjects, with equal care.

If the gentleman – for so he was, despite his lodgings – *had* been a mentath, his difficulty with Polite Society might have been acceptable. As it was, he was generally held to be a most awful dinner companion. Even his patients did not like him, though he was successful in treating some very odd and dire cases. His papers were marvels of blood-less circuitousness, the most amazing theories and conclusions hidden in a hedge of verbiage dense enough to wall a sleeping princess behind for years.

Considering how those theories and conclusions were hooted at by his colleagues, perhaps it was not so amazing.

The small room serving as his office was deep in the bowels of King's, stuffed with paper and specimens on groaning, ancient wooden shelves. Hunched over his desk, writing in flowing copperplate script on one of his inter-minable Reports, a full head of black hair gleaming under the glow of a single hissing gaslamp, Tarshingale muttered as the nib scratched the paper. He dipped the pen again, and the wheeze of his asthmatic breathing fell dead in the choking quiet of stacked paper.

"One moment," he murmured, and the first surprise of Edmund Tarshingale was his voice, deep and rich as his breathing was thin. The second, Clare knew, would be when he rose, and rose, and rose. For the good doctor towered over his fellows in his own lanky way, and some of Tarshingale's troubles, Clare privately thought, was that he towered over them in other ways as well.

It would have been much more just if whatever divine clockwork moved the earth had made him a mentath. But Justice, like Fate, was blind to quality, and never more so than when it came to those whose dedication removed them from a pleasant temperament.

Edmund glanced up, taking in the three men with a single passionless glance, and his dark eyebrows rose. However, he returned his attention to his Report, and Clare used the time spent waiting to compare the room to his remembrance of it the last time he had ventured into the clamour of King's. And, not so incidentally, to examine Tarshingale's coat – reasonably clean at this point in the evening, without the coating of blood and matter that would give it the hallowed surgical stink. He would be in a dashed hurry to get on with the evening's rounds once he finished his notes, and Clare would only have a moment or two to interest him.

As if on cue, Tarshingale spoke again. "Clare, isn't it? Mr Clare. A pleasure to see you again. May I enquire what brings you here?"

*I have very little time to catch your interest.* Still, Tarshie was a stickler for *some* manners. "May I introduce Dr Francis Vance? And this is my man, Valentinelli."

"Sir."

"Sir." Vance contented himself with a slight, correct bow, and Valentinelli was still as a stone.

Clare forged ahead. "I do apologise for my impoliteness, but there is a mystery I believe you may be able to solve. Not only do I believe so, but I have convinced Her Majesty's government of it."

The resultant short silence was broken only by the gaslamp's hissing.

"There are many patients to see tonight," Tarshingale said, mildly. "Surely some of my esteemed colleagues could answer your questions."

"Your colleagues have little experience with the Pathogenic Theory, sir. At least, not enough to be of any use in this particular matter."

"The Pathogenic Theory is not *mine*. It is Pasteur's. And someday it will be shown to—"

*Interrupt him before he gains his head.* "My dear sir, *I* am convinced. It is the only possible theory to explain what I have observed, and I believe you will be of inestimable help in not only this matter, but also proving beyond a shadow of a doubt some of your refinements. There are lives to be saved, Tarshie."

"Very well." Tarshingale conceded, stiffly. The tip of his nose had reddened, as had his scrape-shaven cheeks. The gap between his front teeth had no doubt been wonderful for whistling, had the young Edmund ever unbent enough to do so. "I can spare ten minutes, Clare. Please, do sit, sirs. And *please* do not call me Tarshie."

*It does you good, sir.* Clare could imagine Miss Bannon's arched eyebrows and amused smile, but it was not a proper thing for a gentleman to say. "My apologies." He stepped further into the room as Edmund rose, indicating the two spindly chairs set on the other side of his desk. "Let me list for you the symptoms . . ."

# Chapter Twenty

## An Unseemly Display

The Queen was still Receiving, despite the lateness of the hour. She sat, enthroned, the Stone of Scorn glowing slightly under the northern leg of the jewel-crusted chair, the ruling spirit's attention weighting the shadows in the corners of the Throne Hall. The great glass roof had been repaired, and the stone floor, polished by a few hundred years' worth of hungry feet seeking influence in the sovereign's atmosphere in one way or another, was worn smooth. The roof was a great blind eye, watching everything below with impersonal exactness.

Emma could have perhaps chosen not to hit the Reck Doors at the end of the Hall *quite* so hard with ætheric force, their charm-greased hinges whisper-silent as they swung inwards, the stuffed-leather pads set to stop their motion popping a trifle too loudly to be mannerly.

She further could have chosen not to drag the errant Dr Morris the length of the Throne Hall, his heels scraping the stone and her passage accompanied by crackling sparks of stray sorcery, the simple Work used to ease his dead-weight along fraying at the edges as her temper did. Mikal stalked behind her, wisely keeping his mouth shut, pale and haggard from the effort of controlling two gryphons to the Channel and back. Still, his irises flamed with yellow light, and his appearance was sufficiently disconcerting to have overridden all question or challenge so far.

Her own appearance was likely not decorous enough to inspire confidence. Windblown, salt-crust tears slicking her chapped cheeks, and with every piece of jewellery flaming with leprous green glow, she was the very picture of an angry sorceress.

Which probably explained the cowering among the Court, and the screams.

Her fingers, cramping and cold, slick with seawater, rain, and sweat, vined into Morris's hair and the cloth of his coat equally. Melting ice ran in crystal droplets from her hair, from his skin. Mikal was dry, and his dark hair disarranged; his head came up as some feral current not emanating from his Prima passed close by.

Britannia's attention strengthened. *"Leave Us,"* she whispered, Victrix's lips shaping the hollow coldness of the words, and there was a general move to obey. Emma strode up the centre of the Hall as the Court emptied. Only the Consort remained, his dark eyes round as a child's, his fine whiskers looking pasted on, as if he were a-mumming.

A brush against her consciousness was another sorcerer, a Prime, no doubt, but she was past caring *who* witnessed this. Her arm came forward, and Morris's form tumbled like a rag doll's, fetching up against the steps at the Throne's feet with a sickening looseness.

"He killed my Shield," she informed Britannia, and her voice, while not the power-laden darkness of the ruling spirit's, was still enough to cause every shadow to deepen and shiver. "Justice, Britannia. After You have no use for him, he is *mine.*"

Victrix's ring-laden hand, curved protectively over her belly, tensed, but the ruling spirit rose behind her features, settling fully into its vessel. "And you, Prima, are disposed to order Us about?" Sharply, each sibilant edge a knife, just as the gryphons spoke.

Did Victrix ever guess how like her chariot-beasts she sounded, when the spirit of the Isle filled her to the brim?

*No more than I know what I sound like, when my Discipline speaks.* Emma shook the thought away. "It is no order, my Queen. It is a simple statement of fact." *And you would be wise to understand as much.* Something in her recoiled from the thought . . . but not quickly.

And not far. The sense of another sorcerer, very close and watching, was undeniable but the room appeared empty. Perhaps in the gallery overhead. It mattered little. For right now, Emma Bannon cared only for the woman on the throne and the gasping man on the steps between them.

"Arrogant witchling." But Britannia's smile stretched

wide and white, a predatory V. "We are amused. This is Morris, then."

"In the flesh." But Emma did not lower her gaze and she did not pay a courtesy. *Do you understand what you commissioned from him?*

*Did you not think to warn me of the poison, this illness?*

Of course not. It was ridiculous. Warn a tool of its breaking, or a sword of its meeting another blade? Who would do so?

And yet even a tool could turn in its master's hand, when used improperly.

*I have been so used. But I was willing, was I not? And who am I to question Her?*

"We see." Victrix's free hand, resting on the throne's arm, tapped its fingers precisely once, each ring spitting a spark of painful brilliance. Emma's jewellery did not answer – but only because she willed it not to.

*I do not challenge Britannia. I serve.*

And Eli had paid the price, just as her other Shields had. The warmth of the stone inside Emma's chest, her surety against death, turned traitorous. It was a claw against her vitals, and each of its nails was tipped with a bright hot point of loathing.

Morris coughed, weakly. Both the Queen and the sorceress ignored him. His hollow cheeks were reddened, deadly flowers blooming under the skin. Emma held her sovereign's gaze, Victrix's eyes fields of darkness from lid to lid, strange dry stars glittering in their depths. They formed no constellation a man could name, those stars, and perhaps there was a Great Text that held their secrets . . . but it was not one Emma had ever been privileged to read.

"And this unseemly display, sorceress?" Victrix's tone now held no pity – or, despite her earlier words, amusement.

A hot flush went through Emma, followed by an icy chill. *So you did intend to use him in secret after this. Dear God.* "You wished him returned to you. Here he is." *And that is all I will say before witnesses.*

Morris choked. Blood bubbled in his thin lips, and for the first time he spoke. Or perhaps it was only now that the terrible windrush of fury was no longer filling her ears that she could hear his mumbles.

"*Nomine Patris.*" Bright blood sprayed, and the smell of sick-sweet caramel rose, adding its tang to the sweat, salt and stench of fear. "*Patris . . . et Filii . . . Spiritus Sancti . . .*"

*He's a Papist. Inquisition filth.* Revulsion filled Emma's throat. She turned her head aside and spat, uncaring of the breach of protocol, and Alberich the Queen's Consort inhaled sharply as he hurried down the steps, as if to render aid to the genius.

He was perhaps a decent man, the foreign princeling. But it did no good. Morris shuddered, his heels drumming the floor as his body convulsed, broken on a hoop of its own muscle-bound making, and a fine mist of blood and fouler matter sprayed.

Emma Bannon watched him die. When the last rattle

and sob of breath had fled the corpse, she returned her gaze to her sovereign's face . . .

. . . and found Victrix unmoved. Perhaps she *had* known the manner of research Morris was engaged upon, and at least some of its dangers. Did she guess Morris had died of the same poisonous filth he had been called upon to produce for the purpose of serving Britannia's enemies with terrible, torturous death? Or did she think Emma had somehow crushed him with a toxic sorcery and brought him here to die?

The uncertain young Victrix, new to the rigours of rule and desperate for any bulwark against those who would make her a puppet, was no more.

Now she was truly a Queen.

Britannia was stone-still upon her Throne, and when Emma turned on her heel and stalked away, her footsteps loud in the echoing silence, her fists clenched in her black-mourning skirts, that Queen – Emma Bannon's chosen ruler – uttered no word.

Perhaps she understood her servant's fury. And whoever was witnessing this scene, what tale would they carry, and to whom?

The Consort, however, said enough for all three. "*Sorceress!*" he hissed. "You shall not *dare* approach again! You are *finished*! *Finished!*"

Emma halted only once. She stared at Mikal's drawn face, and his hand twitched. She shook her head, slightly, and her Shield subsided. She did not turn, but her own voice rang hard and clear as an æthrin-scry crystal.

"No, Your Majesty the Consort. When another death is required, or another black deed is to be performed, I am Her Majesty Alexandrina Victrix's servant. As always." She set her jaw, for what threatened to come hard on the heels of those three sentences was couched in terms she could not make less stark.

*And the next time you insult me, petty little princeling, I shall call you to account for it as if I were a man, and this the age of duels.*

She strode from the Throne Room, her face set and white, and her Shield followed.

# *Chapter Twenty-One*

## *A Curative Method*

Tarshingale was very still, his eyes half-lidded, his long legs tucked out of sight underneath the desk. There was a commotion in the hall outside – some manner of screaming and cursing, very usual for King's this time of evening. Perhaps a patient requiring bleeding, or some other dreadful necessity. The surgical wells would be full of howling, with those patients fortunate enough to swoon under the assault of medical treatment the only exception.

Finally, Tarshie stirred. "The implications," he murmured. "The *implications.*"

*For Science? Or for suffering?* Clare decided on an answer that was equally applicable to both. "Troubling, yes. And deep."

Vance had subsided into his own chair, watching Clare as he laid forth the bare facts of the case, then judicious applications of his own observations. He occasionally stroked his fair moustache with one fingertip, and Clare caught sight of an irregular inkstain on the criminal mentath's thumb. The mix of dust and paper, the haze of Tarshingale's living heat warring with the cold stone exhalation of the walls, the tang of carbolic and the effluvia of surgical practice, all was as it should be. Even the ghost of Valentinelli's cologne.

So why did he feel so . . . unnerved?

*Something is amiss here.*

"A rubescent miasma." Tarshingale nodded, as if wrapping up a long internal conversation. "A very bloody illness, this is. A red film over the *ocularis orbatis.* Hmm."

Clare's body grew cold all over. "Tarshie, old chap—"

"Archibald, for the love of God, address me as Edmund if you feel the need to be familiar," Tarshingale snapped, irritably. "*Pray* do not address me as the other."

"A prickly character," Vance interjected. "You were at school together?"

"Two years ahead." Tarshingale rose, pushing his chair back with a weary sigh. The laboured rasp of his breathing evened out. "And he was insufferable even then."

"Pot calling kettle, I'm sure." Vance's tone bordered on the edge of insouciant. "You are not surprised at Mr Clare's tidings, sir. And I detect a breath of sweetness in the still air of this charming hutch, which is *quite* out of place."

"Quite so." Tarshingale did not take offence. "I am afraid I must tell you something very disturbing, Archibald. As your friend has *no doubt* deduced, this contagion has already arrived at King's." He took a deep breath, pushing his shoulders back, and his surgical coat rippled, dried blood flaking from the rough fabric. "We had four sufferers this afternoon. Three died within hours, and the fourth . . . well."

"Dear God." Clare's lips were numb. "You are the foremost advocate of the Pathogenic Theory, Edmund. Do tell me you have some idea of how to combat this bad bit of business."

"No way that does not involve quite a long bit of trial and error." Tarshingale seemed to age in the space of a few moments, deep lines graving his face, and Clare noted with no little trepidation that a faint blush had arrived on the doctor's scrape-shaven cheeks. "Come. He is a drover, our fourth patient, and quite hardy. If he is still alive, we may well have a chance."

"*Damn* it all," Clare breathed.

The ward was full of moaning, shrieking sufferers. It was almost as deadly-chaotic as Bedlam, and Clare's infrequent visits to *that* hell of noise and stench were always more than enough to convince him he never wished to practise the art of Medicine.

The patient – a heavyset, balding Spitalfields drover, carried across Londinium by two of his worried fellows who had left him and a fistful of pence in Tarshingale's care because of Edmund's reputation as a Charity Worker – lay in a sodden lump of blood and other matter, including the foul-sweet pus from burst boils. His empty gaze, filmed with already-clotting red, was fixed on the distant shadowy ceiling, and the indentured orderly responsible for heaving the corpse onto a barrow blinked blearily at the arrival of August Personages, well dressed and obviously healthy, in this pit.

"Joseph Camling." Edmund reached the bedside, and his work-roughened hand covered the staring, bloody orbs. He held the eyelids, waiting until the dead gaze could be for ever veiled. "Do you recall your History, Archibald?"

"I recall rather everything. I am a *mentath*." Clare glanced at Valentinelli, whose attention was fixed on Vance, for all he seemed to be taking no notice of the criminal mentath, whose long fastidious nose was wrinkled most unbecomingly. "Edmund—"

"Some two hundred years ago. You would have had Tattersall for those lectures, I believe." Edmund took his hand away, gazing upon the drover's dead face with a peculiar expression. "My organ of Memory is rather large; though I despise phrenologomancy with a passion as unscientific it is rather useful to be measured at least once. I digress, though. I recall—"

"Tattersall. Lecture one hundred and fifty-three." The blood was draining from Clare's face, he could feel it. There was a disturbing tickle in his throat, as well. A cough caught, or perhaps merely his digestion – excellent as any mentath's, really – was beginning to turn against him. There was, he reflected, very little that could unseat a logician's stomach. But this threatened to. "The plague. But there is no—"

"Nine of the twelve symptoms overlap. It is foolish to discount some things simply because *you* cannot compass their existence." Tarshingale drew himself up. It was his usual, pedantic, insufferable moment of lecturing. "It came to my attention that this was remarkably similar. I spent the afternoon pillaging an excellent library or two, combing for accounts of the Dark Plague and its effects."

*A warehouse hard by the Black Wark. A perfect place for research, but* . . . Clare's faculties raced, and he almost staggered. Vance's hand closed about his elbow, and the art professor steadied him most handily.

"I say, old chap, what is it?" Did Clare's nemesis actually look . . . yes, he did. It seemed impossible to credit.

Francis Vance looked *concerned*.

"Ludovico." Clare shook free of his fellow mentath's grasp. Tarshingale's mouth was a thin line of disapproval, since he had been interrupted before he could gain his stride. "Hurry, man. Fetch Harthell and the carriage. We haven't a moment to lose."

The Neapolitan, to give him credit, did not hesitate, merely vanished into the throng of indentured orderlies.

Edmund's nostrils flared. "Really, Archibald—"

It was Francis Vance who stepped in now. "Very well. I believe now is the moment for a rather bruising carriage ride. Shall the good physicker be coming along, old chap?"

"Bermondsey." Clare found himself actually *wringing his hands*, and almost shouting to be heard over the sudden jarring noise of the ward, intruding on his consciousness. "A plague pit. Of *course*. We may find the original source of the contamination, and a method or means of stopping it."

Vance stepped forward, as if to shake hands with Tarshingale. Whose pride had been touched now, and roundly, too.

"I am no *physicker*, sir, I am a doctor of Medicine, and I shall thank you to—"

"Very good." Vance's grip was bruising on Edmund's arm, and the doctor of Medicine gasped aloud as the mentath's fingers found a nerve-bundle and pressed home, unerringly. "Dear Archibald requires your services, sir, and we shall do our best to send you home in your original condition when he has no further use of you."

"Do be careful!" *I sound like an old maiden auntie. How Miss Bannon would laugh.* His collar was uncomfortably close, but Clare did not stop to loosen it. "Come. A Curative Method, Edmund? Tell me every particular while we hurry for the carriage. It may not be necessary for you to leave King's." He paused, and a rather horrible, unavoidable deduction surfaced. "I rather think," he continued soberly, settling his hat upon his balding head, "that you shall be needed here very badly, and sooner than you think."

# Chapter Twenty-Two

## Unlucky Enough to Live

It was a long way, and she was in no fit condition to be seen in public. Still, Emma kept her head down, cracked cobbles ringing under her boots, and Mikal's presence ensured she was not troubled by catcall or jostle even in the crowd. Yellow fog crept between the buildings, threaded between carriage-wheel spokes, touched hat and hair and hand with cold, sinister damp. It was a slog-souper tonight, the fog lit from within by its own faint venomous glow, and even the air-clearing charm every Londinium sorcerer learned early and used daily could not keep its salt-nasty reek from filling the nose.

She alighted from the hansom, Mikal having ridden with her instead of running the rooftop road for once, and brushed futilely at her skirts. Then she had set off, as Mikal tossed the fare to the muffled driver.

*I am a needle, seeking north.* Except she knew very well what she sought, and it was east. The Eastron End, as a matter of fact. Her jewellery sparked in fitful waves, golden charter charms spinning through metal and stone. Her hair, dressed as well as she could manage without the benefit of a mirror, was still dishevelled enough to annoy her whenever a dangling curl swung into her field of vision. The throbbing pulse-noise of Londinium at night rose and fell, just as the roar of the wind and steady wingbeats had while she was strapped into the chariot.

Mikal must have been weary, but he made no demur. The only mark of their voyage was his windblown hair and his haggard air, his coat hanging from an oddly wasted frame. He would need physical sustenance to repair the damage, and soon.

Still, she walked. The hired hansom had let her loose at Aldgate, where the æther still resonated with the impress of the ancient barrier. The Wall still stood, of course, but the Ald had shivered itself to pieces during one of Mad Georgeth's fits of pique. Sometimes smoke still rose from the blackened cobbles, and traffic – both carriage and foot – was *always* pinched here, no matter the hour.

She hesitated for a bare moment before turning due east, and the buildings rose, the reek thickening at the back of her throat.

Whitchapel swallowed them both, and Mikal drew closer. On a night such as this, even the threat of sorcery might not keep a band of predators, flashboy or other, from trying their luck. The gaslamps sang their dim hiss-song inside angular cups of bleary streetlamp glass, their faint glow merely refracting from the fog's droplets and making possible danger even less visible.

Any carriage or cart rumbling through echoed against cobbles thick with the green Scab, organic matter having long lost its individual character. Excrement – animal and human – foodstuffs too rotted to scavenge, small carcasses, rat, insect, who knew – bubbled as the slime worked at them in its own peculiar fashion . . . there were other less-savoury substances in the coating, and Emma's skin turned rough with gooseflesh as she remembered slipping barefoot through its slick resiliency.

The Scab grew nowhere but Whitchapel, and it thickened at night. It covered a flashboy's footsteps and swallowed a drab's last cries; it clawed up buildings every evening and retreated steaming from the touch of morning sun. If there was any sun to be had, that is, in the alleys beneath frown-leaning slumhouses that almost met over the narrow twist-curved streets. Some bits of Whitchapel were scrubbed by sunshine, and it was those the sorcerously talented unlucky enough to live in the borough clustered in.

Between one step and the next, Emma halted. Her hands, occupied by holding her skirts free of the worst of the muck, trembled. It was a sign of weakness she should not allow, except her traitorous body would not listen.

Mikal was very close. "Tideturn," he breathed into her hair.

A wave of gold rose from the Themis, and the renewal

of ætheric force made her blind for a few precious seconds. The Scab hissed with displeasure as golden charter symbols burned through its hide, and the steam from the touch of Tideturn added another choking layer to the fog.

When her vision cleared, Emma found her hands much steadier and her head clearer as well. Whitchapel seethed about her, an unlanced boil. Someone in an alley was coughing, great hacking retches, and there was the splorch-skim of running feet.

"Mikal?" she whispered.

"Here." An immediate answer. "Prima . . ."

"I feel it." And she did. The disturbance in the æther that was another sorcerer, a vast storm-approach prickling that was another Prime. "Be at ease, Shield."

It stayed with her, the consciousness of being followed. She set off again, and even blinded, she could have found her way.

*There is the church. Barred every night, and there the ragpicker's workhouse. There is Jenny Anydill's doss, and the Mercoran brothers lived there. That was a grocer's stall, and there was the market aisle.*

Now there was a tavern, spilling raucous screams and gin-fuelled hilarity into the fog-soaked dark. This deep into the Scab, the streetlamps were broken or dying, and the yellow-tinged dark was full of stealthy movement. Flashboys, their Alterations metal-gleaming or blackened with soot, stalked among the alleys, and there were wars fought in the country of these bleak nights respectable Londinium never suspected.

She hurried now, nipping between two buildings, through a space so small her skirts brushed either side. Mikal exhaled softly, his worry a burning dull-orange, and she followed the labyrinth twists without needing to see.

So little changed.

*It even smells the same.* The Scab, the cheap gin, a breath of rotting brick, something dying, a raft of excrement reek, the boiled odour of piss left in puddles. The years dropped away and she was six again, a thin scrap of a girl with black-burning eyes and an unlucky streak of uncontrolled ætheric potential.

The buildings leapt away as if stung, and she skidded to a halt. The dimensions of the empty space were unseen but felt by instinct, judged by fingertip and echo. Her breath came harsh and tearing, and Mikal's grasp on her upper arm was a sweet pain. It nailed her to the present moment even as she drowned in memory.

The cobble underneath her left boot was broken. She felt its slide as the Scab worked through it; the slop of Whitchapel's skin against her boots would leave acid traceries on the leather, corrosion on the dainty buttons.

She raised her free hand and pointed. Witchlight bloomed, a point of soft silvery radiance. It was good practice to make it so dim, but it still scorched her dark-adapted eyes.

The tiny point hovered uncertainly, then dashed across the courtyard. It came to rest between two barred doors of old, dark wood, daubed with rancid oil to protect them from the Scab.

"Emma?" For the first time in her memory, Mikal sounded . . . very uncertain. His hand gentled on her arm, but whether his grasp was meant to steady her or halt further flight she could not tell.

"Right there." The words rode a soft sipping inhale. *After the throat-slit and the blood, and all the screaming.* "That was where they found me. The Collegia childhunters. I caused . . . quite a disturbance, even so young."

He said nothing, but his fingers loosened further. The other Prime was very close. She could almost taste the peculiar "scent" of another sorcerer, the personality building delicate overlapping traceries within the disturbance of the æther. It was akin to many layers of gossamer fabric with wires underneath: nodes and lines of force under a many-layered shroud.

*Come and face me, if you dare.* She did not *quite* send the message out in the invisible way available to any sorcerer above Mastery, but the other Prime would feel her quality of attention and remark upon it.

The Whitchapel night held its breath, and Emma let her skirts drop. Pretending she was not mired in filth would gain her nothing. Seeking to become Respectable did not succeed overmuch when one had been born here, and when one's memory held the image of a maybe-mother, her raddled face under a mask of caked powder, her throat pumping bright scarlet blood as the father – or whoever was the father that day – laughed his small whistling laugh, his knuckles greased with grime and blood.

*Then he turned his attention to me, and I ran. And here*

*was where they caught me. I thought they were* his *flash-boys, and I bit one of them – the childhunter with the red thread in his hair.* A shudder worked its way through her. *I paid for that.* "Mikal."

"Emma." Again, an immediate response. Was he worried? She was not acting like herself.

*Who would I be, then?*

"Shall I acquire more Shields?" As if she did not care. She stared at the witchlight, its burning becoming more intense as her attention steadied. "What say you?" Her tone changed, she found the slurring accent that lay beneath every thought. *"I bin a-doight tha' the nanny I get ain' no more; needin' flashboy to dockie m'sweet navskie."*

So easily, the Whitchapel dialect rolled off her tongue. The amazing thing was not that it was still there. No, the amazement of it was that once she began, she could not fathom why she had been forcing her tongue to respectable upper-crust Englene to begin with.

And, as she had suspected, it drew out the other sorcerer.

"Speaking in tongues?" The voice was cold, lipless, and freighted with a Prime's force. It touched the filthy cobbles, slid along the brick walls and the shivering doors, and was obviously charmed to provide misdirection. "Bannon, Bannon. You are a wonder, Prima."

*And youna gen'l'man looksee to fine a drab, roughuntumble from tha sound o'it.* She inhaled smoothly, kept herself still and dark as a deadly pool of Scab itself. Had she drawn the other here as part of a plan, or had she merely, blindly, leapt?

*Does it matter?* It sounded strange to her, the clipped cultured tones of her education. Mikal had gone still as an adder in a dark hole next to her, and he would be waiting for the other's Shields to show themselves.

They did not. The sense of *presence* leached away, and Emma Bannon found herself staring at a sputtering witch-light in a filthy Whitchapel courtyard that held only memories, the Scab burned away from her and Mikal in a several-feet radius of scorched cobble. Had she let her temper loose here? Or had the slime merely reacted?

*It is only the past, Emma. It cannot wound you.*

But she did not believe it.

"Prima." Mikal was pale, and he had her arm in a bruising-tight grip again. "Who hunts you now?"

*I do not know.* "Come." She sought to step away, but he would not turn loose. "Mikal. Cease. I am well enough."

"You . . ." But he subsided as she drew herself up, chin lifting and the stink of Whitchapel suddenly fresher. Perhaps it was just that she had forgotten how to breathe in such environs. And remembered only once the dialect had found her throat afresh.

"Take me home." She shut her eyes, let the mothering dark return. "I . . . take me home."

"Yes, Prima." Did he sound satisfied?

And did she imagine the hissing of the sibilant on his tongue, so like the gryphons'?

*Oh, Mikal. I do need more Shields.*

For she had a strong inkling that Britannia had begun to see the end of a certain Sorceress Prime's use, and had resolved to lay such a tool aside – suitably blunted, of course. And Emma did not intend to be placed in a drawer quite yet – *or* to become unsharp.

No matter how many of her own pawns she would have to sacrifice, in answer to Britannia's gambits.

# *Chapter Twenty-Three*

### *In Cleaner Places*

Clare, shuttered lanthorn held aloft, stood amid the wrack and ruin of Mr Morris's empire, gazing about with bright sharp interest. Miss Bannon, bless her thoroughgoing heart, had provided him with every address she had been availed of for Morris, and he was slightly gratified to find his faculties were not undimmed and that he was most certainly able to deduce which one to visit first.

"Be careful of the glass," he murmured again, and Valentinelli cast him a dark look. "It is, after all, what killed the Shield."

"Really?" Vance, examining a fire-scarred table, very carefully did not remove his hands from his pockets. "Introduction under the skin, I presume. The vestiges left here . . . hrm."

*It was not a gentle death.* "It seems Morris sought to

remove evidence, or cleanse this place. Though why he would remains a mystery; it is *quite* out of character for him."

"A man's character may have hidden depths." Vance turned in a slow circle, his own gaze roving. "We are here, old chap, because . . .?"

*Have patience, sir. All shall be revealed.* His fingers found a starched white handkerchief in a convenient pocket, and Clare stepped gingerly, broken glass crunching underfoot. The cloth, wrapped about his hand, was thin insurance, but all he possessed. Traceries of steam rose from their skin – it was a chill night in Bermondsey, and Londinium's grasping oily fog pressed thick against the walls.

Valentinelli had gone pale, and there was a fire in his close-set eyes that promised trouble. He watched Vance rather as he had been wont to watch Mikal during the first days of Clare's acquaintance with the sorceress and her staff; Clare spared an internal sigh and scanned the floor, dim lanthorn-glow filtering through raised dust. "Should be here . . . somewhere. Close."

He carefully toed aside an anonymous jumble of cloth and splintered wood. Nothing in it should slice the leather of his boots, but still. "Aha."

The trapdoor had seen heavy use, if the marks around it were any indication. The thick iron ring meant to provide leverage to heft it was rubbed free of rust, polished by gloved hands. "This is what we are here for."

"Always down." Valentinelli gave a sigh that would have

done an old woman proud. "Why we cannot hunt in cleaner places, *mentale*? Always down in the shite."

"Miss Bannon is far more equipped to hunt in Society." Clare's amusement did not hold an edge, but it was close. *At least, now it is. Her childhood was perhaps entirely otherwise.* "And that is as it should be. Whether we like it or not, my assassin, *we* are more suited to the mire than our fair sorceress." He wrapped his protected hand about the ring and heaved, and was gratified when the trapdoor lifted, a slice of fœtid darkness underneath dilating. It thudded down, and the draught from below the warehouse was an exhalation of disturbed dust, rot, and the peculiar sourness of earth lain beneath a covering, free of cleansing sunlight, for a very long time.

Rickety wooden stairs under the lanthorn's gleam; he eased the shutters as wide as they would go since there was little chance of a night-watchman seeing a suspicious glow *here*. Vance made a small clicking noise with his tongue, and Clare deduced the man was most pleased.

"What have we here?" Vance's footsteps were cat-soft, but the floor still creaked alarmingly. "Oh, Clare. You are a wonder."

"It is elementary, sir." Of a sudden, Clare was exhausted. "I wondered, why *here*? And I bethought me of the past."

Valentinelli shouldered him aside, a knife suddenly visible in one calloused hand. "What down here, *mentale*?"

"Nothing alive," Clare reassured him. "Everything in this excavation is likely to be mummified as the ancient Ægyptios. But here is where Morris found his prime cause, and no doubt considered himself lucky. The plague was a hardy beast two hundred years ago." His mouth was dry, and as Valentinelli tested the stairs and Clare followed, debated the advisability of explicitly mentioning that here was most likely the original source of the illness that had killed Eli and Tarshingale's patients, and decided against it.

There was no profit, as Vance might say, in stating the obvious.

Down, and down, the sour earth crumbling away from the sides of the passage; shovel-marks were still impressed on damp clay soil. Clare's throat was full of an acid clump, and he restrained himself from coughing and spitting by an act of sheer will.

The earthen strata changed colour, and the first skeletons appeared. Valentinelli crossed himself, and Vance made an amused noise.

"The Dark Plague," the criminal mentath breathed. "Quite. The damp eats at dead tissue, but lower down no doubt there are bodies preserved by the clay. And in those bodies . . ."

"The plague. Which Morris set himself to resurrect, to prove the Pathological Theory or merely to show it could be done. I would give much to know . . ." Clare did not finish the sentence. Anything he wondered now was immaterial.

"Archibald." For the first time, Francis Vance sounded serious. "If I may address you thus, that is . . ."

"For the time being, Francis, you may." Clare lifted the

lanthorn, and Valentinelli breathed out through his nose, the only sign of disgust he would allow himself.

"Very good. Archibald, my friend, we are too late. The genie, as it were, has escaped the lamp."

"You have read Galland, I see. Yes. The dreadful spirit is loose in the world, and our task now is to find a second spirit to oppose it." Clare could see the marks where samples had been scraped from the earthen walls; Morris had a fondness for femurs, it seemed. Scraps of ancient flesh hung on yellowed bone, a rat's corpse worked half-free of the wall and stared with a wide-open snarl, other detritus poured into what had been a grave for the many instead of for one.

Even in death, the space a body took up in Londinium was expensive, and obeyed certain laws of supply and rent, as Locke would have it. Smith and Cournot had refined the principle, of course, and Clare suddenly saw the pages of text before him, clear as a bell. It was an effort to bring his attention to the present moment.

*I am frightened*, he realised, *and my faculties seek to inure me to Feeling*. Did Vance feel this terror? Was a criminal capable of such dread?

"A cure? Dear man, you are an optimist." And yet Vance's amusement might have been a similar shield, for his tone was not quite steady, and he almost tripped on a stair-tread as earth shifted and the rat's corpse twitched. "Ah. Good heavens, not very stable, down here."

"No, Dr Vance. I am no optimist." Clare's fist was damp, for the handkerchief was collecting sweat in his palm. "I am merely a man who sees what must be done. We shall come to Morris's working area very soon, Ludovico. When we do, you shall hold the lanthorn."

*And may God and Science both have mercy upon us.*

# Chapter Twenty-Four

## Burden of Service

Stepping into her own house was tinged with a variety of uncomfortable relief, almost as if she had retired to a bolt-hole. To be Prime was to fear very little, but she was well on her way to seeing enemies in every shadow.

*And for all I know, there may be. Especially if Britannia has another sorcerer dogging my footsteps. And the scene in the Hall probably did not inspire confidence or soothe Her.* After all, Victrix – and Britannia Herself – could not know what Morris's fevered rantings might have told her.

And there was the question of the two canisters, disappeared. Emma sighed, working her fingers under her hair, leaning against her front door.

Mikal echoed her sigh, his shoulders dropping. He finally

broke the silence between them that had held all the way from Whitchapel. "Another sorcerer?"

"A Prime, no less." Wearily, Emma scrubbed at the skin over her skull. It would disarrange her hair most dreadfully, but she was past caring. *Is Clare here? He should be, if I have to stir one step to seek him out tonight I shall be quite cross.* Even the simple act of concentrating enough to discern who was within her walls seemed far too great an expenditure of precious energy.

The house was awake, in any event, and Mr Finch came stiffly down the stairs, his dusty black making the long thin lines of his gaunt body even slimmer. His indenture collar brightened visibly as he laid eyes on her. "Madam." He showed no surprise at her dishevelment – of course, he was phlegmatic in the extreme, as well as accustomed to the various states of disarray she suffered in Britannia's service. "Mr Clare left, with his . . . guest. Shall I have Madame Noyon . . .?" His eyebrows rose, and his face was truly like a death's head.

Starvation left marks on a man, and Finch was unwilling to let them fade. Or he did not possess the capability of letting such things fade. And, it must be said, neither did his mistress, no matter how successfully she hid the traces of her own private dæmons, real or imagined.

*Clare had a guest?* For now, though, she was called upon to tend to the responsibilities of a Prime toward her servants. "Yes, please do. I rather require a hot bath. And rouse the kitchen; Mikal requires sustenance." *Who can he have brought home? Not Sigmund, thank God, he's safe enough.* "I shall not stir forth one *step* tonight, Finch, unless there is a dire emergency. And even then, I shall reconsider." *So Clare had better not be in any danger. I may even be* vexed *with the man, and Ludo to boot.*

"Very well, mum. Sir." A half-bow to her, taking in Mikal at the very end, and he vanished down the hall to the kitchens. Waking the house at this hour was all manner of bother and annoyance, but what were such things to servants? Especially indentureds as well-paid and well-treated as her own.

"Is she at odds with you, then? The Queen?"

How was it possible for Mikal to sound so *indifferent*? "I believe her own cleverness stung her fingers, Shield. But she will blame me." *Or does she know exactly what Morris's madness has done? Perhaps I should have kept my temper in order to discern.* A sigh came from a deep well inside her. "Go. I shall be well enough."

He nodded. In the foyer's gloom, gaslamps turned down for the evening and her unwilling to expend more sorcerous force to brighten the air, his yellow irises held a fire all their own. "Emma."

*Not now, please.* "What?" She sounded ungracious, she realised, as well as peevish.

*Well, at least I require no artifice to cover such things. Not with him.*

"I am only half . . . what you suspect. The other half is different. The whole is—"

"Mikal—" *Curse you, I do not wish to know!*

He dared to interrupt her. "The whole, Prima, is at your command. Of course." He turned on his heel and strode away, disappearing in Finch's wake as a bell jangled in the depths of the servants' quarters and the susurrus of cloth began. At any moment, Severine and the maids would appear to usher Emma into a hot bath, there would be light refreshment, and she could fall into her bed with a sigh of well-earned relief.

Still, it bothered her. Had Victrix any idea what this "weapon" could do? There was also the little matter of the canisters of poison Morris had taken with him; they must be found and dealt with, and where on *earth* was Clare?

"*Madame!*" There was Severine, in a lace cap, shadows under her coal-black eyes and her plump hands wringing at each other. A dark strand of hair freighted with grey slipped from under the housekeeper's cap, and she negotiated the stairs with most unseemly haste. Behind her, Catherine and Isobel hurried, Isobel yawning and Catherine's curls heavily disarranged. All three wore the powdery-silver metal of indenture collars, lovingly burnished and softly glowing. "You are returned, *bien*! And so tired. Come, come, we shall take good care of you."

"Good evening." Her shoulders dropped for the first time, tension easing. "I hope you will, Severine, for I sorely need it. A bath, and perhaps some *chocolat*."

*And I may be able to read half a page of a dreadfully sensational novel before I fall into sleep.*

It was by far the most pleasant thought she had

experienced in a few days. Later, of course, she would curse herself for not sallying forth to find a certain mentath. But for that night, Emma Bannon laid down the burden of service for a few hours . . . and was content.

# Chapter Twenty-Five

## A Congress of War

The following morning began rather inauspiciously.

"What in *God's* name is happening here?" Miss Bannon all-but-barked, momentarily forgetting her usual well-bred tones.

Clare blinked. He had laid his head down on the desk for a bare moment, merely to rest. The stiffness in his back and neck, as well as the uncomfortable crust about his eyes, told him he had instead slept, and quite deeply too.

Valentinelli, his pallet spread near the workroom door, sheepishly slipped a knife back into his sleeve and yawned hugely, stretching. One of his hands almost touched the thunderstruck sorceress's skirts, and she twitched the black silk of mourning away from his fingers reflexively. She was attired as smartly as ever, despite the mourning, and her jewellery – a torc of bronze ringing her slim throat, rings of mellow gold on each finger, her earrings long daggers of jet – rang and crackled with golden charter symbols. Her small arms were full of broadsheets, the ink on them still fresh enough for its odour to penetrate the scorch-throat reek of live experimentation.

Vance had, by all appearances, gone to sleep propped in a corner, very much as an Ægyptian mummy himself. He twitched into wakefulness and caught himself, his gaze distressingly sharp as soon as he rubbed at his eyes. All three men were covered with dust and dirt, the effluvium of a grave below Londinium's surface, and perhaps smelled just as bad as the experiments.

Clare's brow was unbecomingly damp. He coughed, and caught his pen, which threatened to skitter from the desk's cluttered surface. The nib was crusted with dried ink. "I say," he managed, "good heavens. I must have slept."

"There is news." Miss Bannon swept past Valentinelli, and the door moved a fraction behind her, but did not close. "Morris is dead, but his end has been achieved. The broadsheets are full of a mysterious illness spreading with *most* unseemly haste in the lower quarters of town. What *happened*?"

"Morris? Dead?" Vance took two steps away from the wall and halted, his eyes narrowing. "How? When?"

The look Miss Bannon cast at the criminal mentath was chilling in its severity. "Good morning, sir. I do not believe I have had the pleasure." Her tone announced it was a dubious pleasure at best, and her entire demeanour was of the frostiest vintage. "Archibald?"

"Ah. Yes." He cleared his throat again. *This should be quite interesting.* "Miss Bannon, may I present Dr Francis Vance? Dr Vance, our hostess, Miss Bannon."

Clare had very little time to savour Miss Bannon's momentary silence. Vance bowed and his right hand moved as if to lift his hat, forgetting that he wore none. "I am *extremely* pleased to be introduced, Miss Bannon. Mr Clare thinks very highly of you, and your hospitality is simply incredible."

Her response – studying him for a few long moments, from top to toe – lacked nothing in insouciance. "He thinks rather highly of you as well, sir." Her tone managed to express that she did not share such estimation or optimism, and she returned her attention to Clare's quarter with a dark look that promised trouble later. "So. Well. Mr Clare?"

He almost winced. *Oh, dear.* "Suffice to say we are brothers-in-arms in this affair, dear Bannon. The situation is . . . complex. In the lower quarters, you say? Spread of an illness?"

"They are calling it a rosy miasma, and it is spreading quickly enough to make the broadsheets promise another edition at midday. Clare, is it too much to ask for you to grant me an explanation?"

"Not at all. But . . . breakfast. We worked very late last night. I found the original source of Morris's plague. Tell me, what did he die of?"

She all but stamped her tiny foot. "The same poison that killed my Shield. Or is it an illness? This Pathologic

Theory of yours? Really, sir, I *do* require some information at this juncture!"

It rather irked Miss Bannon to be the less-informed of their pairing, Clare thought. Surely it was not quite logical to feel so secretly pleased at the notion. "Breakfast, Miss Bannon. I do not have much of an appetite, but it shall serve as a congress of war. The situation is worse than you may have ever dreamed."

"Lovely." She addressed the ceiling in injured tones. "And now he calls my *imagination* into question. Ludo, if you do not put that knife away *again*, I shall be outright vexed with you. Very well, gentlemen. I expect to see you in the breakfast room soon. Already I have had a request from the Crown for some manner of further explanation, one I cannot give until you share your tidings." Another venomous glance darted at Dr Vance – who looked rather amused again, dash it all – and she spun smartly, twitched her skirt away from Valentinelli again while the assassin stared at her and whistled a long low note, and her retreating footsteps were crackling little snaps of frustrated authority.

Silence fell among the men as they listened to her negotiate the stairs.

"Well." Vance rubbed his fingers together. " A most winning creature, old man, and you have been keeping her all to yourself."

"She singe your fingers, *bastarde*." Valentinelli gained his feet in a catlike lunge. He had, as usual, slept in his boots. "And Ludovico cut them off."

"You're quite a suitor, sir." Vance's laugh carried a note

of calculated disdain, and Clare rubbed at his damp forehead, where a distressing headache was threatening. "Does your wife know?"

*Damn the man.* Clare gained his feet, shoving the uncomfortable wooden chair back, and managed – just barely – to arrive in Valentinelli's way as the Neapolitan leapt for the criminal mentath, whose laugh could have been carved from ice. "None of that!" Clare cried, locking Ludovico's wrist and *twisting*, the knife clattering on the stone floor and his weight driving the assassin back a few critical steps. "*None* of that, Ludo, the man is simply baiting you! Pray do not make it *easier*!"

"Turn him loose, Clare." Vance stood at ease, but with his hands held oddly. Some manner of fighting skill, though Clare did not have enough time to do more than glimpse it, for holding Ludovico back took all his strength and a goodly portion of guile.

*Do not force me to harm you.* But he could not say it.

Ludovico subsided, though he was sweating, and his close-set eyes were hot with rage. He spoke very low in his Calabrian dialect, and there was no mistaking the import of the words – or their meaning. Not even a threat, merely a promise of retribution.

"Enough." Clare cleared his throat again. He rather wished for a spot of tea to ease the scratching. It would not ease the situation to spit, though. "I shall have Miss Bannon separate you, if you cannot behave as gentlemen. We have *much more pressing* problems, and after this affair is concluded you may duel each other with pistols in

Treyvasan Gardens for all I care. But for now, *cease* this foolishness."

He held no great expectation of soothing either of them, but apparently his invocation of satisfaction at a later point was enough. Vance stepped back, almost mincingly, and Valentinelli shook himself free of Clare's grip, stamping for the door. His footsteps were nowhere near as light or dainty as Miss Bannon's, and they vanished halfway up, as if he had recalled his ability to move silently.

Clare let out a sigh. His brow was really quite moist, and sweat had gathered under his arms as well. Exertion was not a marvellous idea so soon in the morning, and his bones reminded him that he was decidedly not of tender enough vintage to sleep in a chair. "That was ill-done," he remarked, mildly enough. "His possible marriage is rather a sensitive subject."

"They always are. And it is not possible; he had a wife once. You should have deduced as much." Vance, supremely unconcerned, set about adjusting his jacket. "Breakfast, you say? And I hate to be gauche, but a watercloset would do me a world of good, old chap."

Clare throttled the annoyance rising in his chest and nodded, sharply. "Do come this way, sir. I believe some shift may be made for you." His pause was not entirely for effect, for a novel idea had occurred to him. "And do be careful. This is a sorceress's house, and Miss Bannon's temper is . . . uncertain, with strangers."

Perhaps it would make the damnable man behave.

Though Clare, wiping at his forehead and cheeks with a slight grimace, was not hopeful.

Clare's appetite had deserted him entirely, for once. He had suitably freshened himself and changed his clothes, but his back still cramped, reminding him of its unhappiness. His joints had joined the chorus, and the broadsheets, spread over a small table brought into the too-bright breakfast room, did not help.

Morris had done his work well. "The remaining two canisters?"

"Disappeared. Either Copperpot was not truthful, or Mr Morris was not quite honest with the particulars." Miss Bannon's colour was fine this morning, but her small white teeth worrying at her lower lip betrayed her anxiety. "I rather think the latter, if only because of Ludo's fine work."

Clare's stomach twisted afresh. He sipped his tea, hoping to calm his digestion, and turned a page. The ink stained his fingers, but he could not find the heart to be even fractionally annoyed. "The ones left in Londinium are now useless. The genie, as Dr Vance remarked, has left the lamp."

"Ah, yes. Dr Vance." There was a line between Miss Bannon's dark eyebrows. "*This* is a tale I am most interested in hearing, Clare. He is *in my house.*"

"I don't suppose there is a method for keeping him here?" Clare blinked rapidly, several times. The words on the pages refused to cohere for a moment.

"I have already attended to that, Archibald." Miss

Bannon glanced across the empty breakfast room as Mikal appeared, his tidy dark hair dewed with fine droplets of Londinium moisture. "Any news?"

"No further dispatches from the Palace." Mikal's lean face was not grave, but it was close. "The borders of the house are secure, Prima."

"Very good. Ludo?"

"At his *toilette*." Grim amusement touched Mikal's mouth, turning the straight line into a slight curve at its corners. "So is our other guest. When shall I kill him?"

"No need for that!" Clare interjected, hastily. "He has a steady pair of hands, and is familiar with the Theory. He will be most useful, and remanding him to Her Majesty's justice at the end of this affair—"

"—will be quite enough to salve your tender conscience?" Miss Bannon's expression was, for once, unreadable. She nodded, and Mikal drifted across the room to fetch her a breakfast plate. The sorceress, settled in her usual chair at the table she shared with Clare when he partook of her hospitality, shook the ringlets over her ears precisely once. "I am gladdened to hear it. But my question remains: what the devil is he doing here?"

"I am not quite certain." Clare forced his faculties to the task at hand, scanning columns of fine print. "Bermondsey, yes. Whitchapel, yes. Lambeth." He noted Miss Bannon's slight movement, slipped the notation into the mental bureau holding her particulars, and continued. "Cripplegate, yes. St Giles. The Strand – why there, I wonder? Ah yes, the Saint-Simonroithe, Morris would of course know the history. And the docks; dear God, it will spread like wildfire. It *is* spreading like wildfire." He exhaled, heavily. "How did he die, Miss Bannon?"

"Of his own creation, sir. I brought him to the Queen's presence; he expired very shortly afterwards." She accepted the plate – two bangers, fruit, and one of Cook's lovely scones – with a nod, and Mikal set to work loading another. "It was unpleasant. Convulsions, all manner of blood."

Clare shut his eyes. For a moment, the idea of swooning appeared marvellously comforting. He was so bloody *tired*. "He died in the Queen's presence? You took him before Britannia?"

"Of course." Puzzled, she stared at him through the fragrant steam wafting up from her scone. "You've gone quite pale."

"Perhaps Britannia will protect her vessel." Clare's lips were suspiciously numb. He gathered himself afresh. "This illness is incredibly communicable, Miss Bannon. The danger is quite real."

"Communicative?" It was her turn to pale as she dropped her dark gaze to her plate. "Infectious? Very?"

"Yes. *Very*. Who else was in the Presence?"

"A few personages," she admitted. "None I care over-much for." Quite decidedly, she turned her attention to her breakfast and began calmly to consume it. "I am still unclear on the exact dimensions of this threat, Archibald. You are to have breakfast and explain. I cannot fend off the Crown's requests for information for very long."

It was, he reflected, quite kind of Miss Bannon that she

did not consider aloud dragging him *and* Vance into Britannia's presence to give an account of the entire mess. "We have found the original source of the illness. Have you studied History, Miss Bannon?"

"My education, sir, was the best the Collegia could provide." But there was no sharpness to her tone. "And I have taken steps to continue it. What part of History's grand sweep do you refer to?"

"Sixteen sixty-six. The Great Plague." *And during it, Londinium burned.*

The silence that fell was extraordinary. Miss Bannon laid her implements down and picked up her teacup, her smallest finger held just so. Mikal settled himself in his usual chair as well, his plate heaped so high it was a wonder the china did not groan in pain.

"A rather dreadful time," she finally observed, taking a small mannerly sip.

"Rather. And we are about to suffer it again, unless Science – in the form of Dr Vance and myself – can effect some miracle of cure. A serum may be possible, if we are correct."

"And if you are not?"

The door opened and Vance appeared, freshly combed, new linens – charm-measured, no doubt, by the redoubtable Finch and his men – taken advantage of, and his eyes peculiarly dark with some manner of emotion Clare found difficult to discern.

"If we are not," Vance said, "then, Miss Bannon, God help Londinium, and the rest of the globe. Your hospitality is most wonderful, though your servants are peculiarly resistant to any manner of charm or politeness."

Miss Bannon blinked. "They do not waste such things on those . . . visitors . . . I have expressed an aversion to," she replied mildly. "Do come and have breakfast, sir. And mind the silver."

"I am an artist of crime, madam. Not a common thief." He straightened his jacket sleeves and stepped into the room, glancing about him with much interest. "Your Neapolitan is close behind me, old chap. Still in a bit of a temper."

*When is he not, nowadays?* "Do try not to come to blows at the breakfast table. Our hostess rather frowns upon such things." Clare sighed, heavily, and returned his attention to the broadsheets. Eating was out of the question, at least for him.

"Good heavens." Miss Bannon took another mannerly sip of tea. "Is there anyone in this house you have *not* annoyed, Vance?"

It was, Clare rather thought, a declaration of war. Vance apparently chose not to register it as such. "Mr Clare, perhaps. And I'm sure there is a servant or two who has not seen me. What news, old chum?"

*I grow weary of the familiarity of your address.* But Clare set aside the irritation. It served no purpose. "Mr Morris fell victim to his own creation, so we are forced to a process of experimentation. Any of his papers or effects detailing his own experiments – Bannon, I don't suppose we could lay hands on them?"

"I have a faint idea where they may be found." Miss Bannon's tone chilled slightly. "I hope the one likely to possess them has not left Englene's shores, or I shall be vexed with *travel* as well. I require as much information as you can give me about the nature of this illness. Perhaps it may yet be Mended."

"If so, I shall be glad of it." Clare closed *The Times* and opened the *Courier*, a most disreputable rag notable for the poor quality of its paper, the hideous shape of its typography, and its absolute accuracy in detailing the grievances of the lower classes. "For I must confess, Bannon, I am not sanguine in the least."

# Chapter Twenty-Six

## A Gift of Any Sort

Saffron Hill hunched colourlessly under morning drizzle. Emma felt just as dreary, her outlines blurred by a slight glamour – no more than a smearing, a delicate insinuation against the gaze, so that her cloth did not tell against her. Beside her, Mikal was utterly still, studying the end of the street where it devolved into Field Lane, and a more wretched bit of dirt would be difficult to find even in Londinium.

The weight in Emma's left hand was a thin, broken chain of cheap silvery metal. Caught in its links was a thread of dark hair, stubbornly coarse. The tiny brass charm attached very near the break held the impress of a double-faced Indus godling, one of the many who made the subcontinent such a patchwork of competing interests and principalities.

*Ripe for exploitation, they are, and Britannia's servants experts of divide and rule. We have done as much since Golden Bess's day. And before. We learned well from the Pax Latium, for all we were slow to apply such lessons.*

What instinct had moved her to quietly pocket the broken necklace she had found tangled in Llewellyn Gwynnfud's spacious purple-hung bed on a summer's morning long ago? Their affair had died a fiery death over a certain French "actress"; while Emma was merely unwilling to share, she was outright indisposed to being *lied* to. The tart had been knifed by her "manager" – Emma had borne the accusation of a hand in that manner nobly, considering she was completely innocent – and had been almost, *almost* willing to forgive.

She was no Seer, and the revelation of the necklace's owner – and the source of the coarse dark hair caught in its strands – had been quite surprising. She supposed Llew was catholic in his buggery, in every sense, and so had quietly left his house and returned to her own with the cheap chain burning in her skirt pocket.

And she had never received him again, or sought his company since. Until Bedlam, and the affair that had brought Clare to her notice, and to . . . yes.

To her regard.

Any idiot with ætheric talent knew how to practise a sympathy. And dear old Kim would not be on guard. She had never mentioned that little incident to another living soul. Kim may well have thought Lord Sellwyth had retained the scrap as a memento Llew may not have even known that his dalliance had been discovered or that a piece of evidence had found its way into her hands.

She held it tightly, her gloved fist bound as well with a silken handkerchief Mikal had knotted with exceeding care. It would not do to lose this sympathetic link. She would be forced to resort to other, bloodier, and far more draining methods to find her quarry.

Grey-faced children dressed in ragged colourless oddments slunk in every bit of shade they could find, and the æther here was thick with misery. In Whitchapel there was anger aplenty, but this corner of Londinium had burned through all such fuel long ago and was left with only cinder-glazed hopelessness. It was a wonderful place to hide, if one was a sorcerer; but the ætheric weight would rather tell on the nerves after a while.

If he had any nerves left, that was.

The chain and charm hummed with live sorcery as she caught the rhythm, her throat filling with a strange murmur, heavily accented in odd places. It was a song of spice and incense, the dust of the Indus rising through the cadences, and the brief thought that perhaps Mikal would find it familiar threatened to distract her.

She waited. Patience was necessary, though the consciousness of precious time draining away frayed her nerves most disagreeably. Clare had not looked well this morning, pale and rather moist, but who would look hale when faced with *this*? As well as that distasteful art professor.

The man had looked very much like the worst sort of

disreputable, with a cast to his mouth that was utterly familiar, especially since Emma had gone recently into Whitchapel and peered behind the dark curtain smothering her pre-Collegia memories. She rather disliked those recollections, and endeavoured to put them as far from her as possible.

The trouble was, sometimes they would not stay tamely in their enclosure.

Another twitch, the sympathetic sorcery testing her grasp. Like called to like, and of course he would have defences, some overt, others subtle and more dangerous. Yet he was not on his home ground, and could not risk a heavy expenditure of ætheric force lest it twist in unexpected ways – and, most likely, cut him alive.

Such was not a pleasant end.

Another twitch, more definite, and she pointed with her free hand, a corkscrew-twisted charter symbol spitting and spilling from her right third finger. Mikal had her arm; he guided her across the sludge of the street, old cobbles and bricks slipping and sliding under a thick greasing of muck. It was not Scab, of course, but it was fœtid enough.

She had a vague impression of warped wood and crumbling brick; the consciousness of being all but blind as she followed the inner tugging struck her, hard. Losing breath, the humming tune failing, she shunted aside the force of the triggered defence and inhaled smoothly, the song becoming a hiss-rasp of scales against dry-oiled stone. Mikal's voice, very low – he would be speaking to soothe her if he suspected she struggled with a defensive ætheric hedge.

It was not necessary, but vaguely pleasant nonetheless.

She came back to herself with a rush rather like the humours rising to the head after one sprang too quickly from a sickbed, and her left hand jerked forward and held steady until the connection broke with a subliminal *snap*. Before her rose a crooked door made glue and sawdust, and the narrow, barely lit hall was full of refuse. Somewhere a baby cried angrily, and there was a stealthy noise in the walls – rats, or the poor packed into these rooms like maggots in cheese. Either was likely.

Mikal had drawn a knife. Its curve lay along the outer edge of his forearm, and his eyes were alight with a fierce joy she rarely saw. Her eyebrow lifted a fraction, and he shook his head slightly. He could hear no heartbeat, no breathing behind the door.

Which meant little.

She stepped aside, very carefully, testing the rotting floor before committing her weight. It was her turn to settle herself and nod, fractionally; Mikal uncoiled. The door shattered, a witchlight sparking into being and flaring to distract and disrupt any possible attack, he swept through with her skirts hard on his heels and gave the small hole one swift, thorough glance before turning unerringly toward the makeshift cot mouldering in the corner.

The room was hardly bigger than a closet, its only claim to light or ventilation a small opening near the ceiling. It was barred, but the bars had been worked loose, their softened bases still tingling with ætheric force, torn free of damp-eaten wood. A scrap of black material caught on one fluttered, and Mikal's fingers darted out, catching and tearing it free as Emma braced herself for more traps.

Which were not present.

The room was echo-empty, and a whiff of brimstone and salt drifting across her nose told her someone had been busily cleaning ætheric traces away. "Oh, *bother*," she whispered, in lieu of something less polite. No reason not to act the lady now.

There was a large damp stain on the floor, and despite the chill a lazy bluebottle had found it and was busily investigating. The cot held scraps of white and green, and she cocked her head, openly staring.

A tussie-mussie of jonquil and almond blossoms, a flowerseller's small silvery dust-powder charm keeping them damp and fresh, lay twined with a red ribbon. Underneath, a folio of new, stiff leather lay, still fuming of the solutions used to tan it.

"Blood," Mikal said, grimly. But softly. "Prima?"

"Not enough to consign dear Kim to the afterworld, I fear." She stared at the flowers and the folio. "And it is unlike him to leave me a gift of any sort."

Her eyes half-lidded. The almond blossom was a sign of promise, and the jonquil's pale creaminess spoke of a demand for the return of a certain affection. The red ribbon – blood, perhaps? But Kim Finchwilliam Rudyard would not leave her such tokens.

*The other Prime? Perhaps.* Probing delicately, she caught no hint or taste of trap. Mikal ghosted forward, waiting for her gesture, and when she sighed and spread her free hand he gingerly touched the nosegay with a fingertip.

Still no trap.

He tucked the flowers under his arm and brought the folio to her; she held it in her free hand while he unknotted the handkerchief and wrapped the broken necklace back into a small efficient parcel, which she slid into a skirt pocket. The folio was so new it creaked, bearing no impress of personality as a well-used item would, and she opened it with a certain trepidation.

Inside, crackling yellow paper, covered in a spidery hand. Her lips thinned as she brought the witchglobe close, uncaring that the sensitised, freshly cleansed æther would hold the impress of even so minor a Work as a simple light for a long while.

And with it, her own presence, like a shout in the night.

Drawings. She riffled through the papers, and her suspicion was verified.

"Well, Clare will be very happy," she murmured. "But I am unsettled, Shield."

"Yes." He held the flowers, gazing at them curiously. Did he understand the message? This was a carefully set stage, and the nosegay had been planned just as the rest of it.

But not, Emma thought, by Rudyard. There was another player at the board. A Sorcerer Prime. One in the service of Britannia? But if so, why would he smooth *her* way?

*I do not like this at all.*

\*     \*     \*

Clare blinked, focused through the lenses, adjusting a small brass knob. "Still wriggling. Nasty little buggers."

"Once they are in the blood, they are remarkably resistant." Vance was hunched over his own spæctroscope, his fingers delicate as he fiddled with the *resolutia marix*. "Even a severe temperature change does not alter their rate of progression. Fascinating."

"Quite." Clare restrained the urge to tap his fingertips on the scarred wooden table with frustration. "The cloracemine?"

"No effect, except to cause the iron in the blood to crystallise. Which I really must investigate further, when this is finished. The applications could be— I *say*!"

"What?"

"Nothing. They're still alive, even as the acidity rises. It does lower their rate of division, but . . ."

". . . not enough," Clare finished. He coughed, wetly, turning his head aside so he did not foul the sample. Traces of steam rose from his cheeks, and he blinked them aside, irritably. It was chill in the workroom, Miss Bannon kindly leaving a charm to keep the temperature fairly steady in order for experimentation to have one less variable.

Valentinelli dozed on a stool near the door. He looked far more sallow than usual, but his scarred cheeks held splotches of bright crimson. His breathing had turned into a whistle, but his dark gaze darted occasionally from under his eyelids, sharp as a knife and more often than not settling on Vance's broad back.

The criminal mentath had taken his jacket off despite

the chill, and his shirt was adhered to his skin by a fine sheen of sweat. He selected another culture and another substance from the racks to his right, deftly sliding the fresh marrowe-jelly full of the original plague organisms into the spæctroscope's receiver. He uncapped the clorafinete powder, measured out a spoonful, mixed it with fresh marrowe-jelly in a small glass bowl, and selected a dropper from the small rectangular *serviette* full of sterilising steam. Two shakes, the dropper cooling rapidly, and the clorafinete mixture was introduced to the original plague. He twisted another knob slightly, and put a bloodshot eye to the viewpiece.

"Blast this all to hell," he muttered.

Clare quite agreed. There was no time, and yet this numbing systematic process was the one that held the greatest chance of working. He himself was no further than wachamile, working from the other end of the elemental pharma-alphabet.

Footsteps on the stairs. The door was flung open and Miss Bannon appeared, high natural colour in her cheeks, her curls disarranged. "Morris's notes!" she exclaimed, holding a creaking-new leather folio aloft rather in the manner of a Maenad brandishing the ivy-wrapt heart of a transgressor.

*Such fanciful notions, Clare.* But his faculties were in rebellion.

"How on earth did you—" Vance halted abruptly as a charter symbol flashed golden between Miss Bannon's fingers, hissing warningly. The Doctor, already halfway across the workroom, approached the sorceress no further. "Ah. I, erm. Well."

Clare rubbed at his eyes, carefully. *He moves very quickly.*

"Will these help, Clare? I confess I cannot make much of them." It was odd, she seemed almost joyous. "But *you* can. There is another message from the Crown, too. I have not opened it either, but we shall be rather in bad odour if I do not make some variety of explanation soon. The streets are full of coughing, and people collapsing in the road – even respectable people. Why is it so *fast*?"

"I do not know." A thought occurred to him. "Did you happen to see any of the victims with an indenture collar? I ask because your servants have not so much as a cough, yet, and—"

There was a soft thud. Valentinelli had hit the stone floor, and Miss Bannon dropped the folio. In that moment, Clare saw truly what she must have looked like as a young girl, and chided himself for thinking he had ever glimpsed the wonder of it before.

She knelt next to Ludovico, tucking her skirts back, and the assassin cried out weakly in Calabrian. The scarlet flags on his cheeks had intensified, and the shadow under his jaw was a swelling – not yellow, as the new plague, but deadly black, as the old.

Clare's beastly conscience pinched. *He knew the risk, I explained it – there are quite deadly vapours here. How did he contract it, though? Did the plague-pit infect him somehow? But it would have infected Morris too.*

The sorceress's house shivered once. Running feet in its recesses told him the servants heard their mistress's call.

Clare's knees creaked as he bent to pick up the folio. A wave of dizziness passed through him; his faculties noted it, allowed it to recede. He was thinking through syrup. "I will not ask how you acquired these, Miss Bannon. Do make Ludovico comfortable. We shall send word should we require more supplies."

"Very well." She was pale as milk, and he noticed her skin did not steam, even in this chill. "I did see some indentureds among the collapsed, Clare. I . . . perhaps mine are simply hardy."

"Or perhaps you have some natural immunity, Miss Bannon. We cannot be certain." *And should we take a sample of your blood for analysis, who knows what might occur?* He opened the folio, hoping his words did not sound too ponderous. His tongue was oddly thick, and the sweat greasing him was most unpleasant. It smelled of treacle, or something similarly sick-sweet, and they had not managed to discern the mechanism responsible for *that*, either. "Do you feel faint at all?"

"I am *quite* well, thank you. Sorcerers do not suffer some things, perhaps this is one." Her gloved fingers hesitated over Ludo's scar-pocked cheek. For once, she did not draw fastidiously away when he moved. "Clare . . ."

"He is quite durable, and he has not Morris's plague." The false comfort was not worthy of her, but Clare did not have the heart to tell her she was perhaps witnessing the last of Valentinelli's eventful walk upon the weary earth.

There was a commotion as the footmen arrived, and such was the devotion of the sorceress's servants that they did not cavil at carrying another very-ill man about, nor did they make avert signs to save themselves from ill fortune or humour. Of course, an indentured servant could not complain . . . and even cadaverous Finch was in proper health, with not so much as a sniffle.

It was *quite* provoking. He brought his attention back to the folio, and noted Vance's hopeful drawing-near.

Miss Bannon noticed too. A few sharp, instantly forgotten syllables left the sorceress's throat, and Vance hopped back in a most ungainly fashion as the air between himself and Clare hardened, diamond-sparkling for a moment, a concave shield of ice. It slid to the floor, shivering into fragments, and Horace grunted as he hefted Valentinelli's dead weight.

"Mum?" the footman asked, in a whisper.

"Take him to his chamber. Ready an ice bath, I shall be along in a moment." The sorceress rose slowly, Marcus the other footman backing slowly up the stairs with his beefy arms under Valentinelli's shoulders. Strange, how small and thin the Neapolitan looked now. "Doctor, must I warn you further?"

"No, madam." Icily polite, the criminal mentath stepped back to his spæctroscope. "I am dependent upon solving this riddle as much as your Campanian suitor; or rather more, for I have contracted Morris's damnable plague. It

may save you the trouble of dealing with me in what is
no doubt your accustomed fashion."

"You have precious little idea of my accustomed—" the
sorceress began, rather hotly.

*Will the two of you cease?* "Miss Bannon. Pray leave
us to solve this riddle. We shall do all we can. If there is
a solution to be found, rest assured you have contributed
everything within your considerable powers towards such
an end."

She studied him closely and he straightened under her
gaze, hoping she could not see the red splotches on his
cheeks or the small tremors running through his bones.
He did not have much time before he suffered a crueller
fate than Valentinelli's.

"Very well." She smoothed her skirts, a woman's nervousness, perhaps. Never mind that she was, in his experience, the female least likely to need such a soothing habit.
"Thank you, Archibald."

"Emma." Clare's throat was full. Feeling, the enemy of
Logic, was mounting. Inside his narrow chest, the heart
she had mended with sorcery such a short time ago settled
into a high, fast gallop.

The mentath watched the sorceress leave, took a deep
breath, and returned his attention to the folio, ignoring
Vance's bright deadly gaze.

# Chapter Twenty-Seven

## A Finer End

She had never entered the room given over to Valentinelli's use before, and saw no reason to now. Mikal hovered at her shoulder as she held the charming steady, her skirts pulled back from the threshold, and Horace and Marcus lowered the assassin into the ice bath. There was a choked cry and Ludovico's wracked body twisted; Alice the blonde chambermaid and her brunette shadow Eunice worked their homely magic upon the monkish, narrow bed and its linens. Their collars were bright, and they cast darting glances at her; when the footmen heaved Valentinelli free of the slurry of ice and water she made a gesture, a drying charm sparked and fizzed, and he was heaved gracelessly into the waiting bed.

"Mum." Finch's discreet cough. He peered around motionless Mikal. "Messenger from the Collegia. Awaiting your reply."

As soon as she loosed her hold, the assassin began to thrash. She gestured again, and Mikal moved forward, stepping into the room.

An iron rack atop a bureau of dark wood, festooned with cooled and hardened wax, held half-burned candles, their wicks dead and spent. There was a small *tau* corpse upon it, made of pewter with sad paste gleams for eyes and side-wound.

*Does he pray?*

The same chest she had seen in his other small rooms stood, closed and secretive, at the foot of his bed. He had chosen this room very near Clare's suite, despite its small size, and she had oft wondered what lay behind its door.

Mikal settled at the bedside, yellow irises gleaming in the dimness. He would keep the assassin contained, and make certain he did not strike an onlooker in his delirium.

The gaslamps hissed, and the servants looked to her for direction.

*Oh, Ludo. Not like this. You deserve a finer end.* There was a dry rock in her throat. She turned her attention to Finch. "From the Collegia?"

"Yes, mum." He did not quite bow, but he did hunch, and she remembered the hungry, sore-ridden wreck he had been long ago, before she had taken him into her service. How Severine had turned up her nose at the distasteful sight, and what had Emma said?

*He has performed signal service already, Madame Noyon. Pray do not argue.* That had been during the Glastonsauce affair: a newly crowned Queen in dire need of defence against a cabal of creaking ministers and competing interests, not the least of which was her mother's determination to keep Victrix dependent and weak. The affair had taught Victrix to almost-trust the sharp-eyed young sorceress who had entered the game uninvited and turned it to the monarch's advantage.

She gathered her skirts. The jet earrings shivered, tapping her cheeks; she took stock of her remaining resources. There was plenty of ætheric force in her jewellery, and the visit to Rudyard's bolt-hole had not drained her overmuch.

The trouble was, there was nothing she could *do*. Except fend off Britannia's ill-humour, and see what the Collegia was about.

*Mikal? He took Shield training, they had plenty of time to notice his . . . distressing talents. They did not. How shall I defend him against a Council of Adepts, one no doubt top-heavy with enemies? Who is likely to be there? What can I muster against them?*

And would she surrender her Shield to the Collegia, as the Law might require?

*Of course not.* Her gaze found Mikal's. He swayed slightly on his chair, a supple movement. *I am Prime. I do not give up what is mine.*

No matter how often she asked herself the question, the answer was unvarying.

Was it more than that? She had undertaken to keep Clare close instead of sending him to Victrix, and undertaken to keep the disagreeable Doctor as well. And there was the matter of a tussie-mussie left for her, and a bloodstain upon a filthy Saffron Hill floor. A promise, and a demand.

*From whom? Does it matter?*

Finch waited with no sign of impatience or irritation. It was a rare man who knew the value of patience, and who was not bothered by silence.

He was such a man, and had behaved with admirable aplomb in the most dire of circumstances. The indenture collar was in no way sufficient reward, but it had been all Emma could offer him. The safety of her service, and the promise that whatever lay in his past would not pursue him past her doors.

For Finch, it was enough.

"Very well," she said, as if the butler had pressed her. "Show the messenger into the study."

"Yes, mum." He glided away, perhaps relieved.

"Prima?" Mikal, the single word a question. Did he fear the Law? Perhaps not. It was, she admitted, far more likely he feared some manner of duplicity. A missive from the Collegia could bode no good.

"All is well." She was conscious, at once, of the lie. It stung her blocked throat, and Valentinelli moved uneasily, murmuring curses in his native tongue. His eyelids fluttered, and his hands leapt up, fighting a shadow-opponent.

Today, his fingernails were clean. An odd sensation passed through her – a hot bolt of something very much like jealousy. She had never known him to scrape the filth of living away while in *her* occasional service. And yet, he and Clare were wonderfully suited to each other, and she did not have to worry overmuch for either of them when they were about chasing whatever prey the Crown set them at.

*Perhaps it is time for worry, Emma. Don't you think so?*

The chambermaids fluttered a little. The two footmen were still watching her for directions. How few people it took to crowd a room.

"Be about your duties," she continued, in a far more normal manner. "Except you, Horace – stay with Mikal, and be ready should he require something for Ludo's comfort. Thank you." She turned and swept away, trying not to hear Valentinelli's moaning.

She was braced for any manner of unpleasantness when she opened the door to her study and sallied inside, breathing in the smell of leather, paper, old books and the richness of the applewood fire laid in the grate, a charm whisking the smoke up the flue but leaving the delicious scent.

Anything, that is, except the youngling from the Hall of Mending, his hands wringing together much as Severine Noyon's sometimes did, his charm-smoothed cheeks pale and his tongue twisting as he gabbled out his news.

Thomas the Mender, Thomas Coldfaith, *her* Thomas . . .

. . . was plagued. And he wished to see her, at once. The message was clear.

He did not expect to live.

## Interregnum: Londinium, Plagued


First a tickle,
then a choke,
then the red rose
lays a bloke.

*The first few cases were ignored. A vast mass seething in rookeries in several districts – the Eastron End, hard by Southwark but not within the confines of the Black Wark, Whitchapel, Spitalfields – swallowed the tiny bits of poison whole, and the drops altered the composition of the ocean. They first complained of a cough, red roses blooming in their cheeks like consumption's deadly flower – and within hours came the swelling. If the boils burst, blood and sourpink pus exploding as eyelids fluttered over their red-sheened eyes, the sufferer might recover. But if the* convulsions started before the boils burst, a winding-sheet was needed.

At first it was called the Johnny-dances, for the convulsions. Then the Red Rose, for the flush in the cheeks, and the Hack, for the thick, chesty coughs. And the sweetbriar sickness, for the sugary smell of the sufferers' sweat. But after a little while, it was simply known as the Red. You caught the Red, hung the Red, danced the Red.

Ships sailed that eve with weakened, coughing sailors; those who were not buried at sea vanished in teeming ports that soon bloomed with deadly roses on hollow cheeks. The Red was a promiscuous mistress. She hopped the backs of gentlemen and hevvymancers alike, and they danced out their deaths in dosshouses and townhouses. Physickers shook their heads in puzzlement, and were often dead as their patients a day later.

And sorcerers fell ill. Some diseases passed the ætheric brethren by, but the Red was not one. In their bodies the Red made illogical sorcery explode in strange ways – one sprouted pinkish fungal growths, screaming as they ruptured his skin, another's body turned to a patchwork of red glass as ætheric force and blood twisted together in an oddly beautiful pattern. Usually so fortunate, the ætherically blessed found the Red invariably fatal.

And some whispered it was only fitting.

Where did it come from? None knew. Charms were no good against it, even those who could afford Mending died under the Red's lash. Some said it was a judgement from on high, others that it was a consequence of Progress and *the filthy conditions of the rookeries and slums of every large city, some few that it was an illness from the hot, newly conquered parts of the globe.*

*Only the dead did not speculate. They mounted in piles, and Londinium for the first time in centuries heard the corpsepickers' ancient cry during times of disaster: "Bring out your dead!" The stigma of corpsepicking vanished, for their habit of taking valuables from the dead lost its impetus once there was a glut of said rags and shinies in the shops that would take such traffic. Instead, they carted the creaking barrows full of twisted limbs, and their cheery singing, interspersed with deep chest-coughs, was the sound of nightmare angels.*

*It was a corpsepicker's duty to sing, while he carted.*

*And on the Red danced, over the bodies of her victims. She bloomed like the reddest rose of the Tuyedor's device. She grew rank and foul, and there was no cure.*

# Chapter Twenty-Eight

## A Footrace with Death

Genius though he was, Morris had not been *systematic*. The notes were a hotchpotch, records of experiments interspersed with bits of weather observation and snatches of old prayers mixed with hand-drawn observations and elongated screaming faces, lists of foods that interfered with Morris's most delicate digestion and constitution, and some most ugly bits of scurrilousness about Queen and Crown.

Morris had not been turned against his country. No, the genius had merely hated his fellow man with a deep, abiding passion and quite *democratic* uniformity, and found a way to cleanse the world of sinners with almost-invisible contagion – very much the hand of his vengeful God. It was an elegant solution to such hatred, and the drawings of the earlier iterations of the canisters were most intriguing.

But the delivery method did not give enough of a clue to the organism's roots, as it were.

Clare went slowly through the folio as Vance continued his testing. There was some small success with dicalchimide, but it quickly faded. The tiny little beings were incredibly resistant, and Clare had a momentary shudder when his faculties turned to the question of what they were likely doing inside his own veins.

*How much time do I have?*

His hand stole towards the secret drawer. Inside was a small silver-chased box, and a fraction of the powder inside would make his faculties sharper. Sharp enough to cut this knotted tangle into manageable pieces, as Aleksandr of Makedon once had in a temple, long ago?

*What a historical thought.*

Near the end, a single, creased scrap of paper drew his attention. The notations on it blurred, and he coughed, thickly. Squinted, cursing the veil drawn over his vision. His nose had dulled, too, for he could no longer smell the experimentation. The thickness of marrowe-jelly, the stagnant reek of disease, the miasma-choke of the autoclave steam-cleansing the eyedroppers. His fingers caressed the knob that would bring the drawer open and reveal the box.

"Nothing with faramide, either." Vance whistled tunelessly, but did not turn. "Do not take your coja, Clare. It will accelerate the illness."

*What manner of deduction led you there, sir?* But it was immaterial. Clare squinted a fraction more; his faculties seized upon the notations on the crumpled, torn farthing-paper. He could almost *see* Morris hunched at his table, scribbling, incoherent with excitement as whatever vengeful Muse or saint waited upon mad geniuses dropped the solution into his fevered, waiting brain.

"Aha," he breathed. "*Ah*." The fit of coughing seized him, and when it was finished, he spat a globule of bright red. It splatted dully on the floor, but Clare was past caring. "Vance. *Vance*."

"Filistune is also useless. I am here."

"Here it is." Clare forced his reluctant legs to straighten, pushing back the wooden chair with a scrape. "Here is the key. It is the alteration process. By God, man . . . by God . . ."

He did not have to finish. Vance was suddenly there, and the other mentath's sweat was as candy-sweet as his own. Vance took in the scrawled notations with a single glance and shut his eyes, the tear filming down his shaven cheeks tinged with crimson. His own faculties would be working through the ramifications and deductions, and when he opened his eyes again Clare found that their gazes met and meshed with no trouble at all.

It was a moment of accord he could have shared with none other than a mentath.

"Muscovide. And not marrowe-jelly." Vance nodded.

"We must have some method of separating—"

"—and an acidic base. Yes. *Yes*." Vance's fists knotted, and he made a short sharp gesture. As if he felt a throat between his fingers, and he wished to *squeeze*.

"It will take time to prepare, to break the chain of

replication. But by God, man, we can halt this dreadful thing."

"Then we must not stand about." A series of wracking coughs seized Vance's body, and he curled around them, shaking away Clare's movement to help with an impatient violence. When he could draw breath again, he straightened, and another of those piercing looks passed between them.

"Indeed." Clare suppressed the tickle in his own throat. With no further ado, he strode for the table and swept a working space clean with one of his trembling arms. *We are in a footrace with Death. But perhaps we may gain a length or two.*

# Chapter Twenty-Nine

## One Word

It was a good thing she had not wasted her sorcerous force duelling with the absent Rudyard. She could not take her carriage, or even the smart new curricle, for Mikal was still at Ludovico's bedside. Harthell the coachman paled at the thought of driving to the Collegia, though he was willing enough; *no*, she had told him, *merely saddle the bay mare, properly, and be quick about it. None of the sidesaddle rubbish.*

It meant she could not wear full mourning, but she suspected Eli would understand. And why mourn, when there was death aplenty lurking in the streets? Her least favourite riding habit, in a shade of brown most dowdy and with newly unfashionable mutton sleeves, at least had divided skirts. She could always turn it over to Catherine and Isobel for reworking; Catherine's needle could no doubt change it into something exquisite.

None of her servants had so much as a cough. The likely reason, of course, was throbbing in Emma's chest; a wyrm-heart Stone that granted life and immunity, extending out through the indenture collars. Such protection would not extend where it was most needed.

Mentaths did not indenture.

Wherever Llewellyn Gwynnfud, Earl Sellwyth, was, he was certainly sneering at her.

What would Llew say of this? But she could guess. And it would be nothing she could give credit to if she wished to retain her self-regard.

She gathered the reins, nodded to Harthell, and the bay clockhorse, shining and lovingly oiled, pranced restively. She was a fine creature, deep-chested and beautifully legged, her glossy hide seamlessly merging into russet metal and her hooves marvels of delicate filigreed power. Wilbur the spine-twisted stableboy darted forward to open the bailey gate, and the mare shot forward, hooves striking sparks from the cobbles. The gate clanged at her passage, rather like a mournful bell, and she was very glad Mikal had not come from Ludovico's bedside.

The witchlight before her spat silvery sparks, but she need not have bothered with the warning of a sorcerer's haste. Those on the streets, handkerchiefs clamped to their mouths, scattered as she cantered past, and the few carriages out and about in the Westron End were easily avoided. Those who could afford to stayed inside, those forced out of doors hurried furtively . . . and three of the scuttling pedestrians collapsed as she rode past, their limbs jerking in a deadly dance.

Morris, damn him, had wrought well.

Riding thus absorbed a great deal of her attention, but what remained circled the same few problems as a tongue would probe a sore tooth. They vied for her attention equally – Victrix, the Duchess and her hangman, the faceless sorcerer who had so generously left Morris's notes and quite possibly injured Rudyard severely in the bargain, Clare's flushed cheeks and sweating, fevered brow, Ludovico's restless tossing, Mikal's hypnotic swaying at the assassin's bedside.

*What am I to do? How may this be arranged satisfactorily?*

For the first time in a very long while, Emma Bannon had precious little idea. Everything now depended on Clare . . . and on other factors she had little say in. For a sorceress used to resolving matters thoroughly, quietly, and above all, to her own liking, it was a d—d *uncomfortable* state of affairs.

Through moaning, fog-choked, eerily calm Londinium the sorceress rode, and she arrived at no conclusion.

As soon as the bay's hooves touched down on the white pavers inside the Black Gate, Emma tasted the chaos and fear roiling through the Collegia's sensitised fabric. The Great School shook, its white spires flushed with odd rainbow tints and its defences, invisible and barely visible, quivering with distress.

She took the most direct route to the Hall of Mending at a trot, and the Collegia servant who took her horse had a fever-bright glare and an oddly lumbering gait. Emma merely nodded and mounted the steps with a stride a trifle too free to be a lady's, the great Doors opening creak-slowly. She nipped smartly between them, rather as if she were a student again . . .

. . . and plunged into a maelstrom.

The white pennants and hangings had been taken down, and the floor was splashed with scarlet. Cots lay in even rows, then jammed into corners, while Menders and their apprentices hurried from one to the next, seeking to dull the pain of sorcerers who lay twisting and screaming as their bodies warped under a double lash of disease and ætheric eruption. Bannon actually stepped back, almost blundering into a young apprentice who hissed "*Mind yourself!*" and scrambled away, his arms full of bloody rags.

The low sinuous altarstone throbbed as well, flushed with pink as its energies, collected over generations, were now plumbed to aid in Mending.

It did not look as if it was doing much good. As she hurried down the central aisle, looking for a particular set of broad crippled shoulders, a lean hieromancer in his traditional blue jacket thrashed off a narrow cot and screamed a high piercing note of pain, and his body disintegrated under a wave of twisting irrationality. His flesh parted with sick ripping sounds, and the blood that spilled out crystallised into what looked like rubies, gem-bright droplets that chimed as they hit the floor.

*Good God.* Emma did not halt, ducking the fine mist

of fluid turned to stone and hurrying past as Menders converged, charms flashing valorously but ineffectively. Sweat had collected along Emma's lower back, and she *felt* the death of the hieromancer, brushing her with soft-feathered fingers.

Her Discipline responded, the deeper fibres of her body and mind twitching. She shuddered, and just then caught sight of Thomas Coldfaith.

His regular ungainly walk, shuffling and pulling his recalcitrant clubbed foot, was even more painful; his twisted face florid with Morris's plague and streaks of pinkish rheum streaking his scar-pocked cheeks. His wonderful eyes were bloodshot, and he appeared not to notice her. His Mender's robe was grey, not white, not his usual jay's-bright plumage, and spattered beside with all manner of fluids. He had just straightened from another cot, where a dead body lay slumped, twisting and jerking as it turned itself inside out and spattered the surrounding area with entrails and foul blackish, brackish semi-liquid.

She arrived before him with no memory of the inter-vening space, the feather-tickles all over her body *most* distracting despite her training's tight reining.

Once or twice before, the Hall of Mending had been full of such suffering. Only then none of Emma's Discipline had been alive to witness it, for those of the Endor had been killed as soon as certain . . . troubling signs . . . were noticed.

Menders, however, had ever been cosseted.

"Thomas." She caught his arm, her gloved fingers

slipping slightly against the slickness coating his robe. "You called for me."

He blinked, bleary, and the red film over his irises and whites turned his gaze to a chilling blankness. "Em?"

"I am here." The same dry rock in her throat. "Thomas . . ."

"And untouched. That is good." A weary nod of his proud, misshapen head. "Though why I am surprised, I do not know."

Her temper and conscience both pinched, but the sea of noise about them overwhelmed both. "There may be a cure. I can bring you to it." *Clare will help. He must be very far along now.* Childish faith, perhaps, but she ignored such an estimation.

More blinking, and Coldfaith swayed, as if undecided.

*Enough.* She slipped her arm through his and began to urge him along. *They can do without you, Thomas. We need a quiet corner, and I shall . . .*

What was she contemplating? The weight in her chest was terrible. Even more dreadful was the shaking through his body, communicating to hers in a flood of loose-kneed, swimming dismay.

"Em." Coldfaith halted. "I wished to see you, before I did what I must."

All her gentle urging could not move him. She clasped his arm more tightly, set her heels, and pulled a little more firmly. "Come with me. Please."

"No." A terrible clarity bloomed in his dark gaze, behind the film of blood. "Emma."

"Thomas – *Tommy*." As if they were students again, young and bright and struggling. "Come."

He freed himself of her grasp, gently but decidedly. "I wished to see you once more," he repeated. "And to tell you I have not been kind to you. Before our Disciplines, Em, I had . . . thoughts." He murmured something she could not quite catch, and as she leaned closer to him among the buffet of the crowd, he coughed. Bright red spattered along her shoulder, but she did not care. "I . . . I must tell you. Em. Yes, must tell Em . . ."

Another ripple through him, and she caught at his elbow again. A Mender hurrying behind her bumped against her skirt and hissed an imprecation, having little patience for the obstruction it represented. A sea of coughing rose through the Hall's capacious entrance, more screams, and moaning.

Even though the Church held the ætherically talented as doomed to a purgatory at best and deep hellfire at worst, the sorcerers still called for God *in extremis*. Some of them even called for mothers they did not remember, for the Collegia was mother and father once a sorcerous child was taken.

None called for their fathers.

Thomas tacked away, slipping through her fingers with a feverish dexterity. He made for the pink-stained altar-stone, and as he did, a vast stillness descended upon the Hall.

Between one step and the next, Emma froze. She strained against air thick and hard as glass, drawing in a torturous lungful of stabbing air as Thomas reached the stone. He stood, his head down, for a long moment, and she knew what the silence and the difficulty in breathing meant.

Here in the Hall of his Discipline, Thomas Coldfaith was about to open the deepest gates of his sorcery. And Emma, an interloper with stinging eyes and a traitorous stone spike in her chest, was pinned as a butterfly on velvet, unable to act.

*No. Thomas, no.*

What had he meant to tell her?

He stretched his arms wide, rather as a *tau*-corpse would, and the silence became unbearable. The Hall's light brightened, scouring Emma's skull, nails through her sensitive eyes and her lungs refusing to work, a crushing upon throat and ribs and bones, her dress flapping and ruffling as streams of disturbed æther swirled past, whipping toward the hunchbacked sorcerer.

It was an act spoken of in whispers long after, how the greatest Mender of his generation opened the gates to his Discipline, becoming the throat Mending sang through. How several of the dying writhed before closing their eyes in peace, whatever hurtful blooming of the irrational wedded to the invisible vermin eating their flesh soothed away. How there was a shadow in the midst of the Hall of Mending's brightness, but it fled as Coldfaith cried one Word, the contours of which echoed and rambled through the Hall's nautilus-curved halls and inner recesses for decades afterwards, a Word like a name, full of longing and frustrated love, a depth of passion scarcely hinted at during a lifetime's watching and waiting.

There was only one sorcerer who could have explained the mystery of that Word, but she did not. None would have listened to her talk of Mending, for it was not her Discipline, and in any case, how could she explain *how* she knew?

She knew, for it was her own name: a Word that expressed a thin nervous fire-proud girl with brown curls seen through the eyes of a misshapen boy. The Word rang and rumbled and echoed, and when the door of his Discipline closed, the Menders found one of their own before the now-dark and drained altarstone, bending and coughing great gouts of scarlet blood that stained the pale flooring and would not be scrubbed away by bleach, carbolic, or sorcery.

Mending, as always, had exacted a price. Thomas Coldfaith's body twisted and shuddered as flesh transmuted itself to smoke-dark glass, particles grinding finer and finer until they shredded into dark vapour that streamed out through the vast open doors and dissipated over Londinium.

He failed, but not entirely. Afterwards, the sorcerous of the Empire did not die of irrationality. They simply, merely, died of the plague's convulsions and boils. A small mercy, perhaps, but all the twisted King of Menders (for so he was afterward called) could grant.

And Emma Bannon, Sorceress Prime, left the Collegia grounds on her bay clockhorse. None remarked her presence there that day, and it was perhaps just as well.

For had they addressed her, she would have struck them down with a Prime's vengeance. In each of her pupils the leprous green spark of her own Discipline had strengthened, and that fire would not extinguish easily.

# Chapter Thirty

## The Island's Heart

The coughing had taken on a wet, rheumy quality that would have been of great concern if Clare was inclined to pay it any mind. The bowl catching their crimson-laced, coughed-up effluvia had to be emptied regularly, else it slopped over onto the stony floor. Even the traceries of steam rising from their skin was tinged with red, or the film over their eyes gave everything a rubescence.

Clare had tossed his jacket and shirt over the desk chair, his narrow chest with its sparse hair visibly sunken as his body, held to its task by his faculties and a mentath's disciplined Will, struggled under the burden. Vance was hardly better, his larger frame scarecrow-wasted and his eyes glittering through the red film. He had stripped down to an undershirt of grey linen, and it did Clare much good to notice the criminal mentath was not quite so fastidious in his underdress as he was in his outer.

They both moved slowly. Past words now, they shuffled about the workroom, its chill that of a crypt. Bubbling alembics as the muscovide was distilled, and they need not culture the new plague, for their own secretions teemed with Morris's deadly gift to mankind. A single glance, or the offer of a freshly sterilised glass dropper, was all they needed.

Outside the workroom, Londinium writhed. The fog, normally venom-yellow, turned grey and greasy with the smoke from the bonfires some of the bodies were tossed onto.

On the fourth day, Miss Bannon appeared. "Clare?" Her gaze was somewhat odd, and he shelved the observation with a mental shudder. He had limited resources, and could not spare them. Not with this matter before him.

Even a mentath's determination would only stretch so far.

"Working." He coughed. "Tomorrow. Come back."

She stood in the door of the workroom, her small hands turned to fists, and after a long while, Clare noticed she had gone. The green pinpricks in her pupils seemed more the product of his fever than of her illogical sorcery. Her house was an island on a sea of chaos, and even the Crown had ceased sending missives.

Britannia, it seemed, was occupied with other matters.

None of the servants took ill, and meals arrived on silver trays and were sent away untouched. They were not quite of the usual quality, but Clare – when he expended any thought on the matter at all, which was briefly at best – realised that Londinium's supplies must be thin indeed at the moment.

An island, yes. But at the island's heart, two small grains of grit, their accretions of bloody phlegm and various odd bits of rubbish from their experiments carted away by pale, trembling servants who nonetheless did not cough and choke, nor grow fevered.

He supposed, when he thought on it – never for very long, there was too much else to be done – that both he and Vance would not live to see the fruits of their labour. There was no word of other mentaths succumbing to the disease, but of course, the broadsheets would not be interested in such things.

On the fifth day, Miss Bannon appeared as he had directed, standing in the door. She wore no jewellery, which was the first oddity; the second was her haggardness, her gaze burning in the peculiar way of sorcerers – as if she had forgotten her very *self*, or some vast impersonal thing was looking out through her skull. It was not the same terrible presence as Britannia peering forth from Her chosen vessel, for Britannia was recognisable in some essential way sorcery was not.

Clare spat at the bowl, accurately. A great deal of practice had refined such an operation – three coughs, deep and terrible, working the weight free of his chest, the roll of the tongue packing the bloody sludge into a compact mass, then the expectoration – just enough of an arc to land it in the bowl with a wet *plop*! It exhausted him, and he leaned against the table, clutching a small glass vial.

Vance swayed. "Muscovide," he croaked. "Who. Would have –" a series of coughs, and he spat as well – "thought?"

*Quite.* But Clare could not speak. His heart, labouring under the strain, thundered in his ears. He held the vial up, and Vance took it, shook it critically.

"Will it. Work?" The criminal mentath – at least he was, Clare thought hazily, a very fine lab assistant – reached for the spæctroscope. It took him two tries to curl his bloodstained fingers about the dial of the *resolutia marix*.

This was the last test, and Clare's faculties blinked for a moment. He surfaced through a great quantity of clear, very warm water to find himself standing, head down, breathing thickly like a clockhorse suffering metallic rheum, staring as Vance eased a dropperful of the thin red substance from the vial into the scope's dish, where a mass of plague was no doubt writhing and wriggling.

"Suction . . . tube," Vance wheezed. "It must be . . . introduced . . . under the skin."

Miss Bannon said something about a needle, and a Discipline.

"Perhaps." Vance coughed again. "We shall . . . see." His breathing failed for a moment, he swayed again, then leaned down to the spæctroscope's viewpiece.

Clare found his head turning. He stared at Miss Bannon, in her severe black, with no jewels swinging at her ears or glittering at her fingers. You could not tell she was a sorceress except for those green pinpricks in her pupils, the smudges underneath dark as charcoal and her curls more unevenly dressed than he had ever seen them. Had Madame Noyon taken ill?

Her lips moved. Something about Ludovico. Was he dead, then?

A vast weightlessness settled on his chest. The relief was immense, and as his knees failed, Clare realised he was expiring.

It did not hurt. That was the first surprise.

The second was Miss Bannon's wiry strength as she caught him, easing his fall, His field of vision swung to include Vance, who was staring down at him with a peculiar, saddened expression.

Had the cure not worked? But that was *impossible*, every other test had been—

Vance's knees buckled. His fingers were at his trouser pocket, and Clare thought slowly that it was *important*, something about that was vitally important.

Miss Bannon did not move to catch Vance as he folded to the floor. Instead, she bent over Clare, and the sound of her ragged breathing was the last he heard before darkness took him. It was perhaps as well he did not hear what followed.

For Emma Bannon, finally, wept.

# ❋ *Chapter Thirty-One*

---

## *Unwise and Unbecoming*

"Put him to bed." Emma's throat was afire, her eyes dry-burning. She had not slept in days, it seemed, and Mikal was just as haggard.

Ludovico still clung to life; the black boils had burst and he merely lay, weak but still breathing, bandages changed every few hours as the suppurating wounds healed. His dark eyes were those of a captive hawk, sullen and hot with weakness he raged against even as his strength gathered and his body fought off the ravages of whatever dreadful illness he had contracted. It was not the Red, that much was certain; his boils had been *black*, and Clare was in no condition to answer any questions.

Marcus hefted Clare's shoulders. "Light as a feather, he is."

Gilburn grunted, heaving the mentath's lower half. "Not from this end, sir."

*It is Clare, do not . . .* She could not even finish the thought. Instead, she stood in the fœtid workroom, staring at the heap of sodden cloth that had been Francis Vance. There was a slow-burning ember still clasped in the man's vitals, but it was more than likely the foxfire of nerves and meat slowly leaching of fevered life.

In any case she did not care. "Put that outside. The pickers will take it."

"Yesmum." Finch's face did not wrinkle with distaste, but it might have been a near thing. "Mum?"

Small flames danced under boiling alembics; the floor was a mess of slippery substances perhaps better left unexamined. Papers with odd notations were strewn about, some crumpled, others merely drifting to scatter on the sludge. The water-closet was likely to be a horror. She could charm it clean, and she would.

But not at this moment. It was terrible to see – Clare was normally so *precise*, even when a certain question or series of experiments took hold of his nimble brain. The only time she had ever seen disorder was when his faculties were underused and he began to suffer the mentath's curse.

Boredom. If not trained and used, logic, like sorcery, *turned* on its helpless bearer.

Finch cleared his throat.

She surfaced. The broadsheets were full of wild speculation. And sending any of the servants out into Londinium was becoming problematic in the extreme. "Yes?"

"Another summons, mum. From the Crown." Was there a moment of fear in his tone, a slight catch to the words?

"Yes." She turned, slowly, in a full circle. The walls were flecked and splashed with various substances. Perhaps a flame-scouring would be in order.

And while she was at it, the entire rotting city could be cleansed, could it not? A small matter, for a Prime. One had only to will it, and the entire world could drown in such a flame.

It was *building* that was the difficult bit.

*You are not thinking clearly.* The heaviness in her chest, the Philosopher's Stone, knocked free of Llewellyn Gwynnfud's dead hands . . . it made her proof against this decay, and was no doubt the reason her servants did not suffer.

But such protection did not extend to Clare. He was not servant or Shield. He was simply, merely . . .

. . . what?

*What is he to me? Dare I name it?*

Horace and Teague appeared; Finch directed them to lay Vance's body outside the gate for the corpse-pickers. "The Lady wishes it so. Come, hurry along, men."

*The Lady wishes it so.* "Finch." Rusty and disused, as if she had not spent the past few days roaming her library reciting cantos until her tongue went numb, to keep from unleashing a torrent of hurtful sorcery.

"Yesmum?"

"Have Harthell saddle the bay again, please. If the maids go a-market with Cook, one of the footmen should accompany them – armed. Mikal?"

"Is still at Mr Ludovico's bedside, mum."

"Send someone to watch Ludo, then, and tell Mikal I require him." *Though he will not be happy; I left him like a pin holding a dress-fold and did not return to retrieve him, or give him lee to depart his post.* "No doubt he will wish the black saddled, as well."

"Yesmum. Mum?"

She turned her attention fully onto him, but he did not blanch. A tilt to her head, and she saw the lines graving deeper into his dry skin, the looseness under his chin, the way his collar cut into the papery flesh.

Finch was ageing, too. But *she* was not. As long as she bore the Stone, she would not, and the thought was enough to send a shiver down her spine.

The butler clasped his hands behind his back. "We are grateful to be in your service, mum. There's talk in the servant's quarters, and right glad we are you . . . well, you are our mistress." His laborious accent changed, and it was the slur and slang of his youth wearing through the words now. "Do you close your doons, missan, an' we shall all stay wit'you."

*Why, Finch.* "I am pleased to hear it. I do not think I shall be required to close the house, though. Britannia dares not imprison me." *For if she did, she would not have me to do certain disagreeable tasks.*

There might be others, though. A sorcerer as invisible as herself, perhaps part of Society, perhaps not, dogging her footsteps and leaving her posies.

"No matter how remiss I have been in answering

summons," she finished. "Thank you, Finch. Please hurry."

He did, and Emma drifted to the door in his wake. She said a single Word, and the lamps dimmed; another, and the flames under the alembics died. She left the workroom in shadow, and when she closed the door, it thudded as a crypt door would, sealing the mess inside.

The pall over Buckingham boiled with the ruling spirit's displeasure. It wreathed the spires of the Palace, it came down almost to the ground, and its thunderstorm-blackness was spangled with flashes of crackling diamond-hard white.

*That is quite . . .* She could find no words. A coughing groom took her horse, and Mikal's too. Kerchiefs knotted around the lower half of many a face, some soaked in various substances, made Londinium into a city full of highwaymen who sometimes collapsed, coughing bloody sputum and convulsing. The corpsepickers sang, and if not for the grey of the fog – for bodies were burning, and the city full of sweet roasting as well as coalstink – it might have been a pleasant day.

After all, it was not raining.

Haggard Coldwater Regiment guards stood at their posts; she stalked past them despite an attempt to bar her passage. Mikal produced the summons, the paper snow-white and the seal upon it sparking just as the blackness overhead did. The sight of the seal answered all questions, or perhaps it was the expression on her Shield's lean face.

Under the pall, the light was wan and anaemic, and the

corridors of the Palace were oddly empty. Though she could hear motion, scurryings in the walls, as it were, she relied on the guards at each doorway to point her to the Queen's location.

Stalking along, her head high and her dress – mourning, again, but this one much more wilted than her garments were wont to be – rustling as she moved, her hair dressed indifferently and bare of any jewellery, she was an unprepossessing figure at best. The charged atmosphere shivered as she moved through it, a Prime's approach through the thick sensitised æther that of a storm approaching.

Did Victrix feel it?

*I hope she does.*

The royal apartments, in contrast to the rest of the Palace, were a hive of activity. Physickers and white-robed Menders, a few scarlet-striped Hypatians, more than one Minister in a wig and some of Court grimly determined to be seen as loyal at this extremity, handkerchiefs lifted to their mouths as Emma swept past, Mikal holding the summons aloft as if it were a banner. It was the bedchamber, she found, and though she had a summons, she might be called upon to cool her heels.

*Then I will leave. I have other matters to attend to.*

As in, watching Clare die? Her skin contracted, a shiver running through her, and she eyed the heavy door to the royal bedchamber, the rose-petalled crest of the house of Henry the Wifekiller worked into the ancient wood and painted over many a time.

"*Bring her in,*" the air whispered, Britannia's tones

shivering through the heads of those assembled without passing through their ears. Emma blinked, but her step did not falter. She passed through the bedchamber doors with her head held high.

Alexandrine Victrix, ruler of Empire, lifted her tear-stained face from the counterpane and fixed Emma with a baleful eye. "*You*," she said, and the word held a long hiss of displeasure. "*I sent for you!*"

Her eyes were black from lid to lid, the dust over Britannia's glare scorched away, the stars burning in that blackness forming constellations that would make a mortal dizzy if he gazed too deeply. She was on her knees next to a high-heaped bed, and the room was littered with physicker's tools, full of a sweet-burning smell, and tropical-hot. The Queen's pregnancy was more visible now, perhaps because she was merely in a dressing gown, and her dark hair hung in rivulets down her back.

On the bed, under the many blankets – they must have thought to sweat something out of him – lay the Consort, the ruby swellings under his chin grotesquely shiny as the fluid within them strained for release. He coughed weakly, a thick chesty sound, and the bubbling of bloody film at the corners of his eyes was the only colour in the room that did not seem bleached by Victrix's fury.

Emma came to a halt as the door swung shut behind her. Mikal stayed outside; her single scorching look had expressed her desire to face this alone.

"*You*," Victrix repeated, and it was curious how certain Emma could be that it was the mortal Queen speaking, though the spirit of rule shone out through her eyes. *"How dare you bring this into Our presence!"*

For a few moments, Emma could hardly credit her ears. Then she realised the nature of the accusation, and her chin lifted. "You sent me to recover Morris, Your Majesty. I did. I even did my best to bring him to you before he expired – at *Your* express command. Had You seen fit to be more open with me about the nature of his filthy '*experiments*', much of this could have been avoided." *There is my gauntlet, Majesty. Return it if you dare.*

For a moment she could not believe she had addressed the Queen so. But the vision of Clare, his sunken cheeks afire and his body held to the task before him with sheer will, rose before her. And it was Victrix's game – the game of empire, of weapons and conquest – that had birthed this monstrosity.

And not only Clare, but Londinium suffered under its lash as well.

*"Our Consort sickens."* Victrix almost howled the words, and the pall over the Palace rattled ominously with thunder. *"There must be a remedy!"*

*She is only a woman, after all, and one with a heart.* Something inside Emma's chest cracked slightly. "I am engaged upon—"

It was, she would remember, the last few moments of the Bannon who had sworn service not just aloud, but in the secret chambers of her very self.

Angry colour suffused Victrix's cheeks, less tender now than when they were crowned. *"Engaged?* Engaged?

*Engage more* thoroughly!" Everything in the room jumped slightly, and Alberich moaned.

*Do I look as if I have been taking the waters at Bath?* Heat mounted in Emma's own cheeks, and the two women were perhaps just as scarlet-cheeked as the Consort now. "I cannot create sheer miracles—"

"*You are a filthy sorceress, what else are you good for?*" the Queen cried, in a paroxysm of rage. "*Creeping in corners, a shameless proudnecked hussy airing before her betters!*" She lifted a trembling, ring-jewelled hand, the gems scintillating with fury, and pointed. "*If he dies, if you have killed him, I will punish—*"

Emma inhaled sharply. The ice was all through her, now. The crack in her chest whistled a cold, clear draught right down to her very core. "*I* did not loose this madness upon the world, Victrix. Your own Crown did that, with no help from me. It is unwise – and unbecoming – for you to speak so."

"*Get out! Do not return until you have found the remedy, and if my Consort dies I will have your head!*"

"You are," she informed the screeching woman, "welcome to try to separate said head from my shoulders." *But it is a task you had best be prepared for the unpleasantness of, and the trouble and expense. I am not some cowering, simpering aristocrat.*

What was she *thinking*?

She did not make a courtesy, either. She turned on her heel, not trusting her voice should she speak further. There were Words crowding her throat and a suspicious looseness at the very lowest floor of her soul – the barred door of her Discipline, ready to open and swallow her whole.

If she loosed it in this fashion, a raging conduit for the power of the Endor, it would not be Thomas Coldfaith's act of sacrifice.

No, it would be . . . otherwise. And the first place that freed sorcery would strike was the suck-sobbing woman crouched at the bedside of her husband, with the ruling spirit watching – coolly, calculating – through her madness.

Victrix beat her small plump hands on the counterpane, and Emma's passage threw the door back, the wood splintering in a long vertical crack as her control slipped a fraction. The material of her dress scorched, a new layer of reek added to the sweetbriar-sickness, the choking atmosphere of the Red.

Mikal's fingers closed about her arm, and such was Emma Bannon's countenance that none dared question or halt them as the Shield, perhaps sensing the danger, ushered her from the room stinking of sweetness and smoke.

# Chapter Thirty-Two

## A Damned Shame

He did not believe in dæmons. Logic and rationality did not admit such creatures.

And yet, while he burned and twisted, sweat-slick fabric clasped in his wet palms, they were all about him. Black-faced, leering, their white teeth champing, they crowded around the bed and laughed, pointing at him.

*Why is this* . . . He could not frame the question. His faculties spun, logic mutating, his heart labouring uselessly inside his clogged chest.

Another crisis came, the convulsion tearing through him, his entire body a rod of iron, the star of his faculties a whirling firework inside his aching, too-small skull. He dimly heard himself ranting, shouting filthy words he would never have uttered had he been possessed of his sanity, and the cotton padding in his ears thump-thudded with his heartbeat.

*Dying*. When the wracking ended, he knew he was. The tide was running away, and once in his childhood there had been the sea along a pebbled beach and his own disbelieving laughter as he saw something so *vast*, and . . .

Miss Bannon's voice. "Clare. *Archibald*."

He was too weak to respond. The sea was all inside him now, its complexity turning to equations, shining strands of logic knitted together so closely they seemed a whole fabric, the vice in his skull and the pounding in his chest dual engines pulling in opposite directions.

"No. Close the door." Miss Bannon, hoarse as if with weeping. "*Close* the door, Mikal."

"What are you—" The Shield, breathless. Another convulsion was coming, and Clare's body was lax in its approaching grip. When its fingers tightened, something in his brain or blood would give way, and the relief would be immense.

*Vance. Is he alive?*

"Prima . . . no. *No*."

A meaty, bone-crunching, *wrenching* sound. A word he could not quite hear, and Emma's voice, raised sharply.

"It is *mine* to give, Shield! And if you will not obey, I will free you from my service *instantly*." It was a tone he had never heard from her before – utterly chill, utterly level, simply factual instead of threatening.

It was dreadful to hear a woman's sweet voice so. The convulsion edged closer, playing with him, stroking along his body with a feather-caress. The dæmons laughed and twisted.

*She does not know, you did not tell her. She does not know.*

"Archibald," she whispered, the touch of her breath cold on his slicked cheek. "Dear God, Archibald, forgive me."

*There is nothing to—*

Then the pain came, and clove him in half. A sudden weight in his chest, as if the angina had returned, and he was never sure afterward if the hellish scream that rose was torn from his own lips . . . or from Emma's.

Archibald Clare fell into a star-drenched night, and the coolness of a summer sea.

Light. Against his eyelids. He blinked, the foulness crusting his eyes irritating as he sought to lift a hand. The appendage obeyed, and he gingerly scrubbed at his face. All manner of matter was dried upon his skin, and every inch of him crawled.

His hand fell back to his side. He took stock.

Weak, but lucid. Again. He blinked several times, and found his familiar bed at Miss Bannon's closed about him. Safe and secure as a little nut in a shell, for a moment he simply savoured the act of *breathing* without obstruction. Such a little thing, and one did not value it properly until it was taken away.

"Alive?"

He did not realise he had spoken aloud until someone wearily laughed, a disbelieving sound. It was Miss Bannon, ragged in a smoke-scored black dress, her hair a loose glory of dark curls falling past her shoulders, tangling to her waist. The hair seemed to have drained its bearer of all strength, for she was wan and hollow-cheeked, the dark circles under her eyes almost painted in their intensity.

Her little fingers were cool against his. Emma picked up his hand, squeezing with surprising strength. "Quite. I worried for you, Clare, but the worst is past."

*We do not know that.* He let out a long sigh. "Ludo?"

"Mending. Swearing at everyone in sight. Londinium is still plagued. It is rather desperate outside, dear Clare, so if you have any news . . . Dr Vance was quite of the opinion that you have solved the riddle?"

*His hand, at his trouser pocket.* "The cure – the cure In his pocket. A glass vial . . ."

She actually paled, though he could not see how she could achieve such a feat without becoming utterly transparent. "He . . . Clare, his body was taken by the corpsepickers two days ago."

"Ah." Clare coughed, more out of habit than anything else. His throat was dry, and Miss Bannon helped to lift him, held a glass to his lips. A wonderfully sweet draught of something tang-laden and cool eased his throat.

Water had never tasted so good.

She settled him back on the pillow. "I can perhaps find his body with a sympathy. It will be—"

"No." Clare felt the smile tilting the corners of his lips. All in all, he had to admit, he felt very fine, considering. A wonderful lassitude had overtaken him, but within it was a feeling of well-being he could not remember ever having before. Perhaps it was simply in comparison to the nastiness of Morris's plague. "I am not a fool, dear Emma. Well, I am in some matters, but not when it comes to Vance. There are extra vials of the cure – they are labelled quite clearly – in the pockets of my jacket, in the workroom." He paused. "Dead, you say? You are quite sure?"

"Dead of the plague." She sounded certain enough, settling back into the chair.

He closed his eyes, briefly. "Shame. A damned shame."

"Well." The single word expressed that she perhaps did not agree, but that she would not argue. Dashed polite of the woman, he thought, a trifle fondly. "The vials hold a cure?"

"And the method for making more is noted quite clearly. I made four copies; one should be in the pockets as well. There is a certain physician – Tarshingale, at King's. He will not only believe, but has the resources to see the cure performed, and can spread the formula and method of manufacture as widely as possible."

"I am told it must be introduced under the skin? Vance mentioned as much, before he . . ."

"Yes. There are many methods . . . I say, Miss Bannon, are you *quite* certain? Of his . . . demise?"

"Very much so, Clare." There was a rustle as she stood. "I shall search your workroom, then, and the matter of disseminating the cure is easy enough. You have done very well, sir."

He nodded, a yawn fit to crack his jaw rising from the depths of his chest. His heart thudded along, sedately observing its beat. Though his ribs seemed a trifle heavy, didn't they? A warmth quite unlike anything he had felt before, but perhaps it was merely a . . .

Miss Bannon breathed a word, the exact contours of which he could not remember as soon as they left the quivering air, and Clare fell into a dreamless, restorative slumber.

# ❀Chapter Thirty-Three

## A Close-Run Race

Tarshingale was easily found, and explanations given; the man's gaze was quite disconcerting and he had given her short shrift until Clare's name was mentioned and the vials and notations – which might as well have been in some tongue of the Indus for all she could make sense of them, though she had prudently retained a copy – shown. She left the man in his bespattered coat with instructions on how to gain admittance to the Palace; no doubt the cure would be administered to Alberich very soon.

If he was not already dead. She had not bothered to check the broadsheets. She told herself it did not matter now.

King's Hospital, bursting at the seams with victims of the Red crammed four to a bed, was also full of moaning and screaming. It reminded her uncomfortably of the one time she had ever braved the halls of Bethlehem Hospital; the cries of Bedlam held an edge of misery this place lacked, though it was a very close-run race indeed. At least the very bricks of King's were not warped as Bedlam's were.

Harthell and Mikal had stayed with the carriage, both were armed with a brace of pistols as well, though the coachman would be of little use except to frighten away the jackals who would prey when the city's forces of order were occupied with other matters.

Besides, she had taken care not to be alone with Mikal since Clare's . . . cure.

The exhaustion was all through her. She had forgotten how weary flesh could become without the bolstering of a wyrm's heart, the Philosopher's Stone granting all manner of immunities.

Even a Prime's strength had limits.

Still, her head came up as her fingers touched Mikal's. Instead of stepping up into her carriage, she dropped his hand and turned swiftly, as if stung, twitching her skirts back and sweeping her hair from her face.

"Penny, madam?" the shambling man asked, querulous, and Mikal moved forward – and halted as her hand, clothed in the tattered rags of a black lace glove, caught his sleeve. "Penny for a poor man? Ha'pence? Farthing?"

The importunate sir was dressed in stinking oddments as well, and under his soft slouching hat the gleam of his changeable eyes was sunken. He had shaved his fair moustache and was far thinner than he had been the first time she had seen him. He halted, and the ghost of amusement on his filthy, crusted mouth was almost too much to be borne.

"Dr Vance." She shook her head, once, sadly. "You rather hoped I would throw your corpse out."

"No other way to leave your tender care, my dear." He had a tin cup with a few thin farthings in it; he shook it and the coins rattled. "We have business, you and I."

She should, she supposed, evince some surprise, but it was useless. "Indeed we have. Pray do enter the carriage, sir. We may at least speak privately there."

He stretched out his legs. Harthell cracked the whip, and Mikal, settled watchfully next to Emma, was tense as a wound clockspring.

As badly as the resurrected criminal's clothes were tattered, he did not *smell*. Which was either an oversight to his costume, a mark of his fastidiousness . . . or the sweetstink of Londinium roasting under the Red had deadened Emma's nose.

"You introduced the cure under your skin in some manner while I was occupied with Clare." She nodded, once, slowly. "You must have been very amused at my questions about that method of applying said cure."

"I expected no less than brilliance from you, my dear, which you have amply demonstrated. I shall be on my way, soon, to sell the lovely cure I helped create at a high price before it becomes common. Profit does not linger."

*The missing canisters are in your hands.* She was suddenly quite certain of that, though she could not tell if it was intuition or simple logic. *But you had no choice but to work for a cure once you were trapped in my house. Interesting.* "Nor does vengeance."

"I rather suspected you would feel so, yes." He tipped the slouching hat back with one soot-blackened fingertip. "You do not strike me as a forgiving woman."

*I have never been. Least of all to myself.* "The thought of striking you dead at this very moment amuses me mightily. Why should I not?"

"Because you will calculate that the dissemination of this marvellous remedy, no matter what profit I gain from it, is worth letting me go unhindered. Especially since it has reached the Continent, and no doubt the shores of the New World as well." And d—n the man, but he sounded so very certain.

Just as Clare did, when he knew beyond a doubt what calculation should be attempted to bring the world to rights.

She tapped her fingers on her knee, exactly once. Her back had straightened, and she felt almost herself again, despite the heat of the day. It was uncomfortably *close* in the carriage, and her underarms were damp. Her corset, filthy as it was, scraped against her skin. It had no doubt worn her into a rash. "The satisfaction of knowing you will no longer be a bother may outweigh that philanthropic interest."

"It will not, Miss Bannon. You are a creature of Justice, however odd your method of applying it." He leaned back against the cushions. "I must say, you have a splendid carriage. I quite admire it."

She raised an eyebrow. "Thank you."

The silence that fell was not quite comfortable. Her breathing came a trifle short, but she could attribute that to her damnable corset.

Finally, she sighed. The weariness that had settled on her pressed deeper, into her very bones. At the moment, she very much missed the warmth of the Stone in her chest.

And yet she did not miss the crushing upon her conscience that bearing the Stone had brought her. How Llew would laugh, were he alive to guess such a weakness on her part.

"You shall cease being a nuisance to Mr Clare." She eyed him closely. "Or I shall cut out your heart, sir, and feast upon it." *There is more than enough of your bodily fluids – and your clothing, sir – left at my house for me to practise a nasty sympathy or two upon.*

"That," Dr Francis Vance said, with a wide white smile on his haggard, Red-ravaged face, "is my promise to you, dear lady. Do take care of Clare, he is a giant among mentaths."

With that, he reached for the carriage door and was gone even as the conveyance rolled. Emma caught Mikal's arm.

"Let him go," she said, and surprised herself.

For her pained, unamused laugh turned into a deep, wracking cough, and her forehead was clammy-damp.

Mikal had turned pale, even under his dark colouring. "Prima . . ."

She gestured for silence, and he subsided. Emma studied

his face as the carriage rolled, Harthell gaining as much speed as he dared on the choked thoroughfares, moans and cries and coughs rising in a sea around them. The cup of the city brimmed over, and she found she could not say what she wished.

*I am sorry, Mikal. For you shall very shortly be cast adrift, and I am selfish, for I cannot cling to this manner of life any more. No matter my responsibility to you, to them . . . to Her . . .*

She coughed again, her fingers in their torn and stained gloves pressing over her mouth, and they came away dripping with red. "Oh, dear," she murmured, and pitched aside, into Mikal's arms.

# Chapter Thirty-Four

## A Stone is a Stone

The house rang with terror and footsteps. Clare tacked out into the hall, the weakness in his limbs quite shockingly intense despite his rather extraordinary feeling of well-being. He fumbled at his jacket buttons, finally inducing the little beasts to behave, and looked up to see Madame Noyon, her grey-streaked hair piled loosely atop her head and her face tearstained, hurry past with an armful of linen.

"I say," he began, but the housekeeper vanished down the hall. *I say!*

One of the lady's maids – Isobel, the scarred one – leaned against the wall by Valentinelli's door, dumbly staring after Noyon with glittering eyes. Her cheeks were wet, and she had the look of a young woman who had just been rather viciously stabbed in the heart.

"I say," Clare approached her. "Isobel, dear, what is it? What is the—"

"It's Missus," she whispered, through pale, perhaps-numb lips. Her indenture collar was oddly dark, the powdery metal's radiance dimming. "She's taken the ill, she has. We're likely next, she wot was holding it back an'all!"

*What?* For a moment, his faculties refused to function, despite the tests he had administered to them that very morning, lying in his freshly made bed and quite comfortable at last. He stood very still, his head drooping forward and taking in the girl's feet in their pert, sensible boots.

*Bannon does have a weakness for sensible footwear, for herself and her servants alike.* He shook his head, slowly. "Ah. Well. There is not a moment to lose, then. I must—"

*"GET OUT!"* It was a scream from the top of the stairs leading to Miss Bannon's chambers. Mikal's voice, and it shook the entire house in quite a different manner than Miss Bannon's return or her anger.

Madame Noyon came hurrying down them, paper-pale and shaking afresh. She babbled in French, Horace and the blonde Eirean maid Bridget behind her chattering in proper but horribly disjointed Englene, and it took quite some time for him to gather a coherent picture of what had transpired.

The Shield had evicted them from his mistress's chambers, quite rudely. While Clare rested himself, Miss Bannon had taken ill; she had passed through the swellings and the convulsions were upon her.

*It is too late.* The pain in his chest was not angina, it was . . . something else.

He did not have time to discern its source, or so he told himself.

Clare bolted for the workroom.

The stench was terrible. He reeled into the stone room, and it was a very good thing he had not been able to stomach much of any provender lately, for his cast-iron mentath's digestion did not seem to have survived the illness quite as well as the rest of him.

It was dark, and his boots slipped in a crust of God alone knew what on the floor. How had they *stood* it down here?

He found his way by touch to the desk, slipping and sliding. His hip banged a table and something fell, shattering. Perhaps it was a fresh load of plague-freighted marrowe-jelly, but he cared little, if at all.

The drawer slid open, and his questing fingers found nothing but a small jewelled box. He swore aloud, a series of vile terms no gentleman should give voice to, and fumbled more deeply in the drawer, and still his sensitive fingertips found nothing but wood, dust, and the box of coja.

The vials he had hidden here, as well as in the pockets of his jacket . . . gone.

He turned, sharply, snatching up and hurling the tiny box across the room. The crack of its breaking was lost in the sound working free of his throat.

It could not be a sob. Mentaths were not prey to Feeling in such an intense fashion. Feeling was to be examined, thoroughly in some cases, then accounted for and set aside so one could function.

He swallowed something that tasted of iron. Staggered for the door, his legs a newborn colt's. Retraced his route through the house, and found a hall crowded with servants. Ludovico was there too, leaning on Gilburn, haggard and swearing steadily, monotonously, in pure noble Italian. He was pale, his pitted cheeks so thinned his face had become a skeleton's grin. *La strega*, he would murmur, then *demone maledetta*, and finally *donna dolce*, and other terms that would have been quite revealing, had Clare cared to apply deduction to them.

They clustered at the foot of the stairs, Miss Bannon's collection of castaways, the servants making a soft noise every time the light of their indenture collars dimmed. Clare pushed through them, blindly.

*No. Please . . . dear God, not Emma. I thought she was immune!*

"The Shield," Finch whispered, grabbing at Clare's sleeve. "He is beside himself. He will—"

"I do not care," Clare said, almost gently, and freed himself of the man's grasp. He put his hand to the balustrade, lifted his foot.

He was halfway up and heard it, her laboured breathing and soft choked cries as the convulsions came. The hall stretched away, as in nightmares, and the entire house shivered again, a chill racing through each plank and bit of plaster, from foundations to high lovely roof. The door to her dressing room was open, and gaslamps hissed. The witchlights in their cages of silvery metal dimmed, hissing as well, turning bloody-hued as the indenture collars dimmed, brightening as they brightened.

*She fights for life, our dear sorceress.* The dry barking sound from his throat had to be a laugh. It could not be otherwise. For what other sound could he make? Mentaths did not weep.

There was another sound – a dry sliding. There was light from underneath what had to be Miss Bannon's bedroom door. An odd scent, too – smoky and musky, a resinous incense, perhaps, but of no kind Clare was familiar with. And the sweetness of Morris's plague, its sickening candy-touch burning through her slight body.

Even a will as indomitable as hers could not stave off this catastrophe. Clare's knees weakened. He forced them to straighten, and later he was vaguely surprised that he had been inside her dressing room . . . and not seen a single thing other than that door of pale wood with a stripe of violent yellow light leaking from underneath it.

The sound became a slicing, a wet noise as if flesh was pulled from flesh in a slaughteryard. Clare shuddered, reaching before him for the handle. He was weaving as if drunk, his feet leaving dark crusted prints. The incense smell turned thick and cloying, and he heard Mikal's voice, singing in a queer atonal hissing manner.

*What is he doing?*

There was another cry, and this one raised every hair

on Clare's shivering body. The bright yellow light stuttered, thundering as a runner's pulse, and Clare found himself on his knees, shaking his head, not quite aware of what had happened.

Silence, thick and velvet.

The hinges creaked slightly as the pale door opened. Behind it, all was dark. A viscous blackness as if of an Indus midnight, its face a sheer wall, almost . . . alive.

Staggering out of the gloom came the Shield. For a moment he looked oddly . . . transparent. His eyes burned, a yellow fire brighter than Londinium's usual fog, and the reek of musk-burning smoke was so strong it nearly knocked Clare flat.

"*Nå helaeth oavied, nagáni.*" The man stumbled, caught himself, and swept the door closed behind him with such violence it almost splintered. He leaned back, his shoulders meeting it with an oddly light thump, but as he slid down to sit on the carpeted floor he gained solidity.

Clare blinked. It had to be a trick of his recovering vision.

Mikal's eyes half-lidded, their yellow gleam dimming for a moment. "Ah." He coughed, but it was a dry sound, not the wet thickness of the plague. "Clare." As if reminding himself who the mentath was.

Clare's breath caught in his throat. "Emma," he whispered. The silence was deathly. 24½ Brooke Street held its breath, too.

"She . . . will live." He flinched as Clare leaned forward, though there was a great deal of space between them. "*Do not touch me!*"

608      *Lilith Saintcrow*

Clare subsided. Below, at the foot of the stairs, a susurration. Sooner or later they would creep up – Valentinelli first, most likely – to see what had transpired here.

"Mikal." He wet his dry lips, settled back on his dirty heels. Winced as he thought of what he had tracked over the carpets and flooring. "What . . . what did you . . ."

The man's grin was a feral baring of strong white teeth, the canines curved and oddly distended, and Clare recoiled from its cheerful hatred. For a moment, the Shield's pupils appeared . . . different, but when Clare examined him afresh, he found they were circular, and normal.

*Only a trick of the light. Only that.* The witchlights strengthened in their cages, losing their deadly sputter-hissing and growing steadily more brilliant.

"Mentath." Mikal shut his yellow eyes. His calloused hands, empty and discarded, lay to either side of his body. "Remember what I am about to tell you."

"I hear you," Clare muttered numbly.

"There is a proverb among my kind." Another dry half-cough, but he was already looking better, his colour improving. "*A stone is a stone, and a heart is a heart.*" A long pause. "Do you understand?"

*What on earth . . .* "No," he admitted. "No, I do not."

"Good." Mikal settled more firmly against the door. "Tell them she lives, she *will* live, and not to come up the stairs. Or I shall strike to kill."

He cleared his throat. "Erm, yes. Well, they will be relieved, but—"

"Go." Mikal's frame twitched once, terribly, as if his skin were merely a cover over something not . . . quite . . .

Clare did not remember gaining his feet. He recoiled, and stumbled down the stairs. They caught him at the bottom, and he managed to give his message. And afterwards, he remembered nothing more until he awoke two mornings later in his own bed.

"You told Her Majesty?" She was propped on several pillows, wan and too thin, her hair loosely pulled back but still glossy and vigorous. There was an uncomfortable vitality burning in her gaze, but Clare ascribed it to the tonics Madame Noyon insisted on dosing her with at two-hour intervals, from Tideturn dawn to Tideturn dusk.

"That the missing canisters had been attended to? Yes, quite." *Though I do not know where you found time to attend to that detail. You are a wonder, Miss Bannon.* "I *also* told her I shall cease chasing chimeras," Clare continued, settling into the chair. Miss Bannon's hands lay in her lap, and the dressing gown was quite pretty, a froth of pale lace at her neckline. He tried not to glance too obviously about her bedroom, fighting back a quite uncharacteristic smile as he saw the stack of sensational novels on her nightstand, next to a globe of what had to be malachite in a brassy stand. The books had dust upon their covers; Miss Bannon had not been at leisure to read much lately.

Near the door, Mikal lurked. He kept himself to a patch of convenient shadow, and Miss Bannon's gaze often wandered in his direction, as if he were a puzzle she sought to solve.

"Chimeras," she repeated, softly. It was not quite a question, but Clare made a *hrrmph* noise as if it were.

"Since Dr Vance is dead, of course. I did not tell her so; it would only create . . . questions. I have been settled with an estate or two, I gather; signal service in saving the Consort's life. He is still sickly, but shall recover."

Miss Bannon's upper lip curled slightly. "Britannia rejoices," she commented, quite properly. But there was an edge to the words.

He fought back the urge to raise an eyebrow. "Indeed. The method of cure is spreading with as much speed as possible. Tarshingale is quite the man of the hour. Publicly, of course, it is *his* triumph. I am content for it to remain so." He lifted the package from his lap. "And this . . . Her Majesty sent it for you, expressly. She was quite concerned for you."

For a long moment Miss Bannon examined the linen-wrapped item. It was heavy, and no doubt a costly gift of thanks from royalty. He would have expected the sorceress to be pleased. Instead, she studied it as if it were some manner of poisonous creature, one she rather feared was about to strike.

Finally, her fine little hands moved, and she took it from him . . . and set it, unopened, on her nightstand. "Thank you, Mr Clare. I shall no doubt pen a note of immense gratitude to Her Majesty."

"Well, that's that, then." But he made no move to depart

her bedroom. He found himself wondering what had transpired between Queen and servant while he lay unconscious. It must have been an event of surpassing magnitude . . . but he had a different question that required answering. "Miss Bannon."

She settled a little more comfortably, and her gaze met his. The quality of directness she possessed was even more marked now, and her earrings – dangles of amethyst in silver filigree, matching the small simple necklace that nonetheless glowed with charter symbols – swung slightly as she did so, then nestled lovingly against her curls.

It was very good to see her so accoutred again. And none of her household had taken ill.

There would never be a better time to ask.

He cleared his throat. "You performed some feat upon me while I was fevered, Emma. Do not bother to deny it."

She did not, merely regarded him levelly. Finally, a hint of a smile crept onto her childlike features, but still she did not speak.

So he was forced to. "I have been most exercised upon the problem, and cannot find a solution."

Her dark eyed positively danced. Did she look . . . why, yes.

The sorceress looked *relieved*, and she finally spoke.

"I shall tell you in twenty years' time, sir."

*Dash it all.* "I am not a young man, Emma. I may not be in a position to hear such news at that time."

Her smile broadened. "Oh, I think you will be. What can I tell you of illogical sorcery? For all you know, I had the method of the cure from dear departed Dr Vance, and introduced it under your skin in some fashion." Was she . . . yes. Her dark eyes danced, and the merriment lurking in her expression was quite out of character. "I would be *quite* vexed to lose you, Mr Clare."

The heat in his cheeks was like the plague-fever, and he stood in a hurry, clearing his throat. "Likewise, Miss Bannon. I shall be along now, I have a workroom to tidy, and some fascinating avenues of enquiry to apply myself to." *For example, the Alderase reactions. Very intriguing.*

"Very well. I believe I shall see you at dinner, sir. In very short order, I shall be quite well." Damn the woman. She *was* laughing, now. It did her a world of good, thin and pale as she was. Still, she looked . . . yes, younger. Though how he could draw such a conclusion Clare was not certain, for she had always seemed childlike, to him.

Then again, Clare himself felt younger and lighter, as if the plague had burned away age and infirmity. No doubt the feeling would fade. His hair seemed to have gained new strength as well, or perhaps the looking-glasses in Miss Bannon's house were ensorcelled. "Delighted. Very well, then." He shook his head, treading by Mikal's shadowed form with a light step. He passed through the dressing room, Madame Noyon bustling in the opposite direction with a covered tray, and halfway down the stairs, he began to whistle.

# Acknowledgements

As always, I am grateful to Devi Pillai, who did not throttle me during revisions, and Miriam Kriss, who told me I could indeed do this. I am indebted to Mel Sterling and Christa Hickey for putting up with me, and to my children for cheerfully going along with my research experiments. Special gratitude must also go to the ever-patient Susan Barnes and the incredibly tolerant Joanna Kramer, who both deserve some sort of medal. (And booze.) Last, as always, dear Reader, thank you. Come into another one of my little worlds, and let me tell you what happened next.

# THE
## RIPPER
# AFFAIR

*Alone in a crowd*

# Chapter One

## A Messy Method

The trouble with dynamitards, Clare had remarked to Valentinelli that very morning, was the inherent *messiness* of their methods.

Of course, the Neapolitan had snorted most ungraciously. Anyone who killed with such a broad brush was a bit of a coward in his estimation – a curious view for one who named himself an assassin, certainly. Still, Clare had not meant merely their means of murder, but everything else as well. It was just so dashed *untidy*.

This Clerkenwell courtroom was packed as a slaughter-yard's pens, and the lowing crowd stank of rotting teeth and stewed potatoes, violet or peppermint cachous and sweat, wet wool and the pervasive breath of Londinium's yellow fog. It had been a rainy summer, and even those venturing into the countryside to pick hops had been heard to grumble. The weather did not fully explain the crush; there were hangings elsewhere in the city that served the lower classes as better amusement.

However, the public – or at least, a certain portion of that great beast – expressed *quite* an interest in these proceedings. It did not take a mentath's faculties of Deduction or Logic to answer why – the Eastron End of Londinium's great sprawl was slopping over with both foreigners and Eireans; Southwark crammed to the gunnels with Eireans as well. Twenty or more to a stinking room and their blood-pricked fingers, Altered or not, largely responsible for the gleaming, expensive mechanisterum shipped out each Tideturn.

It was no wonder they were restless, given the ravages of the Red, cholera and tuberculosis as well – and the rampant starvation on their Emerald Isle, where their over-lords, most of supposedly healthy Englene stock, behaved more like petty feudal *seigneurs* than benevolent citizens entrusted with the task of dragging Papist potato-crunchers from their ancient green mire.

That was, however, not in the purview of a lone mentath to speak against. He was merely present to give evidence. He could not allow Feeling to intervene with Logic *or* Truth.

Sometimes, even a mentath could wish it were otherwise.

"The device you refer to is unquestionably the work of the accused," he said, clearly and distinctly, and ignored the rustle that went through the courtroom. Whispers and hisses rose. "For one thing, the manner of twisting the fuse is very particular, as is the signature of the *chemica vitistera* used to make the bomb itself. Had it not been defused, it would have been rather deadly for anyone visiting Parliament that day."

"A modern Gunpowder Plot, then, sir?" the judge enquired, his cheeks flush with pride at his own wit.

Archibald Clare did not let his lip curl. Such a display would be unworthy of a soul dedicated to pure Logic. Still, the temptation arose. Under the powdered wig and above the robes of Justice, the man's petty chuckling and drink-thickened face was a florid insult to the very ideal he had theoretically been called to serve.

Still, one could not have shaggy brutes blowing up Parliament. Once that was allowed, what on earth was *next*? He had no choice but to send the young Eirean, shackled in the Accused's box and guarded by two sour-faced bailiffs, to the gallows. There would be a crowd of murdered souls waiting for the lad in whatever afterlife he professed, since he had already been twice successful – the explosion on Picksdowne, and another at the Bailey. Now *that* had been a horrific event.

The question of how these events could be traced to the Great Blight wracking the young man's homeland was an open one. There were whispers of the Eirean spirit of rule struggling to manifest itself – a blasphemous notion, to be sure, but even such blasphemy found a ready hearing when the staple crop rotted in the ground and the tribes of Eire found themselves starving as well as browbeaten and outright terrorised. Could such a thing excuse this young man, or mitigate his murders?

When, Clare was forced to wonder in some of his private moments, could a man, even a mentath, cease unravelling Causes and concern himself only with Effects?

The young Mr Spencewail was accused of treachery to the Crown, both as a dynamitard and as a member of a particular Eirean brotherhood that called its members Young Wolves. Eireans were subjects of Britannia; but the Englene's privilege of a trial by jury did not apply to them as a whole, and the Crown had not seen fit to intervene or offer a pardon.

Distaste for the whole affair, finished or not, was a sourness against Clare's palate. "Perhaps," he said, carefully. "That is outside my concern, sir. I may only speak to what I witnessed, and what may be deduced."

As a sop to his conscience, it was not quite all Clare could have hoped for. As Emma Bannon sometimes remarked, conscience was a luxury those in service to Crown and Empire did not often possess.

"Quite so, quite so," the judge bugled, and fetched a handkerchief from some deep recess of his robe. He sniffed loudly, affected to dab a patriotic tear from his deep-set eyes, and launched into upbraiding the young Eirean.

Clare turned his attention away. He was not given leave to go *quite* yet, but experience told him this particular judge would not ask anything resembling a question for a long while. Mr Spencewail had no solicitor: he might as well have been a sullen lump, voiceless and inert.

Miss Bannon would have been watching him with bright

interest, though, ever unwilling to let a potential danger go unobserved.

Upon Clare's thinking of her, the small crystal and silver pendant tucked under his shirt on its hair-fine chain – a Bocannon's Nut, meant to warn the sorceress when Clare was in dire danger – chilled sharply. Wearing it while engaged upon investigations of a somewhat dangerous nature had become routine, even if the thing seemed to have some variance of temperature even when he was not in any difficult strait. He had not yet had a private moment to take the necklace off, *or* sleep. It was a bloody miracle he had possessed a few spare moments to wash his face and shave said countenance before appearing here, and once he was excused there was more work to be done.

As far as the authorities were concerned, the culprit was caught and further danger averted, but Clare was not so certain. He would not rest until he *was*. His faculties – and his quality of thoroughness, however inconvenient – would not allow it.

The courtroom, packed to the gunwales as it was, positively wallowed every time a fresh piece of evidence was introduced or a rise in the judge's voice denoted something of interest. Somewhere in the high, narrow, stone-walled room – a leftover from the Wifekiller's time with the rose of his royal dynasty worked into chipped, cracked carvings near the ceiling – was Valentinelli, who had flatly refused to cool his heels in Mayefair or at Clare's often-neglected Baker Street quarters. Mrs Ginn, redoubtable landlady that she was, sometimes complained that Mr Clare kept the rooms so as to gather dust, but allowed that a gentleman was sometimes allowed to live as and where he pleased, even if he was one of her blessed lodgers.

Another ripple ran through the crowd. Were they bored with the lord justice, as he was? Did they think his refusal to speak outside his purview as a sign of support for their Cause? Did they have anything so concrete as a Cause, or was their dissatisfaction that of the mute beast?

*What is this? Feeling, in place of Logic?* It was not merely the press of the crowd; for a moment Clare's collar was far too tight. He did not lift a finger to loosen it; the Bocannon was a chip of burning ice. The curious internal doubling a mentath was capable of held the crowd in a bubble of perception, while his faculties raced under the surface of his skull to pinpoint the discomfort.

*What is amiss?*

*Observe.*

Sweat. Beads of sweat, a slick brow under the brim of a wool hat; far too flush even for a man caught in this press. High colour on scrape-shaven cheeks, but a pale upper lip told Clare the young man had possessed a moustache just this morning, and the line of his jaw was very familiar. His cloth was wrong as well – the coat was ill fitting, and too rough for the shoulders of a clerk unaccustomed to a drover's work. Besides, there were traces on the sleeves, smears of familiar blue chalk, and the connection blazed into life.

*Ah. So Spencewail* does *have a brother!* The satisfaction of having his deduction proved correct was immense, but at the moment Clare could not luxuriate in it, for the man in the chalk-smeared coat undoubtedly had explosive sticks strapped to his torso.

The man ripped his coat open with blistered fingers, a single horn button describing an arc as it fell. A familiar brass dial attached to strips of leather gleamed against his sunken chest and the stained cloth of his workman's shirt.

Spencewail, standing in the dock, had not yet realised what was afoot. He still glared at Clare, who had already begun to shift his weight. The blast would be quite vicious if they had solved the problem of sputtering in the catch-dial—

"*Bastarde!*" A familiar cry, Ludovico Valentinelli's voice catching halfway, and the Neapolitan assassin appeared from the crowd, his pox-pocked face alight with fury, his lank hair still plastered down from his morning's hurried ablutions.

Clare had enough time to think *oh, dear* before the Eirean rebel in the dock screamed something in his ancient Isle's equally ancient tongue. The crowd, not realising what was afoot, was busy shouting its own discontent, for the judge had reached another pitch in his denunciation.

A simple twist of the Spencewail brother's wrist, and not only would the nitrou-glycerine soaked into sawdust and pressed into sticks tear its bearer to shreds, but also everyone around him.

Including the mentath who had brought the accused to this pass.

Clare's hand slapped the flimsy wooden barrier behind

which a witness gave evidence, and his legs tensed. A single leap would bring him to Valentinelli's aid.

It was a leap he did not have time to make. A great ruddy light bloomed as the Eirean student's ink- and chalk-stained fingers found what they sought and twisted, and they *had* solved the problem of the stuttering fuse.

A soundless sound filled the courtroom, and a great painless blow hammered all along Archibald Clare's body.

His last thought was that death had come while he still had his faculties intact, and that, strangely enough, it did not hurt.

# Chapter Two

## A Remedy for Concern

Morning at 34½ Brooke Street thrummed with orderly activity. The kitchen bubbled with preparations for luncheon, tea, and the evening's dinner; footmen hurried to and fro in preparation to accompany a maid or two a-marketing; a bath had been drained; and the mistress of the house, in a morning dress of amber silk, stood in her conservatory, her fingers infinitely gentle as she parted a tinkling climate-globe of golden ætheric force over a struggling hellebore.

The experiment was not going well, and Emma Bannon probed delicately at the plant with several nonphysical senses, seeking to find the trouble. She hummed softly, finding the proper series of notes, and winced internally at the dissonance in the plant's response.

A slight cough near the door informed her that her lean,

yellow-eyed Shield was not finished with his own troubleseeking. He had already ruined breakfast by almost quarrelling with her.

Or, perhaps not quarrelling. Perhaps he really did believe her in need of coddling, or maybe he was truly anxious that his mistress was sinking too deeply into eccentricity. Primes were notorious for their oddities, which grew more pronounced over the course of a very long life. In some instances, the peculiarities turned deadly.

In any case, he chose exactly the wrong way to express said anxiety, phrased as a command. "Sooner or later you must face the world."

If she were charitable, she would concede that it was not *quite* a command, and most probably intended as a statement of fact. Her skirts rustled – this morning dress, with relatively loose corseting and an unfashionably small bustle, had the advantage of being almost comfortable. "I will," she replied, absently. "Not while *she* reigns, though. At the moment I am very busy with events occurring under my own roof."

Mikal subsided, but not for long. "You are unhappy."

*Why on earth should that matter?* She untangled an ætheric knot, her concentration firming and the pleasure of sinking herself into a task almost enough to soothe her irritation. "I am *quite* content, except my Shield continues yammering while I am engaged upon an experiment. You were trained to act more appropriately, Mikal."

She sensed the flare of unphysical heat from him, denoting his own irritation and further sensed a tightness in his limbs. Did he perhaps wish to strike her?

It was a novel idea. It would certainly save them both from boredom.

*If he wishes to, that is all very well. As long as he does not attempt it in fact.*

Boredom, too, could drive a Prime to experiment too rashly with certain facets of the irrational arts. She was not yet at the point of seeing certain necessary precautions as mind-numbingly time-wasting, but she was perhaps very close.

"Now, what are you about?" she murmured to the hellebore. The plant was carrying on gamely, but traceries of virulent yellow and twisting black ran up its stems, down the central spine of each drooping leaf. Leprous green sorcery sought ineffectually to contain it, but the yellow would not be halted. Even loosening the invisible knots did not help.

*Bloody hell.* The ætheric tangle was growing worse, and strangling the life out of the hellebore's tissues. *I wonder why it does that. Hmm.*

Unravelling the sorcerous threads required a light touch and considerable patience. The problem was a resonance; she caught herself worrying at her upper lip with her teeth. *A lady's face should not make such a display*, Prima Grinaud would have said, and the thought of the wasp-waisted teacher and her whispering black, watered-silk skirts was enough to smooth Emma's expression while she hummed a descant, seeking to find the vibration responsible.

*Ah, there.* Her humming shifted. A tiny thread of ætheric

force spun down, the ring on her left index finger – a confection of marcasite and chrysoprase – glowing sullenly. Yellow veining retreated as the hellebore lifted its drooping leaves, the stems firming and the sudden *rightness* of a correct bit of sorcery sending a delightful thrill all the way down to Emma's toes, encased in dainty button-up boots that also were unfashionable, but reasonably comfortable.

"Very satisfying." She brushed her fingers quickly against her skirt, flicking away a tiny crackling of excess force. The climate-globe sealed itself, singing its soft muted bell-tone; the plant would survive. Not only that, it would downright thrive, and the manner of its cure gave her a fascinating new vista to experiment upon.

*Clare would approve.* Chartersymbols flashed along the globe's shimmer, naming its confines and its function; a spatter of rain touched the conservatory's windows.

Mikal, tall in his usual olive velvet jacket, the knives worn openly at his hips and his dark hair freshly trimmed, stood to one side of the door. Perhaps inevitably, he was boiling with carefully reined irritation: a lemon-yellow tinge to Sight. "You have not left the house in months, Prima."

Which was true enough, she supposed. At least he was not asking *why*. "I have seen no need to go gadding about. Should you wish to visit the Zoo or perhaps take a turn in Hidepark, you are more than welcome to." She clasped her hands, tilted her head and felt the reassuring weight of her lapis earrings as they swung gently.

"The Palace sends you dispatches."

She decided the familiar tone he currently employed could be borne only so far. "Which I return unopened, Shield." *The Empire has not crumbled without my help to prop it up. I cannot tell whether to be pleased or vexed.* "And," she continued, "no doubt you are relieved I am no longer in any possible danger, feeling no urge to step outside. It must be wondrous calming for a Shield when his charge behaves so."

"I am . . . concerned." The thundercloud knitting upon his brow might have cheered her own darkening mood, had she let it.

"Ah. I believe there is a remedy for your concern." Her tone dripped with sweet solicitude. "You may leave the worrying to me, Mikal. Your head is simply not fit for it."

"Your temper, Prima, is as sharp as your tongue."

She took a firmer hold on said temper. "And you are speaking out of turn."

"Emma." His hands spread slightly, and she wished he would not look so . . . downcast, or so pained. His presumption she could easily parry.

His affection was another matter entirely. It took a long while to undermine a citadel with kindness, but it could be done.

She was saved the trouble of responding by a sharp, almost painful internal *twitch*.

The sorceress stilled, her attention turning inward, and her Shield's sudden tense silence was a familiar comfort. *What on earth is that?*

It had been a long while since she had felt that

*particular* sensation; she flashed through and discarded several invisible threads before finding the one that sang like a viola's string. Plucked by a long, bony finger . . . he had marvellously expressive hands for such a rigid logician, though Emma had never told him so.

*Clare. In danger. But he has the . . .* The string yanked sharply again, a fishhook in her vitals, and Emma almost gasped, training clamping down upon her fleshly body's responses to free a Prime's will to work unhindered.

She returned to herself with a rush, the walls of her house vibrating soundlessly. Her indentured servants, well accustomed to such a sensation, would be calmly pursuing their duties.

Mikal leaned forward, his weight braced, ready to move in any direction. "Prima?" Carefully, quietly – no matter how he might test her temper, it was best not to do so when there was sorcery to accomplish.

She supposed it was a small mercy that he was, at least, willing to cease his questioning when an emergency threatened.

"It is Clare," she heard herself say, distantly. "To the stables, saddle two horses. *Now.*"

# Chapter Three

## *Stillness Descending*

Moans and cries, an acrid reek, blood crusting or fresh, the throat-coating nastiness of scorched stone. There was no ventilation, and the crush of the crowd had only worsened.

"Move *back*!" Clare coughed violently, a painful retch bringing up a dry thick gobbet of something he spat to the side with little ado. "He cannot *breathe*, give him space!" The Bocannon was a cicatrice of frost upon his chest; his shirt and jacket were in tatters. His bare knees grated against shards of smoking wood, and somewhere a woman screamed, high-pitched repeating cries piercing Clare's aching skull. "And for God's sake clear the doors!"

"*Bastarde*," the wreck of a body in his arms muttered. "Cold."

"All will be well," Clare lied numbly. "Ludo—"

Whistles sounded, shrill and useless. Help had arrived outside, perhaps, but the shouts and curses amid the struggling mass at the door sought to bring a deduction to surface amid the porridge his brain had become.

*Ludovico* . . . The struggle to think clearly stung his eyes, or was it the thick smoke? Blood, hot and slippery over his hands, and the foul stench of a battlefield. He knew what it meant, knew he should gaze dispassionately at the shredded flesh and shattered bone he clasped, so heavy.

So, so heavy.

Deadweight.

*Do not think such things.* "All will be well," he repeated. "Help is coming."

Half the assassin's face was a scorched ruin. Well, he had never been pretty, even on the best of days.

Why had he thrown himself upon the dynamitard?

*He thought to do his duty. As always. Quite remarkable sense of honour, for an assassin.*

The body in his arms stiffened. Ludo's dark eyes dimmed, blood bubbling at the corners of his shredded mouth. There were spots of soot on his pitted cheeks, and dewdrops.

*Do not be an idiot. There is no dew.* His eyes were burning, blurring. It had to be the smoke.

The crowd screamed and surged for the doors again. Ludo's lips moved, but Clare could not hear through the din. Trampling and thrashing, the courtroom had become a seething creature with its own panicked mind. The pressure against the inward-opening doors would preclude those outside from offering aid.

Nevertheless, a great stillness descended. Clare stared down, into the face he knew as well as his own, horribly battered now. A shudder heaved through the floor – no, the body he held? Or was it his own frame, stiffening against the onrush of irrational emotion?

The Bocannon gleamed, clearly visible now that Clare's shirt and jacket were in tatters. Ludo's gaze fastened on that spark, and his lips moved again. The pendant gave a last flare of fiery ice, and Clare's nerves were alight all through his skin.

His whole, unbroken skin. He had survived, fantastically, unbelievably, suffering only rent clothing and the stinging of smoke. "Ludo—"

"*Stregaaaaa . . .*" the Neapolitan sighed, and Clare bent forward over him, unheeding the illogicality of his own broken sobs.

*No. No, no no—*

No protest would avail; no exercise of deduction would halt this. The mentath closed his eyes.

He did not wish to see.

There was a sound. Low and vicious as a blade cleaving wet air. The noise of the crowd was pulled away, a curtain swept aside by an invisible hand. The Bocannon gave out a high tinkling rill of notes, and a breath of sweeter scent cut through the reek.

Clare could not look. He crouched over the body,

even heavier now that its occupant had fled. The quiet was immense, crushing, the blackness between stars, and when they found him he was no longer weeping.

# Chapter Four

## Some Order Here

It was, as a Colonial might say, a bloody horrific *hell* of a mess.

By the time Emma half fell out of the bay clockhorse's saddle – her morning dress was never going to be the same – into Mikal's hands, the narrow street leading to the Clerkewold was jammed with a milling crowd, straining carriages and a great deal of nasty smoke, as well as policemen blowing their damnable silverwhistles and clacking blocks together instead of doing anything *useful*.

In short, it was a situation only a sorceress could remedy, and Emma Bannon stalked forward. The tugging of the Bocannon had crested and subsided, and why it should lead her *here* she had no idea, except that Clare was somewhere in this disorder and needed her aid. She had not seen him for a week or two, but that was normal, when he had an affair engaging his attention.

The fog was not bad this afternoon, pale yellow and merely unpleasant instead of choking. Still, Londinium's great bowl seethed differently, as if potent yeast had been added during her absence. Or perhaps it was merely that she had lost the habit of familiarity with crowded, odiferous streets and high-pitched cries.

First, a bit of quiet. A half-measure of chant slid from her lips, spiked with ætheric force, every inch of jewellery on her flaming as she drew upon its accumulated charge. The screaming, both human and equine, cut off sharply. It was a moment's worth of work to clear a path to the Clerkewold's set of high narrow double doors, but three of the four were fastened shut and the stream of people fleeing whatever disaster had taken place had dammed itself to a mere trickle.

Emma paused, the crowd exploding away as it realised one of sorcery's children was present and quite likely irritated. Mikal was at her shoulder, having no doubt attended to the clockhorses in some fashion; she set her heels, her hands coming forward, fingers curled around empty air.

She *pulled*, a second rill of notes issuing from her throat, and expended a little more sorcerous force than she strictly had to. The doors exploded outwards, shards of wood whickering as they sliced the air, and smoking bits peppered the crowd.

A torrent of persons issued forth, stumbling down the

stairs, their cries shrill and tinny as they met the blanket
of silence Emma had laid over the street. She unknotted a
single strand of the first spell with a discordant note; it
would unravel on its own and slowly return clamour to
this part of Londinium.

She picked up her skirts, suddenly acutely aware of
being outside her domicile with nothing even approximating gloves, a shawl, or a hat. Her hair was likely disarranged from the ride here as well, and familiar irritation
at being dishevelled rose inside her.

At least the escapees, singed and shrouded in foul
smoke – had Clare been conducting experiments in a
courtroom? – had the wit to give her space as she climbed
the worn stone steps; dividing around her much as a river
embraces a stone.

The Bocannon's tugging was faint now; whatever had
occurred was now largely finished. Its bearer was still alive;
beyond that, she could sense nothing.

*He has Ludo to guard him. And he has . . . it. The Stone.*

She discarded the thought as useless. Besides, why
would she wish to be reminded of that nasty affair? It had
cost them all dearly.

The vapour was foul, and there was a sick-sweet odour
of roasting. What manner of disaster had he embroiled
himself in *now*? She should have paid closer attention to
the affairs he was engaging himself upon.

It was no use to scold herself now.

Mikal's hand touched her shoulder. He pointed, and
there was another set of doors, old wood rubbed with so

much oil it had turned black. The walls teemed with the rose of Henry the Wifekiller's family crest, worked over and over again, an explosion of arrogance. Of course, the man had been an apotheosis of pride, almost rivalling a Prime's traditionally large self-regard. It was a very good thing a reigning spirit would not deign to inhabit a vessel with sorcerous talent. A double measure of such over-weening vanity might well leave whatever Empire it graced a smoking ruin.

It was another moment's work to shatter the blackened wood, widening the aperture through which more smoke-maddened human beasts poured. She was spending force recklessly, and found she did not care one whit.

*Where is he?*

Some manner of legal proceeding had been in session; paper fluttered, blackened and torn. The stink of a battle-field roiled out with the smoke, but she could spare no attention for an air-cleansing charm.

Because there, amid the shattered bodies, knelt Archibald Clare, a lean man past his youth whose sandy, greying hair was flame-crisped at the ends. His shirt and jacket had been blown away, ribbons hanging from the cuffs, and his trousers were just short of indecent.

He hunched over a horribly burnt and battered form.

Emma, who had seen many a death in her day from illness or . . . other events, halted. The sorcery she had been gathering to restore some order and breathable air to the room died unformed, her rings sparking and sizzling, the bronze torc at her throat warming dangerously as ætheric strings snarled, tangling against each other just as the fleeing crowd had.

*No. Oh, no.*

There was nothing to be done for the shattered body; no spark of life left to seal into the violated flesh. Even had she been a Mender, there was no help for Ludovico Valentinelli now, and Emma let out a shaking breath.

"Clare?" She sounded very young, even to herself. Firmed her expression and strode briskly through the wreckage. In the remnants of the judge's bench another well-built man torn by the force of some ungodly explosion – though there was no trace of fiery sorcery lingering in the room, merely the quivering shreds of truthtelling and inkwell charms unravelling as their physical bases lay broken – bubbled and croaked, probably close to dying. She paid him little mind. "Archibald. Dear God."

He did not move. Muscle under the flour-pale skin of his narrow back did not flicker, and for a moment something black lodged in her throat. Was he . . . despite the Stone's gift, was he . . .?

"I hear his heartbeat," Mikal murmured. "But not . . . the other's."

*Ludovico.* It was unquestionably the assassin she had blood-bound to Clare, the most intelligent and reliable of his ilk she had ever come across during her erstwhile service to the Crown. One of his hands was whole and uninjured, slack against the stone pavers lining the floor. His fingernails, of course, were filthy, and for some reason that detail caused a great calm to descend upon her.

*Who did this?*

For the moment, it did not matter. First things must be tidied, Clare must be made safe, and . . . Ludo. There were arrangements to be made for his eternal rest. She owed him as much, at least.

*Then,* she told Clare silently, *I shall visit vengeance upon whoever did this.*

Mikal's hand had tensed, fingers digging painfully into her shoulder. Did he think she would buckle? Swoon, like some idiot woman? Or was he relieved at the fact that it was the assassin who lay dead, and not the mentath? Who knew?

"Turn loose of me," she managed, and her tone was ice. The words echoed in the suddenly empty room, and the wreckage quivered. She rearranged the ætheric strings that had become tangle-frayed, and the air-cleansing charm crackled as she set it free. "Help Clare. And for God's sake let us have some order here."

# Chapter Five

## Quite Possibly Your Regard

There was a sense of motion, and jolting.

*A carriage?* For a moment the protective blankness his faculties were swathed in threatened to thin – or worse, shatter completely.

So he withdrew, and for a long while there was nothing, until he heard her voice again. Cultured and soft, and yet brisk as ever. "Yes, there . . . Carry him to his room. Mr Finch, there are arrangements to be made. Alice, please tell Madame Noyon I require her – I shall be wearing mourning. Horace, fetch wax and parlieu, I shall be sealing a room. Mikal – oh, yes, thank you. Quite."

More motion, outside the cotton-muffling. Sadly, his flesh would not allow him to retreat much longer. Certain pressures were building, not the least the urge to avail himself of a commode or its equivalent. Even a stinking alley would do.

Memory rose – Valentinelli, his eyes a-glimmer in the dark of a filthy dockside lane, amused at Clare's distaste for such quarters. *When you are done pissing, mentale, there is work to be done.*

The choking sensation must have been leftover smoke. For a moment his brain shivered inside its hard bone casing and the edifice of Logic a mentath built to house the constant influx of perception and deduction threatened to crumble. If it failed him, he would be lost – his fine faculties a useless mix of porridge and ash, the irrelevance every mentath feared even more than the loss of mental acuity descending upon him.

Mentaths did not go mad, but they could retreat into phantasies of logic, building a rational inward castle that bore no relevance to the outside world at all. A comfortable room in some asylum would be the rotting end of such an event. He would no doubt have every manner of care – *she* would do no less – but still, it was a fate to be feared.

Softness about his frame, and familiar smells. Leather, dust scorched away by cleansing-charms; linen and paper, and a breath of Londinium's acrid yellow fog. His body was demanding to be heard. He turned away, into the blackness. It was his friend, that mothering dark, and something in him shivered once more.

*Impossible. It is impossible, irrational, miraculous—*

On that road, however, lay something very close to madness.

"Archibald?" Quite unwontedly tender, now. Miss Bannon sounded weary, and breathless. "If you can hear me . . . I am attending to matters. You are quite safe. I . . ."

*Tell me it is a dream. A nightmare.*

But mentaths did not dream. There was no room for it in their capacious skulls. Or if they did, such a thing was not remembered. It seemed a small price to pay for a rational, orderly world that performed as expected.

*You suspect the world is not rational at all, Clare. Therein lies your greatest fear.*

A rustle of silk, a breath of spiced pear. She had worn this particular perfume for quite some time now, and it suited her well. The smoky indefinable odour of sorcery, adding complexity. Another scent, too – the mix of flesh and breath that was a living woman.

Living. As he was.

*Everyone about me was injured fatally. Perhaps I am grievously hurt and I cannot tell? Shock?*

Yet he could feel his fingers and toes, the flesh he was doing his best to ignore. There were cases of those who had lost a limb reporting phantom pain; were there also other sensations? A ghost-limb . . . perhaps the nerves, enduring a shock, struggled to re-create the lost wholeness?

The horrible bubbling of Valentinelli's tortured body struggling against the inevitable refused to recede into memory. Paired with the utter gruesome silence of death, the two set up an echo that threatened to tear him asunder.

"I am attending to everything," she finally repeated. Had she paused, or had he simply lost track of Time, that great semi-fluid that could stretch at will? No matter how a clock sought to cage it, that flow did as it pleased.

"Mum?" A discreet cough, and printed on the back of Clare's eyelids came the cavernous face of Mr Finch, the indentured butler's balding pate reflecting mellow light from the sorcerous globe depending from the ceiling. He could tell from the slight lift at the end of the word that Finch considered the situation rather uncomfortable but certainly not dire. "Carriage, from Windsor. Requesting the honour of your presence."

A short, crackling silence. There was a soft touch to the back of Clare's hand – he shut it away, Feeling warring with Logic again. If he allowed any quarter in that battle, he would be defeated into sludge-brained uselessness in short order.

Her reply, measured and thoughtful. "Give the coachman a dram and send him on his way. Say that I am indisposed."

"Yesmum?" It was all the question Finch would allow himself.

"Thank you, Finch." In other words, she was *quite* sure she did not wish to be transported to Windsor. Inferences began to tick under the surface of Clare's faculties, but he did not dare give them free rein. "Archibald, if you can hear me . . . simply rest. You are safe."

A whisper of silk, the sound of bustling, and no doubt one of the footmen would be sent to sit with him and make certain of his continued breathing. Murmurs and hurrying feet, and Clare finally let himself face the unavoidable conclusion.

*Miss Bannon performed some miracle long ago, while I was ill with the Red and expected to die. She has not spoken of it since, and neither have I. But now . . .*

*Now I rather think we must.*

As a means of wrenching his attention from the memory of blood and dying, it was not enough. The tide of Feeling arose again, and this time he could not contain it. His body locked against itself, and a scream was caught in his stone-blocked throat.

Nobody heard. For he did not let it loose.

He woke to dim light, and for a long while stared at the ceiling. Dark wood, familiar stains and carven scroll-work. He heard the breath moving, in, and out. In, and out, the sough of respiration less than a cricket's whisper. Just one pair of lungs, small and dainty as the rest of her.

Her Shield was not standing inside his door, which was not normal but by no means completely unusual. It could mean she was cautious, or disposed to privacy.

Whatever she wished to say, she wanted no witnesses. It suited him as well.

*Start with a bare fact.* "I was untouched," Archibald Clare heard himself state, dully. The ceiling did not move, and he did not look away from its curves and hollows. "I should have died."

Her dress made a sweet silken sliding as she shifted. "That would distress me most awfully, Archibald."

"And Valentinelli?"

A long silence, broken only by a single syllable. "Yes."

It was, he decided, not quite an answer. Was he likely to receive more from her?

This room was part of the suite he used while availing himself of Miss Bannon's hospitality. Dark wood wainscoting and worn red velvet, the shelves of books and the two heavy wooden tables littered with papers and glassware for small experiments, both like and unlike the larger tables in the workroom she made available for him.

It had taken him some time to enter that stone-walled rectangle again, though. After the affair with the Red, it had taken him a long while to look through a spæctroscope, too. Flesh remembering the nearness of its own mortality, despite Reason and Logic pointing out that at least he was still alive – the inward flinch when he heard a wracking cough, or the sick-sweet smell of some spun-sugar confections, were also troublesome.

He wrenched his attention away from that line of thought. This bed was as familiar as an old pair of slippers. Wide and comfortable, and his weary, aching body sank into it with little trouble.

Questions boiled up. He attempted to set them in some approximation of order, failed, tried again. When he had the most important one, he finally set it loose. "What did you do,

Miss Bannon? What manner of miracle did you perform upon me?" Stated twice, so she could not possibly misunderstand.

"Are you certain you wish to know?" It was the first time he had ever heard her sound . . . well, *sad*. Not merely downcast, but weary and heart-wrung. She was altogether too brisk and practical at any other moment to sound so . . . female?

*No, Archibald. The word you are seeking is* human. *Instead of* sorceress.

"I think I have some small right. I should have died, and I have not so much as a scratch upon me."

She did not demur. "And you have no doubt noticed you are far more vigorous than your age should permit. Even your hair is thicker than it was, though no less grey." A slight sound – her curls moving, she had nodded. "I thought you would remark upon that. I am amazed you did not press for an explanation sooner."

He held his tongue with difficulty. Long acquaintance with her had accustomed him to the fact that such was the best policy, and that she was on the verge of solving the mystery for him. She very much disliked being compelled, or harried. The best way of inducing her to speak was simply to be attentive and patient, no matter how time or need pressed.

"Do you remember when we met?" Her little fingers had crept upon his hand now, and the intimacy of the touch surprised him. They rested, those gentle fingertips, upon his palm, just below the wrist. "The affair with the mecha, and the dragon."

*How on earth could I forget?* He permitted himself a slight nod. His scorched hair moved against the pillow, crisp white linen charm-washed and smelling of freshness. His throat moved as he swallowed, dryly.

Her words came slowly and with some difficulty. "There was . . . during that rather trying episode, a certain artefact came into my possession. I bore it for a while afterward, but when the plague . . . Archibald." Her tone dropped to a whisper. "I could not bear to lose you. And the weight of the artefact . . . the method of its acquisition . . . it wore upon me. I sought to expiate a measure of my sins, such as they are, by ensuring your survival. You are proof against Time's wearing now, and your faculties will suffer no diminishing. You are immune to disease, and to all but the most extraordinary violence."

He waited, but apparently she had finished.

His most immediate objection was at once the most pressing *and* the most illogical. "You should have *told* me."

"I said I would."

"In twenty years' time. Had I known, Miss Bannon, I would have taken better care with Ludovico's slightly more tender person."

"No doubt." Her hand retreated from his, stealing away. A thief in the night. "It is my doing, Clare. Perhaps I all but murdered him."

What must it cost her, to admit as much? The tide of Feeling still threatened to crack him in two. "You should have told me." Querulous, a whining child.

"I feared your reception of such news."

*Rightly so, madam.* "Can it be reversed?"

"Perhaps."

"Would you reverse it?"

"No." Quickly, definitively. "I am loath to lose you, Archibald."

"But Ludovico is expendable?" For a moment he could not believe he had said such a thing. It was brutish, ill mannered, illogical.

"We are all expendable, sir. Have I not often remarked as much?" She stood, and it was the brisk Miss Bannon again. "No doubt you are quite angry."

*I am a mentath. I do not anger.* He closed his lips over the words. His body informed him that it had been held passive long enough, and it had a rather large desire to attend to some of its eliminatory needs. *Anger is Feeling, it is illogical. It is beneath me.* "Your Shield performed a miracle upon you as well, Miss Bannon. You lost nothing in that transaction."

She became so still even his sharp ears could not find the sound of her breathing.

There was no crackle of live sorcery, no shuddering in the walls of her house as he had sometimes witnessed, her domicile responding to her mood as a dog responds to its master's tension.

Finally, she let the pent breath out. "Nothing but Ludovico." Each word polished, precise. "And, I suspect, your regard. I shall leave you to your rest, sir."

Hot salt fluid dripped down Clare's temples, soaked into

the pillow and his scorched hair. He lay until she closed the door with a small deadly click; he slowly pushed back the covers and shuffled to the incongruously modern privy. There was a mirror above the sink-stand, but he did not glance into its watery clarity.

He did not wish to see the wetness upon his cheeks.

# Chapter Six

## Too Winsome and Winning a Place

She had never thought to be glad there were still Papists left in Londinium. As always, where there was Religion there was also a man whose palm was amenable to greasing. Consequently, even a wayward son of a Church such as Ludovico Valentinelli could be laid to rest in Rome-approved fashion. Emma paid for masses to be sung for his soul, too, though it was her private opinion that Heaven would bore him to a second death and Hell was entirely too winsome and winning a place to hold him for long, did he seek amusement elsewhere.

Yellow fog wreathed the gates of Kinsalgreene, elbowing uneasily with the incense puffing in clouds from swinging censors. There was a choir of small urchins, and the roly-poly Papist in his black cloth, scarlet-crossed stole, and long supercilious nose looked askance at her as she stood, clearly not willing to leave as a woman traditionally did before the coffin – the most comfortable that could be obtained, for he would not rest in a beggar's box – was lowered and covered.

The Papist muttered something and glanced at Clare, who stood leaning upon Horace the footman's proffered arm. Finch was there too, in his dusty black – appropriate despite himself, it seemed – and her housekeeper, Madame Noyon as well, dropping tears into a small, exquisitely wrought lace handkerchief. Even broad genial Cook, whom Ludo had tormented shamelessly, stood solemn and sedate. The footmen wore their best, indenture collars glowing softly, and the maids, both lady's and common, scullery and all-work, sniffed and dabbed.

Of course he had been at the maids too, but they seemed to have forgiven him.

The hearse and attendants, not to mention the pallbearers, constituted quite a crowd. Pages, feathermen, coachmen, mutes, how he would have hated the attention.

If she raised his shade through the lead sleeve and oak covering, he would sneer and spit.

Or perhaps he would not. That was the trouble – how could one ever be sure what someone would do, could you restore them to a manner of breathing? Memory was an imperfect guide, and Ludo in all his changefulness could not be compassed.

It was, she suspected, why she had kept him so close.

Mikal was at her shoulder, and she denied herself the faint comfort of leaning against him. There was a toll exacted here, and she paid it as Madame Noyon and the maids retreated, as the coffin was lowered and the footmen clustered around Clare. She paid double when Clare did not so much as glance at her, staring at the coffin's mellow polished gleam with his bright blue eyes narrowed and intent.

*You should have* told *me*. Of course, even a machine of logic trapped in flesh would feel disturbed, or even outright betrayed, at such a secret. Sometimes she wondered if other mentaths were as thin-skinned as her own. They had alarmingly sharp faculties of Perception and Deduction, and were said to have no Feeling whatsoever. Indeed, it was supposed to discommode them quite roundly.

Sometimes, though, she suspected that a *lack* of Feeling was not quite the condition Clare suffered.

Her mourning-cloth was not quite appropriate, for what proper lady would feel the need to mark the passing of a man who was, strictly speaking, a hireling?

Yet she chose to wear something close to a widow's weeds for him, if only to silently tell Clare . . . what?

Black henrietta cloth, an unfashionably small bustle, a crêpe band holding tiny diamonds to her throat, long silver and jet earrings thrumming with Tideturn's stored charge, matched silver cuff-bracelets ice-burning under her sleeves and gloves. She had not worn these earrings for years, not since the last time she had been in grief. .

*Thrent. Harry. Jourdain. Namal. Eli.* Now another name to add to the list. *Ludovico.* A *rosario*, perhaps, like the one the Papist clutched as he mumbled his prayers, sealing the baptised body of one of his God's children into eternity.

There were other matters to worry over, chief among them the richly appointed carriage that had lurked behind the cortège and even now squatted, toadlike, outside Kinsalgreene's high, flung-open iron gates, their spikes wreathed with anti-corruption charms and deterrents most – but certainly not all – grave-robbers would hesitate to cross. She had paid to have the Neapolitan well armoured against the theft of his shed mortal cloak. Time and rot she could do little against now, but she could make certain nothing else interfered with his resting.

Whoever was in the carriage, well, she would deal with them after this ceremony.

Clare's paper-paleness. The thin bitter line of his mouth, drawn tight. Tiny tremors running through him, as well as the haphazard haircut – he had trimmed the burnt bits himself, shrugging aside Gilburn, who would have been more than happy to perform a valet's duty.

Ludovico's duty.

Though the bowl of the sky was a blind eye of cloud, the rain held itself in abeyance. It had been a cold, damp summer even for Londinium, and some whispered Britannia was unhappy.

Had Emma not been so painfully aware of her surroundings, she might have made a restless movement.

*If she is unhappy, it is no concern of mine. Not now.*

The thump of the oaken cask settling sent a shudder

through her, one she quelled even as Clare's face crumpled and smoothed itself, soundlessly.

*Yes, I should have told you. I was afraid of the illogic unsettling your mind. I was afraid of . . .*

Such an admission could not be borne. A Prime did not *fear*.

"Prima?" Barely a whisper, Mikal sounding not quite happy with her movement.

She had taken a step forward.

Hushed greenery and glowing marble mausoleums, their cargoes of quiet rotting hidden behind the gleaming façade and held safe in nets of ancient barrowcharm, to ensure they slept soundly.

Her Discipline roused slightly within her, and even the weak sunlight stung her sensitive eyes. She was glad of the veil's obscurity, and still miserably compelled forward.

Wet earth full of mouldering, the open grave and the stone sleeve within it, nestling the coffin and its inner lining of charmed lead. A box within a box, within another, and inside them all a kernel that had once been . . . what, to her?

More than an acquaintance, more than a hireling, not quite a friend, caught in some space for which there was no proper word.

The first time she had ever engaged his services, he had played, catlike, as if she were a mouse under his paw. When the mouse turned out to be a lioness, the cat had merely blinked once, and afterwards still practised a cool disdain. There had been another woman involved, and sorcery, and plenty of blood. The sounds he made as he almost choked on the gallows, before she cut him down.

*Strega.* Whispered, like a curse, afterwards. She had paid him double, though he had sought to refuse her. *You should have let me die.*

Her own reply – *That, sir, would not please me at all –* greeted merely with a knife driven into the wall beside her head, and a muttered curse. Mikal had come very close to killing the Neapolitan, the first great test of his obedience to her will as her Shield . . . and the first moment she had begun to think that perhaps she might not have erred in accepting his service and sheltering him from the consequences of murdering his previous master.

She blinked, rapidly, grateful again for the veil. Later, glowing marble would rise above the nested boxes, and the stonewrights would chip a farewell into its gleaming face. Building a house for a dead man required time, even if one could pay double or triple for the best.

Her throat closed as she stared at the polished oak.

*I am of the Endor. Did I will it, he would rise even from this . . . but it would bring no comfort.*

The dead did not grant absolution. They merely answered simple questions of fact, and to ask them of Feeling was a waste. Once, one of her Discipline had brought a spirit fully to flesh to answer a king's questioning, but such a feat was beyond Emma, Prime or no.

*Or is it?* There was little comfort in finding, at last, an act of sorcery that she did not dare attempt. It had merely taken her entire life so far to discover it.

*Ludovico.* Her back held iron-straight, Emma Bannon extended her hand. A sharp flicker of sorcery, the fabric of tangled æther that condensed into physical matter shivering, and her glove was sliced neatly open.

The black glove – and the flesh underneath.

*"Madam!"* The priest, scandalised. She ignored him. The barrowmancer, standing ready at the periphery, stepped back nervously.

*Ludo. I am sorry.* Blood dripped, and her housekeeper, as the women obeyed custom and retreated, let out another sob. Emma did not move.

Mikal hissed in a breath as a spatter of scarlet drummed on the polished lid. Its pattern trembled for a moment, the sensitised fabric of reality rippling. Here was not a place for one of sorcery's children to shed blood.

It mattered little. For this, nothing but blood would do. There was no vengeance to be had: Ludo's killer had vaporised himself with the explosive as well. Were she to hunt down every last one of his accomplices, or even take her rage to Eire's green shores, the scales still would not balance.

After all, hers was the hidden thumb upon one side. A cheat so accustomed to thievery it becomes habit, a partial judge. A sorceress who chose one life over another.

*I am sorry, and I shall pay penance.* She stared down at the bright scarlet spots. Mikal snatched her hand, and she let him. His fingers folded around hers, and she resisted only when he sought to draw her away from the graveside.

"Fill it in," she said, each word a dry stone in her throat. "For God's sake, as you cherish your lives, *fill it in.*"

There was a soft commotion. Clare had faltered, Horace and Gilburn caught him. There was a tingle up her arm as Mikal applied healing sorcery, a Shield's capability. Part of a Shield's *function.*

That was worrisome, too. *Your Shield worked a miracle . . . you lost nothing in the transaction . . .*

All this time, she had thought her survival stemmed from a different source; from the sorcery worked by the greatest Mender of his age while the city lay wracked under the lash of a plague let loose on the world by the very Crown Emma had sworn to serve. If her recovery had not been of Thomas Coldfaith's making . . .

Troubles thick and fast, and she could do nothing but stand and watch the open mouth of the grave as the diggers bent their backs to the work, the lone barrowmancer in his long black gown and traditional red stripes still eyeing her nervously as he felt the disturbance spreading from her.

A Prime was a storm-front of ætheric force, sorcerous Will that brooked precious little bridle exercised and fed until it became monstrous.

A woman with a Prime's will and corresponding ætheric talent, monstrous indeed. If she lost control of herself here, in this place of the dead, what could she set loose? If she opened the gates of her Discipline in this place, she could well shatter every stone and coffin. She could hold the door wide for a long while, and fuelled by this, what could it bring forth?

A spatter of earth hit the lid with a hollow noise, each shovelful another barrier between her and . . . what?

She could not name what he was to her, even now.

*Ludo, Ludovico, I am . . . sorry.*

It was not enough.

#  *Chapter Seven*

## *Not Well at All, at All*

The carriage ride to Mayefair was silent and extremely jolting. Clare, marginally restored by an application of salts and a mouthful of brandy from Cook's surreptitious flask, held grimly to consciousness despite the roaring in his ears. Across from him, Miss Bannon sat, her childlike face composed and wan under the veil's obscuring net, the sliced, bloody glove on her left hand wrinkling slightly as her fingers twitched.

A fraction of coja would help, perhaps. He had not availed himself of its sweet burn since the plague incident, seeing no need to sharpen his faculties against that whetstone. And, truthfully, he had not felt the craving to do so. Was it a function of whatever illogical feat she had performed?

*A certain artefact*, she said. Did he dare ask further questions?

She might very well answer. In that case, was he a coward not to enquire?

The coffin, lowering into the earth. The bright spatter of blood, and Miss Bannon not even glancing in his direction. Had he thought her indifferent to Ludovico's . . . passing?

*Call it what it is. Death.*

The roaring in his ears intensified. It took actual physical effort to think through the wall of sound.

"Clare?" Where had Miss Bannon acquired this new, tentative tone? "Are you well?"

*I am not at all well, thank you.* "Quite," he managed, through gritted teeth. "You made certain of that, did you not?"

It was unjustified, and the slight stiffening of Miss Bannon's shoulders told him the dart had hit true. She turned her head slightly, as if to gaze out the carriage window. Her left hand had become a fist.

"Yes." Softly. "I did."

Nothing else was said as they inched homeward, and when the familiar clatter of iron-shod mechanical hooves on the echoing cobbled lane leading into the carriageyard resounded she began gathering her skirts. She wore very deep mourning, and if she did not weep and wail as a woman might be expected to, perhaps it was because she was not inclined to such a display.

Or perhaps she felt a loss too profoundly to risk making any further comment upon it.

He was given no time to remark upon this observation, for as soon as the carriage halted she reached for the door, and it flung itself open as if kicked. There was Mikal, his lean dark face set, breathing deeply but with no difficulty. Whatever method he used to move as quickly as a carriage – granted, Londinium's streets were usually congested enough to render that no great trick, but still – Clare had not yet deciphered, even after all this time.

She accepted the Shield's hand as she left the carriage, and Clare found himself in the position of having behaved in a most ungentlemanlike manner, again.

*What is the* matter *with me?* Feeling or no, there was hardly any excuse for treating a lady so.

Of course, if what he suspected of Miss Bannon's origins was correct, she was not of a quality to feel the lack of such treatment.

*She is of a quality of character you have witnessed several times, and you are behaving abominably.*

Clare climbed from the carriage as an old man would, despite the fact that he did not feel in the least physically decrepit. No, the problem lay within the confines of his skull.

She had assured him there would be no dimming of his mental abilities. Very kind of her.

*Cease this nonsense.* His shoes struck the cobbles, swept twice daily by the disfigured stable-boy, and the jarring all through him dislodged the roaring in his ears for a moment.

Miss Bannon swept ahead, her head bowed as if walking into a heavy wind. Mikal had not followed. Instead, the Shield paused, watching the black-veiled figure whose faltering steps clicked softly.

Then his head turned, with slow terrible grace, and he examined Clare from top to toe. Weak sunlight picked out the nap of the black velvet he wore instead of his usual olive-green – perhaps because Miss Bannon had insisted. The Shield's opinion of Valentinelli had always seemed to hover about the edges of condescension mixed with outright distrust, and Clare had finally decided it was Miss Bannon's fondness for the assassin that . . .

The chain of logic drifted away, for Mikal's tone was quiet, pleasant, and chilling. "Mentath." A slight pause, during which Miss Bannon disappeared through the side-door. "I do not know what has passed between you and my Prima."

*I suspect that is a very good thing.* "No?"

A ghost of a smile curled up one corner of the Shield's mouth, and for an instant it seemed – no, it *was*. His pupils flickered into a different shape.

Clare all but reeled back against the carriage's side. The edge of his calf struck the step, a deep bruising blow. *No more irrational wonders for today, please. I am quite finished.*

"No, sir, I do not." The honorific escaped on a long hiss of air. "Pray I do not discover it."

"Do you *threaten* me, sir?" He meant it to sound less fearful.

"Not a threat, little man." Mikal's smile twisted further, a hideous drooping movement. "A warning."

With that, he was gone, striding across the carriageyard.

Harthell the coachman cooed at the gleaming black

clockhorses, and the stable-boy, his wide, black eyes gleaming as his hunched and corkscrewed body twitched out from the shadow of the stable, scurried to help. The beasts snorted and champed, gleaming flanks married to delicate metal legs, their hooves chiming almost bell-like as sparks struck from the cobbles.

Clare leaned against the carriage's mud-spattered side. A thin misting rain began to fall, and the low venomous smell of Londinium's fog filled his nose. His calf throbbed, his head was full of noise, and he began to suspect he was not very well at all, at all.

A fraction of coja would set him right in a heartbeat. First he must change his clothes, then tell Ludo to hurry . . .

But Ludo was gone, closed in cold earth with a sorceress's blood spattering his coffin. It was perhaps what the Neapolitan would have wanted. The only thing better would be a burning boat, as the pagans of old in cold countries had sent warriors into the beyond.

Clare's eyes were full of hot liquid. He hurried into the house, creepingly thankful few of the servants had returned from the graveside yet, to see him in such disarray.

# Chapter Eight

## I Shall Enlighten You

"Person to see you, mum." Finch's face had squeezed in on itself in a most dreadful fashion. Rather as if he had sucked a lemon, which could either mean he was impressed by the visitor's status, or *quite* the opposite.

Emma lowered the chill, damp handkerchief over her eyes. Her study was very dimly lit, and the leather sopha she had collapsed upon was a trifle too hard. Still, it was not the floor, and if furniture witnessed her *déshabillé*, or behaving not quite as a lady should, it would not speak of the matter.

Nor would Finch, and she took care to answer kindly, "I am not receiving, Finch. Thank you." The shelves of leather spines – each book useful in some fashion, if only for a single line – frowned down upon her, and the banked coal fire in the grate gave a welcome warmth without the glare of open flame.

Finch cleared his throat. Delicately.

*I see.* "A rather fine carriage, following us from the graveyard," she murmured. "Yes. Did they, perchance, present a card?"

"No mum."

*Of course not.* "Mikal?"

"Is aware, mum."

*I certainly hope he is.* "And what do you make of the carriage, Mr Finch?" For though her butler appeared a gaunt dusty nonentity, he most certainly was not thick-headed. *Or* easy to ruffle.

His lemon-sucking face intensified, his collar pressing papery neck-flesh. The indenture collar would grant him a longer lease aboveground, but he was ageing. "Not so much the carriage as the guards about it. All of Brooke Street's under their eye, mum."

"Indeed." They were all aging. Severine Noyon sometimes limped, old injuries stiffening her thickened body. Isobel and Catherine, once bonny young maids, were past the first flush of youth now, and would perhaps marry if she settled a dowry upon them. Bridget and Alice as well. She should attend to that, and soon.

A Prime's life was long, and enough of a burden without a Philosopher's Stone taken from a dead lover's wrack and ruin to weigh upon one. She had intended to make Clare proof against time, and also to assuage her damnable conscience in the matter.

And yet.

Finch brought her back to the matter at hand. "The watchers arrived just as Cook and the girls did."

*In other words, they did not wish to be remarked by a sorceress or a Shield, knowing one or both of us would sense a watch upon the house as we returned. I should feel insulted.* An involuntary sigh worked its way past her lips. "The servants?"

"All accounted for, mum. The carriage is a fine bit of work, but without design. Clockhorses worth a pretty penny. Black as . . . well, black, mum."

*Black as death.* "How very interesting." She crushed the scrap of lace and cambric between her fingers and her sweating brow. "Very well, send word I shall receive *one* person, and one only."

"Shall I bring tea?"

*A cuppa would do me a world of good.* "No. Rum. And *vitae*."

"Yesmum." He sounded relieved, even though he would know the very thought of violet-scented *vitae* would unsettle his employer's stomach most roundly.

"Thank you, Finch." If the carriage held what she suspected, the drink would come in handy.

For *both* of them.

"Yesmum," he repeated, and shuffled out. The set of his thin shoulders was profoundly relieved, no doubt eased by this intimation that his mistress knew exactly what she was about. As usual, her own steadiness provoked calm and assurance in her servants.

Emma allowed herself one more deep, pained sigh.

Of course Clare was . . . upset. The wonder was that he had not bethought himself to ask such questions before. For a logic machine trapped in distracting flesh, he certainly seemed a bit . . . well, naïve.

She rose, slowly, her hands accomplishing the familiar motions of setting her dress to rights. She lowered the veil – a tear-stained face and dishevelled curls was not how she wished to face whatever manner of unpleasantness this was likely to be.

Blinking furiously, Emma Bannon lowered her head and strode for the door.

Pale birch furniture, indigo cushions, the wallpaper soft silken blue as a summer sky. The mirrors glowed faintly, though the curtains were drawn – a strip of garden before a stone wall was not the *best* view, though sometimes Emma thought of a Minor Seeming – a lakeside, perhaps? The trouble with such a fancy was that it weakened any ætheric defence, though glass was wondrous when it came to building illusion upon a physical matrix.

She stood by the cold fireplace – no flame had been laid, and the room was chill. It reflected her feelings toward the entire day, she supposed, and cast a longing glance at the settee. But, no – standing, and the presumed advantage of being afoot, was called for.

The air vibrated uneasily, and the door opened. "Mum," Finch murmured, showing the visitor inside.

Another heavily veiled figure in black, and for a

moment the sensation was of falling into a reflective surface. Or the past, that great dark well. But this woman, while slightly taller than Emma, was considerably rounder. Her black was very proper widow's weeds, and jewels flashed as she smoothed the veil aside with plump fingers.

There was another soundless flashing, the light that preceded thunder, and Emma's mouth turned itself to a thin, bitter line before she smoothed her features.

But she did not make a courtesy. Pride, a sorceress's besetting sin.

*Perhaps I have simply learned to value myself.*

The face behind the veil's screen was rounder too, and beginning to exhibit the ravages of time, care, and rich food. The girl she had once been had vanished. Pressures of rule had hammered that girl into this woman – weak-chinned, yes, but the eyes were piercing, as well as black from lid to lid, and spangled with dry constellations not even a sorcerer could name. Her cheeks were coarser, and slightly flushed, and perhaps it was a blessing that Alexandrine Victrix, Queen of the Isles and Empress of the Indus, bearer of the spirit of rule, did not know how much she resembled her deceased mother.

The drawing room trembled like oil on the surface of a wind-ruffled pond. A Prime's temper could tear this entire house – and a good portion of Mayefair, did it become necessary – asunder, leaving only a smoking hole of chaos and irrationality. The scar would be long in healing.

Why stop there? Londinium itself could bear some cleansing. Perhaps if stone was pulled from stone, the trees blasted and the birds silenced Emma Bannon might find some peace.

*Is peace my aim, then?*

Victrix's lip twitched, perhaps a sign of disdain. Certainly it was not amusement, as it might have been once. "Emma."

As the first blow of a duel, it left rather something to be desired. "Your Majesty." *Do you see your mother's face in the mirror? Gossip holds that you were reconciled to her on her deathbed, even though you found certain proof in Conroy's papers of some terrible guilt.*

What was it like, she wondered, to host the spirit of rule, to be the law and will of the Isles incarnate . . . and to find your own mother had plotted against you? Then there was the matter of the Consort, whose health had never been fine after the Red had swept Londinium. Emma would have thought the widow's weeds a silent rebuke, but for the fact that a queen would feel no need to *rebuke*, certainly . . . and the ancillary fact that it was Victrix's own government that had loosed that particular scourge on the world.

The method of making a cure was known far and wide now, and Emma had held her tongue.

For after all, Clare had survived, even if Emma's Shield, Eli, had not. He had rendered faithful service, and she had failed to protect him.

*I am not calm at all.* Harsh training sank its claws into her vitals, a vice about her forehead as well. A tiny tremor rippled through her skirts, making a soft sweet sound.

That was all.

Victrix's chin rose slightly. "We are here to speak with you."

"Obviously." Emma did not have to search for asperity. She was slightly gratified to see the woman's chin wobble: a very small, betraying movement.

The queen's face shifted, like clay in cold running water. Emma watched through the veil as Britannia woke, Her fleshly vessel filling like the Themis in its stony bed during the autumn torrents that would soon start and drown Londinium as the summer had failed to do.

The spirit of rule peered out of Her chosen bearer, and Victrix's jewels flashed again, with a power different than sorcery.

"Arrogant witchling." The voice was different, too, and Victrix's expression a stony wall. "Is it a grudge you bear?"

"What good would that do?" Emma lifted one shoulder, dropped it in an approximation of a shrug. An unladylike movement, but it expressed her feelings perfectly. "What is it the spirit of Empire requires?"

For a long moment Britannia studied her, the spirit's gaze sharpening further. "Do you still obey My vessel, witchling?"

*I return every communication either of you see fit to send me unopened, and have for a long while now.* "Does she still see fit to insult me?"

"Petty." Britannia narrowed her eyes, the glow above Her veiled, grey-threaded head the most evanescent crown of all, a sign of the spirit fully inhabiting its vessel, all its attention brought to bear. "Who are you, to take *insult*?"

*I am Prime. You should know better, Britannia, even if Victrix does not.* She simply gazed through her heavy veil, willing the wine-red fury within her to retreat.

"We are weakened," the spirit finally said, its cold lipless voice somehow faintly obscene, issuing from a stout woman's throat. "We have . . . there is a draining of Our vital energy. A threat."

*A draining? Weakened?* Emma frankly stared. The world seemed to shift a bit beneath her. "Ah," she managed, finally. "I see."

"No." Britannia drew Victrix's mouth back, into a rictus. "You do not. But We shall enlighten you."

# Chapter Nine

## How Many Acquaintances

A few effects stuffed higgledy-piggledy into his trusty Gladstone, and Clare halted to stare at the bed. It was neatly made, the linens snow-white and the red velvet counterpane as familiar as the worn quilt covering his narrow Baker Street bed. Here the furniture was heavy and dark, of a quality to last; his flat seemed rather shabby in comparison.

How many times had he slept here, though? Contemplated a case at Miss Bannon's dinner table, had a companionable tea in the solarium – both of them silent except for a *Pass the marmalade, if you please* or a *How droll, this article claims thus-and-such*? How many times had Miss Bannon quietly arranged matters to suit him, or anticipated his need for a particular item? *A woman's sorcery*, she would remark, brushing aside his thanks.

He was behaving most shabbily. The voice of Logic demanded he halt and consider, and he would heed *that* dictate before pausing to even consider the voice of Manners.

His breathing came heavily. His heart thundered in his chest, the heart she had repaired – Valentinelli had dragged him here, spattered with ordure and in the throes of a severe angina. Miss Bannon had not questioned or demurred in the slightest. Instead, she had thrown her considerable, if illogical, resources into working a miracle to keep Clare alive. It was Miss Bannon who had brought him to Ludovico in the first instance, during the affair with the army of mecha. Protection for Clare's tender person, indeed.

He would not, if he understood her correctly, have to fear a repeat occurrence of the angina, or the slow clouding of old age. His faculties would remain undimmed. The greatest fear a mentath could suffer, set aside with breathtaking speed.

The fear of physical harm, never overwhelming for a mentath used to calculating probability and setting aside Feeling, was now non-existent.

The possibilities for experimentation were utterly boggling.

He could, no doubt, find a fraction of coja at an apothecary's, and begin there. Clare snapped the Gladstone closed. He glanced at the door, opening his mouth to tell Valentinelli . . .

. . . absolutely nothing. The Neapolitan's place was empty, and would remain so.

Now *there* was an avenue of thought best left unexplored: dealing with how many acquaintances Clare would outlast.

*If I had known, I would not have allowed him to attend the trial. The danger was clear.*

How could he have halted the Neapolitan, though? Stubborn as a brick, that man. And why had Miss Bannon not inflicted this burden on *him*? They were two cats, the sorceress and the assassin, disdainful but never far from each other, sidelong glances and mincing steps. Valentinelli had been married once, but the name of his wife was a mystery, just as so much else about him.

His last word, *strega*, whispered the way another might take a lover's name into the dark.

The dark Clare would not experience for a long, long while. How long? Was there any way to tell? Questions! Questions that required answers.

He sank his sweating fists into the velvet counterpane. Bent over until his forehead touched the bag's use-blackened handles, and attempted to impose some order on his scattered thoughts.

It came slowly. The rest of him was wet with sweat by the time he braced his arms and straightened, his knees creaking.

"I should apologise." It was not quite the thing for a mentath to speak to himself. It was rather a sign of uncertain faculties, wasn't it? "I treated her most dreadfully. Yes."

He found himself at his chamber door, clutching the bag with a sopping hand. A great undifferentiated mass of

Feeling rose again, swamping him, and he dropped the Gladstone with a solid, meaty thump that unseated his usually excellent digestion.

He could not remember breakfast, but he bolted for the water closet and evacuated it in a most decided fashion, pausing to suck in deep breaths between the heaves and wincing at the taste of his own bile.

# Chapter Ten

## And Nothing Came of It

Emma sighed and indicated the settee, faintly surprised when Britannia did not take offence. The ruling spirit settled her vessel carefully, and for a long moment her face became Victrix's as she arranged her voluminous skirts. Drawn despite the doughiness, careworn as well, Emma could not find the young queen she had known in the matron's features.

Did it disturb Victrix, to find her former servant so unchanged?

If it did, she did not show it, merely pursed her lips with distaste. When she spoke, there was only a faint shadow of Britannia under her words, a chill wind mouthing the syllables. "There have been . . . events. In the Eastron End of Londinium. Whitchapel."

"Events." The blood crusted on Emma's left glove was

irritating. "In Whitchapel." The thought of that filthy sinkhole, the Scab covering its floors and cobbles with thick green caustic sludge, was unpleasant, to say the least.

"We *felt* these events, Lady Sellwyth. In Our very core." One plump hand waved, diamonds flashing. "And now there are . . . disturbing signs. A weakness, such as We have not felt since . . ."

*Since when?* But the practice of holding her tongue in the presence of royalty had always stood Emma in marvellous good stead, and she found it easy to adhere to at the moment. And *Lady Sellwyth*, as if Victrix sought to remind her of the fanged gift of a title set as a seal upon Emma's faithful service, and the Sellwyth ancestral lands held in Emma's fist, guarding its secret.

Victrix's mouth barely opened far enough to let the words loose. "Since those ingrates sought to disturb the taproot of Our power."

*Which ingrates? History is full to the brim of those who would supplant a vessel.* Perhaps it was Cramwelle's reign she referred to – the shock of Charles the First's execution must have been a nasty one. Or perhaps she meant Mad Georgeth's reign, though Britannia had held fast to even that ailing container.

She could even have meant the affair with the dragon, given her mention of Sellwyth.

Interesting as that avenue of questioning might prove, the issue of what the taproot of a ruling spirit's power consisted of was even *more* intriguing.

A heavy sigh, and Britannia retreated from Victrix's features. Her shoulders rounded, a flicker of expression crossed her broad face — what was it?

Almost *haunted*, Emma decided. "Your Majesty." She aimed for a soft, conciliatory tone, and perhaps did not succeed. Still, the effort had been made. "This seems to trouble you greatly."

"Can you imagine, sorceress, what it would be to lose your powers?"

*I do not have to imagine.* "Yes." Memory rose – dripping water, smell of stone, the manacles clanking and her own despairing noises as she struggled fruitlessly – and Mikal's steady breathing as he throttled and eviscerated the Prime who had trapped her and sought to tear her ætheric talent out by the roots. His *own* Prime, the one he had sworn to serve . . . a vow broken for what?

*He hurt you,* was all Mikal would say of the matter. She had never sorely pressed him on that point, for a variety of reasons. Clare's accusations rose before her again, unwelcome guests indeed, in the crowded room her brain had momentarily become.

"Yes," she repeated. "I can imagine it very well."

"Then you know how difficult it may be to speak of." Then, a crowning absurdity. "We ask your patience."

There was a tap at the door, and Mikal ghosted in. He held a silver tray – the rum, and a small fluted bottle of *vitae*. Just the sight of the glowing-purple glass was enough to unseat Emma's stomach a little.

His irises flared yellow in the dim light, and, for the

first time in a long while, she found herself slightly worried about her Shield.

Victrix studied him closely; her gaze had lost none of its human acuity. "We remember your face. You were with Us during the affair with the metal soldiers."

He glanced at Emma, who nodded slightly but perceptibly. Which freed him to answer – and also made a subtle point.

"I was." Two brief, dismissive words, and he set the tray down with a small click on the tiny, exquisite Chinois dresser, the three other decanters and crystal glasses already perched atop its gleaming mellowness.

"So long ago." Victrix sighed. "Emma."

She found her shoulders tight as canvas sail under a full gale. Took care to speak softly. "Your Majesty."

"We ask you to investigate. These . . . events have caused disturbance and threaten to rob Britannia of strength. What may We offer you for your service?"

"I am not in trade, Your Majesty." Stiffly. *You could offer an apology, but I think it unlikely indeed.*

"Did We treat so ill with you? You are still of the Isle, witchling."

"Perhaps I dislike travel, Your Majesty." *And consequently have not left.*

"Impertinent hussy. Do you think I do not know your origins? Your pretence at Quality is merely that."

*And your pretence at graciousness, Victrix? This house is clearly in mourning. As you still are, mourning that petty Saxe-Koburg you married.*

She held her tongue, and accepted a tumbler with an inch of rum from Mikal. One of his eyebrows lifted fractionally. The meaning was plain – whatever else lay between them in private, he was her Shield, and no onlooker would be allowed a glimpse of any tension. A burst of relief filled her chest so strongly she almost rocked back upon her heels.

Such a betraying movement could not be allowed. So she composed her features, tucked aside her veil with her free hand, and tossed the rum far, far back without waiting for Victrix to be served a thimbleful of *vitae* by a ghost-silent Mikal.

"And who are you, to treat with Us so?" Victrix's lip actually curled. "We are your sovereign."

*You* were *my sovereign, and I would have done much more for you, had you not used me as you did.* The comforting, soothing heat of a drink most ladies would not dare bolstered her. *I did not mind being a glove for your hand, my Queen, but a Prime does not brook being* insulted.

Emma chose the next few words carefully. An outright refusal would not do. "There must be other Primes in your service."

"None with your . . . efficiency." Her face twisted as if the admission hurt.

*I hope it does.* "Quite a compliment." *Now will you tell me of the other Prime, the one dogging my steps after the plague was released? The one leaving me posies and presents?*

Even now, there were secrets to keep.

"Sorceress." Britannia's voice filled Victrix's mouth, the sibilants long and cold. "You try Our patience."

"What would you have of me, spirit?" Deliberately hard, each word pronounced with the crispest of accents. Her Discipline sent a heatless pang through her. Those of the Endor were held in some caution, even among the Black. Even a Prime could not hope to strike down a ruling spirit . . . but she could certainly inconvenience one.

And do so mightily. If only by inaction.

"Someone in Whitchapel has committed murder." Victrix, now, using her own voice.

"That is hardly an event," Emma observed.

Mikal had gone very still, standing by the Chinois dresser in a Shield's habitual attitude, hands clasped loosely and the readiness clearly visible on him.

Carrying weapons in the queen's presence.

Victrix had come inside, alone, though the street was watched.

The realisation was a slap of cold water, stinging Emma into functioning properly. She continued, with great deliberation. "Starvation, Crime and Vice walk the Eastron End every night." *Every morning, too.* "Someone is always violently shuffling off a mortal coil there, with assistance and without."

"We are aware of such things."

Emma let silence cover that remarkable statement. Her gaze met Mikal's. It would be so easy to cross the room, open the door and step into the hall, consigning this whole conversation to the realms of *Such a thing occurred, and nothing came of it.*

She weighed the idea and found much to recommend it.

When Victrix finally spoke again, her tone was no more than a weary mortal woman's – middle-aged, a desert of hopes lost and the knowledge of grief. "We – *I* – witnessed a brace of murders. It is unspeakable. They have been savaged, Emma. We *felt* it. It was done with intent, and it tapped the source of Our power in some fashion. The weakness is . . . horrid. We do not know how or why. *You* must discover this, and quickly."

For a moment, Emma simply stared. Who knew what she might have said had the door not been thrown open and Clare staggered through, his hair wildly disarranged and his jacket askew?

"Emma, I must apolo – Dear God in Heaven, Your Majesty, what are *you* doing here?"

# Chapter Eleven

## Complete His Cowardice

"Dear heavens," Clare repeated, vainly trying to smooth his wild, greying hair down. His blue eyes were bloodshot – he knew as much – and he was in no fit state to be before royalty. "I had no – mum, I mean, Your Majesty—"

"Sit down." Miss Bannon was at his elbow. She all but dragged him across the drawing room and pushed him firmly into his wonted chair, a walnut affair with high curved arms he tapped thoughtfully when a complex case had his undivided attention.

"In front of the *Queen*?" He sounded genuinely horrified, even to himself.

"I care little who is present, sir, *sit down* before you collapse."

She held an empty glass, and his sensitive nose discerned the odour of rum.

*Her nerves must be frayed, indeed.*

The remarkable fact that the Queen of the Isles was on the settee, without a guard or a minister anywhere in evidence, impinged upon his consciousness as well. It did not bode well at all, and thankfully gave him something new to busy his faculties with. "What dire news is it this time? The dynamitards, have they struck again?"

"No, indeed." Victrix essayed a pale smile. "It is quite a different danger, and I am begging our redoubtable sorceress's aid with it."

"Begging? Nonsense. Miss Bannon is always more than huppy to . . ." He blinked up at the lady in question, whose expression had shifted a few critical degrees. "I say, Emma, I am well enough. Do tell me, how may I be of service?"

"You may sit where I place you, and cease being ridiculous. Mikal – yes, thank you." She pressed a snifter of brandy into Clare's willing hands, and the amber liquid suddenly seemed the best remedy in the world for his pounding head. "And – yes, very good." She lifted her replenished glass of rum, and tapped it against his. "Come now, sir. Chin up, buckle down."

"And devil take the hindmost." The familiar refrain, usually uttered when an affair they were pursuing had reached a breaking point of urgency and strain, comforted him. "I am sorry, Emma. I was dashed brutal about Valen—"

"Let us not speak of that." She eyed him for a long moment before straightening and glancing at Mikal. The Shield's face was a bland, closed book; he did not even spare a moment's worth of attention on Clare. "Now, stay there." She turned, regarding the Queen with a level, dark-eyed gaze.

It was odd to see such a childlike face so set and pale, the tiny diamonds on the crêpe band about her slim throat ringing with sorcerous light. The Queen, round and stiff in her mourning – the Widow of Windsor's sorrow was rather a mark, Clare thought, of a certain calcification of character – wore more jewels, and certainly more costly, but they did not seem as expressive as Miss Bannon's oddly matched adornments.

He noted the tremor in Queen Victrix, the hectic colour of her cheeks and a fresh scratch on the outside edge of her laced boot. Gravel, meaning she had hurried into a carriage, most likely on a wide walkway. And there, behind the careful mask of a middle-aged matron's face, was a flash of Feeling.

He peered more closely, disregarding the rudeness of staring, to verify the extraordinary evidence of his senses. Yes, he was certain he could identify that flash.

Fear.

"I shall investigate these occurrences," Miss Bannon said, formally. "If possible, I shall remove the danger to Britannia. I shall require every scrap of information there is to date; running after every murder in Whitchapel will only muddy the issue."

*Whitchapel? Murder?* Clare's faculties seized upon the extraordinary words with quite unseemly relief.

Victrix's mouth compressed. "The first body was buried

a-pottersfeld, the second is at Chanselmorgue. Her name was Nickol, I am told. More I cannot speak upon here."

*How very odd. It galls her to request Miss Bannon's services. Miss Bannon has not stepped forth on the Crown's business for . . . quite a long while now, really.* He had become accustomed to such a state of affairs, he supposed; Accustomed was a set of blinders where Logic and Reason were concerned. Just as befogging as Assumption and Comfort, and just as dangerous.

The tastes of bile and brandy commingled were not pleasant, and his head still ached abominably. But the storm seemed to have passed for the moment, and Clare had a rich vista of distracting new deduction before him to embark upon.

It would serve quite handily to push the distressing news, distressing *events*, firmly away.

"Did you view the bodies yourself, Your Majesty?"

Miss Bannon . . . was that a flicker of a *smile* hiding behind her steely expression? Had he not been so thoroughly acquainted with her features, he most certainly would have missed it.

She was enjoying Victrix's discomfiture, it seemed. Highly unusual. His estimation of the relationship between queen and the sorceress was incorrect. Perhaps said relationship had shifted by degrees, and he had missed it? For Miss Bannon did not speak upon the Queen much, if at all. Especially since the Red affair.

How very intriguing.

"We did, witchling." Soft and cold. "And now *you* shall.

Do not fail Us." The Queen rose on a whisper of black silk and colourless anger, and Clare scrambled to his feet. Neither woman acknowledged him. Victrix stalked through the drawing-room door, which opened itself silently to accommodate her passage. Miss Bannon's fingers did not twitch, but Clare was suddenly very sure that she had invisibly caused the door to swing itself wide. Mikal slid through after the Queen's black-skirted, sailing bulk.

The sound of the front door, shut with a thunderous snap, was a whip's cracking over a clockhorse's heaving back.

Miss Bannon turned to the mentath, and she wore a most peculiar smile. Tight and unamused, her dark eyes wide and sparkling, colour rising in her soft cheeks.

He downed the remainder of his brandy in one fcll gulp, and grimaced. Medicinal it might have been, but it mixed afresh with the bile to remind him that he was not *quite* himself at the moment.

*That is ridiculous. Who else would you be?*

"Emma." He wet his lips, swallowed harshly. "I am sorry. I should thank you for your pains, and apologise for my behaviour."

The sorceress shook her head, and her little fingers came up, loosened her veil. "It is of little account, Clare. I expected you would be angry. But you are alive to feel such anger, which is what I wished."

"And Ludo?"

"Do you think he would have thanked me for such a gift?" Another shake, settling the veil firmly. Her features blurred behind its weave, yet Clare's quick eye discerned the tremor that passed through her. Only one: a ripple as subtle and dangerous as the shifting of rocks heralding an ice-freighted avalanche. "No. Death was Ludovico's only love, Clare; he would not have been happy to have her snatched away."

*Yours was the name he spoke when she came calling, Miss Bannon.*

There was no purpose in telling her so. If a sorceress could keep secrets, so could a mentath. Were he a lesser creature, he might feel a certain satisfaction in the act of doing so. As it was, well . . . "I deduce your torpor has been shaken, Miss Bannon."

"Certainly my leisure has been disrupted. Would you care to accompany me? I am to view a body, it seems, for our liege."

What was the sudden loosening in his chest? He decided not to enquire too closely. "Certainly. Do I have a moment to change my cloth? I am a trifle disarranged."

"Yes." She paused. "I rather require another glove, I should think."

"I shall make haste, then." And, to complete his cowardice, Clare escaped while he could.

# ❋ *Chapter Twelve*

---

## *Corpses Rarely Are*

C hanselmorgue's spires pierced the waning daylight, thick ochre fog gathering about its walls as it was wont to do in the afternoons. It had been a Papist church long before, one of the many taken by force in the Wifekiller's time and pressed into service in the most secular ways possible. There was rumour of scenes within its walls during that uncertain time that verged upon the blasphemous, but the Sisters of Chansel kept their archives locked. They still had a convent or two tucked in an inhospitable locale, moors and unhealthful swamps where children and young women of a certain regrettable condition were sent to meditate upon their sins – usually of resistance in some fashion to their disappointed elders. Or, truth be told, if there was an inconvenience in the matter of their drawing breath while an inheritance was in question.

A Chansel Sister was a formidable creature, if only for the chainmail she was suspected of wearing under her habit. Not to mention their particular set of charter symbols. Of all Papist orders, only they and the Templis openly and regularly admitted sorcery's children. Oh, some of them made it clear they would not turn away a sorcerer or above possessed of the requisite wealth and connections. The Domenici and the Jesuiri were remarkably accepting where filthy lucre or influence was involved, and the Franciscis and Clairias made it a practice to accept the sorriest wretches they could. For most of them, though, the workers of wonders and their defenders were *quite* beyond the pale.

Feared, respected, allowed to survive in most countries . . . but beyond.

Chanselmorgue was a four-spired hulk now, with sheds sprouting from its backside in the manner of the huge bustle fashionable some few years ago, like a ridiculous growth. One could still remark the *tau*, with a writhing corpse nailed to it, worked in the stone over the front doors, and also see the chisel marks where blasphemers had taken advantage of the Wifekiller's feud with the Papacy to wrench bits of coloured glass and other shiny objects from the facing.

Apparently Emma was expected – perhaps Victrix had been certain of tempting her into action, or had she thought Emma would crumble in the face of a personal visit? Did Victrix have that high an opinion of her own persuasiveness, or of her erstwhile sorceress's pride?

*Do I care? Whatever she thought, I did not agree to more than "If possible". I wonder if she noted as much.*

In any case, it took very little time for a narrow-eyed barrowmancer and a hunched, scuttling morguelrat to guide them to the shed containing the body in question, as well as five others.

As soon as she stepped inside the enclosure – waiting for Mikal's nod, and followed by a pale Clare holding a handkerchief under his long, sensitive nose – she had no difficulty discerning which one was Nickol.

The barrowmancer – a milk-cheeked young man with greasy dark hair and long fingers, the traditional red stripe on his trousers and his slouched hat pulled low – nodded as she halted, her eyes no doubt widening.

"Aye," he said, a broad nasal Cocklea accent reverberating around the shed's flimsy walls. "Enough to put a sour in ye belly, ennit? Doctor co'nae feel it, but he the skullblind. Wasn't til I saw 'er that anyone realised muckie'd been æther'd aboot."

"Indeed." Emma stepped past Mikal, who examined the body of what appeared to be a costermonger laid on a chipped, traditional marble slab, hands and feet pierced with true iron and the gashes scorched with charter symbols to ensure the corpse's peace. The heavyset man's mouth was pried open, the funnel for pouring salt or wine into the cavity laid aside. No flatscraper for pitch to seal the spirit away, so the barrowmancer judged him unlikely to have died by violence. "The report?"

"Ah, yes, will fetchit. Ye're nae gon swoon?"

"I think I may be able to avoid swooning, thank you. In any case, I have plenty of assistance."

"Aye." He paused, studying Clare, then shot a dark glance at Mikal. "Ye're nae gon turn a fillian?"

"I most likely will not be calling her spirit forth to answer questions, never fear." She tried not to sound amused. "And in any case, I would not do such a thing *here*. I am not so irresponsible."

"Well, tha's mun fair." He nodded, and touched his hat. "Will fetch tha report, then. Mind you, she's not decent."

"Corpses rarely are, sir. Thank you."

He hurried out, followed by the morguelrat, whose filmed gaze betrayed precious little excitement. Of course, morguels were taken from the workhouse's lowest strata, since a self-respecting beggar would hesitate to spend his days with the dead. For all that, they had room and board, if they did not mind sharing it with said corpses, and the peculiar blindness that struck after a few years of such work did not seem to bother most of them. Perhaps by then they had seen enough that sightlessness was a blessing.

Odd, how barrowmancers were not feared, though their Discipline was only slightly less Black than Emma's own. To shake hands with morguelrats was considered just slightly less lucky than with chimneysweeps.

"I do not think I shall ever become accustomed to that," Clare muttered darkly.

"To what, sir?" There was much in the current situation she herself did not wish to become accustomed to.

"To how casually you speak of bringing a shade forth to answer questions."

"I have never done it in your presence for a reason, Clare."

"And I appreciate your restraint." He all but shuddered, smoothing his jacket sleeves. The black armband, secured with a pin-charm, was a mute reproach.

As if she needed more than the weight of her own mourning-cloth. She did not fully indulge in a widow's bleakness; perhaps she should the next time she was forced to see the Queen. Although perhaps Victrix would likely take little notice of whatever Emma chose to wear.

"Are you quite well, Clare?" It was not like him to show such discomfort.

"Quite. I . . ." He shook his head, arranged his hat more firmly upon his head. Mikal, giving the costermonger's body a thorough appraisal, appeared to ignore them both. "It has been rather a trying . . . yes, rather a trying week."

She was about to reply, but her attention fastened afresh on the body she had come to view. *How very curious.*

The æther trembled around it, not the quiver of a living being producing disturbance and energy or the low foxfire of soul-residue. She stood, head cocked to the side, and took in what she could with every sense, physical or otherwise, she possessed.

Mikal appeared at her shoulder, his hand closing about her upper arm. He had noted her sudden stillness, and was ready to act as anchor or defence.

The corpse in question was a middle-aged woman, heavy and inert on a discoloured marble slab. Her mouth was open, and one could see the stubs of rotten teeth, as well as the searing from the preparatory mixture of hot caustic salts that preceded sour pitch.

Clare stepped to the side, his head cocked at a familiar angle. When he had gained all he could from observing the corpse's face, he reached for the ragged sheet covering her and glanced at Emma.

She nodded, a fractional movement, but one his eyes were sharp enough to discern. They had examined other bodies; it was, still, not quite *routine*. Ritual, certainly, though neither of them stood overmuch on ceremony when bodies were involved in an affair such as this.

She closed away *that* distracting line of thought. Attention was called for.

*What is that? There, and there, it moves very peculiarly. And there. Most interesting. I wonder . . .* She extended a tendril of non-physical awareness, delicately, and recoiled swiftly when the æther over the body trembled.

Mikal said nothing, but his awareness sharpened.

Clare twitched the sheet down to the woman's hips. The marks of a brutal life were clearly visible and the sewn-up gashes from autopsy – and the attack that had killed her – were livid. He folded the sheet with prissy carefulness, then took its edge and uncovered the rest of her, tucking the neat package of cloth at her feet. Her knees turned outward, and the ragged aperture between her legs oozed dark, brackish corpsefluid.

"*Most* peculiar," he murmured. "And she was Respectable once, or at least well-fed. Hrm."

Though the skin hung loosely, and one could see the marks of violence and hard living upon her, there were none of the deformities associated with childhood want or neglect.

She had afterwards fallen far, as Emma could clearly see from the wooden box containing the deceased's effects. Workhouse cloth, though mended neatly, her boots sprung-sided, and even through the varied reeks of a charnel-house Emma could discern a faint thread of gin. The woman's round face had begun to blur with drink during life, and a shiver worked its way down Emma's spine.

A horrid gash in the throat. The marks of frenzied stabbing over the entire torso were vicious too, but the cluster of open, gaping wounds about her parts of privacy were the most worrisome.

*That is where the attack was centred, and that is where the disturbance issues from. Her womb.*

Emma's entire body went cold.

This was gruesome news indeed.

# ✿ *Chapter Thirteen*

## *Wholly Unguarded Sentiments*

"Marian Nickol, called Polly, though the inquest will legally ascertain her identity." Clare blinked owlishly at the scrawls upon the thin paper as the carriage jolted. "Found by a carter on Bucksrow, near the Hospital. Slashed throat. Abdominal injuries . . . Omentum, uterus . . . sharp object . . . peculiar, most peculiar."

"Indeed," Miss Bannon murmured. She had a queer look upon her soft little face: distant, as if listening to faraway music.

A copy of the particulars of this and another murder had been prepared in advance of their arrival, and Clare had noticed Miss Bannon's tiny *moue* of distaste when *that* was discovered. Perhaps she resented the Queen's easy assumption of her pet sorceress's service? How could Her Majesty be certain, though, given how Miss Bannon had scrupulously avoided such service for . . . how long now?

When the Consort had died of a fever perhaps typhoid in origin – his health never having been very strong after the Red Plague had wracked Londinium – Miss Bannon had not worn mourning, as many of Britannia's subjects affected. Indeed, she had merely drunk a little more rum than was her wont at supper, and retreated to her study instead of to the smoking room, where Clare was habituated to sit and discuss various and sundry with her afterwards, as if she were a man at a dinner party.

The particulars were an easily solved conundrum. Britannia had more than one sorcerer or mentath in Her service, and the pages could easily have served another. He brought his attention back to the report, which held the details of the body's discovery as well. "The first – Marta Tebrem – was found in Whitchapel, too. Georgeyard Building. Stairs – first-floor landing. Dashed odd, that."

"Not if she was an unfortunate." Her gloved hands were clasped together a trifle too tightly. "I would be surprised if she did not bring a customer to that place more than once. Or if she sheltered there, to sleep."

"Ah." He coughed slightly. "Yes. I see."

She sat bolt upright, as usual, and had tucked the veil aside for the nonce. Two spots of hectic colour burned high up on her soft cheeks, and he was struck by how impossibly *vital* she appeared. Primes had long lives, certainly . . . he had taken it for granted that she would outlast him.

*What an unpleasant thought.* And followed by others equally unprepossessing, much like a steam-locomotive dragging carriage after carriage.

Even steam-locomotives possessed charmed whistles, and sorcerous reinforcement upon their boilers. A triumph of Science, yes, but larded with irrational sorcery.

One would have to go far, Clare had found, to escape such things.

"Out of the rain, and dark," Miss Bannon continued, "though I would chance a guess that the first victim was also much under the influence of gin the night of her misfortune. We cannot rule the choice of venue as hers until we examine it. The murderer may have taken her to the building while she was not quite of right mind, impersonating a client for her bodily services."

Of course, they would start with the first murder, and take the chain of deduction from there. It was how they began an affair such as this if time permitted, seeking the site of the first event they could distinguish. There was a certain comfort in the habit, Clare supposed. "She was last seen with a Guardsman, it says."

"Of course that may have been . . ." When she did not continue, he looked up from the papers. She stared out the window, and her fierce gaze was not ameliorated by matted eyelashes and reddened, brimming eyes. Her left hand had clenched, and she had sunk her pearly teeth into her lower lip, cruelly.

For the first time since he had met her, Clare was witnessing her wholly unguarded sentiments. The moment was so novel he almost crushed the papers as the carriage rocked itself, and his mouth had gone dry.

It took another cough before he could speak, and the sound served to alert her to his scrutiny. She smoothed her expression with amazing rapidity, and reached up to free the veil from its fastening. Her rings flashed, a heatless fire.

"Miss Bannon—"

"The morning has disarranged me." Her face was swallowed by darkness again. "Please, continue. I shall be better shortly."

"Miss Bannon, I—"

"The report, Clare. Please do continue."

He swallowed dryly, and forced himself to concentrate. "The medical examiner, in both cases, was quite thorough. There seems nothing missing from the notes. The most recent gentleman performing that duty – Killeen? Yes, that is his name – shall no doubt be at the Nickol inquest."

"Which you shall attend."

"Should time permit. Will you?"

"No." A slight shake of her veiled head. "I think I shall be hunting for clews in other quarters. There was a great deal of . . . disturbance about the body. I am uncertain what to make of it, and I think I shall be *quite* occupied in ferreting out the source."

"Hm." He digested this, and halted before he could make the quick glance aside that would ascertain whether or not Valentinelli had anything to add. The rattling of pebbles against a coffin's lid rolled inside his skull, deafening like the roar of traffic and crowd noise outside. "You are expecting further unpleasantness, sooner rather than later."

"Oh, yes. The first murder appears, if I may make a ghastly observation, merely a rehearsal. First we shall view the scene of Tebrem's discovery."

Did he imagine the slight unsteadiness of her tone? It could be blamed upon the carriage ride – Clare steadied himself as the conveyance rattled again. "And then?"

"Then we shall view the second, and return home for dinner – I am quite sorry, but we shall likely miss tea. Tomorrow, you shall visit quite another Yard." She returned her now-loosened hands to her black-clad lap, and Clare found himself wondering if her face was contorting again behind the veil. "If I may presume to suggest as much."

"Of course." He looked back at the paper. "I was dashed brutal to you, Emma. I apologise."

"Unnecessary, sir." Yet the words remained thoughtful, rather than dismissive. "I understand a temperament such as yours would find such a revelation quite a shock. Pray set yourself at ease."

He was not quite ready, he decided, to be treated with such cool politeness. He had seen her employ such a tone before, to set an overly familiar interlocutor back on his heels, so to speak. Were he not a mentath, Clare acknowledged, such a realisation might sting. Nevertheless, he soldiered on. "No reason to act so ungentlemanly, indeed. I am . . . I was fond of Ludovico, but—"

"As was I," she said, colourlessly. "Do continue with the recitation of facts from these papers, sir. There is a mystery at hand, and I wish it unravelled as soon as possible, so I may return to my accustomed habits."

# Chapter Fourteen

## For Want of a Pause

The Georgeyard Building had been new a decade ago, and clung to shabby respectability by teeth and toenails. Of course, it was off Whitchapel High Street, so the question of its respectability was an exceeding open one.

The day had brightened enough that the Scab's vile green, velvety organic ooze had retreated under muffled sunlight's lash, leaving an evil oily steam instead of its usual thick rancid coating over the cobbles.

*Not to worry, though. It will return with darkness.* So would Emma, if she gained nothing with this visit. For now, though, she followed Clare, their treads echoing in the dark.

She was glad of the stairwell's dimness; her eyes were burning from even the cloudy sunshine outside.

Or from something else.

*Nothing you need take account of, Emma. Do what duty demands here, and retreat as soon as you may.*

Why had she agreed to this? Merely because Clare had immediately assumed she would, or because she had felt some twinge of fading . . . what, for Victrix? Because she feared eccentricity was pressing in upon her too soon, her mental faculties becoming brittle? Perhaps because if she had not, she would have had to solve the questions gathering about her Shield?

Mikal followed her, taking care not to crowd too closely. The first floor came quickly, and she all but staggered when the disturbance in the æther pulsed sharply. All other considerations fled. "There," she managed, through numb lips, and pointed with a rigid arm. "*Right* there."

Mikal leapt up the last two stairs, caught her other arm. "Prima?"

"I am well enough. It is simply . . . I have never . . ." *I have not ever seen this before. I have never even* heard *of such a disturbance.* A Prime's memory was excellent, her education the best the Collegia could provide, and there was precious little sorcery she had not witnessed or read of. "What *is* this? It is still echoing. And she was discovered last *month!*"

"Miss Bannon?" Clare sounded nervous, for once. "There is a rather definite drop in physical temperature here. Remarkable. And . . ." He bent rapidly, and plucked something from the floor. "How very odd. Look."

It was a small pebble, no doubt carried in from outside, on a shoe or in a cuff. He turned it in his long capable fingers, then flicked it into the corner where the disturbance was greatest.

She stepped forward as well, Mikal moving with her. The Shield's grasp was a welcome anchor as she felt the chill difference in temperature, sharp as a falling knife-blade.

The stone hung, turning, in midair. A simple piece of cracked gravel, rough and clotted with dirt that unravelled in fine twisting threads. Now she could see the canvas-covered floor quivering through a curtain of disturbed, snarling æther. A stained piece of wooden wall, heavily scarred with use, was bleached as its physical matrices warped.

"Mr Clare," she heard herself say, as if from a great distance, "it would be very well if you were to retreat from that spot. Quickly."

"Prima?" Mikal's single word, shaded with a different question.

Her free arm, rigidly pointing at the floating pebble, trembled. "Take Clare halfway down the stairs." Mikal hesitated, and her temper almost snapped. "*Now*, Shield."

He turned loose of her with less alacrity than she would have liked, but he obeyed. At least Clare knew better than to question at this juncture. For a moment it was as if Time itself had turned back and it was one of the many investigations or intrigues between their inauspicious first meeting and the crushing denouement of the Plague affair. The only thing missing was Ludovico's silent sneer as he hustled Clare to safety or took up a guard post down the hall, which he might have done if he could have moved more quickly than Mikal.

*Do not think upon that, Emma.*

Instead, she *focused*, tucking the irritating veil aside as her jewellery flamed with heat, its ætheric charge responding to the spreading disturbance. The pebble still hung in midair, and she wondered if any of those who sheltered here noticed the spot, or if they simply felt the chill and avoided even glancing at something inimical. Even a lowly charter with barely the ability to trace a symbol in quivering air could have sensed the disturbance, and probably found other accommodations forthwith.

If there were any to be had; shelter of any kind was expensive in Whitchapel.

She extended a few thread-delicate tendrils of awareness to discern the true shape of the tangle. It throbbed, an abscess under the surface of the visible, a monstrous root driven deep through the real and almost-real. Emma risked another light touch, as a woman would pass her hand down a pinned dress-fold to discern if it would hang true. Intuition plucked at the knot, finding its shape and the likely directions it would bulge upon being observed.

She could have patiently unpicked it, inch by careful inch. It would have been better to refuse Victrix outright than to hurry now, and yet the sooner she found precisely what manner of disturbance this was, she could leave the entire displeasing mess behind her.

The solution, as ever, was to simply cast her net and see what rose with it to the surface. Training clamped its iron grasp about her body and she exhaled smoothly, stepping deliberately forward into the small pond of concentrated irrationality.

*The gin, false friend, hung thick and close inside her head, veils of welcome warmth. A rancid burp, the simmering smell of her own clothes, as familiar-strange as this wide-hipped body, loose and sagging with despair. Stumbling, falling against the wall, she turned to see him, his hat pulled low and only the suggestion of a chin under its shade.*

*Twas not his features she was interested in, but the pence burning in her hot palm. A man paid before he received, that was the best way of business, even for one as curst as old Marta. He had not demurred.*

*"Le's ha'at thee, then," she slurred, and that was when a jet of light cleaved the gloom.*

*She did not feel the first blow. It was the warm gush down her front that warned her, but her throat was full of that darkness, the same covering his face. It crawled down as if it wished to inhabit her stomach, and the knife came up again.*

*He fell upon her, and her fist clenched, but only because she thought,* "Not m'pence, needs it for a doss I do", *before the void swelled obscenely past her stomach, clawing at her vitals, and she knew no more.*

Emma staggered, the shock of her knees hitting the filthy floor only slightly cushioned by her skirts. Her spine stiffened, bending backward as if on a medieval spikehoop, and she was not conscious of her own voice: a high curlew cry that punched a perfect, circular hole in the bleached, sagging wall. Her jewellery blazed, diamonds at her throat emitting shrieking stress-screams, and the jet earrings shattered, their shards driven outwards as if propelled by burning gunpowder. Later, she would find the silver cuffs heat-rippled and all but useless for carrying ætheric force.

Still, they had performed another service: keeping her from being overwhelmed.

Tension snapped and she was thrown back, hitting something almost-soft and tumbling, a brief moment of merciful unconsciousness before the pain swallowed her whole. Even then training did not fail her, but behaved even more mercilessly, shunting the force of the blow aside as the entire building – and the street outside – shivered like a whipped cur. Her own shrieks rattled the walls, plaster dust falling fine and thin, Mikal's answering curse lost under a wall of rushing noise as he lowered her, his fingers biting cruelly as he sought to stop the wild thrashing.

He had left Clare to see to her, and she did not even recognise the fact.

One of a Shield's functions was to conduct such an overflow away from her, but this was too immense. A high ringing noise, a wet snapping, peeling sound, and the world settled into its accustomed dimensions again with a thump. Emma sagged, vicious-toothed trembling all through her as hot pain pounded between her temples.

Silence filled the dark stairwell. Soon there would be

shouts, and running feet. Even in Whitchapel, such an event as this would not go unremarked.

"Prima?" Mikal, raggedly. "*Emma?*"

One last pang, ripping through her, phantom blade cleaving flesh and breastbone. She curled around the blow, blind and witless, and Mikal held her down. It passed, and the shuddering, great gripping waves of it, began anew.

"*Saw* it," she managed. "*I saw it!*" Which meant the sorcery performed here, driving itself through the physical and ætheric, had found some resonance within *her*, and jolted home with explosive force.

The pebble completed its fall, and pinged against the floor. It did not sound right; the entire area bounded by the cold had been changed smoothly and seamlessly to glass. One could peer down into a dim, narrow hallway underneath, and the circular hole punched in the wall had thin, knife-sharp crystalline edges. A nasty smell boiled through, whistling darkness loaded with the breath of the privy-closet that had hidden behind.

At the moment, the crushing ache in her skull and the savage pain all through her body somewhat precluded examining the damage further. Now she was well and truly involved in this affair – all for the want of a pause before leaping in. "I . . ." She coughed, retching, her stomach threatening to unseat itself. "*Hurts.*"

"*Pax*, Prima. I am here." Was Mikal shaking too, or was it merely her own shivering?

"Dreadful," she managed, in a colourless little voice. "Home. Shield . . . *home.*"

"Yes."

With that assurance she let go of consciousness again, retreating to the deepest parts of herself as her violated mind sought to compass what had happened.

Two ideas followed her, both equally chilling.

The first was *He had no face*.

The second? *But he had a knife*.

# Chapter Fifteen

## Unremembering Such a Thing

The return to Mayefair proved long and tense, the streets
clogged with shouting, heaving traffic. It was also
cramped, for Mikal cradled the sorceress's small form and
ignored Clare entirely, studying her wan, slack face as if
it held a secret and feeling for her throat- or wrist-pulse
at intervals.

Clare did not feel it quite proper to venture forth again
that day, even though Miss Bannon was in no condition
to attend dinner and would consequently care little about
his absence. He was to visit another Yard, and he had an
inkling of which, yet he could not leave while the sorceress,
pale and so unconscious she represented quite a dead-
weight, was abed. Mikal carried her upstairs, and Madame
Noyon fluttered about fussing at the lady's maids to help
tend their mistress.

Clare himself went straight for the smoking room and its heavy walnut sideboard. His hand shook slightly as he poured himself a *very* healthy measure of brandy, and he downed it with quite unseemly haste. It left a burning in its wake, and he had to suppress a rumbling of the rudest sort from his scorched throat.

So much illogic could unsettle even the finest mind, he told himself, and his, while acceptable indeed, was not of *that* calibre. He could have Finch send out to an apothecary's for coja, and yet the thought of its deadly stinging did not soothe as much as it could.

No, the brandy was far better. He eyed the sideboard. This being Miss Bannon's house, there was no stinting in quantity *or* quality. Should he be so unfortunate as to feel a lack, no doubt any of the other liquids in crystal decanters would do, even the *vitae*. He had never drunk to excess – the consequent blunting of a mentath's faculties was unacceptable – but he could at this moment bloody well see the attraction.

*A rather awful day, all told*. The sounds Miss Bannon had made – terrifying, wrenching cries, loaded with horrifying, illogical force. No doubt there would be a great deal of speculation over the burst of sorcery, and her carriage may have been remarked.

Dreadful indeed. The sound of earth hitting a coffin lid again, rattling through his skull vehemently, over a spatter of blood. Even *he* knew that for a sorceress to spill that most precious of vital fluids in such a place was dangerous.

*"Eh, mentale. Drinking to death now?"*

Clare whirled. The room was empty, its heavy dark wainscoting and fancifully painted ceiling – cavorting satyrs and nymphs, perhaps Miss Bannon's comment on a man's ideas – just the same as they always had been. The billiard table, where sometimes the clack of heavy striking reverberated as he cogitated upon a particular matter and Miss Bannon sipped her rum, was just the same, covered with its loose canvas because he had not availed himself of its geometric soothing for quite some time.

His sensitive nostrils flared. A breath of dirt, the smoke of a snuffed candle. And the strong oiled-metal smell of a man who lived by violence, his wits sharp and his pock-marked cheeks sallow.

*Impossible.* The silver globe-lights were not flickering. It was his eyelids, falling and rising with extraordinary rapidity as his faculties sought to discern the evidence of the real from heated phantasy. *Simply impossible.*

There was no Neapolitan lounging near the door, where he was wont to pause before edging in to select a cigar from the silver-chased humidor – long, slender, floral in taste, and utterly strange in his blunt, dirty fingers.

"Merely the strain," Clare muttered, the words falling into dead, heavy air. He had never noticed before how close it was in this particular room without a woman's light laughing questions, a muttered reply in Calabrian when a man forgot himself and the tone of his youth wore through his careful mask. Or the clack of the heavy billiard-spheres providing their own music, smoke hanging in the air before being whisked toward the fireplace with a charm-crackle. "A dreadful day. A dreadful *week*. A touch more brandy, and some rest. For my nerves."

As if a mentath was prey to such a thing as shattered nerves. It was ridiculous to even *suggest*.

And yet.

He wiped at his mouth with the back of his hand, turned back to the sideboard and poured another generous measure. No, not rest. Rest would not do him any good at all. Only work would cure this uneasiness, the feeling that the earth itself would cease obeying its laws of proper quiescence or motion and begin behaving as irrationally as sorcery itself.

"Experiments." He gazed at the hand holding the tumbler of brandy, amber liquid trembling. Familiar as his own breath, that fleshly appendage, and the possibilities began to swirl inside his skull.

He did not realise, as he swilled the brandy and poured himself another, that he had left the crushed papers detailing Marta Tebrem's injuries, and statements given by witnesses, in Miss Bannon's carriage, where Harthell would find them and hand them to Finch without comment, to be placed upon Miss Bannon's study desk. It was a shocking sign of absent-mindedness in so normally precise a man.

Indeed, had Clare even an inkling of unremembering such a thing as said papers, he might have thought his condition warranted no little concern. As it was, he simply poured and swallowed until the decanter was empty, and left the smoking room and its shrouded table with a hurried, slightly rolling gait.

He did not feel inebriated in the least.

# ✸ Chapter Sixteen

---

## Rare and Wondrous

Waking after such an atrociously uncomfortable event could not possibly put one in a cheerful mood. Especially when said waking was triggered by an amazing, thumping bang from the depths of her house, and Mikal's muttered curse as he flung her bedroom door open.

*Without* knocking.

"He will kill himself, Prima." The Shield's eyes were alight and his dark hair disarranged, as if he had run his hands back through it. "Or one of the servants. Or he may even bring the house down around our ears."

Emma sighed, turning over and burying her face in the pillow. Even though the room was dark, her head ached abominably, and any hint of light scored her irritated eyes. "Unlikely," she muttered, "on all three accounts. Go *away*."

He reached her bedside, touched her shoulder with two

careful fingers. "I hesitated to wake you. But he will harm someone, perhaps even himself."

*The last thing I remember* . . . She shuddered as the recollection rose. Yet unconsciousness had blunted its sharp edges, and training had drained the venom. At least, enough for her to consider the vision calmly.

She had experienced Tebrem's death, stroke for stroke.

She had also, more to the point, disrupted whatever that death had been meant to achieve or cement. A spreading, deepening stain, with all the febrile tension of Whitchapel's poverty and violence – even in that semi-respectable building – to feed it. Now began the difficult but less dangerous work of deducing what she could of the murderer's method and intention – then descending upon said murderer with the force of law, and the more considerable force of Emma's irritation.

Speaking of deduction, she finally emerged from the haze of restorative slumber as another thump rattled the house. It was not a sorcerous sound, for the defences on her abode rippled only in response to her attention. "What on earth is he doing?"

"He is locked in the workroom, and since Tideturn all manner of noises have issued forth. The door is solid, and in any case . . ."

"Yes." She blinked, yawned daintily, pushing the pillow and his fingers away with a measure of regret. An attempt to force the workroom door would trigger certain protections and a Prime's will might strike before she was fully conscious. "Very well. Send up Severine and the maids. I shall sally forth and find out what he is about. But only *after* I've a bath and perhaps some *chocolat* – I feel dreadful."

"No doubt. Dare I ask what that was?" He all but glared at her, as if she were an errant child.

She decided she did not wish to have such a conversation with Mikal just at the moment, and so feigned to misunderstand his meaning. "I gather he was chasing a set of mad political dynamitards; no doubt they opened up a fascinating and explosive line of enquiry for his active little brain. You are dismissed, Shield."

For a long moment he stayed precisely where he was, waiting. When it became clear she would not speak further, he sank back on his heels. "Prima?"

"If you are not promising to bring me *chocolat* as quickly as possible, *or* informing me of a sudden disaster levelling the whole of Londinium, I do not think I am disposed to hear you." A stretch informed her of her body's protest over yesterday's – at least, she hoped it was yesterday and that she had not been abed for more than a Tideturn or two – events, and she took stock. Stiffness in the lower back, her arms ached, and her head throbbed as if she had been at the rum a bit too much.

"Then I shall not speak." His face closed in on itself; he spun on one heel, stalking for the door. A bright tang of lemon-yellow irritation was clearly visible to Sight.

Emma exhaled sharply, returning her focus fully to the physical world.

*When we do have a conversation, Shield, it will be on my terms, and mine alone.*

She finished her stretch, tasted morning in her mouth, and allowed herself a grimace. Her eyes were sandy and her hair was a bird's nest, like a witch's tangled mane. All in all, though, she felt surprisingly hale.

That was odd, wasn't it? She had grown accustomed to a feeling of well-being, since she had awakened from the Red with none of the scarring or other ill effects that disease normally entailed. It was similar to the Philosopher Stone's heavy warm weight, but without the crushing burden of . . . guilt? Her accursed conscience had weighed on her more and more, the longer she bore the Stone plucked from Llewellyn Gwynfudd's . . . body?

Perhaps it had not been ejected from his corpse. Had it been clasped in his hand as he performed the movements to aid him in remembering the cantos of his brilliant, earthshaking, and utterly insane act of sorcery?

Her return to the site of his demise had gathered no proof: only hole-eaten, anonymous bones, gryphon as well as human, drained even of the ætheric traces of their living. The shock of such a Major Work unravelling had bleached the environs into a sorcerous null-point; truth be told, she had not wished to find a distinguishing mark that proved some of the bones were *his*. She had seen his corpus shred as his interrupted Work tore him apart; it was enough.

She had privately thought, for a very long while, that his talk of a second Stone had been merely a ploy to cause her some hesitation. In the end, she had always been disposable to him.

Emma settled back among the pillows as another rattling

thud from downstairs rocked the house. *Oh, for God's sake.* A moment's worth of attention informed her that the stone walls of Clare's workroom were as solid as ever, and the door – reinforced with sorcery and iron, just to be certain – was likewise. There was precious little he could *do* to himself, with that single Stone safely wedded to his lean, no-longer-aging body. And just at the moment, she was . . . a trifle peeved.

Did she wish to think upon such a thing now?

Well, at least she had a few precious moments of solitude to pause in reflection.

Clare could not fail to grasp the immensity of her gift. He might have some trouble with the illogical nature of near-immortality, of course – and there was another possibility, that the shredding of Llew's physical substance as his wonderful, completely mad Work had unravelled had not been too much for even a wyrm's-heart Stone to soothe.

*Concentrate upon Clare, and let Llew rest. He is, after all, dead.* How would she appease the mentath?

She did a great deal of smoothing-over when it came to Archibald Clare. He had *some* manners, but a mentath was not an easy companion. She did not grudge him the time and attention, but she very much grudged cavalier treatment.

It was, after all, the reason she had quitted Victrix's service. Not openly, of course. But in the secret chambers of a Prime sorceress's heart, a measure had been taken . . . and a queen found wanting.

Clare was not quite found wanting. He was a most

logical, yet fragile, being, and seeing his limitations went far toward the forgiveness of certain of his regrettable tendencies. Still, it irked her. How could it not?

To be a woman was to be a creature most put-upon and taken for granted, and even those among the opposite sex who meant one well had their moments of treating one otherwise.

Yes, she had to admit, she was outright piqued.

And . . . Ludo.

She shut her eyes again. A precious few minutes of consciousness without the scrutiny of servants or Shield, and all she could think of was . . . what was Ludovico, quite, to her?

What had he been?

Simply a tool, an instrument to be played with fine attention and no little respect.

*Oh, Emma, lying to yourself is still bad form. That much, at least, has not changed.*

She had grown . . . *accustomed* . . . to the Neapolitan, much as she had grown accustomed to Clare. To Mikal, and Severine, and Isobel and Cook and Harthell. They were under her aegis, they were her responsibility, and if she cared for them as hothouse plants, had not such care acquired her certain rights as well as responsibilities? Watering, pruning, adjusting the climate-globes and their charmed tinkles . . .

*They are not plants, Emma.* A Prime's arrogance was a weakness, and one to be reined firmly lest it blind her to real dangers.

*Like yesterday. A bad bit of business, wouldn't you say?*

She exhaled sharply, turned her attention to a more productive avenue. Had Victrix seen and felt what *she* had? It flew in the face of much of what was accepted about sorcery, but Sympathy was an ancient art. What could have made a drab in Whitchapel – because Emma Bannon knew a frail when she saw one, thank you very much – possess enough resonance to cause a reaction in the ruling spirit of the Isle, the Empress of Indus, the queen of an empire grander than even the Pax Latium?

Viewing the location of the second body's discovery should be done, but not until she had taken certain precautions.

She stretched again, tapped her lips with a finger, and sighed. For the moment, enough to accept that a resonance indubitably *had* existed. The murders were not unconnected events, and they had some aim in mind.

Why had Britannia bothered to move Victrix to Emma's door? Why had Victrix come *alone*? Cold reflection would perhaps have assured the Queen that Emma Bannon was, perhaps, not likely to bruit the news of a ruling spirit's weakness about high and low. Even if Victrix disliked her methods and person, Britannia was wise enough not to doubt Emma's loyalty to Crown and Empire, no matter that the first rested on a wanting head and the second had not needed a certain sorceress's efforts to continue widening its sway.

Why had Victrix come to her?

*That is the wrong question, Emma. The correct question*

*is: what is she hoping to gain? From the lowest sinks of the Eastron End to the Crown itself, that is the great secret that moves the world. Finding a man – or a woman – who does not obey its dictates is the rarity.*

And *that* was precisely why Clare could continue to treat her abominably if it so pleased him, and why she had allowed both Ludovico's informality and his pride. It was why she allowed Severine's nervousness and Mikal's secrets and silences. It was why she had paid for Gilburn's Altered leg and retained Finch's services, why she had taken in Isobel and the half-crippled stable-boy, not to mention Cook. Those who did not play the great game of living solely for their own profit were rare and wondrous, and it pleased her to have a collection of them.

Since she was, most definitely, *not* one of their number. Yet it was through her grace and under her protection they could thrive. If one had to bloody and muck oneself in the service of Empire, or even in the business of living in such an imperfect world as this one, sheltering such castaways could take some of the sting from the wound.

"I have grown philosophical," Emma Bannon murmured, with a wry smile, for she heard Severine Noyon's step on the stairs, and further heard the housekeeper fussing at Catherine to *step lively, the mistress waits!*

She arranged her expression into one most suited to a lady's rising, and allowed herself one more luxurious stretch before pushing the covers away and sliding one small foot free of their encumbrance.

It was at that moment a curious thought struck her. She supposed, had she been Clare, it would have already done so.

*This first murder was rather sloppily performed – it was a trial. There have been other trials, no doubt; perhaps the second was as well? Impossible to know without viewing the scene. What is it Clare says – experiment requires small steps? Britannia waited for a repeat of the event before moving Victrix to my door.*

She was still abed, staring across her bedroom at the lovely blue wallpaper, when the housekeeper and lady's maids bustled in to begin their tending.

For the logical extension of her ruminations was chilling indeed.

*There is likely to be another death, and very soon.*

# ✹ *Chapter Seventeen*

---

## *Find the Limits*

Clare coughed, wrackingly, and set the knife against his forearm. He was interrupted by a sound not of his own creation, and he blinked rapidly as he watched the last shallow slice slowly congeal. The more he practised, the faster the superficial wounds seemed to seal themselves.

The ramifications were quite fascinating. What had interrupted him?

One step inside his workroom, despite the locked door – this was, to be sure, *her* house, and should she require entry into a portion of it, well, he could not grudge or gainsay her – and Emma's dark eyes widened dangerously. Of course, the blood spattering the smooth stone walls, the chaos of tools on one of the sturdy wooden tables, and the shattered glass upon the floor – he had swept a few alembics from its surface in his irritation – were not comforting in the least.

"What on earth are you *doing*?" Emma Bannon demanded, her earrings of shivering cascades of silver wire and splinters of jet trembling as she halted just over the threshold.

She was in black again today, and looked none the worse for wear. In fact, with her eyes so wide and her expression so shocked, she looked more childlike than ever.

Clare, blinking furiously through veils of acrid smoke, actually goggled at her for a few moments before finding his tongue. "Experiments! Must find the limits, you see. This is quite interesting." He waved the knife absently. "It will make shallow cuts, but no matter how I try, I cannot so much as lop a fingertip off. Controlled explosives merely toss me about a bit. This is very — "

"You've gone mad. *S – x'v!*" The collection of sounds she uttered shivered the walls, refusing to stay in Clare's memory for more than a moment. When the echoes died, he found he could not move. The knife clattered from his nerveless fingers, and she made a short, sharp gesture that gathered up the thick white and grey smoke, compressing it into an ashen sphere that bumbled over her head and drifted out of sight up the stairs, seeking a chimney. "Good heavens. *Look* at all this."

Mikal appeared behind her, one eyebrow fractionally raised. "Is that . . . what is it?"

"Dynamite." She lifted her heavy skirts, stepping briskly through the litter of glass and splinters. "Nitrou-glycerine and sawdust; it tends to be volatile. Do take care. Clare, what on *earth*?"

He could breathe well enough, but his limbs refused to budge. Invisible bands circled him, gently but firmly, and he had the sudden, quite thought-provoking realisation that she was being rather delicate with him. "Experiments," he wheezed. "Interfering . . . damn nuisance."

"Quite." She examined the walls, wrinkling her small nose. "What are you hoping to discover, sir?"

"What the . . . the limits of . . ." The words fled from him as he stared at her throat. Her pulse beat, a fraction too swiftly. "I say, you are quite agitated. And your dress is fashionable even for mourning, despite the tiny bustle, which means you did not deny what Isobel first proffered. She quite thinks you need a bit more *mode* lately, you have not been yourself. And Madame Noyon is becoming forgetful as she grows older—"

"Clare." She shook her head, the curls over her ears a bit old-fashioned, but she could simply have been a well-bred young miss with a hidebound guardian or *duenna* choosing her cloth. An observer who did not note the fact of her sorcery would perhaps draw such a conclusion. "You will refrain."

*But I do not wish to.* "I must know what the limits are. What the logical . . . what I can extrapolate . . ."

"Did it occur to you to simply *ask*?"

His reply was loosed before he considered its weight or its edge. "Would you answer honestly if I had?"

She made a small spitting noise, expressing very

unladylike irritation. Yet she did not deign to answer more fully, and Clare could hardly blame her. He strained against the invisible ropes holding him fast, and reflected that it was no wonder a woman with her abilities was held in such caution.

It was downright *unnatural* for a female to possess such power.

Miss Bannon examined the workroom once more, turning in a complete circle so as to leave nothing unseen. "You have not slept at all," she remarked.

"No." *There is too much to discern, too much to do.*

"You will likely continue in this fashion until you find some means of harming yourself."

"My dear lady, I cannot—" His struggles increased, and his voice rose. "Turn loose. I *demand* you release me, Emma."

"Have I been in any way unclear? I am *quite* unwilling to see you harmed, Archibald. I shall take steps to prevent it."

"You are not my nursemaid!" Why was he *shouting*? A mentath did not lose his temper. It was unheard of. It could not be borne.

Neither could the restraints, and she watched him curiously as he continued to writhe without moving. Could she feel it? Her expression gave no indication. It was frankly maddening to see a slip of a girl, her head cocked slightly, regard a grown man much as a child might a specimen pinned to a board.

"No. I am most definitely not your nursemaid." She nodded once, briskly, her curls swinging. "But you do need one at this juncture. And I think it best you sleep now, dear Clare."

He was about to protest even more hotly, but a rumbling passed through him. More of those damnable unremembered words, her lips shaping incomprehensible, *inhuman* sounds, and blackness swallowed him whole.

# Chapter Eighteen

## Even if I Do Not Grant

Longing thoughts of rum floated through her head. Emma pressed her fingers delicately against the bridge of her nose. "I cannot keep him in a cocoon."

"No," Mikal agreed. He was maddeningly calm, but the high colour in his lean cheeks told her it was mere seeming. "Prima . . ."

"I know. *You* cannot look after him, I need you elsewhere." She decided to overlook his very plain sigh of relief, and turned the question over in her mind again.

The workroom was a shambles. Clare was propped upright, trapped in sorcerous restraints she kept steady with threads of ætheric force trickling from the chalcedony pendant at her throat. The blood on the walls troubled her, and the wild-eyed man who had outright screamed at her troubled her even more. It was so unlike him, and doubly unlike what she knew of mentath temperament.

"Perhaps . . ." But Mikal shook his sleek, dark head as she glanced at him. Whatever idea he had, perhaps he had discovered a great many holes in it as soon as he gave it voice.

"Finch." She twitched a slender ætheric thread, and the call bloomed subtly through the house. It took less than a half-minute for the familiar light step to be heard on the stairs outside the workroom – he must have suspected she would summon him.

When he stepped through the flung-open door, his cadaverous face betrayed no surprise or irritation at all. It was a distinct relief to find him as imperturbable as ever. His indenture collar flashed once before subsiding to a steady glow.

Her sigh was only partly theatrical. "I've a bit of a quandary, Mr Finch."

"So it seems, mum." There was a hint of a curve to his thin mouth, and Emma allowed herself a rueful smile in return.

"I need a minder for Mr Clare. Someone singularly . . . *useful*. And loyal, though I shall of course require a blood-binding."

Finch absorbed this, his thin shoulders stooped. He did not immediately answer, which gave her cause for hope. Which was roundly justified when he finally nodded, slowly. Sharp as a knife when he first entered her service, he had lost none of that edge in the ensuing years. Age sometimes brought a man more fully into dangerousness, and he had experienced enough of treachery to know even its hidden faces.

He was no longer youthful-quick, but he was exceedingly *subtle*.

To prove it, he produced an impossible necessity once more. "I've a . . . cousin, mum. He might do."

"A cousin?" Her eyebrows rose dangerously high. She could hardly help herself.

"Well, after a fashion. He's, well—"

Was he *blushing*? She forged onward, twitching her skirts absently as she turned to regard the somnolent, propped-up figure of Clare. Who looked rather peaceful, d—n him, while she was required to solve this problem. "If you think he would suit, Finch, it is enough to set my mind at ease."

"He's . . . well, he's a molly, mum. If you catch my meaning."

It was a mark of her distraction that she did not take his meaning immediately. Perhaps Finch was right to blush, though he could hardly think her intolerant of such a thing, considering her acquaintance with, for example, the infamous Prime Dorian Childe, and others of his ilk. Society might very well frown upon the men of Sodom, but Emma had found no few of them bright and above all, *useful*.

If Finch recommended a certain man, it mattered not a whit what that man liked to sport with. Unless said sport could lead him to treachery, but Finch's recommendation would mitigate that danger somewhat. "I see. Well, I care little what he buggers, as long as he does his duty. Do we understand each other?"

"Yesmum." Finch bobbed his head, and she caught a slight movement – as if he would tug his forelock, as he used to before he studied a butler's manners. "I shall go myself and fetch him."

"You are a treasure, Finch. Be about your business, then." *Do hurry. There is much to be done.* She did not add the last, it was unnecessary.

"Yesmum." And he glided out the door.

"A molly?" Mikal sounded amused, at least. He could not fail to be familiar with the term.

She gathered herself, leashed her temper, and paused once more to determine what should be done and what was the most efficient way to accomplish it. "Perhaps he will feel affectionate toward Clare. Heaven knows our mentath seems to need it, and I rather think he would not receive *my* affection gratefully at the moment."

"Then he is a fool, Prima." The warmth of Mikal's tone was somewhat indecent, but they were alone. Or close to alone, as Clare was unconscious. He would rest until Tideturn, and by then she hoped to have made *some* arrangement for his comfort.

And, incidentally, for her own.

"Perhaps. But he is *our* fool." She sighed, set her shoulders, and brushed at her skirts, though there was no need to set them to rights. "I had rather hoped to view the second site today, but that is of little account. Come, help me get him to bed."

The cousin was a lean foxlike youth, a measure of rust touching his dark curls and no shame in his wide dark eyes. His cloth was indeed flash: a waistcoat very fine but the coat a trifle ill fitting, no doubt bought secondhand. His shoes were not quite fashionable but they were brushed very neatly, and the half-resentful courtesy he afforded the visibly relieved Finch was telling. A watch-chain that had certainly started life in a gentleman's pocket before being deprived of such surroundings by quick fingers, the dove-grey gloves, and the pomade in his curls all shouted *rough lad.* The only question was whether he paid for his buggering – or was paid for it.

Just where the line was drawn between an Æsthete (or Decadent, for that matter) and a slightly circumspect Merry-Ann was difficult to tell, since those who affected to live for Arte and Beauty often dressed in imitation of the panthers of St Jemes or Jermyn Street. Often in finer fabric, though the end result was the same.

He passed the first inspection, and Emma motioned them further into the room.

"Mum." Finch inclined slightly from the waist. "May I present my cousin, Mr Philip Pico?"

The drawing room was not the best setting for this lad. He belonged in one of the taverns the Merry-Anns frequented, or along the docks in the darkness wreathed by yellow greasy fog . . .

. . . or in some dark corner of Whitchapel, where the trade was less merry and far more rough. Where a gentleman might go to seek danger to spice his buggery, where the panthers, both of Sodom and murder, prowled.

"Mum." The young man made the same motion Finch almost had that morning – as if to tug his forelock. He caught himself, and offered her a very proper half-bow.

"How do you do," Emma murmured, not deigning to offer her hand, and examined him closely.

It was in the feet, she decided. Placed just so, his weight balanced nicely, one slightly forward. The fact that his shoulders were broad – though he was at pains to appear slender – was another indicator. He was not averse to violence, and he was alert.

"Your cousin has no doubt informed you of my requirements." She nodded slightly, and Finch shuffled away to the sideboard. If she found the lad did not suit, she would give him a drink and send him on his way, with a guinea or two for his trouble.

"Discretion, loyalty, efficiency, so on, so forth." He chanted it sing-song, and she almost missed the flicker of his gaze towards the door as Mikal entered, noiseless. She did not miss the sudden tension in his left hand.

*That is where the knife will be, then.* "Yes. You may be amusing, but I do not countenance impoliteness."

"Your countenance is set very politely, madam." Quick as a whip, and with a winning smile to boot.

She found herself measuring him against a Neapolitan with a sneer and dirty fingernails, and had to eye him afresh, so she would not find him wanting without reason. "I take pains to preserve it so," she replied, dryly. "You have no objection to a blood-binding?"

He paled slightly, but set his shoulders. "None at all, mum. He—" A slight tip of his head took in the attentive Finch. "—tells me you do right by those in your service, and that I'm getting too old to molly much more. The gentlemen prefer younger, even with the rough." A defiant tilt to his chin, watching to see if he could shock her.

Her estimation of his intelligence rose, even though he seemed very young indeed to her. "And just how old are you, Philip?"

"Old 'nough. I don't enjoy the molly, mum. It's just easy."

*Ah.* She allowed herself to feel cautiously hopeful. "Your enjoyment of such things, or not, holds no interest for me. I wish to know if you are capable of discharging the duties of a minder for my mentath. He requires a companion of a certain . . . durability, discretion, and capability to deal with Londinium's nastier areas. *I* require that you keep his skin whole and your mouth closed on the subject his affairs, and my own, to anyone outside this room. Mr Finch has no doubt negotiated your wages, should you be accepted for the position, and has also given you to understand certain . . . peculiarities . . . of said position."

He waited. Mute and stubborn, giving nothing away.

*Very good.* "Mikal?"

The Shield was suddenly across the room, locking the

young man's wrist and striking the knife from his grasp. Finch did not move, a curious expression – part distaste, part amusement – flickering over his graven features. The youth actually almost managed to strike Mikal once, but the Shield finished by holding him by his scruff and shaking lightly, before dropping him to hands and knees and stalking away.

Her Shield retook his place by the door. "Amateur."

Which was high praise indeed, coming from a fully trained Shield. At least he hadn't said *useless*.

Emma found herself suddenly weary, and a sour taste had crept into her mouth. "Very well. You shall do, Mr Philip Pico. Do you wish the hire?"

The youth looked up. With his curls tumbled and high colour in his shaven cheeks, his true age was a little more visible. Yes, he was rather a shade too old for mollying to gentlemen, and a swift pang passed through her. Mikal must be out of sorts, to embarrass the lad so.

He climbed swiftly to his feet, scooping up the knife and slipping it back into its hiding-place behind his left hip. "One condition."

*After that display, I suppose you might be allowed to ask, even if I do not grant.* "Which is?"

He pointed at Mikal. "He's a fair boxer. He teaches me that. I'll not shirk, I'll not talk, and I'll keep your mentath safe as a babe in cradle."

She found herself smiling, and Finch's relief visibly mounted. Of course, she supposed he had to have been very sure of the boy to bring him, and who knew what their true relationship was? "Cousin" was as good a word as any, and it mattered little, if the youth was dependable.

"I think that is quite possible, and even acceptable, though Mikal is a much harsher taskmaster than myself. As long as his tutelage does not distract from your other duties, you shall do very nicely, Philip. While Finch arranges for your effects to be brought, we shall settle you in a room and you shall see your charge immediately." *Clare will not like this. But I cannot watch him day and night, and this young enigma will at least keep him occupied while I seek to discern what nastiness is afoot.*

"Yesmum." Pico bent to retrieve his hat, as well, and darted a venomous look past her, at Mikal. Who would, of course, be entirely unaffected.

The little molly seemed to completely discount her as a threat.

Which was very much how Emma preferred it at the moment. She nodded once again, more to herself than to any man present. "Very well."

#  *Chapter Nineteen*

## *Like a Weathervane*

Archibald Clare woke from a sound, sorcery-induced sleep and sat straight up in the bed's familiar embrace. "Who the devil are you?"

The young man in the high-backed chair cocked his head. "Shh. Listen."

*What now?* He opened his mouth to take this stranger to task, before he noted that the youth's shirt and waistcoat were tailored with familiar, tiny stitches – Catherine's work, beyond a doubt – and the way his hair was plastered down bespoke a good scrubbing. Whoever he was, he had the blessing of the mistress of the house, and had been given attention so his clothing did not offend her sensibilities. His boots were well brushed and sturdy, but their age shouted quite plainly that they were his own, instead of Miss Bannon's largesse.

"Tideturn," the young man breathed, and the vowels placed him as one of Londinium's native sons, born within a few yards of Lincoln Inn unless Clare missed his guess. Or perhaps he had merely been a child in such a place, for Clare's sensitive nose caught traces of . . . pomade? And ash, and old blood.

*What on earth can this be?* "Does she think . . . ?" Words failed him.

The youth gave him a scorching, contemptuous look – and the entire house, from cellar Clare had never seen to whatever attic Miss Bannon saw fit to keep under its trim roof, shook like the coat of a dog shedding itself of water.

Clare did not halt to consider the fascinating conundrum of the lad at his bedside. Instead, he scrambled from the covers, hopping as he found he was barefoot on cold wooden flooring, and hurled himself for the door.

It was not locked, which was a mercy, for he would have bruised himself on its heavy wooden carapace had it been. He scrambled up the corridor, booted steps behind him too heavy to be Valentinelli's, the stairs at the end of the hall heaved, creaking and crackling. Screams came from the depths – the servants, of course – and there was a single hissing curse as he slipped.

The youth's fingers clamped around his upper arm like a vice, and he was hauled to his feet as the house shook again. Up the stairs, the other familiar hall shuddering as its very walls warped.

*What is she* doing?

Her dressing-room door ran with foxfire light, leprous

green, and for a moment Clare was caught in a net of memory: Emma Bannon dying of the Red Plague and his own monstrous, helpless uselessness in the face of that event. But then it had only been the lights dimming and the sobbing of the maids—

A blow, and he was spinning. His elbow hit the hall floor, but he was on his feet again and striking with a bladed hand, just as Ludo had taught him, *strike for throat*, mentale, *if a man no breathe, he no trouble you*—

"*Stop!*" Mikal hissed, and bent back with impossible grace, out of the path of Clare's strike. His fingers clamped Clare's wrist and he twisted, one foot flicking out to double the youth, who was hard on Clare's heels. A chiming clatter – *someone has a knife* – then a keening scream rose behind Miss Bannon's dressing-room door, turning the air frigid and shivering. Clare's breath became a white cloud as he fell once more, twisting to lash out at the Shield's legs with his own. It was an instinctive move, which somehow Mikal evaded as a final grating shock ran through the house, wood groaning and plaster cracking, the floor rippling in incomprehensible, *impossible* ways.

The Shield did not fall. Instead, he leapt backward, fishlike, his own bare feet thudding on the heaving boards. He flung himself at the dressing-room door, carried it down in a tide of exploding shards and splinters. He was gone into the darkness then, and the house settled against itself with an audible *thump*.

"*Pax!*" Mikal screamed, beyond the door. "*Pax, Prima! Emma! Emmaaaaaa!*"

Clare pushed himself up, staggered after him.

Miss Bannon's dressing room was pale-carpeted, strewn with broken wood, and he thought, quite calmly, that she was going to be extremely put out by the mess.

The youth caught at his arm, but Clare evaded him easily enough. There was a very real danger of skewering his feet; when he reached Miss Bannon's bedroom door he was gratified that he had not done so. "Emma?" he called tentatively, into the dimness. It smelled, power-fully, of a foreign, feminine country – perfume, and long hair, and silk. The rustle of dresses and the slightly oily healthiness of a dark-haired woman, the smoky overlay of sorcery, pear-spiced perfume, and a hint of rosewater from her morning ablutions. The impressions whirled through him and away, and he had stepped over the threshold before he knew it, blindly. "Emma, please, say something."

"Clare?" She sounded very young, and breathless. "And . . . Mikal." A huskiness – of course, that throat-scouring scream. Was it merely a nightmare?

Somehow, no matter how given the fairer sex was to vapours, he did not think so.

"Here." The Shield sounded even more sober than usual. "What is it?"

"I am not dead." Wondering, a half-disbelieving laugh. "I . . . Mikal. Clare."

"Yes." Mikal's eyes were a yellow glimmer; Clare's adapted to the darkness. He saw Miss Bannon's bed, the dressing table and its beautifully clear oval mirror, the bulk of an armoire, other shapes he could not quite infer just yet. Mikal's glare was a pair of yellow lamps in the dimness. "Come no closer, sir."

"Mikal." She sounded much more like herself now. "Do *not* be impolite. I am well enough. It was . . . simply a shock. Clare, have you been introduced to—"

"—the young man who was at my bedside? Quite an odd choice for a nanny, madam."

"I suppose I am to let you lock yourself in the workroom and attempt to bring down my house with explosives?" Did she sound irritated? It was, he decided, a very good sign. "Yes, Mr Clare. That sounds *ever so helpful*. Kindly remove yourself from my bedroom, sir, I have little time to quarrel with you."

"You do not need explosives to level your domicile, Miss Bannon. Which is why I am here."

"The damage is temporary. *Get out*. No—" This was no doubt directed at Mikal, for there was a flicker of movement in the darkness near her bed. Light glinting from metal, and Clare's skin chilled. "Mikal. Absolutely *not*."

"Little thief," the Shield said, softly. "Come closer, and lose a limb."

"Just looking after me investment, squire," came the cheeky reply – from right next to Clare, and he was hard-pressed to suppress a start. *How very curious.*

"Investment?" he enquired, blithely. "Did you think to replace Ludovico, Miss Bannon?"

"No." Sharp and curt, material sliding, and a bloom of silvery light from the sconces near the door. A globe of malachite on her bedside table, next to a stack of novels – her taste in bed-reading was shockingly salacious, really – made a soft slithering sound as it turned in its stand, and a shiver ran through the house again. "I thought to ensure your safety, sir. A rather onerous duty, but one I have undertaken. Now leave me in peace, I must dress."

She inhaled sharply, and Clare was confronted with the exotic sight of Miss Bannon shrugging herself into a wine-red dressing gown over her nightgown, lace and satin scratching against plain, high-necked white linen. Her small, well-formed feet were bare as his and Mikal's, and her unbound hair was a river down her back. With her tumbled curls and the high colour in her cheeks, she looked every inch a child up too late on a holiday night. "Mikal, send Severine up and rouse Harthell, have the carriage prepared. We are bound for Whitchapel." She strode for her dressing table, sliding past the Shield with a determined air.

"Whitchapel?" *How extraordinary.* Clare's rebellious faculties strained, turning sharply in a most unwelcome direction. "There has been another murder." *And you have sensed it in some sorcerous fashion. Very extraordinary indeed.*

She glanced over her shoulder, and he stepped back, almost into the nameless youth, who was observing this scene with a great deal of interest. "Yes. There has. And I must go."

\* \* \*

"Philip Pico." The youth offered his hand, a firm shake, and settled into the carriage's upholstery just where Ludovico had been wont to sit.

Clare suppressed a protest. It was illogical; the seat was there, he had to sit *somewhere*, and—

"Absolutely not," Miss Bannon said. Her mourning today was wool, and her hair was in place again. There was no trace of the dishevelled, just-wakened child she had appeared, except for a slight puffiness about her eyes. "Archibald, I do not have *time—*"

"You – and *she* – asked for my aid in untangling this affair." He quite enjoyed her discomfiture. "Which I am determined to provide. And this young man, no replacement for our dear Valentinelli indeed, is nevertheless bound to be quite handy."

The door slammed, Harthell cracked the whip and the carriage jolted into motion.

Miss Bannon closed her eyes, the cameo at her throat flashing once. It was a familiar sight, and he knew a silvery ball of strange witchlight would now coalesce before the gleaming clockhorses, directing the coachman to whatever incident had drawn his mistress's attention – and telling the rest of Londinium a sorcerer was impatient with delay.

So much irrationality he had learned to live with as merely part of his acquaintance with this most *logical* of sorceresses. Had he not often thought that if only all practitioners of the arts of æther were as practical as she, mentaths would have little difficulty with their number?

Now he cast a fresh eye upon her as the carriage jolted, and found she was pale, her veil tucked aside, her gloved fingers entirely too tense, and her chin set.

She met his gaze directly. How had he never noticed before that her manner was of a man facing a duel? So much of Miss Bannon only made sense if one ceased to think of her as a proper woman.

And yet. Her little attentions, her gracefulness, her arranging of matters to suit those about her, her collection of castaway servants – none of those graces bore a masculine stamp.

The woman in question remained silent, still gazing at him with that odd expression. As if she expected trouble from his quarter, and soon.

He drummed his fingers upon his knee. It was past baker's-morn but still grey-dark, Londinium's yellow fog choke-wreathing wrought-iron lamps both sputtering with gasflame and, in the better quarters, held to steadier life by carefully applied wick-charms. Hooves sounded and carriage wheels thrummed, even at this hour. The city did not sleep, and a vision of it as a gigantic coal-fed, sorcery-stroked beast had no room in a mentath's logic-ordered brain.

Still, even mentaths had passing fancies. He leaned forward slightly. "Are you . . . are you quite well, Miss Bannon?"

"I was a-study all afternoon, seeking to discern a clew, ætheric or not, to the identity of our killer, and had absolutely *no* success. I did not wish to view the site of the second murder after a day spent so unprofitably, so I retired."

She took a deep breath. "Then I felt a woman die within my own *corpus*, sir. I am a trifle unsettled." She did not look it. "And do forgive my manners. Mr Clare, meet Philip Pico; he is a cousin to Mr Finch and I have engaged him to perform a valet's duty for you, as well as other small tasks you may require of him. Philip, this is your charge, Mr Archibald Clare. Esquire, I believe. *Do* behave appropriately."

"'Ave no fear, mum." The youth gave her a toothy grin, and stretched his legs out most disagreeably in the carriage's close confines.

Clare suppressed the urge to poke the lad in the ribs. Such uncharitable Feeling could not be tolerated. He told himself firmly not to mind its prodding. "You are not in a tavern, sir."

"No, there'd be drink if I were." A twist of a half-grin, and the attention he paid to paring his fingernails impinged on Clare's consciousness like a silent thunderbolt.

A quite extraordinary further deduction occurred to Clare. He tested it thoroughly, and found it not wanting at all. *A Sodom boy? In Miss Bannon's employ?* "Your taste in domestics, as usual, is most curious."

"So I am told." She tilted her head, slightly, perhaps listening to some sorcerous noise. "Now do be quiet, if you can. I am rather occupied."

Nettled, he sank back into the seat and felt a most uncharacteristic desire to curse, roundly and loudly. This was the deadliness of Feeling: it swung one about like a weathervane, and made Reason so very difficult.

*I was merely seeking to find the limits of this extraordinary thing you have inflicted on me, Emma.* But he realised, as Harthell cracked his whip and Miss Bannon's paleness took on another, more worrisome cast, that was not quite accurate.

He had, for a short while, lost his bloody mind. The longer this state of affairs endured, the more likely it was he would do so again. Unless he found some method of making rational the fact of his unwanted, unwholesome . . .

. . . and, likely to be very *useful*, immortality.

# Chapter Twenty

## *Founded Upon Much Less*

Emma freed her hand from Mikal's and took in the grey light of predawn, the fog sallow and the Scab underfoot slippery enough that she had to take care with her balance.

"What the *devil* are you about here?"

It was a greeting from a direction she would *not* have preferred, but at least the hailer's presence would solve a number of problems. She used her sweetest smile. "Mr Aberline. My, you've grown."

Frederick had thickened since she last saw him, and acquired a very fine moustache and side-whiskers. At the moment he was scowling, and it did not improve his knife-beak of a nose *or* his slightly choleric cast. He had been a very promising lad, a watchmaker's son who rose through the ranks of the Metropoleans by dint of ability and persistence.

It must be something extraordinary to set him a-glower, for normally he was rather . . . sedate. Many of his suspects had learned too late that his solicitor's mien did not make him stupid *or* placid.

And many of his quarries, in his younger days, had learned that a broken head in the service of Justice did not trouble Aberline overmuch. He was rightly feared among the more intelligent flashboys in Londinium's seamier quarters.

"Is it . . . Bannon? Yes. A pleasure." But his mouth turned down, and she rather thought not. "How's our lad Geoffrey?"

"Mr Finch is still in my employ, sir." *If that changes, he will be in another country before* you *get wind of it.* "How is your wife?" *I seem to recall she was perennially sickly.*

"Which one? And, Miss Bannon, what is the occasion that honours us with your presence here?" His sharp gaze drifted over her shoulder, took in Pico and Clare just alighting from the carriage, and he looked even more unhappy – if that were possible. "Sightseeing on the Scab's not for gentlefolk this morning."

*As if you think me an excitement-seeker. How very insulting.* She had never given him reason to think his attempts to be offensive were even noticed, and she saw no need to alter her course now. "The gentle are no doubt still abed. We are left to our own devices in this affair."

"I should have known," he muttered. "He said someone else from the Crown would be along."

Now *that* was interesting. "Who?"

"Oh, Gull. He's become Her Majesty's hangman now, like Conroy was her mother's, God rest that poor woman's soul."

He jammed his bowler hat more firmly atop his dark, slicked-down hair, and she saw, even in the dimness, grey beginning at his temples. His boots splorched and slid through the Scab crusting the cobbles, and she did not have to glance about to know she was upon Hanbury Street.

The smell alone would have told her so, and she wondered if Peggy Razor still door-watched a dosshouse a few doors up; if Trout Jack still ran the child-thieves in this slice of Whitchapel; if the Scab still made fine delicate whorls up every wooden wall before sunlight scorched it away, leaving a filigree of caustic char . . .

*Gull.* Her well-trained memory returned a face to go with the name. Physicker to the Queen, and a singularly bloodless and dedicated man. Rumour had him as one who had always wished he were among sorcery's children, but *educated* rumour simply said he liked a bit of secrecy, and so had joined a certain "Brotherhood of Stone". They played at Ritual and Initiation, with a certain degree of ridiculousness, and, like any gentlemen's club, membership was skewed toward the wealthy, or those who wished influence.

Nothing about said brotherhood interested Emma over-much, but if there was gossip linking Gull and Victrix as her mother and Conroy had been linked, it was a trifle worrisome.

She set the consideration aside; Victrix's troubles, except

in this one small matter, were no longer hers. This affair was to be laid to rest quickly, so she could return to her studies and other concerns.

Chief among those concerns was Clare, who sniffed the soup passing for air in Whitchapel with bright interest. He glanced down, toyed with the Scab's green organic sludge with one boot-toe, and nodded slightly. "Most interesting."

*Would you find it so, if you saw what it does to bodies? Or to rats, on particularly active nights?* Emma turned back to Aberline. "I am gratified to find my coming was foretold," she remarked, drily. "There is a body, sir."

"Yes." The inspector – because he was no doubt one of that august brotherhood now, being neither encased in a bobby's blue cloth nor bearing the ubiquitous whistle – furrowed his brow mightily as he took in the mentath. "There is quite a crowd already—"

"Be a dear and clear them away, so we may examine the premises." She put on her most winning smile again, and saw his flinch with a great deal of satisfaction. "My companion is a mentath, and quite useful. As you shall no doubt be. The Yard's taking an active interest in this?" *Not just at the Queen's bidding, if you are here.*

"Third's a charm. This will be in the broadsheets and dreadfuls before long." The man's face was positively mournful. "I don't suppose you could . . ."

"Mitigate somewhat?" Her sigh took her by surprise, and Mikal's comforting warmth at her shoulder was the only thing on Hanbury Street that did not appear worrisome. "My days of mitigation are somewhat past, Inspector. But I shall do what I can." *Mostly to suit myself, for I do not wish to be bruited about in print.*

"Well, good. Come along then." He did not further insult her, which was a very good sign – or a very bad one. He halted, and she noted the breadth of his shoulders under his jacket. Inspector Aberline had not let the iron go cold, as the saying went. "I don't suppose this is merely a social visit?"

*From me? Now there is an amusing thought.* "Of course not, sir. I shall, however, see whatever unpleasantness this is to its conclusion, and as quickly as possible."

"Good. Because the Eastron End's about to explode."

*Is this a new state of affairs?* "Is that so?"

"Foreigners." His lip actually twisted. He moved through the Scab with a distinctive sliding step. You could always tell Whitchapel flashboys and the like from that step, rolling and settling the weight only after they were sure something under the thick, resilient slime wasn't going to shift. "Have you still a strong stomach, Miss Bannon?"

"You ask *me*?" She shook her head, glad Mikal was following step for step. He had not the trick of moving in the Scab's deep cover, and she could actually *hear* him.

Her skirts dragged in the caustic sludge, and she let them. Scab would eat at the fabric, but there was no use in holding them high; she might need her hands. No doubt this affair would ruin a frock or two by the end. *You can tell a Whitchapel drab by her ankles,* the saying went. Or, if you were raised in the argot, *A nav'Whit slit shews gam, sh'doon.*

She might have let herself consider sending the Crown a bill for whatever cloth was ruined before said end. While amusing, it did not have the savour such thoughts usually did.

Aberline was speaking again. "We've mancers now. At the Yard, and in the station houses." He did not sound pleased by the notion. "I doubt any of them would want to see *this*."

*And you sensitive to sorcery, but unable to hold a charter symbol in free air. How that must grate upon your pride.* "Indeed."

She followed him to a dark cleft, a passage leading to the back of the building. Mikal's attention sharpened. The Scab became much thicker, giving reluctantly under her heeled boots and still coating the cobbles at the bottom of every step. Her ankles ached – she had not lost the trick of easing through the mire, but her legs had grown unused to it. Her skin chilled, remembering slipping barefoot and bare-legged through the sludge, dodging cuffs and curses, a stolen apple clutched to her flat child's chest.

Clare's voice, indistinct behind her. Philip Pico's murmured reply. And Mikal's hand at her shoulder, fingers slightly digging in as if he felt her . . . uncertainty?

The passageway ended, and Aberline pointed. He needn't have, for Emma could feel the plucking in the æther all along her body, down into her core. There was no question it was a corpse, and not a drunkard in stupor-sleep.

"No name yet." Aberline's expression was set. He pointed to the far end of the yard. "There is the Yudic

Workingman's Club, though. Which will no doubt prove a deadly coincidence."

"Yudic?" The ætheric disturbance pulsed as if sensing her nearness. *Twice now he's mentioned the Foreigners.*

"Coming from the east and taking jobs from poor honest Englene, the story goes. And socialist to boot. Bloody anarchists. The End's full of them, and trouble every time one's accused of anything from following a pretty girl to murdering a thief." He shook his head. "Now this."

"Has it truly grown so dire?" *Well, of course. Why else would a full-blown detective inspector from the hallowed Yard be here at this hour?* "Yes. I see. Three corpses and a workingman's club – there have been unwholesome incidents founded upon much less."

"Examiner's been sent for. I hope you've some idea of what to do, Bannon. Can we move the body?"

*I have no desire to endure another vision of murder.* "It should be safe enough." *The Tebrem woman's corpse was moved, after all.* She stared at the mangled corpse, took two steps past the inspector and examined it more thoroughly. Yes, there was the head turned to the side, the ripping-open of the abdomen, entrails flung over the unfortunate's shoulder. Thick legs in striped stockings, the legs obscenely splayed. Two dull farthings lay on a blood-soaked handkerchief by her curled right hand, and her pocket had been slit. The throat was cut, and there was a quantity of blood . . .

. . . but not nearly enough.

She decided it was perhaps time to remind the detective

inspector just who held the whip hand in this particular situation. "Curious," she murmured, and heard Philip Pico's sharp, indrawn breath as he caught sight of the body. "Tell me, Inspector, do you still have dreams?"

He was silent for a long moment. Finally, he shook out his left hand, which had tightened into a fist. "Curse you." Softly, conversationally. "Bloody sorceress."

*Yes. And you have, though not in the way you might think. I merely need to remind you to mind your duty, and your place.* "Indeed. Tell me something else, Inspector. Where did the blood *go*?"

"I know where some went. See that?" He pointed, and she stared for a few moments. Even with her sensitive eyes, it took time for what she saw to become comprehensible.

"Leather. Cobbler's apron?"

"Or slaughterer's. Could have been there already. Soaked in the claret, Bannon, though still not enough. And you don't need to be a mancer to know something's amiss here. Look." He jabbed two fingers at the shimmering over the corpse. It was akin to the heat-haze over a fire, or a slate roof on a hot day. "And underneath."

"Yes." Under the body, the Scab's venomous green had been scorched. *Where blood falls, the Scab greens*, that was the proverb. Here, the blood – or something else – had burned down to ancient, slime-scarred cobbles and blackened, sour dirt that hadn't seen free air in longer than Emma had been alive. "Yet she was not murdered elsewhere."

"I'd ask how you know that."

"And I would tell you I know, and that is enough."

"Bloody sorceress." No heat to it, he merely sounded weary. He scrubbed one flat-bladed hand over his face, precisely once, a familiar mannerism. "I happen to think you're right."

#  Chapter Twenty-One

##  Answers in Other Quarters

The poor woman had perhaps never been as much a subject of attention in life as she was now. The surgeon – a round, jolly little physicker in a dark suit, his hands quick and deft as he performed incisions – muttered to a thin boy in a transcriber's gown, while behind them a sour-faced barrowmancer tended to a charm-heated bowl of pitch, eyeing the body warily as if he expected it to perform some feat.

Which was much the way Miss Bannon regarded said corpse, too, when she glanced at it at all. Most of her attention seemed taken by rumination; certainly there was much in this turn of events to cogitate upon.

It was not like her to seem so . . . distracted, though.

The dank little stone room in this morguelrat warren was noisome enough, but it was also crowded. Clare stood at the periphery of a group clustered near the door, comprised of Miss Bannon, the ever-present Shield, the lad Pico, and the stout detective inspector who addressed Miss Bannon with quite amazing familiarity. The hall outside was packed as well, for the murder had attracted no little attention, and the broadsheets were already crying out its details. A small army of scruffy newsboys were having a fine time selling the sheets as quickly as they could be printed.

Clare leaned a little closer, using his height to advantage as he peered over the examiner's shoulder. "Most curious," he said. "The viscera . . . where has the uterus gone?"

"Don't know," Physicker Bagswell said, cheerily, hunched over the scarred granite slab. "There's a rumour some scraper in Stepney is paying in guineas for them. The ovaries are missing too. Look there, a very sharp blade."

"Yes, and handled with some skill." Clare did not hold a handkerchief to his sensitive nose, but he was tempted indeed. "Scraping the underside of the diaphragm, even. And the kidneys . . ."

"The Tebrem woman." Aberline aimed the words in Miss Bannon's general direction, though his posture shouted that he would rather not speak to her. "And Nickol. Yes, the similarities are striking. Both did work as . . . well, unfortunates. This one, no doubt, did too."

"I know a frail when I see one, sir." Miss Bannon's tone held a great deal of asperity. "Yet this one's farthings were left upon her corpse. *Most* troubling."

"When *you* say such a thing, it fills me with dread." The

inspector sighed, his breath making a cloud. It was unhealthily damp here, and the coolness no doubt kept the bodies from becoming *too* fragrant. Still, it was nasty enough. The victim's entrails – what was left of them – were in a bucket, sending up a stink of their own, and her slack face was nowhere near as peaceful as those who called Death a tranquil state would credit.

"Her fingers are abraded." Clare pointed. "I wonder . . ."

"Rings? And look there, the nicks in the cervical vertebrae." Bagswell tutted over the the steady dripping from the slab into the drain, its black eye exhaling its own foulness up through rusty metal grating. "Note that, Edric."

"Yes, sir." The boy was slated to become a physicker himself, and was remarkably unmoved by the spectacle. "Shall I list them separately?"

"Do, please. There are three. Take care with the locations, sketch if you must. Hm."

"Right-handed," Clare prompted. "And her throat slashed from behind. Now why would that be?"

"She would face the wall and raise her skirts." Miss Bannon, archly. "Much easier than couching upon cold ground."

"Must you?" The inspector was crimson.

Clare noted this, turned his attention back to the body.

"You would prefer me not to speak of something so indelicate?" Her tone could best be described as *icy*. "My mentath works best when given what information is necessary, clearly and dispassionately. Now, you mentioned another attack? Before Tebrem?"

"Might not be related. Name of Woad, seamstress and occasional frail. She was assaulted, said it was two men with no faces, or a single man with no face."

"*Really.*" Bagswell found this most interesting. He turned, his arms splattered elbow-deep with gore. "I saw the body. Collapsed in the workhouse, ruptured perineum. Infection. Faceless, she said?"

Aberline's expression could not sour further. "Quite insistent upon that point."

Clare glanced at Miss Bannon, who had gone deathly pale. He doubted it was the setting, for she had gazed upon much more unsettling *tableaux* with complete calm on more than one previous occasion. *Interesting.* Again, he filed the observation away, returned his attention to the body. "Half the liver missing. No doubt an error."

"Do you think so? He has some skill—"

Clare pointed. "Oh yes, but look there, and there. The marks are quite clear. He was aiming otherwise and slipped."

"Detective Inspector." Miss Bannon had evidently heard enough. "I require you to shepherd Mr Clare to the Yard, and give him every answer he seeks, access to *anything* he might require."

"McNaughton's not going to be fond of this," Aberline muttered, darkly. "Nor will Swanley. *Or* Waring."

"That is beyond my control. You shall give them to understand the Crown's wishes in this matter. I am bound to seek answers in other quarters. Pico? You know your duty."

"Yesmum." The lad had sobered immensely, which was a relief.

"Mr Clare? Try to be home for dinner, and *try* not to experiment too rashly." She smoothed her gloves, and her quick fingers were at her veil fastening. "I shall leave you the carriage and Harthell. Mikal, fetch a hansom."

"Bannon—" Clare had to tear his attention from the body before him. "I say, I rather think—"

"Archibald. Please."

*You misunderstand me. I suppose it cannot be helped, now.* "Oh, certainly. I simply wish to remind you to . . . to take care."

"As much as I am able. Good day, gentlemen." And she was gone, the crowd in the passageway no doubt drawing back from Mikal's set grimace preceding her slight, black-clad form. Did they think her a relation of the deceased? Who knew?

"You might as well tell a viper to take care where it stings," the inspector muttered, his face set sourly.

Clare cleared his throat. "I shall thank you, sir, to speak no ill of that lady." *How odd. Only I may do so? To her face, no less.*

Thankfully, the man did not reply, and Clare turned back to the body and the physicker, who had watched this with bright interest.

The barrowmancer crossed his arms, as if he had felt a chill.

Perhaps he had.

\* \* \*

The detective inspector was an interesting case. A proud nose and side-whiskers that did not disguise the childish attractiveness he must have once possessed, but purple shadows bloomed under his sharp dark eyes. His distinctive sliding step would have told Clare he was accustomed to the Scab's fascinating resilience underfoot, even if the fraying along his trouser-cuffs hadn't. Aberline moved with precision and economy, though he took care to appear more a clerk than one of Commissioner Waring's boot-leather bulldogs.

Added to his familiarity in addressing Miss Bannon, and the evident caution he held her in, as well as the fact that he was rather young to have achieved such an exalted rank as detective inspector . . . well. It bespoke some manner of *history*, and would have served to keep Clare's faculties most admirably occupied, if they had not been so already.

Now Aberline looked rather mournful, planting his feet and staring at the flayed, opened body. "Throat cut from behind, right-handed, and then he gutted her."

Clare's collar was uncomfortably tight. He made no move to loosen it. "Could sorcery account for the vanished blood?"

"Oh, aye, it could. *She* said as much. And she's never about but there's nasty work going." He sighed heavily, from the very soles of his sturdy, Scab-scarred shoes. "Whitchapel's in a fine stew. We'll be lucky to avoid more unpleasantness."

"So I overheard." Clare's brow knitted itself rather

fiercely. Something teased at the edge of his deductions, a nagging thought that would not *quite* coalesce. "We shall do our best. Those are her effects? I wonder . . . why take the rings and leave the coin?"

Aberline nodded. His nose was reddened from the chill. "I've seen men murdered for less, and women too."

The examiner let out a gusty breath of disgust. "He needn't have hurried her along. Lungs, heart, all raddled like the rest of her. Prime example of drink and dissolution."

"The question becomes, why *her*?"

"There are thousands of unfortunates prowling the End, sir." Aberline's mouth was a grim line, only opening barely enough to spit the words free. "Perhaps she was merely unlucky."

*I am not so certain*. What in this unfortunate – or in the other members of Londinium's almost-lowest dregs – would have concerned Queen Victrix so? And the organs of generation removed with a very sharp knife. It was unthinkably crude. "Perhaps. Poor thing."

Aberline's eyebrows rather nested under his bowler-brim at that, for Clare had uttered the words softly. A mentath generally did not speak so.

"Well. Gentlemen, should I stitch the bag up?" The physicker's good humour was almost shocking, but Clare took a renewed grasp upon himself. "Or is there more to be seen?"

Aberline's expression grew even more troubled, if such a thing were possible. "Can you tell if she had, ah, *relations*? Before, ahem, the event?"

"Well, that's rather a curious thing." The doctor scratched his cheek, leaving a trace of gore in his whiskers. "What little remains of her organs of generation seems . . . scorched."

Clare blinked, and leaned closer. "Yes, indeed. How very curious. It seems to follow the blood channels and nerves."

The barrowmancer coughed, nervously. Clare's attention fastened on him. "Well?"

"Nothing, sir." But the man was much paler than he had been when Clare had arrived. "Just . . . well, sorcery follows blood and nerve, mostly. But to sear it . . . nasty stuff, that is. Especially *there*."

"Miss Bannon shall be informed." Clare nodded. "Very well, then. Detective Inspector, I believe we are to endure each other's company for some little while longer."

# Chapter Twenty-Two

## Such Guile to Make Headway

The hansom rattled along, and Emma's chin dipped as her attention turned inward.

Outside the carriage's shell, Londinium seethed, and she felt the drag of the Scab along the wheels lessen. Passing out of Whitchapel might improve her mood, but she rather doubted it.

In any case, the hansom was merely a gesture to misdirect a pursuer, albeit an exceedingly lazy one. Still, it was a matter of habit not to approach some things too directly.

Also, it gave her a small increment of badly needed time to think.

The bodies bore the marks of the blackest of sorcery – not of Emma's Discipline, thank the heavens, but the marks of ætheric force harnessed to an intent so foul even those of the Endor would fain avoid it. The only major

Discipline deeper of the Black than Emma's own was the Diabolic itself, but this held no smoky, addicting incense-ghost of *that* art.

Those of the Endor had once been murdered as soon as certain . . . disturbing signs . . . were noticed during their schooling. Those of the Diabolic still were. Not in civilised Englene, of course, but elsewhere. Especially where the Papists still held sway. Any of sorcery's children unfortunate enough to have a Discipline darker than Diabolic most often became a malformed monstrosity, ending their short lives dead in the womb. At least, that was the current understanding. She could safely rule out such a hapless monstrosity, and likely rule out the Diabolic as well.

And yet. The bodies were merely instruments; it was the *locations* that showed deeper marks. *The taproot of Our power*, Britannia had said.

Which seemed to imply that the power of a ruling spirit was a force that renewed itself, as Tideturn's flow filled sorcery's Englene children twice a day. Or was it otherwise, and the draining Britannia was experiencing more . . . permanent? Was it a longed-for result, or merely a symptom?

*I do not know nearly enough.* Frustration boiled inside her; the rock in her throat refused to be dislodged. And there was the unwelcome chain of thoughts again, rising inside her skull's few inches of private space.

Had Clare expected her to let him die of the plague? What had he expected her to do to ensure Ludovico's survival? Did he think she would wrench the Stone from her mentath and return him to fragility?

For good or for ill, she had chosen Clare. At that moment he had been the one in direst need. Had he not been . . . would she have married her conscience-heavy burden with Ludovico's flesh?

*Another question I do not require an answer for at this moment. Or that I will not answer, even to myself.*

The driver *huphup*ed to his clockhorse, and she took stock of her surroundings. She had precious little time before she alighted and Mikal appeared again.

*The bodies are torn; the womb is the locus. A root is driven down in the location; it is a matrix . . . A root, more likely. Into what? How does it echo with Britannia? Can it be Sympathy? How to target it so effectively, though . . . it makes little* sense.

Of course, Clare would likely chide her for assuming it was so, and Britannia's weakness simply incidental. What proof did she have otherwise?

Britannia's word. Besides, the need would have to be pressing indeed for Victrix to come to Emma's door alone, and lower herself by asking, instead of merely commanding, a sorceress's aid.

It was small comfort that perhaps even Britannia thought Emma Bannon unlikely to simply *obey*.

Clare, now there was another worry to be had – that Pico would not be able to effectively restrain him from descending into another fit. It was all she could do, barring keeping watch on the mentath herself. Finch was reliable, and there was the blood-binding as well – which she had performed on an unconscious mentath, and not spoken of.

Clare would no doubt be quite put out by that, too. When he realised she had done so, or when he questioned Pico closely on the matter, or . . .

The driver chirruped, and the hansom jolted again, slowing. Her moments of precious peace were disappearing. Continuing on too scattered to even *think* properly, she told herself sternly, would only result in more deaths.

*Will it? Unfortunates die every night in Londinium. If their deaths weaken Britannia . . . is that acceptable?*

The woman she had been before the Red Plague exploded into the world would have retreated from such a thought, shelving it as absurd. Now she considered, quite calmly, something absolutely treasonous, as well as repugnant.

Clare assumed she would throw herself upon this mystery and seek a solution as a matter of course.

There was also the little matter of the most recent murder intruding upon her in a most rude fashion. She was sensitised to whatever Work was being performed now, due to her tampering with the site of Tebrem's misfortune. Which could have unpleasant symptoms – yet the work she had done yesterday in her study should have insulated her from such effects.

Obviously, it had failed to do so properly.

The hansom halted. A bare few moments later, the door was released and Mikal's hand was as steady as ever as she alighted. The driver, well satisfied with an easy fare, tipped his hat and was off with a clatter and a crack.

Londinium's soup-thick fog, lit with morning sun to a nauseous glow, walled a busy street-corner, shapes moving in its depths. Mikal did not let go, and she was forced to look up at her Shield.

A Prime normally kept a half-dozen of the brotherhood in service, for physical defence and as a guard against an overflow of ætheric force. There were also other . . . uses . . . for them, quite obviously. She had not seen the need for more than Mikal in a very long while. And Eli—

*Do not think upon that. The dead shall wait; we are concerned with the living at the moment.*

Mikal waited. Of course he would betray no sign of impatience.

The fog was choking-close this morning. For all the sound of traffic, they might have been alone, just outside the north-eastron edge of the Scab's furthest creep. Pedestrians hurried by, almost faceless, for Mikal had drawn her aside, the brick wall next to her scarred and pitted with age.

For a moment, his face was a stranger's, too. Emma gave herself a severe mental shake. "Mikal."

"Prima."

"We are bound for Bucksrow." *I might as well tell you.*

"Just inside Whitchapel again." He nodded. "The site of the second murder?"

"Yes. I wished no witnesses."

He nodded, but still paused, in case she wished to add anything further.

*What did you do, Mikal, when I lay dying? Clare said you performed a wonder. I survived, and you have not mentioned a price for any feat you performed.*

The question bubbled up inside her, was forced back, and she was suddenly aware of the weight of her mourning-cloth; the heaviness of her jewellery; her hair braided, piled and pinned by Isobel's quick fingers; the constriction of her shoes; and her stays – she had never followed the fashion of extraordinarily tight corseting, but they were tight enough – compressing her.

Other pressures crowding upon her flesh, as well. Ludovico. Clare. Victrix. This faceless man with his shining knife. Mikal himself, and all those of her household. Her collection of drifting souls, each one an anchor.

Without those weights, would she rise from the surface of the earth?

And where would she float *to*? There was no escape. The only solution was to arrange her immediate surroundings as comfortably as possible, which meant dealing with this affair quickly, directly and ruthlessly.

She swallowed, her throat obeying with a dry click. "Come along then." She reclaimed her hand, and his expression did not change.

It was not as comforting as she might have wished, but at least it freed her for other worries. Chief among them was what, precisely, she might endure on Bucksrow, at the site of the second murder.

"A cart driver found her." Soft, thoughtfully. Strengthening cloud-filtered sunlight had scorched Bucksrow clean of its thin coating of Scab, but the cobbles and pavers held thin whorls and traceries of its green, burrowing into the cracks between to wait for darkness. "The Hospital is *there*." She pointed at its distant, looming bulk, more sensed than seen through the fog. Her forehead furrowed in a most unlady-like manner. "But there is little trace of disturbance. How very curious."

Cracked and missing cobbles, crumbling paving, timbers blackened with age and paint peeling – where the Scab had not eaten it – from whatever it coated.

Mikal took in the surroundings. "*She* was certain this . . ." It was eminently clear who he meant, both by the stress on the *she* and the suggestion of a lip-curl.

"Was an act by our quarry, yes." Emma drew her fur-lined mantle closer. Its surface glimmered with moisture, and it did nothing to stave off the cold that descended upon her. Autumn had arrived. *Soon after, winter.* A further chill coursed down her back. "I am quite certain this is the place."

"Bloodstain." He pointed, a swiftly elegant gesture, tendons standing out on the back of his hand. "Right before the stable doors."

He did not mention that the Scab had been scorched away there too, and no thin traces of green remained even in the crevices.

Emma glanced at the street again. Something about the angle of the stain was not quite *right*. "Locked after dark, one presumes." A steady, warm exhalation enfolded them both – the dryness of hide and mane, the sharp mechanical tang of oil for clockhorse gears. She extended a tendril of awareness, probed ever so gently. "I wonder . . ."

She stepped forward, directly onto the darkened paving stones. Her *corpus* had braced itself for an uncomfortable experience, and the complete lack of one demanded a response. Her training dug its clawed fingers in her vitals, and she shook the sensation away. "Hm. Mikal?"

"I am here, Prima."

*Of course you are.* But it was the response she had wanted. She closed her eyes, tugging on invisible threads in the tangled snarl of the fleshly world.

*There.* A raw, aching space inside her throbbed in response and she leaned forward, barely conscious of Mikal's fingers closing about her arm. He braced her, and she gave up outward consciousness, plunging *in*.

One string, a spider's thread of *wrong* amid all the myriad twisted, tangled knots.

*Salt against abraded flesh, copper terror flooding a mouth not her own, a rocking motion and the* crack *of a whip.*

Her head snapped aside. Reflex let the blow slide away, her body stiffening only slightly. Impressions flashed through her, a tide of hot sourness and deep-driving pain, a warm gush down her front.

"*Carriage,*" she gasped.

*Another rehearsal. It did not go as well as the preceding, I should think.*

"Here now! What are you aboot?"

It was a florid, stocky man with a coachman's cap, massive side-whiskers and shoulders giving him the appearance of a walrus. He had barrelled from the stable's stinking depths, and as Emma thudded home into her own flesh she was aware of high shrills of equine fright and loud crunching bangs.

Mikal barely glanced at the man. He steadied her, and the faint smile on his lean face would have been chilling even had she not understood its meaning. *No.* She shook her head, fractionally, and his free hand fell away from a knife hilt.

"I say, what are you—?" The worthy took in the quality of her dress and Mikal's coat, and the Shield's knives. The noise from inside mounted another notch, and Emma dispelled a shudder. "Miss, are you quite well?"

A cough to clear her desert-dry throat, and she found her voice. "Yes. Quite. Thank you. The horses seem . . . upset."

He tipped his cap back, scratched under its brim. "Been sparky ever since the bad doins, Miss. Did you come to see that'un? Blood was right there. I says to my mate, I says, *What is this coming to?* Even a frail shouldna be done a' that."

"Was there anything surpassing strange about . . . it?" Her head felt too large for her neck, but the words must have come out naturally, for he considered them, his work-hardened hands dropping to his sides. "Other than, oh—!" A helpless movement, she fell into playing the part of a too-gently-bred idiot with the usual effortlessness. Such a persona would make the man facing her much more at ease, and for a moment she wondered what the world would be if it did not require such guile to make headway in.

"Wellnow." He stuck his thumbs in his braces and took up a widespread stance as the banging and clattering inside mitigated somewhat. "I told the leather bulls, I did. I locked up nice and proper, and came i' the morn to find the nasty had been left here. Paid a pretty penny to get rid of any bad mancy, too. But the one who came out, he said there weren't nothing more than a tangle there, took my coin and off he went."

"Indeed," she murmured. "Was he a fair hand with sorcery, then?" *Since you obviously did not dare refuse payment.*

He shrugged, made as if to spit aside, and visibly reconsidered in the face of her quality. "I'm no magicker. Fellow from two streets over, name of Kendall." He visibly enjoyed telling the story of the body on the doorstep, though it became clear he had *not* been the one to find it, only coming across it while the first on the scene – a rather unfortunately-named chandler – had been running to fetch assistance.

She managed to elicit the sorcerer Kendall's address and soothed the stablemaster as well as she was able with her head pounding badly enough to cloud her vision. He took her welling eyes as a sign that she was affected by the poor unfortunate's fate, and waxed rhapsodic about the quantity of blood, and how the belly had been opened just as a fish's. How the horses still shied coming out, and how his trade had been disrupted by the crowds come to see, of which she was presumably a late member. She appeared to hang on his every word and finally made a subtle gesture, whereupon Mikal stepped forward with a few pence for the man's pains.

The stable had returned to its former quiet, but Emma could taste the high brassy tang of horse-fear.

She could also taste the sourness of her own, as well. Her stays cut most abominably, and her dress was soaked under her arms and at the small of her back.

Mikal turned as the stableman shuffled back into his dark domain, his broad back vanishing like a spirit's. "Prima?"

"This Kendall. Two streets away. It might be profitable to visit him."

"Indeed. You're . . . pale."

*No doubt.* Her mantle, drawn close, could not ease the shudders seeking to grip her. She denied them outright, her jewellery warming comfortingly. "I suspect I shall be much more so before this affair is over. I have a rather curious thought."

"Which is?"

"First, that the body found here was thrown from a carriage. And second . . ."

"Second?" He visibly braced himself, for he knew she would put the more pleasant – or less dangerous – of two tasks first, if only to gather herself for the last.

"I believe it's time to visit Thin Meg."

#  Chapter Twenty-Three

## From the Hind End

Whitehell Street had become a rather brooding organism, having been taken over by the Metropoleans. Robertson Peal's vision of a castle of Order and Detection had spread like a mushroom colony, and his knights were now "Bobbies", an affectionate diminutive of the man who made Bow Street famous. The Yard now consisted of several buildings, with the official entrance – through what used to be a back street – granting the entire sprawl its name. It was perhaps a measure of Londinium's intransigence that it was named for the back street instead of Whitehell; Justice, as it were, always approached its prey from the hind end.

Or was often approached from such by those wishing to enact it.

The detective inspector's office, shared with another

inspector, was a curious place. He was of the few Yard occupants fortunate enough to have a window, but all that could be seen was shifting yellow fog and the base of a street lamp, for the room was half underground. Feet passed by, their owners hurrying or ambling as they pleased, or as they felt the eyes of the Yard upon them. There were windows above as well, blank eyes that often as not held flickering gaslight on dim evenings as the knights of boot-leather and order kept the great beast of Law fed with paper and deduction.

In this cave, the shelves were crammed with redrope files, as a solicitor's office might be, but there were also . . . other things. A scrap of calico, bloodstained from the look of it; a cracked globe of crystal with a tiny point of light in its depths; a curved knife in a tooled leather sheath – its provenance was uncertain, and Clare longed to study it further, but other items cried for his attention as well. A red velvet pillow held a heavy, tarnished brass ring; next to it a small brass dish held a parson's collar buttons; and they were kept companion by a small silver candle-snuffer. There was a wealth of inference to be drawn.

"You have a sentimental nature, sir." Clare turned from the shelves to find the inspector standing behind his desk, his mouth slightly ajar as if thunderstruck. He relished the expression. "Mementos from your cases, I take it."

However, the inspector's next words put matters in a different light entirely. "Clare," the man replied, in a wondering tone. "*Archibald* Clare. I *knew* the name was familiar. If you look to the right and down, sir, you shall find your monograph."

"Is that so?" He glanced down, and there was a familiar blue-marbled cover. "Ah. Well." It looked well thumbed, too, and he felt the pinch of Pride. Another instance of Feeling seeking to lead him astray. "I am . . . yes, quite touched. Who would have thought?"

"I *have* actually read it." Aberline now sounded a trifle defensive. "I perform the recommended Exercizes at dawn and dusk, unless I am in dire emergency. They have been of inestimable value, sir. Had I known it was you, I would not have treated you so coolly. Miss Bannon's acquaintances, while . . . effective . . . are also usually somewhat troublesome."

"I have discovered as much," Clare allowed. *Myself among them.* He glanced at Philip Pico, who leaned against the wall near the door – just where Valentinelli might have placed himself, though without such an insouciant sneer. "She is a singular lady, Miss Bannon. I am glad you have found my poor scribblings of some use. This is, however, not why you brought me here. I gather that even Miss Bannon's threats of the Crown's displeasure would not induce you to bring a stranger into this hallowed sanctum – because you do sleep often at that desk, sir, there is a mark just where your forehead or cheek would rest upon the blotter – without some other pressing reason to do so?"

"Just as I imagined you." Aberline's face lit with a grin that showed the youth he had been perhaps a good ten years ago. Sharp as a blade, Clare fancied, and with a hot, easily touched pride kept under a mask of diffidence. "I say, sir, you are remarkable."

"I am merely a mentath." Clare straightened his cuffs. A sudden thought drew him up short. "You were aware these murders were committed by the same hand long before now."

The man sank into his chair, indicating the other one with a wave. "Yes. Lestraid and I – he shares this office, but right now he's chasing some damn fool in Devon – had an inkling of trouble to come when the Tebrem creature was found. There are . . . I say, do sit. And you too, sir."

"Why?" Philip Pico wanted to know. "I'm just a sodding nursery maid."

"A nursery maid wouldn't have half your long face, and wouldn't be eyeing the exits, and wouldn't be sweating at the thought of the Yard." Aberline cast a small, satisfied glance Clare's way, and the mentath found himself agreeably surprised by the inspector's capability at deduction. "You're of St Georgeth's, or Jermyn Street, but you're too old for the play there. And that blasted sorceress obviously entrusted this gentleman – who she seems rather attached to, since I've never seen her take such an interest in keeping someone's skin whole – to you, so you must be at least halfway dangerous." Aberline nodded, smartly. "You've naught to fear from me, little lad. I know better than to set foot where *my lady* chooses to engage a service."

There it was again: the tantalising hint of a History between Miss Bannon and this man.

It was merely a distraction at this juncture; Clare returned his attention to the matter at hand with an almost physical effort. "As soon as Tebrem was found, you say?"

"Do come and sit down, old chap." Aberline's mouth had compressed itself into a tight line again. He had an inkstain on his right middle finger, Clare noticed, and a thin line of Whitchapel grime had worked its way under his wedding ring.

He was suddenly certain the man had been up very late last night.

Quite possibly, he had not been to bed at all. The deduction caused a sinking feeling in Clare's stomach, which he told sternly to cease being idiotic. His normally excellent digestion choosing this particular time to misbehave was a most unwelcome development.

Clare lowered himself into the appointed chair, a monstrous leather thing with sprung stuffing crouching behind a hunched ottoman which bore the marks of another's boots – perhaps the missing inspector, chasing fools in Devon?

He arranged himself, steepling his fingers before his face, and nodded fractionally. "Proceed, sir."

"Are you familiar with *lustmorden*?"

Clare frowned. *What a curious portmanteau of a word. German?* He thought of his friend Sigmund, who would no doubt be brightly interested in this, as he was in anything that involved Miss Bannon. Dear old Sig was growing visibly older; Clare had not availed himself of the man's company in months. Now, Clare had the uncomfortable sensation of wondering precisely why. Of course, Sig was still tinkering with that bloody mechanical spider of his. "I am uncertain. Do explain."

"There are several cases. The Beast of Dusseldorf, for example, or the Florentine Monster. A man so maddened by uncontrolled—" Aberline shifted uncomfortably. His cheeks pinkened slightly. "Or *uncontrollable* desire, committing murders, each with a distinguishing mark springing from the obsession."

Clare's eyelids dropped to half-mast. "I see. A remarkable theory. Could it not be that some criminals simply desire to murder? That it is in their nature?"

"Of course. But these monsters, when caught – I say, Mr Clare, I am not distressing you by speaking so?"

*If only you knew.* "By no means."

"And it will not distress you if I have . . . unorthodox methods of detecting?"

"My own are rather strange, sir." Clare blinked. "Do go on."

"Very well." Yet Aberline still seemed uncomfortable. "The obsession dictates the murder. I shall now tell you what I have ascertained, Mr Clare. The murderer has practised his deadly art. He will be extremely difficult to catch. He is possessed of a coach or some other conveyance, and he has some aim in mind." He drew a deep breath. "And he is nowhere near finished."

Clare nodded, slowly. "I see. You are certain he has a conveyance? A personal chariot of some sort to travel from one nightmarish deed to the next?"

"I am."

"How are you so certain?"

"I . . ." Aberline coughed, looking even more uncomfortable. "I cannot say."

"*Quite* interesting." Clare nodded again. "Tell me what you *can* say, then."

"The very idea of *lustmorden* is so repulsive, it is difficult to even convince our superiors of its existence. To them, Murder is a product of Insanity and Criminal Character alone, and no room is granted for . . . for lack of a better word, no room is granted for sheer evil." Aberline coughed slightly. "I am of the opinion that those who rise in the world's estimation do not often make the best detective inspectors, but they do make excellent commissioners and mayors and lord justices." A cloud passed over his features, but he waved a hand, dismissing it.

This had all the character of a speech polished over long, sleepless nights, and Clare settled himself to the peculiar state of absorbed attention he often practised when Miss Bannon could be induced to speak at length on a subject she found interesting.

It was the interest – or the outright obsession – of an intelligent subject that often led to the most fruitful lines of enquiry and deduction, even if the subject was blind to them as a consequence of said obsession.

*Oh, so Miss Bannon is a subject now? She is not present; do not think upon her.* He brought his attention back to the matter at hand, and nodded, since Aberline had given him an enquiring glance.

"Proceed," he said, and a prickle of . . . irritation? . . . furrowed his brow.

If it had been Miss Bannon speaking, she would not have needed the glance to ascertain his attention.

"You have rather a listening air, sir, and it is most welcome. Do tell me if I—"

*Let us move on, and quickly, too.* "These murders – *lust-morden* is a very evocative name indeed – are of a variety and species your superiors, if we can call them that, are not equipped to effectively halt. By virtue of your almost daily experience of the effects and settings of Vice and Crime, you have acquired a body of knowledge which grants you certain . . . feelings, if you will, for the causes and prevention of both. Which leads you to conflict within the Yard, for though you have many other fine qualities, you do not have the necessary oil to smooth bureaucratic waters."

The silence greeting his observation might have been uncomfortable if Aberline had not been smiling broadly.

"Quite so," he finally said. "Quite so. Lestraid is much better at it, and without him, I confess, I am somewhat at the mercy of my own temperament. It does not help that my methods are . . . In some cases, I have been accused of being little better than a criminal myself."

*Ah. Now there is a frank admission.* The mementos on the shelves were either tokens of cases where Aberline had known the criminal and mucked himself in order to bring him or her to justice . . . or tokens of victims he had been unable to avenge, even by behaving in a not-so-noble fashion.

Or both. So little separated a bootleather knight from a criminal.

*You have grown philosophical, Clare.*

He turned to another avenue of thought. The man's mien was so sober and exacting, it was difficult to conceive of him as one willing to turn the law so that the spirit instead of the letter was fulfilled.

Which meant Clare must look more closely at him. Appearances deceived, and such a valuable clew into a man's character was not to be taken lightly. Especially when Clare himself was . . . *was he?*

Yes. He was distracted. It boded rather ill.

Aberline shrugged. "The fact that I have some small ætheric talent – not enough to charm," he added hurriedly, "no, not enough to be apprenticed, to be sure! And yet I am viewed with a certain trepidation by every hemisphere of the Yard."

"Sorcerous or not," Clare clarified, "bootleather or bonnet."

"Indeed." Aberline looked gratified to be so comprehended. He settled himself more deeply in his chair, and his gaze focused on the shelves of mementoes and files, leatherbound books and bundles of paper. "Yet I digress. *Lustmorden* all share certain characteristics, which Lestraid and I have isolated by poring through bloodcurdling accounts of deeds unfit for print. These murders share such characteristics—"

"Which include?" Clare prodded.

"Savagery, for one. But that is not enough. A certain

method – the progression is quite clear. The murderer begins with experimentation, though one may see the, ahem, you could call it the marks of his obsession—"

"His?"

"Oh, a woman may drink, and a woman may poison, and there may even be the rare woman like Miss Bannon, who is more a viper in frail flesh than a proper *female*. But a woman does not commit *lustmorden*. It is simply unthinkable."

Clare's silence was taken for agreement, and Aberline continued. He had quite warmed to his theme.

"For one thing, the violence of the attacks is anathema to a woman. For another, the driving force is . . . well, the name says it quite clearly. The driving force is the prerogative of the male."

"I see," Clare murmured.

"The marks of the obsession are very particular, and unique to each criminal. Rather as the Anthropometric school of thought holds that the ridges on each man's hands are unique – are you familiar with Faulds, and Bertillon, dactyloscopy? Very good. *Lustmorden* is merely an outgrowth of the principle that a criminal's chosen vice is an expression of their *personality* . . . the theory is complex," Aberline acknowledged, and pushed himself to his feet. He paced to the window, looking up at the gleam of strengthening daylight piercing layers of fog and falling on his face, shadowing the traces of sleeplessness and care. Driving them deeper.

*How frail flesh is.* Yet Clare's own, now . . . not so at

all. He found the logical consequence to Aberline's pause. "The initial attack, the one that came to such attention recently, was not the first? Is that what you mean?"

"There are plenty that bear the same marks; the avocation of drink and prostitution is a hazardous one. But the site of the Tebrem murder . . . there were troubling . . . would you believe me, sir, if I said I possessed what a colonist might call 'an intuition'? A . . . *feeling*, one sharpened by my . . . experiences."

"I would believe you." Clare sought for the right tone. "You are saying that there may have been others, but the Tebrem murder was successful enough to propel the murderer forward? It stoked the fire of his obsession past the critical point, and we are now—"

"—facing what may become an explosion. Especially since the Eastron End bears a distressing resemblance to a powder-keg recently. The influx of Yudics, the Eirean troubles, the Red, sheer laziness and ill character finding its level, so to speak, and the dreadfuls and broadsheets irresponsibly striking sparks against a very short fuse." He turned on his heel, striding for the shelf, and reached for a redrope folder.

Holding it, he looked even more solicitor-like, and Clare had to quash a moment of amusement. The situation most certainly did *not* call for a smile, and his expression might be misinterpreted.

Had he not spent so long watching Miss Bannon smooth over misinterpretations, he might have unwittingly made the situation precarious.

Aberline took no notice of his expression either way. "And the Crown has now seen fit to muddy the waters by bringing pressure to bear on the Yard. I confess I am rather disheartened by the fact, since said pressure will inevitably make it more difficult to pursue a single murderer through the worst sinks of Londinium. Disturbed silt does not permit clarity in a pond, so to speak."

"Ah." Clare cogitated upon this set of statements for a few moments. "I say, Detective Inspector, you very much seem to view these deaths as a personal affront."

The man had the grace to cough slightly, and redden a bit. "Some cases, Mr Clare, become so."

"Indeed they do." Clare settled himself more firmly in the chair. "I believe the file you hold contains the information you deem particularly worthwhile, and also particularly damaging to public order. I further believe you have every reason to be as cautious as you are. This has all the marks of an affair that could end very badly. And Mr Pico, do come and have a seat. I believe you may be of some use to us."

"Glad to become so, squire," was the cheeky reply, and Clare found, much to his surprise, that he was almost agreeably irritated with the lad.

Perhaps Miss Bannon had not been so wrong to engage him.

No doubt there was a sorcerous component to this case, but vanquishing it with pure logic – and the resources of the Yard, no matter how muddied the waters had become – might indeed be possible.

The question of why such a prospect could warm him so agreeably was one he decided to set aside for the nonce.

"These are murders Lestraid and I believe fit the pattern." The redrope was distressingly thick, and the small table dragged to suit Clare's perusal of it was rather overwhelmed by its bulk. "Tea, while you read?"

"Quite welcome, thank you." Clare's brow furrowed as he opened the file, and his faculties woke even further.

He settled himself for a long afternoon's work.

# Chapter Twenty-Four

## Thin Meg

*K* *endall, two streets over*, turned out to be somewhat misleading. Perhaps the man hadn't meant to be deceptive, but the fog was thickening and Emma's thoughts were of a similarly impenetrable nature. She rather wished Clare was about, for he had the most wonderful way of clarifying matters. At least, he did when those matters did not involve his own tender sensibilities.

In any case, it was the rank narrow reeking of Blightallen, the Scab thick and resilient underfoot – sunlight didn't reach past the sloping overhead tenements, leaning together to confer on business best kept low-voiced – that held their quarry. Or, more precisely, his stinking domicile, which was one low-ceilinged room, with a door that had been shivered to pieces.

There had been more than one murder in Whitchapel

last night. The closet was thick with an ætheric tangle of violence. A small, blood-soaked bed, a strongbox that had been rifled – by murderer or by neighbours was an open question – and torn, faded wallpaper; one sad, frameless painting of a woman with dark eyes and a decided downturn to her mouth, dressed in the fashion of the Mad Georgeth's early reign, powdered curls and a plaid beautymark high on her left cheek. The painting was varnished to the wall at least twice, which solved one mystery, while a round of questioning the foul-haired, slattern of a landlady solved another.

"I runs a respectable house, I does," she repeated, tightening her dirty shawl about her consumptive-thin shoulders. Her skirts were patched, and two of her corset stays were missing; it could have produced unsightly bulges had she not been so wraithlike. "Owner's a Westron End gent, high and mighty as yourself, Missy."

"No doubt." Emma pointed at the bed. "And where was his body removed to?"

"Body? Warnt no body, Miss. This morning there's an uproar, our sorcerer gone and his bed all drenched. Nobody heard a thing but, says I, we're Blightallen, of course nobody hears a sodding thing. Still, he's a magicker, and who can tell? His idearn'a joke, p'raps."

*Not likely.* Emma absorbed this. "Is he much of a prankster, this Kendall?"

"Dour as the Widow, Miss." The slattern's mouth pulled against itself, a tight compressed line. Emma nodded, and Mikal produced a shilling. He offered it, and the landlady reached . . . but his fingers twitched and it vanished.

"Are you certain nothing was heard?" Emma enquired, sweetly.

The woman drew herself up, wrapping the shawl even more tightly. She darted a glance back down the darkened hall, and Emma was suddenly aware of the confining space. There was no window, and with the door shut it must have been oppressive. There was no space for even a Minor Work, and the walls held little trace of ætheric defences. Of course, the reverberations were so complicated and snarled, there was little she could tell without adding to the problem.

To compound the oddness, there was not a single fly to be found on the mangled, shredded, blood-soaked bedding. With no window for them to find their way in, it was not *quite* out of the ordinary . . . but still.

"Nuffink." But the landlady's voice had dropped. "I ent had time to come up and change the sheets neither – none of the drabs'll touch it even for forgiving their doss-money. *None heard a thing*, mum, and first I knows of it was that sot Will Emerich come down to kitchen rubbing his eyes and complaining on the splinters in the hall. I'd've said he was dead drunk only Black Poll Backstearn's room is next door, and she don't sleep well. She ent been on gin for a month, and it shows. Whatever happened, was silent as . . ." She made the *avert* gesture with her left hand, tiny eyes almost lost in their pouches of darkened flesh narrowing further. "An' that puts us all fair off our mettle, mum. Silent it was, and Kendall gone."

Emma nodded again, and Mikal handed over the shilling. The woman bit it with her rotting teeth to test its truth, then glanced back over her shoulder again. "And now you visit," she continued, "lady high and mighty, go straight for his room. It's bad business, it is. Bad business all way round."

"You may tell anyone you like that I appeared as a bird of ill fortune, madam." Emma lowered her veil. A snap of her fingers, more for effect than for actual utility, and her jewellery warmed as she drew on its stored force. The blood-soaked bedding leapt into thin blue witchflame, spitting and hissing like a cat as the landlady shrank back against the shivered door.

"As a matter of fact," Emma added dryly, "I would take it as a kindness if you would tell everyone that a woman in mourning was here, and what she did."

With that, she brushed through the door as a burning wind, speaking the minor Word that would confine the flames to the traces of blood – and not so incidentally, sensitise her to the remainder of that vital fluid, wherever it might have been shed or come to rest.

Several unphysical strings tugged at her attention, most of them probably attached to a trap.

She was beginning to have a healthy respect for the canny nature of her quarry.

Mikal's hand was at her elbow to guide her in the sudden gloom of the rickety hallway, and Emma realised she was shaking.

\*      \*      \*

The Chapelease Leper was now a peeling crumble, clotted with whitewash applied indifferently every so often. Around it, the busy thoroughfare of Whitchapel Road throbbed, the Scab sucking at cart wheels, verdant even under the lash of fogbound sunlight as it crawled up pale walls.

Some held that it was here the Scab had been birthed, but not too loudly.

You never knew what *she* might take offence at, or catch wind of.

It wasn't the peeling or the scabrous clots on the walls that made all give the Chapelease as wide a berth as possible, and had made the road divide around it as a rock divides a river. It wasn't even the way the gaslamps that had been erected near it were warped and blasted by some unimaginable fury – or simply by a slow steady exhalation of malice.

No, those who could avoided the place largely because of its washed-clean, gleaming stairs.

Those stairs were wide and sharp-edged, capacious and sturdy, but they were rarely seen. They were, instead, crowded with huddled bundles of rags with fever-bright eyes ranked upon them shoulder to shoulder, with only a narrow ribbon of scrubbed brightness leading to the rotting-cream doors.

These were Thin Meg's brood, and none dared touch them or move them along until there was a soft thud, and a stick-light body was rolled down into the road to be collected. None pointed at, jeered at, or spoke to them.

They sat in their rags and watched Whitchapel Road go by, and only in the dead of night could a sound be heard from them.

A thin sound, a low sound. A soft, hissing, draining mumble.

Emma walked briskly, her eyes stinging even under the veil's protection. The din of traffic was incredible, and were it not for Mikal she might have been accosted, or worse. He drifted at her shoulder, between her and the gutter, and even the alley-side cutpurses retreated. Shouts and curses from coachmen and carters, the crack of a whip, children screaming as they ran past engaged upon some game or another – or intent on relieving pockets of their contents, for theirs were nimble and desperate fingers.

The drabs had mostly retired to sleep off their work and the gin they deadened its rigors with, but the public houses were open and brawling, flashboys crowding the doors and displaying their Alterations: shiny metal, oiled leather, bits of glass, sellsongs from the wheelbarrows jammed wherever they could elbow a niche and pay the "protection" fee levelled from whoever controlled that slice of paving or wooden-slat walk this week, footsteps, hoofbeats, conversation and cries. Crackles of ætheric disturbance, spat charms, lightfinger wards and oil-charms popping blue or yellow sparks as they reacted to the eddies and swirls of the crowd.

The noise drew away when she stepped over the invisible border between the rest of the world and Thin Meg's domicile.

She had to hold her skirts close to pass through the hunched rag bundles as they leaned away from her. A spill of cold slid down her skin as she stepped up, and up again, Mikal behind her.

The Endor in her woke, and the starvelings' bony hands appeared, fingers of bleached anemone blindly seeking for the disturbance in their cold, silent suffering.

A Prime could not pass unnoticed; there was simply too much ætheric force in them to do so. And any of the Black who braved these stairs would feel a certain . . . trepidation. Still, she lifted her chin and twitched her skirts away from the seeking fingers.

The crop of starvelings was dense at the top of the stairs, where those not yet whittled to apathy hunched, swaying slightly as a wheatfield rippled by a cool wind. The Chapelease doors – massive, oaken things not yet Scab-rotted perhaps because of the rancid renderings poured over them every Twelfthnight – hung ajar, quivering.

They never closed.

Mikal was suddenly before her, and he pushed the left-hand door wide, its hinges giving that same faint hissing noise. Emma quelled a shudder, took a very tight grasp on her temper, and continued on.

The sudden dimness was a balm, lit only by shuddering candleflames atop thick tallow columns, their smoke greasing the painted roof. If one looked up, cripplewing angels and spinning saints could be seen leering through the scrim of rippling soot.

Emma did not. Instead, she passed her gaze smoothly

over the ranks of broken pews marching up the narrow interior, the alcoves on either side full of deeper shadows. Nothing amiss, though thick whitish gauze-mist peeped above the slumping wooden backs, moving cold-sluggish.

"And what is this," a deep voice rasped and slipped between chipped and blackened columns, "come to my doorstep now? A little tiny witchling, already slight as a sparrow." A thick, burping chuckle. "More meat on her companion, and a pretty leg he shows too."

Emma's pace did not falter. She continued down the central aisle, and the air grew heavier. Satin and rotting silk shifted, fabric rubbing against itself, and the massive bulk slithering in the well-hole where an altar had once stood resolved into a shape. Just what *kind* of shape it was difficult to say, for there were huge folds and bulges, bright blinking eyes and ivory teeth, yards and yards of cloth piled, buttoned, and stretched about peeping sickly white flesh.

"Marimat the Fallen." Emma put her gloved palms together, halting, and bowed slightly. "I greet you."

"Oh, she *greets* me." Several long, chubby, oddly flexible fingers crawled over the blasted altar-wreckage, and there was a heaving. The many eyes blinked, flashing in their preferred dimness, and the sliding and scraping in the pews were those who had offered her more than just their physical weight in exchange for the starving peace she granted. "Did you come here to trade, wee witchling?" A thick, groaning laugh, cold as leftover black pudding.

Emma cocked her head. Mikal was tense and silent. The

pews behind her would be full of gauzy movement by now, phosphorescent suggestions of cheek and hand and shoulder, supple smoky coils. "Careful," she said, mildly enough. "Your starvelings appear restless."

"Do they?" A long groaning noise, and the gauzy whispers retreated. More bits of her bulk bubbled up, winking with jewels, both paste and real. A hen's-egg sapphire in tarnished silver – probably real – chimed as it boiled over the edge of the stone cup and rolled away.

Emma ignored it, and therefore Mikal did as well.

"I think," the thing in the well continued, hauling and shifting even more bits of herself, "*you* are the restless one. Or is the word 'troubled'? An ill wind brings you here."

"That should delight you." The next few moments were very delicate, so Emma gave herself a pause. "Ill wind and misfortune usually does."

A great rolling, rippling shrug. "*They* seek me out, little witchling. I do not stir one foot to seek *them*."

*And you fatten on their despair, a little at a time.* "Yet all Whitchapel feels your fingers, Thin Meg." Very quietly. "Every dark corner, and every crevice between cobbles."

Stillness filled Chapelease. The walls groaned a little as the creature's attention constricted.

The eyes narrowed, their gleams intensifying. Finally, the creature shifted again, heaving still more of her bulk up toward the lip of the depression where the shattered altar had once stood tall and proud. More fingers splatted dully in dust and splinters, grinding against stone.

They were plump, and they looked soft, but those tiny appendages could find the smallest crack and slide in. Stone crumbled before their persistent fingering. It was ever thus with those of her ilk – they had all the time in the world to poke and prod, to cajole and wear away.

"State your business," Thin Meg finally said, and now Emma could see her actual mouth, the V-shaped orifice peeling open to show serried rows of sharp white teeth. "With no riddles, witchling."

*How very interesting.* "Something new has been added to Whitchapel."

More stillness. Mikal's arm lifted, and he gently, slowly, pushed Emma back a step. His other hand lingered at a knife hilt, and Emma's pulse sought to speed itself, was repressed.

"Oh, aye, and not with my leave." Thin Meg laughed, and this time the heavy, ugly sound was truly amused. Still cold, though, a razor's edge cutting the gloom, sparking against creeping fingers made of fine-woven smoke as they inched closer, pressing against Emma's skirts. "What do you know of it? One of your kind, little hands prodding and poking where they shouldn't. Take care lest the lid snap on those fingers!"

"I suppose if the odd bit of information comes to your lovely ears . . ."

Meg found this funny as well. At least, she shook with jollity, bits of her heaving and slopping, flashing dead-white flesh and pinging creaks as the building itself shuddered. Material split, shredding; the tortured souls in the chapel's shadows shrank back from Emma, Mikal, and the stew of flesh and tawdry finery bubbling before them.

Mikal's shoulders were rigid under black velvet; Emma's throat ached to cut the din with a sharp Word, but she did not.

Finally, the heaving ended. Meg's bulk receded, the sucking and shifting quieting as she eased back.

"It suits me to send you a starveling, should I have news." Her mouth was still plainly visible, that stark, sharp smile causing candleflames to shudder and gutter *en masse*. A breath of rank foulness now slid between the columns, disturbing the fluttering smoke-hangings, which had quieted as they pressed back against the door, half-seen faces writhing with dismay. "You shall pay me by stopping *him*."

"Him." Emma nodded. "The faceless one."

"He has no need of a face," the creature crooned. "He's a sharp canny jack, that one."

Mikal stamped sharply, and there was a wet splattering. Thin Meg hissed, a long indrawn sound of pain, and Emma found herself pushed back further, blinking and shaking her head.

Her Shield shook the green, sticky sludge from his boot, and the pale, wriggling tendril retreated into the cauldron. "Prima?" Soft, but the edge of leashed deadliness under the word made each flame straighten and dance.

"Can't fault me for trying." The creature bubble-hissed, chuckling thickly. "But sparrow-slight she is. Now you, *you* are a finer morsel."

"Not for your dining, madam," he returned, equally enough.

Emma found her tongue. "Very well." She turned, despite the fact that her skin was alive with revulsion – imagine feeling one of Meg's grasping little fingers curling around one's ankle, nudging upward, and the lassitude that would follow . . .

Her footsteps tapped with their usual authority as she set off down the central aisle. "Thank you, Maharimat of the Third Host. We shall be on our way."

"He knows your name, sparrow-witch." There was no laughter now, and the foul breath of a fallen creature that had once sung of and to holiness in other spheres was darker than sewage. It was difficult not to gag, and Emma took her air in tiny sips as she made for the doors. "You have more enemies than you know."

"Pray you do not find yourself among them, bonny Meg," she returned over her shoulder, finding she had enough breath for a parting sting. "For I might decide to let him finish his work, and weaken *you* as well."

The doors creaked open, and she might have tumbled into the ranks of starvelings if Mikal had not caught her again.

Their clutching, brushing fingers were feeble, easily pushed aside, but she did not halt until they were a good distance from both the Chapelease *and* the creeping, cringing, venomous green tendrils of Scab.

#  Chapter Twenty-Five

## Beyond Your Ken

"I am no donkey, sir." Philip Pico bridled, as Alice took his gloves and hat with a sniff.

The other maid, Bridget of the slightly lame left leg and the engaging gapped-tooth smile, took Clare's, and he held his peace until they had both vanished into the depths of 34½ Brooke Street. "You bear a suspicious resemblance to a stubborn ass. And yet it is *me* saddled with *you*."

"Keep him in one piece, she said. Welladay, I will, sir."

"Oh? And what else did she say?"

"Naught that would interest you."

"Oh, I think it would. Did she mention your predecessor?"

"The one you were in love with, sir? No. She said nothing to me about *him*."

Clare halted, and the heat in his cheeks was new and

unwelcome. "His name was Ludovico, and I was not *in love* with him. Mentaths do not—"

"Good evening, gentlemen." A rustle of black silk, a breath of smoky sorcery laced with spiced-pear perfume, and Emma Bannon halted on the stairs, eyeing them both with arch amusement. "A drink before dinner?"

"Rid me of this *encumbrance*, madam," Clare managed, stiffly. "This is insupportable!"

"Oh?" One eyebrow, elegantly arched. "Philip?"

"About to go slumming with the detective inspector, he was." The bratling straightened his sleeves much as a gentleman would, and matched Clare glare for glare. "And on such short acquaintance. I thought it best we come home for dinner."

"It is not *slumming*, it is searching for clews! And, had you not rudely objected, *Philip*, we would have had Aberline here for questioning during dinner, and added his considerable talents to our—"

"Inspector Aberline is not welcome at my table, Clare." Very softly. "Philip, you did well. Go and dress for dinner, if you please. Mr Clare and I have a few matters to settle."

"Oh, I shall say we do." Clare straightened as the youth made that same abortive gesture – as if to tug his forelock – and made for the safety of the stairs. He passed Miss Bannon, giving her as wide a berth as possible, and Clare almost did not note that she did not bother to twitch her skirts back as if he suffered something contagious.

As she always had with Ludovico. Did this young annoyance have Valentinelli's room as well?

Why, Clare asked himself, should he care?

Miss Bannon rested one hand on the banister, the curve of her wrist just delicate enough to make a man think of snapping it.

The idea was a dash of icy water, and Clare inhaled, tensing fruitlessly. He had spent the entire afternoon sifting through papers holding bloodless information about singularly bloody acts, and they had not nettled him one whit. Now, just a few moments in Miss Bannon's company, and he was boiling.

*This is Feeling. It is illogical.* It did not help that the murders Aberline had so painstakingly gathered were clearly not the work of the current madman – except for two, and those two offered frustratingly little in the way of fresh insight.

"Do go on." She was maddeningly calm, but her fingers were tense. A girl who could snap a word that immobilised a grown man, and yet she appeared so fragile.

Clare had seen this woman perform illogical miracles, and they had left no mark on her youthful face. Was this what the churches of the world, both Popish and Englene, meant when they raved of Woman's diabolical nature?

He gathered what he could of his dignity. It was a thin cloak indeed. "I am not a pet, nor am I your ward."

"I agree." She nodded once, her dark curls swinging. "Were you one, I would cosset you, and were you the other I would not allow you to step forth into the dangers outside for a good long while. You are not well, Clare, and this affair, I am beginning to think, is beyond your ken."

For a moment he could not quite believe his ears. "I am *perfectly* well." He was aware of the lie even as he spoke it. "I have endured a succession of shocks to my faculties, true. And I had some . . . difficulty . . . with the notion of . . . but *dash* it all, Emma, this case is fascinating, and work is the best cure for a completely natural . . . loss."

"Except you do not consider your loss natural at all, sir, on either account. This is a matter best left to sorcery. I have discovered much today, and it quite disturbs me."

He could have fastened on *that* little tidbit, but the tide of Anger had him now. "So, I am to be set upon a shelf? I think not. Aberline and I do get on very well, and he is the best man to investigate—"

"He is a slightly useful tool, nothing more, and will serve to distract my quarry quite handily with his bumbling about." Her tone cooled, and the movement on the stairs above her was Mikal, a gleam in darkness. "You would do well to be cautious of the good inspector, Archibald. If he may do me a disservice through you, he shall no doubt try."

"And what did you do to earn such treatment from a gentleman?" Unjustified, perhaps, but the way she rocked slightly back onto her heels, paling a shade or two – though she was already much whiter than her wont, almost drained-looking – made a certain hot bubble rise under his breastbone.

No trace of paleness in her tone, however. "I saved a somewhat-soiled innocent from his clutches, and consequently he bears me a grudge. It nettles a certain type of petty man to be denied something by a woman."

Did she mean it as a return cut? Clare's head had begun to pound as he struggled to lower his voice. "What baseness you attribute to a gentleman who—"

Her chin lifted, and her eyes were flashing dangerously now. "On what do you build your assessment of his good character, mentath? Let me hear your logic."

"I would grant you a full explanation, if I could be certain of your understanding it." Was he actually *sneering*? Clare had the exquisitely odd sensation of falling into a hole, watching himself from its bottom as his face twisted and took on a rather ugly cast.

"Likewise, sir." A dot of crimson had appeared on each soft cheek, yet she was iron-straight. "You are relieved of the need to give any further attention to this matter. *Do* try to stay out of trouble while I attend to the Crown's business."

With that, she swept down the stairs, turning so sharply at the foot her skirt flared and almost touched his knee.

Mikal drifted in her wake, but her pace was such that he had no time to do anything but glower in Clare's general direction, the flame in the Shield's yellow irises waking.

*She goes to her study, instead of to the drawing room. Angry? Perhaps. Nettled? Hurt?*

What on earth had *possessed* him? A mentath did not behave so. Nor did a proper gentleman.

He found he was wringing his hands, and forced himself to stop. To let them hang loosely, fingers throbbing and the appendages afire because he had driven his nails deep into palmflesh. His shoulders loosened, and he cast about for something, anything, to distract his aching head.

Nothing was to be found. He made it to the stairs before sinking down, dropping said tender head into his hands, elbows on knees, and there he stayed until Philip Pico found him an hour later, to bring him to the dining room, where Miss Bannon – and Mikal – were both absent during a long, exquisite, and tortuously silent dinner.

# Chapter Twenty-Six

## With Whatever Means Are to Hand

"Prima?"

"Hm?" She glanced up from the large leatherbound tome, her eyes for a moment refusing to focus as she was pulled away from creaking ropes and singing sails. The book – *Marina Invicta* – which her well-trained memory had dragged forth the remembrance of from a dusty room, contained several passages about Britannia.

Nothing of any real use, however. Just as every other blasted book she had pulled from the shelves was useless in the current situation.

Mikal closed the door: a soft snick of the latch catching and the lock thrown. "Shall you be attending dinner? Or shall Finch bring you a plate?"

"Neither." She waved a hand, her gaze already straying back to the pages. "Rum, perhaps. Thank you."

"Emma." He had approached her desk, soundlessly, and the study came back into focus around her. The shelves were arranged as they should be, though holes had been created by her rummaging, and a stack of tomes large and small lay heaped upon the table she had pulled from its place behind a leather chair she was wont to sink into on certain nights, watching the coal in the grate shed heat and ætheric force while it built its white jacket. Bits of paper covered in her handwriting – sketches of charter symbols and Name-glyphs shifting uneasily as their ink shivered – littered the entire room, but the sopha was bare. It was perhaps where she would sleep tonight, did her researches take her in any promising direction.

She was being rather untidy. And there was a line between Mikal's eyebrows, though his expression was just the same as usual in every other regard. Trouble was brewing in that quarter.

Of course, she had ordered him to cool his heels outside the door and vanished; normally, she did not mind his company while she worked. But she had not wished him to see her discomfiture. Or the tears that had blistered a spare page of notes, tossed unceremoniously into the grate and lit with a hissed imprecation.

To add to her displeasure, every single ætheric strand leading to the fate of the unfortunate Keller *had* been trapped, closing off each avenue of possibly safe enquiry. It took a great deal of power, and a great deal of care, to hide the distinct stamp of one's personality on one's sorcery so completely. Whoever this murderer was, he was thorough, and wickedly intelligent to boot.

She grimaced at the thought, but only inwardly. A lady's face did not twist so. "You have my attention, Shield. Is there some new manner of disaster?"

"Not so much. I merely thought . . . you seem distressed."

"I have undertaken what is likely to be a thankless task. And my library, while normally more than adequate, is of very little use." She blew a vagrant curl out of her face; it irritated her mightily to be so disarranged. "I am distressed only by the bloody *inconvenience* of this entire affair."

"The mentath—"

*Oh, is that what you wish to speak of?* "—is none of your concern, Shield."

"He *distresses* you."

"So do you. Now, if you will not leave, at least be quiet." *Though I have little hope of you doing either. It seems every single blessed thing on the Isle is conspiring to try my temper today, from Marimat to a simple hansom ride.*

"How do I distress you, Emma?"

"Shall I list the ways? And yet, I am very busy right now. *Do* be quiet."

"How long will you ignore—"

"As long as I please, Shield. If you do not cease, I shall force you to do so."

"And how shall you do that, Prima?"

She set the book down carefully, brushing her hands together as if to rid them of dust, and rose. The chair legs squeaked slightly against the wooden floor, and she reminded herself again that a lady did not shout. Then, and only then, she met Mikal's gaze, and the room chilled slightly. Every piece of paper ruffled itself, brushed by an unphysical current.

When she was certain she could keep a civil tone, she spoke. "With whatever means are to hand. Are you weary of my employ, Mikal?"

"Of course not." His hands were loose, and he seemed relaxed. She did not trust the seeming. "You are my Prima."

*Miles Crawford was your Prime; you strangled him as I watched, then mutilated his corpse. Because he hurt me.* The contradiction – trusting her life to a Shield who had done the unthinkable and murdered his charge – was as sharp as it had ever been. Yet he had earned that trust, times beyond counting. Whatever danger he represented, it was not mere murder. "Then why do you take me up in such an unseemly manner?"

"He causes you pain." His chin jutted slightly, and how he managed to look like the defiant, almost-ugly boy he must have been on the Collegia's training grounds could have been mildly entertaining, if she had been inclined to amusement. "Much of it, and I am helpless to stop him. As long as you continue to let him, he will pain you."

"Yes." Anger, tightly reined, suddenly evaporated. Her stays dug into her flesh, and she wondered if she would ever see a day such appurtenances were no longer fashionable or expected.

Of course, Fashion being the beast she was, something equally uncomfortable and ridiculous would likely take its place.

"Yes," she repeated. "He pains me. I am told this is an occasional consequence of having friends. Which is no doubt why so many of my colleagues have so few they use that word to describe. At least, to describe seriously and with meaning."

"And I distress you."

"That is a consequence of having . . . you."

"What am I, to you? If I may ask, Prima."

"You may not." She found her head was aching again, and longed for vinegar and brown paper to soothe the pounding. "We shall have a reckoning, as they say, at some moment. But not *now*, Mikal." She found herself almost willing to utter an absurdity.

*Please.*

A Prime did not *ask*. A Prime *commanded*. But with Clare chasing will o'wisps with the bumbling idiot inspector – and he was too sharp an idiot to give any lee to, indeed – she had lost . . . what? Certainly a resource, and possibly Clare's regard as well.

"I believe a Prime may be behind this series of murders," she said, carefully. Almost, dare she think it, *logically*. "If so, I believe this Prime's aim is no less than the toppling of Victrix, which may please me to some small extent, and the uprooting of Britannia, which may or may not. In any case, *I* am now entangled in this affair, and I may suffer an unpleasant consequence or two if it is not tidily arranged in some fashion." *Which means you – and the rest of my household – may be cast adrift.*

"Ah." A slight nod, and his gaze had grown sharp. "A Sympathy has been created?"

"Perhaps." Yet she was uneasy even as she admitted the possibility. The oldest branch of sorcery, while powerful, was not enough to cause these effects on a ruling spirit's vessel – and if a Sympathy to Victrix had been in effect, Emma herself would not have become attuned to whatever work was being performed.

If it was indeed a *work*, and not a symptom of some other series of events at play. Uncomfortable thoughts were crowding her fast and thick now; Emma returned her attention to the present situation with an effort. "In any case, there is another . . . aspect . . . to this matter."

"Which is?"

At least he did not seek to *guess*.

Emma turned, took two irresolute steps toward the coal grate. Halted. "If not for an accident, I could have been one of them." *Who can tell what makes a sorcerer? Had the Collegia childcatchers not found me, I could have been dead, laid out on a marble slab with a doctor rummaging through me.*

*Or worse.* A shudder passed through her.

"Ah." Thankfully, he added no more. He merely let her know she was heard, perhaps understood. Though *understanding* was much to ask of any man.

She swung back to face him, her jewellery running with

crackling sparks as tension made itself visible. "I need your help, Mikal."

The Shield cocked his sleek dark head. He actually looked thunderstruck, and well he might. Two slow blinks – his yellow irises quenched for a moment – then another.

"You have it without asking, Prima." Formal, and very soft.

*Do I?* But she merely nodded, her face a mask. "Good. Fetch me some rum, and leave Clare to himself for a while. I cannot spare attention to keep him from trouble, I only hope Finch's cousin can."

"He seems capable of that much, at least." A half-bow, a Shield's traditional obeisance, he turned on his heel and was gone in a heartbeat.

The door closed behind him, and she let out a pent breath.

If he sought to reassure her, he had succeeded halfway. She gazed over the wrack and ruin of her study, and brought her hands together, sharply.

The resultant *crack*, freighted with a sharp-edged Word that left her with the sensation of a weight lifting through her spine, echoed for far longer than it should have. The books flew, snapping shut, arranging themselves in their appointed places. A slight lift at the end of the sound shuffled the paper together in a neat pile, stacking it on her desk; ink hissed free of the blotter in venomous little puffs of steam.

What had she not told him?

She held up one hand, counted said and unsaid reasons as if teaching a child-rhyme.

One finger. *I am alone.*

Two. *I suspect I am not drawn into this dance by mere chance.*

Three. *I am matched against another Prime.*

Four. *One I do not recognise.*

And fifth, last but not least, the most galling of all, counted upon her dexterous thumb, the digit that separated man from beast.

*I am afraid.*

# Chapter Twenty-Seven

## A Legitimate Concern

The night passed without incident, and so did the next day, save for the broadsheets screaming of murder in the Eastron End. Those were carried immediately to Miss Bannon's study. Clare was, of course, supplied with his own.

The *without incident* disturbed Clare mightily, for Miss Bannon did not appear. She did not take breakfast in the breakfast room or the solarium; she did not lunch; she did not take tea with him. Trays were taken to her study, and Finch's lean face was grave. The butler gave no information about his mistress's mood, and Madame Noyon attended to Clare's tea with a sombre air that was quite unwonted.

The house was in mourning, and Philip appeared every morning wearing a black armband. *Just to be mannerly, sir.*

His bland good nature was irritating in the extreme, but Clare did not take him to task. He also did not gather his effects and retreat to his own Baker Street flat, for some reason he could not quite name.

The fact that reminders of Valentinelli's presence would fill the rooms there as well was certainly not a consideration, was it?

Late in the evening, Finch tapped at the door of the workroom. Clare had been a trifle surprised at the mess left in that stone-walled room, but Philip had not even blinked at scrubbing the blood off the walls. Tidying the place had taken a day's worth of work, and he was cogitating upon the advisability of a series of experiments involving his own blood and a spæctroscope.

Philip tossed the door open. "Morning, guv! Come to visit the peasants?"

"You are an annoyance, boy," Finch replied, quite unperturbed. "Telegram, sir."

"Telegram?" Clare straightened his sleeves and viewed one of the large wooden tables with satisfaction. A tidy workroom meant a tidy mind, indeed.

"Yes, sir." Finch's tone betrayed nothing but neutrality. However, there was a fine sheen of sweat on the butler's forehead, and there was a slight tremor in the hand that proffered the slip of paper.

It was from Aberline, and the satisfaction of deduction burned through Clare's skull.

*Ah. So it is Finch the inspector would like to pry from Miss Bannon's grip.* It made sense, now – the butler, as one of Miss Bannon's oddities, had a chequered past. He affected a laborious upper-crust wheeze and a slow, stately walk, but his movements often betrayed a knife-fighters's awareness of space and familiarity with tight corners. Several interlocking deductions filled Clare's faculties for a moment – a sweet burn, rather like coja.

The telegram itself was almost an afterthought.

*SEARCHING FOR CLEWS STOP REQUEST YOUR PRESENCE STOP*

"How very interesting," Clare murmured. "Is the boy waiting?"

"Yes, sir."

"Give him tuppence, please. And send for a hansom, there's a good man."

"Yes, sir." Finch retreated, Philip watched with bright interest. His hand twitched, and Finch's fingers tightened slightly, but the young man merely offered a wide grin.

"Finch?"

"Yes, sir?"

For a moment, he wished to utter an absurdity – *Worry not, good man, I shan't bring the inspector home.* Then the likely consequences of such a statement became apparent, bringing him up short. Not to mention the thought of calling Miss Bannon's house *home*. He had a flat of his own, did he not?

*Then why am I still here?* "Do make certain Miss Bannon knows my whereabouts. I do not quite trust the good inspector's intentions."

Finch hesitated. He glided for the door, and Clare

detected a smidgen of relief on his gaunt face. "*Yes*, sir," he said, finally, with a peculiar emphasis on the first word.

*So. It* was *Finch, and I have reassured him.* It would not do to remark upon it, but Clare permitted himself a small smile and a tiny warm glow of satisfaction.

He turned in a slow circle, taking in the view of the workroom, and was struck by the shocking idea that he had been wasting time. Waiting for Miss Bannon to descend from her tower, so to speak, and pass commerce with his mere mortal self again.

*Though how mere a mortal I am remains to be seen.*

"Well now," he murmured, staring at the racks of beakers and alembics, each one shining-clean. "I say, Lud – ah, Philip, I have been imposing on Miss Bannon's hospitality rather much lately."

The lad made a short sound, whether of approbation or complaint Clare could not tell.

Clare forged onward. "You are rather an odd sort, but you are quick and know when to stay silent. I think you may do very well as an assistant."

Philip's nose wrinkled slightly. "A fine compliment, sir."

"And heartily meant. Fetch what you need, we may not return."

"*She* won't like that, sir."

"Nonsense. She has every faith in your capability, or she would not have engaged you to follow me about." He felt, he realised, extremely *lucid*, and the prospect of another tangle to test his faculties against was comforting in the extreme.

He also felt quite calm. Having a course of action to pursue helped to no end.

Philip had no witticism to answer with, so Clare set forth at a little faster than a walk but still short of a run, to fetch his hat and pack a few necessaries.

Perhaps Miss Bannon did worry for his well-being; perhaps this was an affair sorcery alone could untangle. Perhaps she was correct, and perhaps it was dangerous for Clare to accompany the detective inspector into the murderous knots that sprang up thick and rank as weeds wherever illogical sorcery was found.

Yes, Clare admitted to himself as he hopped up the stairs and turned for his rooms. She had quite a legitimate concern, had the lady in question.

*Nevertheless, my dear Emma, I cannot wait to prove you wrong.*

"I say, I wasn't sure you'd come," Aberline said grimly, rising to shake Clare's hand. His desk was littered with piles of paper, his inkstand had seen heavy use of late, and the shelves in his office were disarranged somewhat. The place was full of dust occasioning from that rearranging, and there was a betraying tickle in Clare's nose.

He suppressed the incipient sneeze and cleared his throat instead. "Whyever not? I am quite happy to be of service. This shall keep my faculties tolerably exercised, I should think. Besides, we cannot have murderers running loose. It is an affront to good order."

"Indeed." The inspector's hand trembled slightly, and

there were still dark circles under his eyes. "Many of the public agree. In fact, we are inundated with well-meaning letters, telegrams, notes, scribbles, and opinions. They are certain someone they know has acted suspiciously, or they tell us how we may go about doing our duty and catching the damned man. He seems to have rather caught the public interest."

"Gruesomely so. The broadsheets are full of *Leather Apron* this and *Murder* that." *The less responsible are blaming the Yudics in all but name.* Clare cast about for a place to perch, but there was none. The chair he had settled in last time overflowed with paper – no doubt there was a rich trove of deduction to unearth there. "Do tell me how I may help, sir."

"I would set you to weeding through these, but I rather think it a waste of time and of your magnificent talents. If you can believe it, these are the missives that have been judged to have some merit in other quarters, and are thus passed to me."

*But there must be hundreds!* "Good heavens. Surely there is a better use of your own resources than *this*."

"I rather think so." Aberline tugged on his gloves, of a little higher quality than a mere inspector's, but by no means reprehensibly Æsthete.

Clare noted his walking-stick – Malacca, with a curious brass head that looked rather too heavy – and the overcoat hanging behind the inspector's desk, on a wrought-iron contraption. "I deduce we are going walking."

"Rather healthful, at our age." Aberline shrugged into the overcoat with quick movements.

A flash of amusement passed through Clare, a swift pang, over quickly. He did his best to ignore it. "I further deduce our destination is an unsavoury part of Londinium."

"Will he take cold, our young lad?" The inspector scooped up his walking-stick and thrust his chin at Philip Pico, who held a mutinous peace.

The youth merely let his lip curl slightly, and Clare thought the russet touches to his hair were perhaps natural. Even his eyebrows held a tinge of burning.

"I doubt it. He has overcome his reluctance to accompany me on such salubrious excursions." *There are some advantages to logic, indeed.*

"Very well. He may even be useful." The detective inspector cast a final glance over the room, and an extraordinary flash of Feeling surfaced on his features.

*Observe, analyse.* Clare's faculties seized on the unguarded expression. Longing, disgust, a heavy recognition of futility.

Detective Inspector Aberline was a man who loathed his employment, and yet he would continue in it for as long as possible, devoting his energies faithfully and completely, with little regard for his health or happiness.

Perhaps his dislike of Miss Bannon sprang from the fact that they were, on that level, very much the same. There was no antipathy like that of the familiar. "Mr Pico is singularly useful, sir. I deduce we are bound for Whitchapel?"

Aberline's broad, sudden smile was a marvel of cheerfulness, showing another flash of the youth he must have been. "Incorrect, sir!" He drew himself up, settled his bowler, tested the heft of his walking-stick, and strode lively for the door. "We are bound for Limhoss, and for an explanation."

# Chapter Twenty-Eight

## Tonight, Strike to Kill

"Oh, *blast* it all." Emma's temper frayed still further, and Finch's head drew back between his thin, hunching shoulders, rather in the manner of a tortoise.

A telegram from Aberline, and Clare was out of the door like a shot. At least Philip had gone with him, and she could safely consign the mentath's welfare to the list of problems not to be solved at the moment.

She took a deep breath. "Never mind. They shall distract my quarry admirably for the time being. Thank you, Finch."

"Mum." He paused, ready if she wished to add anything more.

Fortunately, she did. "I am closing the house. Pray let the other servants know, and take care none of the deliveries are allowed to step inside. I do not have time for the bother that would ensue." Not to mention it might drive the prices of some goods up, and while she had a good head for business – a Collegia education rather instilled such a thing – there was no reason to be *flagrant* with what she had accumulated. A second thought occurred to her. "I do rather hope Clare does not bring his new acquaintance to my door. The result would be singularly unappealing."

Finch's posture did not change one whit. "Mr Clare said he did not quite trust the inspector's motives regarding yourself, mum."

"Did he now." A thin thread of amusement bloomed, very much against her will. "Well, Mr Clare is wise to do so." She halted, one foot on the first stair. "Finch . . . *Geoffrey*."

He blinked, and the mild surprise on his thin face might have been amusing as well, except for the sudden flare of fear underneath it. Lime-green to Sight, bitter and acrid, it stung her far more sharply than she dared admit.

"I have not forgotten my promise," she continued. "The inspector may go elsewhere to satisfy the grudges he bears both of us. Should you leave my service or retire, you shall be safely ensconced in a lovely warm foreign country with a comfortable independence before *he* receives a whisper of such an event."

"I would not leave your service, mum." Finch had drawn himself up. "Not willingly, God strike me down if I don't mean it."

Her smile was unguarded, and for once Emma was content to have it so. "Thank you, Finch." She found her gloved hand had rested on his forearm, and her own shock at her familiarity was matched by Finch's sudden thunder-struck expression. "I would be saddened to see you go."

"Erm. Shall you be needing the carriage, mum?"

"No, thank you. I shall most likely return very late, possibly not before dawn. You may all go to bed early, I should think."

"Yesmum." And he glided away, suddenly very small and slight against the foyer's restrained elegance. How Severine had clucked and fussed when Emma brought him home, how the housekeeper had expressed her disdain in every possible way until Emma had informed her tartly that *she* was the resident sorceress and Severine Noyon, treasured and valued as she was, did not have the final say in what or whom Emma pleased to employ.

*If I bring home a dozen cutthroat syphilitic Dutch mercenaries, Madame Noyon, you will be gracious and greet them kindly, and have some little faith in your mistress.*

Her smile faded, remembering how poor Severine had quailed, going cheese-pale, her plump hands waving help-lessly. Emma had gentled her, of course – *You must trust me as you did before, Madame. Have I ever led you astray?*

Still, it was . . . unworthy. Frightening the soft and broken held no joy. Given the habits of Severine's previous employer, it was no wonder the woman still cowered.

"Prima?" Mikal appeared, striding from the drawing room.

"I am closing the house." She shook herself into full alertness, and set aside memory. "Finch shall warn the servants; I hope Clare will not bring his new friend home like a street-found cur."

"If he does, the result will no doubt be satisfying."

"Very. And yet, messy, and no end of inconvenience." She breathed out, softly, and drew her mantle closer.

The scrap of cloth in her skirt pocket was an unwelcome weight, no matter that it was merely a small strip soaked with *vitae* and sealed in a ball of virgin wax cooled with a sketched charter symbol. *Vitae*, no matter how unwholesome for one of Emma's Discipline, was still a most useful fluid, which could be imprinted with the sympathetic qualities of *other* fluids.

As in a sorcerer's blood, shed in a Blightallen doss.

The Sympathy would be weak, but that weakness would insulate her from another overwhelming vision of murder. Or at least, so she hoped. She further hoped it would not sensitise her further to whatever damnable Work was occurring. Her careful, delicate probing of the æther over the last two days had crushed whatever lingering hope she had held of it being simply a mistake, or of the effects upon Victrix and herself being simply coincidental.

"You could merely stay here." The Shield's irises were lambent in the foyer's dimness, and he was a solidly comforting shadow, at least. "Let *her* taste the fruits of her sowing."

*If those fruits did not echo so loudly inside my own body, I might consider it.* "I could. However, Clare expects me to take a hand in this affair."

He nodded. And, thankfully, did not take issue with the statement.

"Come." *I should do this quickly, before I find another reason to avoid doing it at all.* "And Mikal?"

"Yes?"

"Tonight, strike to kill."

A gleam of white teeth, shown in a smile. "Yes, Prima."

The edge of Whitchapel was already showing thin traceries of virulent green, and the fog had thickened to a soup best strained through a kerchief. Emma found she could push her veil aside without her eyes stinging, but chose not to. She was merely a darker shadow hurrying along, Mikal in his black a blot beside her.

The fog lipped every surface, turning passers-by into shades risen from some underworld described in one of the Greater Texts, strangling the gaslamps' tiny circles of illumination.

The alleys were muffled by Scab already, and there were choked sounds from some of them. A soft cry ahead resolved into a confused flurry of shadows, but when they reached the corner there was only a splash of bright smoking blood on the cobbles, Scab threading busily through its warm nutrition in delicate filigreed whorls.

Emma continued, stepping briskly along, the digging of her stays as well as the stricture of her point-toe boots both welcome reminders that she was *not* a child.

Mikal's presence was noted, of course. There were gleams in the darkness: altered limbs, cautious eyes with no more humanity than a Nile crocodile's, a jet of shivering gaslamp glow reflecting from a knife blade. She was not approached, though once Mikal touched her elbow, drifting a few steps away towards an alley-mouth as she stood, bolt upright and breathing calmly, her training sinking its claws deep in her rebellious vitals as her body recognised the heatless scent of danger.

The gleams retreated, but Mikal still stood, the set of his shoulders somehow expressing reluctance to move further, but equal unwillingness to back away. A silent language, one the knives of Whitchapel understood.

Finally he relaxed a trifle, and paced back to her side. She continued without a word.

Blightallen, where the vanished Kendall had met with such misfortune, was of a different character after nightfall. Her ankles ached with the step-glide that was necessary to keep her footing, for the Scab had thickened. The darkness was a living thing, almost impenetrable, and Emma could not decide whether to be grateful she could discern the shapes around her or nauseous at the filth underfoot. For one whom even candlelight could glare-blind during the deeper use of her ætheric talents, it was an unexpected . . . well, not a gift, but it certainly made visiting this hole *easier*.

For a certain value of "easy", she supposed.

Her gloved hand dug for the wax ball; she drew it out securely caged in her fist. Mikal, his fingers quick and deft, knotted a hank of silk about her closed hand, and glanced at her face. Could he see in this reproduction of Stygia?

"Are you . . ."

Was he about to ask her if she was certain? Or ready? Emma shook her head, acutely aware of curls brushing her mantle's shoulder, the fog making its own whisper-sound as it crept uneasily above the Scab. Occasionally it dipped its fingers down to almost touch the thick coating, then recoiled as the surface of Whitchapel's greediest resident twitched.

She opened her mouth to speak the minor Word that would unleash the Sympathy.

It died unuttered, ætheric force tangling and snarling under the surface of the world as Mikal clapped his free hand over her mouth, his head coming up with a quick, fluid, somehow *wrong* movement.

Footsteps, light and quick. *What is that?* She braced herself, and when Mikal took his hand away they shared a look of silent accord – visible because the cameo at her throat had lit with leprous green brightening as the sound grew closer. There was no *splorch* of the ooze releasing a running foot, nor was there the sliding of an accomplished flashboy who had learned the trick of not breaking the Scab's surface in order to move quickly along.

*What on earth—*

It burst from the gloom at the end of Blightallen, and Mikal was there to meet it, his knives out and flashing dully.

Flickers of motion, a whip-crack of sound – and her Shield was driven back, sliding on the uncertain footing.

It *did* have a whip. Emma's eyes narrowed as she flashed

through and discarded invisible threads. The æther resonated oddly, curdling; she had time to take a deep breath before Mikal was flung aside and hit a dosshouse door with a sickening crack.

Scab curled and smoked, oily steam rising as it cringed away from the tall, square-headed figure – it had a coachman's hat, and the whip was a heavy one meant to sound over several heaving clockhorse backs at once.

She had fractions of a moment to decide what manner of creature it was as it leapt skimble-legged for her. A glamour could kill if she believed in its truth; a bound spirit or a Construct could injure her grievously if its binder or creator had entrusted it with enough ætheric force; a dollsome or Horst's Mannequin could *only* strike physically; a Seeming could not injure her unduly; and there were so many other categories to consider she was almost, *almost* too late.

Mikal let out a choked cry, but Emma had set herself squarely, the cameo sparking and two rings on her left hand – one a bloody garnet set in heavy gold, the other cheap brass with a glass stone that nevertheless held a fascinating twinkle and a heavy charge – flaming with ætheric force.

A violet flower bloomed between her and the thing in a coachman's form: sorcerous force widening like a painted Chinois fan. The Word she spoke, sliding harsh and whole from her throat with a harsh pang, was not of Mending or Breaking or even of Binding. No, she chose a different Language entirely, and one not of her Discipline.

Strictly speaking, Naming belonged to neither the White nor the Black, nor the Grey besides. Its only function was to *describe*, but such was a law of sorcery: *the Will makes the Name*.

Had she not been Prime, she perhaps could not have forced the creature's dubious reality to temporarily take the form most suited to her purposes. The Word warped as the thing fought her humming definition of its corporeality, and that very twisting and bulging gave her indications of its nature.

But only indications.

*A tricksome beast you are, indeed.*

It hit the shield of violet shimmering and Emma was driven back, her heels scraping long furrows through crisping, peeling Scab. Her gloved hands flew, describing a complex pattern, and the violet light snapped sideways and forward, again fanlike. The edge slashed up, sharply, and the thing's howl blew her hair back, cracked the folds of her mantle, stung her watering eyes.

She ignored the irritation. It *was* a coachman, its yellow and red striped muffler wrapped high to conceal a void where the face should be and its high collar doing its best to shade the face as well, its coat flapping open, worn and patched in places with tiny needle-charmer's stitches; its boots caked with manure and street-scum. The hat was of fine quality, a jaunty black feather affixed, the waistcoat of embroidered purple and gold a proud bit of flash. It was not liveried, but the boots and the hat said *servant* instead of *hire*, and who would send a creature like this in a livery which could be identified? The clothes were no doubt pawnshop acquisitions, probably corpsepicker gains.

It fell, splatting dully onto the Scab-covered cobbles. More vile steam rose. Its fingers had torn through the ragged woollen gloves, being far too long and corpse-pallid, each sporting an extra joint that no doubt helped the thing wield a knife.

Or its whip, which clattered on the cobbles beside it.

Emma set her chin, bringing the fan-shield back smoothly. The creature's advantage of surprise was lost, and she had successfully driven it down. But where was Mikal, and what precisely *was* this unholy thing?

It hissed, scrabbling at age-blackened cobbles with malformed hands to find its weapon, and she had a moment to be grateful Clare was not further involved in this matter before it twisted upright with inhuman speed and flung itself at her again.

# *Chapter Twenty-Nine*

*A Babe in Woods*

The saying *Foul as Limhoss breath* was marvellous apt. Whitchapel had its own stench, and Limhoss no Scab, but in Archibald Clare's considered judgment there were few places in Londinium to outdo the latter in matters of fragrance. Perhaps it was the Basin, or maybe the mariners who congregated in its dens and dosses, the tar of the ropes or the tight-packed press of alien flesh – for the Chinois population of the Isle was concentrated here, and their suffusion of odours was foreign as well as rank.

Ginger and spices, the starch of their rice and boiling of their odd oils, different fish than an Englene would eat, the dry rough note of raw silk, and an acrid smoke enfolded them. Even the fog was a different shade here, its billows assuming the shapes of their odd writing, their crouching, painted charter stones near the doors alive with weak saffron light so they could practise their native arts of minor charming without the risk of nasty side-consequences.

Aberline knocked twice at a collection of splinters masquerading as a door, which shivered and opened immediately. Perhaps he was expected, or perhaps, Clare thought as he ducked to pass through the tiny opening, *anyone* was expected after dark.

Down a close, reeking passageway and into a womblike dimness, the light turned red by the paper lampshades it passed through, and Clare realised it was a poppy den.

Long shapes reclined on bunks built into the wall, giving a rather nautical flavour to the room. A brown fug rose from winking scarlet eyes as Morpheus's chosen flower carried its devotees into fantastic languor. The eyes were the bowls of the pipes, a beast with a thousand gazes.

"Your methods are indeed unusual," he remarked, breaking the hush. Coughs rose in protest, weakly; he had not adjusted his tone for the confined quarters.

The bent, blue-garbed Chinoise who had bobbed ahead of them into the room made a *shush* sound, but not very loudly. Clare could not quite decide what age the crooked stick of a woman had attained, for her thinning hair was still lacquer-black – as were the few teeth she still possessed – and the skin of her face had drawn tight. She scuffed along in embroidered slippers, threading through those on the floor gathered around the long poppy-pipes, beckoning them along and bowing repeatedly to Aberline, who appeared a giant in a toy shop next to her.

"Nodders all," Philip Pico muttered behind Clare. "Ripe for rolling."

"Not here," Aberline whispered. "*Do* be a good sport, little lad."

Of course, the prickly little russet took offence. "I'm no nodder. Not with the filthy Chin—"

"Silence is good for your health." Aberline cut him off, and Clare observed him handing the Chinoise a handful of coins. He received a key and a packet in return, and she pointed them up a rickety staircase.

"Surely there are more wholesome dens than this." Clare found himself walking stiffly, avoiding the chance of the surfaces of this place brushing against his clothes.

"But here, dear sir, I am certain we will not be overheard."

*Is that a danger?* "Are we plotting, then?"

"We are engaging in a method, Clare. Have you ever ridden the dragon?"

Philip caught at Clare's arm. "*She* won't like this, sir."

Was it Annoyance Clare felt? He shelved it, stepping to avoid a limp hand lain along the floor. "It is a good thing she is not about, then. And really, this is no place for a lady."

A slight cough from Aberline, but thankfully, the man restrained himself. He murmured to the Chinoise crone in what seemed a dialect of their strange tonal language, and she retreated past them, her loose trousers under a long, high-collared shirt fluttering forlornly. She gave Clare a wide obsequious smile, blackened stumps on display, and was gone into the red-drenched gloom below.

The heavy iron key fit a door in a high narrow hallway, which led into an equally high but not very spacious room. Still, it was quiet, the soughing of Londinium outside merely a suggestion of pressure against the eardrums.

Two low sopha-like things heaped with tattered bolsters, rather more in the style of the Indus than the Chinois, a wretched oil lamp Aberline put a lucifer to and turned down as low as possible, and four poppy-pipes on a small round table of glowing mellow brass and mahogany.

Clare took in the dust upon the table, the marks about the rim of one pipe, the dents in the upholstery and pillows on the far side, set where the smoker could recline and watch the door.

"You come here often, Inspector."

"As often as necessary." Aberline indicated the other sopha, and Clare found himself sharing a look of silent accord with Philip. It was a moment's work to move the other divan to a more salubrious position, which manoeuvre Aberline watched with a tolerant smile. "I am afraid, little man, that there is only enough here for two."

Philip bristled. "I am no nodder. I'll take my laudanum like a civilised gent, thank you." He rattled the door. "This wouldn't stand a good beating."

"It doesn't have to with you standing watch, now does it?" Aberline settled himself on the sad wreck of furniture that was, Clare saw, a broken-backed chesterfield that could not even be salvaged for Eastcheap's sorry hawking. Its just-moved companion was sturdier, but much dirtier. "Do sit, Mr Clare. You are about to view a marvel."

It was not at all like smoking tabac.

*A small amount to start,* Aberline had said. *We are not here to enjoy but to learn. To plumb the depths.*

Perhaps the man fancied himself a poet.

A blurring across the nerves. A deep hacking cough. What did it smell like? Acrid, certainly, resinous. A faint amount of spice. Was he already . . .

The couch was quite dirty, but it was also comfortable. Clare leaned back, and the problem burst in upon him in all its dizzying complexity.

*Some manner of sorcery, making me proof against an explosion. Proof against knives, and Time. My faculties will stay sharp.* Yet the poppy had a distinct effect upon him. What would coja do? He had lost the taste for it, but he could experiment.

Later.

The walls, their dingy paper peeling, suddenly took on new breath and interest. Each rip and fleck, each bit of plaster showing, gave rise to a host of deductions. They split and re-formed, the history of this sad little room unreeling in a gorgeous play of light and shadow, logic and meaning.

*Why, this is marvellous!* The urge to laugh rose from his navel, but he set it aside. Irrational, messy, uncertain Feeling had no place here . . .

. . . but, still, the poppy blunted the painful edges and the outright *sloppiness* of Feeling, and he could consider the entire situation rather calmly.

*Ludovico.*

It was grief, of course, and the world became a mist of rose shot through with crimson. He had read of this, the welter of contradictory emotion when death struck; he had not felt it as a young man when his parents had succumbed to mortality. Had it been a blessing, that numbness? What was different now?

*No, Clare. You felt it.* He remembered the nights of working straight through, studying for the Examinations in his draughty, cramped student lodgings. Burying the Feeling, because it was a distraction, and after all, he was young and just coming into his faculties' full bloom. After a long while the ache had retreated, because he was a mentath and Feeling was an enemy to logic.

*Yet one must account for it, in all one's dealings. How odd.*

Aberline was speaking, but Clare could not distinguish the words through thick rosy fog. It was like Londinium's vaporous breath, except it smelled of some sweetness. Spiced pear, smoke . . .

*Emma.* His faculties painted her image against the inside of his eyelids. Her soft face, steely with the force of her character or slack in sleep as he had seen it once. Her small hands, and the fire in her dark eyes. The way her footsteps echoed, and the brush of her skirts.

The images came one after another, tumbling in their rapidity. Emma bloody and battered at the end of some dangerous bit of business, her mouth set tight and determination burning in her gaze. Tucking a stray curl up into the rest of her complex hairstyle; she did so hate to be dishevelled. Poring over a broadsheet or two in the morning, making quite serviceable deductions, writing in her firm, clear hand at her morning desk in the solarium.

And finally, Emma at his bedside. *I am loath to lose you, Archibald*.

Grief for Ludovico, and the sweet sting that was Emma Bannon. It was the sting that wrapped crimson threads through the fog and pulled it tight.

Here, with the poppy smoke burning his lungs and rest of his flesh a loose soup, he could admit the waves of Feeling. He could let them slide through him and away, and when the poppy dream ended he would be whole – and *rational* – again.

Or so he hoped. His eyelids lifted, and Aberline was speaking again.

The inspector, instead of relaxing into languor, had leaned forward. He was still speaking, and Clare sought to grasp the words, but they slid away as well. There was a reply – Philip Pico, near the door, a light amused tone. Why had she bothered to engage such a person to look after him? If he was immortal now – but perhaps she feared not for Clare's physical frame. Perhaps she feared for Clare himself, and what the double blow of grief and irrationality would do to him.

*This is ridiculous. Preposterous.*

Yet the idea had some merit. It was, he decided, a

deduction taking into account a weight of Feeling, and not sinking in the process.

The glow was leaving, draining away too quickly. The crimson threads gave one last painless twitch and were gone, the rosy fog evaporating, and he became aware of a hammering sound.

Aberline had reached his feet. He swayed slightly, and Clare realised the man had been speaking of the murders. He blinked several times as Philip gave a curt command, *None of that now*, and Clare found himself on a broken sopha in the middle of a Limhoss poppy den, the world a sudden vivid assault after the rosy fog.

"Inspector Aberline, sir." A whip-thin young man in a brown jacket, but his hair cut too short for a labourer's. From the Yard, then, judging by his shoes, and out of breath. "There's another one."

Clare's stomach turned over, queerly.

"Another murder." Aberline nodded. "Yes, Browne. Hail a hansom, there's a good man."

The brown-jacketed Browne gasped, red blotches of effort on his sweating cheeks. There was a fog of smoke in here – how much had Aberline produced? The inspector was not only standing, but moving about. Clare gathered himself, an odd burning in the region of his chest.

Philip Pico's face was a fox's for a moment as he bent down over the mentath. The sharp black nose wrinkled, and his ears were perked, alert. "Come on, nodder."

"You, sir, are a fox." Clare's flesh moved when he told it to. It was an odd feeling, thinking of himself inside an imperishable corporeal glove, his faculties simply observing the passage of time. There was a certain comfort in the notion.

"And you're a babe in woods, sir, for all your bright-penny talk. Come along."

Aberline glanced over his shoulder; it really was quite irritating that the man seemed so unmoved by whatever quantity of poppy he had smoked. Instead, he was merely haggard, drawn, the dark shadows under his eyes ever more pronounced. Soon they might swallow his gaze whole . . .

*Wait.* Clare searched through memory, grasping for whatever the inspector had said into the smoke-fog. *He did something, something quite alarming. He spoke of . . . what?*

The tantalising memory receded, and Clare's head began to ache.

*I suspect this was a very irrational event.*

# ✵ Chapter Thirty

## Profit in Reminding

The coachman-thing darted forward. Violet light flashed as Emma brought the fan-shield up smartly, slashing it across the chest. Blightallen was alive with cries and running feet, yellow fog thickening and swirling in a most peculiar manner as the residents of this sorry street realised an extraordinary event was occurring in their midst.

She snapped the shield sideways again, her throat swelling with a rill of notes. Her rings were fading as their stored ætheric charge drained, and the end of the street was fast approaching. She could not give much more ground before she was forced to think of an alternate method for dealing with this creature. She had forced it into precisely the correct proportion of physicality, so it could be hurt, but confining it thus was taking *far* more of her resources than she liked, and it was only a matter of time before its creator noticed her refusal to politely die and perhaps took steps to free the thing from her strictures.

Where was Mikal? How badly was he wounded?

*Tend to him later. Right now content yourself with not dying, for this thing wishes to kill.*

It made no noise now, save whip-cracks and the stamping of its feet. The whip flickered, the fan-shield snapped closed as she trilled a descant, turning on itself to force the flying tip aside. The whip wrapped around a teetering wrought-iron lamppost, its cupola dark since the lighters rarely came to a street so thickly padded with Scab. Emma skipped forward, bringing the shield low and snapping it open again, its edge sharpening as her concentration firmed.

It fell back, and under its curved hat brim were two coals that had not been there before. The whip twitched, iron shrieking as the lamppost bent, and she knew she would not be able to bring the shield up in time. The notes curdled in her throat, breath failing her.

*Oh dear.*

It shrieked, the sound tearing both æther and air, as Mikal's face rose over its shoulder, his eyes yellow lamps. A knifepoint, dripping, protruded from its narrow chest and the Shield wrenched the blade away, his other hand coming up to seek purchase in its muffler. If he could tear the thing's head loose—

Emma spun, the whip's sharp end tangling in her skirt as the fan-shield blurred, becoming a conduit to bleed away the force of the strike.

A vast noise filled Blightallen, Scab-steam flooding up to mix with cringing yellow fog.

She fell, *hard*, knees striking cobble and her teeth clicking together jarringly. Folded over as silence fell, the inhabitants of the street temporarily stunned into mouth-gaping wonder. What could they see through the fog? Anything?

Through the sudden quiet, the thing's receding footsteps were light and unholy, and Mikal's hands were at her shoulders.

"Prima? *Emma?*"

Hot blood against her fingers. Emma winced, drew in a sharp breath, and brought her fist up sharply.

It was barbed, so it tore even further on its way free of her thigh and her skirts. A small, betraying sound wrung itself from her as she finished wrenching it loose and found she had not lost the wax ball either. *Oh, good.* The traces of Keller's shed blood would serve a useful purpose now, giving her a chance at triangulation rather than mere fumbling direction-seeking.

She looked up to find Mikal's face inches from hers, striped with blood. He was filthy – no doubt he had rolled in the Scab – and there were splinters and brick dust liberally coating him. Her hair had come loose, falling in her face; he brushed away a curl and his fingertips found her cheekbone.

*How comforting.* A cough caught her unawares, then her voice decided it would perform its accustomed function. Scraped into a shadow of itself, it nevertheless was tolerably steady. "Are you hurt?"

His expression went through several small changes she could not decipher, before settling on relief. "Only slightly. My apologies. I was . . . briefly stunned."

"Quite a stunning experience." She caught her breath. Looked down again, found herself holding a sharp, barbed metal weight from the end of the coachman's whip, torn free. Catching it in her own leg had not been the best of ideas, she had to admit, even if it had served its purpose. "But still, educational, and *so* entertaining."

"If you say so, Prima. Can you stand?"

"I think—"

He took further stock of her. "You're bleeding."

"Yes. Mikal, I rather think I cannot stand without help."

"You never do anything halfway, Prima. Lean on me."

"Mikal . . ." The words she had meant to say died unuttered, for in the distance there was a bell-clear cry cutting Londinium's yellow fog.

"*Murder!*"

And Whitchapel . . . erupted.

The crowd was a beast of a thousand heads, and its mood scraped against every ache in Emma's tired body. She leaned upon Mikal, letting the press wash about her, and listened.

*Cut her throat . . . side to side, a sight, found in a yard . . . no doubt it's him, it's him! A leather apron . . . Leather Apron . . . foreigner . . . drinking our blood, they are . . .*

If the bloodied apron outside the Yudic workingman's club had been a ruse, it was a clever one. If it had been merely a bit of refuse, it was still serving the author of all this unpleasantness tolerably well.

Her left thigh throbbed, the healing sorcery Mikal had applied sinking its own barbs in. "This will not do," she murmured. "Is the entire Eastron End mad now?"

"Another murder, they say."

"I felt nothing." She clutched at his shoulder, jostled and buffeted. The churchbells were speaking, Tideturn was soon; she could feel it like approaching thunder.

Half past one, of course not a single hansom in sight, and the crowd, spilling out into the streets as word leapt from doss to doss. "Mikal. *I did not feel it.*"

"I know." He steadied her. "Prima . . . that thing—"

"It was a coachman. And it had a knife." *What manner of creature was it, though? I shall know soon enough.*

"Yes." He pushed aside the rags of his bloodied black velvet coat, irritably. Underneath, his skin was whole but flushed in vivid stripes. "A very sharp blade. I hardly felt it."

"I shall wish to . . ." The world tried to spin away underneath her. She had expended far more sorcerous force than was wise, and lost *quite* a bit of blood. The Scab was probably growing over it now, green and lush, not scorched away as it had been under the coachman-thing's feet. "I shall wish to examine the exact pattern of the cuts."

"Yes." He propped her against a wall. Peered into her face, uncertain gaslight flickers turning his eyes to shadowed holes. "You're pale."

"I am well enough." She even managed to say it firmly.

Across the street, a flashboy tumbled out of a ginhouse, his right hand a mass of clicking, whirring metal. He was greeted by derisive laughter as a gaptooth drab with her skirts hiked around her knees shouted, *"Leather Apron's aboot tonight, watch yerself!"*

The crowd gathered itself, and Emma shivered, suddenly very cold. Her breath was a cloud, and she stared into Mikal's familiar-unfamiliar face. "There is about to be some unpleasantness," she whispered.

"I understand. Here." He ducked under her arm, his own arm circling her waist. Her stays dug most uncomfortably, but at least she was alive and drawing breath to feel them. "Close your eyes."

She did, and Mikal coiled himself. He leapt, and below them the street boiled afresh. More screams, and the high tinkle of breaking glass.

The riot bloomed, a poisonous flower, but Mikal held her, slate and other tiles crunching under his feet as the rooftops of Londinium spun underneath them. This was a Shield's sorcery, and very peculiar in its own way, managing to unseat the stomach of those without the talents and training of that ancient brotherhood.

Which explained why, when he finally set her on her feet in a Tosselside alley, the riot merely a rumble in the distance, she leaned over and heaved most indelicately.

Londinium turned grey around her, and she surfaced from an almost-swoon to find Mikal holding her upright again.

Her mouth was incredibly sour, and she repressed an urge to spit to clear it.

*A lady does not do such things.* "The unrest will spread. And likely foul any trace of where that thing went."

"Yes. You are very pale, Prima. Perhaps we should—"

She discovered she did not wish to know what he would advance as the next advisable action. "The decent and sane thing to do would be to go home, bar my doors and wait for this affair to reach its conclusion without me. The Coachman was set upon my trail, just as a bloodhound."

"I thought as much." Did he sound resigned? "I rather think you will not retreat, though."

Indecision, a new and hateful feeling. The temptation to retreat was well-nigh irresistible. Her left leg trembled, and she felt rather . . . well, not quite up to her usual temper.

In the end, though, there was quite simply no one else who could arrange this affair satisfactorily. It was not for Victrix, nor for Britannia, and not even for Clare so high and mighty, looking down upon her for daring to give him a gift sorcerers would use every means they could beg, borrow, or steal to acquire.

No, the reason she could not retreat just yet was far simpler.

The Coachman-thing had made her afraid.

For a Prime, that could not be borne.

"No," she said, and took a deep breath, wishing her stays did not cut so and that her skirts were not draggled with blood and Scab-muck. "I shall not retreat. I require a hansom."

"Where are we bound?"

"The Yard, Mikal. They will not venture into Whitchapel until the riot burns itself out, and there may be certain profit in *reminding* one or two of Aberline's superiors of certain facts."

*Chief among them that I am acting for the Crown – but I am not particularly choosey about how I finish this bloody business.*

# Chapter Thirty-One

## A Somewhat Durable Cast

A thickset man in bobby's blue, his whistle dangling from a silver chain, put up both hands to halt the detective inspector's headlong rush. "Whitchapel's ablaze, sir. We're not to go in. Orders."

"Oh, for the love of . . ." Aberline looked almost ready to tear out handfuls of his own hair. "Clare?"

Clare blinked, cocked his head and sought to untangle the various cries and crashes rending the night air. "Who would order—"

"Commissioner Waring, no doubt." Aberline all but bounced up on his toes to peer between two other broad, beefy bootleather knights, who were viewing the traceries of Scab on the cobbles with studied disinterest. "*Candleson!* Over here!"

The bobby who glanced up and sauntered to join them

was a mutton-chopped and gin-nosed bulk with an oddly mincing gait. His knees no doubt gave him trouble, judging by how gingerly he stepped, but Clare caught a steely twinkle in the man's deep-set eyes and the calluses on his beefy paws. Candleson carried a knotty stick, much in the manner of an Eirean shillelagh, dark with use and oil. A leather loop on his broad, creaking belt was its home on the few occasions, Clare thought, that it was not in his hands.

No doubt it had cracked many a criminal's skull in its time, too.

"Evenin', sir. There's a bit of the restless tonight." His accent was a surprise – reasonably educated, though with a lilt to the consonants that bespoke a childhood on a farm, most probably in Somerset.

"Your understatement, dear Candleson, is superb as always. Let me guess, Waring says to wait for morning?"

"Bit dark in there," was the laconic reply. But Candleson's mouth turned down briefly, and the crease under his chin flushed.

"Another murder." Aberline's eyebrows rose.

"Still bleeding when she was found. Dunfeld's, Berner Street. There's another of those clubs there. Workingmen, foreigners." He looked even more sour at the notion.

"Good God." Aberline did not pale, but it might have been close. "They will kill each other in droves over this."

The noise intensified. Whitchapel buzzed as a poked wasps' nest might. The entire Eastron End might well catch fire, figuratively *or* literally. Clare twitched at his cuffs, bringing them down, and took stock of his person. He did not even have his pepperbox pistol or its replacement, and no doubt the quality of his cloth would attract unwanted attention. He glanced at Philip Pico, who stood with his arms folded and feet braced, watching him with a peculiar expression.

"Well." Clare drew himself up. "There is nothing for it, then."

Aberline rounded on him. "Sir, I—"

Clare set off for the line of venom-green Scab. The onlookers did not expect trouble from his quarter, so he was through the line and marching onwards when Aberline caught at his arm. "What in God's name—"

"I must examine the site of this new event before it is trampled by a mob, and daylight will only bring more of them. Stay here, if you—"

"You shall not go alone. I should warn you, there is tremendous risk to your person."

"I rather think there is." The noise had intensified, and he had to raise his voice to be heard. "I am sure you will find it reassuring that I am of a somewhat durable cast, though. Philip?"

"Oh, she's not going to like this," the lad said, but he seemed willing enough. High spots of colour burned in his beardless cheeks, and there was a definite hard merriment to his tone. Rather as Valentinelli had sported a fey grin, when they were about to plunge into danger.

"She has other matters to attend to," Clare said shortly,

and set out afresh. Aberline followed, with a muttered word that might have been a curse.

Behind them, the line of bobbies and a growing mass of curiosity-seekers murmured and rustled. Ahead, there was a cacophony, the fog billowing in veils as if it, too, sought to misbehave tonight.

Clare did not consult his pocket-watch, but he thought it very likely they had been in a Limhoss daze for quite some hours.

The question of just *what* Inspector Aberline had been saying in the midst of that daze would have to wait. For they rounded a slight bend in the cobbled road, and the fog became garishly underlit with flame. Cries and running feet, piercing screams, and a high sweet tinkle of breaking glass.

The poor, crowded together here, needed little enough reason to strain against the bonds of decency and public order.

The wonder, Clare reflected, was that they did not do so more often.

Underfoot was slick and treacherous. Clare kept to the building side, but gave alley entrances a polite amount of space nonetheless. Darker shapes began to coalesce through the fog.

Between that vapour and the choking slickness under his soles, there was precious little for his faculties to fasten on except the noise.

Slip-sliding footsteps, scurrying tip-taps. Excited babble, and rougher exclamations as some took advantage of the

confusion to perform a deed or two best attempted in such
circumstances. A seashore muttering, another crack of
breaking glass. The fogbound shadows became more
distinct, and a clockhorse's excited neigh cut through the
cacophony. A hansom drawn by a weary roan nag lumbered
past, its driver perhaps thinking to escape the unpleasantness brewing behind him as metal-shod hooves struck the
Scab with muffled splorching sounds. To be plying his
custom so early, the driver was probably a gin-headed
muddle, desperate for—

"Watch yourself, squire." Pico jostled him, not roughly.
Clare returned to himself with a jolt, and found that they
were now in the fringes of a crowd. Hike-skirted slatterns
with frowsty hair, gin-breathing flashboys with their
Alterations gleaming dully, barely respectable workingmen
in braces and heavy boots, a kaleidoscope of sensation and
deduction pouring into his hungry faculties.

The entire population of Whitchapel seemed to be
awake and moving. Rumour and catcall bounced through
the mass of people, and the going quickly became
difficult.

Aberline shouldered through, brushing off no few
enticing offers from the ladies – if one could call them
such – and rough *Watch yerself*s from flashboy and workingman alike. Clare followed in his wake, more than once
pushing away fingers questing for his pocket-valuables.
Pico shoved through after him, and it was probably the
lad's care and quickness that kept Clare from being *more*
troubled by said pickpockets and thieves.

*If Miss Bannon were present, she would no doubt find some more efficient way of working through the crowd.* Clare winced inwardly. Could he not keep the damn woman out of his head for more than an hour?

"*Leather Apron!*" someone bawled, and the crowd stilled for a breath before . . .

Chaos, screams, Clare was lifted bodily as the mass surged forward. Pico's fingers dug into his shoulder once, painfully, before being ripped away, and Aberline vanished.

*Oh, dear.*

His jacket was torn and his foot throbbed where a heavy hobnail boot had done its best to break every bone in said appendage. Somewhere in the distance a clockhorse was screaming, equine fear and pain grating across the rolling roar. Clare slid along the wall, a splatter of warm blood already traced with thin green tendrils of Scab splashed high against the rotting bricks.

He coughed at the reek, consulted a mental map, and edged forward. Cast at the edges of the crowd like flotsam, Pico and Aberline nowhere in sight, he found the Scab underfoot thinning and eyed the buildings about him once again.

Logic informed him that he was near the ancient boundaries of the City, its oldest municipal heart. Under the Pax Latium, Londinium had been merely a trading village burned to the ground by one of Britannia's early incarnations.

The spirit of the Isle's rule had not looked kindly upon the Latiums. Still, the legions of the Pax could not be denied, and they rebuilt the town to make a replacement for Colchestre. Londinium's sprawl since then had been sometimes slow – and at other times marked by fire, not to mention rapine and plunder – but, on the whole, inexorable.

One could call the green filth that hugged Whitchapel's cobbles a similar inexorable creeping. For it seemed to be spreading, thin curling threads digging into the valleys between the stones, hauling hoods of slippery green film over the tiny hills. He followed in its wake, leaving the noise and crush behind, meaning to skirt its edges. Between here and Berner Street lay the bulk of the crowd. There was no penetrating its raging at the moment, but perhaps he could hurry along and come at the site from another angle.

As Clare was comparing his internal map and compass to the fogbound glimpses he could gather, he found that he had come too far, though there was a passage likely to take him in the direction he needed to—

A wet, scraping sound intruded upon his ruminations. He turned, peering through the damp blanket of Londinium's yellow exhalation, a raw green edge to its scent that reminded him of mossy sewage, if such a thing were possible. He supposed it was, in a dark place – what botanical wonder might grow from such rich, if foul, nutrition?

*Crunch. Slurp.* A humming, married to a crackling Clare

had heard many times before, during his acquaintance with Emma Bannon.

Live sorcery.

The fog drew back, for he was approaching, impelled by curiosity and a nasty, dark suspicion. There was another edge to the fog-vapour now, brass-copper and hot, that Clare recognised as well.

Blood.

He realised he was moving as silently as Valentinelli had taught him to, a flood of bright bitterness threatened to overwhelm him. The poppy, lingering false friend, opened a gallery of Memory and Recollection he could not afford to pay attention to, for a shape crouched before him, in a darkened corner of a square.

The gaslamp overhead was dark, burnt out or simply cloaked by the shame of witnessing what Clare now viewed.

A small, dirty, blood-freckled woman's hand, cupped but empty, fallen at her side. The rest of her was an empty sack, her head tipped away and a black bonnet tangled in its greying mass. Dead-white thighs, spattered with dark feculence, flung wide. A section of greyish intestine, poked by long thin spidery fingers. Those fingers returned to the abdominal cavity, plunged and wrenched, and brought a dripping handful up.

Wet slurping sounds underscored by a hum of contentment, like a child or a dog face-deep in melon on a scorching summer day. The figure – a coachman's cap tilted back at a jaunty angle on its blurred head, a red and yellow muffler wound around its throat more than once

– bent over again, the mending on its coat small, skilled needle-charmer's stitches. Its arm came up again, there was the bright flash of a knife, and the blade cut deep into soft flesh. It wrenched the resultant mass free as well and gobbled it.

A rushing filled Clare's ears.

The fingers were gloved, but no trace of blood or matter seemed to adhere to the material. They unravelled at each fingertip, for the thing had extra joints on each phalange. It rooted in the mass of the woman's belly again, and found what it sought. Still smacking its unseen lips, it lifted a clot-like handful – rubbery, pear-shaped, Clare knew there was no way he should be able to discern such a thing, but he knew what it was.

*It is eating her womb. Dear God.*

The crackling of sorcery intensified. The thing hunched, and its figure blurred more. Cloth rippled as the shape underneath it swelled in impossible ways.

*Observe, Clare. Observe. Miss Bannon must know of this. You must give her every particular.*

Blackness rippled at the edges of his vision. He was holding his breath, he realised, for the figure's head had come up, a quick enquiring movement. He was just barely in the range of its peripheral vision – assuming it had human eyes, which, he realised, was not at all a supportable assumption.

It was dark, and he was utterly still, hoping such immobility would hide his presence. Yellow fog swirled uneasily, a tendril sliding between Clare and the . . . *creature* – for nothing human could crouch like that, its knees obscenely high and its head drooping so low, its spidery extra-jointed fingers spasming as it twirled the knife in a brief flashing circle.

The Scab had arrived behind Clare, its wet greenness creeping forward. Tiny tendrils, their sliding almost inaudible under the wet smacking sounds of enjoyment. The quite illogical idea that perhaps some feral, inhuman intelligence was *guiding* the nasty green sludge occurred to Clare, the poppy still blurring the edges of rationality.

Now, when he needed sharp clarity most, it had deserted him.

Fascinating that the drug would linger, even in the face of whatever miracle Miss Bannon had performed upon him.

A rasping, as of a scabrous tongue over chapped, scraped lips. The creature's head made another quick, enquiring movement. The woman – the *corpse* – had worn, sprung-sided boots, and her stockings were soaked with foul matter. Her petticoats were mismatched, and torn to bits. Those white, white thighs, spattered, and the *smell*, dear God.

Had she suffered?

*Does it matter at this particular moment? Stay still, Clare.*

Valentinelli's sneer, echoing through dim memory. *Stay where Ludo put you,* mentale, *and watch.*

His lungs cried for air, even though the soup around the creature became foul enough to see. Or perhaps it was the blackness crowding his vision as his flesh, even if functionally immortal, reminded him that it did still require respiration and all its attendant processes.

A wet sliding. The Scab darted forward, and the creature tumbled aside, fluidly. Steam rose, and Clare caught a glimpse of the thing *under* its clothes. Cracked hide runnelled with scars, terribly burnt as if acid had been flung upon it, and two glowing coals for eyes.

One pale hand came up, the knife blade a star in the dimness, and Clare stumbled back. He felt the slight *whoosh* as the sharp metal cleaved air an inch from his face, fell with a tooth-rattling jolt on a thick carpet of oozing green. A hiss, a whipcrack, Clare's arm instinctively flung up to shield his eyes and suddenly a stinging, a patter of warm blood.

The thing fled, light unnatural footsteps tapping on cobbles, a grating sound, roof tiles shattering as they were dislodged and hit the ground.

Clare scrabbled for purchase, thick resilient slime dragging him as it retreated. It carried him a good ten feet before reluctantly releasing him, his jacket smoking against its caustic kiss and the wound along his forearm smarting as it sealed itself.

The gaslamp above the body burst afresh into feeble flame, and when he gained his feet, Archibald Clare bolted for its circle of glow, telling himself it was merely so he could examine the body in its uncertain light. Certainly not because he felt anything irrational, though his mouth tasted of copper and his sorcerously repaired heart laboured in his chest. It was merely the sudden activity, he told himself, not anything so illogical as *fear*.

And certainly not because as the Scab retreated, it made a low, thick noise, somewhat like a chuckle from a sharp-toothed mouth.

# Chapter Thirty-Two

## Error of Provocation

Even if one could *find* a hansom when one required conveyance, there was always the chance of said hansom being as slow as a newlywed's knitting.

Since Mikal was loath to leave her alone, even though with her safely inside a hansom he could watch over from the rooftop road, she did not even have the luxury of a few moments of solitude to collect her scattered thoughts.

It was ridiculous; a Shield was not the same as *company*, the ancient brotherhood had been trained to discretion and a certain abnegation. And yet . . . it was Mikal.

His hand was on her wrist, perhaps to anchor her. Yet she was attempting no sorcery at all. Perhaps it was the odd, trembling feeling in her legs, the clawed healing sorcery working its way into deep layers of muscle, that made his gaze so worried and disconcerting at the same moment.

She freed her wrist and took the opportunity, in the small, jolting carriage, to push aside sliced black velvet and examine the bright red marks upon his torso. Not claw-marks, which was interesting, and yet the creature had to have been inordinately quick to strike so many times with a single blade. Those long, spidery fingers could wield such a blade, she thought, with amazing delicacy. Very sharp, curved just enough, possibly a physical focus for the creature? Knife and whip.

For a moment, an idea teased at the back of her consciousness. She waited, but it was not yet fully formed, and it retreated into shadow. "How very intriguing," she murmured, and settled back into the dingy seat-cushion. _I suspect I shall never look upon coachmen in the same fashion again._

The hansom jolted, and the hunched, well-wrapped man holding the reins chirruped to the worn-down clockhorse. Emma's vision blurred for a moment, and she breathed out, sharply, dispelling the weakness.

She had lost quite a bit of blood, but so had Mikal. A Shield was exceedingly hard to kill, and yet if the Coachman had stopped to actually fully eviscerate him instead of simply slashing to bleed him out she might be adding his name to the list of her failures.

Obviously she had been judged the larger threat. Or the creature – though she had forced it into exactly the proper proportion of physicality, she still was not entirely certain what it *was* – had not judged her *enough* of a threat to warrant more than incapacitating Mikal for a few crucial moments.

Either way, it had been set upon her by the Prime she faced.

She knew the Primes resident in Londinium, of course; this bore none of their particular stamps.

At least, as far as she could tell.

Not *every* Prime on the Isle was known to her, she allowed. Yet this was indubitably native work. A sorcerer would not risk the possibly calamitous side effects of performing so major a Work in a country not his own.

Even if a foreign sorcerer wished to attempt such a thing, he would have to find a space enclosed by charter stones, and any Major Work, if it did not shatter said stones and make a very public noise, would be bounded by the charter boundary. No, a foreigner would not do such a thing.

Unless, of course, he was insane. She could not rule out that possibility. Still, even the most lunatic of Primes would baulk at performing such a Work in a foreign land and accepting the double risk of side effects and failure. True, one could spin the irrationality of such a Major Work away and evade the confines of charter stones, but there was always the chance of the flow returning, filling the one who cast it to the brim with warping irrationality, with all that would entail. A Shield could handle some overflow, certainly, but still, the risk was enough to send a shudder down any Prime's spine.

She was so sunk in her own reflections she almost missed Mikal's fingers closing about her wrist again. Irritation rasped under her skin, she reined it, sharply. "I am well enough."

"No doubt." His reply was maddeningly equable. "I am merely reassuring myself."

*Of what?* "I am not likely to expire at any moment. Unless it is with sheer pique."

"Comforting." He tilted his dark head, the gleam of his irises a peculiar comfort in the enclosed space. "There is unrest."

*On many fronts.* "Where, precisely?"

"Behind us, and before." He tipped his chin towards the hansom's front, but a glance out the night-fogged window told her very little. The d—d thing was slower than cold pudding.

Just as she was about to knock for exit – she could, she thought, at least have the benefit of moving her limbs freely if she were to be baulked at every turn tonight – the hansom slowed, and she gathered they had reached their destination.

Mikal's tension warned her, and as she alighted, she sensed the disturbance. A glaring note against the low brassy thunder of approaching Tideturn, and several of her nonphysical senses quivered under the lash of fresh tugging on already sensitised ætheric strings.

Whitehell Street was alive with much more activity than it should have been, and Emma sighed, squaring her shoulders. It would be too much to hope for that Aberline and Clare were about, ideally in Aberline's office – perhaps Clare had even returned to Mayefair, though no doubt if he thought she would be relieved at the notion he might well stay away. Of course Aberline should have been at his own home at this hour, or, more likely, trawling Whitchapel in search of trouble.

Perhaps Aberline had even been caught in the riot she had left behind. While that was acceptable, she sighed at the thought of just whom Commissioner Waring might inflict upon her as a replacement. Furthermore, if Aberline was in Whitchapel, it was likely Clare was caught in the riot as well.

*He is as safe as I can make him. Do pay attention, Emma.*

The hansom-driver's whipcrack as he guided his sorry nag away jolted her into stinging awareness. Tideturn was approaching; it would give her fresh strength to follow her course. For the moment, though—

"*Priiiiima.*" A long, slow exhalation, backed by a draining hiss.

Mikal, a knife laid along his forearm, was between her and the alley-mouth. Emma shook her fingers, a cascade of sparks dying as she realised there was little threat.

Her dark-adapted eyes discerned a skeletal shape, wrapped in tattered oddments. The head seemed too big for its scrawny neck, and the hair was scanty. It leaned against the alley wall, and its pupils were full of green phosphorescence.

Scab-eyes, full of an alien intelligence. Bare feet, horribly battered. The starveling had been driven far from

Chapelease, and it coughed weakly and croaked again. "*Priiima.*"

"I listen," Emma said, cautiously setting a gloved hand on Mikal's shoulder, easing him aside. He did not resist, though the stiffness in him told her it was a very near thing.

His nerves were on edge as well, it seemed.

"*It feasstsss on flesssssssh.*" The starveling's reedy little piping strengthened slightly. Impossible to tell if it had been female or male, or what its station in life had been. "*A new thing, under the sssssssun.*"

Questioning the starveling would only confuse it. So she waited, and it did indeed have more to say.

"*Where the beggar burned, where the dial ssspun, there you will find the road to your quarry.*" For an instant, the thing's skeletal face stretched, becoming broader, the mouth becoming a V. Sharp white teeth flashed, as Thin Meg spoke through one of her hapless, consumed slaves. "*If you find him, he will kill you.*"

Interesting indeed. Mikal was almost quivering, leashed violence ready to explode. She kept her hand on his shoulder, fingers biting in. Emma nodded slightly. "I hear." Brief and noncommittal.

"*You hear, but do not hear. You sssssee but do not sssssee. Find the dial again, sssssparrow-witch.*" A trill of burbling laughter, and the starveling's body crumpled, twitching. Its eyes collapsed, thin green tendrils racing outwards from the corpseglow sheen they had been filled with, and the body settled into a twisting, jerking dance as Scab consumed it. It would not last long, here outside Whitchapel.

Or perhaps some vestige of it would, and Thin Meg's reach would eventually extend even this far.

*That is a problem for another day.* She unclenched her fingers, and patted Mikal's black-clad shoulder soothingly as the starveling's bones crackled, foul steam rising. Flesh liquefied, the ragged material clinging to it unravelling under caustic sludge, and soon very little was left.

Emma, however, forced herself to watch. She did not look away until there was merely a verdant patch of Scab, gently sending up thin curls of black steam. There were lumps in it – whatever fragments of rotted teeth the starveling had possessed would be last to dissolve.

"Very interesting," she said, finally. "What do you make of that, Shield?"

"A riddle?" A single shrug, lifting and dropping her hand. "Couched in a threat?"

"And wrapped in Scab." A cool finger of dread touched her nape, she shook it away with an unphysical flinch. "Come, let us see what has the Yard roiling like an anthi—"

*Wait.* The cool fingertip against her nape returned, and Emma spun, ætheric force gathered into a tight hurtful fist. She did not strike, though, for that end of Whitehell Road was deserted. Yellow Londinium fog was a blank canvas, and the streetlamps had begun to sputter, their carefully applied wick-charms fading as dawn approached.

Mikal stepped away, to give himself room in the event

of attack – and a chill throatless chuckle bounced up from the cobbles and the side-paving.

"Emma, Emma." The voice was faintly familiar, for all the simple, elegant sorcery used to disguise its location and waft it to her ears. "You are a wonder."

She opened her mouth to reply, but the brass thunder of Tideturn rose from the Themis, filling Londinium's crooked streets and teeming warrens. It descended upon her, stinging as she fought the sudden helplessness, and she could only hope the other Prime would not recover from the flood before she did.

And that the other Prime's Shields had not been given orders to strike at Mikal.

She surfaced in a rush, ætheric force filling her and staving off physical weariness for a short while longer. The world wheeled underneath her, and she found Mikal's fingers bruising-hard about her arm again as he held her on her feet. She exhaled sharply, setting her feet on solid ground, and spoke a Word.

"*D'sk—zt!*"

Ripples spread, ætheric force disturbed in concentric rings about her. They broke and refracted, her attention sweeping vigorously through, rather as her gaze would slide down a page of text searching for a wrong penstroke or figure. Or a dress, searching for inadequate stitching, a badly pinned fold, a—

*There you are.* Her heart leapt, sought to hammer behind her ribs, was ruthlessly repressed. Sorcerous force became a clamp, a vice, but he slid aside. A knight's move on a chessboard, but she batted the distracting thought aside. It was a clever feint, but her instincts were still sharp from years of hunting treachery at Victrix's behest. A clatter and a ringing sound — his Shields would be Mikal's to deal with now that she had full control of her senses again.

"Not so fast," came the directionless whisper again. "I am merely visiting, dear one."

She found her voice. "Do not be so familiar, sir."

"Most harsh."

There were more clatters, breaking sounds, and Mikal's tone was passionless, crisp authority ringing in every syllable. "Come closer and die."

"No need." The voice shifted direction again. "I simply wish to speak to your mistress. Hear me, Prima. There is a new spirit rising."

She marked the words in memory, set them aside. Hot water leaked from under her lashes, dawn's strengthening scoring her tender eyes. The more force she expended now, the worse they would smart. It mattered little. "I take it you are the one unseaming frails in Whitchapel, sir."

"Necessary."

"Are you mad?" She allowed her voice to rise, as if she had become distracted by his gruesome calmness. She was close, so *close*, a few more moments and she would find him. He had to be physically nearby, possibly within sight of her.

Once she located the source of the sorcery distorting his voice, she could strike.

"Not mad. Merely ambitious. Help me, Emma."

*He is most familiar with me, this masked Prime.* "I find you rather presumptuous, sir."

"Do you like bowing and scraping to that magical whore? Does it please you to be held in contempt for your power and pride? I know what moves you, Prima, and I offer you alliance. And more."

She remembered the nosegay left on another sorcerer's narrow bed, a bloodstain upon the floor, and the same trick used to distort a voice in a filthy Whitchapel yard.

This was most likely the same Prime who had mysteriously moved to aid her during the Red affair, and she had thought it quite likely he was another in Victrix's service.

Now, she wondered.

Did he know his sorceries weakened Britannia? What was his aim?

*A new spirit rising.*

"Do you think," she began, choosing her words with care, "that a new spirit will be more amenable than the old?"

"Amenable?" The laugh was chilling, and another sound of breakage intruded. What was he *doing*? "Perhaps not. But certainly weak, for a long while. And grateful."

It was one thing to privately compass such a thing, but quite another to hear her adversary speak of it so blithely. She relaxed, abruptly, all her considerable attention brought to bear. "You know little of royalty and rule, sir, if you expect gratitude from either to be of any duration."

"And you know far too much to be allowed to become my enemy."

Another shattering sound, Mikal's exhale of effort. What on *earth* was occurring? She did not open her eyes, every inward sense twisting through a labyrinth, following shifting ripples as they doubled back upon each other, circling ever closer to the artfully camouflaged well of disturbance that would be her opponent.

"Think upon it, Emma. Would you rather serve, or be served?"

*I would rather be left to my own devices, thank you very much.* But she did not reply, for her attention snagged on a single flaw in the pattern, a break in the ripples, and she *pounced* without moving, plunging through the matrices of ringing æther. Snake-quick, but he was quicker, and sorcerous threads snapped as he cast his coat of camouflage aside. More shattering sounds, and she was driven to her knees by the expended force of her own blow, reflected back at her.

*Oh, how very droll.* A great ringing in her head, she shook to clear it, her skirts ground against something sharp and powdery.

"Prima?" Mikal, longing to give chase.

"No." She could not find the breath for more. *If he has laid his plans so thoroughly, he will have an ambush waiting, and I shall not lose you to such idiocy.* She fumbled for her veil with fingers that felt swollen-clumsy. Blinking furiously, she found herself kneeling before a heap of . . . shattered tiles?

Yes, they were roof tiles, of the old red clay in use on the sloped top of the stable opposite, which was ringing with the sounds of clockhorse distress.

The equines did not like this Prime, or his works.

Mikal crouched easily at her side, his hands covered in vicious, shallow slices, bright beads of blood against thick pink dust coating his skin. "Good practice," he said, tilting his head as he deciphered her expression behind the veil. "Simple locometry, I should think. And triggered from afar." He pointed to another rooftop, with a half-shrug that told her it was his best guess. "Crude. But effective."

Had she possessed another Shield, she might have also possessed a chance of catching the mad Prime while one stayed to protect her from the assault of flung tiles. But now was not the time for guilt or remonstrance. Her stays cut, her dress was covered with dust; her skirts were torn and stiff with blood. Mikal was a sight too, rolled in Scab and covered with various substances. His coat was shredded, and the glimpse of his muscled belly crisscrossed with angry red scarring – perhaps irritated by his exertions in the last few minutes – caused her a pang she did not care to examine more closely.

"Your hands," she managed. Her throat was very dry. She coughed, delicately, and reacquired her customary tone. "And . . . oh, h—lfire blast it *all*. This rather changes things."

"They are already healing." He held up his palms, and the sight of his flesh closing, sealing itself under the not-quite-ætheric glow of a Shield's peculiar healing sorcery, sent another bolt through her. "See?" Very gently, as if she were a still a student at the Schola, unfamiliar with a Shield.

"Yes. Help me up." She was glad of the veil, and doubly

glad of his strength as he steadied her. Her legs were not quite as strong as she would like, and her left thigh trembled, on the verge of turning in its resignation due to savage overwork. She swore, vilely, in an exceedingly low voice, and was further grateful Mikal was accustomed to her somewhat unladylike language upon certain occasions. She finished with a few scathing terms directed at whoever had thought to tile-roof a *stable*, though she knew such a thing was perfectly admissible, and when she ran out of breath, she inhaled sharply and fully, shaking her head, feeling the quivering all through her. She had expended a great deal of the force Tideturn had flushed her with.

It was small comfort that her opponent had, as well.

Mikal paused, making certain the storm was past, then turned to glance down Whitehell Road. There was a great deal of to-ing and fro-ing: clockhorse hooves and excited voices through the rapidly greying fog. "What next?"

She took stock. She simply *hated* to be so dishevelled, but there was no help for it, and a few cleansing-charms would waste what limited strength of hers remained.

"Next," she said grimly, "we find Clare. And Aberline." She took advantage of the moment to tuck a few more curls away under her veil, and blinked away fresh, welling hot salt water.

"That sounds too easy."

*Indeed it does.* "It is only a first step, Mikal."

"And then?"

"Then," she continued, setting her chin and taking an experimental step, her heeled boot catching and grinding on broken tiles, "we return home to repair ourselves. Afterwards, I avail myself of every means necessary to track down this mad Prime and halt his insanity. I must confess, Shield, that I am more than peeved." She took another step, leaning on his arm, and found she could walk. "I am downright *vexed*."

"Heaven save us all," he muttered, and she let it pass, leashing her temper tightly.

This mad Prime, whoever he was, had finally managed to anger her. She would teach him the error of such provocation soon enough.

# Chapter Thirty-Three

## In Sorcery, as in Science

C lare wrapped his hands around the thick, glazed mug of fragrant tea. It was not a mannerly attitude to take, but he found he required the heat *and* the support to brace his shaking fingers. The ripples in the surface of the liquid could be blamed on the tension outside – and inside – Inspector Aberline's office.

Young Pico had settled himself, one hip on Aberline's desk, and was glowering fiercely at him. "She'll have my hide," he kept muttering, between inspecting the sleeves of his torn jacket and his similarly injured waistcoat, at great length.

Clare affected not to hear him, though he had been immensely glad to be found by the rufous lad, who bore all the marks of a rough passage through Whitchapel's burning riots. The entire Eastron End was still heaving with unrest, the Metropoleans simply standing at every major ingress and egress to keep the disorder from spilling out. As soon as dawn was fully risen, no doubt the Crown would send Guard and sorcerers to quell whatever unrest remained, no doubt with a bludgeon or two to sweetly kiss the pates of anyone whose excitable nerves failed to settle.

Fortunately, the riots did not seem to have been directed at the Yudics, despite the simmering in the more irresponsible dreadfuls and broadsheets. Clare was of the opinion that such uncivilised things as "pogroms" did not belong upon the Isle; however, uncivilised behaviours were piling upon his Englene with distressing regularity at the moment.

It was probably best not to engage upon *that* line of thought, though.

Inspector Aberline had left them to their own devices after calling for tea, and Clare was glad to be so neglected. For one thing, once Clare gave his report, he rather doubted Aberline would still be attached to the investigation of this affair, between Miss Bannon's dislike of his person *and* the rather dangerous complexion Clare's experience put on the whole chain of events. For another, Clare was bearing in mind – cowardly as it was to have such a consideration – that Miss Bannon, despite their differences, was far from the worst ally to have when faced with something of this nature.

He all but shuddered, thinking of the wet, crunching sounds and the creature's horrid, uncanny speed. Its . . . *irrationality*.

Aberline had been gone more than a quarter of an hour, yet the trembling in Clare's hands refused to settle. The Yard was alive with hurrying and excitement, but it was oddly peaceful in this half-buried room.

A mannerly knock, and the door was flung open with quite unnecessary force. In stalked an incredibly dishevelled Miss Bannon. Her colour was dreadful, her skirts were tattered and crusted with blood, ombre petticoats underneath likewise rudely treated, and her veil torn. Her hair was a tumble-mess of dark curls, and despite Tideturn's recent occurrence, her jewellery did not spark as it usually did when she cared to appear in high dudgeon. She was also coated with a peculiar pink dust Clare's faculties identified as from broken roof tiles.

Mikal, at her shoulder, was hardly in better form. His velvet coat was sadly misused, and the sight of flushed, newly healed knife-marks on his belly might have fascinated Clare had he not seen the knife and extra-jointed appendages responsible for such damage very recently. The Shield was coated in roof-tile dust as well, but underneath it was a layer of straw, dirt, and foul-smelling remainders of the organic sludge coating Whitchapel's floor.

Another shudder worked through Clare. His gaze held Miss Bannon's for a short while that conversely seemed an eternity, and he was comforted to find he did not have to speak for her expression to change, as she instantly compassed – or deduced – some measure of events befalling him since his leaving Mayefair.

She swayed, and Clare might have thought his own

appearance was such as to discommode her. Mikal stepped forward, she took his arm with alacrity, and Clare realised the blood on her skirts had to be her own.

He had already gained his feet. So had Pico, who was first off the mark.

"It ent as bad as it looks, mum." Did the lad actually sound *abashed*?

"I certainly hope not." Her tone was dry, and an immense relief. "Whitchapel?"

"Limhoss first." Pico shrugged when Clare glanced at him. "Not like she wouldn't guess, squire."

"Ah." She leaned heavily on Mikal's arm. The Shield swept the door closed with a curious hooking motion of his foot, and the slam reverberated. "Aberline's habits have not changed. Is that tea?"

Pico hurried to the service, and her gaze returned to Clare's. They studied each other for a long moment, again.

"Good morning, Clare. Your arm . . .?" Even her lips were pale, and her childish mouth had lost its usual determined set.

"Yes, ah – good morning, yes. A whip." Another shudder worked through him, he denied it. "The creature is deuced unnatural."

"Ah." She nodded, slightly, and Clare remembered his manners. He motioned her towards the huge leather chair. "It has been rather a trying night for both of us, it seems. Please, take the chair."

She chose instead the overstuffed hassock, and sank down with a slight grimace. Iron-straight, as usual – but something in the set of her shoulders told Clare she remained upright through will alone. He had rarely seen her in such a state before.

Pico brought her another thick glazed mug of tea. "No cream, mum."

"It shall suffice, thank you. Have you had breakfast, Philip?"

"No mum. Wasn't time. Shall I?"

"See what you can find us; I declare I could eat an entire barrowful of pasty, no matter how rancid." She nodded, then turned her attention to Clare as Mikal handed the lad the requisite funds. "Did you find Aberline's method of seeking connexions between crime and criminal enlightening?"

"Was that what he was about?" The faint, poppy-hazed memory of Aberline's lips moving, quite strangely, rose before him. "I confess I was rather busy with my own reflections at the time."

The door closed behind Pico, and Miss Bannon shut her eyes, inhaling the steam from her cup. She really was quite awfully pallid. Yet her dark gaze was as disconcertingly direct as ever when she reopened her lids. "I am about to tell you something which cannot leave this room, Archibald."

"I shall be discreet," he returned, a trifle stiffly.

"I do trust you shall, and yet I must make absolutely certain you understand the gravity of what I am about to say." She inhaled deeply, for all the world as if steeling herself. "I believe we are facing a mad sorcerer."

"Again?" He could not help himself.

She acknowledged the sally with a tiny, wan smile. "Who has managed to find a means of creating a new genius of rule, draining the resources of Britannia in order to do so. He means to supplant the ruling spirit of Englene, Archibald."

He dropped into the chair. Its stuffing groaned in protest, and lukewarm tea slopped out of the rather rustic mug. He frankly *stared*, and Miss Bannon was too busy gazing into her own mug to notice.

Mikal, near the door, was a statue with burning yellow irises.

"And I very much think," she continued, after taking a prim sip and grimacing slightly at the harshness of the reboiled tea, "that he has quite a chance of succeeding."

Whatever reply Clare might have uttered was lost in Mikal's murmured warning. The Shield moved aside, the door opened with far less force this time, and Inspector Aberline hurried through, his jacket as torn as Pico's but his sturdy shoes in much better order than they should have been.

He noticed the two new occupants of his office and stopped short, his greeting dying somewhere in the region of his throat.

"Dear God," the inspector said. "You two look *dreadful*."

Clare expected Miss Bannon to give the inspector short shrift. Instead, she surprised both of them by giving Aberline the same news, preceded by the same dire warning of secrecy.

His reaction was no less marked than Clare's own. The man actually staggered; Mikal was at his shoulder in a heartbeat, holding him up.

Miss Bannon took another sip of tea. "Take him to his desk, Mikal. The inspector thinks better in familiar surroundings."

It was, Clare supposed, rather a mark of Aberline's intelligence that he did not waste time on superfluous questions or doubt. Instead, he settled himself behind his desk rather creakily, as if afflicted by old age. Mikal glided to the tea service, and poured two more mugs.

Apparently the Shield required a cuppa for bracing as well.

"This is extremely grave," Miss Bannon continued. "If it becomes public knowledge – or even not-so-public knowledge – every sorcerer with enough ambition and corresponding lack of scruple shall attempt such a thing."

"How many, precisely, would that be?" Clare's hands had steadied. "I am not attempting any merriment," he added hurriedly. "I am very curious."

Miss Bannon's weary shrug made her ripped veil tremble. She had tucked it aside, and her red-rimmed eyes seemed to be troubling her as they often did. "All it takes is one among sorcery's children, in any country possessing a spirit of rule, to cause chaos. Strife will inevitably follow, and competing spirits may well tear the map of Europa asunder. Who knows what may happen in Chinois or the Indus? The New World may be safe enough, but the method of creating such a spirit can no doubt be adapted. In sorcery, as in science, the mere knowledge that such a thing is *possible* means sufficient determination will find a way."

"Bloody sorcerers," Aberline muttered.

"Quite." Miss Bannon's soft tone did not alter. "No doubt you are lucky to not be among their number, Inspector."

Aberline's response was even more interesting. His throat and cheeks turned an ugly brick red. "And curse you too, you foul-skirted little—"

"Inspector!" Clare had not meant to say it loudly. Nor had he meant to leap to his feet, whereupon he slopped lukewarm tea out of its mug again. "*Mind* yourself, sir!"

Silence filled the office. Miss Bannon sighed, and slumped wearily. To see her posture crumble was shocking enough, but to see Mikal's reaction – he dug his fingers into her delicate shoulder cruelly, hawk's talons on a small soft piece of prey – was simply dreadful.

She straightened, and took another mannerly sip of tea. "Much as I would dearly like to hold an accounting with you, Aberline, it serves much better to use your particular talents – including those you wish you possessed more than a pittance of – otherwise."

"And who are *you* serving?" Aberline's colour had not faded. "*Any* sorcerer could do this, you say—"

"It requires a Prime, not that such a distinction matters to *you*. Nevertheless, I shall overlook your rather base and certainly groundless accusation. I could retreat behind my walls and let this affair take its course. Indeed, I am rather tempted to. It *does not matter to me*, sir. To be perfectly frank, neither do you."

"Likewise," Aberline managed, in a choked whisper.

"Then we understand each other." Miss Bannon did not look at him. She studied her tea as if it held a secret, and Clare began to feel faintly ridiculous, but unwilling to sink back into the chair. His foot had stopped throbbing, and he realised with a certain relief that he was finally free of the poppy's effects.

*Make a note, Clare. It lingers for hours. Acceptable in some cases, but not in all.* His faculties shivered inside his skull, and the irrationality of the creature in Mytre Square receded into a mental drawer for further study later, if necessary.

His straightening and throat-clearing focused every gaze in the room upon him. "Such discussions do nothing to impede this madman," he observed. "Miss Bannon, it appears you have a plan, or at least the glimmerings of one. Be so kind as to tell us our parts."

"And you will perform them without question or qualm?" The words quite lacked her accustomed crispness. She sounded rather as if she doubted the notion.

"Yes," Clare said, immediately. "And so will the good inspector, and I do not even have to wonder upon your Shield's willingness. Each of us in this room is a loyal subject of Britannia. Besides, this affair is an affront to public order. One simply cannot have this . . . *thing* . . . running about, murdering as it pleases."

"And yet women die every night, in the Eastron End

and elsewhere, under the lash and the knife." Miss Bannon shook her head. "Forgive me, Clare. I am weary enough to be unnecessarily philosophical."

A curious tightness had built in his chest, as if he were suffering the angina again. "That is beyond my purview." Stiffly, as if he were in the courtroom again, Valentinelli a silent presence in the crowd. "But at least we may halt this *particular* killer. I saw it – this spirit, I presume, that would replace Britannia – feasting upon the body of its victim, rather as would an animal."

A peculiar look drifted over Miss Bannon's dirt-smudged, childlike, tear-streaked face. "Not so surprising . . . do sit, Archibald, and tell me everything."

"Glove, or Recall?" It was an old jest, and her shadow of a smile rewarded him. "I suggest we repair to our homes, Miss Bannon, and that you lift your ban upon Inspector Aberline at your dinner table. This rather has the earmarks of an extraordinary situation, and I assure you, for the moment Mr Finch is the last thing on Inspector Aberline's capacious mind."

Aberline made a strangled sound, but his assent was clear.

Miss Bannon studied Clare, over the rim of her mug.

He suppressed the urge to cajole, settled instead for bare, dry fact. "We could all certainly use a spot of rest; we shall no doubt perform our parts better for it." He paused, but she still wore that extraordinary expression. Thoughtful, certainly, her eyebrows arched and her head tilted slightly, bright interest in her gaze and her weariness put aside for the moment. "And we may discuss our next moves at your excellent table, where we are unlikely to be overheard or disturbed. It is the logical path to take."

"I am convinced, sir." She handed her mug to Mikal, who had turned loose her shoulder and hooded his yellow eyes, whether from exhaustion or displeasure was difficult to measure. "Inspector. Present yourself at my door at half past five; I dine early and I believe we should discuss some aspects of this affair privately before we do so. The moment you treat Geoffrey Finch with *anything* less than complete courtesy, I shall learn the look of your blood." She rose, arranging her torn skirts as smartly as possible. "Mikal? Two hansoms, please, engage one to wait upon Clare and Philip. Good morning, Inspector, and I wish you luck with clearing up this mess. Should you need to, invoke my name with Waring and he will prove slightly more amenable; I have already prepared the ground for you in that regard."

Her timing, as usual, was impeccable, for at that moment Philip Pico flung the door wide without bothering to knock.

He was loaded down with a burlap sack full of bulges Clare's fastidious nose identified as sausage and cheese, filched from Heaven alone knew where. "Had a spot of luck, I did. You'll have to use your own knife on the bangers, sir and madam – ah. We're leaving, then?"

"Quite." She had retreated into her shell of calm precision, and swept towards Pico in the manner of a frigate swooping upon its prey. "Half past five, Inspector."

The lad hurried aside, Mikal shut the door behind his

mistress, and Aberline let loose an oath Clare chose to ignore as Philip Pico's eyebrows nested in his hairline.

"And you feel emboldened to make a promise upon my behaviour, sir?" The good inspector was outright fuming, and had gained his feet with a speed that was, considering the night's events, quite astonishing. "Why, I've a mind to—"

"You use the poppy in the manner the Grecque oracles used laurel fumes, to amplify your small sorcerous talent in some manner." Clare nodded. "Quite interesting. I must confess I was not taking notes, but Memory will serve me when I have a few moments to gather myself. Such a thing is not quite legal, sir."

The strength visibly left Aberline's legs. He sat down again, heavily, and the choler had fled his cheeks.

"I have," Clare continued, "been acquainted with Miss Bannon for a very long time, despite certain . . . variances . . . in our natures. On one point, however, we are emphatically *not* at variance, and that is in our service to what I would once have called Crown and Empire, but am now forced to name a very odd brand of Justice." He realised he was pontificating, cleared his throat again. The tea was dreadful, and cold now to boot. "I have noted that the lady in question does not, as a matter of habit, overstate her case. Quite the opposite. I believe we are facing a threat to the very foundations of Britannia, and you, sir, are a loyal son of the Isle. It is your *duty* to be pleasant and forthcoming while pursuing this matter under Miss Bannon's direction, and should it become necessary, sir, we shall settle like gentlemen after its conclusion." He fixed the inspector with what he hoped was a steely, quelling look. "I would be quite happy to meet you."

"Likewise." Aberline exhaled sharply. "And if I am not pleasant and forthcoming, you may go to Waring and drop a word in his ear about my dissolute methods. Using such substances to artificially strengthen sorcery is quite scandalous."

"There are laws against such things, no doubt Miss Bannon would know them with a fair degree of precision." Clare gave up seeking to straighten his jacket. It was hopeless. "I would not stoop to blackmail, sir. Instead, I would appeal to your better nature."

"Funny, that." A sour, pained grin. "I am here, Mr Clare, because I have precious little *better nature* left. Now do leave my office."

"Gladly," Clare said stiffly, and suited actions to words.

Pico, his eyes suspiciously round, said not a word. He merely clutched his burlap burden and hurried in Clare's wake.

# Chapter Thirty-Four

## Very Precise Conditions

The broadsheets screamed, their ink acid-fresh. *Double Murder In Whitchapel. "Leather Apron" – Two More Victims!* Speculations of the most vivid nature shared the columns with sober warnings against Vice and breathless tales of the want and violence flourishing just as the Scab did. *On the Recent Events in Whitchapel.* Drawings of the discovery of the bodies – Clare was not mentioned. Naturally, his discretion would have been easy to secure.

Waring's discretion had required no little amount of threat and blandishment in equal proportion. The commissioner was in an insufferable position, and it matched his temperament roundly. Still, he was useful, and she was fairly certain he would be the public face for whatever triumph or tragedy this affair would end with.

Emma glanced over the headlines, directed Horace to

deposit the broadsheets in her library, and fixed Finch with a steady gaze. Her head throbbed and her filthy dress was likely to give her a rash, she *ached* to be clean. Duty demanded she deal with Finch's nerves first. "You are perfectly safe, Geoffrey."

"Oh, I know that, mum." He had only paled slightly upon hearing the news of their dinner guest.

"Do you?" She made a slight movement, checked herself. Finch regarded her steadily, and she searched his features quite closely.

Madame Noyon appeared at the head of the stairs and bustled down, clucking over the state of her mistress's dress.

Finch nodded, slowly. "Yesmum. I do." There was a hint of a smile about his thin mouth now. "Rather pity the man, mum."

Relief filled her; she turned to the next order of business. "Then you are a kinder soul than I. I shall leave dinner in your – and Cook's – capable hands. They shall be in the smoking room afterwards; *do* make certain there are the cigars Clare prefers. And your nephew as well. He has rendered very tolerable service indeed so far."

"Glad to hear it, mum." He waited, but she had nothing further, and he consequently glided away.

"A *mess*," Severine Noyon fussed, her plump hands waving as she arrived at Emma's side. "Good heavens, *madame*, what did you do to yourself? A bath, and quickly. *Chocolat.*"

*I could eat a hanging side of beef and ask for more.*

"And something substantial for breakfast, Madame, I have a quite unladylike appetite."

"*Mais oui, madame.*" The round little woman in her customary black wool ushered Emma toward the stairs. "Catherine! *Chocolat*, and much breakfast for *Madame* in the solarium. Sunshine, *oui*, to make her strong. Isobel! *Attendez!*"

The house filled with efficient bustling, a bath was filled, and Emma sighed with contentment as she sank into hot rose-scented water. There was no time for soaking, however. In short order she was drawn forth, chafed dry, laced loosely into fresh stays and a morning gown. Fresh jewellery was selected, her hair arranged by Isobel's quick fingers, and *chocolat* was there to greet her in the solarium. A hearty platter of bangers, scones, fruit, and a bowl of porridge were arranged in her favoured morning spot, and there was a bottle of nerve tonic set conspicuously to one side of the *chocolat*-pot.

Emma suppressed a grimace. Cook must have glimpsed her in the hall, to be so worried about her condition. Her servants did sometimes make small gestures.

The solarium was full of strengthening morning light, filtered grey through Londinium's fog. Spatters of rain touched glass, puffing into thin traceries of steam when they touched the golden charter symbols scrolling lazily through the transparent panes, reinforcing and defending the fragility. The charm-globes over those of her plants more tender or needing training tinkled softly, each one a different note in the soothing symphony of morning.

Unfortunately, Emma's nerves were not soothed.

Hard on breakfast's heels Mikal also arrived, freshly scrubbed and only a little pale from the night's excitement.

Emma had settled herself, let him stand for a few moments, filling her plate with measured greed. Fortunately her domestics were accustomed to her sometimes-unlady-like appetite, and she needed to replace a great deal of physical energy if she was to carry out her plans.

She had reached a number of conclusions in the past half-hour. Arranging one's person was often sufficient to grant one solutions to certain other problems the physical actions of proper dress and accoutrement tidied the mental faculties as well.

When she finally deigned to notice Mikal, he wore a faintly troubled expression. Perhaps he expected what was about to occur, or at least the nature of her mood.

Emma took a small, delicate bite of scone. Crumbly, dripping with melting butter, *delicious*. "Attend, Shield."

His unease deepened, a low umber glow to Sight. "I attend."

She was, truth be told, a trifle relieved to sense his discomfiture. Perhaps she was not viewed as *predictable* just yet.

*Good.* "There is a conversation we must have, and I have decided this is the proper moment."

"Have you." It was not a question, and his flat tone warned her.

Her own measured softness was a similar warning. "Indeed. You performed some feat while I lay dying of Her Majesty's thrice-damned Plague."

"Prima—"

"*Silence*." Her weariness did most emphatically *not* mean he was given leave to interrupt her, and she was a little gratified to hear the resultant ringing quiet in the sunroom. Even the climate-globes had hushed themselves. "You were aware of the Philosopher's Stone, and my gift of it to Mr Clare."

"Yes. Prima—"

"Confine yourself to answering my questions, Shield. If I wish further detail, I shall *tell* you so. Now, you performed some manner of feat while I lay upon my deathbed. Correct?"

"Yes."

"Does that feat have any lingering effects?"

"Yes."

"On you, or on me?"

"Both."

"Ah." She absorbed this. Whatever effects they were, they had not affected her sorcery. The only evidence she had to build assumptions or guesses upon was her feeling of quite-uncalled-for physical well-being. And, let it not be forgotten, a certain resistance to injury that she had grown quite accustomed to with the Stone married to her flesh. It was not as complete as a Stone's protection. Her left thigh twitched, reminding her. "It would seem I am somewhat more physically durable than a Prime usually is."

"Yes."

"How extensive is this durability?"

He was silent for a long moment. "There is very little I may not heal you from."

*Ah. That* he *may not heal.* "Dismemberment and death, I presume."

"I have an hour's time after your death. Less, if your . . . body is not . . . whole."

*Fascinating.* "I presume this has somewhat to do with your ancestry."

A shrug.

She restrained her temper yet again, but her purpose had been served, so she changed direction. "How did you evade detection at the Collegia?"

"I passed their Tests." His chin lifted, and she decided his defiance was not yet of the punishable variety.

"Of course you did, or you would not have been . . ." An odd thought occurred to her. She set her implements down, poured herself a cup of *chocolat*, and settled into the chair with it. "You are rather wayward, as Shields go. One might almost say, headstrong."

"Disobedient."

*Quite the word I would choose.* "Are you?"

"No."

"Hm." She took another sip. The almost-bitterness coating her tongue had two sources, now. "This places rather a different complexion on our . . . relations."

"Have I given you cause for complaint?"

Ætheric force jabbed, a sudden hurtful compression. She had precious little of Tideturn's force available to her now, but her sorcerous Will clamped about him. He was driven to his knees, not slowly, but not as quickly as she could have otherwise.

"Do not," Emma said, very softly, "*presume*, Shield. I did not give you leave to ask questions."

Perhaps he would have made a reply, but she lifted a fingertip delicately from her cup. A short Word, and his mouth was stoppered as well.

The solarium's glass walls had misted with condensation, for a feral heat now moved through the small room. She loathed this display, but her plans now depended upon a few very precise conditions, and she was determined to arrange them to her liking.

"Mikal." She felt the struggle in him; he sought to rise but was held immobile. "You displease me, and as a consequence, you are Confined. *C−x'b*."

The Word drained her, savage exhaustion running through her marrow. Tiny nips of pain in her fingers and toes, but training held her still and apparently unmoved by the expenditure of force. The house shivered once, sealing itself against the egress of one of its inhabitants.

Until she decided otherwise.

Mikal's irises flamed yellow. He ceased struggling, and instead, watched her.

She returned her attention to her *chocolat*. "You are dismissed to your quarters, Shield."

Woodenly, his body rose, a marionette's jerking motion. Turning inward, she sought for any indication that he was merely acquiescing instead of compelled. None was to be found, and her jaw tightened as he disappeared.

His progress through the house was slow and stilted, and it was only when he was within his dark, narrow room

– she had left it to be modified according to his whim, and rarely entered it – that she relaxed her grip even slightly. The slam of his door flung closed with sorcerous force was the snap of a wineglass's stem in clenched fingers.

Emma blinked, her eyes watering. Surely it was only her Discipline. Tears would be a weakness.

She settled to her breakfast, eating with mechanical good manners. She needed the fuel. Her cheeks were wet, and her morning dress, black watered silk as wasp-waisted Prima Grinaud had always worn, was dotted with tiny splashes of hot salt water.

Now, many years after her graduation from under the grand magistrix's thumb, she wondered who – or what – Prima Grinaud had been mourning. Or if the redoubtable lady had entombed herself at the Collegia alive to escape the world outside.

How long would it be before Emma herself was tempted to do the same?

# Chapter Thirty-Five

## Quite Confident Indeed

Falling into bed, Clare decided, had done him a world of good. His Baker Street flat was indeed dusty, and full of the ghost of a Neapolitan assassin, but he had not cared. His narrow bed smelled rather vile, but he burrowed into its familiarity and was lost to darkness. Pico could have breakfast; Clare wished surcease.

He woke at early teatime when the lad nudged him, and made his toilet with the focused inattention bred of habit and familiarity. Pico exhibited the instincts of a good valet, fussing over Clare's clothing in a manner that was almost familiar. He also charmed the redoubtable Mrs Ginn, sweetening the landlady much more than Valentinelli had ever cared to. The tea tray was not up to Miss Bannon's standards, but Clare welcomed it nonetheless, and Pico confined himself to remarking upon the weather and asking Clare's opinion of this or that waistcoat.

It was not until their arrival at Miss Bannon's gate that Pico betrayed a certain nervousness, rubbing at his freshly shaven cheek. "*She* might not be happy."

"That is exceedingly likely," Clare allowed, straightening his cuffs. They were a trifle late – a hansom, he thought irritably, was *never* about when one needed it. "She does prefer punctuality."

"Well, at least you're alive, right? And in one piece. My heart fair gave out when you vanished in the riot, sir. Never been so glad to find someone in my life." Pico blinked sleepily, his sharp foxface pale as milk.

"No fear on that account," Clare murmured. The thought no longer sent a sharp pang through him. Quiet and familiar, Brooke Street nonetheless had the appearance of a foreign country. Perhaps he was simply seeing it with fresh eyes.

The cadaverous Finch took Clare's hat, and he was imperturbable as usual. "The drawing room, sir."

"Thank you." There was an odd sensation just under his breastbone. "Has, ahem, the inspector arrived?" *And were you prepared to face him?*

"Yes, sir." Finch's manner betrayed no discomfiture.

"He, erm . . . he did not upset you, Finch?" Enquiring in this manner was so bloody *awkward*. Finch gave him a rather curious look, and Pico coughed.

"No, sir." And that, apparently, was that. Finch motioned for Pico to follow him, and the lad went without question or qualm.

Miss Bannon had taken steps to reassure him, apparently. It was entirely like her.

The drawing room was full of clear, serene light, its mirrors dancing and the fancy of waterlilies and birch stems never more marked. There was even a subtle freshness in the air, but perhaps that was Miss Bannon's perfume – for the lady in question had settled herself on the blue velvet settee, and Inspector Aberline, his hands clasped behind his back, stood gazing into the fireplace, where burning coal had developed a thick white cover.

Miss Bannon's dark eyes had crescents of bruise-darkness underneath them, yet her posture was as straight as ever. She was markedly pale, though, and her mien was of careful thoughtfulness. Only her hands, lying prettily in her lap and bedecked with four plain silver rings on the left and a large yellow tourmaline on her right middle finger, betrayed any tension.

Inspector Aberline's colour was high, and his coat and shoes had been given a thorough brushing. He had obviously repaired to his home at some point, much as Clare had.

He was long to remember this moment: the peculiar brightness of the light, Miss Bannon's exhausted face, and Aberline's clenched jaw.

Clare braced himself, and shut the door.

Dinner was superb, of course, but Miss Bannon ate very little. Nor did she take anything but water. "It used its whip upon you?"

"Yes." Clare set his implements down properly, indicated the length of the slash along his forearm. "It seemed quite put out at being disturbed."

"What on earth *is* it?" Aberline wondered aloud. "What method was used in its construction?"

"I believe it may be similar to a Charington's Familiar." Miss Bannon took a mannerly sip of water from a restrained crystal goblet. The gryphon-carved table legs were not restless, as they sometimes were when her mood was unsettled. "At first the Prime would have to kill on his own account – Tebrem, for example, he chose to cut in a relatively sheltered location. Afterward the spirit could commit its own foul acts – but only at night, I should think. There is some physical focus for this spirit, some piece of it that held it to the fleshly world while sorcerous force was poured into it, and until it may walk in daylight that focus is vulnerable. Additionally, each location has become a taproot driven deeply into Londinium to gather force from the city's essence, if you will . . . I do wonder, why a coachman?"

"It seems rather . . . plebeian . . . for a ruling spirit," Aberline observed.

"The spirit of our time *is* rather plebeian." Clare savoured a bite of roast; the sauce held a flavour he had not yet defined. "One only has to take the train to ascertain as much, or a turn about Picksdowne."

"Some hold that Britannia was once the local spirit of Colchestre, a humble minder of pottery." Miss Bannon regarded her plate with a serious, thoughtful expression.

"Books which speak of such a possibility are difficult to procure, for obvious reasons."

"That's all well and good." Aberline had a remarkably hearty appetite, for a man sitting at table with a woman he regarded as a viper. "How do we stop this bas— ah, this mad sorcerer?"

Miss Bannon glanced at the dining-room door. Not for Mikal, certainly, for he did not attend dinner. Nor for Valentinelli. Pico would dine with the servants tonight; Miss Bannon had given orders.

Clare found his busy faculties turning these few facts about and around, seeking to make them fit together. There was a missing piece.

"There is . . . well, there is fair news, and foul." Miss Bannon ceased to even pretend to consume her dinner, pushing her plate back slightly with a fingertip. The tourmaline ring flashed. "Much was decided with the first murder. Every death since then has narrowed the possibilities, so to speak. Such is the way of such Works of sorcery. I believe this mad Prime is very close to achieving his purpose."

"That's foul enough news." Aberline took another mouthful of roast, and Clare, troubled, set his fork and knife down.

Miss Bannon's small smile held no amusement. "That was actually the fair news, Inspector. He requires a very specific victim for the culmination of his last series of murders, and I believe he has settled on one."

"Then how do we find her? Whitchapel teems with drabs."

"Finding her is my task," Miss Bannon returned, equably enough. "*Do* enjoy your dinner now, Inspector. Afterwards I shall inform you of your part in the plan."

Aberline's gaze darted to Clare, who began to have a very odd sensation in his middle. The inspector looked ready to object, and visibly thought better of it. "You are confident in your ability to find, out of all the unfortunates in Whitchapel, the one our Leather Apron has settled on?"

"Quite confident." Miss Bannon's faint smile bore a remarkable resemblance to a grimace of pain. She took another sip of water. "Quite confident indeed. I would explain, but sometimes a Work must not be spoken of." She pushed her chair back, and both men leapt to their feet as she rose. "My apologies, sirs. My digestion is somewhat disarranged. Please, enjoy the remainder of dinner, I implore you. The smoking room is ready for you afterwards."

Her black skirts rustled as she swept past Clare, and he discovered that she was not, as he had thought earlier, wearing perfume.

*How peculiar*. He settled once more into his chair, and Aberline applied himself to the roast in earnest. Finch was not serving tonight; Horace and Gilburn would bring the next course in due time. It was, Clare reflected, almost as if the house were *his*, and this a quiet dinner with a colleague or a fascinating resource.

"Have I been pleasant enough?" Aberline did not wait for a reply. "What do you make of that?"

"I am quite puzzled, I confess." *It is not like Miss Bannon to have a troubled digestion. Where is Mikal?*

"No need to let it ruin one's appetite. She dines well, if early."

Clare almost replied, but another thought struck him.

*It will be growing dark, and Tideturn is soon.*

His faculties woke further, seeking to weave together disparate bits of information and deduction. Some critical piece was missing, and had he not been so . . . uneven . . . lately, he might already have it. Feeling did its best to blur Logic and Reason, and he had indulged himself too far in its whirling.

Did it matter, what irrational act Miss Bannon had committed upon him? It did not, and with the clarity of Logic he could even see why she had not told him. She had been . . . right, it seemed.

The vegetables arrived, and the sorbet. Dessert, and the savouries were savoured. Clare grew quieter and quieter, and Aberline saw no reason to draw him out. It might have been quite a companionable meal, had Miss Bannon been there – and the inspector absent.

It was not until he had entered the smoking room afterwards, its familiarity somehow smaller and more confining, that Clare realised he had been quite a buffoon, and Miss Bannon . . .

. . . was gone.

*Oh, bloody hell.*

# ❃ *Chapter Thirty-Six*

## *Where the Dial Spun*

Under a thick woollen blanket of vile buttery fog, Whitchapel seethed. The great hazy bowl of Londinium's sky had darkened rapidly, yet the Scab had not come creeping out. There was oddness about, of late. From Kensington to the Dock, Caledonia to the Oval – and beyond each of those landmarks – the great smoky-backed beast was curiously . . . hushed.

As if it dozed.

Yet the shadows in Whitchapel were darker than ever. Ink-dark, knife-sharp, and even those who spent their brief violent lives using every scrap of shade to pursue survival felt a cold breath upon their napes. The Scab always came out at dark; it was like Tideturn or bad luck. Since there was no escaping, one made merry in the face of the reek, downed what passed for gin to soothe the sting, and snatched what one could.

To feel the absence of that familiar terror was to feel worse than uneasy.

She kept to those cold, sharp shadows; a short slim woman with a shawl over her head. Oddly, she passed unmolested through the darkness. The flashboys never bothered to catcall or demand a toll for passage; the young, unAltered blades seemed not to notice her. Once in a while an unfortunate glanced at her, taking her for one of the sisterhood braving the thoroughfares and alley-ways early to earn a few pence for doss or gin, or more likely, gin and more gin, and one last customer before staggering to a narrow bed if one was lucky.

If not, well.

*Leather Apron*, they whispered to each other, and each time they did, the shadows deepened. As if the fear and trepidation, the passage of rumour, somehow . . . *fed* that darkness.

The glamour should not have been so difficult to maintain. Emma was weary, disciplined Will alone kept her upright. Tideturn would be soon, she could already almost-hear the approaching, brassy thunder. The dozing beast of Whitchapel drew her in, a tiny particle in its vast pulsing, and she was *quite* content to pass unremarked.

Finding and engaging a hansom had been the difficult part. Now that she was here, a minnow in deep waters, it was . . .

Well, it was as if she had never left.

It was marvellous, how the intervening years fell away. Struggle, striving, experience, all of it so many shed garments, dropping away from the nakedness of memory.

The starveling's words, of course, had made a mad manner of sense. *Where the dial spun, where the beggar burned.* How did Marimat know?

More importantly, who might have paid her enough – and in what coin – to divulge such things? Of course, the Scab witnessed black acts every night in Whitchapel. What might it whisper to the fallen creature in her pit?

Was her opponent Diabolic after all?

Emma put her head down. Tideturn grew closer, and she moved slowly because the rushing had filled her ears. Without Mikal, she would be blind and vulnerable when the golden flood from the Thcmis filled the city.

A sorceress, even a Prime, could vanish into the sinks of the Eastron End; but once, long ago, she had not feared these streets. Did a fish fear the water it breathed? The danger was simply air or rain, and when she had been plucked from it by the Collegia childcatchers she had suffered the gasping every fish performed when torn from its habitat.

*Where the beggar burned.*

She remembered, oh yes. A sweet-roasting stink, the crowd's laughter, flames. After that, her mother – was it correct to call that poor creature a mother? She had fallen far, the woman who birthed Emma Bannon; her respectable husband's death in a fire started by a drunken brawl meant poverty, shame, hopelessness. The men she gave herself to, while her youth lasted, had perhaps been kind enough. Some of them even spoke of marriage again, but it all came to naught.

Emma, grown weedlike and stunted in the Scab's blight, learning to scurry and steal. Learning the cant and argot of the flashboys and the unfortunates, cuffed when she was noticed and learning to be watchful. Inside her, a spark of ruined pride, and the deeper flame of sorcerous talent.

The last man – one of many, she thought perhaps he might have been a carter or even a flashboy, though she could not remember any Alteration on his gin-thickened frame – had announced his intention to sell Emma into a bawdyhouse if one could be found that would take a skinny brat, and the mother had turned on him with drunken fury. Whether it was because some spark of natural feeling for her burdensome child remained, or simply that said burden represented a shilling or two the raddled woman felt should not go to the broad-faced, rotten-toothed *monsieur* who had paid for their doss that long-ago night was unclear.

What was perfectly clear was the blade as it flicked, unseaming the mother's neck. A horrid scarlet necklace, a spray of crimson, and the burning in a thin child's chest had ignited.

The man had dropped the knife and screamed, beating at leprous-green flames erupting suddenly, sorcerously, from his skin and clothes.

A second beggar's burning, there in the reek and the dark. The child had run away, and been caught in a net other than the one she had feared.

Emma halted in a pool of darkest shadow, the glamour held close. Brass thunder unheard by most filled the air, and from one end of the street, a flood of ætheric force roared from the direction of the Themis's cold, deep lapping.

Tideturn.

Golden charter symbols crawled over Emma's skin. The shadows did not hide their flashing, but the malodorous passageway she stood swaying in was luckily empty of any witness. When the flood receded, she blinked and shook her shawl-covered head, expecting at any moment to feel Mikal's hand upon her arm and his quiet word of orientation.

Instead, she heard the scraping of tiny paws, a muffled squeak. Her skin sought to crawl, training clamped upon the waste of energy and it passed. She knew that sound, of course – grey whip-tailed rats with beady dark eyes, sensing in her stillness a possible weakness. The scuffing sounds retreated, and her nose wrinkled slightly, fresh strength filling her limbs.

She took careful stock of her surroundings again. Dorsitt Street was not strictly as she remembered it. Emma was uncertain whether this was a comfort or a danger, and took another few moments to study what she could.

Of course even squalor would change over time. It was still cramped and clotted with refuse, but the carts that had crouched here selling all manner of items were gone. The public houses thumped with the sounds of drunken revelry, but the flashboys did not congregate in their doors here, as was their usual wont.

Even a fast, murderous, well-Altered flashboy might well fear the creature hunting in Whitchapel.

A door slammed, raucous laughter and yellow gleams of gaslight spilled onto the street, and Emma drew further back into shadow. Three women, shapes very much like her own, with bonnets instead of shawls, hurried tipsily down Dorsitt toward the other ginhouse; the one in the middle had evidently been their first stop.

"Lea' *off*, Nan," one slurred petulantly, and her companions laughed.

"Black Mary, Black Mary," one chanted, with a lisp that spoke of missing teeth. "High-mighty *Jinnit*."

"I'us in France ons't," Black Mary retorted, hotly. She sounded young, and would be successful while that youth lasted. "I'en spek Westend dravvy, I may."

A small smile touched Emma's lips. The slurring song of Whitchapel cant was strangely soothing. *I was in France once. I even speak proper Englene, I may.* Perhaps her sad little story was told to draw custom. Or perhaps she *had* been to France, such a thing was not impossible.

Emma's slight smile faded as she turned away from Dorsitt, picking her way with care further down the passage. The smell, oh, it was familiar. Coal and grease, rotting vegetables, spoiled meat. Rancid, unwashed bodies crammed into tiny rooms, the sooty trembling flames of rag wicks in fat.

The only thing missing was the thick greenness of Scab.

She caught herself placing each foot carefully, a slip-sliding movement because the resilient ooze underneath should have been thick in this darkness.

She could feel ancient crumbling bricks, cobbles in some places. Her throat was so dry. The walls of the passage were only hinted at by some sense that extended around her, invisible fingertips brushing. Even her sensitive vision could not pierce this gloom.

Her skin chilled. Her skirts dragged; the quality of the cloth would outweigh the slight value of her life in this slice of Londinium. Yet she let the glamour unravel as she stepped carefully, shedding one more garment between herself and the past.

There, on the left, was the door. A window with a broken pane – it had been whole once. Another door had been cut further down the passage, but there was no true exit to the street save the one she had entered.

She remembered running, bare child's feet slipping in thick Scab, bursting out into the whirl of Dorsitt Street on a late-summer evening, gold in the air and the rank ripe heat simmering all of Londinium on a plate.

The child-catchers had felt the ætheric disturbance, a powerful burst of untrained sorcery. Given chase, and finally brought her to bay in a blind court not far from here. How she had struggled, and bit, wild with terror, thinking only *He has come to kill me too.*

The door was locked. Emma cast a glance over her shoulder, then regarded the broken window for a few moments. A whispered charm, a breath of sorcery, and the lock yielded. She felt a twinge at her trespassing, set it aside. Foxfire light glimmered from her necklace, just an edge of illumination to show the dimensions of the sad little hole.

*Where the dial spun*, the starveling whispered again, and to Emma's relief, the room was changed. A different bed was placed in an opposite corner, and the shabby hob had a cheapmetal kettle on it and nothing more. The floorboards were familiar, though a dark stain had been scrubbed away in one rotting corner.

She went unerringly to that corner. Knelt, her fingers just as deft as they had been in childhood. *Perhaps*, she thought, and her lips shaped a different word.

*Please. Let it be gone, and me a fool.*

If what she sought had vanished, she could call Marimat the Fallen's whispers a feint, and retreat into her house's safety. Let Clare think what he would, let Aberline go his merry way, and make to Mikal some manner of restitution for the display she had forced him to endure.

Leave Victrix – and Britannia – to her fate. At this juncture, such a thing would please her, and if she felt another murder within her frame, she would view it as a last unpleasant reminder that she had once served one who secretly despised her.

*Magical whore*, the mad sorcerer's disguised voice sneered, and the term was so familiar. It teased at memory, but she set it aside. That was not the slice of the past she wished to consider at the moment.

It took a special pressure to lift the edge of the

floorboard, and her hand wormed into the space underneath. Her fingers touched rotting cloth; she shut her eyes and fished the small thing out, settling back on her heels.

It was still wrapped in a scrap of cambric, the threads so rotted they fell apart at her gentle touch. Her skirts would no doubt collect all manner of dust and unwholesome things from the boards, but she did not care. Her fingers trembled as she brushed thin fabric aside, and the pocket-watch, its casing grimed with the passage of years under the boards, gave a slight gleam.

Its chain was short, and it was no doubt a corpsepicker's bargain, but it had seemed so flash and fine to a young girl, once.

They had both been in a stupor when Emma's fingers had relieved the man of his watch. She had slid it into the hiding place, intending to pawn it for perhaps enough pence for a pasty, or even a flower for her weeping mother.

But when *he* woke, he had noticed the theft, and threatened to beat them both to a pulp. The mother wailed that she had been next to him the whole time and her daughter said nothing, despite being prodded and her child's shift searched thoroughly. Shivering, she had heard the man pronounce his doom: he'd get his pence back from a bawdyhouse, if they would take such a stick of a thing.

Then the cries, the red necklace, the fire.

Emma rose, a trifle unsteadily. The watch hung from its short chain, and she twisted her fingers to spin it, feeling the old childish fascination with its motion. If she wound it, would it work?

Who could tell?

*Where the dial spun.*

Old guilt rose, its edges sharp, and it was almost a relief to hear the soughing of air moving as the door drifted open.

She stood, very still, watching the spinning. Who cared how Thin Meg had known this secret? What mattered was that Emma had been brought to exactly the right place, and of her own will.

He approached, softly. Did he think her unaware?

When he was close enough, she drew in a sharp breath. "All in, all in," she said softly, as if they were children playing the perpetual game of tag in the alley.

He halted for the barest moment. Approached, step by step. "Why have you ventured here, Emma?"

His voice, familiar, teased at her memory. She held very still. *Come now. Stop speaking. I am offering myself; let it be quick.*

"You are so clever, my love," a dead man breathed in her ear, and he clamped a foul-smelling rag over her face. "Too clever by half."

Emma's body slipped her control for a moment, but any struggle was useless. The clot-thick vaporous substance on the rag filled her lungs, and the effect, purely physical, was perhaps the only one that would deprive a wary sorceress of her senses.

She felt, after it all, a certain relief.

Then, darkness.

# Chapter Thirty-Seven

## And if Not, Vengeance

Aberline hammered at the interior of the front door of 34½ Brooke Street, using quite colourful language, while Clare made himself comfortable on the stairs and, in defiance of all good manners, puffed at his pipe. No servant hurried to find the source of the noise; Miss Bannon had no doubt given orders.

There was no use in seeking to escape until the mistress of the house released them. Little good would be done by exhausting oneself as the good inspector was currently doing, but at least if the man was shouting and hammering he was exactly where Clare could see him.

It was the other man who gave Clare some pause.

Mikal had appeared in the smoking room just after dinner, looking grey and drawn as he did on those rare occasions when Miss Bannon left him to cool his heels.

Just behind him had drifted the cadaverous Finch, who did not even deign to glance at the glowering inspector. Instead, he had presented Clare with a folded missive of familiar creamy paper, a delicate, feminine hand – also familiar – on its outer flap, his own name traced with her usual care.

The note inside the folds was extremely simple.

*Come and find me.*

Which was all very well, Clare thought, but locking them inside her house so deliberately was rather a bar to her stated wish.

The inescapable conclusion, since it was unfathomable that Miss Bannon had not planned this to a fare-thee-well, was that she intended them to issue forth . . . but not quite yet.

So, he smoked. He had taken the precaution of changing from dinner-dress into something a fraction more suitable to chasing a sorceress across night-time Londinium. Philip Pico, having apparently arrived at the same conclusion, had done the same. Or perhaps he had not dressed for dinner at all.

The rufous youth had settled himself easily on the stairs below Clare, and gone still as a stone. He eyed the inspector's display with an air of faint condescension, but when his gaze drifted across the silent, haggard Mikal, it became troubled indeed.

Tabac smoke, fragrant, drifted up and was sorcerously compressed near the ceiling into neat spheres that bumbled off in search of a chimney. Clare had arrived at a number of conclusions, but the nagging sense of a missing piece would simply not cease.

Aberline finally left off hammering at the door. He whirled, and fixed Mikal with a baleful glare. "*You*. Where is she? Why, I've a mind to—"

"Cease your chatter," Mikal returned, amiably enough. "Or I shall *make* you."

Clare puffed again, thoughtfully. Quite a riddle the lady had posed. Quite.

Aberline clearly thought better of provoking the Shield any further; he cast about for a new target. "Where's that knife-throwing son of a whore? *Finch!*"

"Do be quiet," Clare remarked. "And *do* leave Mr Finch be. In any case, he will not answer your summons. There is only one being who commands that man, and she is not at home." He puffed again. "When you have calmed, sir, we shall proceed."

"Proceed? We are sitting here while . . . what on earth can she be doing? What could have *possessed* the bit—"

It was, strangely enough, Pico who interrupted. "*Watch* your tongue, guv." He actually bounced to his feet as well, and his hands were fists. "I've had about enough of your high'n mighty."

Clare sighed. "This solves nothing."

Whatever Aberline might have replied was lost in a soughing sound.

Clare tilted his head, and the massive clock at the end of the entry hall spoke. In the midst of its chiming, a subtle pressure drained away, and Clare gained his feet with another weary sigh.

Midnight, precisely, and the crackle of live sorcery could only mean one thing. "I believe the door will open now," he observed. "And our murderer will strike again tonight. I further believe Miss Bannon rather desperately requires our aid."

Mikal nodded. "Yes." The word was chilling in its flatness. "The house is no longer sealed. I am no longer Confined. Yet I cannot sense my Prima."

"Bother." Archibald jammed his hat firmly onto his head. "I had hoped you could find her in some sorcerous manner."

The Shield looked positively sick under his dark colouring. "If she is . . . alive, I could. But *I cannot sense her.*"

Clare stared for a moment. Aberline's mouth hung open, and the inspector blinked several times. Mercifully, he remained silent.

"She could have set the house and my Confinement to release at this moment," Mikal continued. "Or . . . not. It would release if she . . ."

Clare cleared his throat. *Down, Feeling! Logic. Logic must serve here.*

But . . . *Emma.* She had been so pale, and taking only water. So certain she would have no trouble finding the next victim.

She betrayed a certain familiarity with Whitchapel. The listening look she wore, when inside its environs. Her origins, however obscure, were no doubt of a sort to make her familiar with Want, Vice, Crime, and other unsavouries. She was also connected to Victrix, and hence Britannia, in numerous ways. Not to mention her rather incredible ability to find a treasonous criminal once she set herself seriously about it.

It would make quite a bit of sense for this lunatic sorcerer to see her too great a threat to continue breathing.

It would *further* make quite a bit of sense for Miss Bannon to wave herself before such a man in the manner of a rag waved before a bull to engage its fury.

She had such a distressing habit of disregarding her personal safety.

*Emma. For God's sake. Do not . . . do not be . . .*

He forced himself to think upon it, the cold tearing in his vitals savagely repressed. "She is not dead," he said, finally, conscious of the lie. He told himself it was necessary, that the Shield would be of more use if he held to faint hope. "She is most likely incapacitated in some manner. Pico, my pistol." He accepted the weapon with a nod. "Now, gentlemen, I trust everyone here sees the course we must take."

"I am afraid I most certainly do *not* see—" Aberline began.

Clare fixed him with a steady gaze. "Your knowledge of the worst sinks in Whitchapel, where I have deduced this monster is no doubt hiding, is very valuable. We may even, should we be forced to, find a poppy den and hope your small talent at sorcery will help. I am *quite* prepared to be ungentlemanly about this, sir, and furthermore, Mr Mikal will take it badly should you give anything less than your full effort to finding our sorceress."

Aberline had gone the colour of milk. He glanced at Mikal, opened his mouth, shut it, and nodded. There was a fire in the back of his dark gaze that promised much trouble later.

At the moment, Clare did not care one whit.

*Emma.* He had to examine his pistol, critically, as if assuring himself of its readiness.

*Bulldog. Made by Webley, very fine. Gift from Emma, to replace the pepperbox. Fully loaded.* His faculties replayed the loading procedure, but just to be certain, he checked the chambers. Five shots, .450 Addams cartridges, and there were more in his pockets, should he need them. *For emergencies*, the sorceress had said with a smile, presenting him with the walnut box.

He swallowed, very hard, and slid the weapon into its holster. A moment's work had it buckled to his belt, and the familiar weight was not nearly soothing enough.

Archibald Clare drew himself up to his full, if somewhat lean, height. "Pico, lad, go and tell your uncle we shall be taking the carriage, if Miss Bannon left it for us. On the shelf in my workroom you will find a decent purse for just such occasions as this. Mr Aberline, come with me; you shall be clothed properly for our descent. Mr Mikal—"

"I know my part," the Shield replied, and turned on his heel.

"If you feel any inkling of Miss Bannon's, er, location—"

"You shall know. And if not . . . vengeance." He disappeared to the far side of the stairs, no doubt heading for the stable to rouse the coachman. "Hurry."

"Never fear," Aberline commented sourly. "The sooner this is finished, the better."

"I hope she's alive, Inspector." Clare paused. "For your sake."

The man actually bristled. "Do you mean you—"

"No, you need not worry about me. You do, however, need to worry about Mikal. Come, let us find you more suitable cloth."

"*Stop!*" Aberline cried, and almost threw himself from the carriage. He would have landed ignominiously face-first on cobbles if not for Pico's lightning-quick reflex to grab at his jacket; Harthell cursed roundly as he pulled the vehicle to a juddering halt. The clockhorses, unhappy at being roused at this hour and further unhappy at such treatment, let their displeasure be known.

"*Canning!*" Aberline hailed what Clare, blinking, perceived to be a hurrying shape on the pavement. "I say, man, halt!"

"What the devil – oh, it's *you*." The voice had an odd lilt, possibly Eirean. "Where have you been? Don't you know?"

"Obviously I do *not*, sir." Aberline motioned the man closer. "What news?"

Clare squinted, and made out what had to be a fellow inspector. The man's hat plainly shouted he was of the

Yard, and his serviceable shoes held steaming traces of Scab's kiss. He was bandy-legged and thick-necked, and when he stepped under a sputtering gaslamp, Clare could see bright blue eyes and a reddened nose. Fog-moisture clung to his jacket and hat, and the steaming from his shoes added vapour to the choking mist.

*How very odd.* He had not, in his small experience of the organic sludge coating Whitchapel's floor, seen it behave in just this way.

"Another murder. The worst yet. Dorsitt Street. And the Scab . . . well."

"The Scab? What of it?"

"It hasn't come out. And where it has, it behaves oddly."

"As if it ever behaves in a different manner." Yet Aberline looked troubled, and he did not pursue this fascinating tidbit. Instead, he turned the conversation in quite another direction. "Where are you bound?"

"I'm to the Yard to report to Waring. There was some chalk on a door – something about the Yudics. He ordered it rubbed out, but too late. The entire Eastron End is up in arms again. There's a Yudic church burning, mobs looking for Leather Apron all the way to the Leae. Even Soreditch is restless."

"The murder in Dorsitt?" Aberline prompted, as the horses stamped and champed.

"It's dire, Aberline. It's inside a doss, for once, but that meant he had time to do his work. A real artist, our ripping lad."

"How bad is it?"

A bitter laugh greeted this query. "I'd say, don't dine before you view it, sir. Everyone's been at six and seven trying to find you, sir. Shall I tell Waring you've been sighted?" His tone plainly said that he expected a refusal of this generous offer.

Surprisingly, though, Aberline nodded. "Do, there's a good fellow. Tell him I am at the scene already. Dorsitt Street, you say?"

"Aye, between the Bluecoat and the Britannia. The ginhouses are near to empty serving the thirst of every blighter in the Eastron End come to view the scene, and it will only get worse. I'd use a whip for the crowds, if I were you." A half-bitter sound of amusement, and Canning touched his hat. "I'll be off then. I'll tell Waring you were already there. Fine carriage, by the by."

"Do you think so? Many thanks, sir, and regards to the missus."

"You should perhaps think on your own, there's a letter on your desk from her."

Aberline winced visibly. "I see. Good evening, Canning."

"Good evening. You'll need one." The man took himself off at a trot again.

"Dorsitt Street, as fast as you may," Aberline called to Harthell, whose reply was a snort saying that *he had heard, thank you, and mind to shut the door.*

Clare eyed Mikal, who had not moved during the entire exchange. The man's eyes were downright unsettling, catching some flash of random illumination and glowing gold. His hands had been loose and easy on his knees, but they had slowly tightened over the duration of the conversation. Aberline settled back next to Clare as Pico shifted a trifle uncomfortably.

*I would be uncomfortable too, next to that stillness.* Clare cleared his throat. "That does not sound encouraging."

Aberline made as if to wring his hands, thought better of it, and sighed deeply. "I have never heard Canning refer to a crime in quite such terms before. No doubt our mad sorcerer has surpassed himself."

The whip cracked and the carriage jolted forward. Clare still examined Mikal closely. The Shield's gaze had fixed on a point over Aberline's head, and the only thing more disconcerting was the slow unclenching of his fists.

"You did not ask for particulars," Clare noted, finally. *A description of the victim might aid us at this moment.*

*Or are you afraid?*

"I did not think it wise." Aberline dusted an imaginary speck from his borrowed trousers; the carriage jolted them all most rudely. "We shall see what Leather Apron and his creature have left us soon enough."

# Chapter Thirty-Eight

## You Will Give Me the World

A chanting, low and sonorous, a faint brushing against her skin as ætheric force crawled over her. She lay perfectly still, returning to consciousness much as a trickle might fill a teacup.

She was not in her bed.

*How odd. I cannot move.* Sorcerous and physical constraints, certainly, and a Prime's displeasure at being held so would no doubt begin to fray her temper before long. The said fraying would loosen her control in short order, and she would quickly become a frantic struggling thing, robbed of much of her mental acuity.

Unless she resisted.

*Do as Clare does. Observe. Deduce. Analyse. I am only temporarily helpless.*

It did not help quite as much as she might have wished.

She slowly raised her eyelids, training twisting its sharp hold deeper into her physical frame as her pulse struggled to quicken and her breathing sought to become shallow sips. *None of that now. Look about you.*

Her eyelids were not paralysed, though she could not turn her head. At first there was only an umber glow, but as she blinked, testing the confines of the restraints for any weakness in a purely reflexive unphysical movement, shapes became visible.

There was movement, and the chanting came to a natural end, dying away.

A slight hiss. The movement became a gleam on a knife blade, and Emma studied the tableau before her.

A black-clad back, one shoulder hitched high with a heavy hump upon it, claw-like gloved fingers. He stood before a large, squared chunk of obsidian, the lighting from wicks floating in cuplike oil-lamps instead of proper witch- or gaslight.

The wall she could see was of rough stone, the masonry old enough to be the work of the Pax Latium. The sounds were odd – what reached her through the distortion of shimmering sorcerous restraints echoed as if they were underground. Of course, Londinium's first burning and rebuilding had been courtesy of the Latiums. Even Britannia had not resisted them completely, or forever.

The shape before the obsidian stone – it looked much like an altar, she realised – turned with a queer lurching motion.

At first she feared the sorcerous restraints were affecting

her vision, or the foul substance he had used upon the rag had lingering aftereffects. But no. Everything else was in its proper, if shabby and worn, dimensions.

She watched his painful movements. Above the black altar – light fell *into* the stone and died, no reflection marred its surface – was a shifting, smoky substance hanging, moving in time to a slow beat very much like a sleeping pulse. She studied it more closely, and caught flashes.

Coal-bright eyes, extra-jointed fingers. Dead-pale flesh peeking through shabby coat and worn, knitted gloves. Neatly coiled atop the obsidian was the whip, the sharp barbs at the end of its long fluid flow pulsing as well with sickly blue-white flashes. The knife, slightly curved by much whetting, stood, quivering upright, balanced on its point. Occasionally, the smokelike suggestion reached down to stroke the rough, leather-wrapped handle, and a bloody flush would slide down the gleaming blade.

*Ah. I see.* It was a marvellous thing, to bring a spirit from nothing in this manner. All it took was the will to do so, and enough ætheric and emotional force. The trouble was, most such spirits tended to be malformed things, working only in a very limited way, as a golem or a Huntington's Chaser or even a *necros vocalis*.

Sorcery's children were cautioned to never let such a spirit grow too strong, for the trembling border between slave to a sorcerer's will and sentience could be breached after enough time and force had become the creature's ally.

And then . . . well. Better to create a new slave than have one grow too powerful and turn against its Maker.

Yes, she decided. Quite interesting. It was most certainly a Promethean. Difficult to create, a thousand things could go awry during the process. Also, it approached sentience very quickly. Why had she not thought of this possibility?

Because a sorcerer would have to be mad to attempt such a thing. It had to be fed, frequently. When those of Disciplines blacker than the Diabolic, malformed but drawing breath just the same, had achieved the status of gods among some benighted primitive clans, the accepted food for such constructs was the most tender and innocent of all, plucked from grieving mothers' breasts. Without such regular nourishment, the spirit would turn on its creator and roam free, gathering strength from casual, wanton murder. The æther around it would tangle and grow clotted, and it would eventually collapse under the weight of that curdling. Some whispered that the sorcerer queen of Karthago had created such a spirit to wage her desperate war against the Pax Latium, and that the blight surrounding that fabled lost city was a result of her death before she could bring it to a second, monstrous birth.

For there was one thing that set a Promethean apart from other created spirits. It could, if certain conditions were met, merge with its creator, and become something . . . *other*. Emma strained her well-trained memory, for once ignoring her own pulse as it quickened. She had, of course, under careful Collegia tutelage, studied several pages of books those of Disciplines other than the Black could not open. Her own Discipline, deeply of the Black, twitched slightly inside her as it recognised something akin to it.

*That is why, when I disturbed its feeding-site, it became attuned to me. How very interesting.*

"She's awake." There was a harsh, grating laugh, and the hunched figure straightened, stretching. Creaks and crackling, bulging and rippling, and parchment-pale hair fell to his shoulders. A terrible raddled face slowly came forward into a circle of smoking lamplight, and she recognised him afresh. "And so prettily, too."

She knew him. How could she not? The questions that had nagged at her for so long now had an opportunity to be answered.

Broad shoulders, one hitched much higher than the other. The black-clad chest bulged obscenely on one side, the cloth cut away to show a latticework of Alteration: arched ribs of scrolled, delicate iron and the dull reddish glow of a stone, curved on one side and flat on the other.

She recognised that as well.

For before she had wrenched it free of her flesh and married it to Archibald Clare's, she had borne one just like it. A Philosopher's Stone, made from a wyrm's heart. Wyrms were held outside of Time's river by their very nature, and a youngling's heart was powerful proof against most ills.

So he *had* possessed two after all.

Llewellyn Gwynnfud, Lord Sellwyth, returned from the dead, creaked as he bent over her.

Now she could see the thin, fleshy filaments spinning out from the ruins of shattered ribs, the wet gleam of organs rebuilding themselves under a carapace of Alterative sorcery. His gloved fingers reached down, most of them broken stubs coming to small points as they regrew, and he reached through the blurring of sorcerous restraints to touch Emma's hair. It was an oddly gentle caress.

Had he ever bothered to remain so tender, he might have had Emma's loyalty, instead of a young queen who would eventually insult her past bearing.

She sought to speak. Nothing came out – of course, she was gagged and silenced. A trickle of saliva slid from the corner of her cruelly bound mouth, pooling under her cheek. She could feel splintered wood underneath her, a hard surface holding her up from the floor. From the wet sound he made when he moved, she supposed she should be grateful.

"And she recognises me," he croaked. No wonder he had gone about muffled up to solicit the Coachman's initial victims. "You should see your expression, darling one."

Her brain began to race, furiously. The beginning of the Plague affair; she had felt another Prime in Victrix's receiving room. She had assumed – oh, how Clare would chide her for that! – it was one of Victrix's creatures, as she herself had been. The sense afterwards she had of being watched, the unseen hand that had aided her in unravelling the whole affair . . . of course, he would have wanted her safe and whole for his own plans. How he must have laughed. Perhaps he knew she did not possess the *other* Stone at this moment. Did he guess? What could he know?

The most likely solution was that he had bargained

somewhat with Thin Meg. Or found some means to exert some pressure upon that unlovely creature.

What could such a Prime, who had been torn apart by his own sorcery after his erstwhile lover had literally stabbed him from behind, not accomplish, if he possessed the will to rebuild his shattered body?

The pain must have been incredible. She had found only bleached bones scattered about the tower in Walcs where he had sought to bring one of the Timeless to the surface. Had some of them been his, twitching towards each other as he gathered strength?

What must he have *felt*?

"I have followed your career with much interest." His teeth had regrown, straight and pearly. His lips were scarred, but the scars would no doubt recede, given enough time. As his body regrew he would no doubt shed the Alterations. Had he performed them himself? The Transubstantive exercises would surely yield to his patience, if not his skill or Discipline. "You broke my heart, you know."

*Oh, I doubt that. You were dallying with that French tart and later with Rudyard, while you amused yourself with me. Had you been honest, we might have made an agreement. And had you not accused me of a hand in said tart's death, I may have forgiven you.* She calmed her pulse, drew in what air she could slowly and deeply. Thankfully the sorcerous restraints kept her nose clear; he did not wish her to suffocate.

*Yet*, she reminded herself.

"Do you wonder why I have not simply killed you outright?" His chin bobbed as he nodded, fat snakes of his matted hair brushing his shoulders with avid little whispers. "You have been well guarded for a very long time. That thing you keep as a Shield, oh, my dear. Quite resourceful, and quite dangerous." He smiled fully, a tear in his cheek widening before sealing itself with a wet sound. "But that is *not* the reason. I have plans for you, my love. Wonderful plans. I am going to give you a gift." The smile widened. "And then," Llewellyn Gwynnfud continued, "you will give me the *world*."

# Chapter Thirty-Nine

## Once the Temptation Is Large Enough

The tiny little court growing from Dorsitt Street was crammed with bluecoated bobbies and others, jostling and elbowing. It was better than the crush outside, where it seemed every criminal, unfortunate, or poor tradesman in Londinium had come to gawk. Aberline's authority carried them to a hacked-apart door guarded by a very pale young man in bluecloth. There was a large wet stain to one side of the door, and a broken window.

Clare's heart sank. He shook off sentiment, steeled himself, and peered into the darkness.

Beside him, Pico made a strangled noise. The lad turned, fumbled past the bobby, and heaved just where a similar viewer of the scene had, right onto the wet reeking splash that should have been covered by Scab.

The lad's eyes had been better than his. He took two

uncertain steps, lifting the lanthorn one of the Yard men outside had surrendered to Aberline.

There was a low punky glow from the fireplace. The kettle on the hob had melted, warped by unimaginable heat.

Beside him, Aberline cursed softly. There was a rancid burp rising in Clare's throat, he denied it.

Behind them, Mikal's step was soundless, but his presence pushed against Clare's back, along with prickles of gooseflesh.

The glimmers described . . .

Long dark curling hair, knocked free of its womanly confinement. Nakedness, indecent enough, but the gaping hole and shredded flesh . . . flayed thighs, the white gleaming of bone, the marks where a dexterous knife had dug in and the thing had feasted . . . feasted upon . . .

*Control yourself, Clare.* He realised, quite calmly, that he had handed the lanthorn to Aberline. Crazy shadows danced over the rotting walls. There was a hole in one corner of the room, the floorboard wrenched up.

He found his busy fingers working his left glove off.

There was very little that could shock or disgust a mentath. He realised, foggily, that he had perhaps found one way to do so. His faculties shivered under the assault, and he was very, very close to becoming a useless, porridge-brained idiot.

He brought his left hand to his mouth and bit in, savagely.

The pain of teeth in flesh was a bright arrow, striking the centre of his brain. It shocked him into some manner of rationality, and he found himself with a mouthful of bloody saliva, staring at the battered body on the bed.

Aberline had said something. Mikal's reply was a short, grating curse. The Shield had approached the bed, his shoulders rigid, and bent closer. How he could stand to have his face so near the . . .

Clare bit down again. It worked, but only just. He blinked, furiously, shutterclicks of dim, roseate light striking him as fists. The face had been stabbed, cheeks laid open, the teeth . . .

*Wait.*

Mikal's gaze met his. The Shield had turned from the bed, and the colourless sizzle around him was rage.

The teeth. They were not pearly little perfect white soldiers standing on their curved, rosebud-pink hills. They were discoloured, one or two under the opened flaps of cheekflesh decayed. The shape of the ear he could see was wrong as well, and it bore no hurtful little mark of piercing for bright earrings to dangle from.

The relief threatened to do what the sight of the body had not, and drive him to his knees. He swayed, the lanthorn swinging crazily again as Aberline caught his arm.

The hand that lay curiously unmarked to one side was small and delicate, but it was not soft, nor did it bear the indentation of rings. Chapped and reddened, it was a hand that had seen much weather and some measure of hard work.

His faculties, shocked, began functioning again. "Ah." He cleared his throat, again, and the smell struck him. The bowels had been opened . . . had the creature eaten them, too, and whatever offal they contained?

*How very interesting.*

Mikal read his expression, and the Shield actually staggered as well. When he regained his equilibrium, he strode across the room. He brushed past Clare like a burning wind, sparing Aberline only the briefest of glances, and halted in the doorway.

"Mentath?"

Clare found his voice. "It is . . . it is not. Her. It is not her."

Mikal nodded, once. "Work quickly." He stepped outside, and Clare wondered if he would lose whatever dinner he had partaken of as well. There was a murmur – Pico, and Mikal's toneless reply.

*What work is to be done here?* But he knew. There had to be some clew, some small detail that would lead them in the proper direction. Miss Bannon evidently had faith in his abilities, and was trusting her life to him.

Unfortunately, a mentath suffering irrational waves of Feeling would have even more difficulty untangling a sorcerous crime than one who was not so burdened by . . . relief? Hope? What *was* the dashed word for it?

It did not matter.

"Are you certain?" Aberline, curiously hushed. "Or did you tell him so because . . ."

"I am quite certain." Clare drew in a deep breath, wished he had not. He examined the kettle on the hob, melted and scarred. Scraps of charred cloth – had he burned her dress to give himself light? Or was it sorcerous in nature? "What do you make of this?"

Aberline drew the lanthorn closer. He cast an uneasy glance at the bed, with its hideous cargo. "Perhaps to delay her identification? Or some sorcerous reason . . . or perhaps he needed light to work by."

"The creature preferred darkness before. What sorcerous reason?"

"See the rings in the metal, there? And there? Chrysfire. Untraceable, unlike witchflame." Aberline dug in his pocket, wiped his forehead with a wilting handkerchief. "It bears little stamp of the kindler's personality. Sorcery is a distinctly *personal* art."

"Miss Bannon often remarked as much." Clare crouched, Aberline holding the lanthorn higher to shed some gleams upon the charred mess. "Quite a bit of cloth. None of it the quality that a lady might wear."

Aberline glanced back at the bed, struck by a thought. "Her teeth. Of course. It cannot be her. I am a fool. Well, what do we do now? I confess I am at a loss."

"You will not like the direction my thoughts are tending."

"I fancy I won't."

"Most poppy users reserve a small amount, rather in the manner of a talisman against want of the substance." *As do most users of coja.* Perhaps a fraction of that sweet white powder would help. Clare shut the thought away. "Do you?"

"You are correct." Aberline had gone pale. "You wish me to . . ."

A gleam caught Clare's eye. He leaned forward. *How odd.* "A button," he murmured. "A very familiar one, at that."

"What?" Mystified, Aberline nevertheless lowered the lanthorn a touch.

"Why on earth would the creature burn its own coat, too?" He settled on his heels. "Mikal. He might know." The ashes were still warm, but Clare's fingers had lost none of their deftness. He tossed the button from palm to palm, rather like a baked potato, and saw with some satisfaction that he was correct. It had the faint impress of a ship's anchor upon its false-brass face, and though deformed by heat it was indubitably the same button the Coachman-thing had worn upon its coat.

"In any case," he continued, "this is an item from the creature's coat. I believe a physical object can be of use in finding a certain person's location?"

"Sympathy? I have none of the power for such an operation." Aberline had gone quite pale.

"Let us hope Mikal does." Clare straightened, rising. "For he may compel you to attempt, power or no."

A few questions elicited the most likely name of the unfortunate upon the bed – Marie-Jinnete, surnamed Kelly, also called Black Mary. She had retired to her room after dark with a customer, and not been discovered until one of her other suitors or customers returned to batter at her door and make quite a scene, thinking her unfaithful.

Which of course she was, and had paid harshly for it.

She had been many shillings behind on the rent for the sad little corner she inhabited, which no doubt led to the decision to peer through the broken window, and consequently force the door.

The missing sorceress had most likely been nowhere near this corner of Whitchapel during the night.

The Shield's face was as white as Aberline's, and just as set. The Yard men in the small court – named after a miller, though there had likely never been one of that persuasion plying his trade here – were at the other end, doing their best to hold back the crowd. Mikal's long coppery fingers turned the small lump of metal over, thoughtfully. "He does not have the power," he said, finally, jutting his chin at Aberline. "And I may only use such a Sympathy in close proximity to my Prima."

"How close?" Clare all but hopped from foot to foot.

Mikal shrugged. "Within her very presence. I do not understand, though – if she is alive, I should *feel* her . . ." His pause was matched by a curious change in expression. "Unless . . ."

"Unless?" Clare prompted.

Was it hope, dawning on the Shield's features? Weary, disbelieving hope, perhaps. "Unless she is far underground, or behind certain defences. Hothin's water-wall, for example, or a muirglass."

"Underground?" A little colour had come back to Aberline's face. "Hm."

The silence that grew about them had all the crackling urgency of the breath before a storm's breaking.

Clare let them cogitate. Beside him, the lad Pico had tensed too, as a bloodhound scenting prey.

"Scare's Row." Pico sported feverish spots on both cheeks, and kept wiping his mouth nervously. His shoulder touched Aberline's, and neither moved away from the contact. The situation was rather beginning to paper over their personal differences, and it was high time, too. "Fan End, too."

"Crithen's Church." Aberline nodded. "That's where I'd go."

"*Do* speak clearly, sirs." Clare eyed the crowd at the end of the court. There was an air of carnivorous festival about the whole scene he did not quite like, even if he was heartened to find all four men upon whom Miss Bannon was now depending finally behaving reasonably

"Tunnels. From the Pax Latium, it's said. Sometimes they're rumoured to have beasts living in them, like near the Tower." Pico made as if to spit, reconsidered. "Bad business, all of them."

"Dark holes. Worst sinks in Whitchapel. Some of them host ginhouses; if the drink does not blind you, a knife may." A fey light was slowly dawning on the inspector's features. "Why did I not think on it before? A mad sorcerer, hiding there . . . sending his creature forth . . . using the tunnels as a means to move undetected . . . hm. Yes, Crithen's Church is where I would start. The deeper holes are all about that location, the ones even the flashboys and Thin Meg's starvelings don't venture into."

Clare jammed his hat more firmly upon his head. "Then

there we shall go. Mr Mikal, once we are underground, will you be able to sense Miss Bannon?"

"Perhaps." His hand flicked, and the button disappeared. "This may be useful, if we draw close enough."

Clare struggled with himself, and lost. "Can Inspector Aberline's powers, such as they are, be magnified in some manner?"

Mikal stilled, and so did Aberline. "There are ways," the Shield admitted, and viewed the inspector afresh. "Blood, for one."

"None of that." Aberline backed up two steps, his steps loud on the Scabless ground.

"We have other methods," Clare said, hastily. "You have a small amount of poppy, Aberline."

The man's reply was unrepeatable, but it satisfied Clare that he did, in fact, possess a small lump of said substance. Not that it mattered – any apothecary could be induced to part with enough laudanum to replicate the effect, should it come to such a thing.

*Finding Miss Bannon outweighs any injury to his pride*, Clare told himself. He did not care to think further upon the chain of logic – what else did it outweigh? His life? Clare's? Or, it could not, for Clare was made proof against such things.

Sacrificing another was so easy, was it not? Once the temptation was large enough. Once the Feeling outweighed pure logic. How did Emma bear such storms of emotion, without a mentath's skills to shield her? How had she borne his accusations? And Valentinelli's death – how could he have thought her unmoved?

*Concentrate, Clare.* "Very well. To the carriage. Pico, climb up with Harthell and direct him to this church. Mikal, do bring Inspector Aberline, and make certain no harm comes to him."

He set off for the mouth of the court, and his face crumpled for a moment before resmoothing itself. For he had realised something.

First, that he had sounded *exactly* like Miss Bannon. And second, he had no particular qualm about shedding the good inspector's blood.

Should it become necessary.

# Chapter Forty

## The Cap to His Ambition

The painful, twisted wreck of a Prime shuffled away, and Emma was left to her own devices, her gaze roving over what little she could see without moving her head. Her pulse struggled to rise, again, the fact of confinement looming, a Prime's will finding such a thing unbearable.

*It is no different than a corset,* she told herself. *It is no different than being a woman in a world that seeks to chain every woman it can find. It is no different than your entire life, Emma. Be still. Be logical. Plan.*

Did Clare feel this distress, when irrationality loomed? Perhaps they were the same – he was logic trapped in an illogical world, and she was a Prime's will trapped in a woman's flesh.

*Enough to base a Sympathy on, I should think. Will they*

*guess where I have been taken? I am underground. Mikal
. . . he may not . . .*

It was immaterial. Whether they accepted her invitation
to find her or not, she had a duty here. Not to Victrix, not
even to Britannia. She had *chosen* to be confined in this
manner, offering herself as a sacrifice.

He had taken the bait. It was now her aim to become
poisonous.

*And you shall give me the world.* What did he *mean*?
How many times had she thought him dead? The simulacrum in Bedlam, the tower at Dinas Emrys . . . it reminded
her of certain novels, wherein a villain was a mad reflection of the hero, and escaped death through the most
fantastic of means.

The Promethean, in its egg of smoke over the lightless
obsidian block, moved sluggishly. Rather like a swelling
spawn in an ungodly womb. Of course it had eaten and charred
the organs of generation. They were incredible sources of
ætheric force, both because of their biological purpose and
the importance accorded them by custom and human instinct.

If Llewellyn sought to marry the Promethean to his own
regrowing flesh, why would he need *her*? And why, oh
why, would it have such an effect on Britannia?

For the ruling spirit had been afraid. And Thin Meg, in
her pit, had neatly placed Emma in a trap – or had she?

*I do not know enough. Logic, Emma. Imagine Clare is
here. What would he say?*

Perhaps it was the wrong question. Her body twitched,
her will flexing against the bonds. They held fast.

Now she remembered, unwillingly, the last time she had been held fast so completely. Dripping water, her despairing, unconscious sounds of rage and pain, and the choking as Mikal strangled his former Prime, slowly, and the horrid sounds of him tearing flesh asunder, before freeing her from the bonds.

*Miles Crawford.* The name of her captor. All the rage, all the terror in the world held in those syllables. She had been outplayed by him, and her Shields had paid the price. If not for Mikal's disobedience—

*Remember your purpose. Which is not to relive that moment.*

Then why had she done this? Perhaps for no other reason than the one she had given a man who had not listened.

*If not for luck, I could have been any one of them. All of them, or more. Or less, as the world would have it.*

Perhaps he did not mean to marry the Promethean to his own flesh. And yet, marrying it to hers would be problematic as well. He could not tell, of course, that she had given the second wyrm's heart to another, or even if she had taken it for herself. The beauty of the Philosopher's Stone was its ability to pass undetected by even the finest unphysical senses. Just as a wyrm could lay undetected beneath a tower for aeons, as the world turned about it. Would the Stone bar another item's introduction into the body it protected from harm and decay?

*You shall give me the world.*

Perhaps . . .

The connection trembled just out of reach. Something,

some symmetry, was escaping her. Just as the nature of the Promethean had—

*Wait*.

If Llew had created a Promethean, and fed it on unfortunates in Whitchapel . . . no. That was wrong.

The only certainty was that a Promethean had been created. Perhaps it had chosen its own meat and drink, as it were.

*You have more enemies than you know, sparrow-witch.*

A Prime always did.

Ætheric force twitched restlessly. Come Tideturn, she might be able to find a crack or a chink in the restraints. They felt supple, slightly elastic, but any pressure against them would make the entire trap harden. Elegant, and just the thing to keep a Prime still and quiet.

If you did not mind said Prime losing her mind from the very fact of being trapped.

She might become just as mad as he was. Except he was not lunatic, really. Simply ambitious. He saw no reason to cap his ambition, any more than Emma did.

*The only cap to my ambition is myself. What is the cap to his, I wonder?*

The gleaming knife trembled upon the stone, turning on its tip rather like a ballerina *en pointe*. Its slight scraping would have sent a shiver down her back, if she could move.

She essayed a slight humming noise, deep in her throat. The gag would keep her from shaping Words, true. Much could be done with tone and—

Blackness devoured her vision. Panic, as her nose was stoppered as well as her mouth. Sorcerous training could not control the fear of strangulation, and she went limp. Air returned, as did consciousness.

There was a soft, mocking laugh. She could not *see* him, and the restraints made the sound echoing and unearthly.

"You think I'd leave you any opening, my darling? No." He scraped back into sight, moving a little more easily. More damp, splashing sounds.

Emma squeezed her eyelids shut. Hot water trickled between her lashes. Then she let them open just a fraction, disliking the dark.

"I *respect* you. Not like that magical whore. It took me by surprise, her luring you into the open. I had hoped to bring you out a different way." A shadow flickered between her and the yellow-rose glow of the lamps. "But here you are. And in such good time, too."

*Think, Emma. Think.*

Unfortunately, he straightened, metal and bone clicking as the ruins of his body shook about him. He reached out, and Emma's eyes opened wide.

His misshapen right hand closed about the knife, and he lifted it free of the stone with a physical and ætheric effort. He turned, and the tenderness on his features was almost worse than the glitter of insane calm in his dark eyes. Thin threads of yellow shone in the muddy irises, a reminder she did not need of Mikal.

Her Shield was most likely frantic by now. How much

time had passed? Was it midnight yet? Could Clare find her? They were underground, could Mikal sense her with any accuracy once he was close enough?

*Do not worry upon them, Emma. You have more than enough to occupy you here.*

Llew shuffled toward her. "*X—ż't'ks'm*," he breathed, a sorcerous Word that bent strangely as it was uttered. The knife shimmered with ætheric force, and the smoky egg containing the Promethean convulsed afresh.

Her Discipline stirred, sleepily.

Too late, she began to understand what he meant to do, and how stupid she had been to use herself as a lure.

He began to chant, the language of Making and Naming alternating as he described what he wished the sorcerous force to shape itself as, how it would affect the tangled fleshly snarl of the physical and the gossamer of the unseen. Stone shivered uneasily as the taproots driven into Whitchapel stirred, only faint echoes where Emma had cleared them but driven deep in many other places. Many, many other victims had fallen – the creature found its own meat and drink, but its creator had been busy with murder, too.

Lines of force coalesced, becoming visible to Sight, and Llewellyn raised the knife. His mouth grinned and slavered over the consonants as he described her death, and what that ending would fuel.

The Promethean was nearing the end of its infancy. It needed a vessel, a mockery of birth. The knife lowered, and a faint piping reached Emma's ears – souls, straining for release, perhaps. Each of the victims crying out, a chorus of the damned.

The smoky egg over the obsidian – it *was* an unholy altar, she realised, another mockery, yet the form was completely appropriate to the Work Llew was attempting – drifted free of its moorings. The two live coals of the Coachman's eyes glared from a suggestion of a face, and Emma's entire body tensed, as if it could deny the coming violation.

The knifetip touched her throat.

# ❁ *Chapter Forty-One*

## *To Crithen's Church*

It was no use. Clare pushed the carriage door open as the clockhorses shrilled. If they went any further, the carriage would become well and truly mired in the crowd, and Harthell's steady cursing was already lost under the noise. Screams of frightened women, breaking bottles and tearing wood, the roiling of men's voices. From somewhere torches had arrived, for the gaslamps were guttering, their wickcharms dying. The throng ahead filled the main thoroughfare of High Whitchapel Road, and the press of the crowd even on this small tributary was becoming rather worrisome.

*Leather Apron! Leather Apron!*

The public, that great beast – or at least a healthy slice of it – had lost patience with the keepers of order.

*In her very bed, he did, and they do nothing, all high*

*and mighty! Heard he opened her up, even her face. Welladay, the Metropoleans don't care as long as he kills poor frails. Our girls, they are, even if low.*

Lining High Whitchapel were shops and better-to-do homes; the crowd pressed uneasily against them. The carriage had not yet become a target, but it was only a matter of time.

Aberline was beside him, casting an eye over the heaving mass. The fog had greyed as if dawn was incipient; Clare's pocket-watch told him that indeed, sunrise was very close, with Tideturn not far behind. More glass shattered, and Harthell cursed again.

"We shall not stir a foot in this," Clare observed. *Soon they may take a mind to upend the carriage.*

"Not without sorcery or a regiment." Aberline, sour-faced, had regained some of his colour. Mikal was silent, but his tension was clearly apparent.

"Ho! Pico, come down. Harthell, take the carriage home." Clare had to shout. "We shall proceed—"

A different sound pierced the seashell roar. High and chilling, a silverwhistle.

"Oh, *blast* it all." Aberline leapt from the carriage, landing heavily on blackened, broken cobbles. "Waring, you bloody *fool*. He's called in—"

"Headcrackers. And possibly a regiment," Clare said, grimly. "Or two. There will be blood shed this dawn."

"Other sorcerers will muddy the waters." Mikal had grasped Aberline's elbow as the crowd surged around them. A toothless beldame in red calico shrieked, falling against a sturdy flashboy with an Altered left hand, metal sharpened and gleaming as he thrust her away with a curse. "How close are we?"

"To Crithen's? A ten-minute walk, were this a fine morning. Today . . ." Aberline indicated the throng at the juncture of Bent and High Whitchapel.

Harthell evidently agreed with Clare's estimation of the situation, for he wheeled the carriage hard right and vanished down Tehning Cross; the crack of his whip sent a chill up Clare's spine. *Set it aside. What may be done? Think!*

Mikal glanced up, studying the rooftops. "I think—"

Whatever he had meant to say was lost in an angry roaring. Beneath it, drumbeats, and the clopping of hooves in unison. Yet it was not from that end of Whitchapel the flaming lucifer that set off a crowd's tinder dropped.

It was from the *other* end, and as soon as Clare heard the sound, his heart sank.

Ever afterwards, none could discern from the conflicting reports who had given the City Streamstruth Regiment the order to fire upon the crowd. The volley was enough to cause a few moments' worth of shocked silence.

There is a moment when a crowd ceases to be a mass of separate beings, when it becomes a single mind and turns upon its tormentor. Or simply, merely upon anything within reach. Once it becomes such an organism, it tramples, heaves, tosses, and smashes with no restraint.

Being caught in the jaws of that monster was not acceptable.

Mikal shoved Aberline to the side of the street, where an open dosshouse door showed a slice of yellow lamplight. "*Go!*" he cried, and pushed Clare for good measure. Pico hopped in their wake with youthful alacrity, and it was Mikal again, suddenly before them, who kicked at the door even as a burly just-awakened stout in braces and a thread-bare shirt sought to slam it against sudden danger.

A quick strike, Mikal's hand blurring, and the dosshouse doorman folded; Pico shoved the door closed and sought a means to bar it.

Clare found himself gasping for breath. *How annoying.* Still, they were out of danger for the moment, and Mikal evidently had some manner of plan.

"Up," the Shield said. "Find a staircase."

"And then what?" Pico enquired, shoving a flimsy chair against the dosshouse door. The entry hall was dingy and smelled overwhelmingly of cabbage and unwashed flesh; on the ground the doorman stirred slightly. Pico thought a moment, then grabbed both the supine man's wrists. Aberline helped him drag him for the door, and Clare's protest died unspoken. The wood cracked and heaved; outside, the sound of the crowd was now a wild howling of pain.

"Then," the Shield said, "we run. And you pray to what-ever god you choose that we find my Prima."

Clay tiles scratching underfoot; timber creaking uneasily when a man's weight touched it. Mikal, impatient with their slow progress, nevertheless shepherded them carefully.

The geography of Londinium appeared much altered when seen from this vantage. Ground became tile and sloped roofs, streets long channels separating thin island-fingers. Crossing the channels was either nerve-wracking – a slide and a leap, Mikal's hand flashing forwards to drag a man onto solid safety – or entirely irrational, a matter of clinging to the Shield and closing one's eyes while he leapt in some sorcerous fashion. Each time he did so, hopping across thoroughfares as if it was child's play, Clare's most excellent digestion threatened to unseat itself.

At least now he knew how the man kept up with Miss Bannon's carriage.

Clare peered at the sky as Pico slithered down the roof-slope behind him, boots scraping dry moss and accumulated soot. Even here, life clung to gullies and cracks; he saw hidden courts, walled off by the rapid building of slum-tenements, with the remains of old gardens gone to seed. Twisted trees no eye but the sky had viewed for years, and even grass and weeds clinging in rain-gutter sludge. Londinium's roofs were a country of mountainous desert, concealing throbbing life and violent motion beneath its crust.

Whitchapel was ablaze, figuratively and actually. Two fires had started, one near the border of Soreditch and another, from what Clare could tell, sending up a black plume from the slaughteryard near Fainmaker's Row. Yellowing fog swirled uneasily, and the virulent green of Scab held to mere fringes and dark alleys.

Cries and moans, the roaring of a maddened crowd, more sharp volleys of rifle fire. Had the Crown authorised such a deadly response? Was it the Old City, nervous at the proximity of the restless poor? Waring was merely a commissioner, he could not have taken the step without approval from the Lord Mayor *or* the Crown—

"Mind yourself," Pico said, grabbing his sleeve. "Look. Crithen's, just there."

Clare peered down. Mikal landed atop the slope with a slight exhalation of effort, and Aberline retched once, quietly.

"Enough power to feel the effects," the Shield said, soft and cold. "And should I need to, *Inspector*—"

"Cease your threats." Aberline sounded pale. "I told you I would do my best."

"Mr Mikal?" Clare's voice bounced against the rooftop. "A moment, if you please?"

"What?"

"It is past dawn."

Mikal was silent for a long moment. There was a flash of yellow as he checked the sky, and Pico moved along the edge of the roof.

Clare cleared his throat. "Do you have any idea why Londinium is still, well, subject to Night? Is this sorcery?"

"Perhaps." The Shield halted, still with a hand to Aberline's elbow. "A Work meant to replace a ruling spirit, or create a new one . . . perhaps this is an effect. My Prima would know. Are we close?"

"The place is there." Clare pointed, as Pico had. "Though I must say, it does not look in the least churchlike."

It was a slumping, blasted two-storey building, set between two ditches that served, if Clare's nose was correct, as nightsoil collectors. Also, if his vision was piercing the dimness correctly, a dustheap or two. "I cannot even tell . . . was it a house?"

"They call it church because Mad Crithen nailed his victims to the walls." Pico sounded dreadfully chipper. "He was popish, he was. Leastways, that's how I heard it."

"Mad Crithen?"

"A murderer." Breathless, Aberline shook free of Mikal. "*Lustmorden*, but with a religious . . . he crucified his victims. I read of it in Shropeton's analysis of—"

"There's a way down!" Pico shimmied lithely over the edge of the roof and vanished. "Here!"

Clare patted his pistol, secure in its holster. "It is extremely likely there will be unpleasantness within. I cannot think this sorcerer will not guard his lair."

"He may not need to." Mikal pointed. "Look."

A subtle wet gleam in the ditches, and stealthy movement in the shadows. Skeletal shapes, in ragged threadbare clothes, and under the sound of riot and mayhem, a queer sliding whisper.

"Scab. In the ditches." Aberline sucked in a sharp breath. "And . . . starvelings? Here?"

"Starvelings?"

"Marimat." Mikal's mouth turned the syllables into a curse. They made little sense to Clare, but he shivered anyway. "Of course. Come, quickly. We must reach the place before they can hold it."

"I don't suppose you—"

But Mikal had already embraced Aberline's stout waist with his arm, and flung them both from the roof with a rattle and a peculiar whooshing. Clare scrabbled for the place Pico had disappeared, and the lad's disgusted curse from below was lost in a rising, venomous hiss.

# Chapter Forty-Two

### No More

The prick of the knifetip made a vast stillness inside Emma Bannon. The world shrank, Time itself stretching and slowing.

*And so I die.*

It pressed further, and the smoke-egg floated free of the obsidian's tethering influence. As it did, it grew heavier, blacker, and the block of glassy stone crackled. Thin fissures threaded its surface, and the lamplight now reflected wetly from its shifting planes.

*Ah.* Much more of the inner workings of Llewellyn's creation became apparent to her. The insistent pressure at her throat mounted, and the following moments were, paradoxically, endless . . . and too quick to contain everything that occurred within them.

Emma turned inward, into that stillness, her eyes forgotten in that quick motion. It was not a physical movement, and her slackened muscles meant the restraints about her loosened.

Raw aching places inside her woke in a blinding sheet of pain, and she trembled on the thin edge of forcing her spirit free by an effort of will, stoppering her lungs and heart before the mad Prime she had once loved could cut her throat.

To do so would deny him his victory – where else would he find such an apt victim for this, the last murder to fuel an unholy transformation?

*No.*

They burst upon her, the murders she had felt and those she had not. Cleaving of flesh and bright copper fear, gin fumes and desperation. Their lives, colourless drudgery and danger, painful except when the gin soaked through and insulated against hunger, the men and their grasping, hurtful hands. A sweet word in the darkness, coaxing them to take one more customer. A faceless thing, and the blade so sharp it almost did not hurt as they were unseamed . . . hot blood, the merciful blackness swallowing them whole.

*I could have been any one of them.*

None knew from whence sorcerous talent sprang. A lucky chance, and she had been lifted from the mire – but her skirts were still draggled, and she would never be allowed to forget.

At the very floor of Emma's consciousness, a barred door.

*He seeks to give life. I am of the Black, my Discipline is Endor . . . and there is no better way to cheat him of his prize.*

Her throat swelled, a trickle of blood tracing white skin. The restraints, sensing a gathering, tightened. The constriction, sudden and unbearable, roused the same blind fury that had once caused sickly green flame to sprout from a drunken man's skin and clothes. The same will, fed and exercised, grown monstrous, able to endure temporary confinement only because she had suffered it, in one form or another, her entire life.

The door at the bottom of her soul creaked. *No more.*

A shattered hulk of a sorcerer, his rasping voice raised in a chant of a Discipline not his own, tensed. Next would come driving the knife home, and the creature – his only issue, a son who might be grateful – would feast upon this sacrifice. And she, *she*, would be given a gift of blackness and no more pain.

Black chartersymbols woke, racing along Emma Bannon's skin. Her eyelids snapped wide, and each pupil kindled with a bright, leprous-green flame. The charter symbols crawled up her legs, rushed over her torso in a wave, devoured her arms – still encased in shredded mourning cloth – and flowed under her hair, smearing across her slackened face in their hurrying.

They reached the knifepoint digging into her flesh, a cascade of pale green sparks fountaining from the contact.

Inside her, the hurtful flower of her Discipline bloomed.

Llewellyn Gwynnfud, still chanting, pushed down.

He dragged the razor-sharp blade across his former lover's throat.

# Chapter Forty-Three

## A Betrayal that Struck One

The starvelings were skeletal corpses, still animate through some feat of sorcery. There were so *many*, shuffling forward with the slowness of the damned, their hands held out. Those soft, insistent graspings could drag a man down, and then they would cluster him, pressing life and breath away with that soft, low, terrifying hissing. They had narrowly avoided losing Pico, and Clare tipped the empty cartridges out of his Bulldog as he sprinted for the door of Mad Crithin's Church.

Mikal wrenched the worm-holed, flimsy wooden door open. It had been chained with iron, and the cylinder-lock dangling from rusted metal links was new, though smeared with grease to disguise any shine. The chain snapped, broken links cascading in a chiming stream, and an exhalation of neglect and rot swallowed them all. Aberline's ankle, twisted just after the man wrenched starvelings from Pico's slim frame with a roaring fit for a lion, was already swollen.

Clare gained the dubious safety and Mikal slammed the door to. "Brace . . . it," the Shield managed, breathlessness the only indication of the efforts he had made so far. "*Hurry.*"

*Does he think we treating this as a Sunday amble?* Clare did not waste his own breath on a sharp reply. Pico, his jacket in tatters and his fine waistcoat ripped, was already shoving a jumble of broken wood that had once been a secretary against the door. Mikal's boots slipped slightly on grime-caked wooden boards, and cords stood out on the Shield's neck as he sought to hold the entry against the soft, deadly pressure from outside.

Aberline hobbled, dragging a sprung-stuffing chair across the uneven boards. Clare's lungs protested, he whooped in a deep breath, reloading his Bulldog. When that operation was finished, he helped Pico drag another piece of shattered furniture against the door; next came a huge, shipwrecked chunk of masonry helpfully fallen from somewhere.

The soft scraping from outside did not lower in volume at all. *That* was quite chilling, Clare allowed, and proceeded to ignore it. He straightened, dusting his hands. "Where now?"

"Down-cellar." Aberline leaned heavily upon Pico. "Good God, is Thin Meg *mad?*"

"Has she ever been sane?" Mikal's laugh was a marvel of restrained rage. "My Prima visited her, she knew far more than she allowed."

"Ah. And Bannon *believed* what Meg said?" Aberline sounded as if he rather did not credit the notion.

"I should think not. She is too wise to believe many things." Mikal pointed at a far corner, between mounds of wrecked wood and marble. "There, I would say."

The walls had been torn through, and there were fittings – brass, copper, other materials – that could have been sold. Yet Clare did not think those who passed through, no matter what crypt below Londinium they aimed for, would take anything from this sad, ramshackle place. There was a faint chill exhalation from every surface, and the darkness seemed altogether too thick to be mere shadow.

"Been two years since I last," Pico breathed, once. "Hasn't changed a bit."

"It never does." Aberline, shortly.

They were making a great deal of noise, but Clare saw no point in quieting them. Mikal was a ghost, and he kept Aberline well within sight.

The cellar was reached through a hole hacked in the floor of what might have been a sitting room, once. There was a ladder made of what looked like nailed-together bits of lath, though it was surprisingly solid.

Aberline made a short pained sound when he landed, and would have toppled if not for Mikal's steadying.

Even here, things were not quite right. A drift of coal, worth good money, clustered against the closer end of the cellar, though the chute it would have been poured through seemed blocked.

*Rather good thing, too,* Clare thought, and shivered at the idea of hearing soft starveling hisses in the dark.

Aberline had struck a lucifer, and Clare saw a yawning hole in the ground opposite the coal-pile. It looked far too large for its own borders, one of Londinium's more irrational corners, and a familiar pain gripped his temples.

Mikal paused. His dark head came up, a stripe of blood and dirt on his cheek black in the lucifer's glare.

Aberline halted as well, quite amazingly pale under the muck and dust he was covered with. He grimaced as he shifted his weight. Pico's breathing was stertorous in the stillness, but the lad was holding up gamely. With his hair knocked out of its careful slick-back and his eyes wide, he looked rather young.

And fragile.

"Mikal?" Clare whispered.

"I think . . ." The Shield shook his head, as if tossing away said thought. "Come."

Clare, his faculties straining under the weight of what he might be about to witness, had a very rational thought. *We should have brought a lanthorn.*

As if in answer, a sound rose from the hole. Long, and loud, it stripped the hair from their fevered brows and brushed against their clothing.

Later, Clare could not think quite *what* the sound had been. A rumble, a moving of earth, the roar-breath of a massive fire, the sea suckling at its rocky confines? No, too much. Perhaps it was the internal shifting of a lie told or found out, or a betrayal that struck one to a heart's core

– but that was *ridiculous*. It was merely Feeling, and Clare should set it aside.

Aberline gasped, rocking back on his heels, but Mikal's reaction was even more marked.

"*Emma!*" he screamed, and leaped forwards into the dark, his footsteps, for once, heavy with reckless speed.

The massive sound did not echo, but it left some imprint on the space around the three left in Mikal's wake, broken only by a thin, light, unholy tapping Clare had heard before: footsteps of a creature that carried a sharp-ended whip. The healed slice along his forearm send a pang up to his shoulder.

Clare also heard, as if in a nightmare, a slow, soft, *draining* hiss.

# Chapter Forty-Four

## In the Final Weighing

*T*he first surprise was that it did not hurt. The knife cleaved flesh, yes, and there was a hot jet of salt-crimson blood.

Then . . . droplets hung in midair, and the blooming within her was a sweet pain. Her Discipline roared, needing no chant to shape it. No, when a Discipline spoke, the entire sorcerer was the throat it passed through.

It required only the strength to submit. As long as that strength lasted, wonders could be worked.

What had she done? Turned inward, yes, and found . . . what?

Not m'pence, *Marta Tebrem* whispered. Needs it for my doss, I do.

They spun around her, sad women and merry, dead on a knife or by a strangle, in childbed or by fever, by gin or misadventure, in hatred or in desperation, by folly or chance. She was of the Endor, but even more importantly, she was of their number, and the spark that rose within her was both negation and acceptance.

Some of them had wished for release from the miserable drudgery and endless pain. There was the acceptance.

Yet even louder, and containing the acceptance as a shell contains a nut, the denial.

No. I will not.

Should not, or could not, those were incorrect. The refusal was a hard shell, wrapped about the tender thing called a soul trapped in a fragile and perishable body.

Beat me, hurt me, kill me, I will not.

Or perhaps the refusal was merely her own, even her Discipline bending to a will grown strong by both feeding and confinement.

They streamed through her, the women of Whitchapel, and their cries were the same as the Warrior Queen Boudicca in her chariot – a vessel of Britannia dishonoured, slain in battle, but still remembered.

Still alive, if only in the vast storehouse of memory a ruling spirit could contain.

No. I live.

The heart struggled, the lungs collapsing with shock. Her murderer crowed with glee, his purpose achieved, his chant becoming the savagery of an attacker's, almost swallowing the sound of sorcery spilling through the bloody necklace of a cut throat.

I live.

*They burst free of her not-quite-corpse – for the throat-cutting does not kill immediately, for a few crucial moments the sorceress, her Discipline invoked, was between living and dead. A threshold, a lintel, a doorway . . .*

*. . . and Death itself, the other face of the coin called Life, for a bare moment gave a fraction of the citizens of its dry uncharted country their mortal voices back.*

*The unsound was massive, felt behind eye and heart and throat . . .*

*. . . and it struck down the man who had sought to give a mockery of Life with a flood of leprous-green flame.*

*He squealed, beating at the fire that erupted from his slowly regrowing mortal flesh, but such is the nature of Death's burning that it consumes metal, red muscle, rock itself, the dry fires of stars and the tenderness of green shoots, all in their own time.*

*He fell against the obsidian altar, and the sound of its shattering was lost in another – the scream of a malformed soul given half-life, brushed with a feather of sorcery and set free.*

*The Promethean fled, shrieking, and on a wooden shelf in a stone womb underneath Londinium, a sorceress's mortality writhed.*

*For a dizzying moment she trembled between, neither alive nor dead, as the sisters of murder and confinement clamoured for her voice to be added to their number.*

No.

*In the end, the choice was hers alone. If she suffered under the lash of living in a world not made for her sex, it was the price extracted for protecting those upon whom her regard fell. Those she protected – did her arrogance extend so far as to think she was, in her own way, their final keeper?*

*To rule is lonely, and there was the last temptation.*

*The pieces of her erstwhile lover's spell curled about her. Her mortal death could fuel its completion, for she had taken from him, again, everything.*

*He had wrought too well, when he sought the perfect victim. In that perfection itself lay his undoing.*

*Oh yes, it was possible. To take the shards and knit them together, to drive the taproot deep into the shimmering field of pain and Empire, and to become what he had wished to create: a spirit of rule.*

*One last, painless lunge, and she would Become.*

*She could be what she had pledged to serve and turned against. She could drain the vital force of the ancient, weary being who charted Empire's course. She could wrap herself in its vestments and strike down the physical vessel of that being, choose a vessel of her own and arrange not merely her household but the world itself to her liking.*

*It would take so little. In the end, only the decision to* do *mattered.*

*And yet.*

*For the final time, the will holding the door open for Discipline spoke. The choice was made, had always been made, for she was as she had been created, and the pride she bore would not allow her to become an usurper.*

*Her answer was clear, if only in the shuttered halls of*

*a human heart – that country where sorcery and even Death are only guests. Tolerated, but, in the final weighing, negligible.*

*I live.*

*I live.*

*I* live.

# Chapter Forty-Five

## A More Difficult Problem

"Curse the man," Aberline muttered. "Curse him, I say." Creaking, groaning sounds. "I am *not* venturing into that hole." He lit another lucifer. He was using them recklessly, having a pocketful of them – perhaps it was part of an inspector's duty, to have one when necessary? "Clare, your pistol—"

"Five shots." He lifted the Bulldog calmly. "Then they will swarm us as I seek to reload. Pico?"

"I've a blade or two." The youth spat aside, still bracing Aberline from the side. The whites of his eyes gleamed. "I don't fancy being suffocated by Thin Meg's children, mind you."

*Who is this Meg? She sounds atrocious.* Then again, Londinium was full of such creatures. Had he not seen a dragon in Southwark, once? The irrationality of the memory no longer bothered him overmuch, in the face of the current situation.

Clare tilted his head. They were drawing closer, those light, unholy, dancing footsteps. "We may have a more difficult problem in a few moments, gents. To the coal-pile, quickly!"

"What about *him*?" Pico's chin jutted toward the hole.

*Perhaps he shall solve that problem for us. Or be solved himself.* "He is well-equipped to handle himself, and he will find Miss Bannon. We are not so durable, and I can hear that *thing* coming. To the coal, now. Come, Aberline!"

Groaning sounds, scraping, from overhead. The starvelings had patiently, inch by inch, pushed the blockage at the door aside. Or they had found some other means of entry. Even the skeletons had some weight, and enough of them could work their way around every obstacle. Those fingers of theirs, dead-white and squirming . . .

A rustling, and a thump. A pale shape fell past the lath-ladder, hit the packed dirt of the cellar floor, and lay there twitching.

*Tiptap. Tiptap. Tip tip tap tap tip tap tip tap—*

They reached the coal. Aberline flung himself upon its hard pillow with a grunt, and Clare whirled, his Bulldog's stout nose coming up. He would at least sell their lives dearly. "Climb the coal," he hissed, fiercely, as the starveling made a convulsive, tired movement. It was insane, to think of anything so skeletal moving, a glitter of mad intelligence in its yellowed, sunken eyes. *"Climb, damn you!"*

*Tiptap. Tiptaptiptaptiptap.*

The Coachman burst from the dark hole Mikal had vanished into, its eyes red coals, and Clare bit back a cry. The thing was terribly solid now, and its face was no longer mercifully obscured. A ruin of runnelled flesh, broken glass-sharp teeth, wide sunken nostrils, hands of clawed monstrosity. It ran with a queer lurching grace, one shoulder occasionally hitching higher than the other as if it was a hunchback, and as it ran its bones crackled.

It paid no attention to the men on the hillock of cursed coal. Instead, it hurled itself on the single starveling that had fallen down – a pebble in the face of a larger avalanche – and buried its face in the skeletal creature's midriff. The howling that rose was a broken-glass scraping against sanity, but Clare, for once, did not look away.

He watched the irrationality unfolding before him as Aberline cursed, Pico let out a strangled noise, and several small soft plops sounded as more starvelings fell through the hole to swarm the unholy thing consuming one of their number.

# Chapter Forty-Six

## Pronounced Once Before

Choking. A clot of soft rock in her throat, forced free, she spat a wad of blood and phlegm aside and inhaled. Her breath died on a scream; the lamp-flames trembled. The altar was grinding itself to pieces, shards of obsidian piercing the body that had fallen across it, and her cry was matched by another – a rusty, horrific sound.

She landed in wet noisome filth, falling from the shelf that had kept her free of the squelching. This far below Londinium, the Themis's puddled feet were at the bottom of every hole. Her skirts and petticoats were flayed to ribbons, but her stays were still intact, and she was glad of their support as she screamed, throat afire with the memory of a scarlet necklace-wound.

A sobbing inhale, she fought the urge to scream again. It *hurt*, ætheric force bleeding through rips and rents, her *self* forced into a brutalised container. Her Discipline receded, the touch of sunheat on burned and blistered skin all along her internal pathways.

Retreating little tips and taps, she heard the Promethean fleeing. Tortured breathing that was not her own echoed as the obsidian shredded, thrusting its fragments heavenward with popping and sharp glass-singing noises.

*What happened?*

The memory of infinity receded, training forcing it aside. Black flowers bloomed at the corners of her vision, and the idea of just collapsing into the sludge beneath her was *wonderfully* enticing.

*Get up. The Promethean is gone. Finish what you came for.*

The question was, just what exactly *had* she endured this for? Certainly not Britannia.

*Oh, d—n it all, Emma. Get UP.*

She levered herself painfully to her feet. Her hair was a tangled mess, full of dirt and heaven alone knew what; her dress was all but gone. She used the wooden shelf she had been lain upon to finish the job of hauling herself upright, and saw with no real surprise that she had been sharing that hard narrow couch with an ancient skeleton. The skull was shattered, the brown bones traced with green – mildew, moss, perhaps even Scab.

A shudder wormed through her. She hunched her shoulders, like a child expecting a sharp corrective blow, and turned her head aside from the skull's grimace.

The second pair of lungs working in this small stone

cube were Llewellyn Gwynnfud's. The shattered block of glassy volcanic stone had turned to fanglike fragments, and speared through his body, regrowing flesh and metal Alterations pierced alike. Steaming crimson blood and thick black oil-ichor coated the larger shards. As she watched, the obsidian fractured again, and the wreck of a sorcerer made another wretched sound as fresh spears pierced him.

*How does it feel, sir? Does it satisfy your hunger?* She coughed again, a second blood-clot forced free of her lungs, and when she spat the hot nasty pellet aside she found she could breathe much more easily.

One thing left to do. She was so weary.

He had taken her shoes off. Barefoot as a Whitchapel drab, she tottered across the intervening space. "Llew." A harsh croak; she would never sing as a lady.

*Oh, I pretend, and I put on a good show. But in the end, I suppose it's taken a Whitchapel girl to bring him down.*

*I wonder if it took one to build an Empire, too?*

Immaterial. She found her voice again. "Llewellyn." What did she have to say?

His mad muddied gaze was a dumb animal's. What must it be like, for Will and Stone to scrape a body together from the wreckage of a Major Work gone wrong? *Had* the bleached bones at Dinas Emrys been host to his consciousness?

Had he watched her stand over them, expressionless, for a half-hour before she turned and walked away? Could he have seen that without eyes?

Amid the broken, metal-laced ribs of his chest, the Stone gleamed.

"*Emma*," he breathed, and his deformed hands twitched. One of them had kept the knife hilt clasped tight, and still knotted about it. The blade was no longer shining, but twisted and blackened. In its heart, a thin line of crimson.

*The whip, and the knife. The Promethean is above, and will begin to murder.* She set herself, and leaned drunkenly forward.

"*Emma!*" A cry from behind her.

Her fingers, blackened by dirt, soot, and her own blood, curled about a warm pulsing.

"Emma," Llew breathed. Had he remembered her name, and forgotten his own?

"Llewellyn Gwynnfud." A wetness on her cheeks, scalding, as the lamplight scoured her eyes. "I loved you, once."

The curled, useless knifeblade twitched. His mouth opened, perhaps to curse her, perhaps to plead.

Emma Bannon set her heels, gathered her strength, and *pulled*, with flesh and ætheric force combined.

A vast wrenching *crack*.

The lamps snuffed themselves as a moaning wind rose. She fell backwards, collapsing in filthy water, the second Philosopher's Stone clutched to her chest.

Very close now, a howling.

*Mikal.*

He screamed her name, but if he had followed her this far, he would be able to proceed in her direction without light.

She clasped the warm hardness of the Stone to her chest, and with the last scrap of ætheric force she possessed, breathed a Word she had pronounced once before.

In the dark, bones ground themselves to powder as the glassy broken altarstone shivered afresh.

Frantic splashing, and he blundered into the darkness, his irises yellow lamps and his hands a clutching relief as they bruised her, wrenched her upward and away.

As she had hoped, though perhaps not in the way she had planned, Mikal had found her.

# Chapter Forty-Seven

## An Echo Within Himself

A snowdrift of pale, emaciated bodies falling through the opening overhead, making very little sound as they dropped upon the Coachman's convulsing form. The starvelings' jaws worked restlessly, clicking and grinding small, discoloured teeth together as they smothered the creature.

It was deadly, and it ripped at their frail forms, but it could find nothing in them to eat. Rancid green dust slid from the rents torn in their stretched-tight flesh, the Coachman's slaver turning vilely luminescent as it mixed with that granular decay.

Clare kept the pistol trained. The scene before him was revolting, but even worse, it was *irrational,* and the throbbing in his temples was his faculties straining to make what he saw obey the dictates of Logic and Reason.

*Do not look away.*

The hissing became the soap-slathered gurgle of wash-water sliding down a pipe. The thing's struggles were weakening, and its whip was lost under an undulating mass of starvelings. Its long, spidery fingers kept seeking for the handle, blindly, but even had it found the braided leather it could not possibly have untangled it from the writhing.

*Keep looking.* The Bulldog's nose trembled. Behind him, Aberline was violently sick; he muttered something about the sorcery, and then wet, crunching noises began.

The Coachman screamed, a miserable baby-cry. It squirmed, and cloth ripped. The starvelings' clever, bony, insistent fingers peeled away scraps of muffler, of a different frock coat than the one the creature had worn before, of shirt. A button shone, describing an arc and catching a gleam from somewhere – where, Clare never discerned, for it was dark as sin, and his night-adapted eyes could only see suggestions lit by the Coachman's glowing slaver as the starvelings commenced their meal.

"Climb," Pico said, his voice breaking boyishly. "*Come on, Clare!*"

He kept the gun's snout level and steady. "Go on," he heard himself say, as if in a terrible dream. Was this, indeed, what dreaming felt like? "I shall hold them back."

For some of the starvelings had noticed, in their wandering, lethargic way, the living meat upon the pile of coal. They dragged each other upright with terrible blind insistence, shuffling across the cellar floor. Closer, and closer, and he had five bullets. They would have to count.

He could perhaps empty the chambers and reload as they retreated up the coal-hill, but there was the blockage in the chute to consider.

*I believe we are all going to die here, even Mikal. I wonder, will they chew me to pieces? Am I proof against that? Or smothering?*

And . . . Emma. They had brought the beast to bay, but what of the sorcerer?

A second faint green radiance bloomed, in the opposite corner. Clare kept the pistol trained. "Aberline?"

A retching cough, before the inspector's calm, hopeless voice. "Yes, Mr Clare?"

"I am sorry to have brought you here." *I am sorry for more, did you but know.*

At least the inspector was a gentleman *in extremis*. "Quite all right, old boy. Couldn't be helped." The words trembled, firmed. "We shan't get out this way, you know. It's blocked."

A series of alternatives clicked through Clare's faculties, discarded as they arose. A means could be found to ignite the coal, but the fumes and smoke would asphyxiate them before doing any good.

He was savagely weary, even though physically unharmed. Apparently, there were limits to even Miss Bannon's gifts.

*Emma. Are you alive?*

The Bulldog barked, and the flash destroyed his vision for a moment. The nearest starveling folded down, its head a battered mess, that green dust sliding out with its terrible, soft hissing sound.

The Coachman screamed again, a wailing infant under a steadily growing pile.

A woman's voice, freighted with terrible power. "*K—g'z't!*"

Slow grinding, the noise of mountains rubbing together.

Clare surfaced with a jolt. He found himself sprawled on coal, Pico's boot in his back, as starvelings cowered at the end of the cellar. The leprous-green radiance at the opposite end of the cellar had intensified, and under it, he could see a thin shape.

It was Miss Bannon, in the rags of her mourning dress and petticoats. The shadow behind her was Mikal, propping her up as her knees buckled. Clare squinted, and saw a glaring scar on her white throat, under a layer of filth. She had clapped one naked hand to her equally naked neck – her jewellery was gone, and it was queerly indecent to see her so. The pale glow, a different green than the starvelings' dust, but equally irrational, issued from about her, a corona of illogical illumination.

"Back," she husked, a dry croaking word. "*Back*, Marimat. They are *mine*, they are not for you."

The starvelings writhed. One final, weak little cry from the Coachman-creature, silenced with a last nasty crunching. A sigh rippled through the starvelings, a wet wind on dry grass.

"*Sssssparrow-witch.*" A thick, burping chuckle; it was one of the starvelings, but some other dark intelligence showed in its empty, rolling eyes. "*Did you enjoy your ssssssojourn?*"

"Quite diverting, twice-treacherous one." Miss Bannon's expression was just as empty, a terrible blank look upon her childlike features. "But I am at home again, Maharimat of the Third Host, and *they are not for you.*"

"*Little ssssssparrow.*" The starveling twitched forward. "*You are flessssh, and you are weak. How will you ssssstop my children?*"

"How indeed." The sorceress's chin lifted. "I am *Prime*." Her tone had lost none of its terrible, queer atonality. "Set yourself against me, creature of filth, and *find out*."

The hush that descended seemed to last a very long while. But the starvelings, cloaked in their mumbling hiss, drew back in a wave. The ones that could not climb the lath-ladder fell and split open, the green dust spreading and rising in oddly angular curls on a breeze from nowhere.

He wondered what might grow from that dust. Was that how the Scab spread?

The starvelings left behind a curled, battered, unspeakably chewed and quickly rotting body curled in the ruins of a coachman's cloth, and a tangled whip shredding itself as it jerked and flopped, the bright metal at its ravelled end chiming before it blackened and twisted like paper in a fire. There was a creaking and a crack, a final obscene wet chuckle, and the lath-ladder plunged down, shivering into sticks.

The Coachman was indisputably dead. Its ruin fell apart with a wet sliding, and green smoke rose. It shredded, making for a moment the likeness of an anguished face, and the soughing that slid through the cellar lifted sweat-drenched hair and a pall of coal-dust.

Coughing, Clare lowered the pistol. Behind him, Aberline retched again, deeply and hopelessly. Pico breathed a term that was an anatomical impossibility, but nevertheless managed to express his profound, unbelieving relief at this turn of events.

Miss Bannon stayed upright for a long moment before crumpling, and Mikal caught her. His expression, before the green flame winked out, was full of the same devouring intensity Clare had witnessed only once before, in front of his mistress's bedroom door, in the dark, after he had worked a miracle to save her from the Red Plague.

What would he call such a twisting of a man's features? Was there a word for it? Did it matter?

It did not. For he found, to his dismay, that he recognised the look, though he could not name and quantify it. It found an echo within himself, one which could not be spoken of or even thought too deeply upon lest it break his overstrained faculties.

So Archibald Clare sagged back against the coal and closed his eyes. In a moment he would set his wits to the matter of bringing them out of this awful place.

For now, though, he simply lay there, and felt the breath moving in, and out, of his thankful, whole, undamaged, and quite possibly immortal frame.

#  Chapter Forty-Eight

## To Sting, or to Soothe

The fussing was not to be borne. "Tighter," Emma said, and the corset closed about her cruelly. "Enough, thank you. Severine, I am *quite* well."

"*Mais non, madame.*" The round woman in her customary black was pale, but she forged onwards. "You can barely stand, and *monsieur le bouclier* said you were to sleep until—"

"Mikal does not dispose of me, Severine. *I* dispose of myself, thank you, and if you truly wish to help, *stop* this fretting and tell Mr Finch I am not receiving unless the widow calls." *He will know what that means.* "And make certain Mr Clare and Philip are properly attended to."

"Stubborn," Severine said, under her breath, and as she flounced from the dressing room Bridget and Isobel brought forth a dress from a tall birchwood wardrobe.

The housekeeper was met at the door by a silent Mikal, who held it courteously for her and slid into the dressing room without bothering to knock.

"She is quite worried." He halted, watching as the dress was lifted over Emma's head. Quick fingers put everything to rights, brushing black silk tenderly, and Emma told herself that the trembling in her knees would fade. This was no time to appear weakened.

"Worry is acceptable." Her breath came short. It was the corset, she told herself. "Ordering me about is not. Loosen the neck a trifle, Isobel. I rather dislike being throttled so."

Isobel hurried to obey. She did not remark upon the glaring scar ringing her mistress's throat. It would pale and shrink, as the Stone in her chest – a familiar, heavy, warm weight, how had she lived without it? – worked its slow wonder.

She had not needed whatever miracle Mikal had wrought – or had she? Would she have survived, even with the flood of her Discipline sustaining her?

Her plan had succeeded. They had indeed come to find her. Now, though, she wondered if she had been quite wise to treat Mikal so.

"Isobel, fetch a bit more *chocolat*, please. And Bridget, I have a mind to refill that perfume flask – no, the green one. Yes. Do hurry along to Madame Noyon and have her do so, then come back to attend to my hair. Yes, girls, off with you."

They exchanged a dire look, Bridget's freckles glaring

against her milky cheeks, but they obeyed. Familiarity could only be stretched so far, here at 34½ Brooke Street.

That left her alone with her Shield, with stockinged feet, her hair undone and not a scrap of jewellery to armour her.

He was just the same, except for the marks of exhaustion about his eyes. Tall and straight in olive-green velvet – he had, apparently, decided he no longer mourned. Or perhaps he wished her to insist.

She wet her lips with a nervous flicker of her tongue. Wished she had not, for his gaze fastened upon her mouth. Her legs were most unsteady, but her stays helped to bolster her, at least to some degree.

"It was necessary." She plunged ahead, for his expression was set and quiet, and she did not like the . . . what was it, that she felt? Uncertainty? "I could not have you following me too soon. And . . . whatever you performed upon me, Mikal, I could not—"

"You do not have to explain yourself to your Shield, Prima." He took two steps towards her, halted.

They regarded each other, Shield and sorceress, and the sounds of movement elsewhere in the house were very loud behind their silence.

*Perhaps I wish to.* Emma swallowed, dryly, acutely conscious of the movement of muscle in her vulnerable throat. "Mikal . . ."

He looked away, at the open wardrobe. Dresses peeked out, in the darker jewel-shades she preferred. She would mourn properly for Ludovico, now. When she shed the black, perhaps there were other things she would shed as well.

Except the names of her failures, the *rosario* she repeated to puncture her own arrogance. *Harry. Thrent. Namal. Jourdain. Eli.*

*Ludovico.*

She braced herself. Lifted her chin, aware that the scar would show. It was time, she decided, for Mikal to receive some measure of truth from her. "I would not care to lose you, Shield."

As if *she* were the Shield, and he, her charge.

A slight smile. "I would not care to be lost."

Did it mean he forgave her? Dare she ask? It was Mikal, why on earth should she feel this . . . was it fear? A Prime did not stoop to *fearing* a Shield. Or craving forgiveness from one of that brotherhood.

Then why were her palms a trifle moist, and her heart galloping along so?

She gathered herself, again. Chose each word carefully, enunciated it clearly. "One day, Mikal, I shall ask precisely what feat you performed while I suffered the Plague. I shall further ask why Clare knew of it, and I did not."

He still examined her dresses. "On that day I shall answer, Prima."

It was not satisfying at all. "Are you . . . distressed? By . . . recent events?"

He finally turned to face her again. The smile had broadened, and become genuine. He closed the remaining distance between them with a Shield's quiet step, and his fingers were warm on her cheeks.

His mouth was warm too; she did not realise he had driven her back until her skirts brushed the dressing table and her shoulders met the wall to its side, her own fingers tangling in his hair and her body suddenly enclosed in a different confinement, one that robbed her of breath and the need to brace her knees.

He held her there, tongue and lips dancing their own Language of fleshly desire, and when she broke away to breathe he printed a kiss on her cheek, another on her jaw, a third behind her ear where the hollow of flesh was so exquisitely vulnerable.

"A heart is a heart," he breathed, against the side of her scarred throat. "And a stone is a stone."

*What on earth does that mean?* She stored the question away, stroked his dark hair. He was shaking, or was it that her own trembling had communicated to him?

"You are my Shield," she whispered, and drew her hands away. Laid her head upon his shoulder, for once, and allowed the will that kept her upright to slacken for a few moments.

He held her, rested his chin atop her tangled curls. His reply was almost inaudible.

"You are my heart."


Like any reprieve, it did not last very long. In short order she had descended to the solarium, her hair finally set to rights, silver chalcedony rings upon three of her fingers, her ear-drops of marcasite and jet comforting weights, and a twisted golden brooch bearing a teardrop of green amber pinned to her bosom.

Finch cleared his throat.

Emma glanced up from the hellebore, which was springing back quite nicely under its charm-globe. "Ah. Finch. Is Mr Clare awake?"

"Yesmum. He is in the drawing room." Finch blinked once, rather like a lizard. He looked grave, but no more than usual. "With a certain personage, mum. *Two* certain personages."

"Ah." She studied the hellebore for a few more moments. "I am . . . sorry that you must endure the inspector's presence."

"Quite all right, mum." Did he sound slightly shocked? "I . . . have every confidence, thank you. In your, erm, protection."

*At least someone does.* She was hard-pressed not to smile. "Good. I take it the second personage is a widow?"

"Quite right, mum. Waiting on your pleasure."

*How that must gall her.* "How very polite. I shall take luncheon in my study, Finch, and we shall go over the household accounts with Madame Noyon afterwards."

"Yesmum." There was a certain spring in his step as he left, and she allowed herself one more moment of studying the hellebore's wide leaves and juicy, thriving green before she made her way to the drawing room.

Mikal was at the door, sweeping it open at her nod.

Clare was at the mantel, studying the mirror over it with

an air of bemused worriment. Inspector Aberline, his wounded ankle securely wrapped, leaned heavily on a brass-headed Malacca cane, but he did not dare sit in the presence of the stout, heavily veiled woman on the blue velvet settee.

Mikal closed the door, and Emma surveyed them, clasping her hands in ladylike fashion. She did not pay the woman a courtesy, instead regarding Aberline with a lifted eyebrow.

"Good morning, Inspector. I take it you're well?"

He glowered. "Fires. Property damage, loss of life. Waring swears he'll have my head, the public is calling for my dismissal."

"How very uncomfortable." *Given your usual methods, I cannot say I mind.* Still, he had aided Clare. "Do you wish to keep your position? Should you not, I am certain those present may be of aid in finding a better one."

"I'm to go on holiday until the fuss dies down." His gaze turned to the veiled woman. "With your permission, Your Majesty, I shall be about my duties."

"We are grateful for your services, during these troubled times." The Widow of Windsor offered a plump, gloved, beringed paw, and he bent over it. "You have Our thanks, and Our blessing."

*Much good may it do you.* Emma held her tongue.

Aberline limped past her, pausing at the door. "My regards to Mr Finch, Miss Bannon. Good day."

*I shall not pass along any of your regard, sir.* "Good day, Inspector. Pleasant dreams."

He restrained a curse, but only barely, and she waited until she heard the front door close behind him before her attention turned elsewhere.

The silence quickly became uncomfortable. Clare appeared to take no notice, until, with a sigh, Victrix pushed her veil aside and regarded the sorceress.

Her eyes were shockingly, humanly dark, the constellations of Britannia's gaze dim and faraway in pupils that had not been visible for years. "Sorceress."

"Your Majesty."

"They tell me it is . . . finished."

*For me, yes.* "It appears so."

Her reply apparently did not satisfy. Colour began below the high neckline of the Widow of Windsor's stiff black gown, mounted in her cheeks. Died away. The tiny points of light flickering in her pupils sought to strengthen. Emma observed this with great interest.

Finally, Victrix spoke again. "We are weakened. No doubt this pleases you."

"It does not." *I wish you every joy of it, though.* "The sorcerer responsible for the recent . . . unpleasantness . . . suffered a hideous fate, Your Majesty. Perhaps that may comfort you."

The Queen hefted herself to her feet. Clare stepped away from the mantel, as if to assist, but she merely stalked to within a few feet of Emma. Their skirts almost brushed, and the sorceress banished the smile seeking to rise to her mouth.

It would not do.

"We are not comforted, witchling." There was no cold weight of power behind the words, but the echo of Britannia's frigid, heavy voice underlay Victrix's words. "We suspect . . ."

*Have you learned nothing, my Queen?* Emma did not blink.

Two women, studying each other, the only thing separating them a wall of trembling air. And, of course, a measure of pride on either side.

Victrix's shoulders sagged. Her hand twitched, slightly, as if she wished to reach out.

*If she did, what would I do? She is not the queen I served.*

The memory of vast weight, the temptation to step aside from her human self and become *more*, rose inside her in a dark wave.

Emma Bannon found, much to her relief, that her decision was still the same, and that she suffered no regret.

"You are the Queen," she murmured, and lowered her gaze. She stared at Victrix's reticule – and what use did royalty have for such a thing, really? She certainly never went marketing. Perhaps it was a touch of the domesticity she had craved with her Consort.

What dreams had been put aside when the spirit of rule descended upon Victrix? Did she curse the weight and cherish it at once, as a Prime might well both curse and cherish the burden of a Will that would not allow rest or submission?

"We are." But Victrix only sounded weary. "We shall not trouble thee again, sorceress."

*Is that meant to sting, or to soothe me?* Emma merely nodded, and Her Majesty swept past, her veil whispering as she lowered it again. The door opened, and Emma turned her head, staring at the velvet-cloaked window. "Your Majesty."

A pause, a listening silence.

"I shall not trouble *you*, either."

There was no answer.

# Chapter Forty-Nine

## You Have Caused Her Grief

*Most intriguing*. Clare cleared his throat. "Emma."

Her head rose, and Clare discerned a redness rimming her dark eyes, a trace of moisture upon her cheek.

The front door opened, closed again, and he was alone with the sorceress.

"Archibald." The high neck of her gown failed to disguise the livid scar about her neck. What had she suffered at the hands of the mad, faceless Prime?

"How . . ." *How do you feel?* The ridiculousness of the question kindled a fierce heat in his cheeks. Was he *blushing*? Irrational. Illogical. "You look . . . well. Quite well."

"Thank you." A colourless reply. She studied him, her chin set, her hands clasped – he did not miss the tension in those knotted fingers. It must pain her, to clench them so. "You do, as well."

"Ah, thank you." He took a deep breath. "I . . . Emma, I must ask. The . . . stone. The thing you . . . can you, *will* you, take it from me? It is . . . irrational. It causes . . . Feeling."

"How interesting." She studied him, dark eyes moving slowly, her earrings swaying a trifle. "That is generally not among its effects. And no, Clare. I will not." She halted, and answering colour burned high on her soft, childlike cheeks. "Not even if you . . . if you hate me."

What must it have cost her, to say such a thing? Hate? He was a *mentath*. He did not . . .

And yet. Was it the thing she had done to him that created these storms of Feeling?

Was it the woman herself?

Or, most unsettling of all, were these tempests somehow . . . his own?

"Emma." Hoarsely. There was something caught in his throat. "I do not . . . I *cannot* hate you."

She nodded. "Thank you." What was her expression? Did he dare to name it? Could he?

"But I am . . . I am leaving. I must learn how to . . . moderate my reaction to this . . ." This was not how he had thought such an interview would go. What had he expected – tears? Cries of remorse? From her? From himself? "To this . . . gift. Of yours. This very fine . . . gift."

Another nod, the crimson in her cheeks retreating. "Very well."

"I cannot . . . I do not wish to cause you . . . pain." How on earth did others bear this illogical, irrational agony?

"Do as you must, Clare." Her fingers were white, clasped so tightly. "Should you ever need my aid, all you must do is send me word."

His throat was alarmingly dry, he forced himself to swallow. "Thank you. I . . . I shall." He could delay no longer, yet the urge to do so rose. He denied it. "Pico has a hansom waiting; I shall pay his wages myself. He is a very useful young man."

She said nothing.

There was nothing more for him to say, either, so he forced his legs to perform their accustomed function. He paused at the door, studying its crystal knob. Slowly, as an old man might, he twisted it, opened the door and stepped outside.

When it closed, he turned and made for the front. In the entry hall, though, was the last gauntlet to run.

Mikal tilted his dark head. His hair was slightly disarranged, and his hand rested upon a hilt – one of the knives at his hips, wicked blades Clare had a healthy respect for his facility in handling.

Clare drew his gloves on, slowly. Settled his hat.

"Mentath." The Shield's words were a bare murmur, but Clare's quick ears caught them. "You have caused her grief."

It was his turn to nod. There was no denial, no excuse he could offer.

There was, however, an answer to the charge. "So have you, sir."

Mikal's hand fell away from the hilt. Clare expected

more, but the Shield was simply silent as the mentath brushed past. Just before the front door, he paused.

*Once I leave, will I ever return?*

There was no answer. He took a deep breath, adjusted his hat, and stepped out into a foggy Londinium midmorning. A spatter of rain touched the small, exquisite garden, and Miss Bannon's gates were merely ajar instead of fully open.

He sallied down the stone path, and when he exited the gate it closed behind him, with a small, definite click. There was a hansom waiting, the driver's face half-hidden by a striped muffler, and a chill touched Clare's back.

It was irrational, so he discarded it, and clambered into the hansom.

Pico, cleaning his fingernails with a thin, flexible knife, greeted him with a nod. "All's well?"

*No.* "Yes. Quite." He settled himself, and tapped th roof. "Baker Street, please, number 200."

"Sir!" The whip cracked. Clare suppressed a shi

What came next? If he thought only of what n done next, he could, he thought, perhaps navi situation properly. "Mr Pico. Miss Bannon you into my service. I trust you have no c

"Course not, guv." The lad grinned. "In Still want to learn from her grim one, though

*I am certain you do, he is most dangerous.* "Wh duties permit. You are a bright lad, and shall be c help. Tell me, are you fond of travel?"

"Can't say as I've ever tried it, guv."

"Well." Clare settled himself, steepled his fingers, and gazed past them at the faded fabric curtains swaying as the hansom rocked over cobbles. "You shall, and very soon." *Very soon indeed.* "There are experiments to be done."

He lapsed into a profound silence, which did not discommode Pico in the least. As the conveyance bore them away from Brooke Street, the lad even began to whistle.

# Note

*A* string of brutal killings in London in 1888 are still a
  subject of unholy fascination to this day. I make no
apology for the allusions to said murders within this wo...
of fiction, for indeed it is difficult to write of Victo...
London without tripping over a mention or two of t...
that gripped the city in that awful autumn. I do, ...
wish to state that there are a number of exce...
and interesting theories about the murder...
availed myself of several.

I wish to further state that though I ...
erately do not address the killer by the ...
have given himself, or the name the nascen...
media" christened him with and that he is known b...
Instead, I shall list other names:

*Emma Elizabeth Smith*
*Martha Tabram*
*Mary Ann Nichols*
*Annie Chapman*
*Elizabeth Stride*
*Catherine Eddowes*
*Mary Jane Kelly*

*There are a multitude of others who also met untimely ends, by violence or poverty.*

*If they cannot be avenged, may they all, at least, be at peace.*

# THE DAMNATION AFFAIR

*Por Gaetano mio.*
*Te absolvo.*

# Chapter One

The stagecoach creaked to a stop, fine flour-white dust billowing, and Catherine Elizabeth Barrowe-Browne gingerly unlaced her gloved fingers from her midriff. Her entire body ached, both with the pummeling that was called *travel* in this part of the world *and* with the unremitting tension. Her nerves were drawn taut as a viola's charter-charmed strings.

For a moment, the sensation of not jolting and shuddering over a bare approximation of something that in a hundred years' worth more of wear might possibly be generously called a *road* was exquisite relief. Then Cat's body began reminding her of the assaults upon its comfort over the past several days, with various twinges and aches.

Also, she was *hungry.* A lady was far too ethereal a creature to admit hunger, but this did not make the pangs of fleshly need any less severe.

"*Damnation!*" the driver yelled, and the coach creaked as the two men hopped off. The fat, beribboned woman in mourning across from Catherine let out a tiny, interrupted snore, spreading herself more firmly over the hard seat.

*Ceaseless chatter for nigh unto fifty miles, me jolted endlessly backward because her digestion won't permit her to share the forward-facer, and now she sleeps.* Cat grimaced, smoothed her features, and heard murmuring voices. The town was not very large, Robbie had written, but growing.

Growing enough for a schoolteacher, apparently. Otherwise her plan would not have progressed nearly so smoothly.

"Damnation!" the driver yelled again, and the stagecoach door was violently wrenched at. Catherine's fingers took care of pulling her veil down securely and gathering her reticule and skirt. There were other thumps—her trunks, sturdy Boston leather, and thank Heaven for that. They had been subjected to almost as many assaults as Cat's temper for the past few days. "One for Damnation, ma'am!"

*Yes, thank you, I heard you the first time.* She slid across the seat, extended her gloved hand, and winced when his fingers bit hers. Feeling for a stagecoach step while half-blind with dust and aching from a bone-shattering ride across utterly Godforsaken country was a new experience, and one she had no intention of savoring. Syrupy golden afternoon light turned the dirt hanging in the air to flecks of precious ore, whirling like dreams of a claim in a boy's fevered head.

*Oh, Robbie, I am just going to* pinch *you.* Her point-toe boots hit dry earth, the burly whiskered stagecoach driver muttered a "Ma'am," as if it physically hurt him to let loose the word, and she took two staggering steps into the dust cloud. *Is there even a town here? It doesn't* look *like it.*

Any place a coach halted would have charterstones and a mage to hold back the uncontrolled wilderness. Still, the sheer immensity of the empty land she had glimpsed through barred train windows and the stagecoach's small portholes would trouble anyone properly city-bred. Across Atlantica's wide heaving waves, the Continent was not troubled by the need for charterstones; but even after almost two centuries on the shores of the New World, civilization was uneasy.

She reclaimed her hand, quelling the urge to shake her most-certainly-bruised fingers. "Thank you," she murmured automatically, manners rising to the surface again. "A fine ride, really."

"Miss Barrowe?" A baritone, with a touch of the sleepy drawl she'd come to associate with the pockets of half-civilization she'd been subjected to in the last several days. "Miss Catherine Barrowe?"

*In the weary flesh.* "Yes." She even managed to sound crisp and authoritative instead of half-dead. "Whom do I have the pleasure of—"

"She's here!" someone yelled. "Strike up the band!"

The dust settled in swirls and eddies. A truly awful cacophony rose in its place, and Cat blinked. A hand closed around her arm, warm and hard, and it could possibly have been comforting if she had possessed the faintest idea whose appendage it was.

"Hey, Gabe," the stagecoach driver called. "No trouble all the way."

"Thanks, Morton," her rescuer replied. "Those her trunks?"

"Yes indeedy. A very polite miss, glad to've brought her. Mail's there, picked up a bag of it in Poscola Flats. And the chartermage's order—"

"I see it, thanks." Now he sounded a trifle chilly. Cat had the impression of someone looming over her—dust coated her veil, and she blew on it in what she hoped was an inconspicuous manner. The sun was a glare, sweat had soaked the small of her back, and she devoutly wished for no more than a chance to relieve herself and procure some nourishment. *Any* food, no matter how coarse. "Godspeed."

"Yeah, well, from here to Tinpan's a long ride and the country's fulla bad mancy and walkin' dead." Creaking, as the driver hefted himself up. "See you." The whip cracked, and the stage began to rumble.

*Oh yes, mention living corpses! That is* just *the thing to do before a journey.* Cat's skin chilled, and she had the distinctly uncharitable thought that if the stagecoach *was* attacked by those who slept in unhallowed ground, at least the hefty woman in mourning would awaken for the event.

Or at least, so one hoped.

"Moron," the man holding her arm muttered. "As if he's not going to stop at the livery and pick up Shake's whiskey. Well, you look rattled around, miss. Let's get you through this."

Her veil and vision both cleared, and Cat found her rescuer to be a lean, rangy man of indeterminate age, a wide-brimmed hat clapped hard on his head and a star-shaped tin badge gleaming on his black vest. Guns slung low on his hips, and the chain of a charing-charm peeked out from behind his shirt collar, glinting blue. The guns gave her a moment of pause—not many in Boston carried them openly. Her own charing-charm, safely tucked under her dress, cooled further.

At least with the charing she could be certain *he* was not of the walking undead. It was faint comfort, given the way he scowled at the retreating stagecoach's back. He looked stunningly ill-tempered.

The cacophony crested, and she realized with a sinking sensation that it was meant to approximate music.

"Good heavens," she managed. "What on earth is that noise?"

The corner of his thin mouth twitched up as he glanced down at her. He was quite *provokingly* tall. "Your welcome committee, ma'am. I'll try to see it don't last too long."

How chivalrous—and ungrammatical—of him. *Oh, Robbie. I am just going to pinch you*, she thought for the fiftieth time, and braced herself.

The town center was a single street framed with raw-lumber buildings, a wide dirt thoroughfare that probably was a sheet of glutinous mud if it ever rained in this hellish place, and the greenery-cloaked mountains in the distance might have been pretty if they had been in a painting. Instead, they were hazy, oppressive shapes, grimacing in distaste.

An attempt at bunting and colored ribbon had been made across the front of a building whose sign proclaimed it to be the LUCKY STAR BAR SALOON, a smaller sign depending from it creaking as it swung and whispered WHISKEY SCALES HOT BATHS. For a moment she wondered just what whiskey scales were, but the sight of the crowd arrayed on the saloon's steps under the bunting and spilling into the dusty street managed to drive the thought from even her nimble brain.

A gigantic banner flapped in the moaning-low, sage-scented wind, and a cord snapped. The banner, its proudly painted length folding and buckling, began to descend upon the motley collection of men beneath it playing instruments with more enthusiasm than skill.

WELCOME TO DAMNATION, the banner read, as its leading edge dropped across a man playing a fiddle and continued its slow descent.

"Oh, dear." She tried not to sound horrified, and suspected she failed miserably. "This is not going to end well."

He gave a short sharp burr of a sound. Was that a *laugh?* It sounded altogether too painful to signify amusement. "It never does around here, ma'am. Jack Gabriel."

"I beg your pardon?" She watched as the banner continued its majestic downward crumple and the music hitched to an unlovely stop. People scrambled to get out of the way, and one or two children crowed, delighted.

So there *were* children in this Godforsaken place. Miracles did occur. Of course, who would she be called upon to teach if there were none?

"Jack Gabriel. Sheriff. Your servant, ma'am." He even touched the brim of his colorless, sun-bleached hat. "I thought you'd be older."

*Oh, really?* "I am very sorry to have disappointed you, sir." She reclaimed her arm with a practiced twist. "Thank you for your assistance. I suppose I'd best restore some order here." She took two steps, found her balance and her accustomed briskness, and stalked for the milling group on the saloon steps.

"Oh, Hell no," the sheriff said, low and clear. "Can't restore what never happened in the first place, ma'am." He fell into step beside her, and she might have been almost mollified if not for the swearing. "My apologies. I just meant, well, we were prepared for ... something else."

*Prepared? This doesn't look prepared.* She tucked her veil back, summoned her mother's Greet The Peasants smile, and told the pressure in her bladder it was just going to have to wait.

The crowd was mostly men, in varying stages of cleanliness; the few women were in homespun and bleached-out bonnets. She suddenly felt like an exotic bird, even though she'd left everything impractical or *very* fashionable at home in Boston.

Home no more. Her chin lifted, and the smile widened. "What a lovely reception!" she gushed, as the banner finished its slow descent and wrapped another portly, bewhiskered fiddler, who was almost certainly drunk, in its canvas embrace. The resultant package blundered into a man with a drum slung about his neck, and the two of them careened into a trio of men holding what looked like kitchen implements.

The first fiddler seemed to think this was an infringement upon his honor, and—uttering a most ungentlemanly oath—swung his fist at a bystander, a man in red suspenders and a stovepipe hat, a moth-eaten fur on his skinny shoulders. Who also turned out to be a mancer of some sort, since he promptly snapped a crackling flash of energy off his thin fingers and knocked his attacker backward.

"Oh, *Hell*," the sheriff said, with feeling, and Miss Barrowe's reception turned into something the locals told her later was named a "free-for-all." A tall, broad-shouldered, and very bony matron in brown descended on Cat and ushered her across the street, toward a lean wooden building—HAMMIS'S BOARDING-HOUSE, according to the sign hanging from an upstairs balcony railing. It was squeezed disconsolately between two other nondescript buildings, one of which seemed to be some variety of shop.

"Very sorry, miss. It is *Miss*, isn't it? I am Granger, Mrs. Letitia Granger—"

*Yes, we corresponded; you are on the Committee that hired me.* "How do you do?" Cat managed, faintly. Behind them, the brawl spilled off the steps and into the dusty street, and the sheriff bellowed *most* impolitely. Charm and mancy crackled uneasily, the dust whirling in tight circles, and her charing-charm warmed a little, sensing the flying debris of malcontent.

She couldn't even care, she was suddenly so desperate for a few moments alone to relieve herself.

*Oh, I hope they have some manner of plumbing, or I am going to explode.* She reached up to straighten her hat, and Mrs. Granger whisked her inside the boardinghouse, which did have a small room for her to freshen herself. That paled in comparison to the watercloset down the hall, of which she availed herself with most unladylike haste.

The room given to her temporary use was an exceedingly small cubbyhole; the vicious sunlight pouring in through a small, dusty glass window had already scorched and faded everything in it. It could have been a palace, though. For one thing, it was not moving. For another, it was *private*, even though she could hear the brawl outside and the furious yelling as stray mancy bit and spread. Much of it was language she would have been shocked to hear, had Robbie not taken deep delight in teaching her certain phrases and their meanings.

Dust had crept into every fold of her dress, and she was far too fatigued to charm it free even if she had a moment of privacy to do so. Instead, she pinned her veil back and stretched with rare relief, and wondered if this would be her lodging. They had mentioned something of a small house—and just then the noise outside faded, and she suspected she was taking far too long and there might possibly be a prospect of something to eat by now. She checked herself in the sliver of mirror, decided she looked as proper as circumstances allowed, and eased out of the tiny room and down the stairs.

As soon as she reentered the hall leading to the boardinghouse's parlour, her hat repinned and some of the dust swept away, she was almost bowled over by a lad of perhaps ten, with cornsilk hair and an engaging gaptooth smile. "*BOXER!*" he yelled, and the slavering biscuit-colored streak behind him was obviously a dog. "They're in here, boy!"

The dog nipped smartly past her into the parlour, feathers exploded, the boy let out a crow-cry and hopped down the hall— and a chicken, its wings beating frantically, knocked over a lamp and tried to flap straight into Cat's face.

The schoolmarm was in blue, with a smart hat perched on slightly wilted brown curls and a smile fixed on her barely pretty face like she smelled something bad. Gabe didn't blame her— Damnation was none too fragrant even on the best of days. Well, *fragrant*, maybe, but certainly not *pleasant*. But even he hadn't been prepared for the melee when Collie Stokes took a swing at Em Kenner.

It was a good thing Gabe was quick *and* light on his feet, especially when it came to dodging flung charms and stray mancy. He didn't have to squeeze off a shot to get everyone's attention—it was never a good idea to start shooting in Damnation—but it was close.

It took a good half hour to restore order, but fortunately Mrs. Granger descended upon the girl and swept her across the street to the boardinghouse. It was, all things considered, the best place for her . . . but still, they'd be lucky if that lolling drunk Pete Pemberton didn't scare her off completely. She'd probably be back on the next coach to Poscola Flats and on the train to Boston without so much as a *how do you do*, and Gabe didn't much blame her.

When he had finally calmed everyone down—including Em Kenner, who was righteously indignant even at the best of times— and had Collie safely stowed in the jail and someone dealing with that fool banner, Gabe settled his hat more firmly on his head and set off for the boardinghouse. The occasion of a New Arrival was giving everyone the jitters, and he silently prayed that big, bony Granger wasn't frightening the poor girl even more.

He clumped up the steps and through the squeaking door, straight into another maelstrom.

He'd forgotten about the chickens the Hammis family kept behind the boardinghouse.

Well, honestly, the chickens weren't bad at all, except for when Boxer was chasing them. Somehow they had all gotten *inside* the boardinghouse, probably one of Tom Hammis's practical jokes on a day when the entire town was all het up.

That kid was gonna be trouble one day.

Gabe's temples were tight with an incipient headache. He later found out Pete Pemberton was safely in an alcoholic stupor upstairs, and that was how Boxer had gotten loose. He also further found out that little Tommy had used a simple chicken-leading charm to bring the poultry inside, thinking it'd be a grand idea to scare his harried mother.

A tornado of feathers engulfed him. The new schoolmarm had Boxer's collar, the mastiff straining against her grip and scrabbling on bare wooden flooring. Mrs. Granger was ranting, and Keb and Lizzie Hammis were trying desperately to corral the charmed fowl. Poor round Lizzie, her red face even redder, swatted at a prize hen. "Oh, for Pete's sake...Keb, grab that one—*Tommy, get down here, I am gonna take you behind the woodshed for sure!* Oh, miss, sorry, Boxer don't bite—"

"*Honestly*, Lizzie Hammis, the *one* day we ask you to be respectable!" Granger had her skirts clutched back as if one of the chickens might foul or bite her.

Gabe almost wished one would.

Boxer made snuffling, grunting, pleading noises, lunging against the schoolmarm's grip. Her hat was askew, and she was flushed. The extra color did wonders for her face, and her wide dark eyes flashed almost angrily before her jaw set and she hauled back on the mastiff's collar again. "*Down*, boy!" she snapped. "I think if we can get him—*oof*—outside, we can restore some—*ouch*—some order here." She brightened as her gaze lighted on Gabe. "You! Get over here and help me!"

It had all the bite of a command, and he decided it wasn't a half-bad idea, either. So he was already moving, striding across the raw lumber, the pale-green rugs askew and everything in the parlour rattling dangerously as Mrs. Hammis started searching for a counter-charm to gather up the chickens and get them quiet. The entire boardinghouse shook with stray mancy as the chickens sent up an ungodly noise and Boxer started moaning. Charing-charms glowed—the marm's bright and clear, Letitia Granger's a glitter of indignation, Lizzie Hammis's sparking as she sought for a bit of mancy, and Keb's barely limned with fox-fire since he had no mancy at all. Gabe could feel his own warming dangerously, and didn't have time for a breath to calm it.

He grabbed the mastiff's collar, the schoolmarm worked her gloved fingers free, and in short order he had the dog outside on the front walkway. Onlookers crowded, but he made shooing motions and they hung back. "Someone find Tommy Hammis for me," he remarked, mildly. "The boy's gonna hafta give his Ma a reckonin'."

"The new miss, is she mad?" Isobela Bentbroad hopped from foot to foot, looking scrubbed and miserable in her Sunday best. Her lank brown braids flopped.

"Well, if the music didn't frighten her off, Ma Hammis's chickens might. Just wait, Izzie. And the rest of you, don't cross these steps 'til we've got things calmed down."

Boxer set up a wail as Gabe finished clipping his collar to the chain bolted to the porch. Most of the time, the dog kept Pemberton out of trouble. But he had a regrettable yen for chasing chickens. He hadn't caught one yet, despite fowls' inherent stupidity, but he was the original Tip Mancinger in the old nursery rhyme—he just kept *trying*.

"I mean it, now," the sheriff said. A murmur ran through the crowd.

He squared his shoulders and strode back into the fray.

Granger was still going. "And *furthermore*, the drapes in here haven't been beaten since this building went up, they're *stiff* with dust! Honestly! *Chickens*, in the *house!*"

The schoolmarm stood against the parlour wall, no longer flushed but very pale, staring at the potbellied iron stove. She cast a single imploring glance at Gabe, and he was only faintly relieved to see the chickens had been dealt with.

"This is *not respectable!*" Granger was getting herself worked up but good. Keb Hammis, his meek face cheese-pale, had his shoulders drawn up like he wished he could vanish, his best suit straining at the seams. Lizzie was probably getting the chickens back into the coop, but she'd be no use here either.

*Oh, Hell.* Gabe sighed internally. A mastiff was one thing, Letitia Granger another entirely.

"Mrs. Granger, ma'am." He had his hat in one hand, running the other back through his hair. "Thank you. That'll be about enough."

It was probably the wrong thing to say. Letty glared at him, her bosom heaving. The cameo pinned at her throat was a sailor on stormy waters, to be sure. The charing-charm on it flashed blue, then green. She didn't talk about where her original charing had gone, but Russ Overton had once commented that it was no wonder Granger was so sour; anyone with her hard luck would be.

Gabe let his hands fall. "Keb. That boy of yours around?"

The new schoolmarm piped up. "Is he about ten, very blond, and quite agile?" The clipped, educated precision of the words made the entire parlour look shabby.

*Well, we do as best we can*, Gabe reminded himself. "That'd be him, yes."

"I saw him heading down the hall, that way." She pointed, her reticule swinging. "I believe he has perhaps made his escape. Will you be placing him under arrest?"

For one mad moment he thought she was serious, before the glint in her dark eyes caught up with him.

Jack Gabriel surprised himself by laughing out loud. Keb Hammis outright stared with his mouth open and his colorless eyes wide, and Mrs. Granger was mute with astonishment, thank God.

"He's a handful and no mistake, ma'am. I don't pity you having him in school." It didn't come out quite the way he wanted it to—he sounded sarcastic instead of amused. "I think we might be able to show you the house now, if you're so inclined. Garrett's already taken your trunks."

Mrs. Granger harrumphed. The house was a sore subject. Or not precisely the house, but the hired help.

The sparkle in Miss Barrowe's eyes was gone. She reached up, twitching her hat back into place. "Yes, I'd quite like that, thank you."

And Jack Gabriel, abruptly, felt like a goddamn fool, for no good reason at all.

# Chapter Two

The house was small and trim, freshly painted white and green, and at the very edge of the "town" proper, though no doubt inside the charter-boundaries. Cat kept her back straight with an effort of will, and groaned internally at the thought of more welcoming committees. There had been a crowd of people, some of them scuffed and bruised, all coated in dust and a layer of sparkling mancy, standing agoggle outside the boardinghouse. Stray mancy still vibrated in the street, and her charm was warm again. Sweat slicked dust to her face, her dress would perhaps never recover from the double assault of dirt and feathers, and her entire body ached. The sharp bite of hunger under her breastbone threatened to make her well and truly irritable.

If she never again sat in another rocking wooden contraption pulled over ground by terribly apathetic nags, she would be *ever* so grateful. Mrs. Granger rocked back and forth in the seat behind them, either too mortified to speak or holding her peace for other reasons.

The sheriff pulled the horses to a stop. "It's small, but it's safe. The town charter covers a couple miles out past here, so you don't have to worry about any bad mancy or otherwise. Plus the girl working here, well. She's a fair girl, in her own way, except she's Chinee. You don't mind that, do you?"

Behind her, Mrs. Granger sniffed loudly. It wasn't quite a harrumph, but it was close.

*That's right; they did mention a girl to charm the laundry and do the cooking.* "Mind? Why on earth would I mind?" The meaning behind his words caught up with her. "A Chinoise girl?" *Does he think we've never seen them in Boston?*

"Name's Li Ang. She's a widow. Good girl, will cook and keep house. She gets half Sundays off, and she's a fair seamstress. Knows some English. Glad you don't mind." It was by far the longest speech he'd given, and he looked straight ahead at the horses while he did so. "There's good people here, and our charter's solid." Still staring forward, as if he couldn't bear to look at her. "May not be what you're used to, but—"

"Sir." She wished she could remember his name. It wasn't like her to forget such a thing, but a day such as this would strain even a mentath's wondrously unshakeable faculties. "If I held the comforts of civilization so highly, I would hardly be here. I am *quite* prepared for whatever this town holds."

For some reason, that made his mouth twitch. "I hope so, ma'am. Hope we ain't scared you off yet."

"It would take far more than this to frighten me, sir. On the contrary, I am roundly entertained. Shall we proceed?"

His only answer was to hop down from the cart. Mrs. Granger cleared her throat. The woman was a serious irritant. She reminded Cat of Mrs. Biddy Cantwell in her everlasting black and disapproval, jet jewelry and her habit of lifting her lorgnette and peering at anything that incurred her considerable and well-exercised displeasure. Biddy's daughter had been a success in Season, and could have had her pick of beaus, but Mrs. Cantwell had driven every suitor off one way or another. It had been the tragedy of the year and was still bemoaned, and Miss Cantwell—none dared unbend enough to address her as *Eliza*, especially in her mother's hearing—was now officially a spinster and would quite probably be her mother's handmaid until said mother shuffled off the mortal coil.

Mrs. Granger shifted her weight, and the cart rocked. "This was not my idea, Miss Barrowe. The girl *is* mostly respectable. She's a widow, and a Christian. But her condition—"

Thankfully, the sheriff again intervened. "Mrs. Granger, ma'am, let's not go on. Miss Barrowe's probably worn down by all the excitement." He offered a hand, and Cat accepted his help. The landing on hard-packed earth jolted all the way through her, and she longed for a bed. Or some cold chicken and champagne. "You look a little pale."

"Quite fine, thank you," Cat murmured. "Merely unused to the heat. Is it always this warm?"

"Except when it's raining. Sometimes even then. And winter's snow up to your... well, that's why the town was named, maybe. For the weather."

"Really?" Now *that* was interesting.

"No. Just my personal guess. This way, ma'am. We repaired the gate." He said it as if he expected a prize, but Cat only had the wherewithal to make a small sound that she hoped expressed pleasure at such a magnanimous gesture. It was difficult to keep her balance, for the ground was swaying dangerously underfoot, as if it had thrown its lot in with the stagecoaches of the world.

The gate in question was painted white, and opened with only a single guttural squeak. There was a sad, spiny attempt at a garden, cowering under the assault of heavy sunshine, and a pump that looked to be in working order. She hoped beyond hope that there was a little more in the way of plumbing *inside*, and swayed as the ground took a particularly violent turn underneath her.

A hand closed around her elbow. "Miss Barrowe?" The man now sounded concerned.

"Quite fine," she muttered. Her stomach twisted on itself, and she hoped it wouldn't growl and embarrass her. "Thank you."

"You don't look fine, ma'am. Let's get you inside. *Li Ang!* It's Gabe, open up!"

The stairs tilted most disagreeably, but she received the impression of a small, lovely porch with white railings, blessed shade enfolding them. The sudden darkness almost blinded her. There was a sound of bolts being drawn back, and she swayed again.

"Aw, *Hell*." Gabriel, she remembered. Gabriel was his name, a herald of woe, and his fingers suddenly bit into her poor arm. "Granger, come on up here, she's about ready to—"

Everything went fuzzy-gray, as if she had been wrapped in a fog-cloud. Her stomach made an indiscreet grumbling noise, and the embarrassment flushed the gray with rosy pink.

Cat returned to herself with a thump, half-reclining on a black horsehair sopha which had seen much better days. The cushions were hard as rocks, and someone held a cup against her lips. It was sweet water, and she drank without qualm or complaint.

Her vision cleared. A scrubbed-clean little parlour met her, lace under-curtains and brocaded green over-curtains, a small table with curved legs, and threadbare carpet worked with faded pink cabbage roses. The sunlight was tamed as it fell past the lace, and Gabriel the sheriff proceeded to try to drown her with the remainder of the water from a battered tin cup.

Cat spluttered in a most unladylike manner, and an exotic face topped with shining blue-black hair rose over the sheriff's shoulder. Sloe-eyed and exquisite, the Chinoise girl was in a faded homespun frock that did *nothing* for her, and the high rounded proudness of her belly suddenly made all the talk of widowhood and respectability much more comprehensible. Mrs. Granger hovered near a doorway cut in the white-plastered wall, her long jaw set with a mixture of what looked to be resignation and apprehension. Feathers stuck to the big woman's bonnet and her quaintly cut brown stuff dress; a completely inappropriate desire to laugh rose in Cat's throat and was ruthlessly quelled.

"Oh, my." She tried not to sound as horrified as she felt. "I am *ever* so sorry."

The sheriff's face had turned interestingly pale, but he snatched the tin cup away and didn't offer an explanation for tossing its contents over the lower half of her face. The Chinoise girl moved in with something like a handkerchief, dabbing at said face, and that was how Cat Barrowe began her stay in Damnation.

The regular card game upstairs at the Lucky Star was usually blessedly monosyllabic, except when there was news of a surpassingly interesting nature.

It was just Gabe's luck that the schoolteacher's arrival was extra-wondrous. It had replaced Jed Hatbush's fence as the preferred topic of gossip, at least.

Stooped Dr. Howard, in his dusty black, dealt with flicks of his long knobbed fingers. "Little Tommy Hammis, the snot, charmed the chickens into the boardinghouse. And set that damn dog loose."

Paul Turnbull, silent owner of the Star, smoothed his oily moustache with one finger. He was a heavy man, stolid in his chair, but quick enough in a saloon fight. And he dealt with Tilson, who ran the girls and handled the day-to-day operations of the Star, well enough. At least, he kept Tils mostly in line, and that was a blessing. "Wish I'd seen Letitia Granger's face at that."

*It was a sight*, Gabe silently agreed, scooping up his cards. Not a bad hand. The whiskey burned the back of his throat, and he tried to forget the dazed look in Miss Barrowe's eyes. Big dark eyes, and surprisingly soft once you got past that prim proper barrier of hers. She probably thought they were a bunch of heathens out here, and she wasn't far wrong.

Russell Overton, the town's official chartermage, scooped up his cards with a grimace. Dapper in his favorite dark waistcoat, dark-curled and coffee-skinned, when he was sitting down you didn't notice he was bandy-legged and had a stiff way about him. You could, however, *always* tell he was aching for a fight, like most short men. "That woman could sour milk. So, what's she like, Gabe?"

"Granger? Still sour." He picked up his own cards, his charing-charm cool against his throat. The schoolmarm's was a confection of lacy silver and crystal; his own was a small brass disc with the orphanage's charter-symbol stamped on the back. There couldn't be a better illustration of just how much she didn't belong here.

*Stop thinking about it. It won't do any good.*

Dark eyes. Brown curls. Not like blonde, blue-eyed Emily.

*Stop it.*

"Not Granger, you buffoon." Russ chomped the end of his cigar as if it had personally offended him. Smoke hazed between the lamps. "The schoolmarm. From Boston, yes?"

"Far as I know." Gabe's mouth was dry. He took another jolt of whiskey, eyed the cards. The room was close and warm, the saloon pounding away underneath them with rollicking piano music and a surfroar of male voices. Every once in a while a sharp feminine exclamation, as the saloon frails and the dancing girls went about their business. It was, Gabe reflected, almost like a steamboat making its way upriver. The noise made it seem like the place was rocking.

"You're asking Gabe? You should know it's like pullin' nails." The doctor showed a slice of yellowed teeth as he examined his cards. "She *is* from Boston. Highly recommended, according to Edna Bricketts. Why a miss consented to come here, only God knows. She's a little thing too; I couldn't see much in the melee. Seemed a bit prim."

*I am so very sorry*, she had kept saying. *I don't wish to put you to trouble, Mr. Gabriel.* After nearly fainting, for God's sake. He was willing to bet it was a combination of hunger and nerves; someone should hold her down and feed her something fattening. Little and birdlike. And she acted like a pregnant Chinee girl was no great shakes, offering her hand to Li Ang and murmuring *How do you do* just as she had to him.

He laid his offerings down. "Two."

For a few minutes, each of them focused on the game. Doc took the round. "Well, I heard Joss Barker's already sayin' he's in love with her. So's Eb Kendall. Two."

"His wife won't like that. Two and a half."

"His wife don't like nothin'. Three, and call."

"You'd feel the same way, married to Eb. Look at this, two Dominions and a Pearl."

Gabe laid his cards down. He took the round, with the remaining Dominions, two Espada, and a Diamond. There was a good-natured round of cussing before he accepted the greasy cards and began to shuffle. "Who else?"

There was a brief silence. Maybe they didn't understand. So he added a few more words. "Barker, Kendall. Who else?"

More silence. He glanced up as his fingers sorted through the winnings, blinking a little, and Doc hurriedly looked away. Turnbull's mouth was open slightly; he shut it with a snap and became suddenly very interested in his own pile of seed corn.

"Nobody," Doc finally said. "You know how Barker is. Mouth two sizes too big for the rest of him."

*Well, that's true.* He searched for something else to say, a thing that might paper over the uncomfortable silence. "Last thing we need is some damn thing else happening to scare away the schoolmarm. Had a hard enough time finding one as it is, what with recent events."

Meaning the boy, and the claim in the hills, the cursed gold, and the incursions. Since closing the claim, though, the rash of walking dead had gone down quite a bit. Even if some damn fool sooner or later would be tempted by the rich veins lurking under the claim's black mouth. Or the bars, each stamped with that queer symbol, just waiting for the unwary to carry them home.

Another uncomfortable silence.

"Well, then." Doc watched Gabe's hands as the cards slid neatly into their appointed places, no motion wasted. "Bad mancy, to talk about women at a card game."

"Aw, Hell," Russ piped up. "What else we got to talk about? Whiskey and donkeyfucking, and claims up in the hills."

"Not to mention undead. How's the charter holding, there, Russ?" Turnbull grinned, and Gabe sighed internally as the chartermage and the saloon owner glared at each other over the cards.

"Charter's holding up fine." For once, Russ heroically restrained himself. It was probably too good to last. "No howlings from the hills that I can tell. Gabe?"

And from there it was all cards and business. But Gabe caught the doctor looking at him speculatively, especially as the night got later and Paul and Russ started sniping at each other again. The night ended as it always did—Paul a little behind, Russ a little ahead, Doc and Gabe largely breaking even.

And the saloon below them rollicking on.

# Chapter Three

It was such a welcome sensation to sink into a bed; Cat almost squeezed her eyes further shut, rolled over, and dove back into sleep. But sunlight gilded the window, and she heard a queer tuneless humming floating somewhere in the house.

*I am here.*

Where was Robbie? Had he seen her, in yesterday's comedy of errors? It wasn't like him not to join in a joke. She'd half-expected the banner to be *his* idea, of course. How it would have warmed his heart. If anyone loved a prank, 'twas Robert Barrowe-Browne.

Cat pried one eye open, wincing as her body protested even such a simple movement. The humming was actually quite pleasant, and she deduced it must be the Chinoise girl. Her charing was blessedly cool, and she rolled over, blinking at the plastered ceiling and stretching gingerly.

All things considered, she was quite well. Merely hungry enough to do shockingly unladylike damage to a platter of breakfast, and sore clear through.

The larger bedroom was at the end of a tiny hallway; the smaller was tucked to the side and held a low corncrib and some few bits of fabric draped on the walls to provide a bit of cheer. Cat made a mental note to find at least a *chair* for the poor girl, and made her way downstairs on slippered feet. The slippers had been set neatly by her bedside, and yesterday's gown hung to air on a press, charmed neatly enough that no dust or feathers clung to its folds.

Which was a most welcome surprise.

Her nightgown made a low sweet sound as she tiptoed along the back hall, following the humming to its source. Which was, as she had suspected, the kitchen.

The Chinoise, her slim back betraying little of the proud belly in front, was humming as she scrubbed, elbow-deep in suds, at something. The kitchen, bright and airy, was full of a wondrous scent. There was a stripped-pine table, two chairs, a steaming kettle, and a washtub to the side. The stove, its heat enclosed in an envelope-charm, spun a fresh globe of golden glow aside; the globe, drifting through the kitchen, bumbled merrily out the open top half of a door leading to a porch and a short breezeway. It bobbed along, the mancy on it crackling, and would eventually rise into the sky, safely dissipating away from anything flammable. 'Twas an elegant bit of work, and a relief. At least the house would not burn down around them.

It was a great relief that charterstones and charings would make mancy work reliably even if one was not properly native-born. The great influx of those from other countries seeking a better life, or merely drudgery in a new environ, could practice such mancy as was native to them within charterstone's bounds. After the Provinces War, the discovery of gold in certain wasted places and the determination to bring the railroad to every corner of the New World had brought all manner of folk to these shores.

It was even quite *quite* to have an exotic as a servant, preferably indentured. The Barrowe-Brownes had not, preferring solid German and French maids, but often her father had spoke of perhaps engaging a Lascar as a manservant, merely to give her mother the vapours.

The Chinoise girl raised a dripping hand, and soap bubbles drifted free into the breezy kitchen. It was a simple charm, meant to amuse, and Cat answered before she could help herself. Her own fingers tingled, and the mancy slid free—light glinting between the bubbles, striking rainbows glittering-sharp as diamonds.

Cat's Practicality was in light; Robbie's had been . . . well, *otherwise*. Light was a very acceptable Practicality in a young lady, indeed, and the Chinoise girl's Practicality was plain as the bubbles drifted on the swirls and eddies of clear air. For a moment the two charm-streams intermingled, light and water a happy marriage—not like air and fire, or fire and water, though true fire Practicalities were rare, and a good thing too. Metal and earth Practicalities were common, and wood was eminently respectable for a gentleman but *not* a young lady. A stone Practicality was considered rather boorish, for it meant one could pass paste jewels for real; a mechanical one was almost as bad as being in trade. New Practicalities shaped themselves as Science and mancy moved forward.

Soon, there might even be Disciplines, as in Englene and the Continent.

The bubbles popped, the rainbows drained away, and Cat found herself facing a pale, heavily pregnant Chinoise girl in a dun frock, who refused to quite meet her nominal employer's gaze.

In short order there was breakfast on the table—Cat gave it to be understood that she wished to eat here instead of in the postage-stamp parlour, and perhaps the girl looked relieved? With a modicum of gesturing and facial expressions, Cat asked if the girl had eaten breakfast yet; receiving a small shake of the sleek dark head, she marched to the cupboard with what she fancied was great determination, fetched a second plate and cup of thick, durable earthcraft, and set it down on the small table as well.

In any event, Cat tucked in with a will, and there was even strong fragrant tea.

Their first breakfast passed in companionable silence, and the Chinoise girl looked rather less pale and peaked by the end of it. Cat settled back with a cup of tea—the cup was actually porcelain, and painted with blue flowers, very fine save for its lack of matching saucer—while the girl collected the dishes and returned to her washing.

So far the morning had proven very satisfactory indeed. The breeze was fresh and smelled of sage, fragrant tea and bacon aromas filled the kitchen, and Cat was beginning to feel almost *quite* again when a shadow fell across the back step.

The Chinoise girl whirled, inhaling sharply. Her little hand flashed out, grabbed a knife that looked more fit for repelling pirate boarders than cooking, and hissed something in her native tongue. Cat let out a pale shriek and started, almost dropping her cup, and Jack Gabriel peered over the half-door, reaching up to his hatbrim. His hazel eyes were bright and wide, and he ducked a glowing ball of heat drawn from the stove.

"For God's sake, Li Ang, put that away. Figgered I'd—well, hello, ma'am. Pleased to see you looking better."

Heat raced furiously up Cat's cheeks. "*Sir!* I am not even *dressed!* Were you never taught to knock before entering a house?"

"I did. Don't reckon you heard me." He took this in, and actually, of all things, *smiled*. "That thing you're wearing could qualify as a winding-sheet, miss. *Avert*," he muttered, right away, flicking his hat to brush away bad mancy or ill-luck. "Beg pardon, ma'am. I'll wait in the parlour."

Cat, her heart pounding, swallowed a most unladylike urge to shrill like a harridan. Her mother would know exactly what to say to this man to cut him to size. "Very well," she managed stiffly. "Perhaps you would care for a cup of tea, while I arrange myself."

He shrugged, leaning lazily on the half-door. Li Ang had gone back to washing, and Cat suddenly noticed the girl's ankles were swollen. Definitely a chair, and some provision must be made for the baby as well.

"I prefer coffee, but thank you kindly. I'll wait."

"I was unaware I had an engagement today," she floundered.

"Thought you might like to see the schoolhouse. But I can understand if you'd rather rest, ma'am. Yesterday was prob'ly enough to turn a lady's nerves to ribbons."

*What a gruesome image. Thank you, sir.* "I am made of sterner stuff than most, sir." Why was she possessed of the sudden feeling that she was coming off very badly in this conversation? "Good morning."

"Morning." He didn't say another word as she retreated, crimson-cheeked and acutely aware she was practically *barefoot*. Her bare ankles were brazenly revealed. And she was in a *nightgown*, of all things, in the kitchen with a servant.

And the day had been going so well.

Li Ang offered him two biscuits and some leftover bacon on a plate; he took it, so as to be mannerly. Besides, his breakfast had been bolted before dawn, and now he couldn't even remember what he'd shoveled in before heading out to ride the charter-circuit with a sore-headed Russell Overton. "How you feelin'?"

She shrugged. She understood far more Englenc than she could speak. Not much escaped those dark eyes of hers, either. She returned to her work, moving slowly, and Jack sighed, leaning against the door while he reflectively chewed on the bacon. He gave it a few minutes' worth of silence, to let her get comfortable.

And also to let himself think about the schoolmarm. Bare-ankled and lost in a nightgown that looked big enough to swallow two or three of her, with her dark hair anyhow and falling out of its braid. He hadn't seen a woman like that in a few years.

Not that it would help him to think about it. He'd spent years not thinking about women at all, and more years trying to forget one particular woman.

It never got easier.

"Any trouble?" he finally persisted, after giving her a decent time to compose her nerves.

Li Ang looked into the washsink like it held gold dust, shook her head. The long braid of glossy black hair bumped her back.

She rinsed a plate, then half-turned, pointed at the hallway, and nodded once, decidedly. "Good," she said, in a high, thin, piping child's voice. She thought for a moment, finding the word in her mental storehouse. "Good charm." Another nod. "Good sense."

Well, that was as close to an unqualified vote of confidence he'd ever heard Li Ang utter. He felt the need to qualify it himself, so she wouldn't think he was . . . what was he? "Bit prim, that miss." *Kind enough, though, and didn't lose her head in Hammis's parlour. "You! Take him outside." Least she's practical.*

*Made of sterner stuff, eh? Well, we'll see. Been too quiet around here. May be another attack soon.* "Keep the doors bolted," he finally added, taking a bite of biscuit. She made them doughy, did Li Ang. For all that, they were food, and he didn't want her to feel poorly. He'd refused to eat her cooking once, and her face had crinkled like she might cry. He still felt a mite guilty over that. "Darkmoon comin' up."

Li Ang shrugged and brought him a tin cup of water, which he swilled gratefully. He wished for some coffee, but Miss Barrowe hadn't precisely offered, and Li Ang was probably mad at him for scaring the bejesus out of her. That knife had come within a hair of being flung, and he had a healthy respect for her aim. "Hate to scare her away," he added, mostly because he suspected the Chinoise girl liked having him make some noise so she could be sure he wasn't sneaking. "Hard enough gettin' a schoolmarm out here, and the young'uns is right savages."

Li Ang made some remark in her native tongue. She could have been calling him a dogfaced monkeylicker, for all he knew; all Chinois sounded the same to him. But at least she said it nicely enough.

"I don't worry so much about little Hammis or some of the othern. It's the older ones." He popped the last bit of biscuit in his mouth. "Like Tommy Kendall, for example. Or that Browis boy. Like to send her home in a sobbing heap. Maybe I should have a quiet word, you think?"

Li Ang shrugged and made another short comment. Jack

sighed, scratching at his forehead. "Well, they're likely to take that nose in the air as a challenge. Quiet word might sort it out, or might make 'em nastier. God*damn*, Li Ang, why do I always end up talking around you?"

"Lo-nu-lee," she half-sang as she charmed the water in the washsink afresh, sparks of mancy crackling. "Jack is lonely."

*Well, shit. I knew that.* His mouth pulled sourly against itself, and he balanced the plate and cup on the door. *I should just shut up while I can.*

It took the schoolmarm a damnably long time to get ready, and his mood didn't grow any brighter. At least he refrained from opening his fool mouth anymore, and Li Ang collected his plate with a dark look and shuffled away.

By the time he heard a light step in the hall, he was half-ready to tell the Boston miss something had come up and he wasn't available to squire her around all damn day. His mouth was dry and he'd already wiped his hands on his pants, cursing himself as the bacon grease made itself felt.

She looked cool and imperturbable in some sort of flowered dress, a pale ruffled parasol at her side and her hat perched smartly on brown curls. As if she was about to go stepping out on a Boston street instead of sitting in a dusty wagon with him, going to look at a one-room schoolhouse that was probably as fine as a chicken coop to her delicate sensibilities.

"Good morning, Mr. Gabriel." She was even wearing *gloves*, for God's sake. She offered her hand as if she'd never met him before. "I must apologize for my previous disarray. Shall we?"

His brain froze like a hunted rabbit and his mouth decided to mumble. "No trouble." Under the gloves her fingers were slim and fragile.

*She don't belong here.* He swallowed, dryly, and her dark eyes mocked him for being dirty and shapeless. Jack Gabriel reclaimed his hand, jammed his hat back on his head, and mumbled something else.

It didn't figure to be a pleasant afternoon.

# Chapter Four

Miss Bowdler's Book of Charms For Frontier Living had been quite adequate so far, but *Miss Bowdler's Book For Schoolteachers* had not prepared her for a ramshackle barn of a building still smelling of raw wood probably hauled from the distant, frowning mountains with a tiny outhouse tucked behind it like a secret. It had a bell, certainly, and a very new slate board. Fine gritty sand drifting over the floor, riding drafts that bore a striking resemblance to a maelstrom. The long rickety seats looked decidedly uncomfortable, and the desks sloped a bit. A rack of pegs for coats and the like, a boot-scraper near the door, a potbellied stove that would perhaps be beyond her powers to keep lit, and precious few windows added to the general air of "barn."

But she essayed a bright smile. "This will do very well, I think. Was it much trouble to build?"

He gave her a look that suggested she was perhaps a trifle soft in the head. "Got to build everything, out here."

*Well, of course.* Slightly irritated, she forced her fingers to unclench. "So it *was* trouble." Ill-tempered of her, of course, but she had the idea manners were perhaps missing in this quarter of the country. Or if not, they were certainly lost on this *inhabitant* of said quarter. "I apologize."

"Didn't mean that, ma'am. Just meant, we were afraid you'd be offended. Not quite what a Boston miss might be used to."

*There are slums in our fair city, sir, that would put this to shame.* Though she had never gone a-treading them. It was not the thing for a young lady; but Robbie had brought back blood-curdling stories more than once.

In the absence of a clear trail to Robbie's whereabouts, the least she could do was attempt the employment she had pursued and was expected of her.

Perhaps a peace offering to this uneasy man would not go amiss. "It seems solid enough. I am greatly heartened."

"Thank you kindly."

An uncomfortable silence fell. How had she set herself wrong with him? If he disliked her so thoroughly, why had he elected himself to show her this place? Mrs. Granger would have been a far better choice, being on the Committee of Public Works as she was, and a matron Quite Respectable to boot.

Abruptly, Cat realized she was alone with a man, miles from civilization, and she had not even asked for a chaperone. How forward did she appear? She took a few nervous steps away, her skirts making a low sweet sound, and a stream of golden sand creaked from the rafters as the wind shifted.

"Damn dust," he muttered, swinging his hat. "Pardon, ma'am. It'll be less thick in here after the rains. Roof's sound, at least, and some of us will come out and stopper up any drafty bits before winter gets bad. We was fair excited about your arrival."

*Oh, good heavens, rain. If God is merciful, I might not be here at the advent of such an event.* She tried another bright smile. "I am glad to have been anticipated. Now that I have some idea of the facilities, shall we—"

"I reckon I might need a dipperful. Well's out front, ma'am. I'll be back." And he vanished out the front door with long swinging strides, dark hair askew and tinged with the ever-present golden grit.

*Well, do as you please, sir, as long as you leave me in peace.*

She shook her head, then eyed the sorry collection of long desk-boards. Slates and chalk, certainly. Rubbing-cloths were in the desk. She spied a familiar shape under a fall of oilcloth and held her breath, twitching the covering aside with two gloved fingers and finding a very sorry-looking upright piano, twanging discordantly as she touched a yellowed key. Well, a tune-charmer could not be that difficult to find even here in the wilderness; if all else failed... well, she had played worse. It might do to teach some of the more promising students a little refinement.

Though they probably needed refinement here about as much as Cat needed the hair ribbons she'd brought. She had not thought much beyond gaining the town; she had expected Robbie to show his face long before now.

*Well, I am possessed of a small independence, and this is not Boston. It is a start.* She sighed, smoothing the covering over the wrecked hulk of the piano. How had it been hauled so far out West? she wondered. Shuttled on the railway, or bumping along on some prairie schooner, finally fetching up here? Had it been sent by dirigible from abroad, perhaps, and washed up in this inhospitable place? Flotsam of a sort, just as she may well turn out to be?

How on earth *would* she find Robbie? Even here at the edge of civilization a woman did not go wandering about a town looking for a man. Perhaps she might engage someone to take a message to him—but his last missives had been rather striking in their insistence on secrecy and that Cat must not, under any circumstances, enquire openly about him.

It was a puzzle, and one Miss Bowdler's books could not help her solve.

A faint scratching caught her attention. She frowned, glancing about. The entire barnlike structure was dead quiet, and she was abruptly conscious, again, of being miles away from anything even resembling civilization.

The back door. It rattled slightly. Perhaps Mr. Gabriel? The well was at the front of the building, a ramshackle affair but one she suspected was a mark of pride, just like the repaired gate at her own dwelling. Cat swung her closed parasol, decidedly, as she made for the back door between rows of mismatched board-desks. It was bad form to carry it inside; but there was no stand, and she did not wish it to become stained.

The door rattled again, groaning, and a fresh flurry of scratch-ing filled the uncanny quiet. Was it an animal? Or perhaps Mr. Gabriel was playing some manner of foolish prank, seeing if the Boston miss could be frightened?

Cat's chin rose. *Robbie could hoax much better than this, sir.* The lock was a pin-and-hasp, sparking with a charter-charm; her charing, tucked under her dress, warmed dangerously. So, it was a prank involving mancy, was it?

*Oh, sir, you have chosen the wrong victim.* She drew the pin, her left hand closing about the knob, the parasol dangling from its strap. She jerked the door in, a small lightning-crackle charm fizzing on her fingers, for she had often dissuaded Robbie by flinging light directly at his eyes—

The rotting corpse, its jaw soundlessly working and grave-dirt sluicing from its jerking arms and legs, plowed straight through the door, its collapsed eyes runneling down its cheeks in strings of gushing decay, sparks of diseased foxfire mancy glowing in the empty holes.

She screamed once, a sharp curlew-cry that he might've taken for a girl seeing a rat if not for its ragged edge of sheer terror. Gabe couldn't remember how he got up the stairs and into the school-house; he didn't even remember drawing his gun.

What he remembered ever after was the sight of Miss Bar-rowe, her parasol cracked clean in half from smashing at the head of an ambulatory corpse, deadly silent as she scrabbled back on her hands, her feet caught in her skirts and breath gone, her face white. And the corpse, of course, chewing on air emptily, greed-ily, making a rusty noise as its drying tendons struggled to work. Some of them were right quick bastards and juicy, too, but this one had been dead awhile, and his first shot near took its head clean off. It folded down in a noisome splatter, and Miss Barrowe had gained her feet with desperate, terrified almost-grace. She kept blundering back, knocking into the edges of the long three- and four-person desks on each side, and if he didn't catch her she would probably do herself an injury.

*Are there any more? Dammit, Russ, the borders were solid this morning!*

*"Barrowe!"* he barked, but she didn't respond, just kept going. So it was up to him to move, and she nearly bowled him over with hysterical strength. The impact jolted a hitching little cry out of her; she whooped in a breath and was fixing to scream again. He clapped his left hand over her mouth, the gun tracking the flopping corpse on the floor. Now he could smell it, dry rot and damp decay, a body left in the desert for a little while. Someone had fallen to misadventure or murder, been buried unconsecrated, and the wild magic had seeped in to give it a twisted semblance of life.

Its naked heels drummed the raw floorboards, and Miss Barrowe tried struggling. She was probably half-mad with fear.

He didn't blame her.

"It's all right." He wished he sounded more soothing. "Ma'am, just settle down. I'm here, there ain't no need for fuss."

Amazingly, that took some of the fight out of her. She froze, her ribs heaving with breaths as light and rapid as a hummingbird's wings. Her lips moved slightly against his work-hardened palm, and he told himself to ignore it while he eyed the open door, its hinges creaking slightly as the wind teased at the slab of wood. It had been locked with a charm-pin—what the hell had happened?

*Well, first things first.* "Now," he said quietly, "you're perfectly safe, Miss Barrowe, I ain't about to let no creatures gnaw our schoolmarm. You can rely on that. Nod if you hear me."

She did nod, precisely once. Her breath was a hot spot in his palm, her lips still moving soundlessly. There was a scorch to the right of the door, still crawling with mancy—she must have thrown something at the corpse. Looked like her aim was put off by the thing busting through the door.

*That* was interesting. So she had a full-blown Practicality, did she? She could have found a decent living in one of the cities back East; why on earth would a girl with a skill like that want to come *here*?

*That's a riddle for another day.* "Now, I'm gonna take my hand away, and you can faint if you want, or whatever it is ladies do in this situation. But you can't go screamin' or runnin', because that will just complicate things. Nod if you agree."

Another nod. Well. He'd see if she was lying. He peeled his fingers away from her mouth, conscious of the fearsweat on his nape and the small of his back, the smell of horse and exertion that clung to every man out here. She smelled of rosewater and fresh air, sunlight and clean linen and the flesh of a clean healthy woman. Her hat was askew, and she reached up with trembling fingers, her broken parasol dangling sadly from a thin leather loop around her wrist. Her fingers moved gracefully, settling her hat, and she took one step to the side. Gabe twitched, but true to her word, she didn't run or scream. She simply swallowed very hard, lifting her chin, and that spark was back in her dark eyes.

"Good." He almost said *good girl*, as if she were a frightened horse needing soothing, stopped himself just in time. "Did you open the door?"

"I th-thought it was a p-prank." She sounded steady enough, though her color was two shades whiter than a bleached sheet. "M-my b-brother…"

*So you had a brother. Maybe you'll take to the little demons we've got for children out here.* He waited, but she said nothing else. He cleared his throat, and she jumped nervously. He half-turned, his back to her as soon as he judged she was unlikely to bolt, and eyed both open doors. "You heard something?"

"S-scratching." Another audible swallow. The corpse ceased its jerking, but you could never tell with wanderers like this. Even with half their head gone, they were still dangerous. "R-rattling the door."

*That's interesting, too.* "Charter's still solid," he muttered, more because he fancied she needed another voice to steady herself than out of any real need to say it out loud. "Was this morning, I rode the circuit myself. This place was cleaned three times before we laid the foundation. Huh."

"If you are s-suggesting *I*—"

Well, she was brighter *and* braver than he gave her credit for. "You ain't got no bad mancy on you, sweetheart." *I'd smell the twisting a mile away. It's what I do, curse me and all.* He pushed his hat farther up on his forehead, wished he could just decide which one of the two doors was the worse idea. If the corpse had gotten its teeth into her, he would have had to put her down, no matter if she had enough of a Practicality to shield her from the worst effects. "Just stay still a minute while I—"

"Sir." Dangerously calm. "You shall address me as *Miss Barrowe*, thank you."

*Oh, for the love of...* His hand twitched. The gun spoke again, deafening, and the shadow in the door didn't duck. *That's a bad sign.* "Stay *here*." He launched himself for the back door, worn bootheels cracking against the boards, clearing a desk in a leap he was faintly amazed to think about later, and out into the bath of dusthaze and glare that was a Damnation afternoon full of the walking dead.

# *Chapter Five*

Crunches. Howls. Terrible sounds, and gunshots, spitting crackling mancy and thuds against the walls. Cat stood locked in place, trembling, staring at the body on the floor, her gloved fingers working against each other. *Walking dead. Here. Oh, God.*

The graveyards were well-policed in Boston, and bodies properly handled. Still, sometimes the more amenable of the wandering dead were set to work—supervised, of course, but used for brute and drudge tasks. There was a Society for Liberation of the Deceased, but Cat's mother had always sniffed at such a thing. *Liberation indeed*, she would say. *Next they shall be wanting franchise.* And her father would chime in. *Though how that would differ from the usual ballot-box stuffing, I cannot tell. Come, Frances, speak of something less unpleasant.*

She had watched as they put the true-iron nails in her father's palms, but she could not bear to see such an operation performed on her mother. Nor could she bear to witness the other appurtenances of death—the mouthful of consecrated salt, the branding of dead flesh with charter-symbols, the sealing of the casques. Thankfully, the Barrowe-Browne name, not to mention the estate's copious funding, meant her parents would not be set to drudgery but instead locked safely in leaden coffins inside a stone crypt, with chartermages making certain of their quiet, mouldering rest.

*Oh, for heaven's sake, do not think on that!*

Cat squeezed her eyes shut, but the darkness made the sounds worse. So she opened them wide, and counted dust motes in the air. Why she did not find a spot more conducive to cowering and hiding was beyond her, unless it was the sheriff's queer certainty.

*Stay* here.

Said very decisively, the gun smoking in his hand, then he had been gone, moving faster than she could credit.

If this was a prank, it was a very good one. The body on the floor was certainly none too fresh. Would someone cart a corpse all this way, and charm it, too—a dangerous occupation, to be sure—all for the sake of a laugh? Not even Robbie would go so far.

Though there had been the episode with the frogs, long ago in their childhood. And their dry-rusty dead-throat croaking. Robbie's Practicality was just barely acceptable in Society, and their father had more than once reminded him *never* to allow it rein outside the house. Especially after the poor frogs, the nursery full of the stink and...

*Oh, I wish I had not thought of that.*

A shadow filled the doorway. She had to swallow a scream, but it was merely Mr. Jack Gabriel, hat clamped on his dark head, his eyes narrowed and his hands occupied in reloading his pistol with quick, habitual movements. She supposed he must do so often, to be so cavalier during the operation.

"You can move now," he said, mildly. "Don't think there's more, but we should step lively back closer to town."

"Is this..." She had to cough to clear her throat. "Is this *normal*, sir? I cannot be expected to teach if—"

"Oh, no, it's not normal at all, ma'am." His eyes had darkened from their hazel, and his gaze was disturbingly direct. "Matter of fact, it's downright unnatural, and I intend to get to the bottom of it. You won't be setting foot out here, teaching or no teaching, until I'm sure it's safe."

*Well. That's very kind of you, certainly.* "That is a decided relief," she managed, faintly. "I am sorry for the trouble."

"No trouble at all, ma'am. You've a good head on your shoulders." A high blush of color—exertion or fear, who knew—ran along his high, wide cheekbones.

For a single lunatic instant she thought he was about to laugh and tell her it *had* all been a prank, and she was, in Robbie's terms, a blest good sport. But his mouth was drawn tight, he was covered in dust, and there was a splatter of something dark and viscous down one trouser leg.

"Thank you." She tried not to sound prim, probably failed utterly. And who wouldn't sound a little faint and withered after this manner of excitement? "I don't suppose you, ah, know the... the deceased?"

He actually looked startled, his gaze dropping like a boy caught with his fingers in a stolen pie. "Can't say as I looked to recognize them, ma'am."

"Oh." She found the trembling in her legs would not quite recede. Her throat was distressingly dry. "I suppose you must have been...yes. Busy."

"Very. You're pale."

*I feel rather pale, thank you.* "I shall do well enough." She took an experimental step, and congratulated herself when she did not stagger. "Returning to town does seem the safest route. Shall we?"

There was a dewing of blood on his stubbled cheek. Where was it from? "Yes ma'am."

Cat decided she did *not* wish to know precisely what the stains on him were from, and set off for the rectangle of dusty sunlight that marked the front door, her bootheels making crisp little clicking noises. The sheriff caught her arm, his grimy fingers oddly gentle.

"Just a moment, Miss Barrowe. I'll be locking the back door, and then you'll let me go through that'un first."

*Oh.* "Yes. Of course." *Please let's not dally.*

"Just you stay still and don't faint. Don't want to have to carry you over my shoulder." He paused, still gazing at her in that incredibly *odd* manner. "Would be right undignified."

"That it would." She clasped her gloved hands, her heart in her throat and pounding so hard she rather thought a vessel might burst and save the undead the trouble of laying her flat.

*What a charmingly gruesome idea. Use that organ of Sensibility you so pride yourself upon, Cat. Behave properly.*

The trouble was, even Miss Bowdler's books, marvelous as they were, had nothing even *remotely* covering this situation. She decided this fell under Extraordinary Occurrences, and checked her hat. An Extraordinary Occurrence meant that one must take care of one's person to the proper degree, and simply avoid making the situation *worse*.

Her gloves were in good order, though her parasol was completely ruined. Her dress seemed to have suffered precious few ill effects from scurrying across the floor. A few traces of sawdust, that was all.

She found the sheriff still staring. "Sir." It was her mother's *There Is Much To Be Done* tone, used whenever something had gone quite wrong and it was Duty and Obligation both to set it right, and it was *wonderfully* bracing. "Do let's be on our way."

At least he stopped staring at her. "Yes ma'am." Another touch to the brim of his hat—and by God, *must* he wear it inside? It was insufferable.

He approached the body cautiously, grabbed it by the scruff of its rotting shirt, and hauled it outside through the back door. It went into the sunshine with a thump that unseated Cat's stomach, and despite his shouted warning, she fled the barnlike schoolhouse. She leaned over the porch stair railing, and she retched until nothing but bile could be produced.

He wished the wagon wouldn't jolt so much. She was paper-pale, trembling, and had lost damn near everything she'd probably ever *thought* of eating. She clutched at the broken stick of the parasol like a drowning woman holding on to driftwood. Damp with sweat, a few stray strands of her hair had come free, and now they lay plastered to her fair flawless skin. He wished, too, that he could say something comforting, but he settled for hurrying the horse as much as he dared.

He'd lied, of course. There hadn't been just a few undead. He'd stopped counting at a half-dozen, and there was no way a single man could put down that many.

Not if he was normal. And Jack Gabriel had no intention of letting anyone think he was otherwise. Not only would it cause undue fuss among the townsfolk, but it might also reach certain quarters.

The Order did not often give up its own, and he suspected they would be right glad to know his whereabouts.

Her charing-charm glittered uneasily. His own was ice cold, and it should have warned him long before the undead came close enough to sense a living heartbeat. Which was . . . troubling.

Not just troubling. It was downright terrifying, and he was man enough to admit as much.

Had it happened, then? Had he lost his baptism? Did grace no longer answer him?

Loss of faith was one thing. Loss of grace was quite another.

She swayed again as the wagon jolted, her shoulder bumping his. Did a small sound escape her? He racked his brains, trying to think of something calming to say. Or should he just keep his fool mouth shut?

"Mr. Gabriel?" A colorless little ghost of a voice. Did she need to heave again? It was unlikely she had anything left in her. And she was such a bitty thing.

"Yes ma'am." The reins were steady. He stared ahead, most of his attention taken up with flickers in his peripheral vision. If there were more of them, they would cluster instead of attacking one by one, and that was a prospect to give anyone the chills.

Even a man who had nothing to lose.

*They won't get you.* He decided it wouldn't be comforting at all to say that to her, and meant to keep his lip buttoned tightly.

"Thank you. For saving my life." She stared straight ahead as well. The tiny veil attached to her hat was slightly torn, waving in the fitful breeze. The heat of the day shimmered down the track, and the good clean pungency of sage filled his nose.

It was a relief. At least he didn't smell like walking corpse.

"My pleasure, ma'am." As soon as the words left his mouth he could have cussed himself sideways. He could have said, *It weren't nothin'*, or even, *You're welcome*. But no. *My pleasure? Really?*

They'd be lucky if she wasn't on the next coach to the train station in Poscola Flats, retreating to Boston. And that thought wasn't pleasant, if only because of how that bat Granger would complain, and the rest of the fool Committee of old biddies as well.

No, it wouldn't be pleasant at all.

His stupid mouth opened right back up. "What I mean to say, it's no trouble. No trouble at all. Wasn't about to let no corpses get their teeth in our schoolmarm."

Well. That was from bad to worse. Plus, he noticed as he glanced down, there was muck on his pants from the last corpse he'd put down, steel blurring into its throat and its head blasted off with a bullet and a muttered Word. It was rubbing against her pretty skirt, and there was nothing he could do about it.

*Oh, hell.*

"I am very grateful." Her gloved fingers interlaced, pulled *hard* against each other, and she did not wait for him to help her down when the wagon halted outside her trim little cottage. Instead, she hopped down, almost catching her dress in her hurry, and was gone inside the house before he could say *boo*.

Not that he'd want to say boo. Or anything else. Dull heat stained Gabe's cheeks, and he swallowed several times before turning his attention to the next problem presenting itself.

Which was getting the horse squared away, and then finding out just what in hell the walking dead were doing inside the town charter.

*          *          *

He palmed the workroom door open, and Russ jumped about a foot. The mancy he was working spit dull red sparks, and Gabe's charing-charm scorched for a brief second. He ignored it—anything Russ was likely to fling could be countered handily. "Russell Overton, what the hell?"

"What the *hell* the hell?" Russ spluttered. His office was dark, heavy shades pulled in his inner workroom because, like most professional mancers, he preferred the gloom where he could see the sparks. His shirtsleeves, rolled up, showed the pale twisting veined scars of a professional chartermage, raised and ropy on coffee-cream skin dusted with sparse coarse hair.

Even his arms were bandy and tense. Jack was struck with the idea that perhaps the man's color had made him accustomed to taking fighting the world as a given, much as Jack's natural stubbornness had.

Such thoughts occurred to a man out West, he supposed. "Just got jumped by the walkin' dead, Russ. Charter was solid this morning; what the *hell*?"

Russ's palms clapped together, shorting the mancy. It died in a cascade of heatless iridescence, and he was already rolling his sleeves down and reaching for his coat. "Where?"

At least the man didn't drag his feet. "The schoolhouse. They're not rising again, but we need to find the breach. God *damn* it, Russ."

"There *is* no breach. We rode this morning." Russ's eyes closed, briefly. "All the compass markers are in place. I can feel them. Gabe..." He licked his lips, a quick nervous flicker of a dry-leaf tongue. "The schoolhouse, you said. Did any of them—"

"She's safe." Gabe folded his arms, glaring. "Goddamn good thing *I* was there, instead of a passel of kids."

Russ paled further at the thought. It *was* nightmarish, and Gabe normally wouldn't have said such a thing. But *damn* it, if that first undead had sunk its teeth into Miss Barrowe...

Well, it didn't bear thinking of. And he didn't like the sinking, empty sensation in his gut when he thought about it. So he wouldn't, would he? There were plenty of other things to think about at the moment.

He could ignore that sinking sensation. Sure he could.

Russ grabbed his gunbelt, hung over a sturdy wooden chair. Papers stirred on a stray breeze, ruffling as the mancy-laden atmosphere twitched inside the narrow office at Gabe's back, full of shelves of bits and herbs and other things, charmer's books stacked haphazardly on a taboret near the desk. He buckled the belt with quick habitual movements. "I meant to ask if any of them looked familiar."

*Oh, for the love of...* He could have cheerfully throttled the man. "I didn't stop to ask their names. But no, none of 'em looked familiar. Bunch of strangers around here anyway."

"Gabe." Russ halted, his black Gladstone clutched in one hand. His hat was askew, and his blue eyes were shadowed. "What if it's...*that*?"

A cool fingertip touched Gabe's nape. "We sealed that claim up solid. And nobody's been showing up with marked bars recently. Dust and nuggets, but no bars."

"But what if—"

"*It's* gone. And that stupid kid, too." *What was his name? Face like a blank slate, you could forget it in a heartbeat.* The eyes had just slid right over him, and sometimes Gabe wondered if it was a type of mancy that had made the kid so forgettable.

"Well, the markers are all in place, and the charterstone's solid." Russ shook his head, straightened his hat. "Let's go."

Gabe held the door. Russ stamped, his bow-legged gait just like a clockwork toy's. He was through the office and out onto the porch in a heartbeat.

Sweeping the workroom door closed, the sheriff had to shake his head, thinking of Miss Barrowe's wide dark eyes, swimming with tears and terror. The unsteady feeling hit him again, like a fist to the gut.

Then he remembered the kid's name.

"Robert Browne." He actually said it out loud, but Russ was outside already and didn't hear. It was a damn good thing, too.

Because a chartermage wouldn't take kindly to having a dead man's name breathed in his office. Jack Gabriel shook his head, ran his fingers over the butt of a gun, and hurried to catch up.

# Chapter Six

Cat stared at her front door. She had her gloves on, and carried her second-best parasol, the one with fringe that quivered as she walked. Her yellow silk was quite cheerful, and had the not-inconsiderable advantage of being almost comfortable. Her hair was perfection itself, and she had clasped her mother's pearls about her neck. Her boots were buttoned firmly, and there was just a breath of rosewater remaining from her *toilette*.

But there was the front door, and here she stood, unwilling to open it.

"Ridiculous," she muttered. "You're being ridiculous." *How Robbie would laugh.*

But that was just it. No Robbie. Her plans had come to fruition; she was here, hundreds of miles from civilization, and she had not the faintest clue of how to go about *finding* him. She had thought it a dead certainty he would find *her*.

If he had moved on . . . but how likely was that, given what he'd written? No, there was another possibility, one she did not wish to think upon, but which must be faced nonetheless.

Foul play.

And here she stood, stupid as a toadstool, afraid to open her front door because of an irruption of undead. Quite reasonable, actually, given what a bite could do to one even if one had enough mancy to inoculate oneself against the worst effects. But there had been no harm done, because of Mr. Gabriel.

Who had called at the back door during breakfast, *again*, to express his hope that she was not *too* upset by recent events. She had reassured him with brittle calm that she did not intend to return to Boston with her tail tucked like a cur's just yet. Maddeningly, the man had simply smiled, tipped his hat, and vanished.

Li Ang had said something in her native tongue that sounded like a curse, and Cat was forced to agree. The man was a nuisance, and entirely too sharp under that slow, sleepy drawl of his. She was even beginning to believe him of a quality, though he sought to hide it.

Yet he had been practical and helpful enough, when the situation required.

*Catherine, you are being worse than ridiculous. You are, as a matter of fact, being a coward.*

Which, for a Barrowe-Browne, could not be borne. That forced her to move another three steps toward the door. From the kitchen came the sound of splashing water and Li Ang's odd atonal humming. The Chinoise girl was quiet, efficient, and discreet; there would be no trouble there.

*You are being a coward—and Robbie needs you. If he has met with foul play, you are his only hope.*

So much of life was merely doing what one was required to. It smoothed the way wonderfully to have no *choice*.

Another two steps, and her gloved hand played with the locks. The knob turned smoothly, easily, and a fresh morning breeze filled the hall behind her. Her reticule dangled. Her eyes opened, cautiously, and she saw the sun-drenched garden. It would, in all likelihood, be another incredibly, mind-numbingly hot day. She would have to be home before luncheon.

*Then it's best to get started, isn't it? If the undead were in the town streets there would be more noise, one fancies.*

While eminently logical, the thought was not as comforting as it could have been.

Chin raised, eyes flashing, palms sweating, and her dress rustling, Cat stepped over her threshold.

Damnation. A main street with others branching away at right angles, buildings sprawled in the dust and the heat, blowsy and blinking. Horses clopping along; men lounging in doorways, raising their hats automatically when the infrequent woman passed them. The men moved slowly in the heat; ragged children darted between hooves and ran before carts, and the few women in homespun or dark drab walked with chin-high determination.

In her bright yellow, Cat stood out far more than she'd thought possible. The men hurried to raise their hats, and she was greeted on all sides, hailed with an intensity that was a touch embarrassing. Had they never seen a schoolteacher before? Of course, she was a bright bird in a sea of dusty pigeons, and she would have been writhing with embarrassment had she not been so occupied in making polite gestures. Her mother's Greet the Peasants smile had rarely been so useful.

She had not passed more than a few sun-bleached building fronts before Mr. Gabriel appeared, falling into step beside her with a tip of his hat. "Ma'am."

"Mr. Gabriel." She stared straight ahead. "You look well."

"You haven't looked at me enough to see, Miss Barrowe. But yes, I'm well. Pleasure to see you out and about."

*My, isn't he chatty this morning.* "Thank you."

"It ain't much, but it strikes me you might want a guide. To show you, that is. Around town."

*If this were a civilized town, I could perhaps purchase a street map. Or hire a carriage, or... dear God, do you really think me so dim I cannot find my way about this collection of dingy little alleys?* "A very kind offer."

"Not to presume, but... it could be risky around here. For a woman."

*Indeed?* "More hazardous than the walking dead?" She sounded archly amused, and congratulated herself upon as much.

He had the grace to cough slightly. "There's some what might be worse."

What an unprepossessing little phrase. Was it even grammatical? "I beg your pardon?"

"Well, look. You passed words with Tils, right? Short little man in a bowler hat, moustaches he waxes up? Red flannel?"

She frowned slightly, her parasol swaying. None of the other women here carried them, and she was beginning to feel a trifle ridiculous. Again. And yet, she was very glad of the shade. "Mr. Tilson? I don't see what that has to do with—"

"He runs one of the three fancyhouses we have in town. The Lucky Star, and that's more saloon than . . . the other. Though the two are the same. Mostly." Did he sound uncomfortable? His stride didn't alter, a long loping gait that meant a single step for every two of hers. "I'd warn you not to have too many words with him. Man's outright dangerous. To women, that is."

Her throat was suddenly, suspiciously dry. "I see."

He didn't sound convinced. "Then I don't need to tell you to be careful where you step. People come out here for two reasons: They're looking for trouble, or running away from it."

"Really." It was her turn to sound unconvinced. "I must disprove your theory, sir. I did not travel to this lovely town for either reason." *Robbie, I am going to pinch you. Twice.*

Was it amusement in his tone? "Well now, that exercises my curiosity something fierce. I've been wondering why such a gentle miss came all the way out here."

Why on earth did she feel menaced? A glitter caught her eye. Cat turned aside, finding herself before a window. How, in the name of charter, did they bring *glass* out here? Did it rattle by stagecoach, wrapped and shivering?

Shabby velvet and twinkling metal—it was a store of some kind, its brightest wares displayed prominently. Two silver-chased pistols, a fine set of them by the looks of it, with bone on their handles and carvings crawling with true-aim mancy, just as in novels of the Wild Westron. Pocketwatches, a fan of folded silk handkerchiefs. A few rings, tucked on tiny, moth-eaten purple pillows.

"This is Freedman Salt's." Mr. Gabriel's tone was very even. "I'd tell you not to go in here, ma'am. It's a pawnshop."

_I hardly think I shall faint at the news._ "Indeed," she murmured. "I am not blind, Mr. Gabriel. I can see as much."

"Well, then I'll tell you something you can't see. Russ Overton's our chartermage. People want respectable mancy, they go to him. But there's people what want something different, and they come _here_. Haven't quite figgered what Salt ran away from back East." He stood beside her, thumbs hooked in his belt, his chin up, staring through the window as if he wished to shatter it with the force of his gaze alone. "When I do, it might be time for a Federal Marshal to come this way. But until then, I just watch."

Well, he certainly received no points for grace or finesse. "I do believe that's the most I've heard you speak so far, Mr. Gabriel." _And now I believe it's time for this conversation to take a different course._ "Your theory, I presume, must hold true for yourself. What trouble did you come Westron-ward to escape?"

He was silent for a long moment. Sweat collected under Cat's arms, her lower back was soaked, and a thin trickle slid down from her hair. Even under the parasol's shade and the awnings and porches extending from almost every building on this main thoroughfare, the entire town was oppressive. The dust was rising in creeping veils, too.

Still, she was cold all through, and a taste of bitter brass filled her mouth. A wave of shivering rippled down her back, and the fringe on her parasol trembled cheerily. She could not cease staring at the gleam that had caught her gaze.

There, on a pad of threadbare red velvet, lay a square locket. It was small, a golden shimmer, and the _tau_ etched on its surface held a single tiny garnet in its center. The chain was a mellifluous spill, but it was broken, and as she gazed at it, another finger of sweat sliding down her neck, the ends of the break twitched as if the metal felt her nearness.

"Well now." When the sheriff spoke, she almost started violently. She had all but forgotten him. "You start asking that question, and people are likely to get itchy."

*What question?* She remembered, and had to swallow twice before she could speak. "I see."

"Good." He touched his hatbrim. "I'll be around, should you want a guide. Or need help. Ma'am."

And with that he was gone, those unhurried strides of his carrying him neatly across the crowded street and between the swinging doors of the Lucky Star Saloon. Even at this early hour there was tinny piano music coming from the ramshackle building's depths. His shoulders were broad and his dun-colored coat blended with the dust; he did not precisely dodge the traffic. Rather, it seemed that it parted for him, and he waltzed through the chaos like a . . . she could not think of what, for a roaring noise had filled her head.

Cat turned back to the window. Her stays dug in, and she had to force herself to breathe. The glass was streaked with dust, humming with carnivorous mancy. Her charing-charm had gone chill against her throat, again.

*Danger, Catherine.*

Robbie's locket winked knowingly at her. He would never have pawned it, would he? The chain was broken. How had *that* happened? He wore his charing on the same chain—*double the safety*, he had always joked. *For if Mother found out bad mancy had been lodged near an heirloom, there would be an Incident of Temper.*

His charing was not in evidence—of course, if some dire fate had befallen him, it would be broken. Or perhaps he had found another means of securing his charing to his person, and had been forced to sell the locket? And yet that was ridiculous; he had left with plenty of money. What would make him give up an heirloom, especially one he had worn since childhood?

If she could hold the locket in her bare hand, perhaps she could find Robbie. Her Practicality would certainly stretch that far. Further, indeed, if she pricked her finger, for blood always told—though blood-work was *bad* mancy, and not something a respectable lady would dare.

*I have already done something no respectable young lady would do, coming here.* She sought to collect her wits, failed, tried again.

There were too many people about. She was hardly discreet, and who was to say Mr. Gabriel was not still watching her?

The pawnshop's door had a bell attached. It tinkled, and a man stumbled out onto the raw-lumber walkway. He was unshaven, bleary-eyed, and smelled powerfully of rancid liquor. His hat was askew, and he held guns in both callused, dirty hands.

Cat turned and walked briskly away. Her skirts snapped, her parasol fluttered, and she hardly remembered retracing her steps to the tiny cottage behind its freshly painted gate.

She was, as Robbie would have no doubt recognized were he present, far too occupied with scheming.

# Chapter Seven

T hose with true business didn't visit the shop by day.
Every once in a while, Gabe would settle in a patch of
shadow near the mouth of a dusty alley, and watch the chartershadow's back door. It was useful to see who was visiting Salt.
It was also useful to see how they approached—swaggering or
creeping, desperate or slinking.

Very rarely, Gabe found himself collaring one of the desperate
and telling them to go elsewhere. It wasn't his business, and Salt
didn't need to know how closely he was watched. In fact, the less
Salt knew about anything involving the sheriff, the better.

But sometimes, some nights, he couldn't stop himself.

Tonight was not one of those nights. He watched, noting who
came creeping down the alley. And while he waited, he thought
things over.

Here came thin, dried-up Mandy Carrick, keeping to the shadows and paying who knew what for protection when he decided
to jump another claim out in the hills, stealing some other man's
rightful work. That was outside Gabe's jurisdiction, certainly, but
he still took note of it. Struthers slithered down the alley, a blur
of fawn coat and stickpin flashing, looking for cheat-card mancy.
A Chinois man was closeted inside the back of the pawnshop for
quite a while, and Gabe didn't like the looks of that. Their mancy

was different, even if it lived comfortably within charter, and he wondered just what one of *them* would want with Salt.

It was late by the time the trickle to the chartershadow's door dried up. The saloons would be rollicking, and there had been a few crackling gunshots. Nothing out of the ordinary here in Damnation. He'd made sure the schoolteacher's house was in a quieter part of town. Respectable, almost.

As respectable as you could get, out here.

*Will you stop?* Irritated with himself, he took a deep breath and slid out of concealment. *She's just a Boston miss a long way from home, and you're a goddamn idiot.*

He smacked the unlocked door open without even a courtesy knock, almost allowing himself to grin with satisfaction when it banged and Freedman Salt, his lean scarecrow body seeming put together from spare parts and his thick white wooly hair shocking atop such a wasted face, actually jumped.

This back room was low and indifferently lit, and the chalked charter-symbols on the floor were all subtly skewed. Some were scuffed and others redrawn—Salt had been a busy little boy tonight. He wasn't quite a sorcerer, or a chartermage; the man didn't have the discipline. Instead, the twisted drained bodies of small furry things lay at certain points within the diagram, false-iron nails driven through skulls, paws, tails. It stank of spoiled mancy and clotted-thick rust.

"Well now." Gabe rested a hand on a pistol butt. If he had been back East, it would have been a knife instead. He restrained the urge to shake the memory away. "What have we here?"

"Sheriff Gabriel." Salt's thin lip curled. "Pleasure, as always."

"Not fixin' to be. Dead bodies inside the charter this morning, Salt. Start explainin'."

"Since when do dead bodies have shit-all to do with *me*?" As if butter wouldn't melt in his lying mouth.

"These were walkin' around." Gabe eyed the walls, rough boards covered with an intaglio of twisted, slurred charter-symbols. Even the dust in here reeked of blood. "Ridin' the circuit again put me in a bad mood, and the charter was solid. Which means I'm lookin' real hard at you, Salt."

A mockery of innocent shock twisted the chartershadow's lean face. "Me? Maybe you need a better chartermage. That one you got is all tarbrush and no talent."

"So are you, *Freedman*." It was a sure way to nettle the man, and Gabe almost regretted it as soon as Salt's face suffused with ugly maroon.

"I ain't no—"

Gabe's free hand flicked forward, the charm biting and fizzing in midair. Salt backpedaled, his boots smearing unfixed charter-symbols. A twinge of satisfaction burned Gabe's chest just as the choking chartershadow managed to get about half a syllable out. The curse went wide, splashing against the wall and punching a fist-sized hole.

Then Gabe had the man down on the floor, the gun cocked and pressed right behind Salt's ear. This close, he could see the dark roots of the man's charm-bleached hair, and also smell the faint smoke and slippery wetroot rot of the lean lanky body as the bad mancy kept twisting him, one slow increment at a time. Salt's hair frayed, chalked charter-symbols on the flooring writhing as Gabe scrubbed the shadow's face across them.

There was, he reflected, almost too much enjoyment to be had in terrorizing the wicked. The Order did not precisely *frown* on such enjoyment... but it was dangerous.

"Settle down." *Or so help me, I will settle you. That curse could have taken my face off.*

The only problem was, Salt's replacement was likely to be worse. Every town, no matter how small, had at least one charter-shadow. Even when there wasn't a respectable mage to be found, the shadows crept in.

Harsh breathing. The tips of Salt's boots scrabbled against the planking before he went still. Gabe knew better than to think he'd given up.

But for right now, it was enough. "Now." He didn't relax. "You been doing something that brings walkin' corpses into Damnation, this'n your chance to tell me."

"Would I be so stupid?" The words were muffled by the floor. At least he wasn't writhing anymore. "I got a nice li'l nest here, *Sheriff.* Except'n you, it's a bed of fucking roses."

*There's always a thorn somewhere, isn't there.* "Well now. Mighty suspicious, then, that I'm the one who ran across walkin' dead."

Still, if Salt had brought the corpses in or charmed them, he would have been ready for Gabe to come through his door, and would have had a lot worse than a half-measure of curse waiting.

"I don't know. It warn't me." Half-hysterical now, with the edge of a whine underneath the words. Salt could have been a reasonably employable chartermage with enough application and discipline, but he was both lazy and a coward.

And mancy—or grace—didn't forgive cowardice easily.

*Am I a coward now? How would I know?* "You sure, Salt? You don't sound too convinced."

*"It warn't me, dammit!"*

He eased up a little. "And of course you wouldn't know anything about it, would you."

The chartershadow began to struggle again, heaving under him. "First time I've heard, now *leggo!*"

Gabe did. He was on his feet and observing a cautious distance by the time Salt heaved himself up, his face choked with dust and bright beads of blood from several scrapes. The gun was back in Gabe's holster—but his hand still itched for it.

"Evenin', then, Mr. Salt." He touched the brim of his hat.

"What, you ain't gonna shoot me? Threaten me some more?"

"No point. I discover you ain't been honest, it's easy to find you. You havin' such a nice little nest and all."

Salt actually paled, his wasted frame visibly trembling. Whether it was rage or fear was an open question. He wore no guns, but Gabe was sure there was a knife or two handy. It would be just like the little bastard to slit someone in a dark alley.

He would have to be more careful now. Why had he drawn a gun, for God's sake? Salt wasn't enough of a threat to justify that.

*Sir, your head is none too organized right now.* He imagined Miss Barrowe's clipped, cultured tones, how a single eyebrow would lift fractionally, but those dark eyes would hold a different message. She likely thought she was hard to read, the school-marm, but those eyes were windows straight down to the bottom of a clear pond.

*Windows to the soul, Jack? Just like Annie's.*

The door was still open, a night breeze redolent of horse, dust, and Damnation breathing into the chartershadow's room.

"Sheriff?" Salt wiped away the blood around his thin lips. "I saw a new face out my window today. Dressed in yellow, and pretty as a picture."

A cold hand clenched in Jack's guts.

"Wonder if she saw anything she liked," Salt continued.

He kept his expression a mask. "Not likely." And with that he was gone, but the sweat on the back of his neck and the tension in his fists were unwelcome symptoms.

*It's nothing. People love to gossip, and they'll stop talking if you don't give them anything to talk about. Just leave it alone, Jack.*

Unfortunately, he wasn't sure he could. And that was almost as worrying as a Chinois sneaking into a chartershadow's work-room late at night and asking for mancy. Jack headed for Russ Overton's lodgings for the fourth time that day, the shapes of the twisted charter-symbols he'd seen in Salt's back room fresh in his memory.

It was maybe time to do a little book-learning.

# *Chapter Eight*

M iss Bowdler's books had said nothing about *this*.
  It was hot as Hades, dusty as another underworld, and Cat's stays were digging into her flesh with the vigor of bony clutching fingers as her temper frayed and she assayed, once more, a calm but authoritative tone.

There were too many of them to count, and she still had not managed a semblance of a roll call. More than half the tiny savages had no shoes, and could not sit still for more than a moment or two. Less than a quarter had seen some version of soap and water in the last fortnight, and she had the suspicion none of them were literate or numerate even in the most basic sense. The older savages bullied the younger unmercifully until Cat lost her temper and her Practicality sparked. The novelty of an adult throwing mancy in a classroom bought her precious moments to compose herself, and she thought grimly that her mother's experiences with Charity Work and the Noblesse Oblige of a Lady were going to stand her in better stead than *any* d—ned book, as Robbie would say.

At least while she was corralling a group of tiny uncivilized animals, she did not think of Robbie's locket in the pawnshop window, and how to obtain such an item without the entire town remarking upon her movements.

"That is *quite* enough," she informed the group of boys who had been tormenting a younger child. "You are to sit *there*, sir, and you *there*." She pointed, despite it being unmannerly.

"What if I don't?" the largest of them—an oafish blond lump who bore a startling resemblance to the small pug-nosed dogs she had seen in quite a few fashionable drawing-rooms last year— actually *sneered*, and Cat's temper almost frayed. Stray mancy crackled on her fingertip, and she drew herself up. A shadow slid over the room, and each tiny savage she was responsible for civilizing drew a deep breath.

"Then I haul you down to the jail and tell your mother you're sassin' the marm, Dwight Caffrey," a deep voice drawled from the propped-open door. "Afternoon, Miss Barrowe."

The mancy on her fingers died. *What is he doing here?* "Mr. Gabriel." She managed a nod, tucking a stray dark curl up and back. *Have you come to laugh at me?* "What a pleasant surprise."

The spark in his gaze told her the lie was perhaps audible. However, he merely shouldered the door aside and swept his hat from his dusty dark head, and his presence had the most astonishing effect.

Every little savage in the room quieted. The girls grinned and whispered; the boys stared with round eyes. The sheriff moved easily to the last row of benches, and loomed a trifle awkwardly over their occupants. "Thought I'd come out and visit." He halted, gazing at her most curiously. "First day of school and all."

And good heavens, but did the man sound *nervous*? Surely not. Catherine gathered the shreds of her temper and found herself standing at her desk, the attendance book lying open and the pen beside it. "Yes. Well, we have been having a most interesting time all seeking to speak at once and determining whether or not I am serious when I demand a certain measure of decorum."

"I see." Was that a faint smile playing around the corners of his mouth? She decided that it was, indeed. "I could tell 'em you're serious, ma'am, but I doubt they'd listen."

*They're listening now.* "I have not yet had the opportunity to inform them that any of their number who misbehaves shall be visiting *you*."

"Well now, that would fill the jail right up, wouldn't it? I might be forced to keep a few in the pigsty." And yes, that was a gleam in his gaze she had seen before in Robbie's.

He looked, now that she thought about it, downright *mischievous*.

One of the younger boys—it was the small blond miscreant who had been responsible for so much excitement on the occasion of her arrival, little Tommy Hammis—let out a small sound approximating a whimper. Jack Gabriel tucked his thumbs in his belt and stood, looming in a manner that suggested practice at using his size to enforce some manners upon the unruly.

*Take note of that, Catherine. Perhaps you can do likewise, even though you are not nearly as tall.*

"I certainly hope we may avoid that." Cat settled herself in the rickety, uncomfortable chair behind her desk, sweeping her skirts underneath her with a practiced motion. This brown stuff was the dowdiest and most severe dress she owned, but it was still of painfully higher quality than any rag the children possessed. She uncapped the ink, dipped her pen, and glanced up to find every eye in the schoolhouse upon her and the entire room disturbingly silent. "Now, let us be about our business. Mr. Gabriel, if you would be so good as to pause for a short while? When I have given my students their first small lesson, I should be glad of the opportunity to converse with you." *Please tell me you have business elsewhere, and merely came to make certain there are no corpses lurking under the floorboards.*

"I'm here all afternoon, ma'am."

She hoped the children could not sense the amusement loitering beneath Mr. Gabriel's straight mouth and dusty brow. Her own mouth twitched, traitorously, until she steeled herself and fixed the far-left student in the first row—a thin girl of no more than six with messily braided wheat-gold hair, the lone girl on the boys' side of the schoolhouse—with a steady, stern, but kind (she hoped) glance. "State your name please, young lady."

"M-M-M-M—" The child, blushing, stuttered, and a sudden swift guilt pierced Cat's chest.

"That's Mercy Gibbons, ma'am." Jack Gabriel's tone had gentled. "Right next to her is her brother Patrick. The Gibbonses are a mite shy."

"Very good." Catherine wrote, swiftly but neatly. "We shall continue down the row, and should you find it difficult to say your name, Mr. Gabriel will help." She did *not* bite her lip, though the urge was almost overwhelming. She did, however, glance at the girl and hazard a small smile. "The first day of school is always trying, I daresay."

"Reckon so, ma'am." The sheriff's tone still held that queer gentleness.

"Jordie Crane!" a gangly redhead next to Patrick Gibbons almost-shouted, fidgeting. "This is Sammy next to me. Samuel, I mean. Sam Thibodeau."

*Oh, dear God, how do I spell that?* She decided to merely approximate, for the moment. "Thank you, Mr. Crane. You will allow Mr. Thibodeau the chance to speak for himself next time."

All through that long syrup-slow afternoon, Jack Gabriel loomed in the back of the classroom, and even though Cat was heartily sick of him, she could not help but admit that his presence had a most sedative effect upon the most troublesome of her students.

Unfortunately, her nerves were a frayed mass by the time she consulted her mother's watch, securely fastened to the chain at her waist, and informed the willowy, dark-eyed young Zechariah Alfstrache that he had, by dint of being the least troublesome today, earned the right to ring the true-iron bell bolted next to the front door. Near to expiring with satisfaction, he did so, and even the awe of the sheriff could not keep the little savages from exploding into action. Ten long minutes later the schoolhouse was echoingly empty, and Cat sagged in her chair, one hand at her eyes.

Jack Gabriel's steps were measured and slow. "Well. Schoolin' seems as difficult as law-work."

*I rather doubt that, sir. For one thing, there are no flying bullets. Or undead.* "They are quite energetic," she managed, faintly. "Good heavens." *Still, it is very kind of you to say so.*

"Fetch you some water, ma'am?"

*How chivalrous.* "No, thank you. You are quite free to go, I simply wished you to frighten some of the savages into behaving."

"Had business, ma'am."

*Oh?* "And what would that be?"

"Makin' sure the schoolhouse is safe."

*Of course.* "Your diligence does you credit." Her eyes opened, and the outside world was an assault of color and light. "I think we may rest assured the environs are *quite* safe."

"Maybe, ma'am. You look...pale." The odd gentleness again. What on earth possessed him to speak so?

Cat straightened. *Come now, Catherine. You can certainly present a better form than this.* "It is very warm today." She checked the ink on the pages of her ledger—dry by now, certainly, but she breathed across the paper anyway, a slight charm to make certain sparking in the charged air. She closed the book with a decisive snap of binding and pages, and glanced up to find Mr. Gabriel looming over her desk instead of over the last row of benches, the star on his chest glinting sharply. Her stays were *most* uncomfortable, but she set her chin and glared at him. "I am *quite* well, sir. I am about to close the schoolhouse and go home, and—"

"I brought the wagon. You walked this morning." Flat statement of fact, and his pale gaze was most certainly amused, but also...what?

As a matter of fact, she had enjoyed a brisk walk in the morning crispness. She had also entirely misjudged the weather— why, it was not entirely clear, since it had been unbecomingly torrid every afternoon since her arrival in this benighted burg. "I am not certain it is quite *fitting*," she hedged, capping the ink with deft fingers and beginning the process of setting her desk to rights. "After all, Mr. Gabriel, I am—"

"About to faint." His hat dangled from his very capable left hand, leaving his right free to touch her desktop with its finger-tips, in a manner that seemed most improper. She could not think just why. "You're *very* pale, ma'am. I'll fetch you some water."

Cat summoned every inch of briskness she possessed. "Not necessary, thank you." But it was no use—the man was already halfway to the door, jamming his hat on his head as if he sus-pected something within the schoolhouse would dump ordure upon his thick skull.

Sighing, Cat set herself to closing up her desk. Each student's slate hung neatly at the back of their bench-seat on a special hook, and tonight she would make paper nameplates for each section of desk. Pride in their desks, Miss Bowdler was fond of saying, would lead to pride in their *persons*, and that would make them neat and respectable.

Catherine had a notion Miss Bowdler had perhaps not reck-oned on Damnation.

In any case, the environs were tolerably tidy by the time the sher-iff stamped back up the steps and into the schoolhouse. She was taking note of a slate that had disappeared—one of the Dalrymple sisters no doubt, who all seemed more interested in simpering and sneering than giving their names or possibly learning their letters—and a suspicious stain on the floor behind the third row of benches when he appeared, holding a dripping dipper and biting his lip with concentration as he negotiated the rough plank flooring.

Cat's own lips compressed, but not with disdain. He looked very much like one of her young students, especially since he was holding his hat as well as the dipper, and his dark hair had fallen forward across his forehead.

"Very kind of you." She accepted it, and the few swallows of mineral-tasting well water made her suddenly aware of just how thirsty she was. Her lower back had collected a small pond of sweat, and her stays dug so hard she had longing thoughts of them snapping and freeing her enough to take a decent breath.

"Pleasure to be of service, ma'am." His tone belied the words. In fact, Jack Gabriel looked...was it anger, sparking in those hazel eyes? His mouth was a thin line, and that odd gentle tone had vanished as if it never existed. "You should take more care."

*With what?* But she was far too grateful for the water, no matter that her stomach was uneasy at containing it. "If you have made certain the grounds hold no undead, *sir*, perhaps we may be on our way?"

It was, she reflected, a trifle unjustified. Still, the disapproval— for that, she had decided, was his expression—nettled her. It was unearned, and though she knew such was the lot of every woman, she certainly did not have to enjoy it—or give it shrift.

It didn't seem to make much impression on the man. "Best we lock up then, ma'am."

"Indeed." She handed the dipper back and set about putting on her gloves. The thought of loading her tired, sweat-soaked body with more cloth did not appeal, but a lady did not go outside without gloves, even in this benighted portion of the world. "If you would be so kind as to return that to the well, sir, I shall accomplish the rest."

His footsteps were very definite against the raw flooring, and Cat closed her eyes again for a moment. The problem that had been nipping and gnawing at her all day, even while she sought to retain some decorum and control in the face of what was apparently the Lost Tribe of Almanache, returned.

*The locket. How on earth am I going to...*

It was quite simple. She merely had to find a way to enter the pawnshop unremarked.

Or, she merely had to not care what people would think if they saw her entering such a place. It was not as if she had a Reputation to maintain, here at the end of the world. But still.

"Ma'am?" D—n the man. Would he grant her *no* relief from his presence?

"Very well," Cat said, as if he had sought to argue with her. She gathered her necessaries and swept down the central aisle, chin held high and her mother's Greet The Peasants smile frozen onto her features. "Thank you, sir."

# *Chapter Nine*

He began to get the idea the marm didn't like him.

Oh, she was perfectly polite. It was *Mr. Gabriel* this and *Sir* that and *Sheriff* the other. But a woman had a hundred little ways to let a man know he was not welcome, and the damn Boston miss had a hundred and one. There was freezing him with a single glance when he showed up at the kitchen door, and Li Ang's sly little smile. Not to mention Miss Barrowe shooing him out of the damn building the second day of school. Nevermind that she obviously had precious little in the way of experience for keeping the little 'uns from mischief; she was bound and determined to do things according to her own fancy. She didn't even ask him about the gate in front of her house, just engaged Carter, that damnfool, to repaint it and take care of a squeak in the hinges.

It was a *perfectly* good gate. He'd hung it himself.

After two weeks of being snubbed by the miss, as well as riding the circuit not just before dawn and after dusk but at high noon in the heat, his temper was none too smooth. He just grunted when Russ Overton asked him if it was *really* necessary to ride the circuit when the chartermage could simply *feel* the charter was intact, and there hadn't been another irruption since.

The card games above the Lucky Star were no good, either. For the life of him, Gabe could not stop losing, and *that* was enough to make him wish he had never seen this town. Dr. Howard had even asked him, with a sly chuckle, if he needed a charming to repair his luck.

The old coot.

So when the woman came sashaying into the jail early Sunday morn, he was already in a bad mood. It didn't help that it was Mercy Tiergale, tarted up in what might've been her Sunday best sprigged muslin.

That is, if a whore ever went to church. On the other hand, there wasn't much of a preacher in Damnation. Maybe the Boston miss was scandalized by the lack of a man of God around here. Some of the men read from the Book, some of the women organized hymns, and that was about it. Letitia Granger often professed herself absolutely horrified and trumpeted her intention to bring a holy man from a city somewhere.

He wished her luck. As long as it wasn't a Papist who might recognize what Jack was—what he *had* been.

*If it is, I'll just move on.* Gabe reached to touch his hatbrim, but the hat was on the peg by the door. His boots were caked with Damnation's yellow dust, but he had them propped on the desk anyway. There were two jail cells; one held a snoring drunk— Rob Gaiterling, who needed a bender about once a month and went crazy when he got it—and the other stood open and empty, its walls scratched with unfinished charter-symbols and finished graffiti, the iron of the doors glowing dully with imbued mancy. "Miz Tiergale."

Daylight showed the beginning of ravages to her sweet round face, but her chin was high and her dark hair was elaborately curled under an imitation of a fashionable bonnet. He'd been seeing them more and more about town this last week, maybe in response to the schoolmarm.

An inward wince. Maybe there was a charm to get the image of Miss Barrowe, terrified and pale, breaking her pretty parasol over a walking corpse's head, out of his brain. If one didn't exist, maybe he should *make* one. He could turn in some more hours laboring over Russ's charter-dictionaries; unfortunately, whatever black mancy Salt had been working, there was nothing in Russ's small collection that could shed light on it.

"Morning, Sheriff." Mercy's shoulders were rigid, her hands clasped together as if she was six again, repeating her charterchism. "I have business."

*No doubt.* "Yes ma'am?" Was Tilson beating his girls again? Or was there a deeper trouble to add to the mess inside Gabe's head?

He might almost welcome some more trouble, if only to keep him occupied and away from brooding over a silly nose-high Boston miss.

"I aim to visit the schoolmarm before the churching." Mercy took a deep breath, and high color flushed her round cheeks. She was popular among the Lucky Star's patrons, most of whom liked a woman with a little heft. "I aim to have you go with me, to keep it all respectable-like. None of the gossipies in town are like to go, and I aim to have the marm listen to what I have to say."

*That's a lot of aimin' you're fixed on.* "She seems the listenin' type." Gabe got his feet under him. "What kind of business, if I may inquire?"

"*Personal* business, Sheriff." Mercy nodded once, sharply, and that was that. "Not saloon business."

In other words, Tilson didn't need to know. Gabe thought it over. Well, what could it hurt? Besides, there was his curiosity, which had perked its ears something awful. "Yes ma'am."

The saloon girl's face eased, and her earrings—bits of paste glass, with tiny charms flashing in their depths, probably to keep the dye in her hair—danced. Her eyebrows were coppery, and there was a fading set of bruises ringing her neck. She'd curled some of her hair over to hide them, but there was no hiding some things. "Much obliged, Sheriff. If you want..."

There were times when he was mighty tempted, true. "No ma'am, thank you ma'am," he said, maybe a little *too* quickly.

The saloon girl's face brightened with an honest smile, and Gabe dropped his gaze as he stepped past her to rescue his hat.

Women. How could a man ever figure? He'd visited one or two of the Star's girls, when it got to be too much. They were uncomplicated. They didn't twist a man up inside.

And they were welcoming, too. What more did a man need?

His mood had just turned a little blacker, and Gabe scowled. He offered the girl his arm as they stepped outside, and at least she accepted.

Mercy was silent the entire way, her steps light and delicate. They kept to the back row running parallel to the main street, their only witnesses some chickens and stray dogs, as well as wet washing flapping on lines, crackling with dust-shake charms. And they reached Miss Barrowe's trim little cottage just as the marm herself, smartly dressed in a soft peach frock that made her glow in the morning sunshine, stepped out her front door with yet another parasol, this one bearing a ruff of soft scalloped lace.

She was obviously bound for church.

His throat tightened. His face was a mask. The gate didn't squeak, but the painting on it was a little slapdash.

Served her right.

Miss Barrowe didn't seem surprised in the least. "Sheriff. How pleasant. Are you attending church today?"

He had to clear his windpipe before he could say "No ma'am," with anything resembling his usual tone. "Miss Barrowe, may I present Miss Mercy Tiergale? She's some words for you."

"I see. How do you do?" And the marm, pretty as you please, offered her hand with a smile that, for some reason, made Gabe's chest even tighter.

"Ma'am." Mercy was back to flour-pale, and she shook the marm's hand once, limply. A tense silence rose, dust whisking along the street on a brisk fresh breeze. It would be hot later. Finally, Mercy swallowed visibly. "How do."

Miss Barrowe glanced quickly at Gabe, her expression

unreadable. "Where are my manners? Do come in. May I offer you some tea? I know Mr. Gabriel prefers coffee—"

"No ma'am." Mercy's fingers tightened on his arm. A spate of words came out in a rush, like a flash flood up in the hills. "I aim to have you listen. We—some of the girls and me—we wants our letters. I mean, we want to do some larnin'. *Book* larnin', and figures." The saloon girl freed one hand, digging in her skirt pocket. "We can pay you. We want it all respectable-like." A handful of rolled-together bills came up, and Gabe noticed a stain on Mercy's gloved wrist. Looked like whiskey.

Maybe she'd needed it to brace her. He kept his mouth shut, and winced again when he thought of Tils's likely reaction to this. And the money—often, saloon girls didn't see actual cash. More of Mercy's nervousness seemed downright reasonable, now.

Miss Barrowe did not even bat one sweet little eyelash. "I see. Please, Miss Tiergale, put that away and come inside. As I am engaged to teach in this town and my salary is paid by the town itself, I see no need for you to—"

"We're saloon girls, ma'am." Flung like a challenge. "Six of us. In the afternoons before the real drinkin' starts, that's when we have time."

Miss Barrowe nodded briskly. "Then after I finish with my other pupils, I shall be glad to help you and your fellow...ladies educate yourselves. Are you quite certain you won't come in and have some tea while we discuss this?"

"No ma'am." Mercy's arm came up, rigid, and she proffered the bills. "Wouldn't want you to miss church. Do you take our money, and I'll be on my way."

Miss Barrowe's glance flickered to Gabe's face again. Her curls were expertly arranged, and that dress looked soft enough for angels to nest in. A faint breath of rosewater reached him, under the tang of cigar smoke and spilled drink, sawdust and sweat from Mercy. He was suddenly very aware that Mercy had his arm, and that Miss Barrowe might draw a conclusion or two from that.

*I don't care.* But it had a hollow ring, and it was maybe the wrong time for Jack Gabriel to start lying to himself.

"I believe it might be best for Sheriff Gabriel to hold your money." Miss Barrowe straightened slightly, her shoulders going back. A touch of lace around the neckline of her dress was incredibly distracting; he found he couldn't look away. "You shall engage my services as a teacher for a certain length of time— a month, perhaps? Then we shall again address the question of payment, if you are satisfied with my methods and your progress." A slight curve of her lips. "That would make every aspect of this eminently respectable, since Mr. Gabriel is a representative of the town that engaged me."

*Well, now.* "Seems a right fair idea," he offered, but neither woman appeared to pay much heed. Mercy's lips moved slightly as she worked this around in her head, and Miss Barrowe held the saloon girl's gaze. Invisible woman-signals flashed between them like charmgraph dots and dashes, and finally Mercy relaxed a trifle.

"I b'lieve that'll do." She let loose of Gabe's arm long enough to roll the wad of bills more tightly, and offered it to him. "Will you hold this, Gabe?"

"Be right pleased to," he mumbled. Why were his cheeks hot?

"Very well." Miss Barrowe closed her front door with a small, definite *snick*. "Are you accompanying me to church, Miss Tiergale?"

"No ma'am." Mercy stared at the ground now, Miss Barrowe's dainty boots clicking on the steps as she picked her way down to the garden path. The marm opened her parasol with an expert flicker and flutter, and—surprisingly enough—offered her own arm to the saloon girl. "It ain't proper. Leastways—"

"That," the schoolmarm said decisively, "is a great shame. Would you care to walk with me at least as far as the Lucky Star? I believe it is upon my route."

Mercy almost flinched. "No ma'am. There'd just be trouble if...well."

"Don't you worry." Gabe's cheeks would *not* cool down. He

had the attention of both women, now, and he hadn't the faintest idea why he'd spoken up. "Tils gives you trouble, you come right on over to me."

Mercy actually laughed, cupping one gloved hand over her mouth. There was, however, little of merriment in the sound. She knew as well as he did that he couldn't settle down in the Star and stare Tils into keeping his temper permanently. "Mighty kind of you, Gabe. I'd best be on my way. Thank you, ma'am. When are we fixing to start?"

"Tomorrow is Monday." Miss Barrowe now looked faintly perplexed, a small line between her eyebrows. "If that suits you, and the other ladies."

"Suits us fine, ma'am. Mornin'." And with that, Mercy Tiergale turned on one worn-down bootheel and strode off, her skirt snapping a bit as the morning breeze freshened.

He searched for something to say. The parasol had dipped, so Miss Barrowe's face was shadowed. He doubted her expression would be anything but polite and cool. "Right kind of you, ma'am."

She was silent for a long moment. He could have kicked himself. Should have followed Mercy and not given the miss a chance to snub him.

"Is there likely to be trouble arising from this, Mr. Gabriel?" The lacy stuff shivered as she adjusted her parasol, and the honest worry in her clear dark eyes pinched at him.

Just why, though, he couldn't say.

"Not if I can help it." His jaw set. "You just settle your mind, Miss Barrowe."

"I don't mean for me," she persisted. "For Miss Tiergale. She seemed...concerned."

"I said to settle your mind." He half-turned, offered his arm without much hope. "Walk you to church, ma'am?"

Her gloved hand stole forward, crept into the crook of his elbow like it belonged there. "Does that mean I shouldn't worry for Miss Tiergale, as you will assist her and her...compatriots?"

"It means I can handle one whorehouse manager, ma'am." As soon as it left his lips he regretted himself. "Beg pardon."

Her lips had pressed together. Her free hand hovered near her mouth, but her eyes were wide and sparkling. She composed herself, and her smile was almost as bright as Damnation's morning sun as she turned slightly, her skirt brushing his knee as she leaned ever so slightly on him. "Indeed. I have faith in your ability, sir. Forgive my repeating myself, but will you be attending church today?"

He thought of saying he had pressing business, but it seemed all good sense had deserted him. The pressure of her fingers inside his elbow was a popcharm, jolting up all the way to his shoulder. "Yes ma'am."

*Oh, Hell.*

# Chapter Ten

Cat rubbed delicately at the skin about her eyes. It was drowsy-hot, especially in the schoolroom, and the scratching on the board was enough to set even a saint's teeth on edge. Cecily Dalrymple was writing out *I will not throw ink*, her fair blonde face set in mutinous agony. The rest of the children, temporarily chastened, bent over their slates, and Cat took a deep breath. "Once more," she said, patiently, and little Patrick Gibbons almost stuttered as he recited.

"A...B...C..."

"Very good," she encouraged, ignoring the fidgets. The youngest students chorused with Patrick, raggedly but enthusiastically. They made their way through the alphabet, and Cat's warm glow of entirely justified (in her opinion) satisfaction was marred only by the back row's restlessness.

Miss Bowdler's books were very useful, but Cat had learned more applicable skills following her mother about on the endless round of charity work a Barrowe-Browne was obliged to undertake. Not to mention the example of one of her governesses—a certain Miss Ayre, quiet and plain but with a steely tone that had made even Robbie sit up and take notice on those few occasions her patience had worn thin.

It was Miss Ayre's example she found herself drawing on most frequently, especially as every child in the schoolroom was dismally untaught. Ignorance and undirected energy conspired to make them fractious, but they were on the whole more than willing to work, and work *hard*, once she gave them a direction. Perhaps it was the novelty of her presence.

Still, there were troubles. The Dalrymple girls, for one. Turning those two hoydens into respectable damsels was perhaps beyond Cat's power, but she had an inkling of a plan. The older girl's longing glances at the sad, shrouded pianoforte had not passed unnoticed, and Cat suspected that with the offer of lessons she would have a valuable carrot to dangle before the haughty creature.

"That is *quite* enough," she said sternly. Mancy sparked on her fingers, and there was a crackle. Little Tommy Beaufort let out a garbled sound and thumped back into his seat. "Mr. Beaufort, since you are so eager, stand and recite your alphabet instead of tossing rubbish at your classmates. Begin."

"A...B...C..."

Hoofbeats outside. *That* explained the restlessness of the back rows—they had heard the noise before she did. Was it Mr. Gabriel again? Whoever it was seemed in quite a hurry, but she held Tommy to his recitation, nodding slightly.

The horse did not pass the schoolhouse. *Who could that be?* But she stayed where she was, standing beside her desk, and when Tommy finished she gave him a tight smile. "Very good. Now, first form, take your slates out and begin copying from the top line on the board—*A fox is quick*. Second form—"

Thundering bootsteps, and the door was flung open. Cat blinked.

It was Mr. Tilson, the owner of the Lucky Star. She had seen him in church just yesterday, nodding along to Mr. Vancey the cartwright's stumbling reading of the Book. Mr. Gabriel had sat next to her, his hands on his knees and his face as dull and unresponsive as she had ever seen it.

Mr. Tilson was sweating, and had obviously ridden hard. Foam and dust hung on him in spatters, and his suit coat was sadly rumpled. He was red-faced, too, and Cat stared at him curiously. His hat was cocked sideways, and the slicked-down strands of his dark hair were dangerously disarranged.

"*You!*" He pointed at Cat, and spat the word. "*You.* I've words for you, *Miss.*"

*What on earth?* She drew herself up. The children had frozen, including Cecily Dalrymple at the board. Their eyes were wide and round, and quite justifiable irritation flashed under Cat's skin. "Mr. Tilson. You shall not shout indoors, sir. It sets a bad example."

That brought him up short. The redness of his cheeks and the ugly flush on his neck was not merely from the heat. It was also, Cat suspected, pure choler.

He actually spluttered a little, and her fingers found the yard-stick laid across her desk. "Step outside, sir. I shall deal with you in a moment, once I have finished giving the second and third forms their lessons. Miss Dalrymple, you may return to your seat; that is quite enough."

"I ain't gonna be put off—" Mr. Tilson started, and Cat searched for her mother's voice. It came easily, for once.

"*Sir.*" Every speck of dust in the room flashed under her tone. "You *shall not* disturb my students further. Step outside. And do close the door properly, the wind and heat are very bad today."

His jaw worked, but he seemed to finally realize the eyes of every child in the room were upon him. He backed up a single step, his gaze purely venomous, and whirled, banging the door shut.

Cat's knuckles ached, gripping the wooden yardstick. Her heart pounded. She tilted her chin slightly, an ache beginning between her shoulder blades.

*I can handle a whorehouse manager*, Mr. Gabriel had said. Surely a Barrowe-Browne could do no less. At least it was not a shambling corpse at the door.

That was an entirely unwelcome thought, and she did her best to put it away. "Second form, take your slates and solve the row of sums under first form's line. Third form—" *All three of you, who can puzzle out a word or two.* "Take out your primers and occupy yourselves with page six."

"Yes ma'am," no few of them chorused, and Cecily Dalrymple actually sat down without flouncing, for once. Cat suspected she might regret showing leniency, but there was nothing for it.

She passed down the aisle, stepping over the cleansed patch where the corpse had landed—there was no evidence of it on the floorboards, but she still disliked setting her feet in that vicinity—and braced herself for whatever unpleasantness was about to ensue.

*"You."* Tilson pointed a stubby finger at her. "What are you playing at? Them whores don't need to read!"

*So that's it.* Her mother's voice still served her well—the exact tone Frances Barrowe-Browne would use in dealing with an overeager gentleman, or a brute of a salesman who sought to engage her custom. "You will adopt a civilized tone in speaking to me, sir." Cat drew in a sharp soundless breath. Dust whirled along the dry track serving as a road, and the horse Tilson had arrived on hung its head near the trough, its sides lathered. "And your horse requires some care."

"God*damn* the horse, and God damn you, too! Civilized tone my *ass*. What'n hell you think you're doing, teaching whores to read? I won't have it!"

She still held the yardstick, and the image of cracking him across the knuckles with it was satisfying in its own way. Cat gazed at him for a few long moments, her face set, one eyebrow arched in imitation of her mother's fearsome You Are Not In Good Form expression.

When she was certain she had his attention, and further certain that he was beginning to feel faintly ridiculous, she tapped the yardstick against the schoolhouse's ramshackle porch. The shade here was most welcome, though she quailed a bit inwardly at the thought of the afternoon walk back to her little cottage. "The next moment you use such language, sir, this conversation is over. Now, am I to understand you have an objection to some of my students?"

"Your—" He visibly checked himself. "They ain't gonna read! You just tell them that!"

"I was engaged to see to the education of those in this town." Dangerously quiet, and Cat's back ached. "Those in your employ are not heathen slaves, sir; they are members of this town and, as such, are entitled to my services. Additionally"—she overrode the beginning of his bluster, and it was Miss Ayre's example she drew upon now—"I am a charter-free Christian woman, *sir*, and you do not have any leave or right to speak to me in this manner. You may remove yourself from my schoolhouse immediately. If you do not, I shall be forced to seek a remedy against you by applying to the forces of law and justice in this town."

"What, Gabe? He ain't mixed up in this. You mark my word, you little bitch—"

"Good day, sir." She turned on her heel.

Tilson took a step forward, and his broad, callused hand closed around her arm, squeezing brutally. "I am *talkin'* to you, you little—"

The yardstick snapped up, its tip crackling and spitting sparks. She meant to merely startle him into dropping her arm, and heard Robbie's voice inside her head. *Don't let them manhandle you, little sister. That's what a Practicality's for.*

Instead, it cracked across Mr. Tilson's face as he sought to shake her, pulling her toward the three rude stairs leading off the porch. The mancy popped, and blood spattered. She recoiled, his hand falling away from her aching arm, and it was as if Robbie were next to her. The image of the locket in the pawnshop window rose, glittering coldly, and she realized that in this town, she could perhaps sally into such a place without worrying overmuch about such a thing as Reputation.

Still, she was alone with this man, with only a group of

children inside, and Reputation was thin tissue indeed to shield her from violence.

Perhaps she should have been more . . . discreet? Passive? What was the proper word?

The saloon owner tripped, tumbled down the steps, and landed sprawled in the dust. Cat found words, harsh and rude as a lady's must never be. Still, they fell out of her mouth before she could halt them.

"Do not *dare* to lay hands upon me in such a manner, you foul-mouthed *brute!*" She hit a pitch just under "fishwife's scream" and for once, did not wish to writhe in embarrassment. The yardstick fizzed with sparks, and she held it in both hands, much in the manner of a sword.

He scrambled to his feet, dust rising in puffs and golden veils. Cat's heart thundered, her palms sweating, and a curl had fallen in her face. The children had probably heard her. Gossip would run through the town, and—

*You're here to find Robbie. Or find what has happened to him. This brute does not matter one whit.*

And yet Miss Tiergale had been very frightened. Almost trembling. If she lived with *this* man, Cat could see why.

And the knowledge made her sick all the way through. Another session of heaving off the school's porch could not be borne either, so she merely set her jaw and swallowed the bitterness.

Mr. Tilson pointed one thick, trembling finger. "I'll get you. So help me, I'll *get* you."

"Your threats are as ugly as your character." She pointed the yardstick, a single star of light hurtfully bright at its tip. The wood was scorched, and Tilson's face was bleeding, one eye already puffed shut. The blood was shockingly bright in all the dun and dust. "Do not *ever* come near me again, sir. Or I shall hand you more of the same."

He blundered back for his horse, and Cat stood watching as he spurred the beast unmercifully. She tried to tell herself it was because she wished to make certain he would not return and possibly make another scene in front of her students.

In reality, however, it was because she was trembling, and her stomach cramped. She watched the man on the horse recede into the distance toward the smoke-smudge of the bulk of Damnation, and her mouth was full of thick, foul fear.

*If I were not such a lady, I would spit.* A lady did not smash a man in the face with mancy and a yardstick, however.

*I would do it again*, she realized. *Most assuredly I would.*

*I would even enjoy it.*

# Chapter Eleven

As soon as he stepped into the Lucky Star, Gabe knew something was amiss. The hush was instant, and he didn't need to see Mercy Tiergale's badly bruised cheek to tell Tils was unhappy. It wasn't like him to tap a popular girl in the face where it would show, either.

It was midafternoon, so the serious drinking hadn't started yet, and wouldn't for hours. The card games were going full-force though, and Mo Jackson was banging on the tinny little piano, waltzing his way through "She Was A Charming Filly" and humming off-key. Mercy made a beeline for Gabe, and he barely had time to lay his littlebit on the counter and accept a shot of something passing for whiskey before she was at his elbow.

"He left an hour ago," she said, and the bruise was fresh red-purple, glaring and still puffing up. Her breasts swelled almost out of the dress—well, *dress* wasn't quite the word, it was just a scrap of corset and lace, and low. "Gabe..."

"Tils?" He nodded as the 'tender, weedy Tass Coy, slapped his hand over the bit and made it vanish. Coy's jaw was a mess; you could clearly see where the horse's hoof had dug in and shattered bone. Not even the doctor could do much for it, and Russ Overton's mancy didn't extend to fleshstitching.

"He said he was gonna talk to *her.*" It was a strained whisper. "I sent Billy to the jail, but you warn't there."

Coy watched this, his brown eyes neutral. He plucked at one of his braces with long sensitive fingers, and turned away very slowly. There was nothing wrong with his ears.

*No, I was ridin' the circuit, dammit.* Gabe's chest knew before the rest of him. A cold, hard lump settled right behind his breastbone. "Tilson's visiting the marm?"

"He said he was gonna ride right out to that schoolhouse and teach her not to interfere." Mercy's hands clutched into fists. "Gabe...now don't be hasty."

*Hasty is one thing I'm not.* "Tilson. Visiting the schoolhouse." He repeated it slowly, just to make certain he hadn't misheard. "When did he leave, now?"

"An hour, maybe more—Gabe, I—"

He bolted the shot. No use in wasting liquor, even if it was terrible. When he cracked the glass back down on the sloping counter, Mercy cringed like a whipped dog. Did she think *he* was going to tap her, too?

"God*damn.*" He headed for the swinging doors, but he didn't have to take more than two steps before they whipped open as if disgorging a flood. Emmet Tilson stamped through, looking halfway to Hell. Blood and dust crusted his face, and one eye was swollen shut. It looked much worse than what he'd inflicted on Mercy, and Gabe stopped dead.

*What the Hell?* His jaw felt suspiciously loose, and the way his hands were tense and tight-knotted, Gabe was suddenly afraid he was going to break a finger or two.

Tils saw him a bare half-second later, and stopped dead as well. He wasn't wearing a gun, which was a piece of good fortune, because Gabe saw the saloon owner's hand twitch, and almost drew himself.

*Now, don't lose your temper*, something inside him was trying to say. Oddly, it sounded a little like Annie, and a little like an archly amused schoolmarm.

There was a general shuffle as everyone in the saloon noticed the two of them eyeing each other like rattlesnakes, and moved out of the way.

Gabe decided to be mannerly. Why not? "Afternoon, Tilson."

The man twitched again, and Gabe was mighty glad there was no gun on Tils's hip. On the other hand, the saloon owner had gone out to the schoolhouse without an iron? That was very unlike him.

Maybe he thought Miss Barrowe wasn't worth shooting. Course, Tilson preferred to talk to a woman with his fists.

A spike of heat went through Gabe. He realized, miserably, that he was not about to keep his temper. Especially if the whorehouse manager said one, small, *wrong* word.

"Sheriff." Brittle, but at least Tilson wasn't shouting. "My office. *Now.*"

*Since when do you order me around like one of your whores?* "Beg your pardon?" He drawled it nice and slow, as if he didn't understand. Give the man some time to reconsider his tone, as it were.

The garish blood and dust all over Tils was thought-provoking. The cold was all through Gabe now, except for that hot spike of rage in his chest, beating like a heart. He hadn't felt that heat in so long, it was almost comforting.

Whatever was in his expression made the saloon owner back up a step, his spurs jangling a discordant note against the worn wooden floor. If Gabe were still of the Faith, now would have been the moment for him to punish the man for a transgression real or imagined.

But that part of him was long gone, wasn't it? And thinking about its loss was not guaranteed to keep his temper, either.

"I mean, ah…" Tilson coughed, rubbed at his swollen lips with one hand. But slowly. "I mean, Gabe, we've got business. Care to step into my office?"

*That's better. But you're still likely to bite. Cowards always are.* "I ain't aware of any business between us, Tilson. Unless you *want* there to be." It was hard, but he glanced aside at Mercy Tiergale, whose hands were clutched at her mouth. "Miss Mercy. Don't you and the girls have an appointment?"

The silence was so thick you could pour it into a cup. Tils stiffened as if Gabe had just slapped him. The doors squeaked on their hinges, and the wind on Damnation's main street was a low moan as wheels rumbled and horses neighed outside.

A susurrus behind him as he returned his gaze to Tilson. "You look like hell, Emmet."

"Tangled with a she-cat." Tils straightened. The tension leached out of the air, and Mo brought his hands down on the keys again. The tinny crash almost made him jump.

"Is that so." *Looks like she tangled you but good.*

"Gabe…" Mercy sounded as if she'd been punched. Maybe she had. Or maybe she found it difficult to breathe. Mo noodled through the first few bars of "My Old Mother Is Watching," and Gabe wondered if it was the man's comment on proceedings, so to speak.

"You just run along now." Gabe said it evenly, slowly. "Take the girls with you. I'll be along to see all's right."

Tils seemed to have a bit of a problem with this. "You can't—"

"You want to think right careful before you finish that sentence, Tilson." *And so help me God, if you hurt her, I'm going to make you pay.*

It was an uncomfortable thought. He didn't even *like* the marm; she was a prissy little miss, and he had no need to be involving himself in this trouble. It was too late, though. He was well and truly involved, because he had opened his fool mouth.

And besides, he was lying to himself again. *A knight of the Order must never commit that sin, of untruth in his own soul.* The smell of incense rose in his memory, the moment of struggle before the altar before he had turned away, leaving his brothers praying in their plainsong chant, his hands fists as they were now and a single thought burning in his brain.

*Annie.*

Except it wasn't her he was thinking of now, was it.

The saloon owner subsided. But the ratty little gleam in his eye told Gabe there would be trouble later.

*Oh, damn.*

The news had spread like wildfire. By the time Gabe arrived at the schoolhouse the Granger wagon was there too, and he winced again.

Maybe this would all blow over. Tils might not use his fists too much on the girls now that Gabe was involved, but there were a hundred other ways he could make their lives even more miserable. And the miss might find that teaching a bunch of saloon girls was not as easy as the little 'uns—though Gabe didn't know how *easy* the little 'uns were, rightly. About all he knew was that *he* wouldn't care to be trapped in a schoolroom with them all day.

He took his time pumping fresh water for the horses. The sun beat down unmercifully, and even though the water was brown and the bottom of the trough none too clean, he still thought longingly of just sinking into it and letting the entire damn situation play itself out with no help from one tired, head-buzzing Jack Gabriel.

He had just finished pumping and settled his hat more firmly when Letitia Granger sailed out of the schoolhouse door, her bosom—the only soft thing on that big bony body—lifted high with indignation and plump with starched ruffles. The rest of her was in severe dark stuff, and she looked so rigid with disapproval he was surprised her skirts didn't creak.

She sallied down the stairs, head held high and the poor feathers on her hat hanging on for dear life. *"Sheriff!"* she crowed, her lips so pinched the word was a hoarse croak.

*Oh, Lord.* He tried his best not to wince yet again. "Afternoon, Mrs. Granger."

*"Do you know what she's done?"* Granger was fairly apoplectic. Her color was a deep brick-red, and strings of her graying hair stuck to her forehead, wet with sweat. She looked fit to expire right there on the steps. *"Do you?"*

He decided a measure of strategic befuddlement might work. "Last I heard, she was teachin'."

"There are *unrespectable women* in there, Sheriff! On the very seats our children...the seats..." Letitia Granger's jaw worked.

He tipped his hat back a little, scratched at the creased band of sweat on his forehead. He took his time with it, as if he was stupid-puzzled. "Well, where else should she teach 'em? At the church?"

*That* was probably the wrong thing to say, for Mrs. Granger's eyes flashed and she sailed across the yard, dust sparking and crackling in her wake. She was so het up she was throwing mancy even though she had no Practicality, and Gabe at least had the comfort of knowing he wasn't the only one the Boston miss had tied up in a tangle there was no working free of.

"It's *unchristian!*" The woman stopped, her hands fisting at her sides. She probably packed a punch like a donkey's kick under all that starch.

"Well, they ain't no Magdala nuns, I'll allow that." He nodded, slowly. "But they paid her fair and square, and I can't find no law against it."

"Law? *Law?* It ain't a question of law, Sheriff, and—"

"It ain't?" He hoped she couldn't tell the surprise on his face was a mockery. "Why are you all het up, then? And squawkin' at *me*?"

She looked about ready to have a fit right there. "*The town shall hear of this!*" she hissed. "Do you know what she told me? That teaching was *her* business, and she thanked me kindly to keep myself out of it. Why, *I am on the Committee! We'll see her out!*"

*That collection of biddies can't even decide what color the Town Hall should be painted, let alone where it should be built and who's going to pay for it.* But they had put together the subscription to pay Miss Barrowe.

He'd thought about that on the ride here. If the miss didn't watch her step, she could be sent back to Boston without a Reference.

Somehow, he thought Miss Barrowe might not mind as much

as Granger thought. She'd obviously come from money and manners, which was just another puzzle about the girl. What was she doing *here*?

*What did you come here to escape, Mr. Gabriel?*

"Now, how would we get another marm out here?" he wondered, openly. "Was hard enough to get this 'un. Been weeks now, and she's at least kept some of the little 'uns out of trouble." He scratched at his forehead some more. "Why not just let her be?"

Granger's lips trembled. For a moment he thought the woman might actually weep. Instead, she stuck her nose in the air and sashayed past him. He hurried to help her up into her wagon, and she snatched her hand back as soon as she had hefted her bulk up as if his heathen fingers singed. The horses weren't happy to leave the trough, but they obeyed. Her wagon set off down the road for town, raising a roostertail of golden dust, and Gabe let out a sigh that threatened to blow his hat off his head.

*I should have just never gotten out of bed this dawnin'.*

The steps creaked under him, and he gave the door a mannerly tap. He opened it to find six women sitting straight-backed and uncomfortable in long desks just slightly too small, the bottom of the tabletops actually hitting their knees. Miss Barrowe, smoothing back a dark curl that looked bent on escaping, stood tense by the slate board, her fingers almost white-knuckled around a yardstick that vibrated with hurtful mancy discharged not too long ago.

*Bet that's what she hit Tils with.* The sudden certainty made him want to smile, but he banished the notion, reaching up to take his hat off. No reason not to act proper. Besides, it gave him a chance to compose his expression, so to speak.

"Sheriff Gabriel." Low, and clear. "What is it?"

Given the day she'd had, he was probably lucky she didn't say anything worse. "Just checkin' to see all's well, ma'am."

"You may sit quietly." She pointed with the stick, at the very back row. "We are rather busy."

"Yes ma'am." He settled himself into a seat.

Mercy Tiergale hunched her shoulders as she bent over a slate she shared with Anna Dayne. Dark-eyed Belle and sharp-nosed blonde Trixie sat shoulder to shoulder, and the youngest of Tils's girls, Anamarie, hunched next to tall rangy Carlota like she expected Tils to come thundering in any minute. Lace shawls more fit for the saloon than for walking around town, the comb in Carlota's hair glimmering mellow in the late-afternoon light, Mercy's cheap paste earrings swinging gaudily. They were a sorry picture indeed, and as out of place as a sheep in a pulpit.

But Miss Barrowe continued, in the same clear tone, patiently tracing each letter on the board. By the end of the session, the women could write their names on the slates, which Miss Barrowe collected and locked in her desk. "To keep them from misadventure at a man's hands," she said grimly, and the ripple that went through the saloon girls, barely controlled, reminded Gabe of a flock of minnows in a clear stream.

"Very good," she said, standing before them with her hands clasped. "You are all quick, and docile. You are capable of being educated. I shall see you tomorrow, then. You are dismissed, ladies."

They sat and blinked at her for a few moments. The silence was thick, and Miss Barrowe's gaze flickered to Gabe in the back of the room. He should have been in town, looking after whatever mayhem the end of the afternoon would bring, or watching Freedman Salt's door, or any of a hundred other tasks. But here he sat, cramped in a desk the likes of which he hadn't seen since seminary after the orphanage, and he stared at the schoolmarm hungrily.

Mercy let out a disbelieving half-laugh. Carlota breathed a profane term Miss Barrowe pretended not to hear.

Gabe unfolded himself slowly, and he found himself the object of every gaze instead of just the marm's. "Take you back to town, ladies," he said, and wondered why Belle and Anamarie blushed, and Mercy's laugh seemed more genuine this time. Miss Barrowe's smile was like sunlight, but she suddenly looked very... fragile.

"Thank you, Sheriff." Prim as always, but high color in her cheeks. The pulse in her throat leapt, and found an answer in his own chest.

It was at that moment Jack Gabriel admitted to himself that he was in deep water, and sinking fast. He couldn't say he minded.

But Miss Barrowe might.

# Chapter Twelve

Her mother would be scandalized. Her father would be amused, but perhaps also scandalized. If either of them were alive, instead of dead of Spanish flu, she would not *be* here.

But Cat could not find it in her heart to set her course differently.

The charm-hot water in the bathing-tub rippled as she stretched a foot up, her toes spreading as she relieved them of the pressure of being crammed into a point-toe boot all day. Her charing-charm was skinwarm, resting quiescent against her breastbone.

*I struck a man in the face today. Mother would simply die.*

Rather too late for that, though. Her face scrunched up, and she slid down farther in the rude copper tub.

Robbie was all she had left, other than her sufficiency. There was his inheritance, the bulk of their parents' estate; but she had been left quite enough to do as she pleased for the rest of her life, or to make a fine marriage if she wished. Her father's arrangements, as befitted a practical man of the Barrowe-Browne clans, had been most thorough.

She could perhaps wish Robbie were as practical. He might not have gone haring off into the Westron Wastes seeking adventure, if...

She moved again, restlessly. It would simply spoil her bath if she continued in this manner, and after today's events she rather thought she deserved a small bit of relaxation.

A globe of heat from the stove downstairs drifted into the narrow, closet-sized water-room. It hesitated, but Cat's fingers flicked, and she brought it down to meld with the bathwater's trembling surface, sighing with pleasure as it hissed. The water sent up trails and curls of steam as she shifted carefully again.

*Think of something useful. Or if you cannot, Catherine, think on something pleasing.*

There was little pleasure to be had in her reflections, however. Mr. Tilson was a brute, but he was also a figure of some importance in the town. Mrs. Granger, almost apoplectic at the thought of Ladies Of A Certain Class sitting at desks reserved for the children of the hame, was a far greater worry. It was such women who were the keepers of Reputation, and Cat's had perhaps taken rather a beating.

Still, what was she to do? Allowing Mr. Tilson's threats to set her course was unworthy of a Barrowe-Browne. And Cat could not hie herself into the saloon and hold reading classes *there*. Nor was there a space in town likely to grant her leave to do so, now that Mrs. Granger was involved. Her own parlour might have sufficed, but... that would not *do*. Teaching such ladies to read and figure was a Charitable Act; inviting them into one's home for more than a cup of tea was out of the question.

At least the sheriff had not made any trouble. Rather, he seemed to have quite an interest in the literacy of the saloon girls. Perhaps he was... involved? Miss Tiergale had clung to his arm, certainly. This was the Wild Westron; perhaps such things were not frowned upon.

In any case, he was a man, and could do as he pleased.

*May I not do as I please, too?*

No, she could not. Yet certain things that were impossible in Boston—for example, smashing a brute in his pig face with a stick—were possible here. Not only possible, but unavoidable.

What else was unavoidable?

A chartershadow, in a pawnshop. She imagined a fading, balding man, his body twisted by misuse of mancy. In novels, the chartershadow was always a villain, and those who went to him paid a price far greater than mere mancy or Reputation. Of course, one could not take novels as a foundation for one's actions.

*Oh, but wouldn't it be pleasant if one could. For one thing, all ends well in novels.*

Chartershadows were dangerous. Her fingers rested against her charing-charm, and its delicate ridges and whorls were as familiar as her own breathing. A shadow could perhaps break a charing, and where would she be then? Vulnerable to any stray mancy, at the mercy of whoever wished to ill-charm her...

*Think logically. Imagine Robbie is asking you to plan some mischief that must be delicately accomplished in Society. Item one. I must acquire his locket. Item two: It is in a place none should see me enter, if possible. And nobody must connect me with Robbie. Item three: I am not in Boston; I am on the edge of civilization, in a town where the graveyards are, by all appearances, not well-cleansed. Night is likely to be especially dangerous outside a charm-locked door.* Her fingertip tapped one fluted edge.

She must merely plan carefully. And take measures to defend herself, should she wish to go gallivanting about after dark here in the wilderness.

Cat cocked her head. Slippered feet in the hallway, brushing oddly as if the person attached to them staggered. She smoothed away the frown rising to her face and gathered herself, rising gingerly from the tub's depths and sighing a little as cool air hit her wet skin.

She had just barely wrapped a drying-cloth about herself when Li Ang appeared. The Chinoise girl's face was contorted, and her fingers sank into the doorframe as a shudder wracked her. Great pearls of sweat stood out on her caramel skin, and her dress held large sweat stains under her arms. Her belly, held before her like a fruit, suddenly looked... odd. Flattened, almost.

The girl gabbled something in Chinoisie. She bent forward, her face contorting even further, a mask of suffering.

"Good God," Cat breathed, just as there was a gushing patter. The fluid hit the floor, and Li Ang made a small, hopeless noise as her feet were bathed in the hot flood.

_Oh, dear Heaven. She is...is she? It's the only possible explanation._

The Chinoise girl was having her baby.

And just at that moment, a series of knocks thundered against the front door.

It was certainly not respectable to throw open the door while clad only in a flannel wrapper, her hair soaked and clinging. Li Ang made another long groaning noise overhead, and the cottage answered with a groan of its own.

She had managed to get the girl onto the bed in Cat's own room and bolted downstairs, her bare feet slapping the floor so hard it stung. _Please don't go, whoever you are, we need help. Please don't go,_ she prayed. _Please._

"Help!" she choked, as she flung the door open and saw the garden, dipped in dusky purple. And there, at the gate, was a familiar hat and broad shoulders in a dun coat.

A sharp prickle of annoyance—what business did he have here after today? She quickly strangled it, and cleared her throat. "I say, Mr. Gabriel! _Sheriff!_ Please. It's Li Ang, we—"

He was suddenly right in front of her, and Cat almost stumbled back. He caught her arm, work-roughened fingers sinking in, grinding on the fresh bruise of Mr. Tilson's grasp. She flinched, and his hand loosened. Would men never tire of shaking her about so?

"Slow down." His pale gaze flicked behind her. "All's well, miss. I'm here."

It was odd, but instead of improper, the words were...comforting. Certainly he was dependable, in his own rather rude fashion. "It's Li Ang," she managed. "She's having her...I mean, she is with…She is in labor, sir. Fetch a midwife. A doctor!" *I don't care who, as long as they know what to do.*

"Hm." He nodded. "I see. I'd get Doc Howard, but he don't hold with no Chinee. Listen to me." He tipped his hat back with two fingers, looking down at her. "I'll fetch help. You bar this door and the kitchen door, too. Make her as comfortable as you can. Boil water, and get clean cloths. We'll need a lot of linen, and a lot of boiled water. Or at least, so I've heard midwives say. Don't you open this door until I come back. You'll know it's me; I'll shout fit to raise the dead. *Avert.*" He let go of her completely now. "Mind you lock up, and don't you open to anyone but me. Understand?"

"Y-yes." *Do you think I would invite the entire town in for a social while* this *is happening?* "Lock the door, make her comfortable. Boil water. Cloths. Of course. I shall, of course, take responsibility for the midwife's fee—"

"Don't you worry about that now. For right now, go on up and tell Li Ang that nobody's going to take her baby." With that, he backed up, reaching for the door. "*Bar* this door, ma'am. As soon as I'm gone."

"Nobody is going to take her—" *What a curious thing to say to a woman abed.* But he swung the door closed, and Cat lost no time in dropping the bar into its brackets. The kitchen door was barred as well—had Li Ang done so?

Another long groan from overhead, spiraling up into a hoarse cry. *Oh, God.* Cat's palms were slippery with sweat, and the wrapper stuck to her most unbecomingly. Her heart pounded so hard she was half-afraid she would collapse.

The girl was up there alone, and in pain. Cat bit her lip, working the pump handle to fill the huge black kettle. She set it on the stove, stammered a boiling-charm—it took her two tries to remember an applicable one from Miss Bowdler's first book— and ran for the hall.

She halted, staring at the exact spot where Jack Gabriel had stood. He hadn't looked surprised or ruffled in the least. Come to think of it, he hadn't looked ruffled since she'd met him. Such phlegm might be maddening, but it was also strangely consoling. If he said he was going to bring help, then help he would bring, and as soon as possible too.

Cat climbed the stairs on trembling legs. Clammy and damp—she should find more appropriate attire before Mr. Gabriel returned.

Li Ang's next groan spiraled into a scream, and Cat put aside the shaking...and ran.

# *Chapter Thirteen*

Ma Ripp was a mean faced hag with hard claws and a widow's sour black weeds. But inside the birthing room she was efficient and strangely gentle. She took one look at the schoolmarm's preparations and barked, "Good enough. Sheriff, more water. You there, girl, set her higher on them pillows." One yellow-nailed finger jabbed at the marm, whose big dark eyes and pale cheeks threatened to turn Gabe inside out.

The poor girl looked scared to death. Li Ang was propped on pillows on what had to be the marm's bed, her knees up and her hair sticking to her cheeks in jet-black streaks. Miss Barrowe had folded the comforter under her knees, and there was another divot on the bed—where, no doubt, Miss Barrowe had sat, holding Li Ang's hand as the birthing pangs ripped through the Chinoise girl.

"What's your mancy?" Ma Ripp finished, checking Li Ang's fragile wrist for her pulse.

Li Ang moaned, cursing in Chinoisie, and Miss Barrowe flinched. But her answer came, clear as a bell. "My Practicality? It's in Light, ma'am."

Ripp nodded once, her iron-gray hair braided tightly and looped about her large head. "Well, not entirely useless. Can you charm ice?"

To her credit, the marm didn't quail further. "Yes, of course."

Ripp handed her a small, battered tin cup. "Dip some water, there, and charm little bits of ice. Enough for her to suck on. Sheriff, get *moving*. This is woman's business."

Gabe retreated, but not before he caught Miss Barrowe's gaze. She stared at him for a long bright moment, and his insides knotted up again. Her cheeks were incredibly pale, and every time Li Ang sobbed for breath, she flinched in sympathy. Her hair was pulled back into a simple braid, still dripping, and she had managed to insert herself into a dress, though the buttons were askew and she had pulled the damp wrapper back on over it.

*I'm here*, he wanted to say. *Don't you worry.*

She averted her gaze, hurriedly, and dipped the tin cup in a basin of water. Mancy sparked, and Gabe found himself in the hall, his breathing hitching oddly.

The doors were locked, and Li Ang was as safe as he could make her. That was the bargain, and he intended to see it through. He should warn the marm about this, though. There were dangers hanging around the Chinoise girl that would only get deeper once she birthed.

He just hadn't thought it would come so *soon*.

More water was set to boil with numb fingers; he had to try twice to get the right charm to settle into the kettle. The marm was using a powerful but volatile mancy, and it almost singed *him*, too.

He wasn't surprised.

Footsteps overhead. He closed his eyes and *listened*. At least his early training still held, and his ears were plenty sharp.

"Are you *quite* sure?" The marm, anxious.

"Walkin's best at this stage." Ripp, a good deal gentler. "That's it, girl. Good, good."

"Her legs." Miss Barrowe gasped. "And did you see... Ma'am—"

"Shh. We've enough to do now."

Of course she would notice the scars on Li Ang's legs. There were more on the Chinoise girl's back—welt and rope and burn, a crazyquilt of suffering, barbaric lines of ink forced under bleeding skin too. Gabe breathed out, slowly, through his open mouth. They wouldn't come into this part of Damnation after her. Not comfortably, at least—the Chinois stayed on their own side, and once the railroad got close enough they'd camp out to provide labor for its iron stitchery.

If word got out the baby was born, though...

*Gabe, this is a hell of a tangle.*

Li Ang couldn't explain much of where she'd come from, but he'd done some quiet digging. At least, as quiet as he could, being a tall-ass roundeye wandering around in the Chinois part of Damnation. He supposed he should be grateful the marm hadn't taken it into her head to explore *that* shadow-half of town. They had their own chartermage, too, a disgusting piece of dried leather with a white beard and clawlike nails.

Who just happened to be Li Ang's husband. Or, to be precise, Li Ang was one of his wives. The only one to bear him a child to term, if what he'd heard was right.

Gabe was thinking the Chinois didn't hold with divorce.

Ripp kept talking, soothing and low. Li Ang cried out again, but softly, like a bird. Maybe it helped to have other womenfolk with her.

Whereas *he* was useless. He should be out riding the circuit, too. But Russ could handle it on his lonesome this once.

Jack stared at the black kettle and kept his hand away from his gun. It looked to be a long night.

"Push!" Ma Ripp barked.

"Oh, for God's sake," the marm snapped. "She's Chinoise; she can't understand you!"

Jack tried to make himself as small as possible against the hall wall. Inside the bedroom, Li Ang's cries had taken on a despairing note. It was almost touching, to hear Miss Barrowe taking up Ma Ripp on Li Ang's behalf.

"Instead of shouting at her—*ow!*"

"That's it!" Ripp crooned. "Squeeze her hands! Almost there, duckums. I can see the head."

"Oh dear…" Suddenly the marm seemed not quite so crisp. "Is that supposed to happen?"

Li Ang's voice spiraled up into a scream, and she cursed both of them roundly. At least, so it sounded. The harsh, foreign syllables broke, agony and triumph mingling, and Gabe flinched.

"Oh…" Miss Barrowe. "Oh, my God."  ·

"That's it! That's a good girl! Now! Now!"

Li Ang screamed again. A wet tearing sound, a gushing. Slapping, and Ma Ripp's muttered mancy. Popping, cracking, fizzing—and Miss Barrowe, softly now.

"Hush, dearie…oh, hush, all's well, yes, hold my hand…Oh, my. My goodness. My heavens."

*She doesn't know what to say. I reckon I wouldn't, either.*

Then, a thin protesting wail, gathering in force. "A boy," Ma Ripp announced dryly. "Breathin' now, thank the Almighty. And just as fine as can be. Missy, turn loose of her and wash this little 'un."

"I've never—"

"That don't matter. Hold his head, *so.* Just sponge him—that's right. Wrap him up good, I laid the swaddling right there. You had a doll once, dintcha? Just like a doll."

Li Ang cursed again, raggedly. Or at least, it sounded like a foul imprecation, with an edge of beseeching.

"Oh, yes, I'm bringing him. Just a moment." Miss Barrowe, half to weeping. "He's so *small.* Oh my goodness. *Oh*—he's leaking, I do believe he's…oh, good *Lord.*" There was a spray and a pattering, and the baby howled with indignation.

"Healthy little cuss," Ma Ripp observed. "Use the fresh swaddlin', there. Sometimes they pee. Now comes another bit of a mess. Bleeding, too. Ho, Sheriff! Needing another pair of hands!"

*What, me?* But he was already palming the door open.

A squalling little bundle, wrapped tightly but inexpertly in boiled and charm-dry cloth, screwed up its tiny little face and wailed. Li Ang, wan and sagging, her knees hitched high and everything below the waist exposed, closed her eyes and clutched the bundle to her chest. It looked like a little old man, and was quickly turning purple. It produced an *amazing* amount of noise.

"Get the tit in that babe's mouth." Ma Ripp pointed at Miss Barrowe, who was braced at the side of the bed, a smear of blood on her colorless cheek. The Boston miss looked dazed. "Sheriff, my bag. Got to stanch this with mair's root and a charm."

The bed looked sadly the worse for wear, bright blood and a clot of darkness spreading from Li Ang's undersides. *That's an awful lot of blood for such a little girl.*

"I believe, ah, that she wishes you to feed the baby, Miss Ang." The marm's fingers, clutched in Li Ang's free hand, must have been throbbing, but she merely looked pale and interested. "I, ah, think it might be best to ... oh, *dear.*"

"Don't you go fainting like a useless little prip." Ma Ripp accepted her capacious black Gladstone. "Or I'll step on you. Get her to put the tit in that little one's mouth; best thing for them both." Rummaging in the bag now, with bloodstained fingers, the woman looked like a graveyard hag. "And *you*, Sheriff. More cloths. Won't fix itself, and I know *you've* seen the underbits of a woman before."

"Will she be ..." His head was full of rushing noise. Damn, who would have thought the little bitty Chinoise girl would have so much blood in her? Grown men couldn't stand after losing that much.

"Right as rain once we fix this. Seen worse, yes I have." Ma Ripp nodded, pushing back a lank strand of sweat-drenched gray hair knocked free of her braids. "Right fine work done tonight."

"That's it, dear. Oh, he knows what to do!" Miss Barrowe actually sounded delighted. Maybe women all loved this birthing business.

"This child yourn?" Ripp's claws were quick and deft, a charm guttering into life on the pad of fresh cloth she pressed between Li Ang's legs. "You seem mighty interested."

"She's a widow." Jack managed the familiar lie, and followed it with truth. "And it ain't mine."

"Well, her husband, God rest the heathen, has a fine son. At least he'll never have to do *this*." She licked her dry, withered lips. "Don't suppose there's no whiskey in this house."

"Madam!" The marm, genuinely shocked, blinked from Li Ang's side. The Chinoise girl had let go of Miss Barrowe's hand, and was occupied with her new bundle, staring at the tiny little purple-faced thing as if she had never seen a baby before. For all Jack knew, she hadn't. She was awful young, and the Chinois... well. It didn't bear thinking about.

"Keep your corset on, missy. A drop's just the thing after this type of work." The midwife accepted Gabe's flask and tossed back a healthy slug. "Now, let's get this mess cleared. Dawn's coming. You should ride for the chartermage, to fetch him a charing."

"Quite." Miss Barrowe no longer sounded so pale, and the baby had quit its hollering. It was occupied with its mother's breast, in any case, and the sight gave Gabe an odd feeling in the region of his stomach.

*She looks just like any of our girls.* And, compelled, he glanced at Miss Barrowe. Some color had come back into her face, and she stared at the baby, rapt as Li Ang herself. The smear of blood on Miss Barrowe's soft cheek was wrong, and his fingers tingled. He could just wipe it away, couldn't he.

If he could touch her.

*Don't, Jack. You know what could happen. You know what's bound to happen if you start getting ideas.*

"Sheriff." A poke to his shoulder, Ma Ripp shoving the metal flask back at him. "You go fetch the mage, now. Sooner this 'un gets a proper charing, the better."

"Yes ma'am," he mumbled, and backed for the door.

# *Chapter Fourteen*

Tuesday was a blur of half-somnolent anxiety. There were items to be procured for a baby's care, and the midwife's fee to pay, and the news to be spread that her girl had birthed and the school was closed for the day. The Chinoise was only a servant, true, and this event should not cause her to leave her duties.

But Cat had been dead on her feet, and Jack Gabriel had, none too gently, told her to take her rest while he made sure the town knew.

She had no idea if it was quite proper or normal for Mr. Gabriel to take charge of affairs, but was grateful nonetheless. Mrs. Ripp, her terrible yellowed teeth showing in a grin, undertook to provide the things the baby would need—for a fee, of course, and Cat had paid without question. Afterward, Mr. Gabriel had words with the crone, and returned a third of Cat's money.

It was . . . thought-provoking.

*It ain't mine*, he'd said, but it was most odd, that he would take such care over a Chinoise girl's baby. It was none of Cat's concern, though, and there was plenty else to worry about on that day.

There was engaging a charmwasher for the laundry, the short coffee-colored chartermage to pay and the certificate for a fresh charing-charm to fill, a delivery of firewood to be attended to, and

Cat had not eaten until Jack Gabriel had shoved a plate into her hands and told her to sit down and take a bite. Tolerable biscuits, some half-charred bacon, and there was even boiling water for tea.

She had boiled so much water she doubted she would ever forget the charm itself. It was burned into her fingers, along with its catchword. She wondered if it was the way a Continental sorcerer might feel about a certain charm or mancy, never mind that their sorcery worked differently. Mancy followed geography, as the old saying went.

She'd fallen asleep at the kitchen table, staring at the side of her teacup, and only woke when the sheriff shook her shoulder and told her briskly to get herself up to bed. It was Li Ang's pallet she slept on through the remainder of that long, terribly hot day, and so deeply she had surfaced in a panic, unable to discern who, where, or even *what* she was.

Fortunately, the feeling had passed, and she found herself in Damnation, with a baby's cry coming from downstairs and Li Ang singing to her son in an exhausted, crooning voice. The poor girl had been trying to clean the kitchen, and Cat's heart had wrung itself in a most peculiar fashion.

It had taken all Cat's skill to gently but firmly bully the Chinoise girl upstairs and tuck her in with the baby.

*This cannot be so hard.* And indeed the biscuits were lumpy and her gruel left a little to be desired, but it was nourishing. Or so she hoped, but then dawn was painting the hills with orange and pink, and she had to hurry to reach the schoolhouse at a reasonable hour. *Without* her parasol, no less.

Her mother would be not just annoyed, but angered. A lady did not forget such things, much less a Barrowe-Browne.

She had half-expected the schoolroom to be empty on Wednesday, Mrs. Granger having had more than enough time to spread calumny and gossip-brimstone. But the students came trooping in, some of them downcast, true, but others bright and cheery— or sullenly energetic—as usual. Now she knew their names, and a curious calm settled over her.

The children did not seem so fractious, now. Even the Dalrymple girls were no trouble, bent over their slates and newly eager to please. Amy, the elder, even elbowed Cecily once or twice when the younger girl seemed likely to bridle, and Cat rewarded the elder girl with letting her touch the pianoforte's keys during lunchtime. "There are such things as lessons," she had intimated, and the naked hope on the young blonde hoyden's face gave Cat another strange, piercing pain in the region of her chest.

Instead of savages, the children now looked oddly hopeful. Their bare feet and ragged clothing were less urchin than primitive, as if the Garden of Shoaal had been re-created here in the far West, amid the dust and the heat and the incivility. Even the freckles on young Cecily's face had their own fey beauty, tiny spots of gold on fair young skin.

It was there, sitting at her desk and staring across the bent heads as they scratched at their slates, that she realized just how far she was from Boston. Perhaps it was lack of sleep bringing a clarity all its own.

Cat drew in a deep breath, her stays digging in briefly, and wondered if she could march into a pawnshop under broad daylight.

*No, night is best. But more dangerous—if you are seen, somehow...*

But this was not Boston. She shook her head and attended to the third form, laboriously reciting from the eighth page of Miss Bowdler's First Primer. "Very good," she encouraged, though she would have said so if they had been reciting backward chartercantations, or even the Magna Disputa. "You may lay that aside, and apply yourself to tracing your alphabet."

"Yes mum," they chorused, and she surprised herself by smiling.

They waited until the children were gone, then trooped silently in, faces scrubbed and mouths pulled tight. Miss Tiergale took her seat first as Cat brought out the slates.

"Good afternoon, ladies," she essayed. They were so long-faced she half-expected bad news. God and charter both knew it would be *just* the time for it.

It was Belle who spoke first, in a rush. "We don't mean to be no trouble, Miss Barrowe."

*Trouble? Oh, none at all, unless you count the bruise on my arm and the loss of Reputation. It does not seem that I will miss it overmuch here.* Her chin rose. "Indeed you are none. In fact, on our short acquaintance I have found you all to be serious and studious."

"She means with Tils." Mercy's cheeks, one with its fading bruise, flushed uncomfortably. "He's . . . well, he ain't a nice man, miss. And he's been drinkin."

"That does not surprise me." She began handing out the slates, her boots tapping the raw lumber with little authoritative ticking noises. "He does not seem the temperate sort." *In any sense of the word.*

"Well, *you* ain't got to be afraid, not with Gabe looking after you." Trixie gazed at the ceiling. Today they were all dressed fairly respectably, instead of in their frail flash and feathers. "It's us what gots to watch our step."

*There are so many grammaticals I could take issue with in those statements.* "Mr. Gabriel is charged with the safety of everyone in this town." She handed Mercy her slate with an encouraging smile.

Anamarie giggled, elbowing the tall one, Carlota. "Not Salt's, I reckon. He hates that chartershadow."

"Wouldn't you?" Trixie was still studying the ceiling, her cheeks flushed from the heat. "Shadows ain't no good."

*Let's cease this chatter.* "We shall begin with—"

"She's blushing," Anamarie whispered. "I think she's sweet on him, too."

That got Trixie's attention. "Who, the shadow?"

"*Ladies.*" Cat folded her arms. Her cheeks stung, perhaps because of the bruise on Mercy's poor face. "We have much to accomplish this afternoon. I intend to earn every cent of the fee you have graciously promised me. Take up your slates."

That served to bring them to task. Her cheeks still burned, though, and it took a while for the heat to fade. It was entirely different than the dry baking outside, and Cat's head was full of a strange noise. She held grimly to her task, and by the end of the session all the women had firmly grasped not only the basic functions of the alphabet, but also the idea, if not the application, of multiplication.

"It's all groups!" Anamarie finally burst out. "Say you've a fellow buying drinks for you and him. That's two drinks. And he buys three rounds. Three groups of two, six!"

"Unless Coy waters yours so you can keep a clear head to roll the bastard," Carlota said, and their shared laughter made Cat smile before the probable meaning of "roll" occurred to her.

"Language, Carlota." Mildly enough. Cat pulled her skirts aside as she reached to wash the slate board clean in preparation for their practice at writing their names. "Very good, Anamarie. It's all groups. Multiplication and division—"

"Now hold on," Mercy finally spoke up. "Let's just stick with the multiplyin' until I get that clear inside my skull."

"I wanta read my Bible." Belle, suddenly, as she scratched lightly at the wooden frame of her slate with one broken fingernail. "That's what I want."

"I'm a-gonna move to San Frances and open up a bawdy house of my own. Be a madam, not the girl." Trixie waved one airy, plump hand. "Count the money and eat me sweet things all day."

"Where you gonna get the stake for that?" Anamarie tossed her dark head, her earrings—plain paste, like Mercy's—swinging against her curls.

"That's why I said we gotta learn numbers, so Tils can't short us none no more."

"Names, ladies." Cat began tracing them on the board. "Can you tell whose I am writing now?"

A ragged chorus: "A...N...A...M...A..."

"Why, that's me! Ah-na-mah-ree."

"*Very* good. Wait until I've written them all to copy your own name."

"It's like mancy. Like the charters."

"Except these don't glow—"

"Ladies, I know you're eager to be gone. We must finish this first, however. Please contain yourselves."

"Why you call us ladies all the time?" Carlota wanted to know. "We ain't."

Cat's patience stretched, but the clarity that had possessed her all day held. "This is the Wild Westron. Anyone can become anything here." *I can even become a schoolteacher, possessed of patience I hardly knew was possible. And helper to a midwife, and a woman who can teach fancy frails to read.*

For a long few moments, nobody spoke as Cat traced a C, an A, an R. "Which letters are these? Anyone?"

The chorus began again. "C . . . A . . . R . . ."

Cat Barrowe found herself smiling broadly, facing the board. Yes, indeed. *Anyone can become anything here.*

# Chapter Fifteen

Dusk was gathering, purple veils and a breath of coolness stepping down from the hills on the heels of a steadily gathering wind. Approaching autumn tiptoed around the town, but the bank of heavy gray stayed firmly in the north and didn't sweep down any farther. When it did roll over Damnation, the mud would be knee-high. He would have to teach Miss Barrowe to drive the wagon, so she could avoid getting her skirts draggled. That would mean caring for a horse close to her cottage, too, and he was involved in a long train of thought having to do with the possibility of a stall in the Armstrongs' stable when he turned the corner and saw her walking slowly, head down, from the other direction.

School was out, then, and the saloon girls were probably back at the Star. He'd had a word with Paul Turnbull about Tils. That went about as well as could be expected—Paul didn't like trouble, and Gabe gave him to understand that Tilson was fixing to have trouble with Gabe himself if he didn't leave the marm alone.

At least it was something.

She was in blue today, and her nipped-in waist was a sharply beautiful curve. Those little pointed-toe boots with all the buttons, and stray dark curls coming loose under her prettily perched hat. It was the first time he'd seen her slim shoulders anything but straight and stiff. She looked half-dead on her feet, like a sleepy horse.

Well, no wonder.

His stride lengthened. What should he say? *Evenin', ma'am?* Was that too formal? *Hello there?* Maybe something else, a little pleasantry. *Ain't you a fine sight.*

Or even, *God must be kind, because you're here.*

It had been years since he'd felt this tightness in his chest. Annie hadn't made him feel silly and stupid; or at least, maybe he'd been young enough that he hadn't cared. She had been sweet and soft, not prickly and precise as this little bit of a thing with her head down and the leather satchel swinging from her left hand pulling her to the side. She was listing like a ship limping into port, and Gabe swallowed dryly. *Oh, Hell.*

The wind picked up, and dust swirled against her skirts. She halted by the white-painted garden gate, staring at it as if she could not for the life of her figure out what such a contraption might be for.

"Don't fall asleep, now." His hand closed around her elbow, gently.

Her head tilted up, a slow movement. She blinked, weariness etched on her soft face. She searched his features, as if he were a stranger. "Mr. Gabriel?" Wondering. "Is Li Ang well?"

*What?* "Should think so. I just got here."

"Ah." Miss Barrowe nodded. "I see. Well, you may come in briefly to see her, but I warn you, she is still very tired."

*What about you?* "Didn't come to see *her*, ma'am."

"Then what are you…oh, *never* mind." She took her elbow from him, very decidedly, and he reached to open the gate. "Is it a disaster, or some new variety of excitement?"

*What do you expect?* "Neither. Just came to visit before I rode the circuit."

"I hope I am not keeping you."

"You treat all your visitors this way, sweetheart?"

"Sir." Frosty and sharp, now. "You shall address me as *Miss Barrowe*."

Well, now he had her measure. And braving that prickliness was worth what was behind it. "Sometimes, yep. Other times, not so much."

At least the irritation had given her a little energy. She sashayed up the walk at a good clip, and he watched the swing and sway of her skirts. How did women move with all that material tied on? No doubt it weighed like panniers stuffed with gold dust.

Something bothered him, but he couldn't rightly figure it out. Something about gold, and Miss Barrowe.

She reached the steps, gathering her pretty blue skirts with her free hand. "I hope she hasn't barred the door. That would be simply terr—*oh!*"

Her hurt little cry pierced the moan of the freshening dust-laden wind, and he had no memory of the intervening space. He was simply *there* as she stumbled back, her skirts dropping free because she had clamped her hand over her mouth. She turned, blindly, and the thump of her leather satchel hitting the wooden bottom step barely covered his hissed, indrawn breath.

He found himself with a shivering woman in his arms, staring at the shadowy writhing thing nailed to the porch. It had probably been a rabbit once, but bad mancy was all that was left, cork-screwing and flapping the dying tissues. An unholy spark flashed inside the thing's half-peeled skull, and whatever tortured bit of soul still remaining in its tiny bone cage let out a piercing little moan.

She shuddered again, and his fingers were in her hair, cupping the back of her skull, a hatpin's prick against his wrist. "Shhhh," he soothed, only half-aware of speaking. "Shh, don't look. God-*damn*. Easy there."

The wind crested, and he had limited daylight to take care of this thing and get to the circuit. Russ wouldn't take kindly to riding alone at twilight. Dawn was one thing, but dark was another, and Gabe didn't blame him.

"L-l-l—" She gulped, tensed, and tried to pull away. "Li Ang! She's inside—what if—"

He found his other hand was pressed against the small of her back, and the fading whiff of rosewater mixed with clean linen and a spice-tang of healthy female to make something utterly unique. She didn't have any idea how good she smelled. "Then I'll find out. Now come along." He didn't have to work to sound grim. "Back door. Step quiet, and stay behind me."

"What...who would..."

"Don't know." *But I aim to find out. That's bad mancy for sure, and what if I hadn't been here?* "Now you be a good girl and stay behind me, you hear?"

A nod. He was all but crushing her, he realized, and loosened up just a little. Then a little more. She might scream, or faint— no, this miss wasn't the fainting type. Even if she had swooned a little when she arrived. Who wouldn't have?

He trawled through memory and found what he wanted. "Catherine."

"Wh-what?"

"Just sayin' your charing-name. Makin' sure I've got your attention, like."

"I believe you do, sir." With nowhere near her usual snap.

"You can call me Jack."

"Thank you." A little prim, now, which cheered him immensely. She was nice and steady, and she didn't try to struggle away. Instead, she just stood there, and he let her. "Jack?"

"Hm." He kept his gaze on the twisting, flopping thing. It was nailed in solid with what was probably false-iron, and it let out another agonized little sound. *A warning, maybe. God damn whoever did this.*

"It's screaming. Could...could you possibly..."

*I'd prefer to clear the house first, but since you're ask-ing...* "Stay right here, then. *Right* here. This very spot."

"I shall." Her eyes were tightly closed, and she flinched when the no-longer-rabbit thing screeched. Jack's chest cracked a little, and he found, to his not-quite surprise, that everything in him still remembered what came next, as if the intervening years had fallen away and he was still the orphan boy sold to the Ordo Templis and the man who had left the knights behind for a woman's arms.

This, he knew how to do.

It was a moment's work to mount the steps, a trifle more to take a long considering look at the mancy pinning the thing. No use rushing.

It looked odd, and his mouth thinned. He shook out his left hand, keeping his right away from a gun with an effort. A bullet wouldn't end this misery.

He closed away the moaning wind and the falling dark. The sun was a bloody clot in the west, its light dipping and painting Damnation in vermilion. The thought of the schoolmarm at the foot of the stairs wouldn't go away, so he breathed into it. Let it fill his head, and relaxed.

*I release you.*

His left-hand fingers made a curious, complex motion. It was not quite charter-mancy; nor was it sorcery. A trace-map of golden veins lit the flesh of his fingers, and he *saw* the knot holding the tiny soul into violated flesh. Sometimes the best response was to unpick the strands carefully, loosening one a fraction, then another.

Then there were times like these.

*I release you.*

His fingers tensed, the golden light casting dappled water-shadows on the roof and floor of the porch. He had a moment to hope she had her eyes closed—this would create all manner of fuss and undue questions if she saw grace upon him instead of plain mancy—before he jabbed his hand forward, a softly spoken Word resonating with hurtful edges as it sliced the knot of bad mancy clean through.

*I release you.*

False-iron popped blue sparks, and the sodden little rag of fur and meat and splintered bone sagged. His left hand, a fist now, flicked down as if he were casting salt. Fine golden grains of pure light showered over the thing, and the blot was cleansed. A brief burst of fresh green scent, like new-mown hay, washed away on the breeze.

*For others, I may do, by Grace. Amen.*

Grace was never in short supply. Faith, though, was far rarer than the gold they dug and panned for. And he was—was he?—oddly relieved that grace had not left him.

*It ain't grace, Gabe. It's . . . her.*

His spurs rang on the steps, and found Catherine, her eyes tightly shut, hugging herself and cupping her elbows in her hands. Tears welled between her lashes. He had to try twice before his throat would unloose enough to let him speak. "It's done." Gabe's chest clenched around something solid and fiery, thrust under his ribs. "Aw, no. Don't *cry.*"

"I am very sorry," she whispered. "I am *trying* not to. Li Ang." She opened her eyes, blinking rapidly and dashing away a tear on her cheek with one gloved hand. "We must find her."

*I didn't mean . . . oh, Hell.* He bent to grab her satchel, but she was quicker, and straightened with it clutched in tense fingers. "Catherine—"

"Please don't. *Don't.*" She brushed past him for the corner of the house, obviously intending to sashay around to the back door in defiance of all good sense.

"Stay *behind* me, you idiot," he barked, and could have slapped himself on the forehead.

"Then hurry." Like a whipcrack, her pert little reply.

But he was already past her, checking the corner and drawing his right-hand gun. His left hand tingled, the odd pins-and-needles sensation he remembered from his Last Baptism right before his vows. Funny how it never went away.

*Some things pursue a man, Jack. You know that.* "More haste, less speed." The side of the house was as innocent as a newborn babe. He cursed inwardly at the thought. Russ hadn't caviled at giving a Chinois child a charing, so at least *that* was all right. But still.

"The baby." As if she'd read his mind. "Dear God."

"Probably fine. Li Ang ain't no fool. Bet she's got the house locked up tight." *But there might be another little present waiting at your back door, pretty girl, and that is not a happy thought.*

"Sir?" Breathless. At least if she fainted now it would save him the trouble of explaining himself.

"Shh."

She stayed silent, then. There was a rattling, and the back door opened, the stoop dust-scoured and charm-cleaned.

Li Ang peered at them, her son clutched to her chest. She was shaking, and gabbling in her heathen tongue, and Gabe was right glad to hear it. Catherine actually flung her arms about the Chinoise girl, and the baby squalled between them.

He took the opportunity to get them both inside and the door shut tight, then went straight to the house to the front to take care of the carcass.

His hands shook, but not with fear.

Oh, no. Not fear at all.

# Chapter Sixteen

"Bad," Li Ang said. "*Baaaad.*" She clutched at little Jonathan—she called him Jin, but there had to be *something* written on the charing certificate, so he was now Jonathan Liang Barrowe, may God have mercy on them all. Mother would die, and Father might even lose his hallowed temper, but Cat was past caring. It was a proud name, and might do even a Chinoise a fair service.

"Yes, but all's well." Cat sought for a patient, soothing tone. The kettle chirruped, heating water for tea, and she forced herself to keep her eyes wide open, staring at charm-sparking against the metal. "Mr. Gabriel is here."

Odd, wasn't it, how such a sentence could be so comforting. As if she were a child, and this a nightmare banished by a parent's sudden presence.

Except Jack Gabriel was not in the least parental. He was something else. She was far too exhausted to find the proper word.

Little Jonathan burbled a bit, but he had ceased wailing. Which was very nice, now that she thought about it.

It seemed she only blinked, but then the kettle was boiling and she set about making tea. If she focused on the pot and the leaves, the water at precisely the right temperature and the cups arranged just *so*, perhaps she would not think of the little thing on the porch, screaming as some variety of dark mancy robbed it of death's comfort.

*Who would do such a thing? My God.*

The back door squeaked as it ghosted open, and Li Ang inhaled sharply, as if to scream. But it was merely Jack Gabriel, his eyes incandescent under the shadow of his hatbrim.

That was like saying it was *merely* a hurricane, or *merely* an earthquake. Something about him filled up the entire kitchen, made it difficult to breathe. Maybe it was the feel of his fingers in her hair, or his broad chest against her cheek, or the way he'd stood, solid and steady.

She kept her eyes down, and noted with some relief that her hands were steady as well. Her gloves lay neatly on the counter, and one of them was stained near the wrist. Ink, and she should attend to that soon before it set so deeply even a charm wouldn't remove it.

*Shh. Don't look. Easy there.* And a curious comfort in the midst of her fear.

Perhaps she should ask the sheriff about Robbie. But *trust no one*, her brother had written more than once.

And, *the law in this town is worse than the lack of it.*

The sheriff was saying something. She concentrated on pouring. Tea would brace her. Tea solved quite *everything*, or at least, so Miss Ayre had firmly believed. Cat was shaken with a sudden irrational urge to write to her old governess and ask *her* help. Miss Ayre would set all this to rights.

Miss Ayre had gone her quiet way years ago, once Cat was too old to need a governess, and their correspondence had stopped after news of Miss Ayre's marriage to a man in Europa. *Quite a rich man, too,* her mother had sniffed, and there was no more said.

No, there was nobody left to solve this quandary but Cat herself, and she was rather doubting her own resources at the moment.

"Put that baby to bed," he finished, and Li Ang shuffled away. "What are you doing there, Catherine?"

A jolt all through her, as if a whip of stray mancy had bit her fingers. *I should not let him address me so.* "I am making tea," she replied, dully. "I had a governess, once." *And she would have this set to rights in a trice.*

He was silent for a long moment. "I think you should sit down."

"I am *making tea.* Such an operation cannot be performed satisfactorily while seated." She took a deep breath. *Now I must ask questions.* "Who would do such a terrible thing, Mr. Gabriel?"

"You may as well call me Jack."

*For the love of...* The irritation was welcome, a tonic for her nerves. It even managed to give her a burst of fresh wakefulness. "In other words, you do not know, or will not venture a guess."

"In other words, you may as well use my charing-name. And I have an idea or two. Don't trouble yourself over it no further."

*Why ever not? It was nailed to my porch and began screaming as I approached.* "I am quite troubled, and I intend to continue to be. Whoever did that—"

"—is gonna reckon with *me* soon enough, Miss Porquepine. You don't need to worry. And I don't think Li Ang wants no tea."

"We should be civilized, even here. And tea is a tonic. It does very well for nerves, and—"

"I think you should sit down."

"I think, sir, that you may go to Hell." What had possessed her? She was trembling. Well, who wouldn't, faced with this? And why did the man have to be so outright *infuriating*?

Boiling water splashed. She let out a shaky breath, and finished filling the pot. Thank God one could find tea in this benighted place, even though it was *not* of the quality her mother would have found acceptable.

"I intend to, if you get yourself into trouble down there."

*What does that mean?* "You're refusing an invitation to tea, then? I shall be pouring momentarily."

"Sit *down.*" He had her shoulders, big work-roughened hands that had probably touched the thing out front, and she let out a tiny piping sound, rather like baby Jonathan's satisfied little noise when Li Ang set him high on her shoulder and patted his back. "I ain't gonna hurt you, but I am gonna make you listen. We need to have a talk."

There was no use in fighting, so she let him push her toward the kitchen table and her usual seat. She sank down, her corset stays digging in abominably, and glared at him from under her knocked-askew hatbrim. Her hair was too loose, as well, curls falling in her eyes and brushing her shoulders.

Hazel eyes, bleached to a gold-green shine most odd, shadow of stubble on his jaw, his own dark hair mussed. At least he'd taken his hat off. He pulled out Li Ang's chair and dropped down, heavily, and she had the sudden gratifying vision of wood cracking and the chair spilling him to the floor. He rubbed at his face, scratching his cheek, and let out a long sigh.

He was too big for the chair, too big for the *room*. The dun-colored coat, the guns at his belt, everything about him was too big and dusty and foreign. Her heart hammered, because he smelled of healthy horse and heat and healthy male, leather and *tabac* and a verdant green note of mancy. An overpowering aroma, but not at all an unpleasant one.

*Shh. Easy there.* And his fingers in her hair. His hand at the small of her back, and the sense of being enclosed, held safely away from something howling and snapping. Quite comforting, and not at all proper, now that she considered it.

The cottage was deathly silent, except for the stealthy creaks of Li Ang moving upstairs. Had the new crib arrived today? Cat really should have arranged for that beforehand, but it had all happened so *quickly*. And there was still the question of other items that should have been delivered, and arrangements to be made—

"I can't watch you all the time. I got other work to do."

Her annoyance mounted another notch. Her cheeks, no doubt, were scarlet; they were hot enough to boil the kettle afresh. "I do not recall asking you to do so, sir."

He refused to take offense. How could he be so d—ned

*imperturbable*? "No, 'cause it'd be easier if you *did*. Simmer down."

"I am *perfectly* calm."

"No, you ain't. I ain't, either. So just simmer down, Catherine, and we'll do some plannin'."

"I do not intend to do any *planning*. I've done far too much of that, and not enough..." *Shut up, Cat.*

She did, closing her mouth with a snap.

He merely nodded, wearily. "I could put you on the next stage-coach for Poscola Flats, and you could be on a train to Boston in two shakes."

"No." *Not until I have Robbie's locket. Then I will find him, no matter what condition he may be in.*

Could that be the warning? Did someone in Damnation know, or suspect? It was very likely, and the trembling going through her mounted another notch.

*Oh, Robbie. What on earth are you suffering right now? Or are you...no, you cannot be dead. You simply cannot be.*

Jack Gabriel held up one callused hand, as if to halt an obedient dog. "I figure you've got a reason not to go back East. Well, no matter. If you're gonna stay in Damnation, we'll—"

Her temper almost snapped. "You have no right to order me about *or* dispose of me in any fashion, sir."

"No, I ain't got a right, yet. But I'm powerful interested in keeping that pretty neck of yours out of trouble. You could try thankin' me."

"I am sure I am very grateful." She made it as prim and unhelpful as she could, which was *quite*.

"You're a bad liar."

*I hope not.* Oddly enough, though, she felt better. Why? "If you have finished insulting me—"

"Are you the marryin' type, Miss Barrowe?"

"*What?*" Her shriek would probably wake little Jonathan, all the way upstairs.

Jack Gabriel leaned forward in the chair, his elbows braced on his knees. He was staring at her, and the faint smile he wore was not calming *or* humorous in the least. "I mean, are you sweet on anyone, back East or here? Some poor bastard who don't know how to handle you when you get all prickly and proper?"

*I'm dreaming. There's no other explanation. This is all a nightmare.* "I most certainly am *not*, not that it's any of your business—"

"Good. Because I'd hate to have to kill a man over you. Now you listen to me. From now on, you stay in sunshine. I'll get Russ Overton to bring the wagon 'round to take you to the schoolhouse, and I'll walk you home in the afternoons. Tell me you will."

*What is he on about? I shall never get a chance to acquire Robbie's locket if you keep crowding me in such a manner.* "I don't see the need for Mr. Overton or—"

"There's a need."

His tone was so grim she leaned back against the chair, and found her hands were not so steady now. She clasped them together—where had her gloves gone? Her head was a-whirl. If she could merely gather herself for a few moments, perhaps this would not seem so overwhelming.

It did not appear he would let her. "Now, are you gonna give me your word, Catherine? 'Cause if you ain't I'm gonna have to do something you might not like."

"Do *not* threaten me. I will observe all proper precautions. Including seeking legal redress and charter protection against whoever—"

"You just leave that to me." He sighed, rose a trifle stiffly, and settled his hat over his tousled hair. With it on, the steely glint of his eyes lost under the shadow of the brim, he was not quite so comforting. "Do I have your word?"

"Certainly." Fancy that—she had gone from being grateful for his presence to wishing she could heave him out the door with exceeding force. "I shall go with Mr. Overton in the morning, and you may be allowed to accompany from the schoolhouse to my domicile in the afternoons. When it is necessary."

"Good enough." He settled his hat, turned on his heel, and strode for the back door. "Bar this behind me. And for God's sake, be careful. That wasn't a May bouquet sitting on your porch." The drawl had evaporated, and he sounded clipped and precise. "Ma'am."

With that, he was gone, the night outside breathing its dust-spice in for a brief moment. Cat pulled herself to her feet, made it across the room on unsteady legs, and settled the bar in its brackets. She turned the lock too, for good measure. The kettle hadn't even finished steaming, and the teapot sent up fragrant veils as well. Everything else, she decided, could bloody well wait for morning to be sorted.

*I'd hate to have to kill a man over you.*

Dear God. Did he mean there was a chance he *would*?

# Chapter Seventeen

Full dark had fallen, and Russ Overton was in a state, jamming his hat on and scrambling to his feet from his usual chair in front of Capran's Dry Goods. Across the street, the Tin House was rocking with drunken laughter, and there was the high sharp note of glass breaking. "It's *dark*, Gabe! The circuit—"

"You come with me." Gabe barely broke stride. Whoever was smashing glass inside the Tin could wait. "We ain't goin far."

"What the hell—is it an incursion? What's going on?"

The canvas bag dangling from Gabe's right hand swung a little, dripping. His spurs struck sparks, bright blue bits of uneasy mancy. "Someone left a rabbit on the schoolmarm's porch."

Russ's legs were too short, so he outright scurried to keep alongside. "That's very nice, but—"

"Twisted up with a death-charm and nailed in with false-iron." His teeth ached; he was gonna crack a few of them if he kept clenching them this hard. At least he had a charm to fix *that*.

Russ spluttered. "*What?* That's goddamn *dangerous!*"

*I thought so too.* Gabe plunged aside into the alley, and Russ hurried to keep up, their boots grinding against dust and small pebbles. The wind had picked up even more, and it might be another one of the storms that made everyone crazy with a constant low moaning and rasping grit in the air.

Of course, Gabe was halfway to crazed already.

He'd probably scared the life out of the girl; the words had been out of his mouth before he'd *thought*. Now she knew, and not only that. Saying it made it real.

Maybe it was just that the schoolmarm was the first miss who wasn't a saloon girl or someone's spoken-for—but that wasn't it, either. It was *something else*, he didn't have the time or the inclination to define it further.

The important thing was, she was in harm's way. Which meant Jack Gabriel had a job to do.

*What a helluva mess.*

"Gabe, dammit, what the hell?" Russ was out of breath already.

"Salt's." The rage mounted another notch inside his chest, and the ice all through him was a warning. Her curls were soft, a little slippery, and she had trembled against him, soft and frightened. "That's where we start. And if the sonofabitch did this bit of work, I'm putting a bullet in him."

"Gabe, now don't get all—"

He rounded on the man, itching to shake him. Might even have, if his hand hadn't been full of rabbit carcass and false-iron nails. "It was on her *porch!* It started screaming the minute she got near it!" *Why am I shouting?*

There was a spatter of gunfire from the sinks in the southwest part of town. Either that or it was firecrackers from the Chinois parts beyond, celebrating something in their heathen way. For once, Gabe didn't care.

The chartermage was pale under his caramel coloring, and thoughtful. "That's just mighty strange. The Chinee girl was there, right? She didn't hear nothin' troublesome?" Russ had his hands up and loose, and he cautiously took a step aside. "I'm just sayin', tell me a little more about this, Gabe."

*Why are you slowin' me down?* "She heard, and she was feedin' her baby, Russ, and she can't speak much good Englene when she's scared out of her mind."

"It's just...normally, you know, that's not a quiet or short job, something like this. And done near dusk. Are you sure it was meant for the marm?"

*Who else?* It couldn't be meant for Li Ang; the Chinois just didn't come into that part of town. Which was why he'd put her there to begin with, and arranged things so she could stay relatively out of sight. "Well, it's *her* damn house. And Tils is swearing up and down that he'll fix her."

"Tils ain't gonna hire Salt to cross you. Tils'll get drunk and come up sneaky behind *you*. You know that well as I do. Sides, Salt ain't going to cross you by leavin' a death-charm at your girl's door."

"My girl?" *I've been careful, have you been opening your yap? If you have, by Hell I'll...*

He realized the ridiculousness of it just in time, and noticed Russ had stiffened. Gabe shook out his fist, lowering his hand.

*I have to calm down.*

Russ kept a weather eye on his hand, in case Gabe changed his mind. "There ain't anyone in town who doesn't know, dammit; don't act surprised. The betting's been a right nuisance to keep track of."

"Betting?" Some of the ice cracked, and his fingers eased up a little on the canvas bag too. Getting the thing up off the planks had been a job; whoever had nailed it in had driven the iron deep. Had Li Ang been inside, quaking, hearing that noise?

It was a hell of a time to wish he knew some Chinois.

"Odds were ten to one in her favor by the time you took her out to that schoolhouse. Laura Chapwick was locked up in her room crying for a good two days, but now she's making eyes at Beau Thibodeau."

"Chapwick? The redheaded one? Why the hell—oh, dammit, quit changing the subject." *I've got someone to beat the goddamn living hell out of, and you're not helping.*

"I never bet on her. Too docile. Now listen, I'm all for asking Salt a couple questions about this little event. But you put a bullet in him, the next shadow we get might not be so damn incompetent, and we'd *both* have to work harder. In the interests of my laziness, Gabe, let's be a little cautious here."

"God *damn* it." But Russ was right. Some of the steel-hard tightness in his shoulders receded a bit, and Gabe set his jaw. The tingling in his fingers had gone down, and so had the unsteady, explosive feeling behind his breastbone. His spurs no longer struck sparks when he moved, a single restless step. "Fine. I won't shoot the bastard." *Unless he forces me to.*

"That's the spirit." Russ brushed at his lapels, swung his hat a few times, and settled it back on his curly mane. "Then we got to ride the circuit. I got a bad feelin' tonight, with the wind up and all."

*You ain't the only one.* But Gabe shut up and followed Russ. He had plenty to think on, now that he *was* thinking, instead of simmering with fury.

"Just promise me you won't kill the man," the chartermage continued. "I don't want to bury no sonofabitch unconsecrated tonight."

Riding the circuit was a good way to think. Or at least, it could have been if the rising dust-laden wind wasn't enough to choke a mule, and Russ was in a bad temper. He had to keep spitting the charm to keep some clear air around them, over and over.

*It ain't my fault,* Gabe told himself. How could he have known they'd find Salt that way? And he hadn't been the one to break the chartershadow's jaw. Doc was flat-out amazed that Russ's small hands could deliver such a blow.

It didn't help that Russ had been sweet on the widow Holywood for as long as he'd been in town. It further didn't help that Salt had the widow on her knees and had his hands down in his trousers, obviously intent on collecting a payment for a piece of bad mancy. Salt had made the mistake of jeering, and Russ had exploded.

*Go home,* Gabe told the widow. *Go to the mage if you need mancy, just don't ever come here again.*

He could pretty much tell she wasn't going to listen. Whatever she wanted, neither Salt nor the widow would tell—not like Salt could, with his jaw shattered and the rest of him pretty near pulped. Restraining Russ hadn't been easy.

This had all the earmarks of a situation that was gonna end badly. But at least Russ had, after all the excitement, verified that the death-charm wasn't Salt's work.

There'd been enough blood on the floor for *that*.

Gabe flicked a spark of blue-white off his fingers, lighting a gully to their left. Each shadow stood out sharp and clear, whirling dust specks of diamond, but all was as it should be. No shambling figures, no slithering movement. The quiet held.

The last incursion of undead had been at the schoolhouse. And Gabe still didn't have an explanation for how those corpses had ended up inside the town's charter.

He didn't like that one bit.

Russ halted for a moment, his head rising. Breathing through a charmed triangle of cloth knotted around his face, blinking, he peered ahead. Gabe eased his horse forward. If there was a gap or an erasure, Russ would mend it while Gabe stood guard.

Russ's hat shook itself, *no*. He continued, and this was the worst sector—due west, where the sun went to die every day.

There were plenty of gold claims in the hills, yes. All sorts of things out in the hills where the wild mancy roamed. And one particular claim, sealed up tight as a vicar's platebox, the ancient hungry thing inside it deep in its uneasy slumber.

It was about time to ride out and check, to make certain the seal was holding. The tribes before the white man in this part of the world had whispered of something foul in the hills before they disappeared. Those garbled legends sent a cold finger down Gabe's back the first time he heard them, because those of the Order knew how much truth there could be in such whispers.

Yes, he had to go out soon. In sunshine, though. No amount of gold could have made either man venture west in the dark. Not through those hills. Some other idiots might, though, and if they brought trouble back to town it was Gabe who would be setting it to rights.

Thinking about that claim put him in a worse mood, if that was possible. Something was nagging at him, and there was no way to tease it out when people kept misbehaving. Something to do with that claim, and the—

Russ pulled his horse up short, and Gabe's mouth went dry. Sparks flew, blue-white and the lower, duller red of the chartermage's mancy. Russ dismounted, and the rifle was in Gabe's hands, steady and comforting. He covered the hole while the chartermage crouched, teasing together the circuit-strands, binding them with knots that flashed with ancient symbols of protection against malice, ill-chance...

And evil.

The rifle was steady. Dust slipped and slithered, if the wind didn't abate by morning they were looking at a regular old simoun, and everyone who was half-crazy before would go all the way into full-blown lunatic while the wind lasted. He'd be busy keeping some semblance of order, and Catherine—who knew how she'd react? The winds were the hardest thing to take, sometimes.

Russ straightened. The border was repaired. The chartermage's shoulders relaxed a little. He turned back to his horse, and the rifle jerked in Gabe's hands. He worked the bolt again, and the shadow fled, sudden eerie phosphorescence leaving a slug-trail on flying dust. There was a flash of white shirt, braces, and a suggestion of loose, flopping hair.

*Man-shaped, could be anything. Nightflyer, a skomorje—but they don't like it when it's dry—or maybe even wendigo, though there hasn't been any spoor and it's not winter. That would just cap everything off.* The rifle's barrel moved slowly, covering a smooth arc. *Ain't a rotting corpse, though; they don't glow at night. It could be...but we sealed that claim. I sealed that claim up solid.*

"Gabe?" Russ called over the wind's mounting rush, and both

horses were nervous. The charming on their hoods would keep the dust out of sensitive membranes, but no beast Gabe had ever ridden liked a hood.

"Not sure," he called back. "Mount up."

The chartermage swung himself into his saddle with a grunt. He waited until Gabe kneed his horse forward to continue, both animals picking their way with finicky delicacy. The western charterstone was very near, and once they reached it the circuit was finished.

*Man-shaped. Tall and skinny. Flopping hair. Couldn't see much else. The glow, though. That's troublesome.*

God *damn* it. He was going to have to go visit that claim again, and sooner rather than later.

# *Chapter Eighteen*

Mr. Overton was a curious case. His skin was the color of coffee with cream, and his dark hair was slicked down with something that resembled wax. He was no taller than Cat herself, with a long nose, and his full lips were pulled tight as he shook some of the biscuit-colored dust from his bowler hat.

His eyes were odd, too, a variety of light almost-yellow she had never seen before. His charing—a brass ring, denoting some form of servitude in his past—was alive with a soft red glow, showing him to be a chartermage.

No wonder he had come to the West. Even in the Northern provinces a chartermage of his particular color might find it difficult to find proper work—if he did not fall foul of a coffle-gang meant to drag him into the dark South where he could be drained of his mancy and turned into a soulless automaton, living only in name.

Robbie had wanted to enter Army service, but their father had categorically forbade it. The War had been fought to settle the Abolition Question, but even after all the blood and trouble there seemed precious little *settled*. Not when there were still coffle-gangs; she had seen them on the streets of Boston the very day she had left.

It gave one the shudders to think of, although Cat's parents had been firmly of the State's Rights opinion. Now, as she eyed the man before her, she wondered if she should have perhaps paid more attention to the Question. It was an altogether uncomfortable thing to have one who would be affected so intimately by such a debate before one in the flesh.

Li Ang hurried away, her step light on the stairs, and little Jonathan's wailing ceased after a few moments. Cat straightened her gloves. "How do you do, sir."

"How do, ma'am." He moved as if to touch his hatbrim, his gaze roving everywhere but to her face. "Gabe said you'd be needing an escort to the schoolhouse."

"So he thinks." She adjusted her grip on the leather satchel and lifted her chin. "May I offer you some tea? Or coffee; I believe Li Ang knows how to make such an infusion."

"No thank you, ma'am. Best get going, there's work to be done today."

*Indeed there is.* "Certainly." She stepped forward, and at least he was polite—he opened her front door, sparing only a brief glance at the porch outside where the...thing...had been last night.

"I'll be fetching you too," he said over his shoulder as he stumped down the steps, his stride wide and aggressive. "Gabe left at dawn, business elsewhere."

"I see." *Left? Where on earth would one go, here? To another town, perhaps? Why?*

But she could not ask. The wind had died—which was a mercy. The blowing dust and moaning air all night had invaded Cat's dreams, and she had dreamed of Robbie as well. Terrible dreams, full of dark cavernous dripping spaces and flashes of tearing, awful blue-white brilliance.

*My nerves are not steady at all.*

The sky was a bruise, and the dust had scoured everything to the same dun colors as Jack Gabriel's coat. No wonder the garden looked so sad and dingy. She accepted Mr. Overton's hand and climbed into the wagon, and the patient bay horse flicked his tail. He had a curious fan-shaped burlap thing affixed to his head, glowing with mancy. "What does that do?" she wondered aloud, then answered her own question. "Ah. The dust. Are such storms usual, Mr. Overton?"

"Simoun, they call 'em." He hauled himself up on the other side with a sigh. He still did not look directly at her. "Poison wind. Sometimes it goes on for days. People can't take it. They go *back East.*" He gave the last two words far more emphasis than they merited, and flicked the whip gently at the bay, who stepped to with a will.

"I found it rather soothing." Cat set her chin and adjusted her veil. *And why would you suggest I retreat to Boston, sir? This is our first real acquaintance; the difference in our station does not matter nearly so much here in the wilderness. Or does it?*

"You'd be the only one. Can I ask you something, miss?"

*You just did.* "Certainly, sir."

"You're an educated lady, and you've got some mighty fine cloth. So fine, in fact, it's got me wonderin' what a genteel miss like you is doin' all the way out here." Now he cast her a small sidelong glance. "And it's mighty odd you get things left on your porch, too. I just wonder."

"I was engaged as a schoolmistress after sitting for my teacher's certificate," she replied, coolly enough. *Mother had thought I would make a good marriage instead of needing an education. Father thought the governesses and tutors quite enough, and I did not need to attend the Brinmawr Academy, after all was said and done. A simple certificate-course after my brother sent me the oddest letter I have ever received, and I am heartily regretting my actions now, thank you, sir.* "I rather thought my gentility was seen as a benefit." *I paid the Teacher Placement Society for this post, and handsomely, too. An independence is a wonderful thing.*

"You could be in San Frances. Dodge City. A place with an opera house instead of some two-bit fancyhouse saloons. I'm just curious, miss."

*You, sir, are not merely curious but fishing.* "Perhaps I wished for a purer life than can be found in *some places.*"

"Never thought I'd live to hear Damnation called *pure.*" His laugh came out sideways in the middle of the sentence, as if he found the very idea too amusing to wait. Cat agreed, but she had thought long and hard about what reason she might give for her presence in this place, if pressed, ever since Jack Gabriel had stood next to her outside the pawnshop window.

And Mr. Gabriel was gone today, on some mysterious errand.

"My parents fell victim to Spanish flu." She sought just the right tone of bitter grief, found it without much difficulty. "I have no family now, and Boston was...a scene of such painful recollections with their passing, that I fled everything that reminded me of them. Perhaps I should not have."

He was silent. Did he now feel a cad? Hopefully.

The wagon shuddered along the road, its wheels bumping through flour-fine dust. It was a wonder he could find the track in all this mess. The hills in the distance were purple, but not a lovely flowerlike shade. No, it was a fresh bruise; the sky's glower was an older, fading, but still ugly contusion. The sun was a white disc above the haze, robbed of its glory, and the stifling heat was no longer dry but oddly clammy. Or perhaps it was merely the haze which made it seem so, since her lips were already cracked.

The rest of the ride passed in that thick obdurate silence, and the appearance of the schoolhouse, rising out of the haze, was extraordinarily welcome. Mr. Overton pulled the wagon to a stop, and when he helped her down she was surprised to find his fingers were cold even through her gloves.

He dropped her hand as if it had burned him. He mumbled something, and was in the wagon's seat like a jack-in-the-box. The conveyance rattled away toward town, and Cat was left staring, her mouth agape in a most unladylike manner.

"Well. I *never,*" she muttered. Except it was precisely the manner of treatment she supposed she *should* expect from such a man. Chartermages were notoriously eccentric, he was not

Quality, either, and he was no doubt unused to polite conversation with someone of Cat's breeding.

Still, his manners were only one of a very long list of things that troubled her. Troubles were fast and thick these days. She opened the schoolhouse and waited for her students, attending the small tasks that had quickly become habitual, and as she did, a plan began to form.

*If I give myself time to think, I will no doubt find a thousand reasons not to do this.* She adjusted her veil once more. It was no use; she had *plenty* of time to lose her courage on the walk into town.

Dismissing the children at the lunch-hour was a risk. Yet she could legitimately claim that so few had shown up, and the return of the storm seemed so ominous, that she had done so for their safety. And the streets were oddly deserted—or perhaps not so oddly, as the lowering yellowgreen clouds were drawing ever closer.

She could even claim to have come into town to find a means of alerting her *other* students of the school's closure for the day. *That* problem she would solve as soon as she had this other bit of business done.

The pawnshop's door stuck a little, its hinges protesting. She stepped inside quickly, unwilling to be seen lingering, and glanced out through the plate-glass window. Perhaps no one had seen her.

She could always hope.

"Hello?" Her voice fell into an empty well of silence, and the walls seemed to draw closer.

It was dark, not even a lamp lit, and chill. Strangely prosaic for a chartershadow's haunt—clothing in piles, some tied with twine and tagged with slips of yellowing paper, others merely flung onto leaning, rickety shelves. A vast heap of leather tack and metal implements, and two long counters—one at the back, one along the left side—with various items on ragged velvet and silk. Pistols, knives with dulled blades, pocketwatches, hair combs. Jewelry both cheap and fine, tangled together.

She tried again. "Hello? I have come to buy."

Perhaps he was at luncheon?

At the counter in the back, something glittered in response.

Cat glanced in the window, and the oddity caught her attention. The bed of fabric, where shiny wares would be displayed to tempt passersby, was empty.

Her throat closed. Was there no one here?

She glanced at the gleam on the back counter again. Pillows of that same moth-eaten velvet, and the locket glittered, recognizing her. Its mancy sparked faintly; a thrill ran along Cat's nerves.

Her breathing came fast and high. "Hello? Is anyone here?"

*Perhaps he is at luncheon. It would be the civilized thing to be doing at this hour.*

But sure instinct told her that was ridiculous. Such a businessman would not leave his door unlocked and his wares half-secured, chartershadow or no. And, strictly speaking, the locket was hers by right. Surely the need to find her brother outweighed what she was about to do?

*I have sliced a man in the face with mancy and a stick; I am spending every afternoon with frail women; last night I was in the arms of a man who now calls me by my charing-name; and now I am about to steal. Mother would be very disappointed.*

Would Cat's mother even *recognize* her daughter now?

She inched across the floorboards, holding her breath until darkness clouded her vision. Finally remembering to inhale, she reached out a trembling gloved finger and touched the locket's gleam. Snatched her hand back, glancing about as if she expected a reprimand.

Nothing happened. The pawnshop was silent as a crypt.

*Avert*, she thought, and brushed ill-luck aside with a quick motion.

A few moments later, Robbie's locket and its broken chain tucked in her reticule and her satchel swinging, Cat Barrowe closed the pawnshop door behind her with a soft *snick*. There was nobody on the street, and the wind inched its way up from a low whisper to a soft chuckle, sliding dust along the boardwalks with brisk broom-strokes. A skeletal tumbleweed rolled past, and Cat hurried along in the precarious shade of flapping awnings toward Capran's Dry Goods. She could enquire after the delivery of items for little Jonathan and engage one of the store's boys to take a message to Miss Tiergale that school was canceled for the afternoon.

Her heart refused to slow its mad pounding, her hands trembled. But she put her chin up and hurried along, hoping no one had seen her.

*Dear Robbie, I am now a thief. If you are alive when I find you, I am just going to pinch you.*

# Chapter Nineteen

Hathorn was no longer the youngest horse, but she was dependable and Gabe had ridden her out of town before. She didn't get excited easily, but when she did she was fleet and smarter than the average equine. She was also prickly-tempered, and didn't respect a rider who would put up with any foolishness.

Well now, that reminded him of a certain miss, didn't it.

*Don't think about her.*

There was plenty of other thinking to do, and he did it best when he was alone, scanning the horizon and eyeing the tops of ridges for any silhouette that didn't belong. It was daylight, but the sky was too clouded for his comfort.

Still, he wouldn't be able to rest until he checked that goddamn claim.

The dangers out here weren't merely wildlife or some of the miners and panners getting a bit twitchy with a stranger. There were harpies higher up in the hills, and other, fouler things in some of the deep-scored gullies and valleys. The wild mancy out here, without a chartermage or people using its flood to shape and tame it, gave birth to oddities. Even the few remaining survivors of the Red Tribes wouldn't come near this slice of the Territory, and they had coexisted with this continent and its oddities before Gabe's kind had sailed west to find the spices of the Sun.

Disease and war had all but wiped out the tribes, though there was some talk of a hole in the world they had escaped through, into a paradise without invaders. Privately, Gabe hoped they had, and wished they hadn't left any of their kind behind, given how *his* kind by and large dealt with those survivors. All the same, this was a fine land, and he'd been born on its shores. Working another country's mancy would be problematic at best.

He didn't mind. Much. The Ordo Templis was far more active across the Atlantica, and escaping to a country they didn't have their fingers in would be a trick indeed. Unless he wanted to take Chinoisie lessons from Li Ang and keep heading West until it became East.

He found the lightning-blasted tree silhouetted against the sky, and suppressed a shiver as he turned Hathorn's black head toward a thicket of spinesage. She didn't like it, but she went, and when he left her at the edge of the hidden spring with its sweet-crystal bubbling top swirling with blown dust, she was content enough.

From there it was slogging through fragrant junip and wild tabac wilting under the heat, underground water heaving the devilpine trees up to clutch at the sky with their bony fingers. He was sweating by the time he was halfway up the side of the wash, and the midges had found him.

*Damn biters.* He didn't risk a charm to shake them off, though. No need to announce his presence any more than he already had, or any more than the grace on him would.

The going became a little easier, but he slowed as it did. Something had come this way lately, breaking branches and scuffing the ground. Didn't take a genius to read those signs, or to see the mark of a bootheel with nails crossed to ward off bad luck. Didn't prove much, but he went cautiously, his breathing slow and even and a trickle of sweat tracing its way down his spine.

A sharp hairpin bend even a mountain goat would have trouble with, but Gabe knew its trick and leapt lightly. Landed catfoot, and crouched, hard up against an old devilpine whose bark smelled of crushed cinnamon when he leaned into its shade. He was leaving sign too; no way to avoid it. Damn the whole thing.

It was too quiet in this little defile. No bird sang here, and even the wind was muted. The dust didn't reach too far up, the devil-pines sheltering the hillsides wherever there was enough water for them to cling to. Nothing slithered in the undergrowth, nothing nested in the trees, and even the midges hung back.

That would have been a mercy, if not for the cold. His breath didn't frost when it left him, but it felt like it should. The chill wasn't physical. It was *inside*.

He crouched there near the tree, taking his time. Then he inched forward, using his shoulder on the trunk to brace himself, and took a peek.

And ducked back behind the devilpine, swearing internally, clear beads of sweat standing out on his forehead and cheeks, wetting his underarms and making his woolen stockings slippery inside his well-worn boots.

*Oh God, protect a sinner, now and forever. Shine Your light on us, dear Lord, and let us be as lamps in darkness. I am a sword of the righteous and You are my shield.*

Funny how the urge to pray returned, even though he'd sworn never to do it again after Annie died, screaming an undead's unholy grinding cry. Only it was a pair of dark eyes he thought of now, and curls knocked loose, and her trembling against him.

He was shaking, but his hands knew what to do. One of them touched a pistol's butt, the other drew a knife.

Another look, just to be sure. He ducked back again, and this time the fear was high and hard and sharp, bitter copper against his tongue and his heart pounding in his temples and wrists and ankles so hard he thought he might slide into unconsciousness right there on the hillside. And lie there, vulnerable and alone, with the unphysical coldness breathing over him.

That brought him up in a rush, and he stepped out into the open, facing the dark mouth of the unsealed claim. It yawned, a fracture in the hillside full of spilled-ink darkness even broad daylight wouldn't penetrate, and the cold struck him like a wall of flash-flood water in a gully.

And Jack Gabriel, who had once been a priest, went about his holy work.

He slumped in the saddle instead of riding straight. Hathorn knew her way home, but he should have been more alert. Instead he was thinking through cotton. The chill exhaling from the mouth of the seal-cracked claim got into a man's bones.

*Think about something warm, then.*

His thinking wouldn't listen. Instead, it hitched on the boy. What was his name?

He couldn't pull it out of his memory at first, and that was odd. More than odd, since he had a suspicion it wasn't the first time. It was downright *unnatural*, the way the boy's name kept slipping through the cracks.

Jack's fingers were strips of ice; he had long ago ceased shivering. The sky was a congested mass, dust billowing as Hathorn picked her way carefully, the fan-shaped charmhood on her sleek head bobbing. A good horse, even if she was getting on in—

*There it is again. Getting distracted.*

Devilpine trees shook as the wind rattled them. Soon they'd be in the flats, heading for town, and he would see Catherine's face again. Those wide dark eyes, and the sweet way her mouth turned down at the corners when she tried to put on a prim face. The single dimple in one soft cheek when she forgot herself and smiled.

*There. That's it.*

"Robbie Browne." His feet were numb and his hands, too. The cold was all through him, except for the flame in his chest that was the light in a pair of dark eyes. Such a small, still spark to hold back that ice. "That was him."

Just a greenhorn, a boy with a quick tongue and deft hands at cards. An expensive charing and good cloth, but he slid around trouble like grease on a griddle. Dark eyes, a stubborn wave to his dark hair, and a jaw just begging to be set right with a fist when he smiled that easy smile.

With so much other trouble to keep in check, though, Gabe hadn't worried about him. Just another dreamer come Westronward without the sense God gave a mule.

*Like Catherine?*

Damn the woman, dancing into his thoughts all the time. But the thought of her pushed the ice back, gave him space to breathe. He lifted his head slightly, checked his surroundings. The hills were behind him, falling away like a sodden coat.

When Robbie Browne showed up with gold bars and a mysterious smile, there was a certain amount of grumbling. But there was grumbling any time a miner struck anything worthwhile out there. But then there had been the incursion, the circuit broken and something deadly lurking in the junip and wild tabac, something whose breath brought the corpses up out of sandy soil and gave both Russ and Gabe plenty of trouble.

It was the claim, of course. Just sitting there waiting for someone, and the boy had stumbled across it. Tracing the incursion of bad mancy to its source had led Gabe straight to the claim, and he and Russ had arrived just in time to see the boy vanishing into the dark crack in the hillside. Waiting for Browne to come out had been nerve-wracking, but Gabe had been sure he would.

And lo, he had. Seeing a sheriff waiting for him, though, the boy had drawn, and Gabe's gun spoke first.

At least they had buried the kid right. It had . . . bothered Gabe, a bit, to see Robbie Browne's charing gone. It could have been lost in the claim, true. The thing that had chased Browne out into the fading dust-choked light of that long-ago afternoon could have broken the chain of his charing-charm.

Still, he didn't like it. He didn't like it at all, so he had gone out that night and made sure the earth around the hasty grave was blessed as one of the Ordo Templis could make it. If he had enough grace to seal up that hole in the hill again, and enough to take care of the death-charm left on Catherine's porch, then Robbie Browne was sleeping safely.

Jack Gabriel's head came up. The cold receded, its fingers scraping his shoulders and trickling down his spine.

The thought of her just kept coming back. The exact sound of her steps, her point-toe boots clipping along with authority. The graceful lift of her arm as she pointed to the large slate board and helped a child along with a recitation. Her inviting Mercy Tiergale in to tea, as if it were no great shakes. And her holding Li Ang's baby, a disbelieving smile like sunlight on her wan face as she looked at Jack Gabriel.

A look like that could go straight through a man.

The smudge on the horizon was Damnation, and Hathorn picked up her pace a little as the wind's moan mounted. The simoun had just been taking a breather, not spent yet.

If he made it back to town in time, he could see her. Might even tell Russ he'd take the wagon out himself, though with Hathorn's gait that wasn't too likely. It didn't matter; Russ would see her home safe. One of the Bradford boys was riding the circuit with the chartermage tonight, so Gabe didn't have to worry about that.

And tonight was also their weekly game at the Lucky Star. Maybe his luck had changed.

Gabe set his shoulders and rode on, the cold fading even as the hot rasping wind rose.

# Chapter Twenty

Sleep hovered just out of reach, held off by little Jonathan's fractious wailing and the wind scraping at the corners of the house. Pops and sparks of stray mancy danced in the charged air, and Cat's nerves were worn clear through.

She rolled over, pushing down the sheet. At least she had returned to her own bed; Li Ang's cot and the new crib were both in the small room down the hall. The evening was stifling, clammy-hot even though the dust sucked moisture from every blessed thing under its lash. Her hair was misbehaving as well, curls springing free instead of lying in a sleek decorous braid.

The locket was warm against her breastbone. It would rest under her dress, the mended chain longer to accommodate Robbie's larger frame, and the secret of its presence was oddly comforting. After the sun had reached a comfortable distance above the horizon, she could unleash her Practicality on the metal; a simple finding-charm would at least show her what direction to take.

If Robbie had moved on to another town, well, Damnation would be missing its new schoolmarm. She suspected the town would be relieved, and no doubt Cat herself would share that relief. This was *not* what she had expected.

Well, honestly, what *had* she expected? To come sailing into town and find Robbie in some small bit of foolish trouble, and to have everything smoothed over by teatime? An adventure from a novel, full of Virtue overcoming Vice and rescuing the Foolish? A penitent Robert Heath Edward Barrowe-Browne, ready to return home to Boston to take up the reins of the family fortune and, not so incidentally, take some of the onus of being In Society from the shoulders of his younger sister?

Cat sighed, moved restlessly again. Jonathan's cries vanished under the sound of the grit-laden moan of simoun, and she understood now what Mr. Overton had said about becoming crazed by the wind. It was certainly possible.

*Poison wind. What a terrible name.*

It was no use. Whether it was the locket against her skin or the baby's fussing, the wind's sliding scrape or the heat, sleep was impossible. No matter if she would need it for whatever tomorrow held.

There was a thumping rattle from downstairs, and baby Jonathan set up another thin cry. This one sounded frantic, and Cat sighed. Perhaps Li Ang had dropped something. In any case, she was awake; she might as well go downstairs.

At least the Chinoise girl was company. Cat was beginning to suspect Li Ang knew far more of Cat's own mother tongue than she employed, too. There was a steely glint in Li Ang's gaze, a certain something in the way she held her shoulders now, that seemed to say so.

Cat drew a blue silken robe over her nightgown and sighed afresh, sliding her feet into well-worn slippers. Shuffling down the stairs, she yawned hugely, and there was another thumping from the kitchen.

*What on earth is she doing? Throwing the crockery? I would not be surprised.*

It was, she reflected, dreadfully uncivilized here. She outright hated it. And yet, there was a certain freedom to her daily routine that would have been unthinkable in Boston. Was that not why Robbie had left? *It stifles me here, sister dear.* His wide grin as she bade him farewell at the train station—Mother would not come, and Father had not seen fit to leave his club that day. *Don't you worry. I'll send for you soon.*

But he never had.

Cat wiped at her cheek. She pushed the kitchen door open, soft lamplight filling the hall and her slippers noiseless as she stepped through.

Her greeting died on her lips.

Baby Jonathan, in his wicker basket on the table, set up a furious howling. The wind screamed. A man had Li Ang by the throat, pressed against the bar on the back door, and the Chinoise girl's face was plummy-red as she struggled. The man had a long black braid bisecting his blue-cotton-clad back, and odd slipper-shoes, and Cat Barrowe clapped her lips shut over a scream.

There was no time for reflection. Mancy crackled on her fingers, and the stinging burst of bright blue-white hit the man squarely in the back. He yelped with surprise, dropping Li Ang, and Cat had enough time to think *Why, he's Chinois too…*

…before the man was somehow right in front of her, and a stunning blow to her midsection robbed her of breath. She stumbled back, clipping her shoulder on the kitchen door, and went down in a heap, the table jolting and little Jonathan sending up a fresh wail at the indignity of being bumped about so. Stars exploded inside Cat's skull as the Chinois man struck her again, and her Practicality, uncontrolled, bit *hard*, striking through her charing-charm in self-defense.

He made no sound, but the mancy flung him back. Li Ang choked, and the baby screeched. The table waltzed dangerously as the attacker fell against it, and Cat's belly gave a flare of agonized red pain as she scrambled, her fingernails tearing against rough planks. The basket spun, the baby howled, and there was a queer meaty *thunk*ing sound.

Li Ang's scream rose, matching the poison wind's fury. Another meaty thumping, with a crack at the end. The basket was heavy, and its wicker bit Cat's fingers. She hit the ground in a useless lump, all her breath stolen, and baby Jonathan waved one tiny fist as if hurling an imprecation at Heaven. It would have been quite amusing to witness such fury, but Cat could not *breathe*; her body refused and darkness crawled over her vision, spots of unhealthy foxfire dancing in the sudden gloom. She curled around the basket, its fall to the floor arrested by her own body. Some instinct deeper than reason had forced her unwilling flesh to move, to save the tiny newborn thing.

There was a sudden, ugly stench, and Li Ang's face loomed through the dark. Cat tried to gasp, but her lungs would not obey her.

There was a creak, Li Ang's fingers striking her abused midsection in a peculiar manner, and Cat whooped in a grateful, unending breath. The air sobbed out, and she found her cheeks wet and her entire body shaking as if with palsy. Li Ang crouched, pulling the wicker basket toward her, then collapsed. The two women lay, the basket between their bellies, and the baby screamed as they stared at each other, nose-to-nose. Cat's breath mingled with the Chinoise girl's, and the spark in Li Ang's pupils found a matching flare in hers.

Her wind returned in small sips and a fit of wretched coughing. The stench did *not* fade. It was a privy stink, and the moment Cat's nose wrinkled she decided she could, indeed, push herself up on shaky arms. The locket swung free of her chest, sparks dancing on the metal as it struck against her charing, and she could not even clutch at it, being fully occupied with heaving her reluctant body upright.

As if her movement had broken a paralyzing charm, Li Ang moved too. She scooped the baby from his basket. The little thing quieted, his lips smacking a little as he fought for breath as well. Li Ang sat amid the shattered table and unbuttoned the top half of her dress. Her breast, luminous gold in the single lamp's glow, rose like a moon, and the baby latched on.

Cat surveyed the kitchen. The stove was sullenly giving forth heat, and the shelves near the washbasin were knocked askew. The table would be useless unless she could find a mending-charm for two of its four legs, and the chairs were matchwood. A bottle of dyspepsia syrup had broken on the floor, and a sticky red tide spread under the Chinois man, who lay with his head—or what was left of it—cocked at an odd angle, the stain on the seat of his threadbare blue breeches announcing where the reek originated from. The cast-iron skillet propped in the ruins of what had been his skull further announced what Li Ang had hit him with.

Cat found her shoulders against the wall. Next to her, Li Ang crooned to Jonathan, who had fallen silent, suckling and content. The Chinoise girl's hair hung in her face, strands of black ink, and she was sweating. Great pearly pale drops of water stood out on her skin. Crockery lay smashed across the floor, other implements were scattered, and the largest knife their household possessed was rammed into the barred back door, its wooden hilt still quivering from whatever violence had sunk it into thick wood.

Her head lolled a little, and she found herself staring at Li Ang, who was regarding her with narrowed, black Chinoise eyes. Cat swallowed several times, seeking to clear her throat.

"Li Ang." Husky, the name dropped into the kitchen's hush. Outside, the wind mounted another notch.

"Bad man." Perfectly reasonable pronunciation, too. "He come for baby."

*Well, obviously.* "And...to hurt you." *To kill you.*

Li Ang nodded, grimly. "Husband. Wants baby."

*A husband?* "I thought you were a widow." Her entire body was heavy as lead. Her mouth tasted of things best left unsaid.

"Husband sorcerer. *Mage.*" The girl spat the world. "I youngest wife."

*Oh, dear heavens.* "Ah. I see." *Except I do not. Youngest wife. Wants baby. She's hiding.*

Apparently the girl who did her washing and cooked her meals had a secret, too.

Cat coughed. Her stomach cramped, and she doubled over. The pain eased in increments.

Li Ang still watched her. "He no take baby. He want go into from baby, make him young."

*Oh, God.* Cat's gorge rose. She retched once, pointlessly, and only grim strength of will kept her from doing so again. That was mancy of the blackest hue, only whispered of in old faerie-stories of witches stealing breath and body from princesses. "Go into? Into... into *Jonathan*?"

Li Ang nodded. "Brass kettle and herb, and Jin. Fire and mage. Make husband young. I no want husband young. Old man. Nasty. *Bad.*"

*Good heavens.* Cat saw again the marks on Li Ang's legs and back, the ink rubbed under the skin making odd characters, Chinois writing. She recoiled from the memory, her own flesh twitching, and another thought took its place. "Mr.... Mr. Gabriel? He's helping you?"

"Jack help hide." Li Ang's gaze was still steady, gauging Cat. "Li Ang hide. Hide Jin. Hide *both.*"

"I see." The cramping subsided. But the *smell*, dear God, it was terrible. How could anyone bear it? He had... the man had tried to kill Li Ang, and now he was... dead. Dead on the kitchen floor, and Cat had absolutely *no idea* how to begin dealing with this.

But Li Ang was looking at her.

*I am a Barrowe-Browne. I came all the way out into the uncivilized wastes to find my brother, and since I arrived I have done things no lady should ever do. Perhaps I am not quite a lady anymore, but by God...* She coughed again, and decided the pain in her midsection was retreating enough to allow her some leeway.

"By God," she muttered, "I am a Barrowe-Browne."

*How would Mother handle this? Well, there is a dead body on my kitchen floor. This is not The Thing, as she would say. It must be dealt with, and quickly.*

The answer occurred to her in a flash. She braced herself, wincing, and wondered if her legs would carry her.

Gingerly, Cat rose, her nightgown falling in folds of linen, marred with dust and splinters. Her legs were obedient, at least. The silk robe—a present from Robbie—had torn, and she felt a pang as she inched her shoulders up the wall and arranged her clothing afresh. The movements soothed her nerves, and by the time she was reasonably respectable she was at least also able to draw a lungful or two of cleaner air.

Li Ang gazed at her, and the girl's lips compressed into a thin grim line. Did she think Cat was going to march her baby down into the Chinois section of Damnation and get out the brass kettle?

She set her chin. "Very well. I shall dress, and I shall find Mr. Gabriel." *Jack. He'll know what to do.*

Another article of faith, but not as childish as her urge to write Miss Ayre. No, she could all but *see* Jack Gabriel pushing his hat back and surveying this scene of destruction and confusion. And glancing at her, that small reluctant half-smile turning one corner of his mouth up, before he settled into making it all right.

Li Ang examined her from top to toe, and Cat might have felt unreasonably ashamed under such scrutiny. But the Chinoise girl must have found whatever she sought in Cat's expression, for she sighed and sagged against the wall. Livid bruises were purpling on the girl's slim throat, and it seemed a wonder that she could put up such a terrible fight. A lioness protecting her cubs could hardly do better.

And, therefore, Catherine Elizabeth Barrowe-Browne could do no less.

"Very well," Cat repeated. "Can you stand? I do not think we should be apart until I leave. I shall dress myself, and I shall find Mr. Gabriel, and we shall make this right."

Though how it could be made right was beyond her.

# Chapter Twenty-One

The Lucky Star was going full-tilt, rolling like a whaling ship on the North Atlantica. The tinkling pianoforte was spitting out a reel, and miners and gamblers were dancing, either with the saloon's fancy girls or the dancing girls who would cozy up to a miner through "Clementine" or "That Old Gal of Mine," as long as he paid for the drinks.

Doc was the first to arrive, in his dusty black, and he gave Jack Gabriel a narrow-eyed stare. "You look like hell, Gabe. Something been keepin' you up nights?"

"Riding the circuit." *That damn storm's too thick tonight. Wonder where Russ got himself off to, he should be back by now.* Gabe tossed back the shot of what passed for whiskey, set the bottle in the middle of the table. The thumping and jollity from downstairs was enough to give a man a headache.

"Not a pretty pair of dark eyes?" Howard's laugh was dry and rasping as the dust. "Someone should tell Laura Chapwick she's still got a chance."

Gabe stared at the amber liquid in the bottle. The old man would grow tired of baiting if the bear didn't respond.

Sure enough, Doc dropped down in his usual seat. "You *are* looking rough, Sheriff. It isn't like you to drink before the game, either."

"Might make it easier to lose." *Since my luck's been so bad.*

"Might, at that." Doc's spidery tabac-stained fingers drummed the table.

"Well, *Hell*," Paul Turnbull announced, stamping into the room and slamming the door so hard it was a wonder the whole place didn't shake. "Gabe, God *damn* it. The whores are accusin' Tils of skimming, and that goddamn man's been taking it from my cut too. He's drunk, the books are a damn mess, and that Tiergale whore says she'll fix 'em if I pay her. What in God's name is goin' on around here?"

Gabe made a noncommittal noise, and Doc's laugh scraped the corners of the room again, harsh as the grit-laden wind outside. "You're just now noticing Tils is a thief? There's a reason I won't play cards with him, Turnbull."

Paul's footsteps were like to rattle the room. He yanked out his chair, its legs screeching discordantly against the floor, and a shout went up downstairs. Gabe tensed slightly, but it was immediately followed by a flood of drunken laughter. *Seems usual enough*, he decided.

"Hell, I *knew* he was a thief." Turnbull eased his bulk into the chair and sighed, rubbing at his moustache. "I just didn't think he'd steal from the whores. Ain't good business, what with the trouble of getting more of them out here. No reason for the dancin' girls to work like that when they can get what they want for a few turns around the floor."

"Maybe Letitia Granger could take up a subscription." Doc found his own witticism hilarious, and wheezed through another laugh.

There was a tentative tap at the door, but instead of Russ Overton, a corn-gold head poked through atop a pair of massive shoulders. It was Billy, the boy who ran errands for Coy and the girls, and he shuffled into the room with his hat in his broad paws, blunt fingers working nervously at the battered thing. His dark eyes were sleepy and one of them drooped at the corner; whenever he was nervous that cheek would twitch madly like a spider-charm was trapped under the flesh. His charing was a cheap brass disc, barely sparking even when he worked a simple mending. For all that, he was good with those graceless hands, and never touched the booze.

"*Now* what?" Turnbull barked, and Billy all but cowered.

"Guh-guh-guh..." The stammer got worse when he was excited. Nobody knew where he'd come from; he'd just arrived in Damnation and slept out on the main street in the dust until Turnbull let him sweep the boardwalk in exchange for a meal. "*Gabe.* Missah Gabe."

The flash of white he was crumpling along with his hat was a piece of paper, and Billy extended his arm. He stayed where he was, trembling in the face of Paul's glower.

*What the Hell?* Gabe gained his feet and did his best to block Billy's view of Turnbull. "What's this now, Billy? For me?"

"L-l-lady." Billy nodded his head several times. "Lady."

The note was stained by Billy's moist palm, and Gabe clapped him gently on one meaty shoulder. The boy was built like an ox, and it was a good thing he didn't like the liquor. He'd be unrestrainable if he took a mind to go on a tear. "Good boy, Billy. Thank you." He dug in his pocket and found a half-bit, pressed it into the boy's palm. "Good boy. You done good."

"A *billet-doux*?" Doc Howard found this intensely interesting. "Oh, my."

The paper was high quality, and as soon as he touched it he knew *something* wasn't right. His heart gave a thundering leap, because when he opened it, the firm, clear handwriting was familiar.

She had a beautiful hand, that was for sure.

*Jack, I need you. Yours, etc., Catherine.*

He folded it up, deliberately. "She waitin' on a reply, Billy?"

The boy nodded enthusiastically, his hair flopping in his face. "Y-yuh-yussir."

"Show me." He glanced over his shoulder. "Duty calls, boys."

Doc Howard was about to make some sort of rejoinder, but it was lost in Turnbull's exasperated sigh. The silent owner of the Lucky Star threw his hands up in an almost comical gesture of disgust. "Ain't that just *great*. Get the cards out, Doc. I ain't leavin' this room until I've had a few hands."

"Russ'll be along soon." Jack followed Billy out into the hall, closing the door on Paul's curse. Doc would be the one to keep the peace between those two tonight, and it served the old buzzard right.

*I need you.* It was after dark, and she was outside her house. And *Yours, etc., Catherine.* As if he had a right to her charing-name.

There was something in his throat. Gabe swallowed, hard, and wished Billy would shamble faster.

Billy pointed out the Lucky Star's front door, and Gabe had to peer into the dust heaving dark before he saw her.

She was at the corner, a shawl wrapped over her head, blinking furiously against the grit. A charmed handkerchief was pressed over her nose and mouth, struggling to filter the air before she breathed it. Stray curls fluttered on the wind, and he stepped around her, blocking the force of it, without thinking. He leaned down to examine her—she wasn't visibly injured, but her jacket had been hastily buttoned and was slightly askew. Under the shawl her hair was braided and pinned, and she trembled so hard her skirts shook when the wind wasn't flapping them.

He tilted his head to the side and took her arm. She went willingly enough, and the wind fell off sharply as he got her into the shelter of the Skell boardinghouse—not nearly as nice as the Hammises' place, that was for sure. The day's heat had dropped off as well, and with the wind now it was too chilly for what she was wearing.

She shook the charmed handkerchief, a flash of white. "Th-thank you. You c-came."

"Course I did." *What, you thought I wouldn't?* "What is it? Another little somethin' on your porch?" *Because if it is, I will hunt someone down tonight. I'm just in the mood to do it, too.*

"N-no. It's w-worse." The shaking was all through her, and even in this dimness he could see she was paper-pale. "I c-can't even begin to tell you how much worse."

"Are you hurt?" He had her shoulders, and she winced. Was he hurting her? He tried to make his fingers unclench. "Catherine, someone hurt you?"

"N-no. Well, my stomach, but..." She drew in a deep, shaking breath. "It's Li Ang. Someone... he broke in through the parlour window, the shutter was loose. He... he wanted the baby. He hurt... he hurt Li Ang." Another deep breath. "Jack... Sheriff... sir, he is dead."

"Dead." He repeated it, just so he could be sure he'd heard her correct-like.

"Yes, sir." Her pupils were so large her eyes looked black. "Sir... there is a corpse in my kitchen. I don't... I do not know what to do." The shaking in her threatened to infect him.

There was a fist made of cold metal in his guts, and it squeezed. Jack pulled her to him, resting his chin atop her shawl-covered head. He hunched a little, wishing he could close himself around her like an oyster's shell around the meat. "Easy," he murmured, under the wind's low moaning and hissing. "Easy there. I'm here, sweetheart. All's gonna be well. You did right coming to fetch me."

She said something he couldn't hear, muffled by his shirt. Her breath was a warm spot through the material, and perhaps she was crying. He hoped not—maybe she needed it, but the thought of tears leaking from those big dark eyes made him feel a little unsteady. Like he'd been after Annie, powder looking for a match.

He could have stood there a little longer, but she moved restlessly and he had to let her go. She wasn't so pale now, though, and there was that determination on her soft little face again. It was right cheerful to see.

"Thank you." She swallowed, hard, and he could not look away from her lips shaping the words. "I... thank you, Jack."

"Catherine." The rock was back in his throat. It was dry as

the sand in the air, and he suddenly longed for another jolt of whiskey. Digging out his flask now didn't seem like a good idea, though. "No need. Give me that rag of yourn, I'll charm it to keep the dust out and we'll set this to rights."

The transparent relief on her face was worth all the gold in the hills, so he repeated himself as she handed over her handkerchief. "Yes ma'am, we'll set it to rights. You can just rest easy now."

*I sound like an idiot.* But he would say it as many times as needed to reassure her. Which meant a number of things. Not least of which was that he was going to have to have a serious talk with Miss Catherine Barrowe about her future.

And his.

# Chapter Twenty-Two

"Li Ang?" Cat called cautiously up the stairs. "Mr. Gabriel's here. It's safe now."

She had left the Chinoise girl barricaded in her own bedroom, since the door was a solid piece of oak that would stand up most admirably to some abuse. Mr. Gabriel's spurs rang as he strode down the hall, and Cat shut her eyes briefly, listening to him push the kitchen door open. He viewed the vista inside for what seemed an *exceeding* long while, then his measured tread came back as the door's hinges gave a slight creak.

"Li Ang?" Cat called again, and there was movement in the shadows upstairs.

The Chinoise girl appeared, a candle clutched in one trembling hand. Her hair was a wild mess, but Cat's was hardly better. And her other hand held the largest kitchen knife, worked free of the back door and freshly honed. She stared down at Cat with wide dark eyes, and slowly picked her way down the stairs. Her feet were bare and soundless.

"No doubt about it." Jack took his hat off, ran stiff fingers back through his dark hair. "Bastard's dead."

"Language, sir." Cat drew herself up. "What shall we do?"

One corner of his mouth twitched, but he sobered quickly. "Ain't no *we*, sweetheart. You go on up with Li Ang now. I'll take care of this. Thank God it's Chinee." He scratched at his hairline, his stubble showing charcoal against tanned and dust-polished cheeks. "If it was a white man, might've been a mite troublesome."

"Mr. *Gabriel!*" Cat's hand flew to her mouth. "What a terrible...my God, sir! He is *dead!*"

The sheriff shook his head, settling his hat afresh. "I ain't sayin' I hold with it, mind. I'm just sayin' that's how it is."

She forced her fingers away from her lips. "I...it is a body. Dead by violence, and the risk of reanimation—"

"This ain't the first murder we've had in Damnation, sweetheart. I told you to leave it to me, didn't I? Go on up and set with Li Ang. Don't think there's likely to be more of his kind tonight." But he gazed past her as he said it, pale-hazel eyes thoughtful, and Li Ang halted two stairs up.

"No more." The Chinoise girl made a short stabbing motion with the knife. The candleflame danced, a spark of mancy keeping it lit as it struggled with a sudden draught.

*Why, she's trembling as much as I am.* Cat forced her shoulders back. "Well, I am relieved to hear as much. Mr. Gabriel, sir, it is hardly fair of me to retire while you deal with—"

"I ain't havin' my girl hauling no corpses. Go on up with Li Ang, or I'll drag you myself. He ain't gettin' no fresher."

Her jaw was suspiciously loose, and the irritation—dear God, must the man be so infuriating?—was nevertheless wonderfully bracing. *You most certainly will not drag me.* "*Your girl?* Mr. Gabriel—"

*Now* he looked damnably amused. "It's *Jack,* sweetheart, and yes, *my* girl. You think I'd come running like this if you weren't? We ain't got time to fix no plans now, but later we will. You can scream and stamp that pretty little foot of yours all you like." He touched his hatbrim, bidding her farewell. "Now get on up those stairs before I take a mind to *carry* you up."

Li Ang made a small noise. Almost like a smothered laugh.

Perhaps wisely, Cat decided to retreat. "Thank you, sir." She reached for the banister, and found with some relief that her legs were much steadier now. The deeper relief—that there would soon no longer be a dead body in her kitchen—did not bear mentioning. But what was that sharp piercing behind her collarbone?

*I am not "your girl,"sir. In fact, come tomorrow, I am not even certain I shall be remaining in this charming little hole of a town.*

Somehow, it seemed the wrong thing to say. And ungrateful, too. She barely remembered writing the note. *I need you.* Three simple stark words, and he had left the Lucky Star in a hurry, following the boy's pointing finger toward her. God alone knew what he had been doing inside that place—portly balding Mr. Capran, just locking the dry goods store's door before heading home for the evening, had said that was where the sheriff would be, and lo and behold, there he was.

Tall, broad-shouldered, dust all over him and shadows under his bright piercing eyes, and he had hadn't even blanched when she informed him of the . . . the problem.

*Oh, Cat, do not be an idiot. The body. The corpse. The man you helped murder.*

She followed Li Ang back up the stairs, feeling Jack Gabriel's gaze on her like a heavy weight. Another thought occurred to her—Mr. Gabriel had hidden Li Ang here; perhaps he felt responsible in some small way for this turn of events?

After all, the Chinois man in the kitchen could have killed Cat as well. This very unwelcome thought brought her up short, and she half-turned to glance back at the sheriff, who waited patiently at the foot of the stairs, his chin tilted up as he gazed steadily at her.

*Did you suspect this would happen, sir?*

It was a terrible thing to think. And now the dead rabbit nailed to her porch took on an altogether more sinister hue as well. Perhaps Mr. Gabriel thought his manner of rough courtship would keep her quietly providing a safe haven for Li Ang.

Now was not the time to ask *that* question, either. And if the poor mancy-blighted thing on her front porch had been intended for Li Ang, did that mean nobody here knew of Robbie?

"Catherine," he said, quietly, under the moan and rattle-whisper of the poison wind. "If he'd hurt you, I would have killed him myself."

The drawl was gone, and the words sounded clipped, precise, and very educated. She studied his features for a moment, or what she could see of them in the light of the single trembling candle Li Ang held.

She could find no reply, so she simply turned wearily and climbed the rest of the stairs after Li Ang.

Perhaps it was the shock to her nerves. In any case, she was deeply asleep as soon as her head touched her pillow, baby Jonathan cuddled between her and Li Ang, whose warmth somehow dispelled the clamminess and overpowered the rasp of the wind. She woke to the dim dust-filtered light of dawn and the smells of bacon and coffee drifting up the stairs.

The kitchen was set to rights, although there were no chairs at the table. Mending-charms still vibrated in the wood of the table-legs, and the floor was charm-scrubbed, innocent of any stain. Cat paused in the doorway, her braid hanging over her shoulder and her bare feet protesting the treatment they received from the boards underneath.

Slippers had not seemed a worthwhile trouble this morning.

The broken crockery had been swept up and disposed of, and baby Jonathan's basket was set in the corner. He burbled a little, and Li Ang was occupied in attending to a panful of biscuits. The bacon sizzled most fetchingly.

Jack Gabriel was crouched by the table, his eyes smudged with sleeplessness and his callused hands running over the table-legs, making certain the charms had sunk in fast. His dun coat hung on a hook by the door, and his boots had traces of sandy earth clinging to them, grinding as he shifted his weight and frowned slightly. Under the worn pale fabric of his shirt, muscle moved, and his mended braces had seen much better days. The guns at his hips gleamed sullenly in the lamplight. It seemed impossible that so large a man could make himself so temporarily small. He had laid aside his hat, too, and his hair was mightily disarranged.

Cat stood there for a long moment. Li Ang turned from the stove and nodded, her face breaking into the widest smile Cat could ever recall gracing her features. "Morning!" she chirped, and Jack glanced over his shoulder.

Her hand had curled around the jamb. Cat stared at the pair of them, and a yawning emptiness opened behind her breastbone. Robbie's locket was tucked safely under her nightgown, and her charing-charm was warm.

She turned, and let the kitchen door shut itself.

*I have never belonged here.* She swallowed, twice, very hard. There was no point in seeking a breakfast. Instead, she should dress herself, pack her trunk, and draw out Robbie's locket. Her Practicality would spark in the metal, and—

"Catherine?" Did he sound uncertain?

She steeled herself for what she was about to do. Halted, and stared at the front door, barely noticing the parlour opening to her right, full of fussiness and shabby chintz.

*I should never have left Boston.*

"Did it fail to occur to you that I might appreciate a warning, Mr. Gabriel?" It was her mother's Dismissing A Servant tone, and it hurt her throat, stung her tongue, and filled her smarting eyes afresh.

The wind filled in the spaces between each word, and rasped against the house's corners. Dust *everywhere*, and even if she retreated to the Eastron edge of this blasted continent she did not doubt she would hear the poison wind the rest of her life.

*I am a fool. He is, after all, so far beneath me.*

He was silent.

So she spoke, each word precisely polished. "A warning that perhaps the servant girl you had procured for me might be at risk of drawing murderers to my home? A warning that perhaps I should be on guard against evil mancy nailed to my porch? Or perhaps a warning that I was at risk of being slaughtered in my own bed by a Chinois criminal?"

"I didn't think—" Was he breathless? And well he should be.

"Precisely." *I wish I would have dressed for this.* "You may leave, Mr. Gabriel. I do not appreciate, nor will I brook, being misled in this manner. I came here in good faith, sir, and have narrowly missed being murdered for it."

"Catherine—" As if he had been struck in the belly, lost all his air. Just as she had been struck last night.

"You shall not address me, sir. You may leave." Though she rather doubted he would. The man was nothing if not stubborn, and there might be a scene.

*Well, I have done nothing but behave disrespectfully since I came to this awful place; I might as well continue.*

Just at that moment, there was a rather brisk knock on the front door. Cat put her head up and strode for it, not caring that she was in her nightdress. She had the bar down in a trice and wrenched the door open; dust swirled as Jack Gabriel gave a sharp warning sound.

But the locket was burning against Cat's chest, and it was merely Mrs. Grinnwald, the sturdy postmistress. She stamped inside, shaking her head as dust fell from her in rivulets. "Didn't think you'd come check for it, miss; there's a letter for you." Her bloodshot blue eyes greedily drank in the scene—Cat in her undress, the sheriff in his, and the letter in Grinnwald's horny hand was rudely snatched away. Behind the postmistress's ample bulk, the porch was a dim cave, dawn's glow eerie and muffled through the flying dirt in the air.

Cat nodded briskly. "Thank you, Mrs. Grinnwald. I am very sorry to put you to the trouble. How long has this been waiting?"

"Two days, ma'am. Bit of a wind, and—"

"Your devotion to service is no doubt to be commended." *You nasty, gossiping old hag.* Cat drew her nightdress about her as if it were a morning-dress. "Thank you very much. Li Ang is preparing breakfast; perhaps you, as Mr. Gabriel, will avail yourself of my hospitality in the face of this regrettable weather."

And with that, she sallied up the stairs. The silence was almost as satisfying as the odd, queerly breathless tone Mr. Gabriel employed as he told the postmistress to come inside and shut the damn door, if she was going to be nosy.

# Chapter Twenty-Three

"I don't know," old Grinnwald huffed "Some special delivery from Boston. Was paid to take it to her, that's all I know."

*Wonderful.* Although he didn't mind the old bat seeing Catherine in her nightdress and Jack right behind her. The news would be all over town by afternoon, and he couldn't say he had any objection.

*I have narrowly missed being murdered for it.* Well, he deserved that, didn't he. Here he was thinking she'd be grateful, and he could have slapped himself silly for it now. It had seemed so simple. Put Li Ang somewhere he could keep an eye on her, and then he had just hoped... or what? What exactly had he been hoping?

He wished the old woman would just go away and leave him the hell alone. Li Ang stared wide-eyed at this interloper in her kitchen, who stood and shoveled away every damn biscuit on the plate, complaining that there was no jam.

"And in this weather, too!" Grinnwald continued, querulous through a mouthful of biscuit dripping with baconfat. "I came all the way from the posthouse to deliver it. Well. La-di-*da*, the miss dismisses me!"

Jack grunted. What the hell did she want, anyway? He had work to get to. *You shall not address me, sir.*

Well, if Grinnwald gossiped, Catherine would be linked to him anyway, and he would have time to change her mind. Maybe explain. Women were convoluted creatures, and she'd had a shock last night. What Boston miss would come out in a dust storm to get someone to deal with a dead body in her kitchen? She wasn't made for this.

She was made for finer things, no doubt, and he...was not.

"She's a bit too big for herself if you ask me." Grinnwald nodded. "Carrying on so. Why, I've heard those *frails* at the Star are taking lessons from her, high and mighty as you please. You should look into that, Sheriff. They's bound to be a law agin' it."

"There ain't." The words came out sharp and hard. "And that's my girl you're talking about, missus." *She could have died last night.* "Stuff your hole with more of her biscuits if you like, but keep a civil tongue in your head when you're talking about Miss Barrowe."

Grinnwald gaped, biscuit crumbs strewing her dusty bosom, and Jack slid his arms into his coat. Li Ang made a soft smothered noise, almost like a laugh, and the baby replied with a sleepy burble.

And that made him think of Catherine, smiling disbelievingly as she held the little bundle, wan and pretty in lamplight. And her softness last night, trembling against him. *I need you.* Well, he'd shown up, hadn't he? And he'd heaved the Chinois, hands and feet pierced with true-iron and the man's dead mouth full of consecrated salt, over the charter-circuit border himself. Let him rot outside the charter, dammit. He hadn't had time to dig a grave, and the thought of consecrating more earth made him sick.

*Wait just a goddamn minute...* But it was gone. Something important, but Grinnwald had shaken her bustled rear, declaring she'd never *been* so insulted.

"Stay and fill your fat gullet, then," he told her, jamming his hat on his head. "I'm sure I'll have some more to say in a bit."

But he did not exit through the barred back door. No, instead his spurs rang as he climbed the stairs. Her bedroom door was firmly closed, and he would have bet it was locked, too. Which just made it worse.

What kind of man did she think he was? Good enough to deal with a dead body, but not good enough to...

Except she was right. She could have died.

And it would be Jack Gabriel's goddamn fault.

"Catherine." He knocked, twice. Nice, soft, polite raps. "I know you're listening." He caught himself, tried to fix the drawl back on his tongue. It had become a habit, to slur his words together. Just one more way to hide. "I know you're angry, and you have a right to be. I never thought you'd be in danger here. You have to believe me."

Silence. The sound of the simoun scraped at his ears. Was she leaning against the door to catch his voice? He hoped so. His hand spread itself on the smooth oak. Nice and solid. If she had to barricade herself in, it was a good choice.

He tried to think of what to say next. There wasn't a whole hell of a lot. Usually he just chose to keep his fool mouth shut. But she had a way of turning him upside down and spilling everything out onto the ground. There was only so much of that a man could take.

"You can be as mad as you want, sweetheart. You can call me every ugly name you want. You can tell me to go to Hell, and that's fine. I deserve it. But you and I are going to come to an accounting one way or another. I'm giving you fair warning."

Which sounded like a threat. Hell, he was probably just making her even more angry. Was there a sound behind the door? Cloth moving, a woman's skirts?

"I have to go ride the circuit now. I'm going to give you some time to calm down. Think things over, like." *And I hope you don't just dig yourself in even more stubbornly. Though you probably will. Goddamn woman.*

Why was his chest aching? And he was thinking of other things too. The screaming. The gun speaking, and Annie's body, free of hellish undead jerking, falling in slow motion. He'd been careless with her safety, thinking God wouldn't repay Gabriel's service by taking such a gentle creature and making her suffer so horribly.

Except the incursion had happened, and Annie hadn't had enough mancy to shield herself from an undead's bite. Out on the sod frontier, each homestead had a ring of charterstones, and Jack had stupidly not checked them that nooning, instead sleeping under the willum tree while Annie, poor Annie, barricaded herself in the house and the sun sank toward the horizon...

And now there was this woman behind her bedroom door, terrified and angry, who could have died last night. There was just no plainer way to say it. He hadn't learned a goddamn thing. He didn't even deserve to have her spit on his shadow.

Jack's spurs made a discordant jangle as he headed down the stairs. He strode through the kitchen, where Grinnwald was still bleating at Li Ang, who probably didn't give two shits in a rabbit hole about whatever the fat woman would say. He touched his hat to the Chinoise girl and vanished out the back door, into the howling wind.

# Chapter Twenty-Four

Her fingers trembled. The outer envelope was from the firm of Hixton and Bowles, the solicitors she had engaged for all business pertaining to her identity as Miss Catherine Barrowe, neophyte schoolmistress. Her father's solicitor, Hiram Chillings, would have forwarded this letter to the Hixton office to be sent to Cat. Which meant it would have traveled from Damnation to Boston and back again.

It was worn and stained from the journey, but Robbie's familiar hand was on the outside of the folded inner envelope, and the charmseal tingled as she broke it. It had not been opened, and she had a flash of Robbie biting his lower lip as he sealed the outer sheet in his own peculiar manner.

*Dearest Kittycat*, it began, and she had to blink, furiously. "Oh, Robbie." The locket burned against her chest, so she drew it out and held it with her fingertips, spreading the letter's pages as much as she dared on the tumbled bedding.

Two knocks on her bedroom door. "Catherine?"

*Dear God.* She froze, staring at the unlocked barrier between herself and Jack Gabriel. Would he turn the knob and seek to come *in*? Well, should she expect any less of him?

He spoke further, but she looked away at the shuttered window, filling her head with the moan of the poison wind. When his foot-steps retreated, she returned her attention to the letter.

*What I have to set down will no doubt shock and frighten you, but it will also explain why I do not, under any circumstances, want you anywhere near this deadly blight masquerading as a town. I have limited time, but what I do have I will spend here in this boardinghouse, scribbling to you. Dearest Cat, best little sister, I will not be coming home. I am sorry for it—I know how Mother and Father will vex you for news of me. But dear God, Cat, do not wish for my return. The way is closed for me.*

*I thought I was so lucky, finding a claim. It was a black crack in the hillside, and a lightning-struck devilpine showed me the way, due west of Damnation and in those cursed hills. No won-der they call this town what they do. I should have listened.*

*There was something there, Cat. Something in the dark.* Then, two scored-through lines, unreadable—the nib had scraped the paper cruelly.

Was the bed shaking? No, it was the sobs wracking her frame. She read through her tears, her nose filling, doing her best to weep silently. Halfway through the letter she rose and tacked drunk-enly across the floor to her bedroom door, throwing the lock and retreating to the window, where dawnlight was strengthening as the wind's moaning receded.

*The thing in the claim is terrible, and it has a hold on me. It lives inside me, filling my head with whispers and already I have done such things—but that's not fit for you to hear, Kittycat. I shall soon be dead, but not before I have rid the world of one more evil. It will take all the strength I have, but what will give me the will to strike is that you shall be reading this in the future, and you'll know you can be proud of me. At long last.*

*It's just a damn shame I had to come all the way out here to become such a beast as a brother you do not have to be shamed of.*

*My charing is beginning to sear the flesh underneath. It's only a matter of time before that cursed sheriff notices, or the damn chartermage. The chartershadow here—don't faint, I am bar-gaining with the Devil to fight the Devil, you remember that old game—will at least take payment for a weapon to fight the thing. I traded my locket since he wouldn't take the gold from the claim. Wise of him, perhaps. Mother would just die, wouldn't she. Avert!*

*In any event, Cat, keep this to yourself. Let Mother and Father think me the wastrel and the fool. I can do what I must bravely, because I know you will know. You were always better at pleas-ing them than I, and this is my punishment. I should have lis-tened when you begged me not to go. I wish to God I had.*

*I love you, Kittycat. You are best and brightest. Polish your Practicality, and do well. I regret I will not ever see your dear face again.*

It was signed with a simple scrawled R.

Cat read it once more, and once again. The front door slammed—perhaps Mrs. Grinnwald, perhaps Mr. Gabriel. Who knew? She rested her forehead on the windowsill, white-painted wood cool and slick against her fevered skin.

*Oh, Robbie.*

She cried as she had not since her mother's last breath had rat-tled from a wasted body. Father had succumbed the day before, and in her bitterness Cat had railed at her brother. For it was Rob-bie's leaving that weakened Mother so badly, and Father...he had not spoken of it, but he was not right without his son. For all Robbie did not please them, he was the heir to the Barrowe-Browne name.

They had thought he would return. So had Cat...but the silence had grown so unendurably long. Why had this letter not reached her before?

She was somehow at her bed again, her face pressed into the linens still bearing the frowsty smell of shared breath—Li Ang's, and Cat's, and little Jonathan's. *"Robbie,"* she keened into the muffling, mothering darkness, and there was no answer but the poison wind slowly dying...

...and a distant rumble of thunder in the hills.

# Chapter Twenty-Five

"*There* you are!" Russ Overton looked like hell, his hat sideways and his jacket askew, stubbled and red-eyed. It wasn't a surprise—Gabe looked like hell too, he supposed. "God *damn* you, Gabe, where the *hell* have you been?"

*Heaving bodies over the circuit-line and destroying a woman's faith in me.* "Around." He lifted the glass, took another belt. Coy eyed him speculatively, but wisely kept himself over at the other end of the Star's bar, polishing some glasses with what passed for a white cloth in Damnation. "Time to ride the circuit, Russ." And so it was. Since the simoun had died, and the bruise-dark clouds over the hills had loomed closer. There was thunder, and the breathless sense of a storm approaching.

*Approaching? No, it's damn well here.*

"You're drunk." Russ halted in amazement, scooping his hat from his head and running his fingers through his waxed hair. It didn't help—the sharp tight curl in it was coming back something fierce. He was pale under his coloring, too, and his bloodshot gaze was a little too stare-wide for Gabe's comfort.

"Not yet." The Star was a dim cave this early, the dance floor empty and the upper balcony full of shadows. And Gabe had the wonderful, marvelous thought that perhaps he could well *get* drunk. "Not enough, anyway."

Everyone else in the building was asleep, including the fat, snoring Vance Huggins in the corner, who used the Star as his philosophical office every night. As long as Paul took a cut, he was welcome to, and Tils held his peace for once.

"Gabe, we have a problem. A *huge* problem." Russ stepped close, grabbed Gabe's shoulder. "It's the marm. The goddamn schoolmarm."

Jack Gabriel set the glass down very carefully, and Coy, perhaps sensing a feral current in the charged air, ducked through the low door behind the bar, into the cellar's darkness. A spark of mancy popped and fizzled to give him lee to see by, a charter-rune sketched on a small glass disc he kept chained like a pocketwatch, so he didn't have to mumble a catchphrase to light it. His ruined mouth wouldn't shape many phrases, that was for damn sure.

"You be careful, Russell Overton." Gabe enunciated each word very clearly. "Be *very* careful what you say about her."

"Gabe, for God's sake, listen. Remember that claim in the hills? And the boy? The Browne boy?"

*What does that have to do with the price of tea leaves on a Chinoise whore's boat?* "Russ, for God's sake—"

"Robert Barrowe-Browne. That's how he signed the register at Ma Haines's boardinghouse. *Barrowe*. And the other day, when I took her to the schoolhouse? Blood, Gabe. She's his blood." Russ drew in a deep breath, and his paleness was more marked. "I divined all *goddamn* night after riding the goddamn circuit, trying to find the connection. She's his sister."

The world spun out from underneath him. *That* was the familiarity—she had the same way of tossing her head, and the same high cheekbones. In her eyes, too—big dark eyes, similar to Robbie Browne's and thickly lashed. Why hadn't he seen the resemblance?

*You weren't looking for it.*

"It don't make sense," he found himself saying. "What the hell..."

"Maybe he wrote home that he had a sweet claim and then disappeared. We just assumed he had no kin; Ma Hainey never heard him speak of none and neither did any of the whores, right? And *Browne* ain't a name you would remember. He just slid by, and probably *what he woke up* helped with that. So here comes sister dear, looking for him."

He thought it over, alcohol and sleeplessness fogging him. "But she's from money, Russ. Why wouldn't they just hire someone? One of the Pinks, or a Federal Marshal?"

"Who knows? I just know she's his blood. And she's here under that name—Barrowe. What if she knows where that goddamn claim is, Gabe? What if he wrote to her? What if he was supposed to meet her here?" Russ threw his hat on the bar and scrubbed his hands over his scalp again. "What are we gonna do?"

Gabe stared at the bottle on the counter. He'd taken down far too much amber alcohol masquerading as whiskey to be entirely sure of his own ability to deal with what the chartermage was telling him.

"Do?" He sounded strange even to himself. "You're sure, Russ? You'd better be *damn* sure of what you're telling me."

"We have time, right?" The chartermage actually looked *anxious*. "She ain't been out to that claim yet, has she? *Has she?*"

"She ain't had a chance." *I'd stake my life on it.* Funny, but he would, and he was about to. "Things in town been keeping her busy. Russ, you're *sure*? They're blood, that boy and my Catherine?" He didn't even care if he was showing too many cards; it slipped out. *My Catherine.*

Even if she hated him.

"I went back to Salt's and looked in that cabinet in back. There was the boy's charing-charm, looks just like hers; I put it in my pocket, Gabe. Figured it was safest, what with you riding out to check the claim." For some reason, Russ turned even paler—some trick, with someone of his ancestry. "It lit up like a goddamn Yule tree. When I had enough time to concentrate, and handed her down from the wagon, mind."

*That had better be all you handed down, Overton.* "I see." He stared at the bottle. The liquid inside was trembling, for some reason. Little circles on its surface. "The claim was open. I sealed it up again, but..."

Russ swore, vilely, and Jack heartily agreed. He scrubbed at his face, stubble and dust scraping under callused skin, and the thought of just crawling under the bar and getting *real* good and drunk was tempting.

"All right." He dropped his hands. "All right. Let's go have a talk with her. May be time to tell her just what happened to her brother."

"You mean, that you killed him?" The chartermage's hands wrung together. He was probably completely unaware of the motion.

Jack took a firm hold on his temper. "He was dead the minute he set foot in that claim, Russ." *But I don't think she'll understand that.*

*Maybe it's best if she doesn't, Jack. You ever think about that? Maybe it's better if she hates the very sight of you. At least then, you won't be putting her somewhere she can end up dead.*

He took his foot off the brass rail and wished he hadn't sucked down quite so much almost-whiskey. The world reeled again, but he held on, grimly, and settled his hat further on his aching head. "Let's go. The circuit can wait."

He should have known it would be too late.

The schoolmarm wasn't at home. Li Ang merely shrugged when asked where she'd gone, and they lost precious time riding out to the schoolhouse, only to find it empty for the day. Back to Damnation, then; Capran at the dry goods store had seen her dressed in a blue velvet riding-habit, walking past with her head held high. *Didn't even say hello*, he'd grumbled, and Gabe had only restrained himself from swearing by sheer force of will.

A riding-habit meant a horse, and the closest of the two liveries in town was Arnold Hayrim's, the one that *didn't* send rotgut whiskey out with the stage. Arnold was out at Brubeck's farm looking over a few prospective hacks, but his son Joe—big lumbering dolt that he was—rummaged around in his memory for a while before saying that yes, the marm had engaged a horse for the day. She had money, and she knew how to ride, so Joe had saddled a bay mare for her and she had leapt into the saddle neat as you please. *No sidesaddle, that miss*, Joe said, his blue eyes gleaming. *Right pretty seat she has, too.*

When asked which way she went, Joe spat and shook his head. He had horses to care for and the stagecoach was due in later today. He didn't give a damn where she went as long as she brought the mare back before dark.

The whiskey had burned off. Jack's head throbbed, and there was a deeper ache in his chest. Russ took his hat off, eyeing the boiling dark clouds over the hills. Thunder rumbled, growing closer. The betting on just when the rains would come would be in full swing by now.

Russ scrubbed at his forehead with his fingertips. "Today of all days," he moaned. "Do you think maybe... she couldn't know I've got her brother's charing. I was careful."

Gabe blinked. "A letter." *Curse me for a lackwit.* "She got a letter today. From Boston, the postmistress said. God*damn*."

"Maybe it... dear God." Russ looked sick, leaning against the livery's splintery wall. The morning light had taken on the eerie greenish-yellow cast that meant the storm was coming sooner rather than later. "What kind of brother would tell his sister where that claim is? Or... do you think he did? Maybe she's got some way of knowing. She's got *some* mancy."

"Enough to have a Practicality." He wished his skull would cease squeezing itself to pieces. "Let a man *think*, Russ. Just shut your hole for a minute or two."

"We may not have a minute," the chartermage worried. "If she breaks open that claim again, she might get infected. And you know what that means."

Gabe clapped a lid on his temper. "I sealed it up, she ain't gonna break it." *Except where there's a will, there's a way, and she's got no shortage of will.* "Now just shut *up* and let me goddamn *think.*"

Russ wasn't listening. "We may have to put her down like a rabid—"

Gabe had him by the jacket-front, up against the wall, his fists turning in the material. *How the hell did I get here?* "Shut. Up. You hear me, chartermage? *Keep your mouth shut.* That claim was *sealed* as of yesterday, and she ain't gonna break in. You are gonna go check Robbie Browne's grave and see if her mancy led her there. *I* am gonna go check that goddamn claim, and if I find her there I am going to *make* her listen to some sense. One way or another, we are bringin' her back to Damnation." *And I am not letting her out of my sight until we get a few things settled.*

Russ gaped at him. How fast had Jack moved? And it wasn't like him to hold a man up against a wall. His temper wasn't certain, and that was a bad sign.

"All right. All right, Jack, just settle down—"

"I ain't settlin' until I see my girl's safe. You just mind me, mage. That damn schoolmarm is…well, you ain't gonna make any pronouncements about her without my say-so." *And if she does break into that claim…No, she won't. She can't.*

Except he had an uneasy feeling that *can't* wasn't a word he could apply to his Miss Catherine Barrowe. She didn't know the meaning of the term. And if the thing in the claim infected her like it had her brother…

*What, Jack? You'll shoot her? Another woman dead because you didn't do right.*

"All right," Russ was saying, the words under a heavy counterpoint of thunder. "All right, Gabe. We'd better get started." In the distance, lightning flashed, silver stitches under ink-black billows. And that was a trifle unnatural, though it was hard to tell with the way the storms swept through at this time of year.

She *would* go out just as the rains were coming in. If there was an easy way to go about things, the damn woman would arrange it the other way 'round just to spite him.

"Reckon so." His fingers threatened to cramp as he released the chartermage. "You remember the grave, right?"

"I remember." The weird light did no good by Russ's complexion. The man was ashen, and staring at Gabe like he was a stranger. "You just be careful up at that claim, Jack. I'd hate to lose you."

"Got no intention of being lost." *And no intention of losing her, either.*

# Chapter Twenty-Six

A fter the heat, a cool breeze was welcome—until it turned chill, and she realized the clouds were *not* a good sign. She had not brought a coat—what need, when she hadn't ceased sweating since she arrived? The wind held a fragrant promise of water, too, just the thing to tamp the dust down.

The bay mare was sweet-tempered and had a good pace, but for a long while the hills due west of the town seemed to grow no closer. She'd struck out from the western charterstone, the brass compass from Father's desk tucked safely in her skirt pocket and her mother's watch securely fastened. Her veil kept the dust away, crackling with a charm she had seen Mr. Gabriel perform, and the thought of him was a thin letter-knife turning between her ribs.

Perhaps he had thought Li Ang would be in no danger. Perhaps he thought—

*Who cares what he thought? I shall find Robbie, or whatever remains of him. Then... what?*

The locket tugged against her fingers, its chain wound around each one. The finding-charm was simple, and as soon as she had uttered its first syllable, the locket had lit with blue-white mancy, strange knots that were not quite charter running under the surface of the metal.

The ride gave her plenty of time to think, though her entire body began to protest that she was no longer practiced in such things. She had ridden with Robbie, of course—pleasure jaunts, and sometimes a hunt when invited to a country house.

If she found a grave at the end of the locket's urging, what then?

*Then I shall shake the dust of this hideous place from my person and leave at once. Perhaps I shall go to San Frances, or return to Boston.*

Except the thought of returning to the city of her birth was too bitter to be borne. And there was a certain... well, the sand-dust ground, broken only by hunched figures of thorny plants and stunted junips, tumbleweeds scurrying from the lash of the wind, had a charm about it. The stifled parlours, parquet floors, endless rounds of social calls and charity work, the decisions of dress and etiquette and prestige, did not close about her so here. There was, she decided, a freedom to be had here in the Westron wilderness, but the incivility of Damnation was not the place to seek it.

And if she was quick enough, she would never have to see Jack Gabriel's face again. Embarrassment all but made her writhe in the saddle. What had she been thinking?

But the heat of him, and the quiet capability in his hands, and that damnable half-smile when he glanced at her. *Don't think on it any further.*

Except that was what he would say, wasn't it? *Don't trouble yourself.* And he would quietly go about solving a difficulty.

Like a body on her kitchen floor.

A body Mr. Gabriel probably had *not* been surprised by. But still... *My girl.*

A hot flush rose to her cheeks, and Cat muttered a highly impolite term in response. The man was a nuisance, scarcely better than Mr. Tilson and his bestial rage. He had put Cat in the path of murder—and now that she thought on it, the rabbit nailed to her porch must have been a warning to Li Ang, and therefore to Jack.

*Not Jack. Mr. Gabriel. Thus he is, and thus he shall remain, world without end, smote it be, amen.*

She would do well to remember that. She did not need to feel *grateful* that he had dealt with such unpleasantness. He was, after all, part of its making. It was his *duty*, and she knew of duty, did she not? One performed it with head held high and smile cheerfully set, and it was only in the privacy of one's soul—and sometimes not even there—that one railed against it.

The locket tugged, and she lifted her head. The hills were growing larger, and the sky overhead was full of ink-billows. Flashes of lightning crackled among the clouds farther into the pleated, jagged almost-mountains, and the breeze freshened, tugging at her clothing and her securely pinned hat. The bay was nervous, but Cat's knees clamped home, and she soothed the horse as best she could.

As soon as she followed the locket's urging to its source, she would be free. She could do as she pleased at that moment. Both duty and love urged her to make certain of Robbie's grave, at least. Whatever his ravings of dark things in a cave, or hints of bad mancy, she had to find him.

He was her brother, after all.

Cat clicked her tongue and kneed the bay into a canter. The hills rose around her like teeth, and she suppressed a shiver as she rode into their jaws.

The mare grew increasingly fractious, and Cat sighed inwardly as she held the beast to her task. The locket tugged, and she followed—though finding a path grew more difficult as the sun vanished behind the heavy, ink-dark clouds and the undergrowth thickened. There was evidently some water here, for the junip and devilpine were no longer stunted but thick and clutching. The pines rose, and there was a trail leading up.

Unfortunately, the bay flatly refused to climb past a certain point, and Cat did not blame her much. The trail doubled back on itself in a series of hairpin turns, but a simple charm—one of Miss Bowdler's—found a spring close by and Cat left the bay tied near its hidden bubbling. The locket wished her to proceed in a straight line up the hillside, which Cat was *not* prepared to do. So she followed the path, reasoning that it would either lead her where she wished to go . . . or not.

There was a convenient set of thick-growing, fragrant junips to relieve herself behind, and she was startled into a half-laugh as thunder rattled overhead. In Boston, such a thing—relieving oneself behind a bush while bolts of lightning crackled from the heavens—would have been farce, or unthinkable. Here, it was simply what must be done.

*Mother would simply die.* Avert!

Oh, Robbie.

Slipping and stumbling, she worked her way up the path. Roots tripped her, and devilpine clawed at her hair and habit. When she returned to town, she would be a sorry sight indeed—at one point she fell, scraping both hands and breathing out another curse that would have made Robbie proud. The locket was safely clasped in her fingers, though a bit grimed, and she did not glance up. If she had, she would have perhaps seen a lightning-charred tree twisting against the darkened sky, and guessed where she was.

As it was, she rounded a massive spice-smelling devilpine, shook her head, brushing bits of stuff from her dress, and halted short, tucking her veil aside.

It was a clearing of sorts, a shelf of dirt and stone before a frowning hill-face glowering down at the growth upon its chin. Its mouth was a vertical crack, large enough for a carriage to pass through, but very black. Above, the eyes were full of twisted, wind-scoured junip, and the devilpines around her soughed in the wind, pronouncing sibilants that sounded eerily like laughter. The nose was a ruin, a shelf of crumbling stone, and the locket tugged insistently. But not toward the crack.

Instead, it fairly leapt, the chain biting her fingers, and a clump of junip shook itself as thunder rolled. Cat let out a faint cry, stepping back and almost catching her abused bootheel on her skirts.

Spatters of rain plopped down, and the earth released a heavy fragrance, junip stretching and tossing as the wind loaded itself with fresh moisture and the promise of renewal.

The figure, a scarecrow with dark messy hair, his once-white shirt smeared with crusted filth, leapt back as well, startled. "Who the Devil—oh, damn your eyes, Kittycat, what are you doing *here*?"

Cat stumbled and sat down, *hard*. Her teeth clicked together, and she tasted copper blood. The locket went mad, its chain sinking into her flesh as it sought to escape her grasp and fly to the scarecrow.

"Robbie?" she whispered, but the word was drowned in thunder. "*Robbie?*"

"What in God's name are you *doing* here?" he hissed, and it was unmistakably Robbie. But so thin, and his eyes blazed. Their familiar darkness lit with a foxfire gleam, and another flash of lightning drenched the clearing, turning the face above into a leering skull. "You have to leave. *Now.* Before it takes over again—"

"Robbie..." Her heart pounded so hard she thought she might faint. Tears trickled, thick and hot, down her cheeks, cutting through dust and dry grit. "My God, *Robbie!*"

He beckoned, one pale hand flickering as a fresh spatter of rain fell, warm drops the size of baby Jonathan's fist steaming as they splatted into dust and hit tossing devilpine branches. "This way, dammit. I can't hold him forever...come on, Kittycat!"

She scrambled to her feet and ran for him; he caught her arm in a bruising-hard grip and yanked her aside—

—just as a searing flash lit the clearing afresh. She was tossed from her feet, a massive noise passing through her and a devilpine's trunk rearing to break her fall. Or not quite, precisely, for she hit badly and there was a brief starry flash of pain before unconsciousness.

# Chapter Twenty-Seven

One thing about the weather in these parts: there were no halfway measures. It was either dry enough to parch you in minutes, or it was a solid wall of water fit to drown you even if you were upright and riding through it.

He had a bad moment when he found the bay tied to a tree near the hidden spring, and he barely remembered stumbling up the hill as the storm broke, the rain becoming a curtain and then, thicker. He'd thought to knot a bandanna over his mouth and nose, and the charm to repel dust could be altered easily to give him some breathing room. The rain danced in silver strings from his hatbrim, and his coat wouldn't turn this downpour aside for long.

*God, just let her be alive.*

As if God would listen to *his* prayers. Those of the Templis were sworn to chastity, and he'd betrayed *that*, hadn't he? Along with all the other virtues, one after another, like dominoes.

The lightning-charred tree was no longer a rarity on this hillside; nevertheless, he knew the trail and struggled up, shaking aside the clutching wet fingers of undergrowth. Out here, any scrap of moisture was to be clung to, and Damnation rested where it did because of the aquifer underneath.

Later, when Jack Gabriel thought of Hell, he thought of that battle up the hilly trail, every branch and root conspiring to clutch and hold, the lightning throwing bolts at earth and sky alike, and the sick knowledge beating under his heart that he might be too late. Wet dirt crumbling and the sick taste of failure in his mouth again, his boots slipping and grinding, the guns all but useless in their holsters and his hands prickle-numb with grace that had no outlet.

There was the large trunk of the devilpine, and he rested his back against it for a moment, his ribs heaving. If he kept this up, his heart was going to explode. He blinked several times, his hat-brim sagging under the water, and wished he'd had time to step behind a bush on his way up. Fear had a way of making a man's water want to escape.

He stepped around the devilpine, guns out, and saw nothing but the clearing before the grinning crack in the hillside, deep velvet-black and exhaling a cold draft that turned the rain to flashing ice. Another gem-bright dart of lightning, almost blinding him, and there was a shape at the claim's threshold—a woman's skirts, fluttering as she was dragged by a tall scarecrow into the gaping maw. He was running before he had time to think, a thundercrack of rage lifting him off his feet and his spurs ringing in the moment before he touched ground again, the bright white-hot flash of God's fury scorching all through him before he landed, flung through the entrance and into an ice-bath of torpid bad mancy. He collided with the scarecrow, and the thin man threw out an arm. The blow tossed Jack Gabriel aside, against the cave wall, and he slid down with red pain tearing a hole in his side.

*Cath—*

But the thought cut off, midstream, and a black curtain descended.

"I think he's waking up." Hushed, a woman's voice. Very soft, its cultured tones a brush of velvet against his skin.

Jack blinked, or tried to. There was something crusted in his eyes. A damp, cold, clammy touch brushed against the crust, but not hard enough. You had to scrub to get dried blood out of crevices.

"Just keep him over there." Harsh, a man's voice, but oddly familiar. "I can smell it on him."

"Ah, yes. You were saying?" Another tentative brush. She was touching him, and his head was pillowed on something soft but damp. There was a living warmth underneath it, and he tried to clear his eyelids of the crust. Sound of running water, thunder rattling above a roof of stone and earth. Hard ground under his hip, he was half on his side, and his hands were flung out, empty.

"He buried me in consecrated ground, Cat. So...here I am."

"The consecration kept you whole. So you're...dead. And... not dead."

"Well, yes. You keep *saying* that."

"Pardon me for having a tiny amount of trouble with the idea, Robbie. It is rather unholy."

"Mother would just..." A heavy sigh. "But she has, hasn't she. I'm sorry, Sis."

Catherine shifted slightly. "Well, what are we to *do*? He's a sheriff, after all, but perhaps he will see things in a reasonable light."

*What's reasonable?* Jack wondered. It was the longest span of time he'd been close to her, and he was loath to move. *That you're alive, or that we're inside that goddamn claim and you're talking like it's a tea party?*

"I don't know. I didn't think much beyond keeping *it* contained. Now it's getting out, and God alone knows what will happen. When does the stagecoach come?"

Tension invading her. "I am *not leaving*, Robert. I thought I would find your grave, but instead, well, here we are. In any case, we are Barrowe-Brownes, and I am not leaving you to the mercy of...whatever happens next."

Jack tried blinking again. It was no use; his eyes were crusted shut, and if he could get hold of whatever rag she was using, he could scrub the crust free. But that would tell her that he *was* awake.

And listening.

"I swear, I will carry you into town and throw you on the stagecoach myself. You should go back to Boston."

"*Do* try it, Robert. I shall take great pleasure in teaching you not to manhandle a lady so. I struck a man in the face with a yardstick recently, and was also party to a murder by skillet. I advise you not to try my temper."

A shuffling sound, and a sigh. "Have I told you lately how deadly annoying your stubbornness is? It's unladylike, Kittycat."

"I would curse you, darling brother, but I suspect you have heard worse. And he *is* awake." She shifted again, dabbing at his forehead now. "Hello, Sheriff Gabriel."

He cleared his throat, harshly, felt new tension invade the chill air. "It's *Jack*, sweetheart. And is that Robbie Browne I hear?"

"Yes sir, Sheriff sir." The same edge of mockery, the same irritating *I am of quality, sir, and you are not.*

Yes. It was most *definitely* the boy Gabe had shot. "I thought I killed you. And you, Catherine, have been keepin' secrets."

Her stiffness now was *quite* proper, and she ceased dabbing at him with whatever rag she had been using. "No more than you. I would call you a murderer, but I suspect you would take it as a compliment."

The prickly tone cheered him immensely. At least she was well enough to bristle at him. "You're the one who asked me to get rid of a corpse, sweetheart." He found his arms would work, and his hands were clumsy but obedient. Scrubbing at his eyes rid them of crusted blood, and he blinked furiously several times before his vision cleared and he was treated to the sight of a pale, fever-cheeked Catherine Barrowe, her hat knocked most definitely askew and her curls all a-tumble, hovering above him. Her dark eyes glowed, the sleeve of her jacket was torn, and she was so beautiful it made his heart threaten to stop.

"He seems quite familiar with you, Kittycat." The boy sounded like he was enjoying himself immensely, for a dead man. "I don't know about his family, though."

"Robbie, if you do not cease irritating me, I shall *pinch* you." She sighed, and her gaze rested anxiously on Jack's face. "Mr. Gabriel, you buried my brother in consecrated ground. He is... as you see, he is not dead—you saved him from complete contamination, he tells me. I would ask you to—"

*I doubt I saved him from anything.* "Give me a minute." He didn't want to, but he found his body would do what he asked, and he rolled onto his side. From there it was short work to get his legs under him, and he gained his feet in an ungraceful lunge.

Unfortunately, his guns were missing. One of them was in Robert Browne's skeletal white hands. The boy was so thin his bones were working out through his dead-white flesh, but he was remarkably steady as he pointed the six-shooter steadily in Gabe's direction.

"Move away from him, Sis." Robert Barrowe grinned, his lips skinned back from very white, pearl-glowing teeth. His canines were longer than they had been, and wickedly pointed. "I think it's safest."

Catherine, her riding habit sadly torn and her curls damp with rain, still on her knees on the sandy floor, gazed steadily at her brother. "There's no need for that. If he promises to—"

"You'd *believe* a promise from the *sheriff*? That's rich. He's the enemy, Cat. We have larger vexations, too, in case you haven't noticed. *It's* loose, its attention is away from me for the moment. But Damnation is the first place he's going to visit, once he can get back in through the cracks in my head. We have to leave, and now."

"He? *It*?" Jack's fingers found the source of the blood crusting his face. Head wounds were messy. Other than that, he seemed just dandy. Except his ribs were none too happy, and his head felt like it was going to roll off his shoulders. "Just what did you wake up in here, Browne?"

"Yes." Catherine tilted her head. Two curls fell across her wan little face, and he saw how thin and tired she was. She winced as she moved, as if her ribs were paining her as well. "I was waiting to hear *these* particulars too, Robbie. What is ... *he*?"

Robbie Browne's laugh was a marvel of bitterness. "Can't you *guess*? Coming into the wilderness has softened your brain, Kittycat. It's—" Thunder tried to drown his next few words, but Jack had heard enough. He went cold all over, even colder than the ice breathing from the back of the cave, where the claim spiraled down into the bowels of the earth.

*God have mercy.* He stared at Catherine's brother, his hands filling with the pins-and-needles of grace again. If he could close the distance between them...

The schoolmarm rose slowly, brushing off her skirts. "Then," she said briskly, as the thunder receded, "we shall have to find a priest. Come now, Robbie, don't be a dolt."

And she stepped toward her brother, whose finger tightened on the trigger.

# Chapter Twenty-Eight

Cat was never quite sure afterward what happened. There was a flash, golden instead of blue-white like lightning, and a roar of rage. She fell, *hard*, her handkerchief—stained with Jack Gabriel's blood, and full of rainwater and dirt—knocked out of her fingers. The cave's rock wall was so cold it burned, and the crack of a gunshot was lost under another huge rumbling roll of thunder.

*No, don't*—

But they would not listen to her, would they? Just like her parents, or really, anyone else. The simple, sheer inability to *listen* to anything Cat said seemed to be a hallmark of the world at large. It was not ladylike to shout, but the thought occurred to her that perhaps, just perhaps, it was the only way to be heard.

"Catherine." A scorching touch on her cheek. "God in Heaven. Say something."

*I fear I am quite beyond words, sir.* "Robbie?" Wondering, the name slurred as if she had been at Mother's sherry a bit too much. "Oh, please, *Robbie?*"

"Gone. Think he didn't fancy hanging about once I took my guns back." Mr. Gabriel sounded tightly amused, and as the clouding over her vision cleared, she found herself propped against cold stone, with Jack Gabriel crouched before her, his green-gold gaze disconcertingly direct and his face decked with dried blood, grit, and speckles of rainwater. "Enough time for him later. Are you hurt? Did he ... tell me now, Catherine, did he hurt you?"

*Robbie?* "He would never," she managed, though her tongue was thick and dry. "Sir... please. *Please.* He's trying to keep the thing trapped here, so it doesn't harm the town. Please don't hurt him."

"If he is what I think he is ..." But Mr. Gabriel shook his head. "Don't trouble yourself. Here. Stand up, now. We've got to get you inside the circuit before dark."

But she pushed his hands away, weakly. "Sir. *Sir.* Please don't hurt him. He didn't know what he was waking, and he has been seeking to keep it bottled—"

"Well, he didn't make a good job of it. Claim was open as recently as a couple days ago, sweetheart. Now give me your hands and let's see if you can stand up. If you can't I'm of a mind to throw you over my shoulder and carry you down that goddamn hill."

"Language," she managed, faintly. "He is my brother, sir. Please don't harm him."

"For the last goddamn time, it's *Jack.* Not sir, not Mr. Gabriel, and for God's sake don't push me, or I might do something I'll regret. Now, if you can't stand up, just lean on me."

Her head hurt most abominably, and so did the rest of her. She found herself staring at a battered, still bleeding, and incredibly sour-looking sheriff, who nevertheless helped her to her feet with remarkable gentleness. The floor of the cave was sandy—well, what was sand but dust, and this horrible portion of the world had that in awe-inspiring quantities. He steadied her when she swayed, and had even rescued her handkerchief from somewhere, for he proceeded to dab at her forehead with it while biting his lower lip, quite uselessly on both counts.

She took it from his fingers, and swallowed several times. "I suppose you are rather angry."

"I've had more pleasant days, sweetheart." But his mouth, incredibly, turned up at one corner. That same infuriating half-smile bloomed as she watched, and the sound of the deluge outside was like a gigantic animal breathing. "But not by much. Hope the horses ain't run off."

"Horses?" She seemed to be thinking through syrup. "I do think you are perhaps furious."

"I'm none too pleased, if that's what you mean. But I am damn glad to find you in one piece, and this goddamn claim empty. No wonder it sealed up so nice and easy the other day. *It's* already found—or reinhabited, is my guess—a vessel, and escaped."

*Reinhabited? Oh, dear. That does not sound very nice.* "Does that mean you *knew*—"

Now he looked annoyed, the smile fading. "Only thing I know is that I've got to get you back inside the circuit before dark. And it ain't gonna be easy with this storm on, but God help me, I'm gonna. You can scream at me all you like, Catherine, and you can stamp your foot and throw things at my fool head, I'll listen. And duck. But you ain't gonna go haring off into the wild after no goddamn—"

"*Language*, sir—"

She barely had time to say the words before his mouth met hers. There was a tang of whiskey and the copper note of blood, fear and pain and her teeth sinking into his lip, and the bulk of his body pressing hers against cold, cold rock. But it gentled, and she had time to be amazed and breathless as her fingers worked into his hair and his hands were at her waist, and the storm outside fell away into a great roaring silence.

It was like drowning, only not quite. It was like waking from a nightmare and finding a soothing voice, but not quite. It was as if she were alone on an isle in one of the novels of the Southron Seas, but inside her skin beat two hearts instead of one. It was as if the world had shrunk to a pinpoint, and expanded at the same moment.

And when it ceased she was left bereft, except for the fact that he leaned against her, her head against his collarbone and the weight of him against her oddly bearable. "Catherine," he whispered into her hair. "Don't leave me. Don't you leave me."

She could make no reply, other than to hold him while the thunder overhead roared its displeasure.

The bay had broken free and fled, and Jack's horse was a sweet, older black mare who did *not* like the thunder, but bore it well enough. Cat's foot found the stirrup, and she was in the saddle after a heave or two. Her ribs ached dreadfully.

"I got business here," Jack shouted, over the drumming rain. "Hathorn knows the way home. You just go on now, and bolt your door, and *don't open it* until I come back. You hear me?"

Her cheeks had to be burning. Cat nodded. "But what are you going to—" She had to scream to make herself heard.

"Don't you worry about that," he yelled back. "*Ride*, dammit, and bolt your doors!" And with that, he stepped aside, smart as you please, and slapped the mare's haunch. She took off, affronted by such treatment, and Cat bent low over the horse's neck. Branches freighted with cold water clawed at her; it took all her experience and strength to hold fast as the mare, deciding she had suffered far too much indignity, settled into a bone-rattling canter.

Damnation was a very long way away, and Cat could only pray she made it before the faint sun gleaming through the stormclouds set.

*He's old and hungry, Kittycat. And there's no use killing it; he just comes back. That thrice-damned chartershadow cheated me. There's no weapon that can kill it. I thought I had it contained, but...*

What was Jack going to do? Her mouth still burned, and other parts of her too. Had Mother and Father ever felt—

The black mare burst out of a tangle of junip, and the storm fell over them both with incredible fury. Lightning sizzled, the devilpines tossing their spiny green arms, and Cat was suddenly acutely aware that in a short while they would be free of the hills and the trees; she and the horse would be the tallest items on a broad chessboard dotted with loose scrub and sand probably made treacherous by this second Flood.

# Chapter Twenty-Nine

The rain had slacked to a penetrating drizzle, but the gullies were full of flash-flood, brown foaming water like beer but without John Barleycorn's kindness. It was a mixed blessing, because Gabe had found the bay mare from the livery at the edge of one of the gullies, unhappy and shivering with fear. It was a job to catch and calm the horse, but he managed, and then the problem became getting back to the town.

As long as he thought of it that way—the next problem to be solved, and the next—he could push aside the sick fear under his throbbing ribs and the lump in his throat. The cold crawling on his skin was nothing new, and the habit of shoving it aside so he could work was nothing new either.

But the warmth of grace, pins-and-needles in his extremities but a bath of balm to the rest of him, was a new thing. For a few terrible moments, standing before the leering cave-mouth as the storm moved farther east, it had refused to answer him. He'd gone to his knees on the soft-squish ground, and instead of rage that God had failed him yet again there was instead a terrible fear that he would no longer be able to consecrate anything—and that meant his best weapon, his best way of protecting what he had to protect, was gone.

*Faith doesn't leave*, he had thought, staring through the

falling water, at the churned-up earth and the darkness. *It just goes underground.*

And then the grace had come roaring back, because of the feel of Catherine's mouth under his, the slim curves of her described under his aching hands, and the sweet dazed look she wore when he'd finished all but kissing the breath out of her. Easy and warm, not a painful swelling to be excised because he no longer fought it. It simply *was.*

The claim mouth was sealed again, and this time, he thought it just might take.

*What am I gonna do about her brother? She won't take it kindly if I put him down. But he's infected, and...but I buried him consecrated, which means he might be well-nigh unkillable. And to hear her talk, all we need to do is find a priest. It ain't that simple.*

And God alone knew what she would think if she found out about *him.* The Templis were not regarded kindly in many quarters. And she was such a decorous little thing, too. Would she even consider a man who had broken his vows?

It was too dark, as if night had come early. That was worrisome as well, and the bay mare was tired and still shuddering. Still, he couldn't leave her out in the wild, with God-knew-what roaming around and the storm still heaving its way across the flats.

At the foot of the hills, he turned north instead of plunging straight to the east. It took him a mite longer than he liked, but he found the stand of crying-jessum trees, their long silvery branches flickering and tossing droplets as they shivered in the knifing wind.

The grave was there, at the foot of a once sand-crusted boulder serving as a headstone. The slightly sunken earth still resonated underfoot, meaning it was still consecrated, but Russ Overton was nowhere to be seen. The ground was a mess, not a lot of sign to be found, but Gabe thought there were two sets of hoofprints— one coming from Damnation, the other heading back.

Well, the mage could probably feel something rising to threaten his town and his charterstones. It wasn't like Russ to not come and find Gabe, though. That was...worrisome.

*Just add it to the list.* Jack stared at the dancing trees for a moment. The wash right next to them was full now, roaring along instead of just a trickle of sandy slugwater in its bottom. Everything in the desert was going to drink well tonight, and the mud in the town would be knee-deep before long.

*Won't Catherine hate that.* He stroked the bay's neck, soothing, and realized he was talking to the beast. The thunder had receded, and the horse shivered afresh. "Easy there, we're going back to town now. You'll be having a mash and a combing and some rest soon."

He hoped he wasn't lying to the poor dumb animal, and decided to walk her for a bit. She'd had a terrible day.

*Ain't we all.* Irritation, frustration, and the need to hurry boiled under his skin, but he breathed deep and let out a long sigh. There was no use in exhausting himself or killing the horse. He had just enough time to get back before sundown, even if it was too dark now. Even the worst evil couldn't make the sun sink faster.

But it could thicken the clouds, and do nasty work underneath them.

*Your trouble, Gabriel, is that you can just imagine too goddamn much. Focus on what needs doin' instead.*

Jack Gabriel set off for his town, still talking to the horse. After a while, he realized he was praying.

Old habits died hard.


Damnation seethed under a dark, rain-lashed sky. He came on the town from the northwest, and knew something was wrong the moment he stepped over where the circuit should have been, its invisible hand a weight that said *home* to a tired body. The weight was absent, and his head came up, bloodshot eyes squinting through the drizzle. The mud had begun, sucking at the bay's hooves, and the horse plodded forward thoughtlessly, past caring.

There was a sound, too. He cocked his head, listening intently. A metallic clanging, with a long reverberation. The grace in him responded, painful prickling all over, the warmth intensifying to just short of a burn. He didn't need to look to see his charing would be alive with golden light, but he did reach up and tuck it under the edge of his shirt, just in case.

It wouldn't do to have questions asked.

*That's the charter-bell.* The big iron thing hanging outside and above the chartermage's office, glowing dully every night as they rode the circuit, was usually silent. There was only one reason for it to be tolling.

An incursion. A bad one. The charter-circuit was broken.

He didn't even swear, just set his jaw grimly and urged the tired bay forward. She obeyed, and though he longed to put the spurs to her, it wasn't fair to ride her to death.

*Catherine. Did she make it before the circuit broke?*

He tried to tell himself he'd find out soon enough, that nothing would be served by riding in all a-lather. Everyone knew their duty when the bell rang—women and children locked in the safest place they could find, the men gathering to patrol in groups with any weapon that might serve against reanimated corpses, the saloons to stay open and dispense news and courage, in whatever increments they could, the jail to be manned by special deputies who were probably even now scrabbling for their tin stars and getting their folk to safety. They were good men, and steady, and hard from work.

*Better hope it's enough.*

Still, he was the sheriff. He rode the circuit with the chartermage; the town's defense was his concern. Keeping the peace was a matter of allowing the chaos to bubble just enough, but not overflow; keeping order during an incursion required something else.

So it was that Jack Gabriel straightened his spine, counting the tolls of the charter-bell. It kept gonging, over and over, and that was serious. It would sound until Russ stopped it, like a metronome or a heartbeat, and Gabe almost stood in the stirrups as he peered ahead, trying to guess what the hell was going on.

*The town is the first place he'll go*, Robbie Browne had said.

The thought of that ancient, hungry *thing* crossing the circuit-line was... well, enough to make a man's knees go weak. The town was safe enough during daylight, wasn't it? Even though it was dark under a pall of stormcloud, and the diamond stitcheries of lightning were centered directly over Damnation.

*You have to face up to it, Jack. That thing could be riding inside any flesh it could find. If the thing ain't inside the town, it's just waiting for dark. Which isn't that long off. And it's no doubt sent in some troublemakers to sow chaos and contagion early.*

Still, fending off the thing from the claim on home ground was better than facing it out in the hills. Damnation hadn't been here long, but charters drove deep, and every man in the town would fight. Even the Chinois would, and now Jack could hear their charter-bell ringing too, a brassier sound lifted on a flirting wind from the south, driving drizzle into his face. The rain was intensifying again.

Fighting in the mud. Again. No matter how hard and fast he ran, he always ended up in the filth with his guns to hand.

The bay mare, sensing something amiss, lifted her head. Jack blinked away falling water, his sodden hatbrim drooping, and he wasn't mistaken.

No, there were things rising from the boiling dirt. Claw-shaped things. Hands, tearing at the surface from underneath as the undead rose. He was fairly sure nobody had been buried out here, so that meant these were *gotar*—pure contagion, human-shaped and shambling, their jaws working and their teeth chips of sharp-flaked stone. And of course the thing from the claim would call them up and send them into Damnation. It would be child's play for *it*, now that *it* had found a vessel.

The fact that the vessel might be Catherine herself was enough to send an ice-knife all through him. Had she been caught outside the circuit by a fleeting shadow, holes driven through its shroud by the falling rain? It would be so easy for the *thing* in the claim to snap a saddle-strap or loosen a stirrup, and if she hit the ground wrong and her neck snapped, inhabiting the still-warm flesh would be child's play. Or, maybe Russ had felt the cold breath, and—

*Don't think like that. Solve the problems right in front of you, Gabe.*

Jack breathed a soft curse, the mare began to shudder, and his left hand was at its gun before he caught himself. Bullets wouldn't do anything against mud-things. Cold iron or blunt force to shatter their coherence was the only way—and the half-dozen or so who were rising were already turning blindly in his direction, making wet snuffling sounds under the lashing rain.

*I'm sorry. There ain't no choice now.*

He put the spurs to the mare, and she leapt. Clods of mud flew from her hooves, and he bent in the saddle, urging every ounce of speed out of her.

Joe swore at him, for the bay was covered in mud, shaking, foam-spattered, and probably near ridden to death. Gabe answered with a term that was a near anatomical impossibility, and the chaos enveloped him. Hiram Greenfarb was passing out torches, Capran's Dry Goods was alive with a crowd as he passed out scythes and other implements, and the Lucky Star was a poked anthill. The jail was open, and Gabe arrived at a dead run to find Tils and Doc Howard there already, tin stars pinned to their vests. Tils was red-eyed and smelled of rye, but his jaw was set and he appeared at least mostly sobered-up.

"What we got?" Gabe yelled, and Doc swore at him with a mixture of profound relief and irritation, bracing an ancient shotgun against his shoulder as he watched the street outside.

"Where the hell is Russ?" Paul Turnbull appeared from the back room, a bloody rag tied around his head. "We ain't seen no one from the outlying farms, even though that damn thing's been beating itself senseless. The graveyard looks like someone stirred it with a stick—Salt got us to drag him out there, and he threw down a boundary. Then he passed out, I got him upstairs with the whores. Some wounded, mostly fools hurting themselves. South end of town's a mess; the Chinee are having a time of it too. Guess their chartermage died last night."

*Now that's interesting.* The cabinets set along one wall were all unlocked, he found the one he wanted and shook his hat off. His eyes burned with grit and his heart galloped along far too fast for comfort. "*Shit.* South end of town?"

"South and west. Western charterstone got hit by lightning. Goddamn thing shattered. Where's Russ?"

*I don't want to guess.* "Don't know. Get Granger, he's the closest thing to a chartermage we've got otherwise." *The charterstone was hit? Goddamn. No wonder the boundary's broken.*

Thankfully, Tils just set his jaw and took off when Paul pointed at him. Doc nodded, once. "I'm off for the Star; the girls are making bandages and Ma Ripp's there. So far everything's holding at the south end of town, but I don't fancy the chances of the outliers."

"Serves 'em right, outside the charter!" Paul hollered, but Doc just bared his yellowing teeth and left. The door banged open, and it was Granger—a paper-thin nonentity of a man, but more solid now that his wife was probably locked in the attic of their neat little two-story house and not looming over him.

"Where's the damn chartermage?" Granger's graying hair stood up in wild tufts, he shook the water from his hat and clapped it firmly back on his head. "And Lordy, Sheriff, what the hell happened to *you*?"

"Got caught in the rain." The belt loaded with extra ammunition wrapped around his hips, and he breathed into the sudden weight. He grabbed at the canvas satchel he had checked just last week, settled the strap diagonally across his body, and jammed his own hat firmly on his wet, filthy hair. "You come with me. Paul, stay here and wait for the other deputies. They should be along any moment."

"Not so sure, they all live south of Pig Street." But Turnbull just waved at him. "Nobody's seen the schoolmarm today either, Gabe. Are you—"

*I hope she's at home.* "Well, then, guess I'd better go find her. Come on, Granger. Limber up your charm-throwing and let's see what the hell's happening out there."

"Always in the mud," Granger muttered. "You'd think they'd attack in the dry season. Shitfire."

A hard barking laugh surprised Gabe, and then it was outside again, the storm overhead rattling and smashing every inch of sky. He turned south, peering out from under the flapping awning over the jail's front, and a confusion of men's voices and high horse-screams broke through the rain. He wasted no more words, and behind him Granger puffed to keep up with the sheriff's long loping strides. Mud sucked and splashed, and all Gabe could think about was if Catherine had made it safely to her little cottage.

The sooner he dealt with this mess, the sooner he could find out.

# Chapter Thirty

H er throat ached.

Cat stirred. There was something soft underneath her, but it was so *cold*. The shivering began, great waves of it passing through her, and when she sought to open her eyes and push herself up, she discovered two things.

One was that it made no difference whether her eyelids were open or closed. The dark was complete, phantom-traceries of colors she could not name bursting as she blinked. She could *feel* the lids closing and opening; her eyes were so dry they scraped. Perhaps she was blind?

*Dear God, no.*

The other thing was silence. She could hear her own heartbeat, and a sliding sound when she moved, her riding habit rasping across some other cloth. There was no thunder, no lightning.

*What happened?*

She had been riding; she remembered *that* much. Across the flats, the black mare giving a good account of herself. Then, confusion. Something had happened—a figure cut from black paper rising up, a geyser of earth spewing heavenward, concussive blasts of lightning and an immense sound tumbling her from the saddle. It bent over her, the thing, and consciousness had fled her.

Cat frowned—or at least, she thought she was frowning, her

face twisting on itself. Her Practicality had flashed, blue-white to match the lightning, and the thing had hissed at her. Its breath was so cold the rain flashed into spatters of ice, a chill-fog rising like white steam from the streets of Boston on sunny winter mornings.

Then, nothing.

She patted about her with trembling hands. The softness was a pile of cloth, and the sounds of her movement fell away into the vast darkness. Her throat burned as she swallowed; her side cramped with pain as her ribs protested the treatment she had endured.

"Robbie?" she whispered, and the word vanished, swallowed by the all-encompassing dark. Then, a little louder, "Jack?"

No answer. *Am I dead? No, my heart beats, I breathe. Am I blind? Or...*

She swallowed through the dry pain, held up her fingers. Concentrated, breathing as deeply as she could. Two of her corset stays were broken, and she had to be careful lest they jab at her in a most distracting manner.

The dim glow clinging to her fingers scored her dark-sensitized eyes. Still, she blinked several times, tears of relief welling up. The simplest of light-charms, mancy responding sluggishly to her call, but still wonderfully welcome.

She gazed about her.

The softness underneath her was a pile of discarded, rotting clothing on flat sterile earth. The chamber was large, and its walls were rock. Moisture clung to the stone surfaces, and in the distance she saw a fluid glimmer—water, catching and holding the light she was producing.

*At least I shall not die of thirst. I do hope it is potable.*

She examined the clothing underneath her. There was no rhyme or reason to the pile—dresses, petticoats, frock coats, torn stained shirts, even some articles of children's garb. She tugged the locket free of her dress's neckline and transferred the light-charm to its metal; the shadows danced and spun as she rose on legs unsteady as a new foal's, arranging her clothing as best she could. One of her bootheels was broken, her dress was torn and damp. Still, it was comforting to see her attire was still whole; it wasn't torn *that* badly. She twitched at the fabric, gingerly, and twisted her hair up as best she could. She could find no pins, and her hat and veil were nowhere to be found.

With her person set to rights as much as possible, she stood next to the sad little pile of clothing and sought to calm herself further. Her neck twinged, and when her fingertips explored the pain they found two crusted scabs. She had bled on the front of her dress, and a cold knife went through her as her fingertips brushed the throbbing clots. She was cold, but the wound on her throat burned.

*Oh, dear.* But her charing-charm lay quiescent, and when she gingerly touched it there was no scorching to her skin. *This is troubling. Very troubling indeed.*

*Do not be maudlin,* she told herself sternly. *You have been carried into this place, there must be a means of carrying yourself out of it. Then you may decide what to do next.*

The gleam of water was a large underground lake; this place was a semicircle of sandy beach. The pile of cloth was at one tip of the crescent, and the weeping stone walls gleamed sullenly as she worked her way along the shore, finding more blank sheer stone. She found a handkerchief in her skirt pocket, and washed her face and hands as best she could in the cold, clear water. It had a faint metallic taste, but it slaked her thirst tolerably well. She would be hungry, soon.

Unless the water held something that would gripe her.

Where the crescent of sand was thickest, there was a narrow aperture, and she eyed it for some time before stepping close enough to peer through. Her nose and fingers throbbed with the cold, and she wondered if the chill would kill her before whoever placed her here returned.

The darkness yielded only grudgingly to her tiny light-charm. She pressed forward, uncertainly, one damp hand reaching out to touch the stone. There was a nasty odor, striking her chilled nose and twisting her empty stomach into knots.

She stepped just over the threshold of the door in the stone, breathing a word to strengthen the light-charm—

—and stumbled back, retching, from the twisted pile of meat and snapped bone, a pile of naked corpses pushed against the wall of the passageway like a jumble of unordered firewood. The momentary sight almost drove every scrap of wit she possessed from her, and she went to her knees, heaving as the water from the lake sought its escape.

*And ch-children, there are ch-children's clothes too...* The light-charm flickered as her concentration waned, and the inside of Cat's skull throbbed painfully. If the charm failed she would be here in the *dark*, with that pile of bodies, and oh *God* she could not, *would not* bear it.

She found herself huddled on the pile of discarded clothing again, hugging her knees, rocking back and forth and moaning softly. The broken stays scraped her most painfully, but she didn't care.

"Oh God," she kept saying. "Oh, God. Please. Dear God. Oh, please. *Please.*"

The light-charm did not fail, but it took a long time for Cat to raise her head, her hair falling forward in a distinctly hoydenish manner and the wounds in her throat finally ceasing their infernal throbbing. The stain of bile-laced water she had vomited had stopped steaming, and was only a dark spot in the sand.

Now she could see that the pocked surface of the beach was the result of footsteps. Had others been brought here, and left? How was their clothing removed? And the...the bodies...

A faint scratching sound. Cat scrambled to her feet, stumbling over the mound of clothing, catching her broken heel on a dress of gray linsey-woolsey that looked just large enough for a girl of eleven or so.

A rushing noise filled her head. She found her back to the stone wall, the light-charm's glimmering dying to a low glow as fear threatened to overwhelm her reason. She gripped her charing-charm tightly, the locket's glow full of shadows now, and the scratching became movement.

*Rats, perhaps? What would live down here in the dark?*

The shadows leapt and spun, crazily. A figure melded out of the dark mouth at the back of the crescent, and Cat made a small inarticulate noise.

It stopped dead. A long, shuffling sound, as if something was sniffing. A sharp exhale. Was it a dog? If it was, perhaps the animal could be persuaded to—

"Cat?" A familiar voice. "Are you awake?"

"*Robbie!*" She ran forward, blindly, stumbling through the pile of clutching cloth, and when her brother's stick-thin arms closed around her, Catherine Barrowe-Browne gave herself up to sobs.

"Don't breathe," he told her. "And don't look. Come, we haven't much time. I lost my wits, then I thought I'd come see if... well, never mind. *It* must have caught you on your way back to town, dear Sis. Bad luck, no doubt."

"Robbie... *Robbie*..." *I am not making a good show of this, no, not at all.* She sought to restore her nerves. "What is this? The clothes, and those... those *bodies*."

"*He*'s been calling people here." Robbie's face was graven. He was so dreadfully thin. "For a long, long time. Sometimes, if they were able to go past the corpses, he would hunt them in the dark. There's passages down here, all sorts of tunnels. Do not ask me further questions, Cat, I do *not* want you thinking on it. Come this way, and for God's sake do not... wait." He touched her chin, pushing her hair aside, and gazed at the scabbed marks on her throat. "Dear God. I... Cat..."

It was a shocked whisper, and Cat swallowed, hard. "I do not know what happened. One moment I was riding for the town, the next... I woke here. It was cold." The shudders would not cease, shaking her so hard her skirts made whispering little noises.

"Damn him." Robbie's dark eyes, phosphorescence glowing on the surface of his irises, narrowed. "Damn him to *Hell*. He probably thought this would make me behave."

*If he knew you, Robbie, he would not have thought any inducement could work such a miracle.* She immediately felt much more like *herself* again, and took in a sharp breath. "Behave?"

"No more questions. Come quickly. Do you trust me, Kitty-cat?" His fingers in hers, and her skin was far warmer than his even though she shivered. His fingers were thin flexible marble, and she had never felt such terrible strength in her brother's hand.

"Oh, Robbie, how can you ask? Do not be ridiculous." She found, much to her surprise, that she could summon a crisp, authoritative tone. "What are we to do now? I am not sorry I came to find you."

"I am. I'd have preferred you safe in Boston." He half-turned, and she did not demur as he led her for the grisly doorway. "Will you faint, do you think? If you have to see...that...again?"

"I do not think so." But she was not entirely certain. "Robbie...will my charing start to burn me, do you think?"

"Not until daylight. Look." He faced her again, his jaw working and the mud and dirt on his face not hiding the incandescent fury. His free hand worked at his shirt collar, and he drew forth a leather thong. It was a charing, but not the silver and crystal confection that matched her own. Instead, this was a plain brass disc with a charter-symbol stamped upon it, lit with the same soft glow that sheened his eyes, and as she peered at the skin underneath she saw only a faint shadow and a dusting of wiry hair. Yet it was indisputably a charing-charm, and she found herself unwilling to question its appearance. "The damn chartershadow owed me. Anyway, consecrated ground, you know. It doesn't burn me now. You have to trust me, though, Cat. We have somewhere to reach before dawn, and then..."

"Then what?"

He turned back to the doorway. "Then we will be cursed and outcast, but at least we'll be together."

"Oh." She shut her eyes as he pulled her forward, and stumbled on her broken heel. *Cursed and outcast, but his new charing doesn't scorch him. This makes no sense. Who could consecrate a patch of this wilderness so thoroughly?* "What must we reach before dawn?" The smell filled her nose, and she held back a retch by sheer force of will, trembling so hard Robbie actually drew her forward, sliding his arm over her shoulders. He was as cold as the stone walls, and his flesh was as hard... but he was her brother, and he had found her in the dark.

"A place by some pretty jessum trees, Kittycat. Keep your eyes closed."

# Chapter Thirty-One

The *gotar* shambled forward. *Why are they attacking from the south?* "Give 'em Hell!" Gabe yelled, and the men of Damnation went to work with flails and scythes. The mud-creatures were falling apart; Granger had actually thrown a charm-blessing that spread and sparkled between drops of rain, turning the water fair-holy. He stood upright behind the defense-line, holding the mancy active for as long as he could.

It was bad, but there was hope. Russ Overton had limped into town, madder than a wet cat and all over mud, his clothes scorched from the shattering of the west charterstone. A group of men were hauling a chunk of granite from behind Ma Hainey's boardinghouse—she'd braced two boards on it and used it to chop off chicken heads, so it was already blooded—to the west border in Cam Salthenry's rickety wagon, with Russ perched atop the chunk of stone muttering charter-charms to prepare it. The instant they heaved it upright among the shattered ruins of the other stone, he could repair the boundary—and that same group of men would go with him to ride the circuit and keep any undead off the chartermage.

It was now a question of how long they could hold. They still had the *gotar* bottlenecked south of Pig Street, but there were more of them every time thunder rumbled overhead. At least the rain had slowed.

Jack wasn't sanguine, though. The sun was sinking, and if Russ and the stone didn't get to the west in time, it could get ugly. Underneath the stormclouds, a furnace of gold was turning orange and red, giving the entire town a coat of wet gilding. The *gotar* gleamed like seals, too, but the sunlight raised steaming welts on their dirt-skins.

*Where are all the other undead? Salt put a boundary around the graveyard, but—*

"Sheriff!" A boy's voice, high and piping. "*Sheriff! Sheriff! They're here! Help us, they're here!*"

It was Zachary Corcoran, and he was running down the street as fast as his thick little legs could pump, throwing up clods of mud and dirt. He gabbled, pointing to the northwest, and the pins and needles all over Gabe's body were almost driven back by cold fear.

The dead from outside the boundary shambled, their jaws working, and Gabe finally had an answer for a question that had bothered him a long while. It had to do with the undead in the schoolhouse, and why they'd gone after Catherine.

It was Jack's fault, actually. He'd buried Robert Browne in consecrated ground; Robbie would find charter-boundaries no bar to his passage. The thing in the claim had probably forced the boy to carry corpses over the line, to see if it could be done. Once over, those dead could spread contagion and break the charter-circuit from the *inside*.

They clustered in shadows, some of them freshly dead—he recognized Amelia Gerhardt from one of the outlying farms, her head stuck at a strange angle and her eyes blazing with unholy red pinpricks as she shuffled toward him on bare, flayed feet. The sun flashed, clouds scudding and tearing as the wind rose, and the thing that had been Rich Gerhardt's wife squealed and fell, its flesh smoking.

Zach Corcoran was sobbing with fright. The *gotar* set up a chilling rumble-noise—their version of a battle cry, maybe.

*I have had enough.* Gabe drew in an endless breath. "*Keep them back!*" he roared, and pointed at Granger. "*Protect him!*"

"What are you *doing*?" Emmet Tilson screeched at him.

*What I should have done a long time ago.* He faced north, and walked toward the approaching undead, his boots sinking in squelching mud. Zach Corcoran wailed, and the hiss-rasp of dead throats working as they tried to eat clean air was fit to drive a man mad.

Jack Gabriel spread his arms. The pins-and-needles of grace rose through him, and he stilled the fruitless inner thrashing.

The surprise was how easy it was. He'd spent so long hiding it, avoiding the questions, like a hooded horse, just plodding ahead and refusing to look. But the space inside him that had opened at his Last Baptism dilated, and inside it, the still small voice spoke.

*Not for myself, but for others I may ask.* Underneath the words was a single thought.

A pair of dark eyes and a sweet little face, dark curls and the feel of her against him. Her teeth sinking into his lip before the startlement passed, and then the sweetness and the thundercrack inside him as her name rose like the charter-bell's clanging.

*Catherine.*

Grace burst free, a point of golden brilliance that shrank before it exploded outward. Time halted, and the wetness on his cheeks was not mud or blood or rain.

It was, after all, so easy. The Word spoke itself in silence, and the undead cringed from the sound. Their faces smoothed, the corpseglow leaving them in puffs of gold-laced steam, and Jack struggled to hold the place inside him open.

One question nagged him, though. *From the north. Catherine. Dear God, Catherine. Please, if I have ever served You, let her be safe.*

The golden light winked out, and he fell heavily to his knees with a splash of liquid dirt. The silence was immense, broken only by little Zach's sobbing for air and Emmet Tilson's wondering, breathless curse.

The charter-bell had stopped ringing. And now everyone in town would know what he was.

Gabe shut his eyes. *I don't care. Catherine. I have to see her.*

But when his group of Damnation's citizens reached the schoolmarm's house, they found it afire like half the northern part of town, smoke rising into a rapidly clearing sky.

He stood before the burning cottage, and the whispers rose in a tide behind him. The sun finished dying in the west, the stars peeping through torn clouds as the storm moved away.

*Man of God. Turned the undead back.*

*But we all saw him kill Parse Means that one time, and he drank and visited the whores—*

*Sweet on the schoolmarm too.*

*Maybe one of those Papists. Maybe he's a spy for the Vaticana Arcane.*

*Naw, it's just Gabe. His reasons are bound to be good.*

*Where's the marm? And that Chinee girl?*

*Gone. Nobody can find hide nor hair.*

*Well, maybe there'll be a body in the house...*

The cold closed about him, and the pins-and-needles of grace left him, cold ash after a fire. His face froze, and the flames crackling through the snug little cottage mocked him.

Perhaps she had not reached the town after all. Or if she had, was she inside the flame and the...

"Gabe?" It was Russ Overton. Mud cracked on his face and his bloodshot eyes blinked furiously, a muscle in his stubbled cheek twitching. "The charterstone's solid, it'll hold. What now?"

*Why the hell you askin' me?* he wanted to howl. But it wasn't a fair question. He was the one they looked to. The responsibility was his. "Contain the fires. Go house to house. Deal with every corpse we find." Who was using his voice? He sounded harsh, and savage-sullen. "Get the wounded to Doc Howard and Ma Ripp, and ride the circuit in groups all night. And give Freedman Salt a goddamn tin star; if he hadn't put a boundary over the graveyard we would've been in a world of hurt." He stared at the flames. It was an inferno, and he thought he knew why.

The thing from the claim was not going to be happy with this turn of events.

"Gabe—" Russ's hand on his shoulder, fingers digging in. "Did you find her?"

He shook his head. *Don't ask me, Russ. You don't want to know.* "Later. We need to deal with the dead."

"You..." This was Emmet Tilson, and he was pale under the mud and the blood, his moustache a limp caterpillar clinging to his upper lip. "You're a goddamn priest, Jack Gabriel. Don't you try to deny it, we all saw you. You're a goddamn Papist!"

He didn't think he could explain the history of the Order of the Templis to this jackass whorehouse dandy. Even if he had the urge, he doubted he had the patience. "I was something, once. Then I got married to a nice sweet girl who showed up dead one day." The words tasted like wormwood. "I had to shoot my own wife, the woman I'd broken my vows for. Do you want to give me some grief, Tilson, you're welcome to. And I'll answer." *By God, will I ever answer.*

"That's enough." Russ was between them, for Gabe had turned to face Tils, and the firelight played over both of them as the drenched wind cut through sodden clothing and laid a knife to the skin. "We have *other problems* right now, God damn you both! Tils, take a group of men and start ridin' the circuit."

"I don't take orders from no tarbrush son of a bi—" Tils began, but Gabe stepped forward.

The punch hit clean, with a high cracking sound. It threw Emmet Tilson to the mud, and Gabe had his gun out. It was a damn good thing too, because Tils had drawn, and pointed his own iron up at the sheriff. The skin on Tils's cheek bled, laid open, and his eye was already puffing.

The cold all through Gabe didn't alter one whit. "One more body to put iron and salt in won't be no trouble tonight." He stared at the man, realizing just how small Tilson really was. "You want to meet me, Emmet, you do it at high noon. Say so now, or shut your goddamn mouth and get to work. I ain't havin' no more of this from you."

It was, he realized, all the same to him. He could kill this man now or later; it didn't make a goddamn bit of difference. He'd sent Catherine to her death.

Told her to go home and bolt her doors, and they would probably find her corpse in the flames. Iron and salt in that body he had held, filling the mouth he had kissed; the kiss that still burned all the way through him.

How could the kiss be in him if she was gone? How was it possible? Was the God who had spun the world into motion that brutal? That...that *unrighteous*?

Tilson lowered his gun. Gabe's finger tightened. It would take so little to solve the problem of this irritating jackass once and for all.

In the end, though, he holstered his own gun, and offered Tilson his hand. "Get up. Let's get the town cleaned out, dammit."

But Tilson scrambled to his feet without help, and glared at Gabe. He shoved off through the crowd, and Gabe ended up having wide blond Paul Barberyus gather a group to ride the circuit with a hollow-cheeked, glaze-eyed Russ. Who, thank God, asked him no more questions.

Maybe Russ knew there were no more answers to be had. In any case, Gabe had enough work organizing the shattered town back into some semblance of order.

Then, he told himself as he cast one last glance at the burning wreckage of the schoolmarm's house, it was time to go hunting.

# Chapter Thirty-Two

Perched on the wagon's swaying front seat, Cat peered through the rain. Each time it jolted, her side ached; her bottom was *never* going to forgive her. She clung to his thin, stone-hard arm, and blinked away falling water. Her hair was an absolute sodden *mess*. Neither of them were respectable at this point, and the heaviness of the trunks in the back of the wagon probably kept the entire contraption from flying away in this dreadful storm. "Does it...hurt?"

"No more than living." Robbie's laugh was a marvel of bitterness. "Neither of us will be carrying on the Barrowe-Browne name, I fancy."

*Of course not. The undead do not procreate, even the conscious ones.* "Don't be nasty, Robbie." She sighed, exhaustion swamping her. "But please do answer me honestly: Does it *hurt*?"

"What's pain? For God's sake, would you rather be one of *its* corpses?"

She jabbed her fingers in just under his ribs, and *pinched* him. The skin gave a fraction, resilient stone. He actually laughed, and it was Robbie's old carefree, surprised merriment. "Ow! Very well. It stings, Kittycat. I won't lie, it stings a bit. But that's only until you fall asleep. I'll do it as gently as possible."

"And you're...you're certain I'll wake up?" She suddenly felt very small, and as the rain intensified and the wagon's wheels cut into a sludge of mud, she huddled closer to her brother and wished Jack Gabriel were here too.

*But he won't take very kindly to what Robbie is, and what I'm going to be.* She shuddered a trifle, but her brother was right. The...the *it*, the master, or *him*, as Robbie inevitably referred to it as, had contaminated her brother. A man of Jack Gabriel's stripe would not allow such a contaminated thing to live. He was a *sheriff*, for God's sake. And so irritatingly...well, he was so *irritatingly* Jack. It was the only word she could find.

"I'm absolutely certain." Her brother's tone was so grim she dared not question further.

Now that Cat's throat was throbbing with pain, *she* was contaminated, too. The *thing* had not outright killed her, perhaps because it still needed Robbie's aid. But it had put her in that ghastly underground cave...and the *bodies*, dear God, the corpses piled up, waiting to serve the master's bidding at some future moment—perhaps when it was certain it could overwhelm the town and add to their number in one great mass.

Some of them were merely bones, and older ones, slowly mouldering in the labyrinth's depths, were dressed in strange and primitive costumes. The removal of the clothes was a newer tradition, it seemed, and Cat's shudders were coming regularly now, in great gripping waves.

"I don't feel quite right," she murmured.

"Try to rest. You lost a lot of blood."

"How *gruesome*."

He shook a spatter of rain away, the familiar forelock falling over his pale forehead. "Well, that's what it is. Cattle are good, other animals—but you won't have to bite anything. You can just take from me; I'll hunt for the both of us."

This was a highly indelicate conversation, and her stomach was none too steady. "Robbie..."

"You shouldn't have come."

*Well, you shouldn't have left in the first place.* "I *had* to."

"I know. I just wish…" Mercifully, he stopped. "Should be around here. Why this patch is consecrated, I can't tell you. You'll feel it as soon as we get there. It's actually pleasant. And then, after dusk tomorrow, we'll set out. We'll go to San Frances. If we're careful, we may actually pass unnoticed."

"We won't for long. Or do you think our presence will not spread the contamination, and cause a great deal of suffering?"

"Well, I haven't turned anyone into a slavering undead yet. I believe the consecrated burial is what saved me from…" Robbie trailed off, lifting his head. The rain was coming down harder now, and Cat discovered she was *quite* sick of frontier living, no matter how Miss Bowdler rhapsodized about its purity.

*I will never see my students again. Or the ladies from the Lucky Star.* She found, much to her surprise, that she quite missed them already. And Li Ang's round, now-familiar face, and little baby Jonathan's piping cries. She even missed the heat and the dust. *Any* heat would have been welcome now.

*Is Jack well? He stayed behind at the cave, to do… what? He said he had business there.* Oddly enough, the thought of him—dirty, stubbled, and comforting—hurt somewhere in the region of her chest. A piercing pain, as if she had been stabbed.

Her head ached quite dreadfully, too. "I truly do not feel well." Her voice was high and rather young, as if she were nine and afraid of the shadows on the nursery wall again.

"Don't worry." Her brother tautened the reins, and the horses—thin nags, but tough as bootleather—halted, switching their tails. "We have arrived. Straighten your fan, dearest."

The words—just what he would say before a ball, in the carriage as they braced themselves for another night In Society—made a small, forlorn giggle escape her. How far they were from Boston. Here, in the middle of a wet night in the cold, and her throat throbbing terribly… but still, she clung to his arm until he fastened the reins and hopped down from the wagon.

It was dark, and the rain came down in sheets. She could just make out a roaring river, its curve reminding her terribly of the crescent of sandy beach and the soul-eating blackness on its other shore. But there were white-trunked jessum trees, shaking their jangling bracelet-leaves under the wind, and as Robbie lifted her down she felt a tingle along her skin. It was a comforting warmth, and even though her breath came in puffs of white cloud as the wind veered and cut through her sodden riding habit, she felt it like a blanket about her shoulders.

"Oh," she said, a thin breath of wonder, and her brother laughed again.

"I *told* you that you would feel it. Now, step this way, sister."

She did, holding fast to his arm, and the rain was a curtain of jewels. The jessum trees waved their long fluttering finials in greeting, and there was a patch of sunken earth with a stone at its head.

Robbie drove the shovel in at the foot of the grave, his booted foot stamping it cleanly home. It would wait until needed.

She clung to his arm with all her remaining strength, and when he turned to face her, there was a break in the heavy clouds, and starshine played over his pale, ravaged face.

"Are you quite sure?" he asked her, pointlessly.

"Don't be ridiculous." Her throat really did hurt most awfully, and her head was full of rushing noise. She stepped away, her hands falling to her sides, fisting inside the ruins of her gloves. "We shall go to San Frances. The opera there is quite fine, I've been told." There was a gleam in his hands. The rain slackened. The gleam was a pistol, and the fear was suddenly very large, and she was lost in it. "Robbie..." Breathless, and she lifted her chin. *I am a Barrowe-Browne. I shall not cry.* "Do it, for God's sake. Do not let me become a mindless slave to that thing. I would rather...well." *I would rather die, but I will, won't I? Either way. It is six of one, a half-dozen of another. At least this way I shall not become a slavering hag.*

"I..." His throat worked, and the warmth enveloping her skin was familiar. Where had she felt it before? "I am sorry, Kittycat."

She nodded, strings of wet hair falling in her face. If she ever reached a dry warm place after this, she would stay there for a *month*, she promised herself. Thick woolen socks, and a wrapper, and some of Li Ang's harsh black tea would do very well right at the moment.

The pistol's mouth looked very large as he pointed it at her. Where had he acquired such a thing, she wondered, and decided not to ask if it had been bought in a pawnshop on Damnation's dusty main street.

What else had Robbie bought from a chartershadow, she wondered?

"If this hurts," she managed in a queerly husky, ruined voice, "I shall simply *pinch* you, Robert. *Twice*."

He squeezed the trigger, and squeezed his eyes shut at the same time, and there was a terrific blow to her chest.

*How odd, it doesn't hurt.* The warmth spilled through her, and there was a rivulet of something hot on her chin. She reached up to dab it away, but her limbs would not obey her. A swimming weakness took her, and Robbie cried her name, over and over.

*It is all well*, she wanted to tell him, but the bubble of warmth burst on her lips and she fell. She did not feel it, spilled sideways onto the cold ground...

...and Catherine Elizabeth Barrowe-Browne died.

# Chapter Thirty-Three

"I ain't giving you a horse." Joe glowered, the bandage around his head glare-white in the livery's lamplight. "You rode Bessie near into her grave, dammit, and that schoolmarm—"

"It warn't her fault." Gabe's eyes burned, and he was sure his temper was none too steady. "And I ain't *asking*, Joe. I need a horse, Hathorn's missing, and after the night we've had, you'd do well not to question me."

"Give him a goddamn horse." Russ coughed rackingly, leaning against a stall door. "He's got business."

Gabe pulled his hand away from the gun-butt. "How long you been standin' there?"

"Long enough." The chartermage fixed him with a piercing glare. Russ looked about ready to fall down and sleep right there against the stall door, but his gaze was clear and his hands were loose, leftover mancy popping and sparking about him. "She might not have been in her house, Gabe. And that thing in the claim..."

"It can't have her." The words had to work their way around a wet rock lodged in his throat. "By God, if I have to, I will put her in a quiet grave. But *it won't have her.*: And if it killed her, I will return the favor. I have grace enough for that.*

*I have to.*

Russ nodded, wearily. His hair, free of the wax and grimed with mud, stood up anyhow. He'd lost his bowler hat somewhere, and the guck smeared all over him was thick enough to turn aside a curse. "You want some help?"

*As if you could give me any.* "I ain't askin'."

"But I am."

Joe set about saddling a big white cob-headed beast of a horse, mutiny evident in his every line. He cast both Russ and Gabe reproachful little glances, but neither of them paid attention.

"Damnation needs you more." Gabe considered the charter-mage for a long moment. "I'll take the ammunition you're carrying, though."

For a moment there was silence, as Russ unbuckled the belt full of cartridges and leather boxes of stacked bullets. He handed it over, and Gabe weighed it. Almost full; Russ's battle had not involved gunplay.

"I was of the Templis." The words surprised him, and the fact that he could say it so calmly surprised him as well. "I was a Knight, full-made and Baptized. I left them to marry Annie, but it follows a man, don't it."

"Fate tends to do that." Russ leaned back against the stall door. The exhaustion had turned him gray, even in the warm lamplight. "I didn't think the *Ordo Templis* still existed."

*Oh, they do.* "My...my wife. She...died." Why had he not told the man before? *I had my reasons.*

But were they good ones? Was it too late to offer an explanation, or even ask for...what? Forgiveness?

*My way is to cleanse, not to forgive.*

"So I gathered." Russ coughed again. "I ain't gonna see you again, am I."

"Maybe not." But Gabe paused, taking the reins from Joe as the big pale animal snorted and eyed him nervously. "You're a good friend, Russ Overton. I wish to God I'd told you what I was."

"Shitfire, Gabe, you think I didn't *guess*?" The laugh was

worn and threadbare, but it still made the chartermage look years younger. "Go on now. Do what you got to."

*That's all I ever do. What I got to. Some days I wish it weren't.* His foot found the stirrup, and he heaved himself up with a grunt, his entire body protesting. "This ain't, by any chance, that man-eating bastard of a horse your dad was swearing to put down, was it?"

Joe's gaptooth smile was pure malice. "*Hyah!*" he yelled, and slapped the pale beast's flank.

The horse lunged for the livery doors, and Gabe cursed.

The sun had long since set, and riding outside the circuit at night was a fool's game. Just like everything else in Damnation. The rain had become an intermittent mist and drizzle, and the roaring of water in the desert mixed with the rolls of receding thunder.

He set his course west-northwest. The thing from the claim would likely return to its hole to lick its wounds, but Gabe wanted to check Robbie Browne's grave first. If the consecration still held, he wanted to know.

*What are you thinking, Jack?*

Not much, he admitted. You didn't need to think when you had a job to do, or so he had always told himself. When he started thinking, that was when the trouble happened. It was thinking that got him tangled up with Annie, because he couldn't get her out of his damn head. It was thinking that had gotten him all the way across the goddamn continent to this Godforsaken place, and thinking that had landed him the sheriff's badge. Nobody else would take it, and Jack didn't care, so why the hell not? And it was thinking about Catherine that had led to...what? Being silly and stupid, and costing another woman her life.

*She might be alive. She might not have been in that house.*

Then she was wandering out in the wilderness during a storm, with the thing from the claim wandering loose, too. And nobody had seen hide nor hair of Li Ang and her baby; he could add that to the list on his conscience.

Yes, if the ground was still consecrated, Jack wanted to know. He would need somewhere to rest after killing the thing.

Especially if the battle ended badly.

There was a swelling of cold light on the horizon, and as a waning moon shouldered its way clear of the hills and began peeking through the tatters of flying cloud, Jack Gabriel began to sing.

It was an old tune, one he had heard over and over in the dimness of his orphanage youth. A hymn to the Templis Redeemer, its notes full of sonorous dolor, meant to be chanted plainly by plain men whose task was to cleanse and revenge.

If the thing from the claim was anywhere near, it would be maddened by the syllables. And it heartened a man to sing a bit before the battle began.

*Come find me*, he thought, and felt the prickles rise all over his skin again. His charing flashed gold, a challenge he didn't bother to hide under his shirt anymore. *God damn you, come and find me.*

*If you don't, I will find you.*

# Chapter Thirty-Four

It was cold.

She could not *breathe*, there was a weight atop her, and she clawed at wet dirt. *Out, get out—*

The intent to rise ran through her bones like dark wine, and she found herself exploding from the ground in a shower of wet dirt and small pebbles. Coughing, retching, she fell and lay full-length on cold soaked ground, and the sky was so *bright*, dear God, it burned along every inch of her, smoking through rips and rents in the riding habit, driving needles in.

Something landed atop her. It was a blanket, followed by a warm living weight. A thundering filled her ears, and she went still.

There was a voice, too. Familiar, and piercing the thundering thudding beat like a golden needle, a queer atonal screeching. There was another thump-thump, a very small one, some distance away.

*What on earth... I am not dead. I am... oh, no. No. But yes. Robbie, where is he?*

"Quiet," Li Ang said, finally. "You quiet."

Another set of racking coughs. Her throat was dry paper, and she suspected that very soon, she would be very thirsty. "Yes." She blinked and recognized the blanket—it was the quilt from her very own bed, and it stopped the terrible burning all over her. She could *sense* the heat and light just outside, waiting to score her sensitive skin, scrape at her eyes. "Li Ang?" Wonderingly.

"Good." The warm weight of the Chinoise girl's body rolled away. "They think us dead. We go now."

*I* was *dead. Perhaps that's beside the point.* She took stock of herself—her arms worked, and her legs. Her hair was a filthy mess, and the ruins of her riding habit were scarcely better. The pain in her chest was a metronome ticking, and she realized the thudding was Li Ang's pulse. The smaller one had to be baby Jonathan's.

*Catherine. I am Catherine Elizabeth Barrowe-Browne. I am...alive. No, undead. Something. Robbie shot me.*

She groaned, the inside of her skull unhappy with the memory, refusing to contain it. "It's...dawn?"

"Sun soon. There is wagon. Heavy boxes. Yours?" The girl's hands were strong and slim as the rest of her, and she dragged Cat to her feet, wrapping another blanket around her. "Horses, too. My horses better."

*Boxes of gold bars. Robbie took them from the claim. Not cursed now, he said.* "The boxes...yes. There's...they are important. Li Ang..."

"You save Li Ang and Jin. Li Ang save you. We go now."

"How did you find—"

"Li Ang *quiet*. Not *stupid*." The Chinoise girl trailed off in a spitting, atonal song of curses. Cat stumbled, her broken bootheel throwing her off-balance, and she was evidently much heavier than she had been, for the wagon groaned most unsettlingly when she heaved herself up into the back and collapsed next to the corded trunks. There were scraping sounds, and more cloth settled over her body, merciful dimness easing the pain of inimical daylight.

*I shall quite miss the sun. But at least I am alive, and Robbie...*

Where had he gone? He was free of the thing in the claim, or so he said. And the gold, its curse lifted, would buy them all breathing room in San Frances.

"Li Ang?" Cat swallowed. The thirst was dreadfully bad, pulling against her veins. "I fear I may not be...quite safe."

"*Jiang shi*." Li Ang spat as she heaved herself into the wagon's high seat. "You no hurt Jin or Li Ang."

*I certainly do not wish to.* "No. I would never." But the burning all through her, different than the heavy horrible weight of day, made her not so sure. She was *thirsty*, and the heartbeats were so distracting. Her broken stays grated against her skin, and every inch of her crawled under the weight of drying dirt. At least it did not seem overly warm this morning. The afternoon would likely be a welter of sweat and unpleasantness.

"Good." The Chinoise girl chirruped to the horses and flicked the whip, and baby Jonathan burbled. The wagon jolted, and Cat, wrapped in quilts, found herself tossed about most hideously.

"Li Ang?" There was no answer, just the steady grind of wagon wheels, and Cat closed her eyes under the smother of quilts. It promised to be a *very* long day. And she still had no idea where they were bound. "Li Ang, my dear, where are we *going*?"

"Train," the girl called cheerfully. "You buy ticket. We go Xiao Van-Xi."

It took her a moment to decipher what the Chinoise girl meant. Cat let out a half-sobbing sigh of relief. "Yes. San Frances, indeed." For Robbie would find her there if they were somehow separated; they had agreed upon as much last night.

*Was it last night? It must have been. And now I am...*

Cat's fingers crept to her throat. The wounds in her neck were gone, and her charing-charm lay cool and unbroken against her skin. And...Robbie's locket, its metal familiar and still tingling with mancy.

*Why did he leave me the locket?* "Oh, Robbie," she whispered, and hugged herself under the blankets. The wagon jolted, baby Jonathan burped and burbled his way to sleep, and after a short while Li Ang began to sing. It was then Cat Barrowe discovered she could not shed a tear.

Whatever clay her body was made of now, it refused to weep.

# Chapter Thirty-Five

The moon's cheese-rotten grimace rose through spilled clouds; its sullen light turned the flats into a treacherous chiaroscuro. The plainsong had burned its way through Jack's throat, and he coughed and spat once, breaking the monotony of its rise and fall.

When he did, the shadows pressed close, and he hurriedly took up the thread again, despite the scraping to his voice and the vicious nips of pain all over his body as weary flesh told him just how thoroughly he had abused it. His head tipped forward, and when he glanced up he saw with no real surprise gleams of paired eyes in the ink-black shiftings, oddly colored like beasts' eyes.

He was not merely being watched, for when the massive, ill-tempered white horse pranced restively, some of the shadows would dart in, nipping at the gelding and making him difficult to control. Only the song kept them back, and he heard the sliding sound of mud-beasts rising from the wet earth. By tomorrow, the flats would be a carpet of wildflowers, seeds that had lain dormant springing into brief, gloriously colored life.

His course had veered, but by the time the jessum trees shook their long tresses in the moonlight, he had an idea of what was waiting for him.

The darkness was more than physical, but when the horse stepped over the invisible boundary of consecration it lifted, and the white gelding discovered his usual ill-temper again. He had to work to convince the damn horse that Jack was the one in charge, and the disdainful laugh from the shadow-figure crouched atop the charterstone at the head of the grave nearly drove the beast out of its mind with fear.

Through it all, Gabe kept the song's measured cadence. When, sweating and shaking, the horse stood with its ugly head hanging and lather dripping from its sides, he let the song die gratefully in his burning throat.

Silence. A faint brush of wind over the new life sprouting amid the ruin and mud.

"You've got a choice," Robbie Browne said, finally.

Jack Gabriel dropped from the saddle with a purely internal sigh of relief. *I just want to get some goddamn rest, kid.* "So do you, Browne. Or is it Barrowe?"

"Both, actually." The boy—or the thing wearing the boy's likeness—shook his head, tossing the forelock with a curiously familiar motion. "Barrowe-Browne. Old names, sir. Not like yours."

*My name's old enough.* "Where is she?"

"My sister? Far beyond your reach, Sheriff. Which brings us to the choice."

"You ain't Robbie Browne. You're *it*. The thing in the claim."

"A lamentable misunderstanding. The *thing* in the claim lives in me, Jack Gabriel. A marriage of minds, you could call it. Except I'm not willing to give up my bachelor status."

Gabe dressed the horse's reins. If the animal bolted, good riddance. Plus, Joe would likely welcome its return without him. "So who am I talkin' to?"

"Right now, on this ground, it's Robert Browne. The consecration you so thoughtfully performed made *its* hold on me…uncertain." A sigh, as Jack Gabriel's gun cocked with a slight, definite *click*. "If you shoot at me, sir, you shall never see my sister again."

The fear was claws in numb flesh. "I likely never will anyway."

"I wouldn't be so sure. She's been bitten, and buried in

ground you so thoughtfully made sacred. For better or worse, dear Cat's just like me now. Little sister, always tagging along behind." Another pause, and the scarecrow-figure shivered atop the charterstone, a quick, liquid, terribly *wrong* movement. "She shouldn't have come."

"Nope." In that, at least, they were in complete agreement. Jack took a single step forward, wet pebbles and sand grinding underfoot. Another. "She ain't fit for this."

"Let me be frank, sir."

"I wish you would be." Another step.

"That's close enough." The light, laughing tone was a warning, and the white horse made a low unhappy sound, shivering. "Here is the bargain, Mr. Gabriel. I shall make you eternal, you shall leave me for daylight and the crows to feast on." Robbie's face was a white dish in the moonlight.

"Now why would you offer me a good deal like that, Browne? You ain't the charitable type."

"I am not. At least, I never was." The boy hopped down from the charterstone, stepping over the freshly turned earth below. "Did you ever have a sister, sir?"

*Something's buried there. Buried nice and deep so sunlight won't touch it.* "Orphan."

"Ah. Well. Then you don't know." A pause. "Sir, I wish... Catherine is all I have left. I wish for her to be proud of me. I would prefer her not to know I... am as you see me."

"Funny way of showing it."

"I didn't know she would *follow* me. I had to alter my plans rather quickly once she appeared. As usual, you know, she always was rather a disturbance. Now, are you going to be reasonable?"

"There are good people in town dead because of you, Robbie Browne."

"Would you like to add my sister to the list?" The boy's laughter faded, and he reappeared to Jack's left. Quick little bastard, slipping through pools of moonlight and shadow. And he was so damnably tired. "You're Templis, aren't you? The Order of the Redeemer. You know more about what she is than she ever will."

Well, and there it was. His worst fears, confirmed. "The undead at the schoolhouse. They weren't meant for her."

"I knew there was something about you. The thing in the claim recognized you, but it's . . . distracting, to have that much knowledge. It's like a lumber room; thing wanted often buried—"

Jack *moved*. He hit the boy squarely, the knife sinking into the thin chest, and Robbie Browne laughed. Rolling, wet dirt flying and his exhausted body betraying him, the knife slapped out of his hand and the boy's limbs closing around him like a vise. He struggled, and the prickles of grace burned unholy flesh. Robbie Browne hissed, his breath a sudden foulness . . . but even though Gabe's spirit was willing, the flesh enclosing it had endured quite enough. Grace ebbed, and the struggle ended with a greenstick crack as bone in Jack Gabriel's right arm gave way. He screamed, but the thing had its teeth in the juncture of his neck and shoulder. Tearing and ripping, a gout of hot blood down his shoulder, and his left hand was full of the gun he had loaded with charter-blessed ammunition.

Rolling again, the barrel jammed into the boy's ribs. The thing inside Robbie's flesh gapped and leered, and when the gun spoke, the white horse screamed to match Gabe's cries and fled, trumpeting its fear as it tore through shadows and undead mud-substance alike. Another shot, and Gabe's prayer rose like a charter-bell's tolling, grace washing through him in a last hot flood of *in extremis*.

*Catherine*, he thought, deliriously, and Robbie Browne's body sagged aside.

Jack curled himself into a ball, whisper-screaming as edges of broken humerus grated together. His lower arm had snapped in two places, too, and the pain ate him alive. Everything he had ever thought of eating rose in his throat, escaped in a series of retches.

Robbie's body twitched. It hissed, a viper temporarily dazed. It wouldn't be down for long.

*I wish for her to be proud of me.*

*Me too*, Gabe might have said, only he was busy trying to breathe. On his knees, left hand dropping the useless gun, and his fingers scrabbling through dirt for the knifehilt.

He found it, and the thing with Robbie Browne's face glared up at him, its mouth working, black with Jack's blood. "Do... it..." it hissed, and Jack didn't hesitate. The broad blade bit deep, a tide of blackness gouting, and he hacked grimly at the thing's neck until the head fell free, spurts of unholy ichor steaming in the chill night. The jessum trees rattled as they shook their fingers, just like slim graceful women letting their hair down, and the sound of the undead and the mud-creatures outside the consecrated ground falling to bits as the will that had impelled them decayed into dissolution was a whisper fit to haunt nightmares.

There was a brief starry period of blackness, and when Gabe regained consciousness he found himself lying under a cloudless sky, the stars a river and a graying of dawn in the east.

There was a wooden shape to one side, and two slumped corpses that were probably horses, drained to feed Robbie Barrowe's unholy thirst. Jack didn't care. He lay for a little while, until, blinking away dirt and crusted blood and nastier decaying fluid, he found the last gift Robert Barrowe-Browne would ever leave.

It was a second grave, dug just to the side of the freshly turned earth with the charterstone at its head. All Jack had to do was crawl, and pull some of the dirt over himself.

It should be enough. He prayed it would be enough.

His right arm hung useless, and the gun was left behind. He clutched the knife, its blade running with bubble-smoking black ichor, in his left fist as he crawled, scratching along the pan of the flats under Heaven's uncaring vault. In the predawn hush, the scrape and rattle of his boots digging against damp earth were loud as trumpets. When he tumbled into the hole, the sides gave loosely, scattering over him.

*It ain't so hard*, he told himself. *All you have to do is put the knife in the right place.*

He set the fine-honed edge against his own throat, and arranged his feet. His right arm throbbed and screamed, but he disregarded it. All it would take was a single lunge, jamming the hilt against the side of the grave, and he would bleed out.

But he had to do it before the sun rose.

Jack shut his eyes.

"Cath—" he whispered, and his legs spasmed, pushing him forward.

# *Chapter Thirty-Six*

*Four months later*

San Frances was a simmering bowl of smoke, dust, filth, mist, corruption, lewdness, and outright criminality.

It was, Cat reflected, merely Damnation writ large.

Her arms were too thin; she had not yet recovered from the agonizing thirst of the desert. She no longer felt the dreadful heat, and every drop of moisture they had been able to scavenge had gone to Li Ang and little Jonathan. One of the horses had died, so they traveled at night, Cat's boots slipping and sliding as she heaved the wagon along like a mindless undead in a quarry. Next to her, the other horse had lost its fear of her predator's scent, and had merely endured that terrible passage.

The thirst had consumed every excess scrap of flesh, leaving her slim and breastless as a boy. Still, she possessed enough inhuman strength to lift both heavy trunks, and settle them on the wagon. It was a far finer vehicle than the one that had carried them out of the desert; the bars of un-cursed gold from the claim had proven *most* useful. There were even solicitors who could be paid to transact business after dark, and Cat's experience had built a fairly unassailable comfortable independence for a certain Li Ang Cheng Barrowe-Browne, as the widow of one Robert Barrowe-Browne.

How Robbie would laugh.

Not only that, but Catherine Elizabeth Barrowe-Browne and Robert Heath Edward Barrowe-Browne, both deceased, had named Jonathan Jin Barrowe-Browne their heir, and all papers were in order.

Mother would be horrified, and Father might be angry...but it was *right*, Cat thought, that it should be this way. At least the wealth would shield Li Ang and little Jonathan from some of the unpleasantness of life.

Her dress hung on a too-wasted form, scarecrow-thin as Robbie's. Now that the thirst raged through her, she understood a little more of his bitter laughter. She refused to think on the slaking of said thirst, of the lowing of the cattle and the stink of the slaughteryards. Overcoming her disgust at such feedings would help her survive...but dear God, it did not completely erase the terrible burning. Another manner of blood was called for.

Human. It was a mercy her parents were dead.

She sighed as she surveyed her work and found it as proper as she could make it. "It's safest this way, Li Ang."

The Chinoise girl, heavily veiled and mutinously quiet, shook her head. There had been argument, and the throwing of a butcher knife...but really, it had taken only one instance of Cat standing over baby Jonathan's new cradle, shaking and dry-weeping with the urge to sink her newfound, pointed and razor-sharp canines into the tiny, helpless pulse, for Li Ang to become convinced of the wisdom of Cat's plan.

Little baby Jonathan, tucked safely in his mother's arms with charter-charms on red paper attached to his swaddling, was fast asleep. Cat stepped back, not trusting herself, and bit her lower lip.

But gently. The teeth she now sported were *provokingly* sharp. "I shall miss you," she said, softly. "The gold shall help, and do *not* let anyone take advantage of you. Especially solicitors. Jonathan is the heir to a fortune in Boston, and you shall be safe enough there. Though I advise you to go overseas."

She had expected Robbie to follow her before now. That he had not, and that he had not met her at any of the appointed times... well, it did not bear thinking of.

*If I could survive Damnation, I can very well endure this.* She set her chin. "Come now. You shall just make the station, and mind you do not overtip the porters. I shall be watching, to see you off safely."

Li Ang refused to answer. She did accept Cat's help into the wagon, and Cat melded into the shadows as the nervous horses were chirruped to and the whip flicked. *I would have liked to embrace her, at least once more.*

But it was too dangerous, when she could hear the mortal heart working its cargo of precious, delicious fluid through Li Ang's veins.

It was no great thing to pass unnoticed, her shawl over her head, keeping the wagon in sight. She did not ease her vigilance until the veiled woman carrying her baby was helped aboard the huge, steam-snorting train by a solicitous conductor, and Cat moved aimlessly with the crowd at the station, the soft press of their flesh and the many heartbeats a roar of torment until the cry of *Allll aboooooord!* echoed and the metal beast heaved itself forward. Slowly at first, then gathering speed, handkerchiefs fluttered from windows—and there was Li Ang's slim hand, waving a red silken rag that fluttered from her fingers and landed at Cat Barrowe's feet. The woman with the shawl wrapped about her dark, pinned-up hair snatched up the scrap of fabric and held it to her mouth as she watched the train disappear into clouds of steam crackling with stray mancy-sparks.

There was nobody to remark when the shawled woman vanished. One moment there, the next gone, as the next train heaved and screeched its way forward to disgorge its weary passengers.

# Chapter Thirty-Seven

It was a fairly respectable boardinghouse, and the rooms were at least clean. Nevertheless, a fastidious hand had been at work among the draperies and at the two beds, and there was a space between a large armoire and the washstand just large enough for a cradle. The marks on the floor showed where the armoire had been pushed aside, no doubt by two strong men.

Or by an entirely different strength.

A key rattled in the lock, and the darkness was complete. It was silent, though the street outside throbbed with catcalls and wagon wheels, clockhorse hooves—for here, the citizenry could afford the pens to marry metal to living equine flesh and bone, instead of the wilderness where plain flesh was good enough.

She sighed as she stepped through the door, locking and barring it with swift habitual motions, and shaking out her shawl. There was a heavy mist from the bay tonight, and its salt-smoke scent clung to her skirts. A dark, unassuming brown, but the cloth was of very good material and the cut was new, if not fashionable.

Quick, decisive tapping bootsteps, crackling and pert. She did have such a distinctive step.

The lucifer hissed as he struck it, and the lamp's sudden golden glow swallowed her indrawn breath.

Her shoulders hit the door behind her, and he stared for a long moment, settling the glass lampshade and turning it down so it wouldn't sting her eyes further. She'd probably been feeding off cattle, and looked like it. Too birdlike-thin, her cheekbones standing out sharply, and the way her throat worked convulsively as she stared at him made him long to speak.

But he'd waited so long. He could wait a little longer.

"Jack?" she whispered.

He nodded, once. "You get into *more* trouble, sweetheart."

The sudden leap of hope in her dark eyes was enough to break a man's heart. "Robbie..." A mere breath of sound, and he could not look away from her lips shaping the two syllables.

"He killed the thing in the claim." The lie came out easily. It should—he'd had plenty of time to practice the words, tracking her down, thinking of what he would say. What he would do, if he ever saw her again. "He...you can be proud, Catherine. He did right."

Her gaze flicked to his chest, where the tin star still gleamed. It was easier to say he was a lawman, and precious few questioned him. Her throat worked again as she swallowed, and he was surprised to find out some things about his body still worked, even if he was technically...undead.

"Are you..." She set herself more firmly against the door. "Are you here to..."

"I'm only here for one thing." Now was the time to rise, the floorboards squeaking sharply underfoot. Measured steps, his spurs striking stray sparks of mancy as intent gathered in the tiny room, the washbasin rattling in its stand. "And that's you, Miss Catherine Barrowe."

"I..." Had he finally struck her dumb? Not likely, because that chin came up, and her dark eyes flashed with familiar fire, through the sheen of phosphorescence on the irises. "I cannot hear your heartbeat, sir."

"Technically, I'm dead. Undead, more like." He shrugged. "Your brother and I agreed it was best."

"Oh, *did* you?" She folded her arms, and he had never been

so glad to see the prim mask of politeness. He approached her as carefully as he would a nervous horse, and when he was finally within reaching distance, he stretched out a hand.

*Please.* He couldn't say it out loud. *I've followed you over half the goddamn earth. I'll follow you over the other half, but give me something, sweetheart.*

Instead, his mouth ran away with him again. "I've been getting what I need from the guilty, sweetheart. There's ways to take what we need and not spread the ... not spread the bad mancy. I can do it for both of us, if you like. There ain't no need for you to—"

"It's still murder." Deadly pale. "And you're a sheriff."

*I was something else before.* His shirt tore, and he tossed the star. It pinged as it hit the floor, rolling under the bed. "I don't *care* about no goddamn law, sweetheart. I care about keeping us both alive. I don't care if we're goddamn cursed. I ain't going to see you die. Not if I can help it."

"Language, sir." But her shoulders dropped, and a trace of color crept into her thin face. "There ... Jack, we're *undead*. We're ... I don't even know what to call it, unless—"

"I know what to call it. I'll even tell you, if you like. I'll tell you anything you want to know. But you have got to tell me something too, sweetheart."

"Sir." Frosty now, and her hands dropped to her sides, became fists. "Must you address me in such a manner? I hardly think—"

"God *damn* it." That did it. He closed the last bit of space between them, and when he had restrained the urge to shake her, he found himself nose-to-nose with a deathly tired–looking, trembling, paper-pale, absolutely beautiful woman.

Dead, undead, or alive, she was all that remained to him of grace.

"You'd better be willing to marry me," he told her.

"We're *undead*, Jack. Somehow I think the question is moot." But she smiled, and the tips of her long pearly canines dimpled her lower lip, fit to drive him mad. "But if you're proposing—"

"I ain't proposing, sweetheart. I'm *telling* you. Now pack your things. This ain't no fit place for no lady."

The silence stretched between them as she studied his features. The stolen blood in his veins burned, and he didn't care if it turned him to ashes, so long as he immolated right where he was, with Catherine's beautiful, stone-cold hands creeping up around his neck and clasping sweetly.

"Don't you think," she said quietly, "you had better kiss me first?"

In the distance, a train's long mournful whistle sounded. And outside a slumped, barely respectable boardinghouse in the sinks of San Frances, the moon rose higher in a soot-darkened sky.

## *Finis*

# Acknowledgments

Thanks to Mel Sanders, who encouraged me to head for the finish line, Miriam Kriss, who encouraged me to consider it for sale, Devi Pillai for not throttling me when I dug in over the brass kettle, and Susan Barnes for sheer good humor. Last but not least, thank you to my dearest Readers. Hopefully you will have as much fun with this one as I did.

# extras

orbit

# meet the author

Daron Gildrow

LILITH SAINTCROW was born in New Mexico, bounced around the world as an Air Force brat, and fell in love with writing when she was ten years old. She currently lives in Vancouver, Washington.

# interview

**The Iron Wyrm Affair** *is your first experience with writing* *steampunk. How was it compared to writing your previous* *books?*

To be honest, I didn't think it was "steampunk" when I was writing it. I tend to view steampunk more as an aesthetic than as a genre. For me it was a variety of alt-history mixed with urban fantasy. It was incredibly fun to write, and just happened naturally once the initial image—of Archibald Clare in his study, disheveled and bored almost to literal death—came to me. From there it was a race to uncover things as the characters did. I literally did not know what would happen next until Bannon's Ride, near the end of the book.

*Where did the inspiration for* **The Iron Wyrm Affair** *come* *from? Were the Sherlock Holmes books a big influence?*

I loved Sherlock Holmes and Encyclopedia Brown as a child. The idea that the power of observation could be used like that...it was like a superpower ordinary people could polish. Also, when the recent *Sherlock Holmes* movie hit theatres, there were a couple scenes that were just such fun, so tongue-in-cheek, that they really fired my imagination.

# extras

*There is a wonderful spark between Emma Bannon and Mikal. An unusual choice since Clare is the other point of view. Why choose Mikal over Clare for the love interest?*

My goodness, Clare would *not* be attracted to Emma. Plus, he's a mentath. Logic machines are hard to live with, as are Prime sorceresses. Initially, Mikal wasn't even a love interest, and I hesitate to say he's one now. He was simply an almost-socially-acceptable way for Miss Bannon to relieve, shall we say, a little pressure. He and Miss Bannon have a relationship more founded on mutual respect and a variety of trust than anything else.

Clare, on the other hand, wouldn't know what to do if he did have tender feelings for *anyone*, let alone Miss Bannon.

*When did you come up with the idea of jewels and jewellery as a source of power?*

Jewellery has always been a source of power and fascination. It's very human to adorn oneself, and have that adornment carry power and significance. I realised about halfway through the book that Miss Bannon's jewellery was a character in its own right, and during revision had to go back and write out every set she wore. It was almost like dress-up.

*Emma Bannon is such a fascinating character. So tough... and yet so proper at times. Where did you get the inspiration for her?*

Her influences are manifold, from Kage Baker's Edward Bell-Fairfax (probably the biggest one) to Rudyard Kipling's Kim, as well as *Jane Eyre* and a huge, choking load of Charles Dickens. I wondered what a woman, especially a woman who had escaped the confines of a lower class, would do with the phenomenal power of a Prime. There was also a very interesting tension in her character—Miss Bannon is, after all, expected to act in certain ways because she is a woman, and sometimes she doesn't. There's always a price to pay for that. It would be anachronistic to have it otherwise. The arrogance and willpower of a Sorcerer Prime and the powerful social strictures of gentility and gender roles make for interesting complexity.

# if you enjoyed
## THE COMPLETE ADVENTURES OF BANNON & CLARE

### look out for

# AFTERWAR

### by

## Lilith Saintcrow

*America has been devastated by a second civil war. The people have spent years divided, fighting their fellow patriots. Now, as the regime crumbles and the bloody conflict draws to a close, the work of rebuilding begins.*

*One lonely crew, bonded under fire in the darkest days of battle, must complete one last mission: to secure a war criminal whose secrets could destroy the fragile peace that has just begun to form.*

*Bestselling author Lilith Saintcrow presents a timely and all-too-realistic glimpse of a future that we hope never comes to pass.*

# Chapter One

## Details Later

February 21, '98

The last day in hell ran with cold, stinking rain. A gunmetal-gray sky opened up its sluices, mortars and bigger artillery shook the wooded horizon-hills at 0900, and roll call in the central plaza—down to two thousand scarecrows and change, the dregs of Reklamation Kamp Gloria—took only two and a half hours. Pale smears peered from the red-painted kamp brothel windows, disappearing whenever the Kommandant's oil-slick head and unsettling light blue gaze turned in their direction. Stolid and heavy in his natty black uniform, Kommandant Major General Porter stood on a heavy platform; the raw edges of its boards, once pale and sticky with sap, were now the same shade as the lowering sky. The skeletons in dun, once-orange dungarees stood unsteadily under a triple pounding—first the Kommandant's words crackling over the PA, then the thick curtains of rain, and last the rolling thunder in the hills.

*Not just partisans,* some whispered, their lips unmoving. Convicts and kampogs learned quickly how to pass along bites of news or speculation, despite the contact regulations—worth a flogging if you were caught talking, a worse flogging if more than two kampogs were "gathering."

*Nope, not just partisans. Federals.*

Feral rumors, breeding swiftly, ran between the thin-walled Quonsets, bobbing over the reeking, sucking mud like balls of ignes fatui down in the swampy work sites, drifting into the empty stone rectangle of the quarry, flashing like sparks off the sicksticks the uniforms and jar captains carried. Raiders, Federals, knights riding dragons—who cared? Hope wasn't a substitute for a scrap of moldy potato or a filched, crumbling cube of protein paste.

On the second floor of the joyhouse, in a room with dingy pinkish walls, cheap thin viscose curtains twitched a little, and the narrow bed underneath them shuddered as he finished. The bedspread had been freshly laundered, and the white, sharp smell of harsh soap and dead electrical heat from the industrial dryers filled Lara's empty skull. It was a darkness full of small things—a glimpse of the dusty silk flowers in the tiny vase on the nightstand, a twinge from her discarded body, the burn of slick soylon fabric against her cheek, the indistinct mutter of the PA as Kommandant Porter, the God of Gloria, spoke. Someone would later tell her the Kommandant, his hair swept back and his mirror-shined boots splattered with that thick, gluey mud, had made a speech about how the shivering pogs had paid their debt to society and were to be taken to a Re-Edukation Kamp. Porter audibly hoped they would remember the struggle and sacrifice the uniforms had suffered to remake them—brown immies, any-color degenerates, white politicals since the brown ones were shot, traitors all—into productive members of the Great United States of America First.

It didn't matter. Nothing mattered then but getting through the next sixty seconds. Lara heard all sorts of details later, without meaning to. Right now, though, she lay flattened and breathless under the weight on her back, life and hope and air squeezed out.

"I love you," the Kaptain whispered in her left ear, hot sour breath against her dark hair. It had grown back, first in the sorting shed and now here, though the ends were brittle and fraying. She was lucky to be in the pink room; the plywood stalls downstairs could see as many as six, seven an hour between first roll call at 0500 to midnight, no breaks, no lunch. Up here in the rooms named for colors, though, there were special clients. A special diet too, more calories than the average kampog, especially a twenty-niner, could dream of. Exemption from even "light" labor in the sorting sheds.

Some of the uniformed guards, or the jar kaptains—the highest class of kampog, because why force a uniform to work in the stinking jar-barracks, where you lay three or four to a shelf-bed—brought "presents." Tiny containers of scent, either liquid or paste, not enough to get drunk on. Lipstick—it was edible, more welcome than the damn cologne. They often brought food, the best present of all. Cigarettes to trade. Some of the girls here drank the colorless, eye-watering liquor the uniforms were rationed, instead of trading it away for more substantial calories.

It let you forget, and that was worth a great deal. A few minutes of release from the tension was so seductive. The poison dulled you, though, and dull didn't last long here. Soaking in bathtub booze was a good way to drown.

"I love you," the Kaptain repeated, the hiss of a zipper closing under his words. The mattress had finished its song of joyless stabbing, and it barely indented under her slight, lonely weight. "I've organized a car, and gas. A good coat. I'll come back and get you." He bent over to arrange her, pushing her shoulder so she had to move, wanting her to look at him.

Rolled over on her back, Lara gazed at the ceiling, the damp trickle between her legs aching only a little. More raw lumber. Paint was a luxury—the red on the brothel's outside was left over from something else. The only other painted building was the Kommandant's House on the outskirts, with its white clapboard walls and picket fence. Lara had even seen the high-haired, floral-dressed wife once or twice, sitting on the porch with a glossy magazine back when the war was going well. Some kampogs used to work in the house or the garden, but that stopped when the siege of Denver was broken. Even the Kommandant's family had to go back to the cities, retreating eastward.

The Kaptain was blond, his bloodshot blue eyes showing his worry over the war. He was her special client, and his status meant she didn't have others. Black wool uniform with the special red piping, the silver Patriot Akademy ring on his left third finger mimicking a wedding band, the back and sides of his head shaved but the top longer. He'd begun growing it out a little while ago.

When the war turned.

He examined her while he buttoned his outer jacket, settling his cuffs, made sure he was zipped up completely. A hurried visit, for him. How many hours had she spent in this room, blessedly alone, and how many with him talking at her, unloading his worries, his thoughts, words dripping over every surface, trying to work their way in? Most of her energy went toward being impervious, locked up inside her skull. Building and maintaining walls for the steel bearings rolling inside her, so their noise could drown out everything else.

"I'll be right back." The Kaptain bent over the bed again, and his lips pressed against her cheek. There was almost no pad of fatty tissue over her teeth—still strong, they hadn't rotted out yet. Childhood fluoride had done her a good turn, and with McCall's crew there had been pine needles. Berries. Ration bars with orange flavor and minerals all in one nasty, grainy mouthful.

She was lucky, really, and how fucked-up was it that she knew? The question was a waste of energy. Here, you couldn't afford to ask. Every effort was channeled into one thing only.

Survival.

"I love you," he whispered yet again. Maybe he needed to convince himself, after all this time. His breath made a scorch circle, a red-hot iron pressed against shrinking flesh. Branded, like the Christian Courts were so fond of decreeing. *B* for "bandit" or *P* for "partisan," or the ever-popular *A* for "scarlet woman," because "adulterer" could possibly be the man, and you couldn't blame *him*.

The Kaptain slammed the door on his way out. Yelled something down the hall—an order, maybe. Quick, hard bootsteps, scurrying back and forth. Looked like he was clearing the top floor. The girls up here might be grateful for the respite, unless they were waiting for a special to bring them something. If they were, they'd assume Lara had pissed the Kaptain off somehow, or something. They didn't quite dare to band together against her—it wasn't worth the risk—but the top-floor joyhouse girls were pariahs even among kampogs, and she was a pariah even among *them*.

Exclusivity, like luck, was suspect.

*I'll take care of you*, he'd promised. *Wait for me.* Like she had any sort of choice. So Lara just lay there until he went away, his presence leaching slowly out of the small, overdone, dark little room. Nobody wanted bright lights in a joyhouse. A lot of the specials may have even honestly believed the girls in here were glad to see them, glad to be somehow saved.

1258

As if anyone here didn't know it only took one wrong move, one glance, or even nothing at all, and into the killing bottles you went.

It didn't matter. She drifted, letting her ears fill with the high weird cotton-wool sound that meant she was *outside* her skin. Just turned a few inches, so she could look at whatever was happening to her body without feeling.

After some indeterminate period of time—maybe a half hour, maybe more—the throbbing beat of the ancient wheeze-box downstairs thumped-ran down to a stop. Without that heartbeat, the expectant hush inside the red-painted building turned painful.

When Lara pushed herself up on her sharp starved elbows, stealing back into her body bit by bit from the faraway place where not much could hurt her, the first rounds took out two of the watchtowers, splashing concrete, broken glass, slivers of red-hot metal, and rags of guardflesh down into Suicide Alley along the electrified fence.

The Federals—and Swann's Riders—had arrived.

# Chapter Two

## Regret

It took longer than Adjutant Kommandant Kaptain Eugene Thomas liked to finish his arrangements for a retreat, mostly because Kommandant Major General Porter, unwilling to delegate *or* make a goddamn decision, kept Thomas for a good half hour, going on about paperwork. Maybe Porter never thought the Federals would have the unmitigated gall to actually interfere with his little slice of republic cleansing, or maybe the old man had cracked under the pressure. He was certainly sweating enough. There were dark patches under the kommandant's arms, sopping wet, and his flushed forehead was an oil slick under the crap melting out of his dyed-black hair.

At last, though, Gene saluted and was released with a packet of "sensitive documents" to take east, flimsies and digital keys rustling and clacking inside a tan leather pouch. The stairs outside Porter's office were choked with guards, but no officers—Gene's fellow shoulderstraps would know better than to possibly be sent on some bullshit detail while the degenerates were already so close. If Gene hadn't been such a believer in prudently covering his own ass at all times, he would have already collected her from the pink room and would be speeding past the gate in a shiny black kerro, watching the girl's face as she opened the box and the fur coat, vital and black and soft as a cloud, rippled under her chewed fingertips. Even her habit of nibbling at her nails was enchanting.

She'd be grateful for the coat and the escape—she would *have* to be. He'd finally see her smile.

The Kaptain accepted the salutes of the black-clad guards still unfortunate enough to be on duty with a single, frosty nod as he passed, keeping his step firm and unhurried in shining, scraped-clean boots. The ancient yellow lino in the hall of the admin building squeaked a little under his soles; there were no kampogs in striped headscarves or faded dungarees working at streaks of tracked-in mud with their inadequate brushes. One or two of the guards enjoyed smearing the worst filth they could find down the hall and kicking pogs while they scrambled to clean it, but Porter frowned on that.

The smell alone was unhealthy. Just because the pogs lived in shit didn't mean the soldiers, being a higher class of creature, should get it on their toes.

Soldiers. Gene's upper lip twitched as he lengthened his stride. As if any of these assholes had ever seen *real* combat. Kamps were supposed to be cushy jobs, good chances for advancement once your loyalty and capacity were proven. An endpoint like this meant hazard pay and extra alcohol rations, both useful things. So what if combat troops looked down on them, or if his fellow shoulderstraps were a collection of paper pushers and rear-echelon weekend warriors? *He* was probably the only true patriot in the lot.

A thumping impact made the entire admin building shudder just as he reached the side door, and he took the stairs outside two at a time. Mortars. At the *fence*. The degenerates weren't in the hills anymore. They were moving fast, just like the hordes descending upon Rome back in the day. That rather changed things—he had to get back to the joyhouse and collect the girl—

Another *wump*. Something smashed past the fence, and a high whistling drone screeched across Gloria before the admin building shuddered again, hit from the opposite side. There was an instant of heat in Gene's left calf, a flash of annoyance as the world forgot what it was supposed to do and heaved underneath him. Then the world turned over like an egg flipped on a griddle, and after a weightless moment he hit gravel with a crunch. It was a minor wound, all things considered, but the guard he'd paid and left with strict orders to watch the kerro dragged his superior to the now-dusty, low-slung black vehicle. Before Gene could shake the ringing from his ears, he'd been tossed in the back like a sack of processed starch lumps, and the guard—a weedy, pimple-faced youth who had less than twelve hours to live, though neither of them knew it yet—was already accelerating on the wide macadamized road out of Gloria.

Instead of watching the girl with her wide, empty eyes and pretty cupid's-bow mouth and full underlip, Gene had to work shrapnel free of his own leg and grind his teeth, improvising a pressure bandage as the kerro bumped and jolted. The wheelless vehicle wasn't meant for gliding at high speed, its undercells humming and sparking as chips of pressed rock jolted free under the repeller field.

Driving that way would have gotten the kid a reprimand two weeks ago. Now, though, Gene just dug under the seat for a bottle of amber Scotch—the good stuff, imported, he'd been looking forward to seeing her reaction when he produced it— and didn't bother to glance out the back bubble, wasting a bit of the stinging, expensive liquid to disinfect the cut.

One small Rome had fallen, but the rest of the empire would endure. Or at least, Kaptain Thomas hoped it would. He settled in the cushioned back seat, easing his wounded leg, and took a healthy hit from the bottle.

If he drank enough, he might even be able to forget her—and the pink room—for a little while.

# Chapter Three

## Last Bloody Hours

It was the third camp they'd ... what was the word?

Found? Bombed? Liberated?

Each was worse than the last. At least by this time both raiders and regular infantry knew mostly what to expect, and CentCom was moving up supplies—electrolyte drinks, gruel, medics with clean needles, sanitation engineers. The filth was indescribable, and the skeletal campogs could perforate their tissue-thin stomach walls gorging on ready rations. You could kill just by performing the oldest of human kindnesses, sharing your calories.

The shitholes were *all* bad, even the showplace camps closer to the more densely populated sectors. But Reklamation Kamp Gloria, lost in swampy pinewoods, was ... Christ. It was the first Reklamation site, the one where the Central Federal Army found the bath bays, their glassy sides holding deep, shimmering caustic unfluid capable of swallowing flesh, bones, even tooth enamel when a mild electrical current was passed through. That current did double duty, shocking those who tried to cling to the sides, too. If a victim managed by some freak of fate or chance to hang on to a simulacrum of consciousness in the killing bottle, the chute poured them dazed and convulsing into the bays, and they were eaten away in short order. The side products—saponified fat, traces of gold or other valuable metals and minerals from bones, the magchips in left arms, or old-style fillings—were skimmed off and shipped away.

The Quonsets were emptier than at the last camps they'd come across, because Gloria, sunk in the marshland, wasn't really a work site. Though it had a quarry and workshops, the rail spur only led *in*; the side products were trucked out in boxes. Literally and figuratively, Gloria was the end of the line.

The Army InfoSecs managed to capture about 60 percent of the records before the digital worms could finish their work. The black-jacket, red-piped Patriot administrators and officers were gone, probably got away right as the Federals arrived. All the Special Group motherfuckers, the hardcore Patriot believers in the Leader and the Flag, were long gone too, probably because the advance had finally sped up since Swann's Riders knew the terrain. And fuck if it wasn't that asshole General Leavy who busted the *other* asshole General Specter, who wouldn't fucking listen to the raiders because they were outside the chain of command.

With Leavy in charge things started to steamroller, what with a raider or two in every damn company telling them what to look out for and how to avoid getting their asses blown off by booby trap, guerrilla action, or rear guards grown brutal after four years of Insurrection Kontrol.

Chuck Dogg, a helmet clamped over his 'fro, was the first of Swann's through the gates, tagging along with the army grunts hopping to secure the damn place. Chuck was, in fact, with the platoon that found the goddamn bath bays, and sometimes

Zampana said he was never really right again after that. He just stood for a while, watching the harsh overhead lighting ripple on the placid, green-glowing surface. It was him and Hank Simmons—Simmons the Reaper, that big blond bootstrap bastard—who rounded up what they could of the uniformed fuckers captured in Gloria's corners and tossed six of them in the bays before they were stopped. It took Swann himself, striding in with his boots almost striking sparks and that goddamn vermin-ridden hat clamped firmly on his shaved head, to get the Dogg to stand down.

Raiders believed in eye for eye, tooth for tooth. You had to, running behind the lines and sabotaging installations or gathering intel. CentCom called them "irregulars," and the Firsters called them "partisans" or "traitors," but they were *raiders*, and the name meant vengeance.

It also meant no quarter.

The InfoSec squad got an eyeful of the prisoner rolls, and one of them grabbed Simmons—who was almost skunkfucking drunk by then, but still ambulatory through some freak of his big old Norwegian constitution—as smoky dusk hung over the swamp, to tell him there had been twenty-eight raiders sent to the camp. Easy to tell who had been a raider: they were the prisoners with a thick band of lase scar tissue across the left wrist, which meant they had to be magtatted instead of chipped.

There was no use wasting a chip on an enemy of the state.

Twenty-six of the raider prisoners had gone right to the baths upon arrival. One died right after liberation, his emaciated body found in the mud of the central plaza, where he'd fallen in the middle of the Kommandant's speech and hadn't been hauled away yet by his jar fellows.

The last remaining raider prisoner was in the two-story building slapped with blistering red paint, transferred there after a stint in the sorting shed where the belongings of each prisoner who hadn't already been processed through another camp were searched, stacked, fumigated, baled for transport, and taken back into the heartland to be distributed to America First party members.

No name and no citizen file, which meant she hadn't broken under any torture and given them any information that would find her in the old gov databases. Just a half-wormed prisoner number—QIP-x834xx16x—and a single note in the locator field: *Remanded to Joy Duty rm 6, Kpt E. Thomas.*

Joy Duty. That was what they called the brothel.

When Simmons found Room Six at the end of the second-floor hall, he also found a hollow-cheeked, painfully thin but not skeletal prisoner—they had better rations in the red house, just like the prisoners forced to work the bath bays did—in a paper-thin viscose slip, sitting primly on a pink soylon bedspread and staring vacantly at the wall. The pink dress she was supposed to wear to match the room had been torn into strips, and she stared at the Reaper for ten very long seconds. Some of the dress's pink soylon was wrapped around her bloody right fist, a rough and nonabsorbent but very capable bandage.

Below, some of the brothel's inhabitants were screaming at random intervals. They couldn't help it—they would stop in the middle of drinking or shell-shocked wandering and begin to shake, and a long cry would ribbon up and out, accumulated terror whistling through vocal cracks. The sound of smashing glass from the bar, which had supplied the uniforms and some of the more favored jar captains, had just petered out; even drinking to blackout didn't stop the random cries of the newly liberated.

A couple MPs at the door earned a lot of heat for keeping even the frontline officers out of the red building, but orders were direct, thorough, repeated, and unequivocal from General Leavy, who might have been an asshole but was not a man who thought troops deserved a little fun whenever or wherever there were cunts—especially brutalized ones—hanging out to dry.

How Simmons got past the MPs was a mystery even to him. Maybe because he was a raider, and they weren't known for rape. Or maybe because he was too drunk to even contemplate getting his pecker swabbed, which was, even for that blond bastard, very drunk *indeed*.

Simmons blear-blinked, trying very hard to focus, his rifle poking over his shoulder and his breath enough to kill a cactus at fifteen paces. He took in the room, the faded silk flowers in a tiny scrap-glass vase on the nightstand, the sliver of mirror over a washbasin—even that sliver was splintered; someone had driven a fist into it, to judge from the bloody mark in the middle of the breakage. She stared at him, the dark-haired woman in the cheap slip, and even through the liquor he saw glaring bruises on her skinny arms. Around her ankles, too.

Her pupils shrank a little, her dark eyes focused, and she coughed, a painful, racking sound. "Lara Nelson," she said, in a cracked, reedy whisper. "Senior medic, Third Band, McCall's Harpies."

Big, pale-headed Simmons stood there, filling up the door, and tried to think of a reply. Any reply.

"Lara Nelson," she repeated. "Medic. Third Band. McCall's Harpies. Captured March twenty-second." Her face crumpled slightly, smoothed. "Year...ninety...ninety-six?"

Simmons finally found his voice. "It's '98. At ease, soldier." It came out crisp instead of slurred. Even a raider couldn't drink enough to get away from the fucking war. You could pour down engine degreaser until you went blind, it didn't fucking matter.

"Ninety..." Her chin worked a little, her mouth trying

to open, closing, turning into a thin line. Simmons watched it, and of all the situations in the goddamn Second Civil, he would later say that was the second worst. *Here's this girl, and she's been... Christ, man. They even had kids in that goddamn house, we found an eleven-year-old boy from Indiana in the stalls downstairs, and here this girl was, repeating "McCall's Harpies. McCall's Harpies." And I couldn't fucking tell her McCall was dead at fucking Memphis.*

Memphis, that graveyard of raiders. Of *course* she knew McCall was dead; she'd been captured during the ill-fated uprising. The one the Federals were supposed to push in and relieve the pressure on, supposed to coordinate with. The one they hadn't helped a tit's worth with, because cooperating with irregulars wasn't part of CentCom's strategy back in '96.

Simmons ended up taking off his rancid camo field jacket—a veteran of both the Casper and Third Cheyenne battles, where Swann's Riders had run supplies for the Federals and bloodied themselves taking out rails and quite a few bunkers—and wrapping it around her shoulders. He picked her up—she weighed less than his kid brother—and carried her out of the red house, straight to Swann.

Who didn't want to fucking *debrief* her, and double didn't want any more goddamn problems... but he poured himself another shot of colorless engine cleaner, downed it, and told Dogg to get the new medic some fucking clothes and whatever kit could be scrounged. There were bales of civilian clothes in the sorting shed, but the girl refused to go in there, so it was Zampana who eyeballed her sizes and went in with Dogg, both of them nauseous at the sheer amount of clothing. Plenty of it had been shipped from other camps to be sorted and packaged here, but still, it was hard to look at all the jackets, shirts, skirts, jeans, and the small mountain of unsorted shoes and not see the bodies tumbling from the gas-filled killing bottles into the placid-looking, caustic bays.

The front elements left Gloria the next morning in a stinking rain that would swell the rivers and make the next set of engagements miserable slogs through sucking mud that sometimes swallowed shells or mortars whole. Swann's folk left too, and the new medic went with them, big-eyed and clutching two first aid kits Dogg had managed to find. The raiders also drew extra ration bars and stole cans of condensed calories from the camp supplies to soak the bars in, and Zampana got her hands on a Firster sidearm for the medic, too.

For a Christer, Zampana was all-fucking-right.

The frontliners were supposed to leave all prisoners in Gloria for critical care, processing, and medivac, but goddamn if Swann's crew was going to abandon another raider in that fucking place. It was probably a mercy, since the second-wave troops weren't kept on as tight a leash as Leavy's boys, as witnessed in DC later that summer.

That was how Lara Nelson, later christened Spooky, joined Swann's Riders in the last bloody hours of America's Second Civil War.

orbit

## Follow us:

/orbitbooksUS

/orbitbooks

/orbitbooks

Join our mailing list
to receive alerts on our
latest releases and deals.

**orbitbooks.net**

Enter our monthly
giveaway for the chance
to win some epic prizes.

**orbitloot.com**